Ogya has won complete control of the People of the Savanna through the authority of his avatar, King Laughing Dog. He blazes through the forest consuming everything with his flames; but still his hunger grows ever fiercer.

Elder Cloud leads her group of exiles across the empty lands to the ancient, storm-lashed city of Bogana. Cloud hopes to find help in stopping Ogya, but the dim childhood memories she carries of the dangerous city provide little comfort. The exiles are unaware they are being followed by one of the King's loyal Fire Hunters, carrying his own ghosts of the past.

Fledgling forest god Clay and his mate Doto seek to prevent all-out war between Kwaee, Ogya, and what remains of his tribe. Clay—now trapped with his feet in two very different worlds—must learn to embrace his divinity to reconcile the estranged goddesses of earth, water and forest in a desperate attempt to stop the seemingly unstoppable Ogya.

# God of Fire

## The Fire Bearers: Book Three

by Ryan Campbell

Saint Paul, MN

---

**God of Fire**



Printed in the United States of America

First Printing, March 2021 • POD Printing, June 2023

ISBN 978-1-936689-71-2

Sofawolf Press, Inc.
PO Box 11868
Saint Paul, MN 55111-0868
*www.sofawolf.com*

*David, this dance is for you*

# Chapters & Illustrations

# Acknowledgements

Thanks to the readers in my writing group: Tim Susman and Watts Martin, who gave me water, patted me on the back, and administered the Heimlich several times as I repeatedly insisted on biting off more than I could chew. I'd never have finished the book and structured it as well as I've managed without their invaluable help and support at all stages of writing.

Thanks to Sofawolf for being patient over the four years it took to write this final entry, and for shepherding it through to publication in the middle of political upheaval and a pandemic.

Thanks to the artist, Zhivago, for being willing to return to the series for one final entry.

And thanks to all my fans who waited so patiently as I worked to develop the skills I needed to finish this story the way I felt it deserved. Thank you for taking this journey with me, and I hope it was an enjoyable one.

*—Ryan*

# 1 After the Shot

The sun burned red, an ember rising out of the forest in the east. Yesterday, the skies had been blue and clear, but now they were hazy and clouded with yellow smoke. Mirage sat on Gamewatch Rise and watched the low flicker over the forest. It had been two days.

Two days since King Great Ram and the demon thing that had looked like Clay had been killed. Two days since Laughing Dog had become King. Two days since the People of the Savanna fractured. Two days since Mirage had let go of his bowstring. He felt that he had not truly left the hill since that moment, that still his fingers stung from the pull of the string, that his bow still vibrated.

And in that moment, he had stopped, but the world around him had kept going. Cloud had challenged Laughing Dog for rule, and he had exiled her. So she had gone and taken a third of their people with her: mainly the older folks and the children who depended on them. The village still had its vibrancy: the young, the strong, the energetic, virtually all of their hunters and scouts. But their wisdom had left them. Their memory had gone. Their healer, their Teller of tales, the craftspeople who knew their trades so completely they could work them in the dark, and their connection to their ancestors. There was the flattened track they had left in the grass, heading west along the forest. They had left.

But Mirage had been unable to move. He had stood atop the rise, the bow in his hand, while the world changed around him, while people said their goodbyes, while they wept and laughed and exchanged gifts, while a third of all the people he had known in his life gathered up their possessions and trudged off into the west. While they hefted up the body of Left Rabbit and carried it away. He could not look any of them in the face. The bowstring still burned at his fingertips.

And then the night had come, and he had gone to the tent he shared with his mother. She was asleep, so he ate the food she left out for him and lay in bed where no sleep would come. Just the moments of the day before, over and over. Not always the arrow. Sometimes the weeping. Sometimes the goodbyes of the people around him. Sometimes the terror at the edge of the forest. Surely, he told himself, no one was sleeping well tonight. Other than his mother. Well, she was used to sleeping after terrible things.

The next morning, when he went out, no one would look him in the eye. He gleaned from overheard conversation that the fire hunters had gone early that morning. They'd taken up their spears and bows, but also torches and palm oil. That morning was the first day of the war against the forest god Kwaee and his tyranny. Mirage went back up Gamewatch Rise and watched the heads of smoke begin to peek up from the canopy of the forest like torpid clouds. No one came up to see him that day, to find out if he was all right.

There was a dark patch in the dirt where Left Rabbit's blood had spilled out. There had been no afternoon rains since the Day of Sorrow. Nothing to wash it away.

Evening and morning.

And now the sun burned red.

It was Broken Stump who first came to see him. Not the King, not Mirage's mother, not even his damned father, but one of the fire hunters. He'd never liked Mirage much, had complained about allowing kids to join the fire hunters, even though he had barely ten rains on Mirage. He'd gone grey early and he spoke in the rude cadence of hunters who spent a lot of time away from the village. At least he didn't shy away from meeting Mirage's gaze, though his expression was unfriendly.

"King says it's time to come down and help out."

"Another hunt?"

"Mm. We don't need the meat. Lot less stomachs to go empty now. We got other priorities. The burn. Vengeance on Kwaee. You got yourself a rest day, I reckon, but it's time to work.

Mirage flicked his gaze to the horizon. "Seems like you've made a good start. The sky glowed pink last night."

"Maybe. But there's a lot of forest. We're going to need every hand. And the things the King is doing out there…" He shook his head. "You'll have to see for yourself. You wouldn't believe me."

"How is he?"

Broken Stump shrugged his wiry shoulders. "Who can say? He's different now. Even compared to before."

"The forest murdered his whole family."

"Yeah, that's what he says." A silence. "Proud as parrots of you, though. Keeps talking about how you proved yourself. How he gave the order to all of us, but only you obeyed." A sidelong, assessing glance. "Says he can trust you."

The red sun was a wound in the sky. Greasy yellow clouds drifted up around it. "But everyone here is acting like I did something wrong."

Broken Stump's mouth twisted in disgust. "No, you obeyed orders."

"That's right."

A low mutter, barely audible: "Still a murderer."

"What?" Mirage felt the word like a slap. "I—I obeyed my King. What was I supposed to do? Refuse?"

"No." The shorter man walked up until he was right up against Mirage's chest, and when he spoke, his teeth bared. "You shoulda done exactly what you did. Your King ordered you to. But you still did it. And you're still a murderer."

The injustice of the accusation, of his tortured logic, wrenched Mirage out of his brooding. "I did what was right!" he snapped. "I stopped sedition at a—at a time when our whole village was in danger. I don't know what my King knows. What if he'd been a demon too? A spy sent by Kwaee?"

"Yeah but he wasn't, was he? Boy, you didn't even hesitate. The King says kill and while everyone else is thinking, 'Did he really say that, could I really strike down my brother,' while everyone is having a gods-cursed moment of shock, your arrow is sprouting out of Rabbit's chest."

No. This was unjust. "Why should I be ashamed? I was loyal. I obeyed my King. He gave the order to all of us. He could have given it to just you." He saw the flicker of uncertainty on Broken Stump's face. "And you'd have done it, wouldn't you? You'd have obeyed the order. You'd have had to."

The shorter man set his jaw and stepped back. "Maybe I would. But I didn't, did I? It was you. You're a murderer now, and that's how everyone will see you. Maybe," he added, his voice softening a little, "maybe you drew unlucky stones, boy. But you can't change it now."

No, he couldn't change it. But how could it truly be murder, if it was done at the command of a King, a King who was following the orders of a god? How, if it was to save his people and demonstrate their allegiance to Ogya? There had to be a better word.

The voice of his grandmother, Two Broken Hands, echoed in his head. She'd spoken of older days when the gods had talked directly to humans; when worship of them involved less fire and drums, and more screaming and blood. No other way to appease the gods, she would frequently mutter to him, shaking her head at the traditional dances and songs. You want to prove you serve them? You give them life.

Two Broken Hands was dead now. Kwaee, god of the forest, had sent monsters to attack the village. They'd torn her open and left her bleeding in the dirt. And then they'd gone.

Mirage rubbed at his eyes again. They were beginning to sting from the smoke. His throat burned and his head throbbed with pain. "It wasn't murder," he said aloud. "It was sacrifice."

Broken Stump's face hardened like clay in a fire.

~

"It tastes like smoke," his mother complained between bites of yam. She crouched outside the tent with her dinner at her narrow knees. "Everything tastes like smoke."

The evening sky above Mirage glowed a sickly orange, stirred through with the milky white of smoke. "It's only for a while," he said. "Once we clear this part of the forest, the fires won't be so near. Then you won't smell it as much." He toyed with the bundle of twine in his hands, playing Priest's Procession, an old game his grandmother had taught him when he was a boy. Braid the strands of twine left, right, left, over, over, right, under. The pattern continued in a complex order, but if you wound the cords correctly, you'd have one that would pull all the way through, all the others immovable knots. *You see, boy? If you're clever, then no matter how tightly they hold you, there's always a way to break free.* He pulled the strand, and the whole thing came apart in his fingers. He'd done something wrong.

His mother turned worried eyes toward the forest. "And how do we know the wind won't change and send the fires toward us in our sleep?"

"You never listen, Dry Grass. That's your problem." Knife Strap stood at her side, fingering sorghum mash from a calabash into his mouth and slurping it down noisily. "The King controls the fire. Why do you question everything? Don't you trust him?" He nudged Dry Grass with a foot.

"Don't touch her," Mirage warned him, looking up from the twine.

Knife Strap wasn't supposed to come in contact with Dry Grass, ever, by order of King First Claw. Not anymore. Not ever. Not since the day the King had unwed them both. But he still ate meals with them and kept his tent nearby. To help raise his son, he said. A King could unstitch a marriage, but he couldn't unmake a child. So, like it or not, Knife Strap was always around, making comments. Pushing boundaries. He'd been worse and worse of late.

But he sucked at his fingers as if he hadn't heard. "We've got a new King now," he said conversationally. "Who knows what will change?"

"Yes, and I am one of his fire hunters," Mirage reminded him. "At his right hand. And I'm sure he'll want to reward me for my service. I wonder what I could ask for? Maybe think about that and leave my mother alone." He started the twine again, focusing, trying to shut out the conversation. Left, right, left, over, over, right, under, back, right.

His father hunched up his shoulders like a tortoise. "You shouldn't talk to me like that. I'm still your elder."

"And how much do you think that means these days? We sent all our elders away. Would you join them? They failed us. They let the forest kill us and the savanna starve us. It's a young man's world now, Father." He let the final word drip with contempt.

"Stop it, just stop." His mother huddled back against the wall, crossing her arms tightly.

Mirage kept his focus on the twine, embarrassed.

"I wish we could eat together," she said after a while, gazing out toward the council fire area. There wasn't a fire tonight, and why bother? The whole horizon was a blazing beacon, the air choked with enough smoke already. But even without the fire, people usually gathered there for the evening meal, sharing food as well as stories, songs, and conversation about the day's events.

"Why isn't anyone out there?" Mirage asked, scanning the empty ground.

"Too many people are gone now, I suppose. It would be hard to see everyone missing. Better to eat indoors."

Mirage understood. How could you eat a meal amidst all that empty space? All those seats unfilled. Most of the elders and their families. Many of the children. Cloud. The Teller. Great Ram. Clay. First Claw. The People of the Savanna had been broken and scattered.

Knife Strap stood and stretched up on his toes, flicking flecks of sorghum from his fingers into the dirt. Normally sparrows would hop near their feet hopefully, waiting for the opportunity to dart in and steal a morsel, but since the fires started, all the sparrows had gone. "There won't be any meals together anymore. Not for us." He gave Mirage a sidelong glance. "Our son took care of that for us. Didn't you, boy?"

Mirage recognized resentment in the set of his cheeks and the narrowing of his shoulders and grew quiet and careful. There were no right answers to this sort of question. Protesting that he'd had no choice wouldn't help. Anger couldn't be quenched or satisfied; it had to be abided. Or challenged. Mirage nodded wordlessly.

"Father of a killer." Knife Strap spat in the dirt. "How proud you've made me."

Mirage almost flinched at the word; from his father's lips it was more jagged and brutal. But flinching around Knife Strap was a mistake. So was passive silence. Instead he stood, getting to his feet, reminding his father of the good half a hand of height he stood above him, letting him see the fire hunter stripes across his chest and shoulders. "Let's all just enjoy our dinner, yes?"

Disbelief passed over Knife Strap's face like a break in the clouds. "Well, look, Dry Grass, our killer son thinks he is in charge of the family now. Now that he's all cozy with the boy King, he must be feeling pretty important." A nasty smile creased his face. "Is that how you feel, killer? Important?"

"If I am a killer," Mirage said calmly, "then you ought to be more careful around me." He looked down at his father's tightening fists. "Who knows *what* I'll do."

The sight of barely restrained fury bubbling across Knife Strap's countenance was almost satisfying, almost worth the hundred petty vengeances his fathers would take over the next few days. Knife Strap held back splutters for a moment and then settled back into an easy smile. "You're on shifting sand with this whole village and you know it. Not even the King can protect a murderer for long."

Mirage held his gaze a moment more and then went into the tent. Inside, the air was still stuffy and hot, but it was preferable to sitting out with his father in that mood, preferable still more to walking through the village and seeing people turn their gazes away from his. He opened the vent in the roof of the tent and lay down on his pallet. The window let in a triangle of evening light painted an ethereal orange by the smoke.

Things weren't usually this bad with his father. At times, he could be cheerful, even kind. But he had moods like thunderheads, and they built and built over days, dark and dangerous. Mirage could see all the signs of one building now. It would pass, but in the meantime, someone had to look out for his mother. Someone had to be there to listen and watch, to remind Knife Strap what would happen if he forgot himself.

Exile. That's what the old King had promised. It helped, sometimes, to whisper the word to him, to remind him. But his mother wouldn't do it herself. When the warning signs came, she would fold, crumple. Others in the village used to watch as well. Knife Strap behaved himself around others. But now… Now everyone was avoiding them. Now they looked away from the family of a murderer. Knife Strap would feel safer, more confident.

Mirage fidgeted with the bundle of twine. If anything happened to his mother now, it would be his fault. He had brought shame onto his family, whether ordered to or not. The command changed so little. He'd killed Left Rabbit. Left, right, left, over, over, right, under.

*You never even hesitated*, Broken Stump had said. But when Mirage closed his eyes, he was still there, hovering in that moment, the smoothness of the taut acacia bow pressing into his hand, only the strength of his arms holding back death. The words of his new King still echoed in his ears. "Kill him."

And he had obeyed. How could he not? Laughing Dog was their only protector against the violence the gods waged on the People of the Savanna. He was the only one who had refused to cower, weak and helpless, while the gods beat him down. Mirage would have followed him anywhere, would have obeyed any order. Left Rabbit had been an enemy. If Laughing Dog believed it, then so it was. So Mirage had obeyed his King. There was no going back.

But still, when he closed his eyes, he was there, the gut string of the bow creasing his fingers. Still he hung in the breath between his old life and his new, suspended by the look of fear and confusion in Left Rabbit's eyes.

Still, he hesitated.

~

He woke to the sound of someone calling his name. Broken Stump. He rubbed at his eyes, thumbing grit out of them. The sky was still dark. His sleep had been poor; late into the evening his father had been grousing and sniping at his mother, and when they'd come into the tent his father had aimed a petty kick at Mirage's hip, pretending he'd stumbled in the dark.

Mirage had grunted and ignored it, but all around his hipbone pain flowered into what would surely be a dark bruise the next day. And so between that and the knots of worry in his stomach, he'd gotten very little sleep.

"Mirage."

Surely there was no hunt this morning? It was not his shift. Groaning, he arranged his leathers and crept out of the tent. Broken Stump stood impatiently outside, looking nearly as weary. His eyes were red, but whether from lack of sleep or smoke irritation, Mirage had no idea.

"King wants to see you."

Uneasiness found fingerholds in Mirage's grogginess. "Did—did he say what it was about?"

Broken Stump shrugged. "He told me to come get you. I follow orders. I'm guessing you won't find fault with that."

So it was still going to be like that. "Where can I find him?" Mirage tried to push the weariness from his voice.

"Out on the forest edge. You'll find him easily enough."

Mirage made his way through the still-sleeping village. The scars from the calamity of three days before were everywhere: shattered and flattened homes; the earth gouged out by the path of the bouncing acacia tree that a furious god had flung at them; huge, gnarled branches that had broken off in its path. The wall had already been partly repaired, as everyone feared beasts from the forest retaliating against them in the night, but it would take moons to repair the other damage. The deep gash of the tree's path had severed their village in two, a line drawn in the earth down the middle, as though Kwaee himself had reached out with a giant paw and raked it in half.

The massive trunk of the tree lay splintered and cleft across the council fire circle. It was so enormous that they could not hope to move it, the wood too hard to burn. But what use had they for a fire circle anymore? There was no Teller to remind them of the tales of their ancestors, nor even many remaining elders. The thought made Mirage's skin prickle. What would they do without their past? The death of a single elder was a tragedy. So much knowledge lost, so much experience. And now the People of the Savanna had lost nearly all of their elders.

But then again, what good had all that wisdom and experience done when the gods had turned against them? No one had known how to fight an ever-growing drought, nor placate the god of the forest. They had just accepted Kwaee's cruelty, bowing deeper and deeper under it. Sometimes defiance and bravery were more important than knowledge and humility.

And maybe once this fight was over, once they had beaten back the forest god, then they could go and find their wayward elders, welcome them back to a rebuilt village, one where the people were strong and had no need to fear the caprice of their gods anymore.

He made his way outside the village. The burned forest was a dark hole gouged out of the green. Smoke still swathed the ground like a fog, and around the edges, embers glittered red. The remnants of trees jutted upward, old blackened teeth in the twilight.

Revulsion twisted Mirage's stomach. It was such a waste. All that wood, all that life. All gone. But of course, they had been unable to use it anyway. The forest was their enemy. It would instantly kill any who entered it. Now, at least, the burned land was safe. Mirage knew the old edge of the forest. Everyone did, because no one crossed it and lived. The people had marked its border with stones. Here, those stones formed an arbitrary line across a harmless field of ash. Mirage stepped over it.

An orange glow illuminated the smoke a little distance away. That could only be Laughing Dog, awake before dawn to wage his tireless war against Kwaee. He didn't notice Mirage's approach, but stood naked, his back turned toward the village, his arms raised. From his hands, liquid flame poured in fiery torrents of yellow and white, roaring and crackling as it licked and lit fresh brush and trees. The forest blazed in a halo around Laughing Dog, and he strode across its embering bones without concern for the heat.

The magic of Ogya always filled Mirage with awe and terror. No man on earth wielded power like Laughing Dog did now. He had grown fat with it, his belly wide, his shoulders broad and muscular—the largest man Laughing Dog had ever seen, like in the stories told about the great heroes and the first Kings. His flesh was so tight around his body that he seemed about to burst from within. The flame gushed from him like water, so bright that it left streaks in Mirage's vision.

"King Laughing Dog?" he ventured.

His King turned toward him. It was unusual to see an unclad King, but of course clothing could burn, and the King's raiments were far too valuable to risk to scorch and ash. Behind him, fires licked hungrily up the trunks of trees. A liana burned free of the treetops and fell, a blazing serpent coiling to the ground. The light seemed to burn still in Laughing Dog's eyes, and for a moment Mirage swore there was no man inside that stretched skin. Only an unending inferno.

"Yes, Mirage." His face creased in a smile that, elsewhere, might have looked welcoming, but in the odd shadow of the firelight only frightened Mirage more. "Don't look so worried. I may be King now, but we're still friends."

"That's good to hear." Mirage searched Laughing Dog's face for signs of sincerity but could not read anything in his unfamiliar countenance. "I know you wouldn't forget those who had been faithful to you, but—"

"But you thought you'd better remind me anyway," Laughing Dog interrupted, irritation glittering in his eyes. "I haven't forgotten. And neither has anyone else. That's why you're here."

"My King?" Mirage fought a nervous stammer from his lips.

Laughing Dog put one heavy arm across Mirage's shoulders. His flesh felt tight and sooty, warm as though feverish. He wasn't sweating, Mirage realized. Standing out amid all this fire and he was dry as on a windy night. "You are faithful and a friend, but you are still a killer. I know how people look at you and talk about you. You have taken on a terrible burden for me. Don't think me ungrateful for that. But—"

"But?"

"Perhaps there are tasks you could perform that would not make everyone else so uncomfortable. Even the fire hunters need time to—"

"You're sending me away." Mirage spoke the words as he realized them. His voice sounded distant. Dimly he noticed Laughing Dog's further annoyance at being interrupted, but he couldn't care. He thought of his mother and father, no one in the village looking them in the eyes, her isolation and his rage steadily growing, and no one there to keep it in check.

"It isn't like that. It's not exile. I am handing you an important responsibility. And it will require you to be away for some time, which, let's accept it, will be good for everyone."

"But Prince—but King Laughing Dog, I cannot leave now. My mother—"

"Cannot? Strange. I had you sighted as a man who followed orders no matter how difficult. You kill a man so quickly, and yet you're hesitant to go on a journey? Mirage, if I weren't your friend, I'd wonder myself whether it was something more than obedience that made you kill Left Rabbit."

Mirage couldn't help flinching. Satisfaction sparkled in the King's eyes.

"But I am your friend, so I'll overlook that. You'd be happy to obey your King, wouldn't you? Because you obey him in all things. You've proven that to the whole village. You could hardly find your objections *now*. So listen to me. Cloud and the elders may have left, but I'd be a damned fool if I just *let* them go. They may not be strong or swift, but they are cunning, and our kinsmen as well. They might still make some play for the village or the loyalties of the fire hunters."

Mirage nodded, grateful for the change in conversation. "I agree with you. We can't trust them. They'll try to come back. They might even try to get help."

"So we're of one mind about this," Laughing Dog answered with a warm-seeming smile. "That's why I want you to follow them."

"But—but I'm no tracker." The objection was as flimsy as cobweb.

"I'm not asking you to track a hare through a thicket, you know. I'm *ordering* you to follow a good sixty slow-traveling people across the savanna. I know you're not so incapable a hunter that you can't tell where a third of a village has gone."

He was right, of course. Even a child would have little trouble following such a trail. "And what would I do once I found them?" Mirage asked, barely listening for the answer. He tried to think how he might yet plead his way out of this. He couldn't leave his mother here alone. It was unthinkable. Maybe he could take her with him? But no, she would never leave the village with him—she didn't have the courage for that. And Knife Strap would surely follow them. Out there on the savanna, alone, there would be no other people to shame him into mildness.

"Follow them. Find out what their plans are. And report back to me whenever you have news. Speak your words into a flame, and Ogya will carry them to me."

Mirage started from his worrying, amazed. "He can do that?"

"He can for those who know how to command him."

"But how do you hear these words? Does Ogya himself appear before you and speak them? Or is it like a song playing itself in your mind?" Another worrying thought occurred to him. "Do you hear all words spoken into a fire?"

"You don't need to concern yourself with those kinds of questions. Just follow the outcasts and find out what their plans are."

Mirage gloomily tried to trace the prospective journey. It could take moons, maybe even rains. He'd have to scavenge for his food, somehow hunt and carry water without alerting the people to his presence. Cookfires would be impossible—the smoke would show from a day's journey away.

And there would be no one to talk to. He chewed on his lower lip in frustration. This was a punishment he hadn't earned. All he'd done was obey his King. "And when am I to return, my King? Suppose they found a new village someplace else and settle. Am I to watch them the rest of my life?"

The King rubbed at his chin. For a time he was quiet, his head cocked as though listening to the wind. "I will know your location when you speak to me in the flame. When I am convinced that we need worry ourselves no more with the outcasts, I will send a runner to collect you and bring you home, and by then, perhaps Kwaee will have capitulated. Perhaps I will be able to ask you to bring all our people home again."

"If they survive on their own," Mirage reminded him. Neither the savanna nor the forest had been very hospitable lately. And that was another reason he could not bring his mother with him. Even if he could keep her safe, what if they ran into a great stretch of the journey with no food or water? They would be following in the trampled tracks of scores of people who would eat and drink anything they found. Despondent thoughts of her alone with Knife Strap that had huddled in the corners of his mind now pushed their way into his concern once more. "But King Laughing Dog, if I *am* to be gone for very long…" he trailed off. What if any request only made things worse? But he had to try something. He couldn't leave her alone without help.

"You are my friend," the King said, and Mirage thought that he had never before been reminded of a friendship so many times in one morning. "Anything I can do to give you peace of mind while you carry out this important mission for me."

Mirage made himself ask. "Will you look after my mother?" The words felt weighty and terrible, as though he had asked a lion to watch over his goats. He searched Laughing Dog's face for some measure of understanding or kindness.

The King's smile was unreadable. "Of course. Things must be very hard for your family right now, having a son so dutiful in circumstances so extreme. Mirage, you must know that your loyalty means a great deal to me. I am not exiling you. When you return, you will be my right hand. I will make sure everyone knows it. Your family will be given places of honor at the council fires, and offerings will be made to your ancestors. And while you are gone, I will make sure that your mother is well looked-after. You have the word of a King on that."

"Thank you." Relief settled into Mirage's veins. Laughing Dog had been harsh and erratic lately, but he kept his word.

"I notice you didn't ask me to look after your father as well."

"He can look after himself."

Laughing Dog grinned and gave Mirage's shoulder a playful shove that sent him stumbling. "I think most people here share your feelings about that, you know."

Mirage managed a smile he did not feel. "Yes. But if he should make my mother unhappy..."

"He won't." And his King spoke these words with such confidence and firmness that Mirage felt his worries ease. He clasped Laughing Dog's shoulder firmly, to show trust and kinship. He met his steady gaze to show confidence. Despite all the darkness and suffering of recent days, they were still People of the Savanna. They would still survive. They would still look out for each other. He had not been abandoned after all.

~

Before the sun was high, he had packed all he could think to bring on his journey: his bow and several freshly fletched arrows; salted meat and a bag of jugo beans; his knife and a bit of flint; elder-beard lichen that would make excellent fire-starters; a dipping calabash; his lucky stork foot, dried in the shape of Mother Wem; two water skins; and an assortment of useful items like palm twine and flint needles and feathers. The supplies would not be enough, but he could find more on the way, provided the traveling exiles didn't strip the land bare before he got there.

Finally, he stood upright in the tent, hands at his hips as he considered the belongings spread out over his pallet. He'd gone through everything he owned, but unease still gnawed at him. What had he forgotten? What would he miss only once he'd gone? He was fairly sure he hadn't overlooked any useful supplies, but what about mementos? If something happened to the village while he was gone—and the way the gods had been directing their lives lately, it seemed likely—he might lose something else precious. The amber beads from his grandfather, for example, or the needles from the Stone Wastes for which he'd traded a pair of sturdy shoes to one of the Journeyfolk five rains ago.

He dropped to a crouch, preparing to go through everything again, and then caught himself, swearing under his breath. He was only delaying his journey. He did not want to go. Why were all Laughing Dog's commands so difficult?

His mother's voice. "Have you lost something?" Relaxed, so Knife Strap was not around.

He narrowed his shoulders. He'd not heard her enter and hadn't wanted her to find him mid-preparations. "I don't think so. I'm just…" Now he wished he'd thought of some excuse.

Her gaze flicked to his traveling pack. "Are you going somewhere?"

*Yes, I'm leaving, and you should come, too.* But she wouldn't. Not even for him. He'd known that, always.

"Where are you going?" Her voice took on a dull and emotionless tone. "Is it because of what happened? Because of Left Rabbit? Are you being exiled?"

"No, in fact. I have an important mission from King Laughing Dog himself. I know things have been hard for us these last few days, but it will be worth it. The King trusts me, Mother. He—"

She interrupted, her voice hollow as the trunk of a baobab. "When do you return? How long is he sending you away for?"

He hesitated. "I don't know."

His mother turned away. The little muscles in her neck were taut and bunched. Many little white hairs had joined the black curls there. He didn't remember noticing them before. "Then it's exile. Were you going to tell me? Or were you just going to leave?"

"It's not exile," he insisted, trying to push past that point. "I'm supposed to follow the others, find out where they're going, what they're planning. If they intend to return, we need to be ready. And we need to know what happened to our people. I was going to tell you, of course," he added weakly. "And you're not going to be alone. I've made sure that you'll be looked after."

She was silent. Then her back heaved several times, and he knew that she was crying.

"You'll be okay, Mother. I promise." He squeezed her shoulder and felt the bones, light and delicate, like bird bones, roll beneath her skin.

"Of course I'll be okay. I'm always okay. But you. Who is going to look after you out there?" She turned back, staring up at him. Her eyes were wet, but her mouth was a hard line.

He chuckled uncertainly. "I… don't need looking after, Mother. I'm a hunter."

"My brother was a hunter. He stepped in a hole and broke his leg out where there was no one to help. You think that can't happen to you?"

"No, but I won't be traveling fast. I'll be okay."

"Snakebite. Wildfire. Travelers. Leopards. Maybe you go too near the forest. Maybe something comes out of it after you. Maybe the people you're following sneak up on you in your sleep. You need someone else with you."

Mirage had to admit, it would be far safer to travel with someone else. Not to mention less lonely. "I know, Mother, but the village can't spare anyone else. We've lost too many hunters and craftsmen already. Kwaee Laughing Dog will need everyone available to provide for the people and fight Kwaee."

His mother nodded slowly and looked at the ground. Then she walked across the tent to her pallet and stared down at it, silently. Her breaths came as slow as sleeping. Neither she nor Mirage's father were well-named, people often said. A knife strap was for restraint—it held your knife and kept it out of your hands, but Knife Strap was always ready, always on his toes for a fight. And Dry Grass? Mirage could think of nothing less like his mother than something that kindled so quickly and burned so hot and fierce. Oasis Reed, they ought to have called her. Something trampled by creatures in search of a drink.

Now she knelt at the side of her bed and picked through her belongings, selecting different items from them to make a small pile. Despite himself, Mirage smiled, touched by the gesture. "I don't need any of that, Mother. I have my own supplies."

"You'll be all on your own out there. And maybe it's a better place for you right now. No one in the village… respects what you did for us. For the King. They won't let me work with them."

"You'll be all right."

"You need me." His mother folded the small pile she'd assembled into a hide and tucked it in her travel pack. "So I'm coming with you."

Mirage stared at her. She'd hoisted her pack up onto her shoulders. Her face was as hard and severe as a god mask. "You can't—that's ridiculous! I don't know how long I'll be gone or how far I'll travel."

"I've traveled before," she reminded him. "You think you followed the rains by yourself?"

"But—but it's too dangerous! What if something happened to you? I can't do my duty to the King and make sure you're fed and safe."

"I'm not *helpless*. I can find food. I can do things that need to be done." She must have seen the argument in his face. "Don't you stick out your chin at me. This is my decision. I'm going to come with you. I'm going to look after my boy."

"Mother, when have you *ever* looked after me?" He regretted the words as soon as he spoke them, but by the eye of Wem, they were true, weren't they? Where had she been when Knife Strap had knocked him to the ground time after time? What had she done to stop him from breaking Mirage's little finger in his sleep that time Mirage had called him a dung beetle? It wasn't her fault, not really. She was simply weak and timid, and Knife Strap's brutality could be as sudden and irresistible as a storm.

His mother turned her head as though slapped, but her fingers gripped her pack straps more tightly. "I'm coming with you. And if you don't let me walk out with you today, I'll follow you at night. You've told me where you're going," she added quickly, heading off his protest. "And it won't be hard to follow. But I'd prefer to leave before Knife finds out we're going."

He rubbed at his chin, feeling the patchy beard that had been growing over the last several rains. Perhaps it couldn't hurt to let her come a little ways. Once she learned how arduous and tedious the journey would be, she'd turn around. She'd head back. She might be defiant now, but not after a few days journey through a landscape stripped bare of anything edible or useful by a traveling tribe. The mood would pass. He knew her too well.

~

They didn't speak to his father before they left. In the early afternoon, he would probably be in the flint quarry gathering stone, and that was a good walk east of the village. Dry Grass left something on her pallet for him, but Mirage didn't see it clearly and didn't ask. And though no one lifted their eyes to them or acknowledged their departure, plenty of people saw Mirage and his mother heading out of the gate with their packs.

No one said goodbye—not even the fire hunters—but Mirage caught a few expressions on his way out of the gate. The people looked relieved. So strange to be leaving everyone he had ever known and somehow feeling *less* alone. He was glad, he decided, that his mother had come along after all, if for only the first few days.

She strode ahead, her shoulders back. "We should probably hurry," she said. "They might be slow, but the sooner we catch up, the better."

Mirage was inclined to agree: the less time they spent catching up, the more they'd have to scavenge for supplies. Not to mention putting more distance between them and Knife Strap. He looked back, wondering if his father would care that they had left. Or if anyone would even tell him where they'd gone. Following two people if you didn't know they were walking in the footsteps of sixty would be impossible.

His mother was already a good distance ahead, striding forward with her head high. She never once looked back. Ahead of her, the savanna rippled in the afternoon sun. Midday was certainly not the best time to start a journey, but that was the thing about leaving a place you love. It's never a good time.

He hurried after.

# 2
# Godling

A crack of thunder swallowed up Doto's roar as Clay slammed him against a tree. Rain soaked his fur. The tree broke against his shoulder, sharp wooden splinters jutting into his chest and side.

Clay's fangs flashed in the rain; with a snarl, he bit at Doto's neck. It was surely meant to be a nip of passion, the way mating animals tugged at the other's scruff while in rut, but Clay could not be used to the finger-thick knives that had replaced the flat little seed-teeth that fire bearers were accustomed to. Doto yowled in shock—he had not experienced pain in his own forest since he was a cub and Kwaee had seen fit to punish him.

Clay paused. His breath clouded the rainy air with steam. "I didn't mean to. Are you all right?" Worry tinged his voice, but his eyes were clouded with passion, begging for permission to continue.

"Yes." Doto nestled back against Clay's belly and chest, offering his bent neck again. The bite had healed instantly, though the feeling of his hot blood soaking into his fur with the rain was strange. More strange was the insistent press and thrust of Clay's arousal inside him, a sweet and hungry need, unyielding. Clay had never taken him this way before, and Doto wasn't certain he liked the sensation. There was discomfort, but the feeling was drowned out by arousal, as though a fist had clenched inside him and was forcing him into agonizing lust, making his own erection jut against his soft-furred belly, squeeze, and drip his heat there to mingle with cool rain.

Clay's passion now was fierce and unrestrained; his powerful thrusts seeded a deep and exquisite ache somewhere inside Doto. He clung to Clay, exhilarated by the strength in his mate's new body, just as he was worried by the fresh weakness in his own. How could someone else root this electric pain in him, here, in the forest, where he was god? Why did he shudder and shiver? Why was he lost and confused?

He suspected that these emotions and feelings wracked him because he had surrendered his power. He had given up some integral part of his godhood to resurrect the only person he had ever loved, and as his life and power had filled Clay, so had something of frailty and mortality entered Doto. He was weak. His limbs were heavy. His connection to the forest remained, but less absolute—where once he could have commanded it to obey him, now the force of his divinity was like a wind. It could move the forest, but it could be resisted. God he might be yet, but he had given half of his divinity to Clay, and he had only been half-god to begin with. His mother had been a fire bearer, one of the old enemies of the forest. And that meant that he, Doto, was now perhaps only one-quarter god.

And his mate was now drunk on that immortal essence. Doto knew the storm, at least, couldn't be Clay's doing. Forest gods had never owned dominion over the weather. But no one would mistake Clay for a mortal now. With his urgent thrusting, the forest moved. Roots and tendrils coiled around Doto's body, around his ankles and waist and throat, stroking and tugging at him, resonating with Clay's desires. Tree branches strained with the urge to create life, new leaf buds forming at their tips and erupting into young green leaflets that had never tasted sunlight. Flowers bloomed in the pouring rain, stamens swelling taut and heavy with pollen, cups bobbing as they filled with water and overflowed, spilling onto the ground in heavy streams.

He would have felt distracted from his mate by the shifting, animated world around him were that world not now also partly Clay. He could feel the energy, the life of Clay, in the vines that caressed and clung to him, in the delicate petals that sheltered from the rain under his body and kissed at his exposed flesh, making him shudder and buck his hips. His climax threatened to take him before he was ready. With stubborn determination, he pushed it away. He would not be under anyone else's control. He sent his own will into the world around him, commanding it to leave him be, ordering the cool, smooth leaflets insinuating themselves around his erection to retreat, to respect his divinity.

*Out, out*, he sent his mind. *Into leaf and vine.* But Clay's presence was there to meet his own. It greeted him with an awareness of another. Doto had never felt that in the forest; though he shared power and dominion with Kwaee, they had never confronted each other in that way—neither sent his mind into the forest when the other was there.

Clay felt no such forbearance. He embraced Doto in the divine world as completely as in the physical. No barriers stood between them—the power of one forest god blended and dissolved into that of another, and there, inside the life of the forest, Doto lost himself. He was in his body and in Clay's as well. For a moment they groped, confused, blinking through two pairs of eyes, trying to understand what had happened. They could not remember who they were, but they were connected by something deep and powerful, and it compelled them to mate. They thrust and pushed back against their own rocking need. They gripped themself too tightly. They bit their neck again and shuddered at the novelty of the pain. They rocked against the soft fur and lean, powerful muscle of their bodies. They called the forest to them again; they wrapped themselves in their domain. They stroked at themself; they clenched around their other self, and in unison they released, yowling in twin voices at dual pleasures.

The passion coursing through them ebbed. They were half-astonished that they did not feel exhausted after such exertion, but then remembered they were god now. No, not now. Always. They had always been god. Part of their mind struggled at their unison. They were not one person, but two. Crouching in the pouring rain, they pulled themselves free of each other, physically and mentally.

And then Doto was himself again. He crawled away from Clay and clung to the wet ground, reeling. He clutched at his sides as though with his paws he could hold his spirit inside his body, keep it from spilling out into the world like rainwater through the petals of a flower. He was soaking. The rain never used to fall on him. Without thought he had always directed the air about him to carry those falling drops around him, leaving every strand of fur clean and dry. Now he was drenched. He felt heavy and bedraggled. He was glad not to be two gods anymore, but now he barely felt like one.

He glanced over at Clay, who still lay on the ground, staring up at the thunderous sky, gold-green eyes wide with amazement and, Doto suspected, deep confusion. He'd tasted some of that when the two of them had joined. All these changes were too much for Clay. They'd overwhelmed him, and now he was like a blade of grass caught by a river, rushing helplessly downstream, trying not to drown in his own passions. Fragments of his memories fluttered through Doto's mind yet; images of fire bearers that he'd cared for: a woman with laughing eyes and round cheeks; the elderly fire bearer that had come into the forest calling for Clay; the two brothers, one of whom had murdered Clay in front of Doto. There was fire and thirst and joy in those memories, but they shredded even as Doto examined them, carried away like spider thread in high wind.

He was glad to be rid of them, glad to be himself in his own body once more. He had already lost enough of himself for one god's lifetime. No more, he swore to himself. Not one bit more. If he lost anything else, there might not be anything left.

Clay still lay on the ground, entranced, and so Doto left him there. He was immortal now. He would be fine on his own in the forest.

Crouching, Doto sprang up into the branches of the trees. He shook out his fur, willing the water to leave it. It took some focus to keep the rain from falling on him and soaking him again. He ran through the treetops, leaping from bough to bough, careful to catch with his claws at each jump. After he'd healed Clay's foot the first time, he'd learned that the forest didn't respond to him as quickly. If he wasn't mindful, he could trip on a root or misplace a step and fall. Now he was even more weakened. He doubted a fall could hurt him, but it was… undignified.

For a long while he ran, and he did not stop until he was alone. He huddled on the upper limb of a giant pear tree, sinking his claws into the bark with a bit of vicious satisfaction. This was where he was meant to be: alone in his forest. He felt exhausted, in a way he had not since his trip across the savanna. He was seized by an urge to keep running, to escape, to find some tunnel through the earth to the world before any of this had happened, to the world where he was alone and unafraid and where nothing would ever change.

~

Clay could not find himself. He was carried up the bark of trees by thirsty branches. He cried his confusion from the mouths of startled birds. The earth embraced him as he crawled through it. Somewhere in the forest was a body that was now his, but he didn't know it well enough to find it. He felt a surge of panic and leapt into the air, carried up by a thousand wings, beating with sturdy, urgent flaps; whirring away with whisper-softness.

There were too many sensations now, the world and wind flowing around him. He dizzied with the sight of the forest streaming to him through uncountable eyes: some fracturing into myriad discs; others registering only fuzzy light and darkness; still others feeding the world to him in fine, crystalline detail and in ranges of colors his mind had no names for.

Time, too, split and broke in his senses. To some of his eyes the clouds of the storm funneled through the sky like a flash flood, boiling and churning as no clouds ever had. And yet raindrops hung in the air, massive gourd-shapes, shuddering and rippling as they drifted downward past his whirring flight paths, and through them the forest hung upside down. The separations between racing time and the frozen world tugged his mind farther and farther until he felt he would be torn apart. He screamed in uncountable voices. He tried to close his arms tightly about himself to shut out the world.

He willed it all away. The impossible sensations vanished with an abruptness that was almost painful, like the ringing in one's ears after a thunderclap. And then he was one being again, the ground cool and wet beneath him, his fur heavy and sodden. His arms were clutching around his face, forearms over his eyes, solid muscle that was his now, though still not familiar. How long had he been lying there, lost? Time was—no, he could not think about time. When he tried, his mind began to unspool again like a ball of twine.

He opened his arms. Above him, the trees and plants had knit themselves into a protective shelter, dozens of clasping wooden fingers interlacing themselves into a fist to shield him from the world he'd been lost in. Rainwater streamed between the cracks in the twisted trunks and stalks.

Clay rolled to his feet, crouching in the shelter that had constructed itself around him. The movement felt natural and easy, and it disconcerted him. He ought to be shaking. His heart should be sprinting in his chest; he should be gasping for ragged breaths. But he felt nothing. His body was as calm as though he had woken from restful slumber. It was disconcerting.

Standing upright, he placed clawed fingertips against the tangled plants, wondering if he would be strong enough to push them aside, or if—but even as he considered it, stems untangled, parting like cloth before his touch. With some dismay, he saw that they had damaged themselves in their efforts to shield him, the trees especially. Their trunks were shattered and splintered, and as they shifted to move upright once more, they listed and broke further. One larger trunk cracked and, pouring collected rainwater off of it in cataracts, came crashing to the ground, snapping lianas free, its heavy limbs bouncing at one end.

He'd killed it. Without even trying. Without even being aware of what was happening at the time. Another tree groaned and listed further; it would surely fall before the storm was over. He put his hand to it as though he could soothe it. Perhaps he could? Maybe it could feel the divinity in him, concerned and remorseful. The pads of his fingers pressed against the rough, splintered bark of the fallen tree, softened by rain, and beneath that, something more. He felt the tree's pain. It was not a sensation, not pain as he knew it, but something similar: a registering of damage, a hot crisis in its splintered ends. It sensed things slowly, but it did sense them. Clay's nose twitched. Sharp, desperate odors filled the air around the trees, warning other plants of the damage.

He'd never meant to hurt anything. He'd never asked permission of its spirit. A strange feeling sparked inside his body, a kind of exhilaration, and it rose, growing bigger, more overwhelming. Occasionally, while out hunting, he'd been surprised by storms blowing in from the east with terrible suddenness and violence. He'd lain flat in the grass, covering his head with his arms as the wind rolled dark clouds each as massive as Ogya-Bepow above him and lightning seared the air. He'd trembled in awe and fear at the power of Father Wem.

He felt that same awe and fear now, but this time, the wind was inside him. The clouds roiled in his chest; the lightning sparked behind his fingertips. He clenched his fists at his chest, trying to contain it—but no, he could direct it.

The words formed in his mind: *Out, out.* Around him the wind rose, ruffling his fur. The strange, awed feeling rose inside him, blooming hot and ecstatic in his fingertips. *Out, out. Into—*

A leopard's roar cut through the air, startling him out of his reverie too late to brace for the impact of Doto's powerful, compact body slamming into his side, knocking him away from the broken tree. For a brief, disorienting moment, he was in the air, and then he struck the ground with Doto atop him, sliding through wet leaves and mud. The blow hadn't hurt at all, but it had startled him badly, and before he even realized his panic, he was slapping at Doto with both hands, his fingertips feeling tight and stony. His breath hissed from his mouth, loud and full of warning. He hadn't known he could make a sound like that.

Doto flinched backward at Clay's flailing, but his eyes stayed serious, his paws firmly clamping Clay's shoulders to the ground. He didn't feel as strong as he once had, but his grip was still unbreakable. "What in the name of Wem do you think you're doing?" he roared.

Clay squirmed under Doto, trying to pull free, panic still coursing through his blood. "I wasn't doing anything, I was only… touching the tree, and—"

All of Doto's very large, very predatory teeth were bared, his lips pulled back in a snarl. "I felt what you were doing. You were about to *heal* it."

"No," Clay stammered. "No, I was trying to… to put it… back together." His mate stared at him as though he were no more intelligent than an insect. "Which would be… which would be the same as healing?"

Doto leaned down until his predator's teeth were inches from Clay's face. "Never, ever try to heal anything. Promise me. Give me your word."

Clay's mind scattered down a thousand directions. Moments ago he'd been lost in the entire world, and now the only person who even knew and cared that he was alive was roaring in his face. He couldn't hold onto his thoughts. "But what if… what if—?"

"Do you want to become mortal again? Maybe to die? And to give all that power that I gave to you to some tree?" Doto released Clay's shoulders, clenching his fists. "Do you understand what's happened? I'm less now than I ever was. I gave you so much. And you would throw it away on a plant? Who even knows what kind of god a tree would be?" He knitted his brow and shook his head. "Swear it to me, Clay. You must."

Clay stared up into those gold-green eyes, eyes that stared into him, pinched with worry. They were the eyes of a god who loved him, who spoke to him, commanding a vow, a promise. He wanted to say yes, but his voice caught like a bur in his throat. He bit his lower lip, feeling the unfamiliar jut of his fangs. "Doto, I can't."

The god stared at him in naked exasperation and then threw his paws up into the air. "You can do it and you must! I will not lose you. If I can make a promise never to kill a fire bearer without need, then you can make a promise never to heal!"

Clay slid out from beneath him, rolling to balance on the balls of his feet. "But Doto, what if it's someone I care about? What if it's important? What if it's someone from my village?"

"You would give another fire bearer my divinity? Would they then come and live in the forest with us? Share our temple?"

"Doto, what if it's *you?*"

Doto flattened his ears. He looked away with a dismissive snort. "I will not need healing. Gods are not mortal. Even part gods are not. I am as impossible to kill as my father, or Ogya. And so are you."

Clay stared at him. What Doto had said was a thing too big to fit in his mind. He stood, backing away, feeling the stretch and pull of muscles at the bases of his ears as they flattened just like Doto's.

The leopard god paced toward him, his unblinking gaze steady. "You are behaving very strangely, Clay. You look like a frightened cat. Your fur is all standing out, but I will not be intimidated if you look larger."

"But you said that I—that I—"

"Are impossible to kill. Yes. You will not die. Unless Ogya or another angry god destroys your temple."

"But I haven't got a temple."

Doto tilted his head. "Of course you have. Can you not feel it? It beats within you like your heart. And there I am with you."

Clay put his paw to his chest, sliding his fingers through the white fur that covered it, over the lean, hard muscle that did not feel like his own. He *was* acutely aware of his body now, but surely that was only because everything was so strange and different.

"Not there," Doto said in an irritated voice. "This flesh is not you. The temple is you. *Feel it*, far away, calling you." And then, as Clay felt his mind begin to slip outward into the surrounding world again, Doto added hastily, "Not there. Focus. Feel where you come from. Can you sense it?"

And then Clay could. It was distant from his ears and nose and yet close all the same, as close as his thoughts. It sung to him as though it was the sunrise, and his heart the sun. There was something delicate within him, so *awake* that he could feel the heat of the day on his leaves and petals. The breeze touched him, and he gave before it and released the scent of his nectar into the air. Languorous insects hovered in the warm draughts of his lungs, and cool water poured down his spine and pooled in his belly, where fish idled among his mossy stones.

He settled out into the feeling, exploring the boundaries of this private world. Unlike the terrifying and disorienting sensation of losing himself into the forest, this felt like huddling down at home, of retreating from everything else in the world. Here everything was safe and familiar and gentle. A sublime peace suffused him. He floated in the air of his own being. Coolness spread across him, and the petals of his flowers curled inward, and cricket song stirred his leaves. Then warmth, and he unfolded, naked before the sky, stretching toward the bright and encouraging face of Wem. He spread and grew, expanding in that power, tasting air full of nourishment. He wiggled his fingers and birds burst from his branches in an explosion of color and excitement. He dug his toes deep, deep into the earth, strong enough to crack boulders with them, brushing against the loamy domain of the world's mother, Fam.

And now he remembered her, he longed for her, to speak to her again, like when she'd come to his tent before he died. That was important, he sensed, distantly. There was something she'd told him, something that he was supposed to remember to tell Doto—

"*Clay,*" an insistent voice said in his ear. He flicked it, trying to ignore the voice. "Clay!" Louder this time. Irritated, he gathered himself up and tried to reduce himself back into the small feline body that was newly his own. It felt a frustrating, unnecessary task, like attempting to pack up too much for a trip he did not intend to take.

His eyes opened. Doto was lying next to him with a bored expression, his chin on his paws. "That is enough," the leopard said.

"Oh, Doto, it's so wonderful. Just a few moments more, to grow used to it."

"You have been sitting there for two days already."

"Two days?" Clay repeated in shock, and then he thought of the coolness and warmth. Night and day, so quickly? His tail switched and tugged free of grasses that had grown around it.

"Indeed, and Ogya continues to burn the forest unhindered. Many trees and creatures died of his blaze while you dreamed. It is time now to teach you to be a god so that you can help us to stop him."

"I didn't know it was so long. It was so wonderful there."

"Of course it was. It was your pure divinity, and all gods love themselves deeply. Why do you think my father sits ever in his temple and seldom leaves? I would not see you lost to it as he was, with year after year disappearing. We have a responsibility to Wem's creation now."

Clay disentangled himself from the grass and stood. He stretched out his legs and back, but this was more from habit than any need: there was no stiffness in his limbs. It was as though he had only just sat down.

"Now you have seen your divine self. That is what every god must protect. If your lands were wide and far reaching, you could move your temple at will. But you and I have no lands—all of that belongs to my father. So we cannot move it. Happily, we are secreted deep within my father's dominion. Few could find us there, and fewer still could reach it. We would turn the forest against them to protect it."

"I would give my life to protect it," Clay breathed. He was already dreaming of that place of perfect paradise. How wonderful it would be to lie back inside it once more and let a few days more slip by, or a few months, or years, until he was far away from the deaths of his father and the betrayal of his brother. And he could do it at any time.

Doto snorted. "That is a foolish and impossible thing to claim. Do you not understand? You do not die until it does." His expression softened. "But it pleases me to see you care so much for it. It is right and proper that a god should love his temple and himself."

The heat of flush rose to Clay's cheeks and ears. He wondered if it showed through his fur. "My people teach that to think too highly of ourselves is wrong. That it's vanity."

"They are certainly right about that. They are simple fire bearers. But they worship and honor the gods."

"True," Clay answered uneasily.

"And rightly so. Even you cannot deny what you feel for your temple. You wish to treasure it and protect it. It is sacred."

Clay felt that the tracks of the discussion were vanishing into the tall grass. "But Doto, if I slip and I start thinking of myself the way" *—the way you do,* he barely stopped himself from saying— "the way you mean, that's arrogance."

"A god cannot be arrogant."

"It leads to unkindness. I could begin to think others unworthy of me."

"As they are. They tried to kill you, beloved." Doto's lip curled, showing the daggers of his teeth at the word kill.

"I mean, I could lose myself. I could change. And maybe I wouldn't be worthy of a god's love anymore."

"You were worthy as a fire bearer." His lover's voice filled with fierce and defiant conviction. "As a god, nothing could make you unworthy."

"Even if I change?"

"Even then. Only one thing could lessen you." Doto took Clay's paws in his, spotted fingers closing tightly around them. "If you were to heal another. Then that beautiful place would wither and fade. It would be wrong to let that happen, wouldn't it?"

"Yes." Clay was surprised at how passionately he agreed with Doto, but that place, that temple—he could not imagine anything more beautiful and wondrous. His instant love for it did not feel like the pride of achievement or in physical appearance, perhaps because he did not see himself in it.

"Then you must promise me," Doto said. "Promise that you will not heal another and let that beauty fade. Do not make me lose you, for I have given half of myself to you. If you lose your temple, you could die, and if you die, I lose myself. And how could I ever protect the forest then? Would you send me into mad grief like my father? If you will not promise for love of yourself, then promise for the love of me, and the forest, and everyone who will suffer without you."

Clay felt his ears flatten again. To have Doto's request stated in such drastic terms was almost too much to take in. But Doto *had* once made a promise not to kill. Perhaps a promise not to heal was not so unfair a request, especially if healing something meant he could lose Doto. Still, the promise was not easily made. What if he should be called upon to use his power to save someone important to him, like Cloud, or perhaps even Doto? The old stories were full of unwitting fools making vows that proved costlier than they could ever have imagined. And now he was among gods and magic, in the middle of one of the old stories. Was not this very situation the reason these stories were told?

Doto's tightening grip betrayed his distress. "Please, Clay. Please. I among perhaps all others in the world know what this sacrifice costs. Will you trust me?"

And so it came down to that. Trust. All the ifs and maybes and worries drained from Clay's mind. "Of course I do, Doto. I trust you." He inhaled deeply. "I promise not to heal anyone or anything with magic."

As the words left his lips, Doto slumped in naked relief. "It is good to hear that. You have always revered divinity. I do not understand why you would balk when it is within you." He turned his gold-green eyes back to Clay. "And this is your first lesson of godhood: that you are sacred. You are your temple, and from your temple extends the forest. And the whole world needs the forest to thrive." He pressed a clawed forefinger to Clay's chest. "You are holy and vital. The world depends on you as it depends on all the gods. It is your duty to preserve yourself, and so preserve all the world. Were your power to be lost, the forest would diminish."

The notion stirred unease in Clay's chest. His father, his mother, and the Teller had always stressed humility, that as one of the People, he owed his allegiance and reverence to all the gods, and that he shared his place in the world with all the other animals and plants and stones and clouds. To think his spirit to be greater or more deserving of life than any other was an affront to Mother Fam, who bestowed all life to everything as she saw fit, and to Father Wem, who had shaped the unliving world to his own inscrutable design.

That had been the crime of Laughing Dog, hadn't it? In his arrogance, he thought himself equal to the gods, and had challenged them, contested them, and defied them. And now he had lost himself to their designs, caught up with Ogya in an apocalyptic war with Kwaee. He had imprisoned, tormented, and poisoned his own people, and had even ordered the murder of his own brother. He was lost now, unrecognizable within the thrall of Ogya. That was where arrogance took you.

But it was not arrogance to know your strength. It was not humility to deny it.

Doto gave him an impatient glance. "If you have finished thinking, it is time I taught you to control your presence. It is not very helpful for you to go disappearing into plants or other animals or" —and here his fingers brushed softly at Clay's shoulder— "even into me. Or the earth, or your temple, or into birds, or anything like that, all the time."

Clay nodded. "I don't mean to. I keep… slipping."

"It is easy to do. But usually very boring. Especially for me, when I must stand around waiting for you to return to your avatar."

"My what?"

"You are your temple. This body is your avatar. It is your link to the rest of the forest. Feel it. Know its shape, every strand of fur, every vein your divine blood pulses through. It is yours. Know it perfectly. Hold yourself within it. Can you do that?"

It was such a bizarre question, Clay almost giggled at the absurdity of it. Could he stay within his own body? He'd have laughed if someone had asked if he could leave it at will. But now he kept drifting—losing himself, or losing his body. He wasn't sure which was which. And he wasn't honestly certain he could answer yes.

So he focused. Instead of sending his mind outward, he sent it inward, feeling out the boundaries of his shape, finding his presence in the center of it. He let the wind blow around him, unmoving. The choir of the forest sang past his ears and he let its notes go without straining to catch or follow them. And as he let these other sensations go, the strangeness of his own body became more acute. His ears tilted toward sounds, and the fine fur that grew over them almost tickled as the breeze caught it. Tail. He had a tail. The muscles that controlled it flexed and curled on their own, tight and then relaxed, a weight pulling at his spine, moving always to balance him, as expressive as a face. He carried tension in his fingers and in the toes on which he balanced, and within that tension he concealed curved knives. His tongue felt thick, cradled between smooth fangs, rasping at the roof of his mouth with a blanket of thorns.

He glanced up into Doto's eyes, gold like the sun, green like the forest. "It's too strange," he said. "This body. It doesn't feel like mine. I think—I think that's why I keep leaving it, maybe. I don't feel like I belong in it."

"I think you look very appropriate in it," Doto said a little stiffly.

Clay smiled. "I don't mean it isn't *nice*. Just that it's not familiar. It's not me."

The leopard relaxed, his tail curling over his toes. He gave Clay an appraising look up and down. "Well, you still look very much like you. Only a superior version. But you are correct that it is not you. We have discussed this. You are—"

"My temple, yes. But being like this… I guess it'll take some getting used to."

"You will," Doto said in a knowing tone. "But for now, learn where your own edges are, as you learn the border of the forest and savanna. Call them to mind if you feel yourself drifting. You will anchor yourself soon enough. Once you have, I will teach you to send your mind out deliberately into other things. Not in this accidental sloppy way that you seem to enjoy doing."

Words echoed in Clay's memory: *Out, out, into flesh and bone, into blood and scar.* He couldn't remember ever having heard them; they were like the words to an old song long forgotten. He turned his mind away from the thoughts; right now he felt as slippery as a fish caught in clawless fingers, ready to wriggle away and back into the stream of the forest. No. Find your edges. Hold onto them.

He wrinkled his muzzle and his whiskers twitched, talking to him of the movements of the air. The rich scents of the forest entered his nostrils—*his* nose. Sensory information conveyed to his body. He curled his toes, feeling where the forest floor ended and his skin began. He let the delicate movement of every strand of fur remind him of his own boundaries and anchor him there.

"You are learning." Doto nodded approvingly. "I can tell."

"I do feel more solid. Heavier, I think. Was it like this for you at first? Did you have this kind of trouble?"

Doto snorted. "How should I remember that? I was an infant." A bit more gently, he added, "But I have lost myself in my temple. And on my father's throne, with the whole forest at my toes. I know what it is to forget your body. Now that you have found your own borders, sink your roots into them. Stay in your own hide."

"I don't know what you mean," Clay protested.

"You will feel it with time. Now. Use your ears, your nose, your eyes, your god-sense. Taste the wind. Smell the forest—not only this part, but all of it at once. Listen to the sound of it breathing. A god must be aware of all his domain as much as he can."

"I'll try."

"But stay in your avatar this time," Doto warned him. "Do not stray."

"All right." Clay listened and immediately plunged into a forest of infinite sounds: the calls of birds; the rasp of monkey fingers on bark as they climbed; the delicate footsteps of insects; the furrowing of the soil as things crawled beneath it. He heard the trees moving in the wind, and the creak of their bark as they grew with inexorable but audible slowness. He heard the shapes the breeze made when it blew in circles. His ears twitched around, trying to follow each of them at once and failing.

"You are distracting yourself. Do not hunt an individual sound. Listen to the whole of them at once."

That was an analogy that Clay could understand. When hunting deer or eland with his brothers, it was a mistake to try to follow any single animal, as any individual's movements would be wild and erratic to escape predation. You had to be ready to see everything, hear everything, and follow nothing. So you learned to unfocus, to let your eyes and ears take in the whole of the herd at once, and then discrete movements transformed into an understandable whole. The motions of the herd would become fluid and certain.

As then, Clay mentally withdrew from the sound, letting it pour into him without tracing any one thread. And the disparate sounds dissolved into a whole: not the movement of one tree, but all of them. Not the call of one bird, but an entire chorus of birdsong joined in endless harmony. He heard the movements of insects following hot sunbeams as the sun moved across leaves. The forest now sounded not like uncountable tiny living things, but one massive creature sprawled across the face of Fam.

"It's—it's..." he stammered, the immensity of what he was witnessing stealing the words from his tongue.

"I know. You are hearing it. Good. This is a tiny shadow of what it is like to sit on my father's throne. You and I can observe our forest from a distance. He can dive deeply into it. He can become the forest, all of it at once. It is difficult even for my own mind to handle. But listening like this is enough to observe the forest, to be aware of it and know if something is wrong, and that is a god's purpose." He smiled. "It was listening to the forest that first led me to you. I heard your... drums."

"The Cry of the Dead," Clay said, remembering.

"Yes. Now that you are hearing, breathe deeply. Smell and taste the air."

Obediently, Clay inhaled as deep a breath as he could—and he kept inhaling, as though his lungs were impossible to fill. At first, he breathed in the air around him, smelling the rich earth, the grass, his own curious new scent, sweet and electric, and then Doto's, so like his own, but older, tasting of a thousand deaths and lives. And then he breathed deeper and smelled the grove: every animal that had wandered through it in the past week; the sour tang of centipedes in the soil; the warm, salty pinions of recently molted parrot feathers; the hot sunlight releasing fresh herbal air from leaves of the trees. How he could recognize all these scents when he had never detected them before, he couldn't understand, except that it must be another gift of divinity. And then he was breathing deeper still, taking in the air of their little pocket of the forest, and then deeper, and deeper still, until he inhaled from all the woods at once, and he thought his breath must be the wind in the branches of the trees, pulling the clouds across the face of Wem.

He choked. Pain needled in his throat, burning down the forks of his lungs. He dropped to his hands and knees, coughing. "Fire. Smoke. It burns."

Doto's paw gripped his shoulder. "You blocked your sight from it after I brought you back, remember? I showed you how not to look. But smell is harder to block than most other senses."

The memory of the pain after his revival surged back into Clay's memory and he shuddered, instinctively bracing his mind against that awareness lest it return to scorch him again. "The forest is burning. They're burning it. Your father. They're burning... *us*. That's why it hurts so much."

"And you and I must fight them," Doto answered firmly. "Or we die. The forest dies. And without the forest…"

"Nothing lives." Clay spoke the words with a certainty whose source he could not identify. But he knew—he *knew*—that without the forest, the savanna would wither. The waters of the world would turn to sludge and everything living in them would die. The wind tugged at him strangely and he realized that all his fur was standing on end. "We have to stop them," he said, trying in vain to pat down the bushing fur on his arms and legs. "Whatever it takes."

Doto gave him a pleased smile. "We do. But not yet. You are not ready. You have much training left before you can call yourself a proper god."

Clay coughed again, trying to clear the sting of faraway smoke from his lungs. "My brother will be there, won't he?"

"The one who killed you? Yes. I suppose he will. But he will have the power of Ogya on his side. Do you wish vengeance on him?"

"No!" Clay protested, but then paused, frowning. "I don't know. He killed me. I ought to feel more. I ought to feel… something. But when I remember it, it's like it happened to someone else. The feelings are far away, somewhere in some dark part of me, where I have to grope for them."

"When first I healed your paw, I felt changed. Your emotions were strong. They overwhelmed me. I did not know how to act when I felt them. Perhaps it is a part of being human. It makes you weak and strong at the same time." Doto sighed. "I accustomed myself to it in time, much as I accustomed myself to walking outside the forest without my power. And then after I brought you back, the feelings were even stronger. Again I had to learn how to control them, keep them calm. I think I took them from you."

Clay stared at the ground, not liking this idea at all. He had gained so much: the freedom to be with his mate, the affinity with the forest and the new abilities he was only now learning, the chance to help save the forest and his people. But he had lost those people at the same time, hadn't he? And if Doto was right, had he lost something even more vital?

He groped inside himself for the feelings that eluded him. There they were, within him, still present: joy at being with Doto, deep love for his mate, yearning for his mother, grief for his father, fury toward Laughing Dog for his betrayal, and deep grief and hurt toward Great Ram for killing him—but all of these felt small, difficult to grasp, as though he were trying to pick up beads with fingers too large and clumsy to hold them. Only one was simple to latch onto, and that was his anger. Laughing Dog was burning the forest. In his arrogance he thought to remake the world as he wanted. Never mind what the gods understood about the world. Forget who might be hurt, what systems in precarious balance might be destroyed. Laughing Dog thought himself the equal of the gods. And anger at that conceit rose up in Clay like the fires of Ogya-Bepow.

He curled his fingers into fists, his claws biting into the heels of his hands. "We must go stop them now."

Sternly, Doto answered, "I told you that you are not ready yet. You have much left to learn."

"Now!" Clay roared.

Doto's gold-green eyes widened. "Very well, then. We will go and see."

~

The heat near the fire bearers' nest was intense, and the smell worse. Doto wrinkled his nose, trying to shut out the reek of his domain burning. The scent was tinged with something fouler than fire: the rotten-egg stench of Ogya-Bepow.

Here, the brightness of the flame was little more than a hungry orange glow behind the vast clouds of white smoke that billowed through the trees. Most of the birds and animals had fled this area, but he could feel the pain of burrowing mammals beneath the soil, and the desperate scrambling of insects crawling beneath earth and bark as the heat boiled them alive and split their chitin.

He gave Clay a wary glance. His mate had been behaving erratically since transformation, which was not surprising. No mortal could be expected to handle godhood very well. But Doto needed Clay to be predictable now. Ogya was near, and that meant terrible danger. Perhaps he wouldn't be able to kill Clay so far from their temple, but the fire god had imprisoned Sarmu inside a mountain of flame. And pain and loss could hurt people as much as injury. Doto had seen that with his own father. With himself, even, when he believed he had lost Clay.

Clay was crouched low on the forest floor, his tail switching back and forth, his lips curled in a silent snarl.

"What are you doing?" Doto said in a low voice, slinking over to him. "Are you planning to stalk the fire?"

Clay glanced at him. "I'm keeping low to the ground. The smoke isn't as bad down here."

"It cannot injure you."

"Maybe not, but it stinks. And it makes me cough."

Doto rolled his eyes. "Then do not breathe, idiot."

Clay stared at him for a long time, not saying anything. For a moment, Doto wondered if he had said something wrong again. "You are trying it right now, I suppose."

Clay got to his feet. "I didn't know I could do that. So. How close can we get before it actually hurts us?"

"I would not try to find out. The fires are burning back the forest wall constantly. You would not want to be surprised by it." Doto's fur lifted in memory of the absence of all his powers outside the forest, feeling hunger, thirst, sickness, pain, and even torment. The inside of Ogya-Bepow had been almost unbearable with its suffocating heat and scalding stone. He would not like to think what Ogya's personal touch would feel like outside the forest.

"But we can get closer than this." Clay stepped past him, heading toward the orange glow.

"You should not go closer!" Doto's gut tightened with sudden fear, so powerful he felt he was shrinking into the leaves. How did mortals manage this intensity of emotion? All he could think now was that Clay would see his people and foolishly think himself still one of them. He would run to them, out of the forest, and they would hurt him, or Ogya would trap him. Or worse, they would not, and Clay would leave again. Doto found his mate's motivations perplexing and impossible to predict, especially since his ascension to godhood. He ran after Clay across soil that grew warmer and warmer with each step.

His mate disappeared into a drifting wall of yellow-tinged smoke, a fading silhouette, and Doto could no longer hear nor smell him through Ogya's contamination. He followed Clay step by step through the clouds of dead forest, querying the ground for the paths Clay had taken, and receiving weak, dying answers from earth and plant.

He need not have feared that the forest wall would be difficult to trace. Kwaee's power sent it flailing in helpless rage against the pack of ash-smeared fire bearers. Vine lashed against them as flame crawled up their necks; trees swiped their stiff arms and aimed their charred husks at them as they fell. But none of the attacks could land far beyond the forest wall, where Kwaee's magic failed and the forest lost its animation.

Outside that wall, the fire bearers earned the name the gods had given them long ago. They carried great boughs dipped in burning sap and looked for dead leaves and limbs to set alight and carry the blaze further. Across their mouths and nose they had stretched bits of woven plant or animal material—cloth, Clay had called it. Doto could not divine the purpose of this. If it was to disguise them or mask their features, it did a poor job of it. But perhaps, despite their allegiance to Ogya, they did not enjoy the fire. Doto noted that their eyes streamed with tears, and they coughed as Clay had in the smoke.

Some of them stood further back, carrying bent arches of wood tied with animal gut, and they used some form of power with these to send sticks flying into the trees. These sticks had blazing heads of fire, and spattered sparks where they landed, carrying Ogya's curse well beyond the wall of the forest or the reach of the rest of their pack.

Clay stood still, smoke billowing through his spotted fur, his ears folded back. "The ground is so hot." His voice was distant.

"The fire bearers are too fragile to set foot on it. They would burn. Except perhaps that one." Doto nodded toward the one called Laughing Dog, who strode back and forth among his pack of hunters. That fire bearer housed a part of Ogya under his flesh, a twisted shard of the fire god. It made him very dangerous.

He argued with one of his pack, the ash-striped hunter gesticulating insistently toward one section of the forest. There stood an old and mighty tree, made of hard wood and soft bark that drank the daily rains. It would not burn easily. Its skin stubbornly resisted the touch of the fiery brands the hunters bore. Several of those flying sticks the other hunters used sprouted from its higher limbs, their stony heads embedded, their fires gone out.

Laughing Dog spat in the dirt, his saliva evaporating with a hiss. He shouted at the other hunter and strode over to the tree. He raised both hands over his head and shifted from foot to foot, dancing in place. Words that shook with power fell from his lips.

*Ogya the Hungry grants us flame*
*He sears our meat with his sun-teeth*
*The flash of his eyes puts fear to the night beasts*
*We feed Ogya that we may be fed*
*Let his tongues temper our tools*
*Feed Ogya*

*Let his fury clear the paths that we walk*
*Feed Ogya*
*Let him banish all darkness*
*Feed Ogya*
*Let him burn our clay to stone*
*Feed Ogya*
*That his hunger may never die*

The fire bearer was larger than the others, swollen to bursting with power, and as he sang and danced, the light of Ogya's flame glimmered between his fingers. Brighter, with each line, and brighter still. Then it erupted in twin tongues of fire, slathering greedily over the obstinate acacia.

Doto heard its scream: a million shrieks of steam bursting from a million ruptured cells. Its bark cracked and split in the heat, baring its hardwood to the inferno. The power pouring from Laughing Dog's palms sputtered and waned, but the tree was already enswathed in a column of twisting flame.

So. Ogya had taught Laughing Dog a song of power. Or perhaps Laughing Dog had invented it, as Clay had done for Doto. And as Clay's dance could change field to forest, so could Laughing Dog's transform arbor to ash. If only Doto could kill him now—but Ogya was too clever to venture into the forest on his own. Outside it, Doto would be powerless.

And even if Doto could draw close enough to let his claws taste the fire bearer's blood, Ogya might be strong enough to stop it from dying. And though Doto might kill Laughing Dog, he would not kill Ogya. No. Surely he would be burned to ash or pierced with a dozen stone teeth before he had a chance to save himself. Right now Clay needed him more. How might a fledgling god react on seeing his mate burned to death? Of course, Doto would wake in his temple and return to him eventually, but while he was gone, what would Clay do, to himself or to the forest?

Satisfaction aside, there was little to be gained from killing Laughing Dog, and had Clay not made Doto promise he would not harm another fire bearer without need? Doto doubted very much that Clay would permit an exception in this case. Clay seemed very attached to his siblings, even the one who wore fancy decorations on his skin and talked importantly. The one who had killed him.

Doto did not see that fire bearer anywhere and was glad of it. Much as he wished to stop Ogya and Laughing Dog, he carried a special thorn of hatred in his heart for the fire bearer who had murdered his love and thus stolen his divinity. He did not trust himself not to keep his promise around that one. Perhaps now that Clay was no longer a sentimental fire bearer, he would release Doto from the vow. Doto resolved to ask Clay about it sometime when he was not so moody.

Now was certainly not the time for that. Clay's eyes, narrowed to slits in the brightness of the blaze, were liquid with restrained tears. "I can't believe they're doing this. How can they? Don't they know they need the forest? Don't they see that they're destroying their own world?" He raked at his arms and sides as though trying to scratch away invisible flames burning him, his claws tearing wounds that healed instantly.

Doto snorted. "Their kind have always been foolish, Clay. Do not forget that they allied with Ogya long ago."

"After your father attacked them. They had a right to strike back."

"No mortal has a right to oppose us. They are unfaithful. They should be punished for it."

"After the fires?" Clay snapped at him, his voice cutting through the roar of the fire like a stone tooth. "And the drought? And the poison Ogya fed them, and the animal attacks, and the forest dragging people off into it to tear them apart? I think we've been punished enough."

Doto felt a prickle down his spine as his hackles lifted. "We? You are not one of them anymore." He growled each word as though it were a command.

"I still am. They're still part of me, and I'm part of them."

Still this? Still he clung to them, after everything they'd done? As he witnessed them burning the forest, the body of his father, of his mate, of his own power? Frustration slid the claws from Doto's fingertips. "No. You are divine. Why will you not accept that after everything they did? They killed you to prove it, and I will never forgive them for that." Heat flooded his head, and his eyes seemed to burn. There was rage boiling up inside him, a terrible fury. He had never felt any anger so powerful before. It would burst from his mouth, from his fingertips. The scorched remnants of the forest shuddered around him. "You do not belong with them, Clay. You belong with me."

Clay's voice went quiet, a small animal huddling in the smoke. "They're still my people."

Doto's lips curled back over his fangs. "No they are not. They murdered you. They killed the beloved of a god. Do you know what it cost me to bring you back? Do you have any idea? You do not. And now you stand in front of them as they burn us? As they kill us? It is vile. Profane. And they must be *stopped!*"

He clenched his fists and then flung them outward toward the fire bearers in frustration as though he could hurl all his fury toward them in one fell blast. It was, he realized a moment too late, an echo of his outrage at the wall of the fire bearers' nest, but this time, rather than a massive tree, the forest floor vomited up a mass of black stones and sent them hurtling toward Laughing Dog.

For a moment, Doto hung in the split second between his mistake and its consequences—Clay would never forgive him for breaking his promise. He tried to will the stones back toward him, but a god could not break the laws of nature.

They never struck Laughing Dog. As they flew past the charring boundary of the forest, the big fire bearer's eyes flashed orange, and the flying rocks abruptly glowed white hot and burst into pieces with the sound of many small thundercracks.

Shards of hot stone perforated Doto's body, lancing through his cheek, his belly, his knee and shin. He yowled in shock and pain, knocked backward by the blast. The searing blasphemy of fire burned into his bones and muscles, cauterizing divine flesh before it could heal. Igneous worms of pain crawled through his limbs, his gut, his face. Lying in the ashen grass, he turned a terrified glance toward Clay. His mate lay on his side, jaws gasping breathlessly in the smoke.

A sibilant chuckle hissed above the crackle of fire. "Did you think I wouldn't feel you there, godlings? You cannot hide from me."

Billows of smoke coalesced and coagulated into the shape of a massive hyena crouched at the edge of the forest. Its body glimmered like fallen embers. It turned its empty gaze toward Doto, and the shapes of countless scorpions crawled from the corners of its mouth, out of its eyes, its ears, skittering down its neck and forelegs before being reabsorbed by its caliginous bulk.

"Your father could have spared these people, and all their descendants, and their countless progeny, for a thousand years, had he but chosen to sacrifice a son he does not love. Would I not tell my followers how he forsook them?" Scorpions drooled from the corners of the thing's maw and burst into wisps on the forest floor. "And you come to challenge me here? These are the Ashlands now, foolish kittens. And here I reign."

Doto pushed himself up to a crouch, crawling on all fours toward Clay, who was dragging himself further into the forest, away from the flame. Doto's body was healing, but slowly, the burned spots growing around seared muscle and skin, expelling strips of scar tissue, the fiery worms he'd felt before. Clay paused in his crawl, buckling and clutching his stomach as he vomited up slimy fragments of ash-greyed stone.

The apparition laughed again. "Oh, but it seems I have interrupted a quarrel. Surely you do not believe that you will remain devoted to each other. Life among the gods must have taught you, at least, Doto, that a god cannot truly love. He can only possess. Consume. As you have consumed this little fire bearer and made him yours. Just as I will consume you, and your forest, and your father."

Doto struggled to his feet. His wounds were healing, the pain fading, though the memory of it chewed into him, sparking a primal fear he hadn't felt since he was a kitten and his father had punished him with tooth and claw. "We will… we will stop you," he managed.

"I will make you feel such pain as I devour your little temple," the apparition crackled. "I will consume it slowly. I will savor every petal. Every thorn."

"No. No, you can't." Clay's voice growled through obvious pain. He pushed himself upright and staggered to Doto's side. He had received the worst of it, Doto saw: his belly and throat were seared with a score of slowly healing punctures, fur still scorched black where the fragments had struck him. "Please, Lord Ogya, what happened to you? Why are you like this? In the old stories, you were a trickster. Sometimes gr—sometimes hungering for more than others wanted you to take, but you weren't cruel. You didn't try to—to destroy everything. The forest. Other gods. Your own worshipers. Who made you like this? Maybe we can make it right."

The hulk of smoke fixed its crawling gaze on Clay. " 'Lord Ogya,' he says. Even now, so devoted, so respectful toward the one who will devour his mate and his home. I can see why you chose this one, godling. He would whimper and debase himself before any god at all. The only worshiper you could find, I suppose.

"I remember you little bearer. I remember the savory flavor of your people as they fled my advance across the savanna. Their fat popping in my tongues, oh yes." The smoke creature's tongue slathered over its formless jowls, dropping embers.

"No…" Clay sagged against Doto's side.

Doto put his arm around Clay, holding him up. "Come on, let's go. You don't have to listen to him. His words are poison. He lies."

"Oh, but I know so much," Ogya crooned. "Would you like to know how your father died?"

Clay's fur bristled. "No."

"It was I. I devoured him. Well. I wore your brother's flesh then. The big one who thinks himself crafty. Named after my emissary. He's there now." The beast nodded its head toward the shape of Laughing Dog, a dim silhouette hunched oddly in the mist, limp and lifeless. "Perhaps you should go to him, Clay. Ask him how your father tasted."

"You will be *silent!"* Doto roared at Ogya. Clay had all but collapsed into Doto's grip, shuddering, but Doto could feel the brush of Clay's claws at his leg. Good. Anger was better than despair. All the same, he didn't want to risk another moment in the fire god's presence. He dragged Clay backward across the ash, hoping to draw him out of reach of Ogya's words. Clay hung limp in his arms and let himself be drawn.

"Oh, don't go, little fire bearer," Ogya called after them. "Don't you want to know what became of your *other* brother?"

Clay's muscles tensed in Doto's arms. "What did you do?"

"Don't *listen* to him, Clay!"

"What did you do? What did you do?" The words were practically a howl.

"Oh, it's not what I did. It was Laughing Dog. He strangled your dear older brother all on his own. It's why I chose you fire bearers as allies. You always show such initiative."

Clay bucked twice in Doto's arms and then tilted his head back, emitting a low, wordless wail. And all around them, the forest died. Plants sturdy enough to the ash and heat now wilted and fell. Climbing mice that had scurried into the upper branches of the trees to escape the fire dropped out of the branches like rotten fruit, little puffs in the ash where they fell. Insects too slow to escape curled up and expired.

Doto kept his focus on Clay, murmuring in his ear, "Come on. Do not listen to him. Listen to my voice." Step by step, as quickly as he could manage through the smoke and ash, he pulled Clay away from Ogya, hands clasped around his chest, giving him a steady voice as the forest decayed around them. "Please, Clay. Stay with me. Keep your mind here. Don't slip now. Don't go spread out into the forest. Don't return to your temple. Stay here with your avatar. Stay here with me."

Clay hung motionless in his arms, his gold-green eyes staring out into nothing, but Doto kept repeating the words until the sound of the fire faded, until they were alone in the forest. He lay there with Clay in a small clearing, stroking his fingers through the fur on Clay's head, repeating the words, "Stay with me," over and over. Like a mantra. Like a prayer.

# 3 The Long Wild

Cloud's feet hurt. She focused on the pain and let it direct her thoughts. Think about her aching soles, and she wouldn't have to think about where they were going. Because if she started thinking about that too much…

Fortunately, her feet hurt quite a lot. Her knees hurt too, and her left hip, but her feet most of all. She was accustomed to long walks, but those were punctuated with breaks to dig for roots or cut sprigs from bushes or strip bark from trees. She could stop for a while to lean on her stick and admire the clouds on the horizon or contemplate the foolishness of men.

There was no time for that now. The People of the Savanna were on the move. Not that they moved at any rapid pace. Their ranks included many of the old, the infirm, and the young children of the village. Some still struggled with carts or lugged what possessions they had been allowed to retrieve before their exile from the village, though these were few. Laughing Dog and his fire hunters had been severe, forbidding any of them to return and gather their belongings before being exiled.

But a People divided are still a people. Edicts did not have the power to erase friendships or annul family. Runners, loyal to Laughing Dog but friendly to their kin, had hurried back to the village to retrieve necessities. Most of the travelers had water skins, and there were enough knives, bows, and spears to go around. As they traveled, the People gathered what they could find, never venturing too close to any place it looked like the forest grew too thick. Yams grew here and there in the scrub, and on the third day of travel, several of the children found a patch of horned melon that the birds and animals had not yet picked clean.

Between caring for the young, accommodating the pace of the elderly, and foraging for food and supplies as they traveled, the people moved at a rate scarcely faster than a bored porcupine, but it was still unceasing. Food was eaten on the move, and rest was short. They had all seen the unearthly power that Laughing Dog wielded. They all knew that most of their kin remained behind, vulnerable to a King that had ordered his own to be killed and who had an alliance with a malevolent god. And behind them, filling more of the sky every day, the billowing yellow clouds: a harbinger of the destruction of their world. Few wished to stop for long.

Even days from the village, the thick smoke choked their lungs and stung their eyes. Cloud wished for willow bark to ease the pounding headaches all complained of, but her supplies had been destroyed long ago, and she had seen no fresh sources. She did, however, come across a mass of dry elephant dung that was worth collecting. At night she burned sparing clumps of it and allowed those suffering the worst to derive some relief from the curative smoke as well as from the mosquitos it repelled. Fight smoke with smoke, she supposed.

Still, there were no easy remedies for the blisters that had formed on her feet. There was aloe, of course, and oil squeezed from castor beans to keep the chafing spots from worsening into new blisters, but without rest, they'd not heal properly. She kept her feet bound in her leather footwraps so that no one would see her limping. They could not see weakness in her now. Not so early in their journey.

"Cloud." The firm, brusque voice of Ant with a Leaf jarred her from thoughts.

"Yes. Ant." She looked up at the tall woman. She hadn't even heard Ant approach—though she supposed that was one of the things that made her an excellent hunter.

"Are you well? You're limping."

"I'm old. Old people limp." Cloud leaned on her walking stick for exaggerated effect and then wondered why she hadn't been doing so already, as the pressure on her feet eased considerably.

"And you smell of blood. Your feet?"

"Blistered," Cloud admitted. No hiding blood-scent from the hungry, she supposed. "But I don't mind it so much. It keeps me focused. From thinking about…" Perhaps her deeper concerns were better not shared with the people. No sense worrying them over nothing. "About home."

Ant gave Cloud a coolly skeptical gaze. "And what else?"

"Does there need to be anything else? Here we are out in the wilderness running from demons and angry gods. We're in trouble. Real trouble. And I want to take my mind off it for a while."

"All right." Ant walked beside her, but her legs were long. She had the pace of a young woman, and visibly itched at moving so slowly. "Only," she said when they'd gone no more than a hundred paces, "there's something else bothering you. You can tell me, Cloud. I'm on your side. You know that. If there's some way I can help—"

"You can't," Cloud snapped. She immediately regretted the tone. Ant had been so faithful to her through everything. "I'm sorry. It's only that I wish you *could* help. I wish someone could."

Her friend gave her an appraising stare. "You're worried about where we're going. Bogana."

"Yes."

"Is it dangerous? Are there many predators on the way? Bandits?"

"No." Cloud shook her head. "Maybe, but… I'm more concerned about what happens when we get there. You know, many rains ago, some of the People of the Savanna lived there. I was born there myself."

"And Two Broken Hands. Others?"

Cloud nodded.

"But they left. Why?"

"There was a sickness there. A plague. Worse than anything that ever touched the People. It was—" Cloud's chest grew tight at the remembrance. "It was very bad. So my parents and the others fled before it spread to them."

"Do you fear the sickness is still there?"

*Yes. Of course. I fear it so much.* "I don't think that it's likely. It was too deadly, and too long ago. No one would be alive to pass the sickness to others if it were still around."

Ant with a Leaf made a puzzled frown. "Then what?"

"It was the disease, how it… changed people. Not the sickness itself, but the fear of it. Bogana had dark days in its past. They practiced older ways. There were sacrifices to the gods. Blood sacrifices. Young men. Children."

"They killed their own? But that's—that's…"

"Unthinkable." Cloud sighed. "So it was for us. But you saw what that boy Mirage did. Fear and hardship push people to dark places." She looked back at the clouds of yellow smoke drifting above the forest. "I don't know what we'll find in Bogana. I hope it is a people who have recovered. Who have remembered the songs of their ancestors. I'm hoping for a people who will help us stop the destruction of the forest. And the tales in Bogana go back a long, long time, farther than any of us remember now. They may know stories of men who fought the gods or who allied with demons for wealth or power. Perhaps they can tell us how to reach Laughing Dog and bring him back from whatever forces have corrupted him."

"But you don't know?"

"No one has heard from Bogana since my mother left. It's not so strange. They are sea-traders."

"What is a sea-trader?" Ant asked, looking puzzled.

Cloud reached for her dress to worry it between her fingers, then recalled that she no longer had it. It had gone into supplies for bandages. The people had stitched together for her a garment of leather and beads—not quite a queen's garb, but reminiscent of it, at least. It looked fine, but it was not as comfortable as the dress her husband had brought for her so long ago. "A sea-trader is a merchant who searches for people not across land, but over the great water. The people of Bogana know how to make… a kind of tent or house. It floats on the great water like a leaf on a stream, and they catch the wind to pull themselves along."

Ant with a Leaf rolled her eyes. "Now you are offering false fruit."

"It's hard to explain. You'll see."

"So we will learn how to stop Laughing Dog and perhaps calm the forest?"

"If we're lucky," Cloud answered.

"And if we're unlucky?"

Cloud gathered all her worry into her chest and breathed it out slowly. "A dead city. Or worse."

"What could be worse than that?" Ant asked.

Cloud shook her head. "Never mind," she said. "Let's not go hunting shadows." She tightened her grip on her stick and quickened her pace a little, enough that the blisters on her feet protested with hot, wet shouts of pain.

Enough that the aches almost let her forget the buzzing in her head, the malignant droning of a million crawling, black flies.

~

On the sixth day, the wind changed directly, blowing cool and brisk out of the east and carrying the heavy smoke away from the travelers. Heads cleared, stomachs no longer turned, eyes ceased their stinging, and the people praised Wem.

On the seventh day, Ant With a Leaf and Beetle between them managed to bring down two fat buffalo that had separated from their herd, and the people feasted. What they could not eat right away, they dried in the sun and fire. The hardened meat could then be hammered into powder and mixed with bone marrow and berries to keep the rot from it, but this took an extra day.

Cloud was glad of the time to rest; blistering feet could not toughen if they were overused, and she knew she was not the only one of the exiles walking on the outside of her feet to favor torn soles. The route, at least, was simple: follow the setting sun to the great water. Little chance of losing their way. But the terrain in this part of the land was not flat like the open savanna, and she knew from the reports of those who had made their way before that there would be high hills to travel before they reached Bogana.

She was sitting atop a hill—not a high one, but with the promise of climbs to come—and tracing their next day's journey with her eyes when Firefly found her. He was aging, but still a capable enough hunter, and the death of his son Whistling Thorn by Laughing Dog's poison had set his jaw and hardened his eyes to flint.

"There you are," he said, as he came up behind her. "How does the journey look?"

"Better," Cloud answered, "now that we've rested and can take a full chest of air without choking. We've been lucky so far, finding so much food and water."

"Wem be praised," Firefly answered in agreement.

Privately, Cloud doubted he felt very lucky at all, considering the great misfortunes they all lived through, but in times of privation and suffering, any relief felt like a blessing.

"There is something you should know," Firefly said. He crouched near her, lowering his voice. "I suspect someone from the village may be following us."

All sense of rest fled Cloud. "Do you know who it is?"

"I don't. I'm not even certain it's true." Firefly rubbed his hand through his grizzled beard. "Two days ago I set snares, hoping for hare or fowl. This afternoon I went back to check. Two of them had been sprung. By one I found blood. My twine looked as though it had been cut."

"By a knife?"

"I'm not certain. Some animals, caught in a snare, are clever enough to gnaw free. Or a jackal or other predator might have worked it loose."

"But you don't think so."

Firefly shook his head. "It looked like a knife cut to me. And then yesterday, when the smoke began to clear, I thought I saw smoke from another fire, closer. Perhaps one day's journey back. A long, thin snake of smoke. But the air was still clearing, and I may have been mistaken. By the time the wind changed, it was gone."

Cloud breathed out slowly. "I feared Laughing Dog might send someone after us."

Firefly gave a rueful nod. "As did I. If someone is following, they're clever enough to conceal their presence. I found no tracks around the snares, and I've seen no other sign of anyone behind us."

"So probably a hunter."

"That would be my guess."

If there was truly someone following them, what would Laughing Dog want? To kill Cloud? She wouldn't put it past him, not with that *thing* inhabiting his body. She scowled into the distance. They didn't need to deal with this now. Not in addition to everything else. Still. If Laughing Dog—or the thing inside him—was worried enough to send a scout, then that meant they weren't powerless. Maybe this was a sign they were on the right path.

"Cloud?" Firefly prompted her, putting his hand on her shoulder. "What do you want me to do?"

She bit her lip, thinking. "Don't say anything to the people for now. No sense spreading fear without cause. Tell a few of the other scouts or hunters, those you know can keep quiet. And then keep aware. If someone is following us, eventually they'll leave a trace." One that can hopefully be detected over the trample of a couple score of traveling people, she added silently to herself.

"And if we find someone?"

"If you can capture them, do so. We don't need anyone skulking around our campsites in the dark." *That* was a disquieting thought, and she could tell by the tensing of Firefly's shoulders that he shared her unease. Suppose their food was poisoned, or worse?

"Should we set additional watches?"

She considered this. There were already scouts posted at night with torches to discourage wild beasts from bothering them in their sleep. "No," she decided. "If we change our behavior and someone is watching us, they'll know we've detected them. Just be on alert for now."

Firefly's face was grim. "If Laughing Dog thinks us weak and vulnerable, he's mistaken. He may have kept the physical strength of the People, but we have the experience. Our scouts know how to watch and how to listen. We won't be surprised so easily by some puffed up boy or his soldiers."

"Good. And… Firefly? What I am going to ask next may sound mad, but—"

The hunter dipped his head. "You are our leader. We trust you, Cloud."

"Thank you." She smiled but breathed a silent prayer to Fam that she could maintain that trust. "When you watch for him, when you even discuss him or anything else that might be important, no torches, yes? No campfires. Do not speak of where we're going or anything we learn on the way. Not near fire."

If her words unsettled him, he did not show it. He gave her an unblinking nod.

"And tell the others? If gods or monsters watch us from those flames, then we must be circumspect. You saw what Laughing Dog managed. How the flames poured from his hands. And you remember the tales of Ogya."

"The Listener at the Hearth," Firefly answered. "I agree. We must be careful. But Ogya is no monster or demon. First Kwaee and now Ogya? If both gods truly oppose us, Cloud, what can any of us do?"

"If anyone knows, it will be the people of Bogana. They have kept the stories longer than any of us. If there are any that will help us to appease the gods, they will remember them. Even—" She bit the words off.

Firefly gave her a long, searching look, but let it go. "I'll tell the others," he said. "Quietly."

"Thank you." She crossed her arms behind her head and lay back, picking apart the afternoon clouds with her eyes, trying to find the forgiving face of Father Wem in them.

*Blasphemies. Even blasphemies.*

~

In a village, with time to scout and little concern about squandering resources, a council fire could be a regular and welcome affair. On a journey it was a waste of wood and effort. And few had any appetite for a fire after days of walking in asphyxiating smoke.

So there was no bonfire that night. Nor, Cloud resolved, would there be any more between here and Bogana. But they had their Teller, and bonfire or no, the tales still had power. They connected people and reminded them that they were home. Home was their gathering. Home was their stories. Home was their ancestors listening from above to the refrains that drew them all together.

The Teller stood in their midst and told of Adanko the hare and how he became the god of lies. And he told the story of Makobe the tortoise who forgets where he lives in the afternoon and every night sweeps the desert smooth with his belly looking for it.

And he told of how Wem and Fam fought over the right to rule the earth, and how Wem took the sun out of the sky to blind Fam in the night, but Fam sent up the moon to find her way in the darkness. And then Wem held back the rains to dry up Fam, but Fam tapped wine from her palm trees and got him drunk until he recanted. And every drop of wine Wem spilled became an eternal oasis.

The people heard the stories they loved and were at peace. They went back to their pallets with old songs in their ears and home in their hearts.

Cloud returned to the slope where she had sat before and lay back in the grass, her eyes tracing the shapes of stories in the stars. One day, perhaps, her story too would be written up there, and that of the People of the Savanna, and of King First Claw, and of Great Ram, and of Clay. Perhaps he watched them now and interceded with Father Wem for all of them. Poor boy. He hadn't deserved all the trouble he'd seen. But then, he had traveled with gods and seen wonders she never would.

His eyes had been true when he'd told her the story of Doto and how he'd been loved by a god. Recalling that story planted a thorn of fear in Cloud's breast. What would this Doto do to the people who had killed his follower? If the forest hated them before…

She sat up at a rustle in the grass. The Teller stood there, tall in the moonlight. She knew his silhouette by the bushy ring of hair around his bald head, and by his girth. He had always been pleasingly plump, even in the lean times and their long journey across the savanna.

"You're a long way out, Cloud."

"No tent to hide in."

"You've always been a loner," he said in an agreeable tone.

"Something you want?"

"I'm afraid I've had terrible news."

Cloud could tell by the humorous lilt in his voice that the news was not terrible. "Yes, I noticed right away. Your hair is falling out."

"Is it?" He patted at the top of his head. "Ahh, no! Well. I can hardly worry about that with this latest crisis. We seem to be all out of jugo beans."

Cloud smiled, though she doubted he could see it in the night. "Well you had better find some more. You know I can't abide a skinny man."

The Teller sat down beside her. The night wind carried his warmth to her. He still smelled the same as he had all those years ago: spice and musk and dry grass. "You're leading us well."

"I know."

"Knowing and hearing, not the same. Someone should tell you. They all should tell you."

"You're the Teller. I suppose it's your job."

He turned, leaning over her, his features indistinct in the darkness. "I told you before, long ago. You should be a queen. And here you are."

"Here I am," she agreed.

"It took you long enough."

"I had things to do. But I'm here now." She sighed deeply, turning to stare past him at the sky. "I wish it hadn't taken me so long. So many terrible things have happened. And now I'm so old."

"You are very old. You're full of knowledge and stories. They have filled you up and made you priceless. But to me…"

She reached for him despite herself, her fingers grazing his cheek. "Basket?" His name, the one given to him before he was the Teller, came unbidden to her lips. He'd hated his own name, and she used to tease him with it, but now it was something else. Intimate.

"To me you are still that girl studying in the healer's tent, one who could do anything. I still think about—"

She put her hand to his mouth. She locked away the memories of her husband Wind, and her betrayal of him, and his death. Some stories should be consigned to silence. Not forgotten, perhaps. But allowed to go unspoken, so that new ones could be told.

He kissed her hand, his beard tickling her palm. She let it slide down his chin to rest against his chest. The tight coils of his hair tangled under her fingertips. That was different. As a young man, he'd been smooth and taut under her touch. She withdrew her hand, looking down, and he caught her wrist. "No," he murmured to her. "It isn't."

"Isn't what?"

"Too late."

She wanted to protest that she hadn't been thinking that, but the Teller knew her well. "But there are other concerns now," she said instead. "I have all these people I am responsible for—"

"And should you relax, they will wander off in the night and be lost."

She could hear the smile in his voice. "No," she said, "but—"

"Cloud." Basket put his heavy hand on her shoulder, and she felt unexpectedly fragile in it, as though made up of bird bones. "You don't need to carry the whole world every moment of the day. You don't need to hold yourself apart from us. For once, be incautious."

She reached for him again. Her fingers found the soft flesh of his arms and she pulled him down, and with him, a surrendered lifetime. The rains had come and gone forty times while she slept alone. No one to reassure her in the dark, no one to hold her close and shelter her from the calumnies of the people who did not understand her. No relief. No comfort. No one to stand on her side and be strong in the moments when she needed to be weak. She had surrendered it all, long ago, when she had betrayed her husband Wind.

He had died because of her. And so she had given up Basket. Given up love. It had felt right and just. She hadn't deserved his embrace. The rains came and went, and each time they passed, it had been easier to hold herself apart.

But now his soft arm slid under her back. He pulled her to his chest. And deserve didn't matter anymore. She knew Wind watched her from the stars, but his judgment didn't matter. She *needed* Basket. She was on a journey to a place of dread with all her people relying on her. If she was to travel through this hard world, then she had to allow herself moments of softness. She leaned up and met his lips with hers.

He tasted the same as he had all those rains ago. The scent of him sparkled lost memories in her mind, drawing them into focus, scenes clearer than her real vision could reproduce.

Drops splashed against her shoulder. She broke the kiss and felt his breath uneven against her face. The muscle of his back tensed under her fingers. She kissed his cheek and tasted salt and water. She couldn't see his expression in the starlight. "Basket?"

"I've missed you," he said.

It was only then that she heard the pain in his voice and knew that he loved her, that he had always loved her. After Wind died, she had shut herself away and allowed herself neither joy nor longing for the tryst she had lost. And Basket had withdrawn. He had never pushed, never pleaded. He had never shown her his sorrow.

She could have gone to him. She could have let him love her. But she hadn't. Her reasons for resisting broke apart and drifted away in the winds. They could have had so much time together.

She would not waste what they had left. She kissed him again, and again. She let his arms and his heavy body surround her. She found that part of him that was still youthful and sturdy and took him into herself there, under the stars, in the long wild and the dry wind.

# 4 The Circle Broken

Kwaee's eyes were open, and he did not like what he saw. His forest burned on its northern edge, a ragged wound that would grow, would spread like blight. It had happened before, many rains ago, and the pain now was worse for its memory—a torment returned. Ogya gnawed at him with clicking mandibles of flame, tearing away leaf and branch, stone and soil.

Kwaee's insects burst in their carapaces; his birds dropped from the sky; his beasts collapsed in hollows and dry streambeds, sucking down the last of the air they could find. And he was helpless to stop it. He lashed his vines against the fire bearers. He sent beasts to attack them. But they had fire. They had the power of Ogya. And against that, nothing in the forest could stand for long.

Every day of the blaze was a new tragedy. Butterflies nesting for their egg-laying season burnt like dry grass, those who tried to escape dropping out of the air. Mothers choked to death in their dens while trying to save their young. Today the blaze had reached Ekutan, the only tree Kwaee had named. Hoary and venerable, it was the oldest tree in the forest. Kwaee thought it might be the oldest living thing in the world, but for the gods themselves. It had been ancient when the great bargain was first struck. It had seen the rise of the savanna and the birth of Doto. Kwaee had crouched in its branches in the early hours of creation and from there, watched the rise of his dominion. It had been the pillar of his first temple. When he had surrendered the forest to Sarmu, he had bent the borders around Ekutan so that it might be spared, so that he would not forget the roots of his godhood. And now it perished, its needles blackened around its toes, an unquenchable flame flickering behind its skin. And Kwaee had been able to do nothing.

He fumed and roared. He paced back and forth in his temple, and its walls sprouted thorns and poison. He seized the barbed saplings in his paws, little noticing the stabs of pain, and bellowed to the heavens. "Wem! This is your injustice! You set this in motion. You gave Ogya the power to destroy me. Come down! Face me! Answer for what you've done!"

It was bravado, of course. The Sky-Father never showed his face. None had ever seen him or spoken to him, save, it was said among the other gods, Mother Fam. He stared at his fingers, flexing his claws in and out. Useless. A mockery. What use claws against any enemy a god might possess? Could he tear out a throat made of flame? "You made it all. Life—" he growled. He set his claw tips against the trees of his temple. "—And death." He slashed.

The pain flared up his legs, gashes opening in his hide. He almost mewled at the flash of agony but would not allow it of himself. The pain was worse than that of the fire on the edges of his dominion, but it was his. A pain he could control. He clenched his fangs together, willing his temple to regrow. The bark of the trees knitted back together, but the slashes in his flesh remained, a reminder. Damage a temple and you damaged the god. Such wounds did not so easily recover.

"And life anew. But Ogya" —he gestured toward the north, giving the sky his most challenging glare— "leaves no life at all. Ogya will destroy *everything*. And then your grand world, so perfectly in balance, so carefully crafted, will die. Is that what you desire?"

The clouds in the sky above his temple crept along impassively, their contours rolling in unending circles.

"You left us here," he growled bitterly. "You made us gods and you put us here, *alone*, and you *left* us. To squabble. Fight. Suffer. And we did our best. We tried to keep the world you left us going. It should have been perfect."

He turned his gaze away, padded toward the pond in the center of his temple. Water striders slid calmly over the surface, unfazed by his shouting. "You could have made it perfect."

It had been, at first. There had been no loneliness, no anger, no sorrow. He had maintained his forest in perfect balance. Ogya's fires burned and died. Mpo stormed and quelled. The world had played its delicate chorus in precision, unending, exact, and infinite. A perfect circle, each action leading to the next, and the next leading back inevitably to its cause once more. But that was before the great bargain, the terrible choice they all had made.

Now they were lost. Ogya hungered, Mpo raged, and Kwaee… he yearned. Lusted. Grieved. And the world would end, careening ever more wildly out of balance. He paced the perimeter of his temple. For centuries, it had been his shelter and prison. He had shut his eyes to the outside world, the one that had brought him pain and disruption. It had been so easy to tell himself that the threat was gone. All he had to do was look away. But now his eyes were open. His son and that mewling fire bearer he'd captured had ventured far from the forest. They'd found the lost god Sarmu and learned secrets that Kwaee had wished forgotten. His shame. His weakness. For better or worse, they'd woken him up.

And now Ogya gnawed at him, devoured his dominion, and he could do nothing to stop it. It would be easy to close his eyes again, to turn away. But he would not show that weakness again. Better to face the end of everything with his eyes open and a roar of defiance.

Something rustled near his temple and with a momentary flash of alarm, he turned his attention toward the disturbance. Two ripples in the pool of creation moved toward him—disturbances only the divine created as the world parted and bent around them. His fur settled. It was only Doto and his new… mate.

He smoothed out his pelt and sat down in his throne, curling his tail around his legs, hiding the bloody slashes.

His son entered the temple with his mate close behind. The once-fire bearer was shorter and slenderer, his fur darker in color, and of course no feather sprouted from his brow as with Doto, but he still greatly resembled both Doto and Kwaee. Kwaee's nose wrinkled. A thief, usurping the power of the gods.

He could feel the steps of their paws inside him, in his temple. He had never cared to have any other being enter it. The creatures that lived there were part of it, part of *him*, but to have an alien tread on his holy ground felt unpleasant, a violation. His son he had grown accustomed to over time, though even that intrusion felt unwelcome, an intimacy he did not care to share with anyone. When the fire bearer had first set its grubby little toes inside his sanctuary, he'd felt a physical revulsion. He liked it little better this time. He slouched backward on the moabi tree that was his throne and scowled at the two. "Well?" he snapped in god-tongue. "What brings you both to trouble me?"

They crept forward, the mate a few steps behind, his ears lowered, tail tip flicking. Both noses twitched as they drew close to his throne. They could smell his blood.

Doto bowed low, flattening himself against the temple floor, and the other one followed in kind. At least they hadn't lost their manners as well as their sense.

"Father," Doto said, rising, "Ogya burns your borders. He intends to destroy you. To devour you. And me. And the entire world."

Kwaee gave him a flat stare. "Truly?" he asked drily. "You came a long way to inform me that I am on fire."

Doto's ears pinned back. "I have had to come a long way before to tell you things you should have known already."

The impudence! Kwaee half-rose from his throne, but his son stood unflinching, his gaze steady and serious. His nose and that of his mate twitched again as they sniffed the air. Both of them glanced at Kwaee's legs, and he realized only too late he had revealed his wounds to them.

He sat back on his throne, but his claws dug into the soft wood, little stabs of pain echoing in the flesh of his back. "There is no need to tell me of these things now," he said, keeping his voice cool. "You were right before, son. I should not have kept my eyes closed to the world. I thank you for showing me that. But now that they are open, there is nothing that you can see that I cannot."

Doto's ears lifted. "Then what do we do? How do we fight back? Why are we doing nothing?"

"Fight back?" Kwaee scoffed. "And how would you propose we do that? Ogya keeps his temple deep below the earth where none but he and Fam can reach it, and his power overwhelms hers. What would you have me do?"

"You are a god too. Use the forest." Doto spread his paws. "Somehow. There must be a way."

"A way? There is no way. Ogya's power surpasses my own, by the wisdom of Wem. All I have that I can send his way, he burns."

"But he needs my people to do it, doesn't he? Your, uh, your worship?"

Kwaee snapped his gaze toward the shorter leopard. "You. Usurper. You use your filthy fire bearer language to speak to me? It is like the screeching of a chimpanzee. Speak god-tongue when you address me, or do not speak at all."

The little demigod visibly wilted. "But I do not know how to speak—" he began in god-tongue, and then trailed off, his eyes widening. "I can speak your language." He breathed the words in evident wonder, as though he found the ability of a god to speak god-tongue astonishing. "How do I know these words? I can speak and understand them! Have you been speaking god-tongue this entire time?"

"You have been listening to us speak it since the day you took my son's power." Kwaee's voice dripped with scorn. But he spared a glance for Doto and saw his son's fists clenched at his sides. Loath though he was to admit it to himself, he had been glad of the eased hostilities between himself and Doto. Belittling his son's mate, however deserved, might renew those tensions. He let his breath out slowly. "What was your name, little fire bearer? Dirt, was it?"

"Clay," his son's mate answered in his own language.

"Hardly an acceptable name for the divine. In god-tongue, boy."

His son's mate flattened his ears. "But how can I know my name in this language?"

"The word, boy." Kwaee stifled his own impatience. "Think of the word they used for you in your own language."

"Clay."

"And now in god-tongue."

"D—Doté."

Doto looked over at him sharply.

"It is a coincidence," Kwaee said. "Think, son. Doté is the word for 'clay' in god-tongue, as Doto is for 'copse.' It means little. So, little Doté, you persuaded my son to give you his power. I warned him your kind was treacherous."

"I did not persuade him," the boy answered, a bit stiffly. "I was killed. I was not even alive when he restored me."

Kwaee narrowed his eyes. "Perhaps. Your people have always been devious. Perhaps you deliberately sacrificed yourself so that he would grant you his power."

Doté's fur bristled. "Sacrificed myself? You mean you think I willingly let myself be murdered on the slim chance that Doto would use a power I did not even know he had to bring me back and make me a god?"

"Your kind kill themselves for the gods all the time," Kwaee remarked. "I rather think they enjoy it. And look at you now. Strong. Powerful. Allied to gods like no fire bearer ever before."

"And alone," his son's mate answered. "An outcast from my own people. Doto cares for me, but who else? I miss them. I miss the comfort of my community and my home. And this power? It carries me away from myself. It makes me lost. In some ways, it is wondrous, truly. But it frightens me. I would return it if I could."

"No!" Kwaee started up from his throne, his fur bristling, his voice deep and resonant with divine authority. Doto and Doté both dropped to the forest floor instinctively, crouching flat, their camouflage making their rosettes swim against the sun-dappled floor, going invisible—to all but Kwaee. He took several deep breaths, calming himself. "No, little Doté. Ill-gotten your power may be, but you cannot return it. In the attempt, you could… harm my son. You could put more of yourself into him than you intend. This magic is raw and wild. No god can truly control it, much less an upstart kitten who cannot even keep his mind in his own avatar."

He scowled, disliking the only conclusion to which this could lead. "If you are a thief, you are a trapped one. The power you have taken ties you to my son. He gave it to you, so now you must stay with him and keep him safe and happy. You are not permitted to die, nor to abandon him."

He drifted for a moment, his mind floating to the city of Abansin, full of bones. His own lover's were in there somewhere, and thinking of her renewed a flood of anger and regret that threatened to consume him. He marveled at the pain it could still make him feel, a pain so terrible that he had wished to close his senses forever, to feel nothing. Abansin was decaying rapidly now that he had let the forest return to it. Animals gnawed on the bones. Rain washed their remnants away. But his sorrow remained.

He snapped his gaze back to the two godlings. "If you should disappoint him, I will make you suffer terribly. Remember that death no longer holds any release for you, little one. I can hurt you day after day after day and you will always come back. So attend him well. Give him what he could not find in my forest alone."

Doto's gaze grew ever harder and more challenging over this last order, and Kwaee could not fathom why. Surely his son should be pleased to hear the god of the forest mandate his happiness. Ah, well. Doto had never been easy to understand, even as a kitten. Kwaee had long ago accepted that attempting to please him was futility.

"Clay makes me happy now," Doto said. Why he insisted on using that silly ape-name for Doté was another unsolvable mystery. "He would never hurt me."

"So you think now. But did you not hear him? He yearns for his people. How do you know he will not betray you to them? How do you know he will not change his allegiance and ally with Ogya against us? He knows secrets in this forest now. He can walk unharmed by it, perhaps even lead others through safely. He could take Ogya right to your temple and burn it down."

"I could never—" Doté protested, and at the same time, Doto spluttered, "Why would he do such a thing? It is his temple too! It would kill him!"

Kwaee had not considered that, and under his fur he flushed at making such a simple error in front of the young gods.

"Besides," Doto said, "he would never do that. He loves me. I trust him completely." Doté nodded and put an arm around Doto's shoulder, his tail curling around the other's ankle. The obvious affection softened Kwaee's anger; he recalled Oko holding him like that, her fingers furrowing his fur, her body fragile and warm against his own.

He sighed. "Your trust is foolish. No one can be trusted completely. And you should not have given that ape your power, son. But… but it was strong, as well. Your mother—I failed to save her not because I was wise…" And the admission was like a thorn in his gut, one that had been buried deep for a long time, festering, injuring him over and over. He could not look his son in the eyes when he pulled that thorn free. "It was because I was weak. It shames me that you were stronger than I was."

He let the words hang in the air, wishing almost that he had not spoken them. For a time, the temple was quiet. His birds lost their voices among his branches. The water striders stilled themselves on his pond. Only the wind in his leaves continued its susurrus. Kwaee looked down at his toes, then up at the glimpses of blue sky barely visible through gaps in the canopy. Doto and Doté looked at each other and back at him. He determinedly paid them no notice.

"You. Doté," he said finally. "You must have considered returning to your people. Those no longer with Ogya, that is. No doubt they will now worship you. I imagine that would be very pleasing for you."

"Those no longer with Ogya?" The smaller leopard's ears perked forward. "Forgive me, Lord Kwaee, but what do you mean?"

"My eagles have seen a smaller number of them traveling toward sea and sunset. They do not burn the forest, though they still make little fires. The others do not follow. I have never seen a pack divide itself this way.

At first, I thought it foolhardy—so many old and so many cubs. A hunter would have separated them so to pick them off at its leisure, but they split on their own."

"To the sea? The great water? Why would they be going there?"

"If you do not know, how should I? But they travel slowly in that direction. Asubonten tells me there is a fire bearer nest there, near the place where her mouth kisses Mpo. They seldom venture into my domain, and never since I set my wrath against their kind. You could go and see them. Learn what they're doing."

Doté flexed his fingers, sliding his claws slowly in and out and looking thoughtful. "Many of them wouldn't have stayed if they knew what happened. And with my oldest brother dead, that would make Pataku—" He frowned, seemingly displeased with his use of the god-tongue for hyena. "That would make *Laughing Dog* in charge. Surely by now his treachery is evident. And he cannot hide Ogya's influence any longer. Cloud, Ant, Firefly and No Rocks would likely have left, and most of the elders would have gone with them."

"But why?" Kwaee wondered. "Perhaps it is like with the other apes? When a group grows too large, they divide."

"Maybe. Cloud came from—from the nest by the sea, as did a few others from our nest. Maybe she hopes to relocate there with the others." He stopped. "Or maybe she seeks help. She might be trying to learn the truth about Ogya. Some secret that can stop him."

Kwaee growled low. "There are no secrets that can stop Ogya. But the sea-people are cursed by Mpo. If your people go there, they will find nothing but suffering. Perhaps you should go to them."

"Perhaps," Doté said after a long pause that Kwaee did not care for. "But if Laughing Dog and his fire hunters do not stop burning the forest, we all may depend on Cloud and her people to intervene. If they can get help from the others and make Laughing Dog and the rest of my people stop with this madness, it might be our only chance."

"It might be." Kwaee feigned a casual tone. It was probably little worth worrying about. The forbidden secrets the sea-nest fire bearers had held would be forgotten by now. Mpo had left few alive to remember them, all that time ago.

Doté looked back over his shoulder at Doto. "But I could go and speak with my brother and those who remain. If they see me now, they would—"

"No!" Doto shouted at the same moment Kwaee declared, "You will do no such thing."

"But why?" Doté looked between the two of them in naked confusion. Kwaee was suspicious of the creature anyway. The fire bearers were adept deceivers, and not even a leopard could so easily change his spots.

"They'll hurt you," Doto said, coming to his side. "When Ogya attacked you at the fireside, I could hardly bear it. I can't see you harmed again."

"But I'm a—well, I'm not exactly a fire bearer anymore. They can't hurt me so terribly."

"Precisely," Kwaee said, rising from his throne to his full height. "You are no longer theirs. You belong to the forest now, and to my son. And yet you want to go skulking back to them, away from my sight? To speak where Ogya can overhear you?"

"Not to hurt you or the forest, but to try to save it. Lord Kwaee, I think I can help."

"Clay." Doto came up behind his mate, put his paw on one arm. "We should go. We'll find another way."

Kwaee growled. "You will not go to them. You were one of them before. You cannot be trusted." He bared his fangs, unsheathing his claws, his message unmistakable.

And yet the hapless little kitten disregarded it. "Lord Kwaee, I was part of them. I lived among them when you turned your forest against them. All it did was frighten them and set them against you. They wouldn't be fighting you now if you hadn't…" Behind him, Doto kept repeating his name: Clay. *Clay*. But he ignored him. "My people don't back down when you fight them. They just fight harder! You have to talk to them, persuade them—"

Fury burning in his blood, Kwaee strode down from his throne, his tail lashing. "Only a few days a god and already you defy me."

Doté pinned back his ears, crouching toward the ground, his fur standing up. "Father, don't. Father, please." His son, whimpering like a kitten.

Kwaee seized Doté by the scruff, hoisting him upward, the godling's feet kicking at empty air. Blood welled hot around his claws. "You will not return to the fire bearers. You will never speak to them again."

He gripped the smaller leopard around the throat with his other paw. Doté's vain attempts to swallow flexed against his fingers. It was tempting to squeeze, to snap that neck as the godling's little paws clutched and batted at his own. And it would have been a suitable punishment for him. He'd awaken in his temple a humbled, chastened creature.

Kwaee glanced at Doto. His son was trembling as if in fear, but the look in his eyes said that if Kwaee did this, if he punished his son's mate, the renewed kinship they'd discovered, the companionship, their union in their fight against Ogya—all that would be gone. Doto would not forgive him. It was unfair. Kwaee was lord of the forest. It was his right—his *duty*—to mete out punishment. To rule. His son had no place wielding this kind of influence over him.

He bared his teeth at Doté. "You are not one of them anymore. You are a god of the forest, and you will fight to defend it. Even if that means killing every last one of them. *I* am lord of the forest. I am the god whose dominion you are created to preserve. You will not question me again."

He released Doté's scruff, drew back his arm, and hurled the little leopard out of his temple. The sound of Doté's yowl of shock as he hurtled, twisting helplessly through the air, was deeply satisfying. Far in the distance came the sound of him crashing through leaves and perhaps a few tree branches.

But his blood was still hot with anger. It had felt wrong to back down under his son's stare, to capitulate. It was a surrender of his power, and he had done quite enough of that for one lifetime. He turned to Doto. "Train him. Teach him to kill fire bearers. We must know that he allies with us and not with Ogya and the traitors."

Doto's gaze was hard and unblinking. "When I found you in Abansin, and then, when you came to Clay and me at the edge of the forest and stood up against Ogya, I thought…" He looked away, as though the sight of his father had somehow become poisonous. "I thought you had changed. But you haven't."

So the surrender had been for nothing, as all surrenders were. Kwaee had learned that long ago, when he'd felled his own forest to stop Ogya from burning it and created the savanna. It had done nothing but delay Ogya's advance. Surrender was a self-inflicted wound. It accomplished your enemy's goals for you. He would never do it again.

He climbed back to his throne and settled down into it, allowing the awareness of his forest to soak into him, feeling the brush of the uncountable lives that were his responsibility. And Ogya chewing into it, a wound growing deeper and more terrible with every passing hour.

"Gods don't change, son."

Doto turned, tail lashing, and stormed out of the temple. Kwaee roared after him. "Gods don't change!"

But that, of course, was a lie. The gods *had* changed, all of them. The perfectly balanced circle Wem had put into place had broken. All the world would, one day, come apart. And none of them could do anything to stop it.

# 5 Inferno

The forest burned, and Great Ram murdered Clay.

The forest burned, and it was Laughing Dog's own hands strangling Great Ram to death while he watched in distant horror.

The forest burned, and he gave the order to kill Left Rabbit. The arrow flew through the air and Left Rabbit dropped to the ground.

The forest burned, and he exiled his own people to the unforgiving wilderness.

The forest burned, and he poisoned his people's medicine.

The forest burned, and *something* that he could not discern happened to his father.

The forest burned, and he broke Sara's neck, and smashed Yakeb's head in with a rock.

Ogya seemed to own his body much of the time now, striding around, giving orders to his fire hunters, gouting flames from his palms to slather the forest in unending conflagration. The control was far from absolute. Whenever Laughing Dog wished to exert his will, he could. He could move his limbs whenever he wanted, or speak his own words, the words that he preferred over Ogya's imperious and sneering contempt.

But much of the time, now, it seemed pointless. He was King. He led the fight against the tyrant Kwaee to stop the persecution of the People of the Savanna. But his family was dead, every one of them. His people had turned against him. And his fight against the gods had left him subject to a hostile intelligence that, at its best, ignored him, and at its worst, confused and exhausted and seduced him with hungry words that made him eager to serve it once more.

He seldom fought it anymore. He sat back in his own mind and let it control him while the persistent images of his sins and the world he'd lost smoked accusingly before his eyes. His body floated and moved around him, too large, not his.

*It is time, Laughing Dog.* Ogya's voice crackled with command, and Laughing Dog pulled himself up out of his torpor. *The dance.*

Laughing Dog resumed control of his body and shook his head. "I don't want to dance." Now that he was aware, he saw he was standing in the midst of a field of ash. One of his fire hunters, Broken Stump, gave him a glance. He must have heard. Well, let him. No one dared question him anymore.

*But you do. You love the dance. And you will do as I command. As I request,* Ogya purred into his mind, *or I will leave you. Just you, alone, in the ruins of your village. And then how will you save what's left of them? How will you fight Kwaee and free your people? When they see you have lost your power, what will they do?*

Laughing Dog retreated farther inside himself, into the darkest recess of his mind, where his eyes were but distant windows to the blaze of the outside world. "Does it matter? What do I have left?"

*You have me. The power of a god at your fingertips.*

"*Your* fingertips," Laughing Dog returned bitterly.

*Only when you choose not to wield it. Is this not what you desired? The ability to challenge the gods? Did you think you could handle that power and not be burned? You challenged us, defied us, and now you are unwilling to take the power you sought. Feel what I feel constantly.*

"No—" Laughing Dog tried to beg, but Ogya would not listen. The skies of the god's mind opened and rained starvation into him, a terrible, agonizing hunger. Had he been in full control of his body, he would have screamed, but instead he clutched around himself tighter, vibrating, his soul a fist in the empty dark of his body. The hunger burned and gnawed at him, a hole in his center that grew ever more intense, consuming every thought. He had to feed it with something, with *anything.*

Helplessly, he came back to his body. He buckled to his knees and, hunched over, scooped up great fistfuls of fluffy white ash from the ground and crammed them into his mouth. He tried desperately to swallow, but there was not enough moisture, and he choked, coughing grey clumpy clouds into the air. His throat and eyes stung. And still his stomach was unbearably hollow. He needed food, needed anything he could get to fill it.

Then the hunger vanished, and he was left shaking on his knees, tears clotting the ash on his cheeks. Caterpillar stood to one side, revulsion twisting his face.

"King Laughing Dog, are you—"

"It's the power," Laughing Dog told him wearily. He tried to control his shaking and found that Ogya lent him the strength. His mouth flooded with saliva and he spat thick gobbets of ash. Hatred and gratitude toward Ogya mingled inseparably in his mind. "It makes demands of me."

Caterpillar gave a slow nod. "But it's worth it, right? All of this? What we've… had to surrender? All that we're doing, it still means something, doesn't it?"

*Tell him*, Ogya crackled at the back of Laughing Dog's tongue. *Tell him that you plan to give up my power. That Kwaee will win. That you made a mistake and you will all continue to suckle at the forest god's teat, thanking him whenever he deigns not to murder you.*

Laughing Dog took a deep breath. Unlike the others, he never felt the choke of the smoke. The cinders never stung his eyes. Caterpillar looked back at him, wanting, *needing* reassurance. Behind him, the other fire hunters stood, some watching, others working tirelessly to spread the flames. Their skin was scorched and blistered.

Down the hill, their village huddled, furred with a coating of ash. It no longer bordered the forest. The hostile vines and branches of Kwaee could not reach it, and invading beasts had day after day been deterred by the smoke and flames. The massive tree the leopard beast had hurled into the middle of their village had had its smaller branches stripped away, but it still lay there like a dismembered carcass. Many rains and a great deal of work would be required before they could hack the whole thing into pieces small enough to drag away. But the wall through which it had tumbled had been repaired. No more would die because of the forest god. Everyone down there was depending on him. He had urged them to stand up and be strong, and they had listened to him. He was their King. He was responsible for them.

And Ogya was right. Power was commensurate with pain. Victory required sacrifice. If the gods could handle the suffering that came with that, so could he.

"It will be worth it," he promised Caterpillar. "We will win. We *are* winning. We will be free of the tyranny of gods forever."

The man relaxed, tension going out of his shoulders, the worry from his face. "I know it. We all trust you, King Laughing Dog. We know you love your people."

Ogya crackled in his ears. *You are indeed a wise King. You just need to be reminded sometimes.*

Yes, Laughing Dog thought to himself. This was why he pressed onward when he had lost everything else, when he had done such terrible things. Even if he had no more right to life or happiness, the people depended on him. He was the only one left who could save them from the gods. He could not let all that loss, every sacrifice, every horror, every unspeakable act be for nothing.

His brothers would not have died in vain. This was for the People of the Savanna.

He summoned the song of adoration Ogya had taught him.

He danced.

~

The council circle huddled in the rain. All the elders had been exiled, so the new council consisted of senior delegates from the village: the craftsmen, the hunters, the farmers, the cooks. They had a new Teller, Horned Melon, who knew most of the stories fairly well and dutifully only recounted those approved by Laughing Dog. Yellow Bug, though young, attended too, their only healer now that Cloud was gone.

The circle gathered at the top of Gamewatch Rise to avoid the ash-mud sloughing through it, an oily, thick alluvion that slid tents downward and unseated the village walls. The council members pulled pelts over their heads to shelter themselves from the downpour. None of them looked happy.

Only Laughing Dog sat unsheltered. He'd had his braids tightened and tied back on his head, and they were heavy with rain and clotted ash. He rubbed the water from his eyes. "All right. How is the village? Half Moon?"

The hunter rubbed streaked soot from his arms and shoulders. "There's no game to be found anywhere. We've traveled two days journey out and there's not a sign of any hunting. It was scarce before, but now..."

"You hunted upwind?"

Half Moon gave him a flat stare. "Of course. We always hunt upwind now, much as we can when it shifts with the storms. Even after the rains clean the air, there's not much to be found. Tracks, yes. All leading away from here. No creature cares for the smell of smoke."

Laughing Dog grimaced. "Then you'll have to travel farther. Three days out. Four. Whatever it takes."

"King Laughing Dog, you know as well as I do that three days out, the meat won't keep. It'll be sprouting maggots by the time we get it back."

"So hobble the game and bring it back alive." He knew even as he demanded it that this was a stiff requirement. Carrying or herding live game was difficult even over a short distance. To transport it three days' journey would be an arduous if not impossible task. But what else could he do? His people needed meat, and he and his fire hunters had risen to power in no small part due to their ability to provide it.

To his credit, Half Moon gave no hint of reluctance or dismay at this command. Laughing Dog had chosen his fire hunters well. "Of course, King Laughing Dog. However… if there is no meat three days out, or four, we may need to think about other ways to provide for our people. We can hunt and we can track, but we can't kill game that isn't there."

The others in the circle nodded.

"Suggestions?" Laughing Dog asked.

A big, rough-hewn farmer named Big Storm grimaced. "The people won't like it, but we might have to go to travel rations."

Mumbles and groans went around the circle at that. Travel rations were slim, meant to sustain people through extended famine and long journeys.

"Now, it won't be so bad as all that. We have plenty of water, and we won't be traveling. But—" He broke off, looking down at his callused hands.

"Well?" Laughing Dog asked impatiently. "You're on the council, and it's not to keep secrets."

Big Storm peered at him from beneath bushy eyebrows. Unlike Half Moon, he was clearly a bit cowed by Laughing Dog. "Well, King Laughing Dog, it's the ash, you see."

"What about it?"

"Not so bad on its own. Good for the crops, even, I reckon. But when it rains like this, the mud slides through, sometimes ankle deep. Takes everything with it. We're losing the sorghum, the jugo beans, near everything. Even my yams got stripped away. That's the other reason I say travel rations, King. If there's no game and no crops…" He spread his hands wide.

Laughing Dog rubbed at his temples. Behind his mind, Ogya hissed and groaned, hungry for more of the forest, insisting they go back to burning immediately. He seemed insensate toward Laughing Dog's reasoned response that without the rest of the village supporting them, the work would not get done.

"Replant the crops. Somewhere out of the way. Get whatever labor you need from the village to assist you. Without food, we can do nothing else. Plant them uphill, away from the mudflow. The hunters and I will move our burning farther away to try to avoid further damage."

The farmer's face fell. He rubbed his hands together as though searching for some other answer but caught Laughing Dog's warning eye. "Y—yes, King Laughing Dog."

"If we're talking about the mud…" That was Dawn Come Early, their chief carpenter and tentmaker.

"What?" Laughing Dog snapped. Trying to focus on the endless problems while Ogya simmered in his head the whole time was starting to make him jumpy.

Dawn raised greying eyebrows, but her expression remained calm. Carpentry required patience, and she was a patient woman. "We all know the tents are sliding downhill. When we wake in the morning, our homes have crawled from their spots. Our pallets are soggy and ruined, our possessions lost in the mud. Many have—"

"Yes, yes," Laughing Dog interrupted her. "Stop telling us what we already know. You were supposed to be digging channels to direct the flow."

"And we have. But they aren't working. There is simply too much mud. Even if we carved a canyon into the hillside, it would not be enough. And now the tents are coming apart. I don't have enough workers to repair all of them. The village walls are beginning to tilt, too. I fear they may collapse on someone in the night. And then there is the… tree. The big one, that the forest threw into our village. It's slowly sliding downhill from the mudflows. It's only a matter of time before it rolls over a home and crushes someone."

"Get more people to help you, then! If we don't have as much food, then surely some of the cooks—"

"With respect, King Laughing Dog, most of our skilled carpenters left with Cloud."

"Wem's eye," he swore bitterly.

"And many of the others can barely work. The smoke chokes them."

"It's true," said Yellow Bug. She was young still, too green for such a necessary position, but what could they do? "Cloud taught me a little about smoke before she left, but not much. I have the workers using wetted palm-cloth around their mouths and noses to help with the smoke, but they're getting sick anyway. They have terrible headaches, and their eyes are watering so badly that many of them can barely see. Some can't keep food down. I don't know what else to do but get them away from the smoke."

Laughing Dog rubbed at his face with both hands. It was too much. He wasn't a bad King. He was trying his best to care for everyone. But what King had ever had to deal with this many problems all at once? In his mind, Ogya simmered, muttering the words, *Burn, burn,* over and over. How little the gods cared for them, even those on their side.

"I do have a suggestion," said Horned Melon. "No one will like it, I think. But it might be the only way to solve all these problems and allow you to pursue your, er, sacred mission, King Laughing Dog."

"What is it?" He didn't have much hope for Horned Melon's ideas. He'd selected the young man to be their new Teller because of his devout love for stories, a quality every good Teller required, but Melon didn't just know the stories. He lived inside them. He had never been receptive to Laughing Dog's opinions on the old stories—that they were more parable than literal truth. It was surprising that he hadn't chosen exile with the others, given Laughing Dog's attitudes toward the gods. But Horned Melon valued safety. He liked to retreat, both behind walls and into legends.

"We move the village. Not far," he added hurriedly, as a series of groans and grumbles rolled around the council circle. "Maybe a few days away from the burn site. We'd be closer to hunting, able to farm, and if we're far enough out from the forest, we'd have less risk of animal attacks. But still close enough that you'd be able to coordinate with us for supplies and to conduct your… kingly duties. At least until your burn ventures far enough into the forest. At that point we could move back."

Dawn Come Early slumped forward, her shoulders sagging with weariness. "To move everything again would be no small task. Rebuilding the tents and the walls? It would be exhausting. And everyone has had little food. But it would be less work than trying to keep everything standing day after day, especially if we were out of the smoke."

"And we need to get people out of it," Yellow Bug agreed. "The longer people spend inside the smoke, the sicker they get. I don't know how long people can last."

"We could swap out the fire hunters." That was Wasp, the other fire hunter Laughing Dog had appointed to his council. "We'll be better at facing down Kwaee and showing him who's in charge around here if we can come back fresh every now and then."

"Well, I don't like it," Half Moon told his fellow fire hunter. He cast an appraising stare around the circle. "How's it going to look if we've finally found a home, finally settled down after years and years of wandering the savanna, and then less than one moon after Laughing Dog became King, we all have to pick up and move again? People will notice, and they won't like it."

"How does it look now?" Dawn Come Early returned. "We exiled a third of our people and now we're all starving and sick and our homes are caving in on top of us. You think it's going to get better? It won't. And when it doesn't get better, the people will blame the King. They always do." She hesitated, then dipped her head to Laughing Dog. "Justly or not, my King."

Her obsequiousness annoyed him. He preferred unpleasant truth to this fawning. But Ogya hissed in his mind. *They learn who you are. They speak to you this way because they know you are dangerous. You smell that fear? That is how you know we are growing powerful.*

He rubbed at his chin, thinking.

"My King, I urge you not to do this," Half Moon said. "You will look weak, like your father."

Anger boiled behind Laughing Dog's eyes. An unpleasant but alluring urge rose inside him, the urge to summon Ogya's power by song and dance and slather Half Moon screaming to the ground with tongues of fire. He clenched his fists tight, digging in his nails to stave off the bizarre temptation. "My father was not weak!"

Half Moon flinched. "No. Of course not. But to some, he looked it. After moving the people time and time again, some of us began to wonder if there was a better way. And of course, there was. You found it. That's why people respect you and follow you. But if you move the village now, they will remember the last time they fled fire. And this time, begging pardon for the implications, King Laughing Dog… this time, the fire we'd be fleeing is one we set ourselves. People will talk."

"If they stay here in the smoke much longer, they might not be *able* to talk," Yellow Bug said. She rubbed at her neck with one braceleted hand. "Who here has had a sore throat for days? Anyone but me?"

An uncomfortable series of mumbles resonated through the council.

Horned Melon grimaced. "I think Half Moon is right that it may look weak. But as in the story of the reed and the rod, it is better to look weak than to be weak. We need to know when to bend. Our homes are collapsing. We are sick and starving. Now is the time to bend, or our village will surely break. I know you will remain strong, King Laughing Dog. You and the power that you wield. But if we don't move the village, I fear it will be you wielding it alone against all the forces of Kwaee, and you will have no more subjects to save."

"I concur," said Dawn Come Early, and she thumped the hilt of her knife against the ground.

"As do I," said Wasp. He thumped his own knife-hilt.

And so, around the circle, all the council members struck their agreement against the ground. All but Half Moon, who resolutely folded his arms, his expression growing darker and darker as each vote was cast.

The council's advice was not binding, but Laughing Dog knew only a very foolish or very certain King made decrees against the advice of his council's majority.

"Very well," he said, sitting taller. "The village will move three days out from the burn site. We will stay close to the forest so that hunting and food will be easier to come by."

Wasp nodded his approval. "East or west, my King?"

Laughing Dog hesitated, uncertain. Where did their current path lead them? They'd been burning a broad swath of forest, moving roughly south, but with no particular direction, for some time.

*We burn east*, Ogya crackled hungrily in his mind. *That is where our prize waits. South and east.*

"Take the People west," Laughing Dog said. "Our fire hunters will burn east. Besides, the wind blows eastward these days."

"West," Half Moon said unhappily. "Of course. In the tracks of all those you exiled before."

"Only a few days journey. And soon enough our burn will be deep enough into the forest that the people can move back."

"If we do," Dawn Come Early said. "If we can find a good location to settle, it might be better to think of it as permanent."

Laughing Dog stood. "No. This is our home. Make sure everyone knows that this move is only temporary. We will not let the gods bully us out of our homes again. This is where the People began a new story. Our friends and family have died making a stand here. We won't surrender it to gods or demons or smoke or mud or traitors. We will not falter."

The creaking and groaning of wooden poles rubbing against each other came from behind him. He turned in time to watch the great yellow fence that bordered the upper section of the village where King and council lived sag inward. Twine bindings whined as they strained, then frayed and snapped apart. The support posts, each taller than three men, dipped, sliding in the slate-grey ash mud.

Then, with a moan like a dying elephant, the entire upper section of the fence collapsed. Poles splintered and snapped. The bones of the forest tilted toward the ground, free of their bindings, and bounced, crushing homes beneath them.

Laughing Dog turned back toward the village where, alarmed, people were clambering out of tents, backing out of the work areas and gathering in the middle of the village. The entire fence around it listed to one side.

One by one, the villagers below turned to look up at him, their King, standing over their whole home gone sideways.

~

They burned mostly at night. Morning burns made little progress, as the afternoon rain quenched the fires they started. Night was cooler, and the smoke seemed to rise and dissipate faster. Though the air quality never bothered Laughing Dog, his fire hunters didn't share his resistance and greatly preferred the night work.

Laughing Dog preferred it as well because of the view. In the darkness of night, the fires they spread lit a brilliant orange fringe against the dark forest, and the smoke rose in a flowery pink haze. Behind them, embers glimmered yellow and red along the forest floor, outlining the white paths of ash that were safe to walk. All else faded into darkness except the larger trees, whose hardwood cores burned for days, glowing yellow circles peppering the ashlands.

Far down the hill, the torches of the village remained lit as the People of the Savanna gathered their belongings and fashioned carts and grass sleds out of the ruins of the fence. Horned Melon estimated that everyone would be evacuated by dusk tomorrow.

For all the failures that the village had suffered lately, the burn was proceeding well. Ogya knew exactly where to start fires: when an arrow shot into the branches of a tree would burn more thoroughly than a torch at its base; where to spread their limited quantity of palm oil to start a blaze that would spread far and burn hot; and when and where Laughing Dog ought to dance to summon the fire god's devastating power.

When he allowed himself to forget the terrible sacrifices he had had to make to get here, the dance was Laughing Dog's favorite part of the burn. The feeling of a god's power erupting from his palms, surging through him, burning away everything inside him but energy and the satiation of an endless hunger? That was an ecstasy he both craved and was ashamed to indulge in.

He had no right to pleasure after the things he had done. Of course, his crimes had been for the People, everything for the survival of the People in a world of bullying gods. But they were still monstrous. And growing more and more difficult to dwell on. When he descended into his dark moods, distant inside himself, harried by Ogya's hunger and the memories of his own sins, Ogya would take control, and would say and do things that confused his people and his fire hunters. Ogya cared little for the support of the village, however much he might need them. And when he needed the dance again, he would torment Laughing Dog with hunger until he had no choice but to obey.

It wasn't what he'd wanted, trading the brutality of one god for the tyranny of another, but for now, at least, their purposes were aligned. Ogya's control was not absolute. Laughing Dog would find a way to oust the god's presence from his mind when it was time. And for now, if wielding the power of the flame gave him pleasure, then so be it. He would dance.

He learned things when the fire poured out of him. He tasted what it touched. In consuming it, he knew it. It was as though, for a moment, he became part of it. He basted an old acacia with flames and tasted the years of rains it had thrived in and the years of drought it had suffered through. He tasted its fruiting and its flowering and the seed that had sprouted it. He tasted the beetles in its bark, felt the crack of their carapaces in the heat, the greasy fat of their larvae.

It was a consumption more delectable and satisfying than mere eating, for now he had a thousand tongues, and teeth that could hew through stone. Everything in his world was a delicacy, an exquisite and enrapturing experience. When he channeled Ogya's fire he felt as though he wished to taste the whole world.

It had been a challenge when using Ogya's fire to hunt. He had had to exercise so much restraint, scorching his prey without killing it, tasting without swallowing. The deer he'd licked with his flames had tasted of muscle and terror, the grass it had eaten, the musk of its rut. And in the meat of its body, the plains it had grazed, the silt in the water it sipped. He'd wanted to consume more, but that had been meat for the People.

Sometimes, when alone and certain he would not be interrupted, he fed his meals to the flames instead of his own belly, to taste them more completely. Burning the forest was satisfying, but there was little animal life in it. His fire craved variety.

*I emerge*, Ogya roared in his mind.

"Not now," he urged Ogya, but it was too late, and besides, the god never listened. Out of a sizeable circle in the ash where the embers still burned with a hot and steady glow, one massive pincer of fire erupted from the ground, and then another.

The fire hunters shouted to each other in terror as Ogya pulled the massive bulk of his arachnid body from the ground. The titanic creature stood many times their height, his body composed of bright and shifting flames of reds, yellows, and blues. He had the approximate shape of a man, but with four clawed arms and four unnaturally segmented legs upon which he moved in a sinuous and spasmodic gait. His eyes blazed white and inhuman; they appeared to form and dissipate on his face as though bubbles opening in molten rock, so that Laughing Dog was never certain where he was looking, nor even how many eyes he possessed. He spread his mandibles wide, opened his jaws, and vomited a thick gout of white fire at the forest, and here Laughing Dog could see exactly the limits of Ogya's power: where the edge of the unburned forest began, Ogya's flames spread outward as though encountering an invisible wall. It seemed that his power and the forest god's were matched in this way: as Kwaee's lianas and grasping roots could not reach beyond the edges of his domain, so Ogya was unable to spit his flames into that realm.

But wherever the hunters had sent flaming arrows or ignited torches, there Ogya's eruption could burst through, and the heat and magnitude of his fire was far greater. An old hardwood tree whose bark barely flickered could be transformed into a towering torch of flame, and that fire's heat and flame could spread.

The fire hunters cowered, shielding their eyes and faces from Ogya's fire. The heat and light seared them painfully, and they found the visage of the god's physical form horrific. In private, many of them had pleaded with him not to summon the god again. It would have been unwise for him to reveal how little control he had over Ogya's actions, so instead he had severely answered that everything they were doing was for the good of the People, to take down Kwaee as quickly as possible.

This was only the third time that Ogya had manifested, but each time, his appearance terrified and demoralized the hunters. Several had sworn never to return to the burn if he made another appearance, and this close, the god's enormous shape could be visible from the village, where the People of the Savanna still gathered their homes and belongings for departure. Only the massive, thunderhead-like clouds of greasy smoke concealed the truth of the god—within their obscuring depths he seemed more apparition than creature, and from a distance, only a peculiar and capricious inferno.

After Ogya's second physical appearance, Laughing Dog had reasoned with him, explaining as he had uncountable times before that they needed the help of the people and they could not, as Ogya had hungrily suggested, obtain that assistance using force. He could not tell Ogya, however, his larger concern: that seeing the god manifest before them would erode their faith in their King: a tiny man scampering around the split-toed claws of a titanic fire demon. How could he claim to them that they were fighting the gods when he literally served at the feet of one? They would believe him lost, under its sway. And if they truly saw the power that aided him, they might become convinced that Cloud had been right, and follow after her.

Now, as Ogya loomed over them, his segmented snare of a tail dripping molten fire that spattered into hot beads into the ash, several of the fire hunters fled.

Fighting down a surge of desperation, he shouted, "Stop!" And before realizing what he was doing, he turned the flames he had summoned toward them, trying to cut them off from fleeing. He hadn't meant to use the power against them. He'd only wanted to delay them long enough to speak to them, to exhort them to stay.

Three of the men skidded to a stop, tumbling forward, falling in the ash in great white puffs of cloud before the power of their King's fire. But one was too late. He tumbled into the path of the flame.

He screamed, a terrible, inchoate wail of agony.

And Laughing Dog *tasted* him.

It was Broken Stump. Before he even realized what was happening, Laughing Dog learned the flavor of his friend's flesh as it bubbled and burst in the wake of his divine power. It held the flavors of the sorghum and melon mash he loved, the scent of his father's goats, the shea butter he was fond of rubbing into his skin, the palm oil in his hair. He knew the hard sinew of

Broken Stump's strength and the freshness of his youth. There were flavors of fear and determination and sorrow and a deep weariness.

For a moment, Laughing Dog was lost. And then the screaming of his men reached his ears again. His fire sputtered and went out, as did the light from Ogya's effulgent form. The ash was soft and fluffy under his feet as he ran toward the burned man, thinking at first only that if he didn't help Broken Stump immediately, if he did not display immediate and overriding concern, all the men would turn against him. His next thought was shame that he'd cared first for his men's opinion than the safety of Broken Stump. Then: swift and overwhelming revulsion at what he'd done.

He was at Broken Stump's side in mere moments, and then the sickness in his stomach redoubled. Broken Stump would not stop screaming or writhing on the ground. His garments had not caught fire, but his entire right side was burned horrifically, his dark skin peeling away to reveal red, raw and glistening flesh beneath. The fire had seared off his hair and the flesh across half his face, and his ear was charred black, as was much of the skin of his right arm and hand. He flailed his damaged arm at everyone who approached, his white teeth sawing at the air from behind charred lips, and then he fell suddenly silent and limp.

"He's dead!" a fire hunter shouted.

"No." Laughing Dog saw the man's chest rising and falling with narrow breaths. "Unconscious." He knelt and slid his arms under Broken Stump, hefting him to his chest. The man felt as light as a child. He stood with him cradled in his arms, marveling at how strong he had grown since the day he first found Ogya's gem.

"Quickly!" he shouted to the other fire hunters. "Go and fetch Yellow Bug. Tell her that Broken Stump has been burned and to bring any supplies she needs. I'll be near the village gate."

He gripped Broken Stump firmly around the unburned parts of his limbs and chest and hurried down the hill, his footsteps landing heavily in ash, occasionally crushing still-glowing coals with his heels, making a ring of sparks puff outward.

*He will not live.* Ogya's voice was quiet and resigned in his mind. He sounded almost remorseful. Could he recognize the seriousness of this error? Neither of them had intended this. There would be consequences.

"He might. We have to try. If he doesn't…"

*The others will see your power and fear you. They will follow and obey.*

"*No*. They will flee. They will take the others, find Cloud, and rejoin her." He nodded toward the village below them, all in lights, the people packing their belongings and homes. "They're already leaving. If they find out what I… what has happened, they won't stop a few days away. They'll keep going. How can you be a god and not understand people at all? You and I have taken away everything from them. We have to give them something back. Something that makes them want to stay."

Broken Stump moaned in his arms, stirring.

*It is only because of my power that you have the chance to save him.*

"It's only because of your power that he was hurt in the first place!"

*You made the error, not I. You turned your fire against your men.*

"You manifested in front of all of them and terrified them! I was only trying to keep them from fleeing! How am I supposed to lead these people when you will not let me?"

Ogya's voice grew smaller in his mind, but more intense, focused with furious heat. *You speak to me like this, you miserable little ape? I was commanding armies of fire bearers a thousand rains ago, before any of your ancestors had ever existed. It was I who rallied the forces of the world against Kwaee. It was I who waged the first war your people had ever known. I, commanding at the head of their armies, in all my splendor!*

"And did you win?" Laughing Dog reached the bottom of the village, where the mud flows from the afternoon rains were still wet and thick. He should have been exhausted from running so far with a fully grown man in his arms, but Ogya's strength made him tireless. He knelt down in the mud and laid Broken Stump at his knees. The burned man twisted, moaning in pain even in his unconscious state.

*What?* Ogya's indignance blazed hotter in his mind.

"This war you're so proud of, the one you waged against Kwaee. Did you win it?"

There was silence in his mind. Laughing Dog scooped up thick handfuls of soft, cool mud and began carefully applying it to Broken Stump's wounds. One some, the man twitched violently even at the lightest touch. With others, the worse ones, he did not react at all. Laughing Dog glanced over toward the entrance of the village and saw he'd attracted the attention of those preparing to leave. They were coming in this direction. Behind them, Yellow Bug hurried through the gate, her thin arms full of bundles.

*Kwaee made a choice I did not expect*, Ogya answered finally. *He surrendered his forest. In less than ten days' time, millions of trees fell. Plants died on the vine. His beasts fled or perished. I could not have expected such a surrender, but it worked, for a time. His sacrifice created the savanna. And I…*

Not once had Laughing Dog ever heard Ogya hesitate or admit failure. "You what?" He whispered the words so as not to be overheard by the villagers who, curious, were approaching.

*I was angry. I turned on the people. I consumed them.*

Laughing Dog said nothing to that. Persuading a god to concede an error was one thing. Gloating about it was another. But Ogya had also allowed for a new, terrifying possibility: if Laughing Dog and the People of the Savanna disappointed him, if they failed to bring down his enemy, Kwaee, history could repeat. The god he had brought among them could turn on them all. He could, and perhaps would, kill every last one of them.

*You are right. The people need someone they care for to follow. I require their help.* Ogya was silent again. Then: *I will let you lead.*

And with that, he was gone, his presence utterly vacant from Laughing Dog's mind for the first time in more than a rain. The sensation was unexpectedly raw and hollow. He felt as though he had drunk too much palm wine the night before and woken the next day wine-sick.

The strength blew out of his limbs, drifting away on the wind, and his body felt squat and heavy and clumsy. He could barely hold it up. The hunger was gone too, and the power. And he was alone.

Yellow Bug hurried to his side, slogging through the mud in great, sucking steps. "Oh no," she breathed when she saw him. "Oh no." She set down her baskets and bundles and opened them, drawing out green aloe leaves and powders and palm fiber bindings. "The mud was good, King Laughing Dog, but these burns… are severe. I will do what I can."

He scarcely heard her. His world grew and grew around him, and he knelt in it, smaller and smaller. The grit of the mud scratched at his knees. The smoke stung his eyes and rasped in his throat. His head pounded. His friend, Broken Stump, was dying. His village was destroyed, his people leaving. He was a murderer of his own family. He was King of all these suffering people and there was no one left to help him, no one to look to. He sat alone among his catastrophes and crimes. This was what happened when you fought the gods.

Yellow Bug looked up at him, her mouth a flat line, her eyes both sad and fearful. Why should they be fearful? Had he become that monstrous, that everyone in the village feared him? "King Laughing Dog, I'm sorry. There is nothing I can do. He's dead."

"No!" Wasp's voice, behind him. So the fire hunters had caught up to him. They would tell everyone what he'd done. They should tell everyone. He did not deserve to lead them.

At first he thought it was the sting of the smoke that brought tears to his eyes, but then they began to run down his cheeks. He wept. He wept of despair for their venture. For Clay, who he had urged Great Ram to kill, and for Great Ram himself, who he had strangled with his own hands. He wept for their lost father, and for Left Rabbit. He wept out of exhaustion, his body ready to collapse from weariness, his thoughts a snarled tangle in his mind, raw and confusing in the absence of the flame that had guided him for so long. He put his arms around Broken Stump's mud-smeared body and cradled the limp frame to his chest and sobbed for his dead friend.

But most of all, he wept for himself: unredeemable, lost, alone, and unloved, with no strength left, no one to give him the guidance he needed, to hold him close, to assure him that things would be all right, that they would win, that he could be the great man the People of the Savanna needed. He cried the tears of a child abandoned, clutching Broken Stump tighter to him, never mind the stickiness of the mud and wounds, never mind that the whole village, it seemed, gathered around to witness his weakness and failure. He wept with shame.

"How did this happen?" someone asked. This would be it. The fire hunters would tell the village about the great scorpion of flame that led them all, and how they fled, and how Laughing Dog himself had burned his own men to stop them from leaving. They would call him murderer. Demon. He would be exiled again, or perhaps his crimes were too great even for that. Perhaps they would simply kill him here, knowing him to be too corrupted and dangerous to live.

"It was King Laughing Dog," said Wasp. His voice was hard and flat. "We were burning the forest, and he—"

The voice of Half Moon broke in. "He tried to save Broken Stump. Isn't that right?"

Laughing Dog did not dare look up. He kept his head down, continuing to weep over the dead man in his arms, though in his confusion the tears now did not come so easily.

"The fire got out of control," said Half Moon. "Some of us tried to run from it, and Broken Stump… he ran right into it."

"That's right." Another fire hunter—White Sand. "A burning tree fell on him. He was trapped. King Laughing Dog lifted up the tree on his own.

I've never seen such strength. He pulled Broken Stump free and carried him back here. He sent us to get Yellow Bug, but—"

Half Moon's voice was wracked with sorrow. "But I suppose it was too late."

Laughing Dog finally dared to look up. His eyes were swollen, and mucus ran from his nose with the tears. He knew he did not present a very kingly spectacle. But he had been given a chance. The people would be listening for something from their ruler. He hoped the words he chose were the right ones. "It was my fault," he told them. "I was careless with the burn. The fire got away from me. I am so ashamed."

He turned down to Broken Stump and let his voice crack. "I am so sorry, my friend. We will remember you in our tales forever. And this will never, ever happen again. I promise you. I swear it. Not one more will die because of this war with Kwaee. Not one more."

When he looked up again, the village stood around him, and he knew that something had changed. Faces that had been hard and suspicious toward him were now softened. Many were weeping. Others held their children close. But most now looked at him with admiration and respect. They had not looked at him like this when he had become King, when he had showed them his power, when he had provided meat for them in the famine, or when he had led them in the movement against Kwaee. No, only when they had seen him broken and frail, his power gone, holding the corpse of his dead friend, had they changed. In the end, it was his weakness, not his strength, that had won them over.

None of the people wanted to do anything else that night. Those preparing for travel laid off their preparations. The fire hunters retreated to their homes. Yellow Bug began the preparations of Broken Stump's body for his funeral.

Laughing Dog was so weary he felt he might sleep for ten days. The spark of Ogya had left him. But when he retreated to his tent, he found Half Moon waiting for him.

"I've spoken to the others," the fire hunter told him. "Those that know the truth will never speak it."

"Why?" Laughing Dog asked him. "You could have told them all what happened."

"What happened was we saw our King drop everything to try to save one of his men. They don't need to know the rest. They wouldn't understand it. If I'm being honest, none of us really understand either. But you banished that… monster that comes out of the fire. We all know what happened was an accident. And you tried to save him. You tried your best."

He squeezed at his hands as though lost in thought. "To be honest, Laughing Dog, we had all started to think that… that maybe you didn't care. That maybe this power had… driven you mad. After what happened with Left Rabbit, well, it shook us. And then the village started going bad, and you were talking to—well, it doesn't matter. You showed us tonight, sir. We always knew you were strong. That you were the only one willing to defend the People from the gods, willing to—to fight back. Seek vengeance against them if they wrong us. That takes bravery like I've never seen before. But now you've shown us why you do it. That we matter. That your people matter. And I guess we'd follow you anywhere for that."

Laughing Dog gazed at him in astonishment. And for the first time since his exile long ago, he felt like he was one of his people again, part of them. He was not, after all, alone.

A spark awoke in his mind: a low, spreading crackle of fire.

Ogya.

Ogya was very, very pleased.

# 6 The God's Apprentice

Cursing his father under his breath, Doto raced in the direction Kwaee had flung Clay. He felt his mate before he saw him, the ripples of power radiating away from him, a heartbeat of the forest. When he reached the center of the ripples, he had to look around for a moment before he spotted Clay, who was perched on a tree limb high above the forest floor, his tail swaying slowly.

"There you are," he called up to Clay. "What are you doing up there? Are you all right?"

Clay flicked his ears. "I'm fine. I… landed up here somehow. I was flying through the forest, and I saw the branch, and I… caught it. With my claws." He took a step forward and dropped to the ground, landing gracefully on all fours before standing.

Doto hurried to his side. "I'm so sorry about Kwaee. He—"

"Is an unchanging deity of the forest. I know. I wish I could have made him understand. But the last time I visited his temple, he ordered you to kill me. This time he only threw me out." Clay grinned. "So that's an improvement."

"You aren't angry?" Doto lowered his ears, puzzled. He'd been expecting a fight with Clay. "He choked you and insulted you and abused you. I would be furious."

"Honestly, I think I'm just thrilled to be alive after that. It was a new experience, hurtling through the air like a bird."

"Well, he couldn't have killed you, you know. Not without killing me. I still suspect he would if he could." He took a deep breath. Clay would need to know about his father's command. "Clay—er, Doté," he corrected himself.

His mate put a paw on his arm. "Just Clay. Please. I've changed enough. I don't need a god's name, too. Especially not one that reminds me so much of you."

Doto wasn't sure if he was supposed to be stung by that comment. "And what's wrong with being like me?"

"Nothing!" Clay gestured up and down his own body. "Obviously. But the last few days have been so much, so fast. And all of it feels like I'm… disappearing. Into this body, into your lessons, into the forest, into our temple. I want to hold onto the bits that are me. That's what you love, isn't it?"

"Of course." Doto moved to take Clay into his arms and felt a surge of unexpected arousal. But now was not the time. He breathed in Clay's scent all the same, isolating those aspects of him that remained distinct, hints of the fire bearer in this god's body. That only excited him more. He forced himself to focus. "But Clay, my father, he… he wants me to train you."

"Good." Clay nuzzled his cheek, a low purr-like rumble in his chest. No doubt he had scented Doto's interest.

"In using your divine powers."

"Uh huh." Pointed teeth nipped at Doto's left ear.

He pulled back. "To kill fire bearers."

"Oh." Clay stepped back a step. "I hope you know that I'm not going to do that."

Doto looked around, his ears twitching. "Let's go somewhere we can talk."

"There's nothing to talk about," Clay answered, stone edging his voice. "I thought you understood that."

Doto sighed. "Just… follow me. All right?" He turned and headed toward their temple at the highest speed he could manage, so quickly that the air heated with his passage, little cyclones tearing up in his wake, stripping the plants of their leaves. He knew that he was no longer perfectly divine—nor even perfectly half-divine, if he was being honest with himself. He could trip, or misjudge the distance of an obstacle, or make a wrong turn, and fall or crash into something. Healing Clay had introduced that weakness. It was not an incapacitating one, though. All he needed to avoid error was awareness.

Once, he had been able to run through the forest idly, his movements through it as natural and easy as water flowing around rocks in a stream or the wind blowing around the branches. But his divinity no longer worked unconsciously. Now he had to pay attention. He had to choose his path, watch his steps. He had to be a conscious and deliberate member of the world. Not above it, but part of it.

He had not seen Clay trip or slide or fall once since his change. But Clay was used to moving through the world without it deferring to him or bending aside. Clay was always aware, always participating. A weak person given a little bit of strength could perhaps do far more with it than a strong person who was accustomed to it. And now that success was no longer automatic, Doto found it pleasing. It was one thing to succeed because you could not fail; it was another to do so through your own effort.

And so Doto made a game out of it as he ran, veering near but avoiding the massive trees and stones in his way, or pouncing up into the branches and leaping from tree to tree. And although his god-swift passage caused no small amount of damage to the trees he leapt between, he found the journey entertaining, a welcome distraction from unpleasant conversation he would shortly need to have with Clay.

Somehow Clay arrived at the temple before him; perhaps he'd taken a more direct route while Doto had busied himself leaping about branches and running along canyon walls. But he was standing there, grinning a pointy-toothed grin, right outside their temple, and a split second before Doto could reach it, he put one foot firmly down inside their intimate borders. He felt it along with Clay immediately, a pawprint on his soul.

"Good running," Doto said approvingly.

"I thought I'd be out of breath. I… hope I never get used to this."

"You shouldn't," Doto warned him. "You will fall." He ignored Clay's bewildered expression and followed him inside their temple.

If Clay would never get used to exercising his new powers, Doto thought he would never get used to having him in their temple. It was at once jarring and intimate feeling him inside the space that they shared and that defined them. He had the sensation of standing inside himself and beside himself all at once. Here he had perfect awareness of every part of Clay's body. He felt his breath in their shared atmosphere. Here their heartbeats slowed to match each other's, to beat in perfect syncopation.

He settled down in their grass and it curled around his thighs and calves, brushing softly against his fur with something like intent. "Here," he said. "Here we can talk, and Kwaee cannot hear us."

"All right. But you know that I'm not going to…" Clay trailed off, his expression going vacant. "You do know. I can feel it."

"Here we know each other well," Doto agreed. "Of course you will not kill fire bearers. Neither will I. My father can command and rage all he likes. The fire bearers are—" He took a deep breath, not well liking the words he was about to speak. "They are your people. No. They are *our* people. For you come from them, and they are creatures of this world, which means we are responsible for looking after them as much as any other creature. And… and my mother… was a fire bearer. Part of me comes from them."

Those words felt foul coming from his mouth, reminding him of when he had fallen ill on the savanna from bad meat. His stomach had clenched and sent the foulness spilling from him. But then, after the badness had left him, he had felt much better. This felt the same. Speaking the words was unpleasant, but once they were spoken, their heaviness was gone from inside him.

"So they are my people too. Ogya has tricked them into following him. And you and I, we will save them. We will save the forest. And if you say we cannot do that by killing them, then I believe you. We will find another way."

He stopped. Clay was staring at him, his gold-green eyes wide. And then it was if the entire temple shared that wondering regard, every flower turned toward him as though he were the sun, every tree bending in his direction, every current of the stream coursing toward his shore. And he realized that he, too, shared in that amazement. That something inside him had changed—no scar or wound or new resentment, but an opening, as though he had hatched newborn from an egg or cracked open a chrysalis to let new, wet wings dry in the morning sun.

"Do you mean that?" Clay asked.

"Of course. How could I not mean that here? I trust you, Clay."

He felt, for a long moment, his heart stop beating. It was of no great concern, for of course a god's body did not need a beating heart, but he didn't recall wishing it to do so. It must have been Clay's heart that had stopped, and his along with it, and then he felt the surge of intense emotion radiating from Clay a split second before Clay's clawed toes curled in their temple's earth.

Then Clay was crouched over him, pressing him down into their soft, caressing grass, his lips pressed to Doto's own. This forwardness was unusual for Clay, but Doto supposed it was due to his new divinity, and he kissed his mate back fondly, letting his teeth part when Clay's coarse tongue slid between them to rasp at the roof of his mouth.

Here in their temple, emotion tended to build on itself, echoing between them more and more intensely, and Doto found himself kissing back fervently, lost in adoration. He wrapped his arms around Clay and turned, rolling him over in their grass, eagerly tasting the humanity in his divine mate. Their arousal grew between them in twin pulses, and he slid his fingers down Clay's lean belly to feel the erection there, to grip it against his own in one paw as the plants around them ripened into sexual fruition. The insects in the air released their pheromones; the fish in their stream pursued each other with vigor; their flowers drooled their nectar.

And Clay began to disappear, his consciousness bleeding out of himself and into their temple.

Doto paused, carefully releasing Clay's erection. "Stop," he said, keeping his voice gentle but firm.

"What's wrong?" Clay's eyes were puzzled, hungry, his jaws parted, the tips of his canines visible between his black lips. "Don't you want to—no, you do. I can *feel* that you do, but…"

Doto slid his paw over Clay's head, and then along his muzzle, smoothing back his whiskers. "Stay *here*," he said when his paw was on Clay's forehead. He moved his fingers to his mate's lean, strong chest and pressed down. "Here. Feel the center of your avatar. You control your power. It does not control you. No slipping. All right?"

Clay nodded breathlessly.

"All right." Doto waited a moment more and then moved forward, his knees to either side of Clay, straddling him. He swayed his tail, letting it flick across the tip of Clay's erection and was amused to see him wince and the whole temple echo it in a resonant shiver.

"You are a god," he purred to Clay, and leaned down to plant a kiss on his muzzle. At the same time, he slid backward, letting the stiff root of Clay's erection nestle between the curves of his rump. His own need pressed downward into Clay's belly, aching to be driven someplace tight and deep, but this could wait. "But you must learn. So. Remain inside yourself. Keep your presence here, in your body. If you begin to slip, I stop. All right?"

Clay nodded breathlessly, and the temple bobbed its branches and lianas with him. The fish were frozen in the stream; the gnats hung in the air.

"All right." He let himself expand into their temple a little, enough to curl several flowers down, heavy with nectars on their creeping vines. He dabbled his fingers in them, coating them, letting the honey drizzle over his palm. Then he gave an encouraging smile and reached back to slick Clay's erection with the liquids. Clay groaned and arched his back beneath Doto but stayed within himself.

Doto rose to press Clay's tip against his ring and then settled down slowly, feeling his mate's thickness slide steadily up into him, a rising pressure that increased in pleasure as he sank, aided by the slickness of their nectar. He kept his senses spread wide, a lattice of awareness strung through their temple, feeling for Clay's awareness.

His mate's presence hovered in his avatar, remaining in his form for the most part, but blurring around the edges, inexact, like the reflection of the moon on a wind-stirred pool. Doto wanted nothing more than to press all the way down, to blur the lines between both of them a little more, but he paused.

"Why—why did you stop?" Clay asked between needy breaths. "I'm doing it."

"Almost. Feel your borders. Feel where your body ends and the rest of the world begins." Doto ran his fingers through the fur of Clay's chest. "Don't feel the fur itself move. Feel it pull at your skin as I brush it. Do you feel it?"

"I—yes," Clay said, but he was far more focused on the erection he kept flexing with need inside Doto.

Doto twitched an ear, watching him with patient, unblinking eyes.

"But I…" Clay flushed, the white fur of his throat betraying a deepening pink beneath it. He knitted his brow, took a deep breath, and stopped making pulses of need inside Doto. "Okay. Do it again."

Doto brushed his fingers through his mate's fur again and this time felt the borders of Clay's presence become clearer, his mate more fully cohering within his own form. "Good. It is easy to do this when there are no distractions. You must learn to stay present even when there are many other… stimulations." He sank down again, coaxing a low groan from Clay that he echoed from his own muzzle, the pressure making his bared erection drool with arousal, dripping into the fur of Clay's belly.

This time, Clay's presence slid much more dramatically from himself, and once again Doto paused, giving him a moment to collect and recenter himself. He slid his paws up Clay's sides, gripped his mate's strong, muscled arms, felt the blood pulse in his throat, and brushed lightly at the ends of his whiskers, all stimuli meant to remind him of the limits of his body, his sensations.

Clay responded to his touch, pushing back, but also finding his own boundaries, the nebulous shape of his divine presence pressed and molded and formed by Doto's paws until it learned the shape of his avatar exactly. Doto rocked forward, letting the stiffness of his mate slide backward, and then he pushed down again, his hips rolling with feline flexibility, arching his back and then rutting forward, his own tip dragging tracks through the fur of Clay's tightly muscled belly. And each time Clay began to lose himself, to spread outside of his avatar, Doto paused and reminded him where he was with a kiss on the lips or a squeeze against his hips or by flicking his tail across Clay's toes.

And, motivated by need and pleasure, Clay learned. His divinity responded to Doto's touch, sculpted and fashioned by Doto's paws, by his mouth, by his embrace, into the shape of Clay.

Soon, Clay needed little guidance, fully inhabiting his avatar as he rocked his own hips, his paws on Doto's waist as he moved inside him. The shape of his aura had become distinct, the pool reflecting that moonlight still and calm and clear.

Only at climax did he lose focus—as his seed flooded into Doto, so too did his awareness, and Doto accepted both at once. It was, after all, a moment of release. It was good, he decided, once in a while, to lose control, and as the pleasure gripped him, he and Clay were one, sharing sensations, sharing the pleasure of mating and being mated, the twin ecstasies of spilling into Doto's tight passage and erupting across Clay's face and chest overwhelming them.

They spread out into their temple, inhabiting all its life for a time, before they finally returned to their own panting forms, and Doto kissed Clay's cheeks and throat adoringly, and Clay buried his fingers in the fur of Doto's head and tugged it to his chest in adoration.

~

"You did well," Doto told Clay later, sprawling with him in their soft grasses. "You are a fast learner."

Clay smiled, gazing up at the patches of blue sky that shone between the branches of their temple. The trees arched up and spread their limbs across it like the dome of an enormous tent. Between them, white clouds drifted, herds migrating across an endless blue plain. He had not known that there could be a perfect place in the world, but he had found it, and his spirit was at peace. It would have been easy to forget that there was trouble anywhere, but for the gnawing at the edge of his awareness: the burning wound from his mad brother and the blazing god spreading deeper and deeper into the forest.

He turned his mind away from it and rolled onto his side to stare into Doto's gold-green eyes. "Faster than you?"

The fur bristled around Doto's neck. "Well. This isn't exactly how I was taught."

Clay burst into giggles. "No, that would be highly inappropriate of Lord Kwaee, god of the forest."

"You should speak with more respect," Doto told him archly, but Clay kept grinning at him until finally his stern composure broke and he relaxed into a reluctant smile. "I thought you believed in respecting the gods."

"I did," Clay agreed. "I still do. Treating people—and especially gods—with respect is usually wisest. But things have changed."

"You mean because you are one of us now."

Clay felt his ears fold back. He was never going to grow accustomed to that. "Well, maybe. But look, there's all this stuff about the gods that isn't in the stories. When we hear the Teller and sing the old songs, the gods are these removed, revered beings that… aren't the same. No offense to your father, Doto, but he's kind of like a child. He doesn't try anything that's difficult, he has tantrums when he doesn't get his way, and anything that he doesn't like he tries to pretend doesn't exist. And at the same time, he seems… lonely, maybe. He's not imperious and all-knowing and all-powerful, guiding the forest with an inerrant hand. Paw. He doesn't know what to do about Ogya. He seems as disconnected from Wem as we—er, the fire bearers—are from the rest of the gods."

Doto's tail had begun twitching as Clay spoke, his fur prickling along his spine, and so Clay reached over and rubbed at Doto's shoulders and neck, a touch that seldom failed to calm him, and soon he was leaning into the massage, eyes half-lidded, rumbling in pleasure.

"Anyway, it's not only Kwaee," Clay said. "Sarmu sat stuck in the middle of that volcano and did nothing. Asubonten was boastful, Adanko was a liar, and then there's Ogya. He's vicious and insatiable. Why? Did Father Wem make him like that? Or did something happen?"

Doto was now flattened out so low into the grass that he resembled a bed pallet. "I don't know," he mumbled into the crook of his arm. "They've been that way as long as I've been alive. Though I never met Sarmu or Ogya before you. The only gods I'd met before were Fam, Asubonten, Atekye and the lesser gods of the forest. And Kwaee, of course. But I am not even a thousand rains old. Kwaee claims they have been around more than a thousand times that."

Clay tried to work out a number of that size in his head and surrendered quickly. It was beyond comprehension. "Are we going to live that long?" The thought was dizzying. To simply continue as everyone he knew aged and died, as the rains came and went, generations rose and fell and joined their ancestors. Would he ever see his own ancestors? Would he ever go to the stars and dwell with the Sky-Father? Or were those stories also false—misrepresentations of an afterlife that was itself flawed, or even cruel?

Doto sensed Clay's unease, for he turned his head, one bright eye peeking over his own arm. "If Ogya has his way, none of us will be around for very long. At the rate he is burning, the forest will be entirely gone in perhaps two hundred rains."

"That long? How much forest can there be?" Of course, he could send himself out into it and sense any part of it, and he could feel when distant parts of it were troubled, as with Ogya's flames. But to understand the whole of it at once, all its breadth and scope, was beyond him—and would be, Doto had told him, unless Kwaee allowed him to sit on the moabi throne. Still, Clay remembered their visit to the high places, an endless expanse of forest stretching beyond the limits of his then-human vision. The world was wider and vaster than his imagination could comprehend, like the lifespan of the gods—beyond understanding. And then it seemed impossible that, even with two hundred rains, Ogya could destroy it all. Surely by the time he reached one end, the other would regrow. Trees and plants sprouted quickly in burned soil. He had seen it himself out on the savanna.

Something else occurred to him. "My brother will not live for two hundred rains, unless Ogya has some way to sustain him, and even then, the fire hunters and the rest of my people will not. How would Ogya keep them burning and moving their whole lives? What happens when the forest is so thin that the food runs out? His plan doesn't make any sense."

"Or we have not divined it entirely," Doto answered. "But it's true. He is more impatient than that. Perhaps he plans to recruit other fire bearers to assist him. Or perhaps as he continues to devour more of the forest, his power will increase enough that he will no longer require their assistance. We must stop him before either of these things happen."

"And we'll try to do that first by talking to the people, persuading them?"

"I do not know what we could say. I doubt your brother would listen even if Ogya let him."

"I've been thinking about this," Clay said. "Look, the only reason that the people agreed to fight is because they believe that Kwaee hates them and will starve them out of existence. They didn't come here to hate the forest. They came here to live, and then Kwaee attacked them."

"Which is his right, as god of the forest," Doto pointed out.

Clay sighed. "It may be his right, but that doesn't mean it *is* right. Look where we are now. My point is, if the people think that Kwaee might be willing to make a truce..."

"He never would. A god doesn't negotiate with the creatures he rules. And Kwaee loathes the fire bearers. You saw how he reacted when you tried to talk to him about it. He never, ever backs down from anything."

"I know. But all I said was if the people *think* Kwaee wants a truce. Then they might stop burning. They don't want to do all this, I know it. If they knew that they could live peaceably with the forest, hunting and harvesting wood and fruit when they need it, then they'd never follow Laughing Dog."

Doto's ears perked with interest and he leaned up a little. "But how would we make them think that if Kwaee won't go along with it?"

"Well, no one in my village has ever actually *seen* Kwaee," Clay said slowly. He plucked at a strand of grass, not meeting Doto's eyes. "But you are a forest god, after all, and with a prayer to Adanko..."

Doto's brow knitted in puzzlement. "Adanko? How could the god of lies possibly—" He narrowed his eyes. "*That* is a very, very bad idea. Impersonating a god is—well, it's beyond blasphemy! And no one would fall for it."

"No one's saying you have to impersonate a god exactly. I mean, just introduce yourself as God of the Forest and let the people assume what they will. And if some of them call you Kwaee, you don't have to correct them."

"Ogya would know the difference. If he's there, even a trace of his presence, enough to know what's going on, he'll make sure everyone knows the truth." Doto rolled to a seating position and nudged his nose at Clay's ear. "And when did you become so deceptive? Half the time we run into trouble it's because of your compulsive honesty."

Clay scowled. "Yes, and look where that got me!"

Doto gave a long, meaningful look around the temple of indescribable beauty in which Clay, ascendant, now sprawled with his divine mate.

"All right, yes, but with my people. I told them the truth. I tried to be honest with them. And they wouldn't listen."

"You were the one who said talking was the way to reach them."

"And I meant it. But is there any chance Kwaee will back down before the fire bearers stop burning the forest?"

Doto frowned. "I do not think he would for any reason. Even after they stop, he is likely to be… surly… for a while."

Clay spread his paws. "Well, the fire bear—*my people* aren't going to leave off attacking Kwaee if he doesn't stand down. Laughing Dog's got them all believing the gods are against them and that the only way they can survive is to fight back."

"So we need a truce."

"And if Kwaee won't offer one, I think it has to be you."

"Or you," Doto suggested. "They will hardly recognize you now. They think you are dead."

Clay pushed that uncomfortable thought and all its nasty implications away for now. It didn't belong here in their temple where everything was bright and peaceful. "I could try, but I don't have all that experience being a god. And they might recognize my voice."

"No. It is different now. They will not know the sound of it. Your old voice was very high-pitched and smooth."

"Well, uh, okay," Clay said. "But there's still my manner of speaking and everything. Listen, I think this can work, but I need your help. It's a deception, maybe, but only a little one. Just to get everyone else to stop fighting for a while. And if it could save lives and end this conflict—"

"Then it is a worthwhile deception. Very well. I will not call myself Kwaee. But I will go to your people as a god of the forest and offer them peace."

"Thank you, Doto. Thank you so much." Clay shifted his haunches a little and then pounced Doto into the grass.

Doto laughed and caught him, and they rolled over together in the little meadow, nearly splashing into the brook. "But not yet," Doto whispered into Clay's ear, his breath tickling the fur inside it. "First you have more lessons. No official god missions until you have learned properly how to be a god."

"But I can stay inside my avatar without slipping now," Clay protested.

"Once, you managed it. You must try it many more times." Doto's expression was positively lascivious with those words. "And there are more lessons. Many more."

~

Doto had not exaggerated. Over the coming days, he trained Clay with dogged persistence to use and manage his divine gifts. The training was not limited to the exercise of remaining centered in his form, although Doto emphasized that one strongly, and insisted that Clay learn to manage it not only during sex—though that remained a favored activity—but during other types of distraction as well.

He took Clay to the forest fire and made him sit in the smoke, well out of the range of Ogya's taunts, but not out of danger. There, he had Clay breathe the thick clouds while sitting high in the branches of a tree, challenging him to feel the burn and choking in his throat and the sting in his eyes but not respond to it. It was important not just that Clay remain within his form but that he hold back his influence from the forest around him while ignoring the unpleasant effects.

In Clay's first attempt, he managed not to cough or rub at his eyes, remaining within his form instead of allowing his consciousness to flee into the surrounding world, but around him all the trees and plants grew larger and lusher, sprouting new leaves and suffusing the forest with more clean air for their suffering god. That prompted a number of lessons in shielding his emotions and desires from the world he inhabited.

The second time, he was so focused on *not* prompting the plants to supply him with air that for several paces in every direction around him, they all wilted and died. And so the lessons continued.

Doto taught him how to consciously bend the growing of plants to his will and how to move them as an extension of his body. Moving them unconsciously had been difficult to avoid. Now he struggled with the fine control needed to move a single floral tendril and curl it around Doto's ankle. It took him many, many tries to get it right, and his errors were multitude. Moving only one vine instead of all of them at once was its own challenge, as was nudging it to grow and bend in the ways its structure allowed. Clay could easily prompt a solid tree branch to bend, but even he could not push it beyond the laws of nature, and beyond a certain point the branch would break, fibers of green wood fraying apart, permeating the air with the sharp odor of its botanical blood.

"Little nudges, little encouragements," Doto told Clay each time he killed another tree or shrub. It was not using his power at all that gave Clay difficulty—it was refraining from using too much of it. An attempt to extend a liana might tear it from the tree; his urging a tree to lift its roots might pull it completely out of the ground.

"You are doing too much. Trying too hard," Doto said. "When you wish to move a finger, do you put your whole mind and all your body's strength toward making it stretch outward? No. You simply will it. The tiniest of suggestions and it moves."

"But this is nothing so simple as moving a finger," Clay protested. "You're talking big, incomprehensible magics. I have to focus. I *have* to try as hard as I can."

"The forest here *is* your body, in a way. Let its branches be your fingers, or its liana your tail, or roots your toes. See?" Doto nodded toward a sprouting coil of vine covered with passion-purple flowers. "That is your finger, there, covered with flowers. Don't send your mind into it. Don't focus or fixate on it. Think of it as your finger. Now. Reach out that finger."

And as Clay was making the attempt, Doto reached over and flicked him on the ear hard enough to—well, very little *hurt* him anymore, but it was irritating. He opened his mouth to complain, but Doto held up one paw. "Look." He pointed. The vine had straightened and was reaching outward, its delicate tendrils and flowers undamaged.

By the end of the day, Clay had begun to control the movements of plants with ease, a skill that he quickly put to good use in his play with Doto in their temple. Doto kept the lessons challenging, however: as soon as Clay could master moving one plant however he liked, Doto challenged him with moving five, a trick that made him feel as though his mind would split.

From there, Doto taught him how to send his consciousness into that of other creatures. First with cats, since he claimed they were most like themselves, but eventually birds, fish, and insects. He did not have Clay attempt to control them, as he said this was difficult and stressful for the animal, but simply ride along, listening through their ears and watching through their eyes.

Every experience was surprising and enticing to Clay, and he learned much about the creatures of the forest: seen through the eyes of a serval, the world was blurry and faded, with no red to be seen anywhere; through the eyes of a bee it was pebbled, composed of a thousand circles of light in colors he had never seen or imagined. Back in his own mind, he could not even remember them—only that they had been beautiful and alien.

He learned to ride on the backs of eagles, watching with them as they scanned the forest below for prey. For them, the world sailed by with a crystalline distinctness that astonished him, but they paid little mind to details. They watched for movement, and the scurries and shifts of creatures below glowed as though on fire. He fluttered through the night on the wings of bats, and became part of their endless chorus, singing his own tiny part in it, a song so sweet that the whole world sang it back to him, its voice shining in the darkness and lighting up the landscape like sung moonlight.

He stopped counting days and nights, losing himself in the study of this wondrous magic and finding himself in Doto's arms in their temple. The world grew wider and wider, and he thought he understood now why Kwaee and Doto had thought so little of his people. They were only a few hundred minds in a world of endless experiences. A mouse struggled for life no less than an elephant; it suffered no less acutely; its joy at the flavor of a favorite meal was no smaller than that of a fire bearer's. How, then, to brook the crimes of these hairless apes, who set flames to the forest and induced pain and terror and death to uncountable awarenesses?

Sometimes, if he had been in other minds for long, he found it more difficult to remind himself of the reasons why the fire bearers should be spared and not simply eliminated like a spreading fungus. In these moments, he repeated to himself the tales of his people. He sang their songs and remembered the voices of his father and his mother. His brothers when they were young. That was one thing he had not seen in any other mind in the forest. The fire bearers did not just live stories—they shared them. They connected to each other's experiences. Even if a fire bearer died, their life continued in the stories of others. The beauty of that life and all that they had seen and done continued beyond them in the minds and voices of their companions.

That was why the fire bearers were here now, burning the forest. They were creating untold suffering and death, true, and not for the reasons other animals killed: not for food or shelter or even territory or the safety of their young. They did it all for a story, one they had believed in and shared, even though it was a lie, twisted by king and god.

The fire bearers had not always been this way. They needed a new story—or perhaps an older one, one they had forgotten.

~

Clay did not know how many days had passed since he died and Doto brought him back. Time in the forest was ephemeral, something that could be measured no more than the water flowing by his toes when he hung them in the cool of their brook. Days were for living, not for counting. And yet, it had fled. The shock of opening his eyes to the forest around him felt fresh every time, the way his fur tugged at his skin when he moved was eternally a new thing, and each lesson Doto taught him of controlling himself and his power seemed hasty, desperate.

They had no time for any of it. The gash of the burn into the forest ate its way deeper and deeper, but the progression of the fire bearers slowed as the burn grew wider. The pain and numbness of the inferno ate into his consciousness deeper and deeper, despite his attempts to shield his mind from it. It was like a scar growing deeper into his side every day. He tried to learn everything as quickly as he could, but he feared he would never be ready.

And so he was surprised the night when Doto sat up in their temple and said, "It is time. You have learned much about being a god. Not everything. You are still very clumsy and awkward at it, and I think other gods might laugh at you if they saw it, but it will be enough to impress fire bearers and fight them away if they attack you. Are you ready to go?"

Clay stretched and rose. "Will we be all right, do you think?"

"I do not know. We will have to go out of the forest to see them and talk to them. There, they can hurt us, like the two fire bearers did when we crossed the savanna." Clay flattened his ears, remembering Jai and Ulo, who had bound, tortured, and nearly killed him. "But this time will be different. Then I feared for your life. This time, you cannot die. I think."

"You *think?*"

Doto shrugged. "How can we know for sure unless it happens?"

"Have *you* ever been killed?"

"No."

"Then how do you know for certain that you can't die?" Clay asked.

"All gods know this. A god cannot be killed. They simply return to their temple. You, however, are only part-god, and so…" Doto trailed off, his pupils narrowing to slits in his widening eyes.

"We both are," Clay said. "And what you said about our temple being our real self, I feel that. I know it. But what happens to the part of us that's not god if we are killed?"

"Probably nothing." Doto's voice wavered on the last word, however resolute his expression. "But you are right. It would be wise to be cautious. If there is danger, we will retreat." Strength hardened his voice again. "I could not lose you a second time."

"Nor I you," Clay returned fondly. "Shall we go?"

"Yes. But I warn you: you will not like leaving the forest."

Doto's prediction proved all too accurate. The wall between forest and savanna was more imposing than Clay remembered it. Inside, all was brilliant color and sound and smells, an awareness of all the life around them. That it was night made no difference; Clay could now see as easily in the darkness, and his sense of hearing and smell were so acute that he could have moved about with his eyes closed. But at the wall of the forest, that vibrancy ended abruptly, as though the entire world dropped off into nothing. Beyond its border, all was ghostly images, a dream world shrouded in fog and darkness. Nothing outside the forest seemed real.

Doto tilted his nose up, curling back his upper lip as he tasted the air. "The fire bearers' nest is not here."

"How can you tell?"

"I don't smell it. Can you?"

Clay gave the border of the forest a skeptical glance. "I'm not sure I'd be able to smell anything out there."

"Don't be foolish. Your god-sense will not work out there, but you still have a leopard's nose. Smell for them."

Well, Doto would know better than he. Clay sniffed the air a few times, catching whiffs of something, and then imitated Doto, pulling back his upper lip and letting the air travel over his tongue. Now he could smell the the fire bearers—the carrion-scent of their pelts, the musty hewn wood of their fences, their excrement pit, the musk of their goats and the green of their crops—but it was smothered in the foul stench of ash and smoke. And it seemed an ancient odor, faded, washed away by rain and wind and baking sunlight.

"You're right," he said to Doto. "They were here, but they're gone." This puzzled him. Why would they have left so suddenly? Had they revolted against Laughing Dog? The fire bearers burned the forest still; not only could Clay feel it, but this close, he could see the glow from the blaze and hear the roar of the flames.

Doto travelled a little distance along the border of the forest. "This way," he said after scenting the air again. "They have moved the nest."

Clay followed him through the forest, careful to stay on the inside of the wall of their world. They moved at very high speed, and Clay had little sense of how great that distance was, but he felt sure that it was farther than a day's journey for a fire bearer. He had no way to gauge his own speed for comparison. After a while, the reek of the village grew stronger in the air, and he wrinkled his nose at it. How could they tolerate living in such a foul odor all the time?

"There," said Doto, stopping and pointing toward a spot outside the wall of the forest.

Clay peered, trying to see the ghostly images beyond the brilliance of his domain. It seemed that lights flickered out there, some distance from the forest, tiny and orange in the ethereal darkness. "It's pretty far from the edge," he observed.

"They must have wished to protect themselves from further attacks from Kwaee. Our visit will not be welcome."

Clay nodded. "Have you decided what you're going to say?"

"I will use their tongue. I will tell them that I am god of the forest. I have recognized that great wrongs have been dealt their people and that I am there to call truce and make amends." Doto gave him a sidelong glance. "I would ask that you remain nearby. I may need your help after that."

"All right, but it will be better if they don't see me. If they do, and they recognize me, they may not understand."

"Yes. Your people are very poor at understanding things. We should not make them attempt too much of it." Doto walked up to the wall of the forest. "Are you prepared?"

Clay came up next to him. "I think so."

"Then let us go."

Clay took a deep breath and stepped forward. He had experienced the travel out of the forest before, when the only magic of Doto's he'd possessed had been a transformed foot and the protective magic of the fetish. That had been unpleasant. This was far worse. He felt as though he had been plunged underwater. His sight went dim, his hearing muffled, and his nose stuffed up. His lungs struggled for air that felt both too thick and too thin for them at the same time. Every part of his body ached—there was a tremendous pressure as though he was being clenched in a giant fist.

He fell to his hands and knees, his eyes squeezing shut. Then the pressure was gone, and he felt tiny, helpless, and alone. He gasped for air, and his voice sounded strange to his ears. More frail and high-pitched.

He opened his eyes and saw smooth, clawless fingers and hairless brown skin. Trembling and weak, he got to his feet. The flesh of his soles was uncalloused and delicate, the wood and pebbles of the savanna floor digging in uncomfortably. His legs shook as though he had not used them before. He was a fire bearer again.

"Clay?" The voice was both strange and unfamiliar at once.

He turned. A man stood there, tall and muscled. He stood uneasily, shaking like Clay. His hair was wild and black, his skin nearly as dark, and his eyes had a feline tilt. They were brown, but in the moonlight they flashed a hint of gold.

It was Doto. Doto had become a fire bearer.

# 7 Desecration

Doto had not remained outside the forest and in human form for more than a few breaths. After a moment of standing and staring at his body with a very human expression of horror, he sprang back into the forest, crouching there in leopard form, his tail lashing. "Come back in, come back in!" he urged.

Clay needed little convincing to return to the vivid and lush world of the forest. It was strange to feel so much more at home, so *right* with a tail and claws. Had human existence really been that bleak? Had he adapted to the senses of a god so quickly?

"We cannot go out there," Doto said. "We must remain in the forest from now on." He stared at the forest wall and scooted further back from it as though it might suddenly shrink inward and return him to human.

Clay stroked Doto's back and ears, trying to soothe him, but his whole body shook with terror. "It's not that bad. You knew you were part fire bearer before. Now it shows a little, sometimes."

"It is awful. Terrible," Doto moaned. "I have lost myself. I have lost what I am."

"You've just changed. It's not bad to change. That's how we grow." Clay sighed. "I changed for you."

Doto tilted his head up enough to give Clay a gold-green glare over his arm. "Yes, but *you* became a god. I am… fallen. Lesser."

"It isn't very godlike to feel so sorry for yourself," Clay observed, despite all evidence to the contrary. "Listen. Being a fire bearer, or part one, can't be so terrible. You fell in love with one, didn't you?"

"You know I did," came Doto's muffled reply.

"Well, you wouldn't love anything unworthy, would you? Am I worthy of your love, Doto?"

Doto looked up again. His shaking had stopped. "Of course you are. I would not have loved you if you weren't."

"Do you think I love you any less because of this?"

A long pause. "No. Once I thought you might. I loved you because you are the best fire bearer out of all of them."

Clay laughed at that. "I am far from that. You haven't even met most of them."

Doto flicked his ears. "You should not argue with a god. You are the best."

Clay leaned back, bemused. It still sometimes surprised him how childlike Doto could be. But of course, he was new to relationships of any kind, not just romantic ones. And vulnerability—that was something new to him too. It would take him time to become comfortable with it. "All I'm trying to tell you is that change is all right. You're still you. Trust me. You're still *very* you." He grinned. "And besides, you made a very handsome fire bearer."

Doto straightened up a little. "Well, of course I did."

"I would like seeing that handsome fire bearer again."

"I suppose you would," Doto said, narrowing his eyes. "You are made to like fire bearers best, after all. But we must not go outside the forest again. For any reason."

"But we do need to talk to the other fire bearers somehow."

"We will find another way. Lure them into the forest, perhaps, or talk with them at the edge. But you must not go outside the boundary of the forest, ever."

Clay hadn't expected Doto to extend that prohibition to himself. "I understand if you don't want to, but… well, it's not comfortable going outside, but I don't mind it. I'll be fine."

"But you might not be! What if… what if something happens to you out there, while you're not a god? What if they hurt you, or you get sick or old? You could die, Clay. We do not know if you would return to our temple. Maybe your body would lie out there where I could do nothing to save you."

"It's a risk," Clay admitted. "But Doto, I think we have to try."

"No," Doto said firmly, and he would not budge on the subject. Reluctantly, Clay dropped the topic and suggested they return to their temple. Doto was happy to comply.

Clay didn't feel much like rushing back and kept a slower pace, pondering over their difficulty. They had to speak to the rest of his people and try to persuade them to make peace with Kwaee. Well, if Doto didn't want to risk it, Clay would have to do it on his own. And soon, before it occurred to Doto to make him *promise* not to. He didn't like the thought of creeping out against Doto's wishes, but his mate was intractable on this matter.

The touch of Doto's toes inside their temple nudged him out of his contemplation. Doto took a couple steps in, stopped for a moment, and then hurried to the center of their temple, where he stood very still. Clay could hardly feel Doto's breath on the air. Something must have caught his attention. Wondering what it could be, he quickened his pace, hurrying back to the mountain crevice where their temple was nestled. He didn't have to enter to see what had captured Doto's interest.

A new tree had sprouted in the center of the temple—a baobab. It was far from the girthy giants Clay knew from the savanna, but it was very young, perhaps a little more than twice Doto's height. It was already beginning to hollow, though, and a rivulet of their brook trickled from beneath it.

Puzzled, Clay joined Doto's side. "How can this be? That's not a forest tree. It doesn't belong here."

Doto curled his tail around Clay's ankle. "It does now. This is from you. You are shaping our temple now as much as I am."

"You don't sound upset."

"Why should I be upset? A god shapes his temple, and this temple is partly yours. Besides, it is interesting, and beautiful, and new."

Strange, Clay thought, that he should be so welcoming of this change to the most intimate part of him, and yet so upset that his avatar looked different in the outside world. What was the difference? "Does this mean these trees will begin to grow in the forest now?"

"You have no forest territory of your own. Everything outside this temple belongs to Kwaee. He never allowed me to rule over any of his domain. He never gives it up to anyone. He will certainly never do it for you."

"He did it once, to stop Ogya," Clay recalled.

"Yes, and he's been grousing about it ever since. You will have to be content with being god of this little temple. Kwaee will never give you more."

Clay marveled at the idea of wanting more territory to rule over. What would he even do with it?

"This change you made in our temple—perhaps you are feeling more confident. You are learning how to be a god." Doto switched his tail. "I am a very excellent teacher."

Clay rested his head on Doto's shoulder. "You are."

"It is a big change, but it is not the first. There are others. New plants that I did not know. Like those." Doto pointed to a thicket of long, slender stems whose ends were thatched with circlets of fern-like leaves, and in the center of them, clusters of oddly familiar oblong fruits.

Clay frowned. "That's odd. Those look like—" He sniffed the air. "They're dates! But that's impossible! Dates only grow on palms!"

"I think you are changing that in here. The forest would be a different place if you ruled it!"

"You mean Kwaee makes the shapes of all the plants in the forest?"

Doto stared at him as though he were stupid. "Naturally. What do you think a god does?"

"But I thought Mother Fam creates all life."

"She does. And Kwaee shapes it. Just as Sarmu shapes the life on the savanna according to his nature, which explains these big… fat… elephant trees."

"Baobabs."

"That is a bad name. Big Fat Elephant Tree is much better."

Clay ignored that. "But why did this happen so suddenly?"

"It is not sudden." Doto padded around the baobab, looking through the garden of their temple. "You have been changing things in my temple since *you* changed, bringing things of the savanna. Perhaps things you like? Things that make you who you are? There are these thorny berry vines, and this strange moss. And you have been growing all this clayfruit."

"I thought you were growing that," Clay said.

"You did? You are terrible at being proud of the things you do. Just… very, very awful. I do not know why you do not take credit. You have been growing things for a while. The tree is new and sudden. I cannot think what made you want to grow this… tall, stiff thing jutting up right in the center of our private temple." Doto turned his head very slowly to look back at Clay. He was grinning.

"Doto. Did you make a joke?"

"Yes. The joke is that I *can* think of what made you do it because this tree reminds me of—"

"Okay, yes, I understand," Clay said. He put his arms around Doto and slid his fingers down his mate's belly. "Why don't you show me instead?"

~

Doto slept. Clay could tell not just by the rise and fall of his chest but by the way his flowers in the temple had closed up, the way his birds in their branches settled with their eyes lidded. And of course here in the temple they were connected, feeling everything the other did. Doto *could* sleep whenever he chose to, as could Clay, though this was more like expanding out into their temple and the surrounding forest and letting his senses drift. But since he had restored Clay to life, he periodically became drowsy enough to require real sleep—a fact that made him grumpy and ill-at-ease.

And the forest was dying. The scar of the burn ate ever further into Clay's side. If he had ever a chance to go and speak to his people without Doto trying to stop him, it would have to be now. Instinctively he let his spots dissolve and swim until he looked like no more than a patch of shifting moonlight. It was unnecessary, surely, but it happened on its own when he wished not to be seen. Doto had taught him how to move through the forest soundlessly as well, and he did so now, creeping out of their temple on all fours, the forest bending around him so as not to make any noise, twigs refusing to crack, blades of grass turning aside without a rustle.

Once he was out of the temple and a good distance away, he hurried back to the edge of the forest, tracing it until he found the spot closest to where the fire bearers had relocated and, happily, far enough from the burn that the smoke and fire were not a distraction.

He paused at the wall. Passing through that had been unpleasant before and he did not relish the idea of experiencing it again. But a possible end to their conflict waited on the other side. He had to try. He took a deep breath and passed through.

Again the awful feeling of contracting, of being squeezed, of having his senses plucked away from him. He blinked in the darkness—he could barely see, even after giving his eyes time to adjust. And he had no way to make fire for light, even had he dared risk alerting Ogya of his presence. He would have to get there on his own. From here, he could see the torches of the village, and he moved toward them carefully. The soles of his feet were as soft as a newborn's, and the ground bit into them painfully. Every now and then his toes stubbed against a rock or jutting bit of wood. His hair, now untamed by braids, bobbed heavily on his head. He had a new appreciation for how unpleasant the journey into the savanna must have been for Doto, especially the first few days.

It took him several hours to make it to the village, though it hadn't looked that far away. Perhaps growing accustomed to a god's swiftness was making it harder to gauge distances without it. This relocated village was far smaller than the old, the walls shoddier. Probably there had been much less wood available. A guard was posted outside the gate, half-lit in the flickering light of a torch.

Clay took a deep breath. As soon as he entered the torchlight, Ogya would know he was there, which meant Laughing Dog would as well. Still, as long as his brother was working on burning the forest, he'd never be able to get here in time. It looked like a good three-to-four-day journey from the relocated village to the burn for a mortal. Unless, he conceded, Ogya had infused Laughing Dog with powers that Clay didn't know about.

He looked over his shoulder toward the forest. It remained invisible in the darkness, but it pulled at him as though with cords hooked into his spirit. He would have been able to find it again blindfolded.

Who was the woman standing guard? He couldn't make out her features in the heavy shadow from the firelight. Maybe instead of exposing himself to Ogya's gaze he could summon the guard from here. "Hello?" he called.

The guard nearly fell backward in surprise, but very quickly she had snatched up her bow and had an arrow nocked in his general direction. "Who's there? Who is it?"

He crouched down behind a boulder. It was unlikely that she could hit him in the darkness, but he didn't like having that arrowhead aimed at him. "Please don't be afraid." At the sound of his voice, she turned the arrow further toward him, and the firelight revealed the face of Spiral Horn. Clay felt a little surge of relief. She had been friendly, even kind to him in the past. "Spiral Horn, I know you. It's all right. It's… it's Clay."

He heard the creak of her bowstring tightening. "That's impossible. Clay is dead."

"I know people think that, but I'm all right. I lived." No need making things more difficult with explanations that might frighten them. "Please. You know my voice. You know it's me."

"What I *know* is that I'm hearing the voice of a dead man coming out of the darkness. If you really are Clay, let's see you. Come into the light. And if you do anything to frighten me, I *will* kill you."

There was no way around it. He rose from his crouch and stepped around the boulder, drawing close enough for the firelight to touch his face. Spiral Horn's arm faltered, the bow dipping, but she quickly aimed it again, and this time directly at him. "You look like him," she said, voice full of doubt. "But your hair is different. And you're naked."

"I… didn't have anything to wear. I'm not good at making clothes like you, Spiral Horn." He took several steps toward her.

"Don't come any closer!" She pulled the bowstring tighter. "King Laughing Dog said you were not Clay. That you're a demon."

"He says a lot of things. You don't believe all of them, do you?" That was a gamble. He had to hope she kept her own mind about things.

"All I know is something took our prince a rain ago and everyone said he was dead. Then something else came out of the forest. Something whose foot turned into a leopard paw. And our King killed that. Whatever it was. And now here comes something that looks like Clay again, out of the forest, in the middle of the night. And you're naked and wild-haired and you… move… wrong. I don't know what you are, demon, but you will not enter this village and hurt my people. Run back into the shadows you crawled out of."

That was dismaying. He raised his hands and took one more step forward, lowering his head submissively. "Spiral Horn, please. I know you. I know that all this seems strange. I would be afraid too. But I'm asking you to listen. If you think there is even a tiny chance that I'm the real Clay, please listen. This war between Ogya and Kwaee—it will kill everyone. My brother will never stop. But I think there is a way out."

Spiral Horn backed toward the gate a step. "A way out. What way?"

"Truce. I can… all right, I know how this sounds, but I can talk to the forest god. We can all back down. We can live in peace again. Wouldn't that be better?"

"Truce. You want us to make peace with the monsters that killed Flint and Bramble and Two Broken Hands. That poisoned Whistling Thorn and Red Moth. You want a truce with the demons that killed your father and brother. Now I know you are a demon." Her arms were shaking.

"Kwaee didn't do that! Well, not most of it," Clay amended lamely. "Please, Spiral Horn, listen to me. Or find others who will. We have to save our people. This is the only way." He kept his hands raised, his head bowed, but took another step forward.

"No. You are a demon. Every step you take, I see it. You can imitate our faces but not our movements. I will not let you threaten our people again."

Clay staggered backward.

Something had struck him hard in the sternum, as though he had been punched by a powerful fist. He looked down in astonishment and saw the slim shaft of an arrow sprouting from his chest. He couldn't breathe—he gasped, but air wouldn't come. Instead he coughed, and hot liquid sprayed from his mouth, and then searing pain flooded his chest and back. The strength fled his legs and the world tilted sideways. His head struck the ground and bounced with a ringing thud.

A voice called for help over and over.

He couldn't move.

The sideways world before his eyes was sandy earth and thin blades of grass. Dark, wet patches had spattered across it. They glinted red in the firelight. From those patches, the shoots of young plants sprouted, lengthening and curling as they grew, taller and fuller, white flowers opening toward the night sky.

Footsteps were approaching, many of them.

The plants thickened and spread, growing taller and wilder. The forest was in his blood now.

The world before his eyes grew dim, and distant, and then it was gone.

He was not there. He never really had been. He was his temple. He was trees and grass, vines and fruit, insects and birds and mice and fish. He was joined with Doto, and Doto's avatar was cradled within them, no longer sleeping, but awake, spilling fear-scent into the air.

"I felt it," Doto said, and Clay heard it through the many ears of their temple, felt the words spoken in the vibration of the air. "Clay, please, where are you? What have you done? Please tell me that you're okay."

Clay tried to answer, but he had only the voices of the creatures that were part of his temple, and those were inadequate. He should speak with his mate, but for that, he would require a body. Within himself, he shaped one, formed out of earth and decaying leaves and old bone and water and stone. He shaped it the only way it could be shaped, in the form that belonged to him. And then he filled it.

Earth was in his eyes, his ears, his nose. His earth. Him. He parted himself, clawed free of the ground, gasped for breath.

The dirt fell away from him and then he was crouched on the floor of the temple, next to Doto, shaking with remembered pain and terror.

Doto clutched him in strong but trembling arms, clinging to him as though the world around them would tear Clay away from him. "I felt it," he murmured. "I felt what happened to you."

Clay let himself be crushed into Doto's arms and wept. "My people killed me. They killed me again."

# Minor Prevarications

You all remember me. I know you do. I stick in your memories like happy dreams, the kinds where you can't quite remember what happened, but you know it was good.

Yes! It is I, Adanko, god of escapes and surprises and earth-shattering truths. Fair, fair, some do name me god of lies, but who are you going to believe? Some shiftless rumormonger or a god who can run like the wind and who is very kindly disposed to you?

And your favorite fuzzy god Adanko is busy with the important work in this story. Let the fire bearers and the forests fight each other, let some beleaguered group of exiles wander inexorably toward some grim fate, what care I?

Not a whit, not a tittle. For I serve at the behest of no gods, no, not even Mother Fam herself, though we have enjoyed a nice mud bath together occasionally. And fast as flame may spread, it could never catch up to Adanko, the fleetest and most cunning of all the pantheon. But you know gods. All powerful and sneaky. And they have ways of stopping you from doing things they don't want you to.

Like Sarmu, the elephant-lion. Remember him? Half pleasant, half surly, *all* lazy, and floating around and around in that fire-mountain. You know I think he actually *enjoys* being imprisoned? I tried to seek help for him! I vowed to summon all my hares to swarm the mountain and hoist him out on a bunny chain of freedom, but would he hear of it? No.

"Adanko," he said, "though you are surely the noblest and most heroic of all gods, and though you have long been my fast companion, I must command you not to interfere. Let Ogya have his day." Have his day, he said, as though the fire god was just going to breeze on by like a thunderstorm. Very devoted to the way things are. He sees the rise and fall of the seasons and thinks that life moves in circles and not spirals. Our savanna god is all about repetition. Doesn't like new changes, just wants the same old changes he knows.

Personally, I think it's because he's only a baby god. I'm far, far older than him, you know. We hares were scampering through the forest when the savanna was but a lurking fear in Kwaee's heart.

"Oh great and wondrous Lord Sarmu," I said. It's good to make gods feel special, and that's why I'm always so polite to them. "Surely we cannot let all those poor fire bearers burn up into piles of ash! I must insist in the politest possible terms that you allow me to go and help them."

"Nay, valiant Adanko!" he thundered. "For you are my most valued companion and I would have you here by my side, keeping me company as the savanna burns."

"Oh Lord Sarmu, provider of every feast and withered seed of every famine, I must humbly and with deepest respect insist. I care not for my own people—they are extremely accustomed to dying, and should my all-hearing ears catch the screams of millions of little leverets burning in their dens, I can understand that sacrifice. But the poor fire bearers! And the gods Clay and Doto as well! I cannot let anything bad happen to them. I urge you to allow me to help them, and if you will not, I fear it may severely impact our long and abiding friendship."

The god of the savanna trumpeted at me in ferocious rage. "Nevertheless! Should you thwart my desires on this, I shall turn my savanna against you and your kind. Every creature alive will hunt hares. All living things in the savanna, beast or fowl, shall be your enemies. Your kind will never know a moment's peace or safety."

I am proud to say I did not smirk in this moment. Smirking is a habit of the terminally smug and ugly-hearted and I discourage it in all of you. My response was a humble one: "But forgive me, Lord Sarmu, he who knows all wisdom leads to inaction, what exactly would change?"

I could see my incisive question surprised and intrigued him, but he was not so easily dissuaded. "Then I shall turn even the grass and bushes against your people, just as Kwaee has done with the fire bearers. Your kind will have no place to hide. The bushes will whip and beat them. If they burrow, the roots will strangle them in their dens. Their very meals will choke them in their throats. They will be eradicated."

"Truly, a more terrible fate than if all their homes were incinerated by Lord Ogya's flames, oh wise and benevolent Lord Sarmu. But this seems a dramatic and forceful response from you. Why should you fight so hard to keep us from saving the world? Could not my efforts be merely another part of the cycle you so revere?"

At that, the elelion (for such was his transfiguration at the moment) was surprised. "You are wiser perhaps than I give you credit, Brother Adanko," he growled. "But my answer remains the same. The savanna thrives because it is in balance between life and death. Even if outside forces threaten that balance, its god must never lean too far toward one side or the other. For if Mighty Sarmu should become imbalanced, then all of the savanna would tilt with him, and once the tilt begins, it is impossible to stop. Sarmu would fall, and the savanna would bloom into forest or dry into sand. I would lose myself, and my terrain shift forever toward Ogya or Kwaee. Then there would be no more savanna and no more Sarmu. Is that what you wish, Adanko?"

"All that?" I tell you truthfully, my jaw dropped. "I had no idea that the fate of all the savanna was so dependent on your utter and complete inaction. All that power and you can do nothing at all with it." Had I been a cheekier and less polite fellow, I might have added in dryer tones, "Other than killing all the hares in your domain, which affects that balance not at all," but you who know and love me will remember that I am guided ever by caution and prudence and so kept this criticism to myself.

"Well, that is the end of it, I suppose," I said, and I hung my head in dismay. "I will return to the grasslands and wait to be consumed by flame. Still. It will be a pity, when they all find out about you."

"Find out?" Sarmu snarled. He was shifting toward his leonine aspect now, and that always makes him surly. "Find out what? Why should they find out anything?"

I shrugged. "You know those fire bearers. No deed of the god escapes their stories for long. What will they think, I wonder, when they learn that the great Sarmu is utterly impotent."

"Impotent?" he roared, and he reached for me with snaggly claws, but I kept well out of reach. "How dare you? I shall—"

"Ah-ah," I warned him. "Don't forget about the balance." And indeed, he had begun to drift sideways slightly. "I take you at your word, oh powerful and discerning Sarmu, but when the fire bearers learn that their god can take no action to help or hinder them, they may wonder if he truly exists—or worse, whether it matters. I can hear their storytelling now.

" 'What difference a god who can take no action from no god at all?' their Tellers will ask, and the listeners will cry back, 'No difference!' Then why sing praises, why pray? Their faith in you will dwindle, and those devotions wither and crack like reeds when the oasis has dried up. What becomes of forgotten gods, I wonder? Do you talk to Bew or Obonka much these days?"

Sarmu trembled at my portentous words; I am sure I put the fear of human into him. "They… the fire bearers, they love me. They would never forget me. I tell you, Adanko, I have seen this cycle before. The fires will come and go. The fire bearers will struggle and suffer, but they will multiply once again, when the danger has ebbed. And they will—they will remember me, I'm sure of it. I love them all, and they must know it."

"Oh, certainly," I assured him. "If there is one thing constant and unchanging between the gods and humans, it is love. You must hear their prayers even now, as strong and fervent as they ever were, their songs just as passionate, the dances as vigorous. How I envy you, being the center of all that devotion all the time."

Lord Sarmu drifted in place like a coconut bobbing in a pool for a while. "You could—you could at least follow the fire bearers," he said at last. "See where they are going. Whether they are falling to… to poor influences that might make them forget me."

I gasped. "Would that not be interfering?"

"Do not speak to them. Do not show your true form. Do not assist them in their journey or in their quest in any way."

"But Lord Sarmu, supposing they *do* fall to poor influences that might make them forget you? What then? Might I then—not in my true form, of course, but that of a humble ground hare who speaks only through the majestic power of Lord Sarmu—advise them to sing songs of praise to any gods that might need their attention?"

I had chosen my timing of this question for the moment when Lord Sarmu was ascending toward his most elephantine, for is it not said that this is when he is at his most gracious and kind? And nearly, nearly I had persuaded him, for he began, "I suppose it would be—" but then caught himself. Alas, the savanna god is more clever than I. "Oh ho ho, Adanko, I know your tricks. No, I shall not be deceived by you, little mischief. No, instead you shall report back to me and allow me to decide how to handle things."

I grimaced, for truly he had outwitted me, and hung my head. "I understand, Lord Sarmu, and of course obey. I shall do none of those things, then, I swear it."

And you, my loyal and devoted worshipers, will know that I am nothing if not a hare of my word.

Duly bound and restricted by all the commands Lord Sarmu had given me, I begged my leave of his company and sought out the travels of the fire bearers, those who I could watch over, but with whose journey I could not interfere.

I tell you now, so you will not have too much hope or care about them too deeply, a god knows how these sorts of tales go. We have seen them a thousand times before. Those I follow and watch through the eyes of my many hares are doomed. All of them will die before this tale is out, and the greatest sadness of all is that the only one to bear witness to their struggle is, I'm sorry to say, a notorious liar.

# 9 A Different Kind of Dying

Doto scowled out at the fire bearers' village from behind the safety of the trees. "I cannot believe you wish to return to them."

"I don't wish to. I have to." Clay's ears lay flat, his claws sinking deep into the bark of the tree he peered around. "They can't see us here, can they?"

"They will see only sunlight moving through the forest. Your camouflage is excellent. I am a good teacher." He looked over for his expected approbation, but his mate was too distracted. "You cannot fool me, though. Look at you with your back all hunched and your fur bushing out. You look like a terrified kitten puffing himself up."

"Well, last time they *killed* me, Doto. It hurt so much."

"And that is why you should not go again." Doto filled his growl with blood and vengeance. "They deserve to die for what they did."

"They're afraid," Clay said. "Creatures lash out when they're afraid."

"Not you," Doto pointed out. But Clay was right—any creature in the forest would attack if it felt threatened and could not escape.

"We have to try to reach them. No matter how many tries it takes."

Clay took a deep breath and stepped through the border of the forest. His feline features retracted back into his form in a fluid instant, and then he was a fire bearer again. Doto's heart beat stronger seeing him like this, in the shape he'd first fallen in love with—though there were changes. His head fur was strange: large and fluffy and shapeless, not lying flat in neat little tails like it had done before. And of course he had a perfectly healthy foot where the previous had been mangled. He leaned forward, hands on his knees, panting. "That does not feel pleasant."

"No," Doto agreed. "But I should accompany you. To show those fire bearers that you are not alone and have powerful friends."

"But you would look like another fire bearer to them. They would wonder who you were and why I brought you. I think it's better if you stay, Doto."

"As you wish," Doto answered, secretly relieved. Stepping outside the forest was enormously unpleasant, and moving closer to that stinking fire bearers' nest doubly so. And he had no wish to be attacked and made to feel pain and death.

Clay fastened a vine around his waist. He had grown it himself, with several large, heavy leaves sprouting from it that covered his genitals and buttocks. Doto found this mystifying, but Clay assured him that fire bearers sometimes found it proper to keep covered. Why? Doto had wondered, but Clay had not known the answer. Some peoples wore no covering, he said, but the People of the Savanna did, and it was better to behave with their customs when trying to make peace with them.

Doto had followed very little of that. But Clay was no longer a fire bearer and would not have to bother with such foolishness most of the time.

He had also used his power to shape mahogany wood into a covering for his chest and belly. This, he said, might help if the fire bearers used their stone teeth on him again. He fastened it to his chest with flexible stems and gave Doto a hopeful smile. He didn't look as frightened now that he wasn't a cat anymore, but the acrid odor of his fear hung in the air like a storm.

"This time will go better," he claimed, and he leaned inside the forest wall to plant a kiss on Doto's muzzle. Then he left, picking his way gingerly among the sticks and rocks to spare his soft feet.

Doto paced back and forth between the trees. At first, he was anxious for Clay, but quickly he grew bored. It was taking *so long* for Clay to reach the village with his baby-fresh feet, and the further he traveled, the harder Doto had to peer to see how he was doing. Within the forest, he could see any distance. Beyond, his vision went muddy and indistinct. Finally, annoyed, he waited until a passing eagle glided near and sent his mind into it, urging it to perch on a tree close by, where he could watch through its sharp eyes.

After a period of agonizing boredom as Clay crept his way inexorably across the terrain like a dying ant, he finally drew close enough to the village that someone ran out to meet him, carrying one of those stone tooths on a stick that they called a spear. Clay spoke to the other fire bearer, but Doto could not hear the words. Curse these eagles! They were fine for watching but their ears were all but worthless. He tilted the eagle's head, trying to make out the words from their lips, but had no idea what they were saying. There was a black spot on the ground that Clay stared at, but Doto could not discern from this distance what it was, even with the eagle's acute vision.

The other fire bearer opened its mouth wide and banged its spear on the ground, and then more fire bearers ran out of the village, also with spears. They pointed them at Clay in a very angering manner, and if Clay had slashed or bitten a few of them after that, Doto would not have blamed him at all.

Clay said something back to them, waving his arms up and down, and then he got down on his knees, spreading his arms wide. This seemed to confuse the other fire bearers, because they lifted their spears and began to talk to each other.

Then another, his skin grey as an elephant's, came out of the village and acted like he was the dominant fire bearer. He pointed at the others and then pointed at Clay and shook his finger. The others waved their hands and said something back to him and then Clay reached up and they all shouted and turned their spears toward him again.

But Clay lifted the wooden chest covering he'd made and pulled it free. Doto wanted to shout at him: Why are you doing that? Put that back on now! This is why you made it! Now you are exposed and vulnerable, showing them your belly like a meek jackal!

This made the other fire bearers wave their spears back and forth and argue further. Clay held out his arms toward them, pleading, but then one of them turned and jabbed at him with his spear.

The eagle voiced Doto's fury and dismay in a scream that made the fire bearers flinch and stare in his direction. He wanted to leave the forest, run to Clay, pull him to safety, and then savage those worthless creatures with claw and fang. But there was nothing he could do. Out there, he would be a weak and helpless fire bearer, no more capable than Clay. He could only watch from the eagle's eyes as Clay slumped to the side, dark blood spilling out of his belly.

Another fire bearer threw his spear and it hit Clay in the chest and he fell backward, jerking. Doto screamed through the eagle again. His mate was suffering. His mate needed his help.

Again the fire bearers stared toward the forest, hunching low. Then they crowded Clay, blocking Doto's view; he could see only the movements of their arms and their spears. When they withdrew, they left a carcass of brown, black, and red lying on the ground. A field of green was sprouting around the body, sprinkled with red and yellow flowers. The grey fire bearer pointed back into the village and two of the others ran back inside. When they returned with torches, Doto knew they intended to burn the carcass.

He had seen enough. Clay would be waking in their temple any moment. He would need someone to comfort him.

~

Clay took longer to reincarnate this time. His presence dwelt within the temple, and Doto could feel him watching and listening, but the sun crawled a good way across the sky before bone and flesh formed beneath their soil again. When Clay pulled himself out of the earth, he crouched flat for a while, his ears pinned, his eyes darting about warily, and when Doto approached, he shook his head and slunk backward into the grass. The temple responded as well, with branches pulling away, petals closing, and the creatures hiding.

Doto felt a little hurt at that. Why wouldn't his mate want comfort from him? But he supposed that dying must be very unpleasant, and the attack the eagle's vision had shown him had looked more painful than most deaths. So he let his calm flow through their temple and through Clay's awareness, trusting that being still and present would be enough to restore Clay.

After some time, he felt Clay relax a little, and his mate sat up. Gingerly, he began probing at his chest and stomach as though expecting pain or injuries. His breathing slowed, and when he finally looked up at Doto, Doto opened his arms. Clay slunk over and sank into them. His tense muscles relaxed in Doto's embrace.

"It was so awful," he murmured. "They all did it—several of them at once, all stabbing me."

"I saw," Doto said. "I wanted to help."

"I called them by name. I begged them for mercy. It hurt so much, Doto. I didn't know anything could hurt so badly. It was so terrible that…" he looked away, biting at his lower lip.

"What?" Doto stroked at Clay's ears and neck.

"Doto, at first I didn't want to come back. I didn't want a body if it could feel that much pain."

"You do not ever have to feel that again." He felt the muscles of Clay's neck and shoulder tense under his fingers. He was learning his mate's body language—that meant an argument unspoken. And that argument could only be… He scowled. "Clay. You cannot mean to go back there again. Not after what they have done."

Clay lay in his lap for a time, not saying anything. Every now and then, he would draw in breath as if to speak, hold it for a moment, and then let it go, his body relaxing into Doto's embrace again. They lay that way into the night, and now Doto noticed something new Clay had added to the temple: rings of lichen encrusted to many of the trees that, in the total darkness of night, glowed a deep and radiant green. Neither he nor Clay needed assistance to see at night, but the glow was pretty and, he supposed, reassuring for Clay.

"I do have to, though," Clay said finally.

Doto sat up and turned Clay around by his shoulders. He gave him his steadiest, most serious gaze. "No. They will only hurt you again."

"Doto… this is hard for me to force myself to do. It's hard even to say I should, to think about it."

"Because it is not something you *should* do!"

"I have to, Doto. What other choice do we have? They're my people."

Doto's fingers tightened on Clay's shoulders. He wanted to shake him. "No. They. Are. Not! Not anymore!" he growled. "They are not your people, Clay. You are better than them. Not because you are a god. You were *always* better than them. They have killed you three times. Three! Is that not enough? Leave them be. Let them earn their own fate. They do not deserve you."

"They're just afraid of me, Doto. I'm something new. Something different. I come from out of the woods and there is magic, and it frightens them."

"I came out of the woods once," Doto said. "And I found you. And I threatened you and showed you magic and kept you from your own people and forced you to walk even when you were hurt. Weren't you frightened? But you never tried to hurt or kill me. You were kind and curious and you… you danced for me." His chest felt too small for his heart, remembering it. "You are better than them."

"But that's why I have to keep trying. I tried so hard with you and for so long, and I won you over. You changed for me. We found something good with each other. If I can win over a *god*, then I can win over my people too. It will just take patience and" —he flinched in remembered pain— "a little hardship."

Doto tried much of the night to convince him not to go, but Clay was intractable. And so he held him in his arms and tried to enjoy the time they had. The next morning, he watched with mounting dread as Clay once more stepped out of the forest, again wearing a leaf garment and his wooden armor. The fire bearers were waiting for him this time. They pinned him to the ground with cords and stakes. Then they set him on fire.

He had to hold Clay a long time after that. And still Clay would not give up. The next morning, he went out to the village again. And again they killed him. Doto had no idea what drove him to the edge of the forest over and over. The fire bearers slashed him open with knives. They beat him to death with stones. They held him down and forced poison into him. They held their hands over his nose and mouth while he struggled. Each time a new torment. Each time he hesitated before forming his body again. Each time he clung to Doto.

And each time, Doto learned to hate the fire bearers a little more. Clay was right about so much, but he was wrong about them. You could not talk to people so full of hatred and fear. They would not change. The only thing you could do was fight them.

The trauma, day after day, was destroying Clay. He looked sad and distant much of the time, his movements slow, but would also jump and cringe at sudden movements. Doto could not explain this. Outside the forest, when he wore his fire bearer skin, Clay was vulnerable, certainly, but nothing in the forest could hurt him. He explained this over and over to Clay, but Clay only shrugged. And flinched when Doto reached for him, which made Doto angry for reasons he couldn't understand, and then two people's emotions were frustrating him.

Worse, though, were the changes he noticed in their temple. As Clay grew more guarded and jumpy, new flora sprouted that mirrored his attitudes. Delicate flowers wilted away to be replaced by thorny vines, sturdy stems, and prickly burs that clung to Doto's fur. One morning, he noticed that the fish had gone from their brook. In their place was a large, vicious-looking snapping turtle. The golden gnats that hung in the daybeams remained, but were joined by a swarm of gangly wasps.

These changes were terrible not because Doto had been fond of the beauty of their temple, although he had—these new developments possessed their own beauty. But the temple was an expression of Clay's soul. If it had changed this much, this quickly, then the attacks by his people were not just making him sad and jumpy; they were harming him in deeper ways.

In one quiet afternoon, Doto lay with Clay, stroking at the fur on his chest to calm him. It had been two days since he had last visited the village. They had burned him again. It had become their preferred method of killing him. Clay had spoken little about it, and Doto hadn't wanted to hear. Knowing the details only filled him with hatred toward their kind.

Clay lay with his arms crossed behind his head. "My brother was there that time," he said after a while. Doto remained quiet, letting him speak. "I saw him standing inside the village, watching. It's a sad place. A lot of the people are gone. Cloud is gone. Ant with a Leaf. Most of the elders. I think everyone who might have listened to me left. No one stands around Laughing Dog. I can't tell if they're afraid of him or if they just dislike him. I suppose he's King now, but… I don't think he's enjoying it."

Doto busied himself swatting at Clay's whiskers until Clay finally twitched his nose. "Quit it." A hint of a grin. That was good.

"He stood and watched the whole time. I thought he might come out to—to hurt me himself. I was glad he didn't. It's hard to see him like that. I loved him, you know?"

"No. I do not know. He is the worst fire bearer I have ever seen, and I cannot imagine what loving him must have been like."

Clay sighed. "It hurts less now, I think. Dying, I mean. At first it was agony. But I think I'm getting used to it."

"That is why I am going to stop you from going back again," Doto said with sudden conviction.

"Because it hurts *less*?" Clay gave an incredulous laugh.

Doto sat up, curling his tail across his toes. "Yes. Life is supposed to hurt."

"Spoken like someone who's never felt pain. How did you come to decide that?"

"I *have* felt pain. When I traveled outside the forest. When my father punished me. When I—when I thought I had lost you. When I fear it is happening again. Clay, each time I changed you, it changed me back."

"I remember your sulking about it!"

"Yes, but—" Doto scowled at his paws, stalking words that remained hidden from him. "You get the good and bad together. If nothing hurts you anymore, then—then nothing makes you feel good either. Remember? Remember what you told me about running through the grass and what you felt?"

Clay breathed out slowly. "Joy."

"I never felt it until I changed you. Once I was weak, once I could fail and fall, that's when I first understood. I do not want you to stop feeling things." He rolled in the grass to crouch over Clay, gazing down at him. Clay liked his eyes.

"You have to stop, my love. You have to stop letting them hurt you. It will not make them listen. It will not make them understand. Look at our temple. Look what they are doing to you. This hurt will go deep and it will not get better. Being a god does not mean you cannot be wounded."

Tears welled in the corners of Clay's eyes. "So I just can't do it? I can't help my people? All this… all this power and I'm still weak?"

Doto sat up, snorting with distaste. "You are talking like someone weak. But you are strong, Clay. No one else would do what you have done."

"Strong, ha. You know you're the second god this…" Clay's brow furrowed, and Doto braced himself for a tedious argument. But instead, Clay squirmed backward and sat upright. "Doto, I'm such an idiot."

"Well, sometimes," Doto granted, "but you *are* very—"

Clay grabbed his shoulders. "I had forgotten because of everything that had happened. I mean, dying and becoming a god and all that. Mother Fam! She came to me!"

Puzzled at this sudden shift, Doto asked, "When? In the forest?"

"No, outside! Back before I… changed. When I was tied up in the village and they were planning to push me into the forest! Mother Fam came and talked to me! She said I was strong!"

"She hasn't been talking to me," Doto said, feeling a little put out. He only had very faint memories of the goddess of earth, from when he was a cub. She and his father had not gotten along well.

"Lord Sarmu told us your father banished her from the forest to keep you from finding out who your mother was. But she said" —Clay frowned, thinking— "though she's not allowed to come to you, you could come and find her. She said that she's waiting in the mountains!"

"But why would she want that?"

"She said she misses you. And she knows things, Doto. Things about the fire bearers. She called me all these strange names. Like world-dancer and god-kin."

"Well, those make sense for you," Doto pointed out. "You became a tiny part god when I healed your foot, and you can make the forest grow when you dance."

"Yes, maybe." Clay sounded doubtful. "But I think it might be more. We should go and see her, Doto. She said she would explain things. Maybe she knows something that can help."

Doto opened his mouth and then closed it again. He'd been about to protest. Mother Fam was up in the mountains and he'd never been there before. But more importantly, she was outside the forest. He'd have to step beyond the wall and become weak and fleshy again. He'd have to take on the form of the enemy. And then he and Clay would be subject to all the frailties and vulnerabilities of the fire bearers. The idea of facing that hardship and discomfort for just the possibility that a goddess he hadn't seen since he was a kitten might have useful information would have been enough to make him object strenuously.

Except that Clay had been facing that every day. Day after day he'd struggled across harsh terrain to endure certain torment. He had died over and over trying to save them, and nearly destroyed himself doing it. Doto could hardly protest now over simply having to take a walk outside. He'd look weak and selfish.

He sighed. This trip would not be pleasant. It would hurt. But then, he'd just told Clay that it was *supposed* to hurt. "If we go to see her, we would need to talk to Kwaee first. He banished her from the forest. Maybe he had a good reason." He ignored Clay's blatant eyeroll at that. "And if we're gone from the forest for a while and he doesn't know why, he might be angry when we return."

"Angrier than he is already?" Clay asked in a disbelieving tone.

"*Yes.*"

"Oh. Well, all right, we could go to see him. But he had better not throw me again."

"He had better not," Doto agreed with a low growl. "Very well. We will go to see Mother Fam in the mountains."

Clay threw his arms around Doto and squeezed him tightly. The chance to see her must have meant a lot, Doto thought, because a large yellow and blue butterfly flitted lazily through their temple and lit atop a large thorn vine. Or perhaps that had come from him? It was becoming harder and harder to tell.

~

"Absolutely not." Kwaee sank his claws into the gnarls of his moabi throne. The whole tree bent toward them, its branches clutching. "Fam is controlling and manipulative. I won't have her turning my son against me."

Doto folded his arms.

"This was *his* idea, wasn't it?" Kwaee pointed one massive arm toward Clay. Clay flinched despite himself; every instinct told him that terrible pain was imminent. "And why is he cringing like that? What have you been teaching him? You were supposed to be instructing him in how to be an effective—and *deadly*—forest god."

"Clay has learned much over the past days," Doto began.

"But not to abandon that fire bearer name of his, apparently," Kwaee said, arching a brow so high the plumage on his forehead folded backward. "If he is to be a god in my forest, he will use his divine name."

Clay could see the muscles in Doto's jaw tense, but Doto simply inclined his head and began again. "*Doté* has learned much over the past days. But killing fire bearers is proving to be more difficult than we expected. They are clever enough to avoid any place the forest can touch them."

"Well do I know that," Kwaee growled as if to himself.

"And when we go out of the forest—" Doto gave Clay an uneasy glance. Clay understood. There was no telling how Kwaee, with his complicated history of love and murder with the fire bearers, would respond to the news. Doto let his breath out. "When we go out of the forest, we both change. We become like them."

Kwaee's expression darkened further. "This foul healing magic. I warned you not to use it, son. Didn't I tell you that it was dangerous? And now you are corrupted by the very enemy we seek to destroy."

Doto's ears went lower and lower at these words. "If we leave the forest, we are weak. Their shape is soft, with no claws or fangs. The ground hurts our paws. They find—they would find it easy to kill our avatars."

"Well, perhaps you should fight them with their own methods. What of those tools they use? Their bows and spears. Can you make them?"

"I can," Clay answered uneasily.

"Well then. Teach my son to use them, and the two of you can fight the fire bearers safely from the forest, where they cannot hurt you. It will simply be a matter of patience. They must approach my forest to burn it, and that is when you attack them."

"With respect, Lord Kwaee, even if we could kill them, there would only be more. And it is violence against them that has provoked this conflict."

He slitted his eyes. "You seek to lecture me about old history? I suppose this is where your plea to talk to them—to *persuade* them—to surrender comes from."

"No, Lord Kwaee. I only point out that trying to fight my—fight the fire bearers has gone on for… more seasons than I can imagine. Uncountable. And still they trouble you. Maybe it is time to look for another solution. I do not know what Mother Fam has done to anger you, but surely she cannot be worse than the advances of Ogya. You have lost so much fighting him on your own, in your own way. It is not weakness to ask for help or advice. It is strength."

"Implying that it is weakness *not* to ask for advice, I suppose. Your words are nectar and poison mixed, Doté. You will deceive me into drinking too deeply of them. But," he added, just as Clay had begun to despair, "it will not hurt to seek her advice, I suppose. She was the first of us, after all. The first Wem created. With her aid the rest of us were made. It may be that she knows the secrets of unmaking."

Kwaee's eyes lit, his plumage spreading. "Yes. She has always had a weakness for life and for the fire bearers. If she knows that Ogya plans to destroy it all, she will help. With the right magics, perhaps we could not only stop Ogya, but strip him from this world entirely. No more fire, anywhere, ever."

"No more fire?" Incredulity hastened the words past Clay's lips before good sense could catch them.

"You do not like that plan, *fire bearer?*" Kwaee asked in a knife-edged voice.

Clay lost himself for a moment in a world without fire, one where no one could see in the darkness, cook or preserve food, harden their pottery or tools. They would live in fear at night, unable to see or fend off predators, or—

*They held him down against the rough ground. A fire hunter stood over him, gourd in hand. He tilted it, and warm palm oil splattered across Clay's body, soaking him. Then another hunter struck Clay with the torch. Blinding agony engulfed him.*

"We don't need fire," he said. "We can see in the dark, and do not need to cook or use tools. And we fear no predators. The fire bearers are not the same. They were taught to bless their tools. To use them in accordance with the will of the gods and honoring the spirit of the wood and stone and flame the tool came from. Fire was a gift. If the fire bearers wanted to keep that gift, they shouldn't have abused it. They can learn to live without it, like any other beast."

He saw Doto's ears flatten at that, but Kwaee raised his brows. "Well, well. Perhaps you *have* been teaching him something after all, son." The forest god settled back into this throne. "Then you have my blessing. Go and see Mother Fam. But be wary of what she tells you. Do not act on her advice without coming to see me first, do you understand?"

"Yes, Lord Kwaee."

"Yes, Father."

"She would have stolen you away from me, once. She tried, you know. She's cunning, and she believes the whole world belongs to her. She thinks we're seeds. All of us. Gods and beasts alike. Seeds she would plant in her endless garden."

Clay gave Doto a curious glance, but Doto only shrugged.

"Go then," Kwaee commanded. "And hurry. My dominion diminishes every day."

"I feel it," Doto confessed. "It is a stone in my side that grows ever deeper. I feel that it is moving ever toward my heart."

Clay glanced at Doto. So he did feel it, too. That terrible absence of feeling where part of them had died, moving from his side up toward his chest. Moving ever toward some terrible design.

"Heart?" Kwaee wrinkled his nose. "Son, you are addled. You know not the forest so well as I. The burn consumes us, but it moves toward our belly. And Ogya will have no more of it. And if we are fortunate, one day he will be gone. Completely gone."

He tipped his head back and sighed. "A world without fire."

A rustle moved through the branches of his temple. They creaked as they stretched and spread, sprouting broader leaves and thickening the canopy, casting the temple into shadow.

~

"So what was that about?" Doto asked. He ran at Clay's side, moving at high speed, raising a cloud of leaves and earth behind him.

"What?" Clay vaulted over a rock, enjoying the strength and grace of this form, especially after days of creeping across the savanna ground on tender human feet.

"You sounded like you *wanted* the fire bearers to suffer. You called them beasts."

"They *are* beasts. You've called them that yourself."

"Yes, but you haven't. You've changed, Clay."

"Clever of you to notice," Clay said wryly. A wide canyon approached, deep enough to contain the entire fire bearer village. At this speed, he could vault over it easily, he was sure. He sprang, leapt, and for the briefest moment flew through the air, the wind in his fur. He landed lightly on the other side and kept running, Doto at his heels.

"You know I do not mean your shape. Or your power."

Clay didn't respond to that. What he knew was that he couldn't think about the fire bearers without a wave of revulsion rolling over him. His stomach clenched. His claws flexed. He fought the instinct to squeeze his eyes shut, as if when they were closed he would not see the faces he'd grown up with twisted in hatred, screaming at him, lips flecked with spittle as they jabbed at him with spears or cut him with knives or brought stones crashing down on his bones. But he wasn't angry at them, not really. They were doing what came naturally to them. They were behaving like cornered beasts, lashing out in fear.

The anger he felt was toward himself. He'd let them do it. Not the first time, not back when he was still one of them, and his brother had cut his throat. But every time after? Every time he'd given them another chance, had reached out with an open paw? He was to blame for that. And he had gone back not once, but over and over and over. *He* had let them hurt him terribly. *He* had let them damage him, murder him, ruin him. He would not make that error again.

What was it Doto had said? Life was supposed to hurt. Yes. But that didn't mean you were supposed to just let it hurt you. It didn't mean you shouldn't protect yourself. That you shouldn't fight back. He owed no more kindness to the fire bearers, no more forgiveness. He owed them nothing.

"I know what you mean, Doto. I know that I've changed. But I have to. It's like you said: I'm a god now. I can't pretend that I'm one of them anymore. They're not my people, not anymore."

He slowed to a stop, staring at the landscape ahead. They'd been climbing higher and higher. He should have noticed, he thought. It should have exhausted him. The trees had begun to thin, and the underbrush even more. The ground rose high before them in many mountainous peaks. The air had been growing colder and colder. He had felt cold before, when he and Doto had journeyed to the high places on their first trip through the forest, but this was more intense and aggressive. The air bit at his nose and the tips of his ears. "Is it supposed to be this… uncomfortable?"

Doto blinked his gold-green eyes slowly, tilting his head. "It's colder in the high places. You know this. The higher we climb, the further away from the heat of the world."

This sounded unlikely to Clay. "So we're farther away from the things that make heat now? But we've been climbing higher and higher. We're closer to the sun! Shouldn't we be getting *warmer?*"

The slow advance of blank confusion that slackened Doto's face was more than a little satisfying. The leopard god finally wrinkled his brows in irritation. "Yes, but high places are different."

Clay had his doubts, but as they ascended, the air nipped at him more and more, and his fur began to stand on end. Doto must have felt the same chill; his body looked thicker and fluffier. Later, to Clay's astonishment, tiny clouds began to form in his breaths, but Doto assured him this was not some new divine weather-creating ability. It was, he said, merely an aspect of the cold, and all warm creatures did the same.

The word *cold* in god-tongue summoned images that were strange to Clay: animals slowing and sleeping; the death of plants; the dimming and lowering of the sun in the sky; seasons not of rain but of a long darkness; a white dust that sifted from the heavens; the prickling numbness and drowsy death of things that could not hold their heat. All these were foreign and bewildering to Clay, but he sensed also that they were part of his world.

He stopped at Doto's side. The wall of the forest shimmered before him, and nausea cramped his stomach. He knew that when he walked outside this wall, it would not be to face the fire bearers. No one would murder him and burn him. But his stomach didn't know that. His bones didn't know it. His body shook.

"You cannot be suffering from the cold yet," Doto said, frowning, but then he sniffed the air and caught the sour reek of Clay's fear. Clay was surprised it had taken him this long; the stink of it burned in his own nose and made him ashamed. "What are you afraid of? Is it Mother Fam? She will not harm you."

"No, I—" Clay turned away from the shimmering wall of imminent death. "I know it doesn't make sense. I shouldn't be afraid of going outside the forest. But every time I've done it…"

"Oh, that. That makes sense," Doto said. He came and put an arm around Clay, pulling him close. Clay's shaking eased a little in his grip.

"It does?"

"That is how fear works. It is powerful, but not very specific. You just have to show yourself that this is not something you need to be afraid of." Doto gave him a smile. "Here. Take my paw."

Wondering, Clay took Doto's soft-furred fingers in his own.

"Now we will go through together," Doto said. "It will not be pleasant, because we will both be fire bearers and we will lose all of our god powers and everything will be very uncomfortable. But you will see: nothing bad will happen to you. And I will be there to travel alongside you. All right?"

Clay nodded. He clenched Doto's fingers tight, fighting away the wave of fear. There were no fire bearers waiting on the other side. He would not be killed. They were traveling through the mountains to find the mother of all creation. He took a deep breath, and they stepped through.

His body ached as it warped. Immediately, the cold in the air became a shocking, attention-commanding force. With no more fur—or divine power—to protect him, the wind pulled the heat away from his skin. He felt it tighten again, prickling into bumps. His genitals shrank and retracted into him. The sensation was almost a physical pain—it stole the warmth from him. Every instinct told him that he should not be standing there—that he should immediately return to the warmth and safety of the forest.

He looked over at Doto, who stood to one side, his tall and handsome fire bearer form hunched over in the cold wind. He clutched at his sides with both arms, squinting into the harsh and biting wind.

"Well," he said, "this is terrible."

# 10 Formicide

"Ogya!" The voice that called out of the forest was high-pitched but full and hearty. Laughing Dog started, the fire from his palms sputtering as he lost his concentration. He looked about for the speaker. It would not be one of his fire hunters; most of them retired during the heat of the day, which did not bother him.

The voice called again, but in words Laughing Dog could not understand, full of clicks and chitters.

Laughing Dog took an uncertain step back, but Ogya's voice crackled with laughter in his mind. "I know who this is. He calls me traitor and demands that I come and face him. Do not worry. He can be of no harm to you. Go to him. Burn a path through the forest. I will show you where."

Laughing Dog followed his directions, muttering the song and skipping through the dance whenever the flames began to die. The power of the fire he could generate was stronger the more energy and feeling he gave to the dance, but for this, he did not need to scour whole swaths of land clean. He needed only to burn a trail wide enough that the forest would not come to life and seize him. He was deep enough now into the forest that he had to be cautious, though. A narrow trail might prevent vines and bushes along the ground from attacking him, but overhanging trees could still whip their branches at them; his cheek bore a series of welts from the lash of a liana he'd noticed only too late.

"Ogya!" The voice cried out again, and this time Laughing Dog could see the source of the cry. He recoiled—the thing was horrible. It was an ant, or at least an ant-like thing, but much, much larger, its antenna waving almost at the height of Laughing Dog's knee. It walked upright on two legs, and was continually in motion, but it had four arms—or were they legs as well? Laughing Dog couldn't tell. Its whole body was encased in a black carapace, except for two round, empty black eyes and horrific twitching mandibles between which sprouted bristling orange hairs.

"A demon," Laughing Dog breathed in revulsion.

Ogya sneered in his mind. "Why must you fire bearers call everything you do not recognize demons? There are no demons but by your own invention. This is Atetea, god of ants. You will speak to him. I will tell you what to say. Use my fire. Move closer."

Unwillingly, Laughing Dog burned a path closer to the horrid creature. As he approached, he saw that a long trail of ants followed it as it marched in an endless, wandering route across the forest floor. If he peered closely, he could trace its entire journey through the leaves, over a stump, up a tree and a vine, until the trail extended down into an ant mound it could not possibly have fit into. The thought of this repugnant thing crawling around under the soil, unknown to anyone, made him shudder.

The thing croaked a long string of unintelligible syllables. Ogya spoke the words into Laughing Dog's head, his voice merry with amusement. "So, you finally show your face in the forest. Or should I say the face of your lackey? You will find no welcome from me here, not after you have roasted so many of my followers with no apology to me."

"Speak the words I give you," Ogya's voice commanded.

"Lord Ogya has no interest in your welcome," Laughing Dog repeated dutifully. "He does not come to parlay but to conquer. He finds your demands for apology pitiful."

The thing that called itself Atetea let out a hissing shriek of anger. "You would dare speak that way to a god? Even if you repeat only the words Ogya whispers to you, this is blasphemy."

"The animal gods are low, barely divine at all. What cares Ogya for the adulation your insects offer you? You have no power over him. Your godhood means nothing to him. You are no more threatening to him than a fire bearer."

Laughing Dog paused after hearing himself utter those last words; he'd spoken them before they had registered. He had no illusions that Ogya considered him or his people as worthy of divinity, but to be used as an example this way was demeaning. Especially in their war against Kwaee. The forest god needed to respect them. Fear them.

Atetea's thin arms slid over his flat black eyes, rubbing them or cleaning them. Laughing Dog couldn't tell. Perhaps it was the creature's lidless way of blinking. "Then you require a warning, oh great Ogya." Laughing Dog could almost hear the sarcasm in its chittering voice. "Listen."

Laughing Dog stopped, and the voice in his mind fell silent as well. For a moment, he heard nothing but the crackle of spreading flames from the burn. But then, from the direction of the small camp he and his fire hunters had made, rose a raw, howling cry of terrible pain, then another.

"You sack of monkey piss," he snarled at Atetea. "What have you done?" In his mind, Ogya hissed in annoyance at his having spoken words unbidden.

Atetea tilted his head toward Laughing Dog, still walking in an endless trail, followed by a train of ants. "Sack of monkey piss?" he said, and this time his words were in Laughing Dog's language, though hideously mutated by the clicks and chitters of his unearthly voice. "So, the puppet speaks on its own. Well, fire bearer, I have sent my saifu ants to visit your fellow hunters. Their bites are terribly painful. Even in death, they will not let go. This was just a little pain to remind you that you toy with gods. If you show respect, if you stand down now, your men will live."

The screaming in the distance had faded now.

"Kill him," Ogya crackled.

Atatea marched a looping trail. "I warn you, fire bearer. We can discuss how you might achieve your own goals without harming my people. I bear allegiance to all major gods, but I would protect my own first. If we can come to some arrangements, perhaps your subjects might be spared."

Laughing Dog still seethed at being cornered like this by a tiny bully, by an *ant*, but he could hardly decline such an offer. "What terms would you suggest?" he began.

"I ordered you to kill him. Kill him now." Ogya roared with fury all around him. "Go to him. Summon my fire."

Laughing Dog didn't move. Saifu ants were deadly. You didn't approach them—you ran from them, lest you be swarmed. If there were more around…

"I said go!" The heat of Ogya's anger began to boil under his skin, first a warmth, then an escalating pain.

"No, Lord Ogya, he could kill us! And my men!" Laughing Dog said out loud. Atetea's head tilted toward him at that outcry.

The words of Ogya's rage were almost incoherent around him, as though growled by wind and thunder. "You will allow nothing to defy me. Punish that creature or I will burn myself out of your body and find someone else who will. Just as I did your friend Sedjet."

A flash of memory. A fire in the dark. A man who came out of the darkness, but not a man. A demon who walked backwards, with a beast's head growing out of his hair. A demon who fell into the fire and was consumed.

The memory fled his attention as the pain of Ogya burning through his body became too intense to endure. He spoke the words and summoned the flame. Fire vomited from his palms.

"Burn them," moaned Ogya in hunger. "Burn them all."

At Ogya's behest, Laughing Dog strode forward, turning his flames toward the trail of ants, keeping an eye out for hidden anthills from which the saifu might emerge to attack him. But no attack came. He tasted the crunch of their carapaces and the acid in their blood as he enveloped their bodies in fire.

"You will pay for this," Atetea shrieked in anger and, Laughing Dog detected beneath it, panic. "You dare attack a god directly?"

Then came another scream from the fire hunter camp, this time raw and terrified. It was followed by another, and another. All his men were screaming, hoarse, shrieking wails unlike any he had heard from another man.

"I dare," he said, and again they were not Ogya's words. Freed from fear of reprisal, he now felt only rage at Atetea's attack on his men. This was his anger now, his punishment. It was he who would take on the gods and make them suffer for his people. He turned his fire onto the ant god, bathing him in flames.

The thing emitted a horrifying shriek of agony and fell over, its six limbs and antennae rapidly flailing about. It tasted like the others, but richer, nuttier, so full of flavor that it almost overwhelmed him. He clenched his fingers together as though closing his jaws and focused the fire on it. It shrieked louder. Its shell cracked and hissed as its insides boiled and steam escaped. Then he sunk his power into its syrupy guts, turning them to ash. His tongues of flame licked out its eyes, cracked apart its mandibles, snapped off its antennae.

His flames guttered and died. The god of ants lay dead, its split shell at his feet. Laughing Dog stood over the carcass, panting with exhilaration. "I killed him," he breathed. "I killed a god."

"You sent him to his temple," Ogya muttered. "He is not dead. But he will not bother us again. The lesser gods do not recover from the deaths of their avatars so quickly. Now you may go. See to your men."

Annoyed at having his victory so cavalierly snatched away from him, Laughing Dog made his way back to the camp. He how his men had fared against the ants. They had not all died—he could still hear hoarse wailing in the distance. And those would now see that he had been right about his campaign against the gods. They would know the stakes of what they faced. They would have a brother to avenge. They would never stop now, not a single one of them.

Kwaee would fall.

Movement caught Laughing Dog's eye. He looked down at the forest floor. As he traveled, all the ants in every direction were fleeing his path, their movements crazed and erratic, unguided. Abandoned.

He crushed as many as he could.

# 11 The Prodigal Son

Nearly a full moon had passed, and Dry Grass's pace was unwavering. Mirage had been certain his mother would turn around after a few days. She hated being alone even for a few hours, always preferring to sit with people talking or working or watching over children. Three days following the trail of the exiles should have been too much for her.

But she'd walked alongside him, sometimes taking the lead, sometimes following. She would try talking with him sometimes, about the people she missed, about the trouble he'd gotten into as a boy, about whether the village missed her hands at harvesting. Other times she would sing softly to herself or remain quiet.

Each day they traveled further from the village, she relaxed more. She began to walk with her shoulders back and a purposeful stride. A stoop to her posture that he'd never even noticed before dissipated. It was as though she had been carrying a heavy bundle on her shoulders all her life and had only now set it down. When she spoke of their plans, her voice was bright and optimistic, as though nothing could stop them.

At times, though, she retreated back into her old self, holding her elbows and growing pensive, the lines deepening on her forehead, and then she would turn and stare back in the direction of their village with a troubled expression. In these moments, he wasn't certain whether she missed their old life, or whether she worried that his father was following them.

The days passed, and her pensive moments grew fewer and fewer. Eight days out, she asked to borrow his knife and shaved her head bare. It seemed to shave ten years off of her age as well; suddenly her face looked as it had when Mirage was a young boy.

Their hardship on the journey was not as great as Mirage had feared. He had been certain that the exiles would strip the countryside bare, leaving little for them to eat or use for supplies. But Dry Grass was an experienced harvester and could find food the exiles had overlooked, as well as articles they had forgotten or abandoned during their journey. So while the travel was hardly comfortable, it was not the journey of privation Mirage had expected.

Partly this was due to the slowness of their travel. To remain undetected, they had to stay at least one full day's travel behind the exiles. Mirage and Dry Grass had caught up to them after only a few days, the group slowed, no doubt, by the large number of elderly and infirm traveling with them. A herd moved only as fast as its slowest beast, as they said. Mirage knew he should be patient, but the tedium was getting to him. As his mother grew cheerier and happier, his impatience with her grew.

Even this morning, she'd woken up earlier than he'd cared to, bustling around, humming to herself while he tried to sleep. He'd groaned at her to go back to bed, but it was too late—he'd woken, and so he'd stumped off to go check the snares he'd set the night before.

He'd had good luck with snares—crumbs and morsels of food dropped by the exiles tended to attract birds and other scavengers, but this morning, all but one of his snares had remained unsprung, and that one had been chewed through by a squirrel or other rodent. Swearing, he turned to head back and saw what was unmistakably a thin plume of smoke rising into the western sky.

He dashed back to camp and found his mother settled next to a small campfire, resting her elbows on her knees.

"What are you doing?" He rushed to the fire and dug up several large handfuls of earth, dumping them on the flames.

"Mirage, no—please, oh no, oh no, now you've ruined them."

"What were you thinking?" he shouted at her.

She didn't look up at him, but began picking through the earth he'd thrown on the fire. "I don't like it when you talk to me like that." She dug a little around the edge of the fire circle with her fingers, gently probing the soil. "I was *thinking* that you'd like some guinea eggs for your breakfast. Oh, they're not ruined after all. Look."

She held up her cupped hands, in which were nestled three cream-colored eggs, holes poked in their shells to vent the steam while they cooked. Despite himself, Mirage found his mouth watering at the sight of them.

"They were always your favorite when you were a boy. We haven't found any in a while." She looked up at him then, a hopeful smile on her face.

Something inside Mirage cracked at that, but he couldn't soften now. He needed to be firm with her. "Don't you know what you could have done? What if someone had seen the smoke? The exiles could already know we're here!"

His mother's eyes went soft and sad. "I didn't think it would matter all that much. They're a day's journey out—"

"And they have scouts and hunters! They will be expecting Laughing Dog to send someone after them. They will be watching!"

"Well, all right. I won't start a fire again. But there's no point in wasting the eggs, is there?" She held them a little higher. He could smell the fat in the yolks.

Reluctantly, he took two of them, leaving her the third. "I appreciate it. But mother, you have to be more careful."

"All right," she said, but she said it in the voice she used to mollify his father, which irritated him all over again. She peeled the egg delicately with her fingers; inside it was not completely cooked, but hot and jelly-soft, just how he liked them.

He sat down next to her and cracked one of his own open, and as he sucked out the soft, hot flavor, she asked, "But would it really be so terrible if the exiles found us?"

Suspicion crept through his mind. She hadn't done this on purpose, had she? Trying to get the exiles' attention so that they could go back to be with the people? "You know I'm here on the King's orders, don't you? That's why we're here."

"That's why *you're* here," she corrected him. "I'm here to look after you."

"And to get away from Father."

She gave him a long stare. "I thought perhaps we both might be escaping cruel men."

"It doesn't surprise me that you mistake strength for cruelty. King Laughing Dog is doing what needs to be done. He's giving our people a chance, not just hunkering down and giving up like Cloud and those other fools. Not like… like…"

His mother's voice was very calm and very quiet, as though she could still the air itself by speaking. "Like who, Mirage?"

He scowled at the ground. It felt wrong to say the words when his hands were full of the food she'd found for him. "It doesn't matter. Maybe a long time ago, it did. Not now."

For a time, they ate in silence. When his mother spoke again, it was as though she had to force the words. "You don't ever know who you'll be when someone hurts you. You think you know, but you don't."

"Well. You were the wrong person."

She took a deep breath and let it out again. "It doesn't surprise me that you mistake cruelty for strength."

~

They sat together atop a high hill, far enough away from the exiles' camp that they could not be seen, but the fires and movements of the people below were easily discernible. The exiles didn't look like a people scheming or planning an attack. They spent their days as they had when in migration: scavenging for supplies and food, repairing handcarts and tools, preparing meals and caring for children. Mirage found himself wishing they *would* do something especially treasonous, but that would surely come when they reached their new destination. Were they looking for simply a new place to settle? Or something else—other peoples, perhaps, or following rumors of dark magics? Whatever it was, he hoped they found it quickly. He had been kept away from the companionship of his fellow fire hunters far too long, and for, as far as he could tell, very little reason.

His mother had been quiet since their argument that morning, and he felt irritatingly guilty over it. He was in the right here. It was better to stand up to bullies like Kwaee and fight them. It was better to be strong.

He found himself hoping that the exiles would actually attempt to muster an army and fight back. That would be a move worthy of respect. Far better than simply accepting defeat and retreating to Bogana to live whatever life they could.

"Our whole life has been surrender," he said out loud. "Don't you get tired of it?"

His mother rubbed one hand over her shaved head and said nothing.

"I mean, when I was a child, the fires came, and we all just left."

"You can't fight fire," his mother pointed out.

"But then we kept running, over and over. We had no power. And Father—he would act like it was our fault. For a long time, I thought it *was* my fault. That maybe I had set the fires in my sleep, or that they were coming after me and making everyone have to run."

Dry Grass fixed him with a serious gaze. "You know they weren't your fault. Nothing that happened was your fault. Not the fires. Not your father. Not what he did. Not who he was. You must understand that."

"But that's what I'm saying. Fault doesn't matter. What matters is what you do next. Yes, Father did bad things to us. But you and me? We did nothing."

"You can't—"

He cut her off. He had no patience for more of her excuses, more of *oh you don't know what it was like.* It didn't matter. "And then we got to the forest, and we thought we were safe. And we weren't safe. People *died.* Grandmother *died.* Horribly! And while everyone else wanted to cower down and hide from the gods and what they were doing to us, King Laughing Dog stood up. He was the only one. He told us that we could be strong. That we didn't have to let people hurt us anymore. That we could fight back! Everyone else cowered. Everyone else said, 'Oh no, we'd better pray harder. We should give more offerings. Let Kwaee hit us a few more times and then maybe he'll forgive us.' "

He rubbed at his eyes. "King Laughing Dog was the first person out of the entire village who made me feel like I didn't have to be afraid anymore."

The sound of broken breaths came from his side. His mother had buried her face in her hands, her body shaking. A drop of water crawled down her wrist. "I'm so sorry," she said. "I'm so sorry I let you feel afraid."

He turned away from her in disgust. He'd asked her for strength, and this last moon, he thought he'd begun to see it in her. But now she proved herself still fragile. Broken.

~

They climbed another hill, higher than the last, and heavily forested, though not inside the forest proper, as none of the vegetation animated to attack them. Discerning the border was difficult, though. The line between savanna and forest seemed arbitrarily drawn, some immeasurable density of trees separating one from the other. In general, Mirage and his mother were safe traveling in the tracks of the exiles, but their scouts had been journeying further and further from the camp, so finding discreet locations to settle had become a daily task.

This hill was extremely steep, and the climb arduous, so Mirage was surprised to see his mother ahead of him at every step, tirelessly moving forward. The first ten days of their journey, she'd been slower, her steps more delicate, but since then she'd discovered some stone in her resolve he'd never seen, and reluctantly admired. She crawled upward ahead of him and left a red-smeared footprint on a boulder.

"Mother, stop. Your foot is bleeding."

"I'll be fine. It's just a little cut."

"A little cut on your foot can be a big problem. Let me take care of it for you."

"Once we're at the top." She pressed on, not even wincing with her steps.

Mirage had no idea where this new grit had come from. He wished she had discovered it sooner. At the top of the hill, the view of the exile's camp was excellent: closer, and with plenty of foliage for cover. He pressed his mother to sit down on a log and used spare water from his skin to clean the small cut, wrapping it in a spare bit of baobab cloth.

"They're moving more each day," his mother observed, scanning the camp.

"Maybe they're afraid of something."

"They're growing accustomed to travel. This happens every time the People migrate." She let out a low breath. "West always. They are going to Bogana. I'm sure of it."

Mirage followed her gaze toward the setting sun. "They are going to the great water? Do you think we'll see it?" Hope stirred in him at the thought. The great water was supposed to be a miraculous and unsettling sight: so much water that you could not see the end of it. And all of it undrinkable, poisoned by the tears of Mpo. And Bogana itself, the home of his ancestors. His grandmother had traveled from there before he was born. His father had been a child during that journey.

"If we do end up there, you must not go to that city." His mother's voice had gone hard and wary.

"Why not? Did my—did Knife Strap tell you something about it?"

His mother glanced down at him. "I want to ask you something, and you won't like it."

"All right."

"You mumble in your sleep. You're restless. You say his name sometimes."

"Who? King Laughing Dog?"

"Left Rabbit."

He turned away, folding his arms, as though they could squeeze down the hollow sourness in his stomach. He didn't want to think about this. That was one of the benefits of not being in the village any longer: not having to be continually reminded that he was a killer.

"Mirage. I love you. But I need to know. Why did you do it?"

"I was ordered to. By our King. After our village had been attacked by something terrible in the forest."

"You were ordered to," she repeated to herself softly, sampling the words. "One thing that I was always proud of you for, even admired a little: you were always a rebel. You never accepted orders, even from your own parents. You always fought back. But when a man—nearly a boy—told you to kill another boy, you did it. Without hesitation."

*But I did hesitate*. And the words took him back again to that moment, that choice. "It was the right thing to do," he answered firmly, putting more passion into the reply than he could muster. "Why are you asking me this?"

"People talked about you. Not to me, never to me. But I overheard. They say you used another word about what—what happened to that boy."

"Oh."

"Is it true? Did you tell people that Left Rabbit was a—a sacrifice?"

"No! I mean, I mentioned it, maybe, but I didn't mean…" He swallowed a knot of frustration. "There were things grandmother said about the way things used to be."

"Your grandmother—listen to me," she said firmly when he groaned. "Listen to me. Two Broken Hands was a cruel woman and the world that she came from was sick."

"How do you know? You were never there. And you shouldn't talk about grandmother that way. She died because of the forest god's treachery."

His mother shook her head, her mouth a hard line. "How she died doesn't change how she lived. She was a mean-spirited and violent woman."

"She was always kind to me," Mirage said, but he knew that wasn't really fair. She'd treated him with favor, certainly, selecting the best bits of a meal for him, or singling him out for compliments, but these moments had often been at the expense of someone else. Praise for his manners would come after his father had offended her, and the gifts she gave him were frequently those that his father had desired even more. It hadn't been fair, but it had often been satisfying. His grandmother was the only one who had seemed to hate Knife Strap more than Mirage did.

"Maybe you think so, then. But you don't know what that woman did to him—"

"He deserved it."

"Do you think your father was born cruel? Mirage, it doesn't come out of nowhere. She was terrible to him, and I've heard her speak of things her father did to her. Proudly. As though she thought it made her better. Violence doesn't stop with one person, son, it spreads like—like fire…"

The comparison annoyed him. Another little reminder that she thought him siding with Laughing Dog was wrong. "It doesn't excuse what he did! What kind of man he was! Whatever she did to him—"

"I'm not excusing it." His mother reached out to put her hand on his arm. "You're right. Nothing excuses that. But I'm trying to explain it. Mirage, what your father did to you, to us, what your grandmother did to him, what their ancestors did? It all starts in Bogana. And it starts with words like sacrifice. You have to be careful. Please." Her fingers tightened on his arm. "Don't let that cruelty spread to you, too."

He pulled his arm away. "I don't know who you think you're becoming now that you're away from Father. You shaved your head and you're leaving bloody footprints behind because you're so tough now that *he's* not around. But for rain after rain you sat by and let him hurt me. Hurt *us*. So whoever this new Dry Grass is, you don't suddenly get to start being my mother."

She gave him a steady, unreadable stare. "Yes," she said. "I do."

~

The edges of the sky were paling with the grey hues of morning. Mirage sat huddled under the low cover of a thicket of elephant grass. Over the last few days, his snares had been repeatedly chewed through. No one had ever mentioned a savanna creature that was savvy enough to gnaw through set snares, and he was determined to first find out what sort of creature it was, and then cook and eat it. Even if he had to watch for it all day. Besides, he'd managed to get up and leave without waking Dry Grass.

In the days after their last conversation, his mother remained frustratingly unflappable. There were no moments in which she broke or seemed uncertain. She didn't cry or smile sadly at him. She spoke and moved with a quiet resolve that Mirage found unsettling, because he wasn't sure what she had resolved to *do*. He caught himself making sideways verbal jabs at her, trying to provoke her into an emotional response, but she answered these, when she didn't ignore them outright, with a calm and steady tone that deflected any insult.

He didn't know what to make of it. It was as though she had simply decided to be someone else entirely. And she insisted on following him everywhere. As though he couldn't take care of himself. "Shouldn't you be scouting for food and supplies?" he'd snapped at her once, but she'd only answered that she could do that at his side as easily as on her own. Besides, she'd pointed out, in this wilderness, it was foolish to travel alone if they didn't have to. That was a point he reluctantly agreed upon. Isolation in the wilderness could easily mean death.

The early light was waking birds all over the savanna, and their calls would rouse the morning fauna eventually, but for now, nothing else stirred. Mirage plucked stems of grass and began tying them into the Priest's Procession: left, right, over, over… Forming the pattern usually calmed him. It was something to center his mind on, to give him stable ground amidst the turmoil of family. But now, weaving it reminded him of the grandmother who had taught it to him, and that led his thoughts back to the conversation with his mother.

His father was responsible for his own actions. Grandmother had nothing to do with it. He looked down and realized he had lost his count with the Priest's Procession. He couldn't focus on it. So that was gone, too. He scowled and dropped the bunch of grass, but then a flicker of movement caught his eye.

He held still, lifting his gaze. A hare crept toward the loop of his snare, its ears perked forward in curiosity, whiskers twitching. The snare was constructed of a loop tied to a sapling bent down and held in place by a loose catch. The design relied on the animal not realizing it was there and springing through. The loop would catch around its head and pull the snare free of its catch, and then the sapling would spring upright and kill the hare, leaving it dangling from the sapling, out of reach of scavengers such as jackals.

But somehow, this animal had detected his snare. Step by step, its nose working rapidly, the hare crawled forward. It leaned up and stood on its hind legs, sniffing all around the edge of the loop. It lowered back down to all fours and crept around the snare. It must be something to do with the scent, Mirage reasoned. Something on his hands—maybe the smoke from fire hunting day after day had cooked into his skin and left an odor that transferred to anything he touched.

The hare stopped by the anchor that held the catch, keeping the sapling bent low. Then it leaned up on its hind legs again, found the bit of cord that tied the whole thing down, and gave a little nip. With a *whip*, the sapling lashed upright again, waving back and forth before settling, a little more bent than before, the ruined snare falling to the ground.

Mirage almost fell backward in surprise, but then the hare turned right toward him, its ears perked, brown eyes staring off to either side. It reared up, lifted one paw, and *waved* to him, wiggling the stubby appendage as though saying hello.

"Eye of Wem," he breathed aloud, and then with a thump of its foot and a sudden puff of dust, the creature was gone.

Mirage jumped to his feet, half in amazement, half in fear. Animals did not behave like that if the gods were not involved. Could he have strayed into the treacherous forest by mistake? But no vines slithered around his ankles. No thorns clutched at his flesh. He scanned the twilit horizon, searching for the creature, but there was no sign of it.

What he saw instead was an orange glow and a column of smoke, dark against the dawn, back in the direction of his camp. Fire. His mother had lit another fire. Swearing in fury, he got to his feet and ran as quickly as he could.

There was no way around it, he told himself. She jeopardized his assignment. What was he going to do, return to Laughing Dog and confess that he'd failed as a spy because his mother kept lighting fires? He'd have to send her back. But that would be a long journey on her own, on a trail that had already been stripped clean twice over. It would be isolation. And then she'd be going back to Knife Strap. If she would even go at all.

It might be better to send her ahead to join the exiles. They could come up with a story about how she'd been isolated and Mirage had disowned her or something, and she'd spent days catching up. And then he'd have someone inside the group who could tell him what was happening. Though that was assuming he could trust her. And if she was building fires and alerting them to their enemies after he'd expressly instructed her not to, how trustworthy could she be?

He squinted toward the campsite as he approached. Making out distinct shapes was difficult in the early morning light, but he could see someone squatting a short distance from the camp. His mother, maybe. But if so, then who was that crouched right next to the fire?

He slowed, then dropped low to the ground. Someone else was in their campsite. It could only be one of the exiles. They must have come when they saw the flames. Now wary, he resumed a hurried pace but crouched low. What would they have thought when they found his mother? Would the scout who found them be observant enough to notice that there were *two* matted spots of grass near the fire? What would she tell them she was doing there?

If she was smart, and kept the reason for her journey secret, this might all work in his favor. The exiles would take her along to their own camp and care for her, and Mirage would be free to follow at his own pace, his mission uninterrupted. But he'd need to know exactly what she was saying to them, so even though he risked being caught, he had no choice but to draw close enough to overhear what they were saying. And he would have to do it quickly, before dawn light made stealth impossible.

He skirted around to the west so that his silhouette wouldn't stand out against the yellowing sky and ran closer. It wasn't until he drew near enough to overhear the voices in the camp that he recognized the other person standing there. It wasn't one of the exiles at all.

It was his father.

Curses rose to his mouth anew; he barreled toward the camp as fast as he could. His father looked up as he approached and backed away from the fire, raising his hands. "Whoa, whoa, easy, little rhino."

Mirage dropped to his knees next to the fire and scooped dirt over it with both hands. "What were you thinking coming here? How dare you?"

"Hey!" The word was a jackal bark, sharp and angry. "That's my breakfast you're ruining, boy. You going to go catch me another?"

Only belatedly, Mirage noticed the cleaned carcass of a monitor lizard, skewered on a stick and half-scorched, now with heaps of earth covering it. He pulled it from the fire pit and tossed it out into the savanna. "Go and fetch it."

Immediately, he knew a moment of quiet terror. His father couldn't have done much to him back in the village. But they were far from the village now. Far from a threat of exile having any meaning. He tried to scan through the fire pit for any branch sturdy enough to use as a weapon.

But his father only laughed, a genial, friendly laugh, like he was passing palm wine around a group of his fellow stone cutters. "Well, now, killer, there's no need to get nasty."

"You shouldn't be here. King Laughing Dog wouldn't like it that you came." Mirage spared a glance toward his mother. She looked small, terrified, shrunk in on herself. She clutched at her knees with both arms and stared at the ground. So much for her transformation. One sunrise around his father and she was the same old pushover she'd always been, quiet and immobile as a terrified hare.

"Well," Knife Strap said, grinning at Mirage lazily, "what your dear King Laughing Dog doesn't know won't hurt me. He'll never miss me, I can promise you that. The whole village got up and moved, and your grand high madman barely notices. He's up on his hill, fighting his little war against every tree that ever dared offend him."

*That's not how it is.* Mirage swallowed the words. That was the argument his father wanted him to have. "So you thought you could come out here and… what? Get your family back?"

Knife Strap sauntered over toward the bushes and poked around for his half-cooked lizard. "Can't a father be worried about his son? And his wife, who disappeared without telling anyone?"

"She's not your wife anymore, you goat carcass."

His father looked over, but only laughed. "I'll give you this, boy, you grew the family fists. No one would ever argue you're not my brat. Now here's what's going to happen. I'm going to stick around and spend some time with you and your mother, out here away from annoying Kings and people who don't understand our special relationship."

"No. You'll leave now. We want nothing to do with you."

Knife Strap sauntered back over to him. "Or you'll do what, boy? Put an arrow in me like that boy back in the village? You'll never set foot among the People of the Savanna again. You'll be exiled."

Mirage clenched his fists at his sides. This wasn't the beaten down, petty man he'd grown used to ever since King First Claw annulled his parents' marriage. That man was vicious and mean, but also withdrawn. He preferred to spit his insults from dark corners, to save his little kicks and jabs for when they might be mistaken for accidents.

No, this man was his old father, smug and gloating, sure he could get away with anything. "Besides, I'm not going to hurt you and your mother. Not anymore. Those days are done. You, me, her, we're going to work it out. We're going to find a way to be happy again. Now, we've all done some things—"

"Not her," Mirage spat back at him, pointing at his mother. She still sat in the same place, hiding her face in her hands. No, not her, he told himself. She never did anything.

"We've *all* done things. I've lost my temper. I've hurt you and your mother, and I'm genuinely sorry for that. And I can promise you, that those days are over. As long as… well, as long as the two of you own up to your own mistakes. I've thrown a punch or two in my time, boy, but her? She knew just how to make me do it. She's got a tongue like a knife."

"That's sick." Mirage noticed he was shaking. Was it fear? Anger? He couldn't tell. "She didn't make you. You did it. You chose to do it."

Knife Strap ignored him. "And you, my boy, do you ever have problems. You killed a man. Just murdered him with an arrow, quick as lightning. Shamed me. Shamed our family. Ruined us in the village."

"That's different. King—King Laughing Dog, he ordered me to—"

"What?" His father almost purred the word. "Did he *make you?* Own it, boy. You're no better than the rest of us." He grinned. "Why, you might even be the worst."

"That's not true." The words came from Mirage's mother, soft in the morning chatter of birds.

"What a surprise. Dry Grass has an opinion. Well, speak up, wife. Let's hear it."

His mother got to her feet, staring down. Her hands clenched, her knuckles pale. "He's… he's a good boy. He got confused. You can't say those things to him."

Mirage was waiting, just waiting, for the moment when his father went after her. These moments had been common in his boyhood, when the air felt charged with lightning, and the past and future stripped away. All that mattered was the present. When would he try to hurt her, or both of them?

Knife Strap nodded slowly. "All right. That's fair. We're all trying to get along now, aren't we? We're going to make things better. And as a father, I am resolved to be a kinder, gentler man. To both of you. But what are you going to do, Dry Grass? How are you going to be better?" He pointed a knobbed finger at her. "You see, it hurts me—it pains me deep—that our son is a *murderer* and you say, 'oh, we have to be nice to him, we can't make him feel bad about it.'

"But me? What did I do? Felt passion like a man should? Slipped once or twice and took my anger out on someone who didn't deserve it? Yes. Was it wrong? Absolutely. But Dry Grass, I never killed anybody. I never did anything that wouldn't heal. So where is my forgiveness, eh? How do you know I didn't 'get confused'?"

"No. No forgiveness for Knife Strap. You don't even say goodbye to me. You sneak out in the middle of the night and disappear!" His teeth were bared now, spittle flecking his lips. "You take *our son* and disappear on me. And I had to go to the King himself to find out where you stole him away to. You know, he forbade me to come after you? He seemed to think *someone*" —and here he whirled on Mirage— "wanted to keep me away from you."

"I'll tell him." Mirage said. "The King didn't want you to come after me? I'll tell him you did. You'll be exiled for good."

"You're going to run all the way back there, for days?"

"The fire. I can speak to him through the fire. He told me how."

His father's eyes went a little wider at that, his mouth stretching like a frog's. Then he burst into laughter. "Well, go ahead, boy. I got the fire burning bright. Oh. No, where is it? Did you put the fire out? Now why would you go and do that?" He turned toward the west, making a show of shading his eyes with his hand. "Lot of sparkly little fires out there, aren't there? Would those be the exiles?"

He clapped his hand over his mouth. "Oh no. They're not supposed to know we're here, are they? Seems like a pretty big risk making a fire. Or a lot of noise. Hm?" He chuckled. "Oh, lose the sour face, son. I'm here to make amends, not trouble. I promise to get along. I'll help you hunt and find supplies. I can keep watch at night."

Mirage shook his head. "No. Get out. Go back to the village."

His father took a deep breath and let it out slowly. "Life back there wasn't so bad, was it? It was tolerable, at least. I know I didn't make things easy, but that's all over now. We're free of all of that. And I will show you—I will prove to *both* of you—that I'm going to be a better man. And when you see it, I know you'll both be better to me, too. And we can be a family. That's all I want, son. That's the only thing I want. So unless you want to kill me, or risk causing a ruckus that might interest your friends over there, I think you're stuck with me."

He grinned again. "Huh? So why not make the best of it?"

~

They followed the exiles in the late afternoon, when they would be too tired from travel and the heat of midday to keep a sharp eye out. Mirage was sure they were too far back to be seen, but it was better to be cautious, especially now that they had an extra traveler. He doubted his father would willfully attract attention, but it was better not to give him the chance.

Knife Strap was in high spirits, sometimes walking with a little skip or singing old Boganan songs. Mirage hadn't heard any of these in a long time and had never cared for them. The tunes were wrong, skipping notes or reaching unusual pitches, and there were no places for a chorus of people to repeat important words or answer the questions of the song. And they were in the Boganan language, which sounded both chattering and guttural. Mirage remembered barely any of the words from his grandmother teaching him, but there were dark themes to them: a thousand wings, the sleeping dead, a flood that would wash the world clean.

The songs were unsettling and alien, and eventually Mirage had had enough. "If you have to sing, can't you sing something else? Why those songs?"

His father shrugged. "The songs are from Bogana. And that's where we're going, isn't it?" Catching Mirage's annoyed look, he added, "Don't act surprised. It's my mother's birthplace. Your grandmother's. Your ancestors came from there. Aren't you excited to see it?"

"We're not going to see it," Mirage told him. "Once we're sure that's where they're going, I'll report to King Laughing Dog. He'll send a runner to me and I'll go home. With Mother."

His father laughed and spat in the dirt. "Boy, you may have inherited your father's fists but you sure didn't get his wits. Your King isn't going to send for you. You're not here on an important mission!"

Mirage stared at him dully.

"You're a killer, son! He couldn't have that in the village. Not when he became King under such… bad signs. He sent you out here to get rid of you."

Fighting a flash of hot anger, Mirage demanded, "If he wanted to get rid of me, then why didn't he exile me like everyone else?"

His father shook his head. "No wits at all. Use your head, son. The King can't exile you for following his orders. Who would want to obey him after that? No, he needed you to fly, and fly willingly, and you strung yourself for him, shaft and string! You're such an obedient little weapon, aren't you?"

Mirage stared at the ground, his face hot. It couldn't be exile. Not really. He could return… but the King had ordered him to stay out here until he sent for him. What if it never happened? What if they got all the way to Bogana and the King never sent a runner? How long would he have to wait? Moons? Rains?

His father's smile grew more confident. "Ah hah, ah hah, I can see you're thinking now. You fell for some stupid, stupid goat dung, didn't you? Were you really going to lean over and talk into a fire? Did you really think that whelp Laughing Dog could hear you?" He cackled. "Oh, Wem's tears, you've done it already, haven't you?" He bent over and cooed into his cupped hands, "Oh, save me, King Laughing Dog, I'm out here talking to a fucking fire like the huge fucking idiot I am."

"You—you keep quiet!" Mirage shouted at him. "You're talking about things you don't understand. You saw what he can do. You saw the power of his god! You want to blaspheme that power? You want to get *that* god angry at you?"

Knife Strap rolled his eyes. "Oh, relax, son. I'm having fun with you. We're having fun together, aren't we, Grass?"

Mirage looked back. His mother was walking a good distance behind, her gaze on the ground. She said nothing. As usual.

His father clapped an arm around his shoulders and he had to resist the urge to shrug it away. "Look, son, I'm sorry this is all such a surprise to you, but I thought you knew. You're not going back. No one there thinks you are. They all talk about you like you're gone forever. And if I'm being honest, they sounded glad. So I figured you saw how things stood. That you were gone for good, with your mama. That's why I had to come after you. I couldn't lose my son forever. So I came to get you."

Knife Strap gave Mirage a cheery smile. "But there's a new life waiting for us. Our old family home. Bogana! You'll see. We'll go there together, and we can all be a family again. A family in a place where we belong, where they understand… people like us. And nobody will ever separate us again."

A numbness spread throughout Mirage's body, starting at his fingers, toes, and lips, and reaching into his gut, his heart. There had to be a way out. He would drop back a discreet distance, find a hollow and build a tiny sheltered fire where the smoke might not be seen. Then he'd tell the King everything. He'd swear the exiles were going to Bogana. He'd explain about his father. He'd beg to come home.

And then what? Wait endlessly? Wonder nonstop if his father was right and he was stupidly talking to inanimate flame?

The numbness was turning his body to stone. He looked back at his mother, walking with heavy limbs and an empty gaze, and he realized, distantly, that he had begun to stare and move the same.

His father swayed from side to side, a smile on his face as he sang a song about the deep, deep mother who would clean away all the suffering of the world.

~

They bedded down without saying much else. Though he loathed the thought, Mirage lay down near his father, as much to look out for his mother as to help guard against night scavengers that might hassle a single sleeper. He lay awake a long time, listening to the raw snore of his father as his mind turned over and over.

They could flee, go back to the village. But if they did that, King Laughing Dog would surely exile him as punishment, and he would be no better off.

Maybe this was all some dark imagining. The King had never given Mirage any reason to doubt him. He was strong, capable, a leader. He'd hunted alongside Mirage and shared his kills. And why should Mirage believe his father, a liar and a bully? These fears were perhaps born of exhaustion and isolation.

That notion calmed him considerably, and he held onto it. It was no use dwelling on questions he had no way of finding the answers to. Things might look different in the morning. And he would have a long time to think of a way to get himself and his mother away from Knife Strap. Or to get Knife Strap to leave on his own.

His father wasn't old—less than forty rains—but he wasn't young and strong like Mirage. And he was mean. He hadn't changed, no matter what he said. He would try something again, with his feet or his fists, and when he did, well, self-defense was hardly a crime. It would be a shame if something happened to a knee or an ankle and he couldn't keep up with Mirage and his mission. He'd have to go crawling back to the village on his own.

There were ways out of this. Mirage had to be patient, and rest. He settled his mind around these reassurances as he drifted to sleep.

〰

A soft crunch in the gravel woke him. He had never been a heavy sleeper, and so was scrambling backward from his sleeping spot even before he saw the shape lunging for him in the dark. The figure lurched past him, arms outstretched.

"Where is she, boy?" His father's voice, muzzy with sleep and anger mingled.

No point asking who. Mirage cast about in the dim light—the horizon was a deep blue in the east, only the promise of dawn. There, the divot in the grass where he'd bedded down. There, the shape of his father's sprawl. And there… his heart sank. His mother had slept there, a little distance away. And she was gone.

He tried to tell himself she'd crept away in the pre-dawn to set snares. Or perhaps to make water. But he knew her. He knew his mother, and who she became around Knife Strap. All the new toughness, all the serenity, just an act. She'd fled. She'd left him with *him*. Just like always.

"Well?" Knife Strap snarled. His voice cut through the quiet of night and was answered by the sudden cries of birds out in the bushes.

No reason to give his father the satisfaction. "Why would I ever tell you—" he began and then his father's fist sent his head whipping back. He stumbled backward, nearly losing his balance, shards of pain digging into his skull. His eyes streamed, and heat ran from his nose down his upper lip.

"I knew you were with her."

Mirage couldn't see. His sinuses pounded with heat and pain, the pulse of blood in his ears too loud to hear if Knife Strap was moving closer. He tried to rub the tears from his eyes and then he felt an impact in his stomach, heavy enough to lift him from the ground. He fell backward, sprawling in the bristly grass. The wind had been struck from him; he sucked for air and nearly choked on the blood in his mouth.

"She always knew how to make me feel like nobody. Like nothing. Cutting me down with her words, with her—with her gods-damned mouth. Or worse, with her silence. And you were always on her side, every fucking time." He punctuated the curse with his foot, the kick knocking Mirage sideways again.

Mirage fought the dull numbness in his hip, found his breath, and tried to crawl away in the grass, though he knew, wounded and stunned, he had no chance of escaping. His father had hit him before, had broken his finger, had kicked him while sleeping, but this time was different. This time they were out in the dark, in the middle of nowhere, and no one would be able to see and stop him.

"Trying to leave me again." The hiss of grass against legs as his father followed him. "You and her, always trying to leave me behind, always happy to let everyone think I'm some kind of monster. Like you two were innocent, like you didn't know how to hurt me in secret. You ruined me. You let everyone hate me with your—your one-sided stories about what I'd done. Everyone. And then ignoring me? And then leaving me alone. Ruined me. Now I'm the man who has to be kept away from his family. And you? And her? Any blame for the way you drove me to it? The subtle, sneaky, superior little ways you both had, the way you could *make* me hurt you, *make* yourselves the victims so everyone would feel sorry for you. You miserable little pile of monkey shit."

Another kick. This one missed, but the next one surely wouldn't. Or the next. There was no use begging for mercy. "Simpering" only enraged Knife Strap further.

His father's voice dripped with disgust. "My own flesh and blood. I ought to—"

"All right. That's enough." The voice belonged to an older man. Familiar. Someone from their village, and very close. Knife Strap made a wordless shout of surprise. For one brief, crazed moment, Mirage thought it was his ancestors, come to rescue him. He pitched sideways in the grass and rubbed the tears and blood from his face. Several figures stood around, holding spears. The points were fixed on Knife Strap.

"This—this is a family matter. It's none of your concern!" He took a few steps backward, tripped over Mirage's heels and went sprawling.

"I reckon it might be." One figure came closer and crouched in the grass. "Are you all right, boy?" He peered. "Ah. It's… you."

In the dim pre-dawn, still blinking away tears, Mirage could make out the face of Firefly, the man whose son had died of Cloud's poison. He had still sided with her. Mirage had never been able to understand why.

"So you're the one Laughing Dog sent to spy on us. Well, that's over with, and I guess you have us to thank for it. You're coming back with us. Can you get up?" He reached out a hand.

Reluctantly, Mirage took it and allowed himself to be pulled to his feet. His hip wasn't too bad, and the blinding pain in his nose was beginning to dull, but there was a raw, pounding ache in his stomach still. All in all, not too bad. Not the worst beating he'd taken from his father, but he could not remember one more terrifying.

And now they'd been caught by the exile's scouts. They must have seen his father's fire and scouted them after that, creeping up on them in the middle of the night. He wondered how long they'd watched him being beaten before they'd stopped it.

"You can walk, or we need to carry you?"

He took a few steps. His hip moved all right. "I can walk."

"We bringing this one, too?" The other scout stood over his father—Mirage recognized the voice as belonging to Beetle.

"Fuck you, I'm not going!" his father's voice snarled.

"Yes, of course, him too," Firefly said. "You think we're going to take one of Laughing Dog's spies and leave the other?"

Mirage turned in time to see his father take a swing at Beetle—a futile one considering he was still seated.

Beetle lifted his spear and gave Knife Strap a sharp tap on the forehead with the haft. "Enough of that. Let's go."

As Knife Strap cursed and swore and clambered to his feet, someone else—a third scout, someone he hadn't seen—wound leather cord tightly around Mirage's wrists. This was it, then. His mission was over.

"Come on, let's get going. Get their things."

Firefly held up Mirage's pack and knife. "Is this it? Is this everything?"

In the darkness, his vision blurred, he couldn't tell, but he had it all together when he went to bed, so he nodded. "I think so."

"All right then, come on. Let's go. You're going to have a lot of questions to answer."

He stumbled as the scouts shoved him toward the twinkling lights of the distant camp of the exiles. He wasn't sure if he was grateful to have been saved from the beating or not. So soon in his mission he'd been caught, and it was all his father's fault.

No. Not all.

His mother was to blame, too. His mother, who had once again left him alone. Once again run away. Or had she gone to the exiles herself? Was that how they'd been found? Could she have betrayed them all?

Some days, he almost understood why his father hit her.

# 12 The Stone Wastes

The scouts had sent for Cloud, and now she looked forward into a land of death. The savanna behind them was, if not lush with life and food, at least somewhat green and forested. But ahead the land sloped down and down into a massive, discolored plain. The grey columns of what might once have been trees jutted up all through the valley, but they bore no leaves or branches. Piles of jagged stone surrounded the bases of each, as though their limbs had long ago fallen and shattered like clay fragments. The plain extended and merged with the forest to the south and reached as Cloud could see to the west and north. There would be no going around.

Basket came up behind her, leaning on his staff, and surveyed the terrain ahead. "Ah. So we're finally here."

"Yes." Cloud sighed. "The Stone Wastes. I had almost hoped we had invented them."

"Not impassible," Basket said.

"No. I've come through before, as a child. Traders can navigate it too. But it won't be easy, especially with this many people. No food, little water, no wood for torches. The nights will be dark."

"And the days hard. How long do you think it will take for us to pass through?"

Cloud looked back at the encampment gathered on the other side of the hill. "You know the stories better than I. I remember crossing it as a girl, but not how long it took us. Just being very tired and growing very thirsty. My father carried me much of the way, I think."

Basket straightened a little, lifting his chin as he did when he remembered his role as the Teller. "There are a few stories. Petal, who wandered the Stone Wastes for three rains, and Grey Locust, who raced Adanko and managed it in the span of one hundred breaths. But stories are known for their exceptional events. If I go by the stories, I can only say it is a journey somewhere between a hundred breaths and three rains. If I ask the traders, who are known to boast, it can be crossed by a single, capable traveler in under ten days. But who knows whether they tell the truth? Or how our progress will compare? Few tell the story of the People of the Savanna, who crossed the Stone Wastes in twelve days, which was slightly slower than usual."

"Maybe you'll have to tell that one after this journey," Cloud suggested with a smile.

"Maybe. If I can find the truth in it."

"I'm thankful we have you here. I mean, not only for me. The people need someone who can guide them through this journey. Remind them of those who have gone before. How to be strong. But I worry about the ones we left behind. Maybe they need a Teller more."

Basket sighed. "I worry about them too. So many good people left to be deceived by that dark spirit. But they're telling their own tale now, so loudly that they've drowned out all others. And the people here need me. If I thought I could have done more good there, I would have stayed."

"Would you?" Cloud asked with a smile.

He returned it. "That is the tale I have chosen to tell for now."

"You lying old scoundrel." She leaned into his side.

~

She had difficulty getting the attention of the people as they prepared their shelters and meals for the night. Her nightly announcements had become routine, and so had the habit of giving her only half an ear. That was something she would have to change. She plucked a blade of grass from the ground, pressed it between her thumbs and blew, making a shrill, sharp whistle.

"I want to begin with good news," she said, but she could hear that her voice was not carrying among the crowd. She clambered up on a nearby boulder, its surface still very hot from the afternoon sun, and tried again.

"My good news for you all is that we have come more than halfway through our journey." She pointed to the west. "That way lies Bogana, the city of my ancestors. Despite us all being tired and grieving for our home, we have all pressed forward and kept a good speed."

Heartened smiles and genial murmurs passed through the crowd. Those stooped with weariness stood a little taller and put back their shoulders. Now, though, Cloud would have to disappoint them.

"But a difficult part of our passage begins. On the other side of that hill lie the Stone Wastes. Some of you have heard of this cursed place. It is a hard land, where little food grows, and the ground is sharp and may cut your feet. There will be little water, and no wood."

The smiles had soured into scowls or depressed stares as quickly as they'd appeared. Well, it couldn't be helped. As a healer, Cloud had grown accustomed to delivering bad news. As a leader, all the bad news would be seen as her fault. She was prepared for that. "You must all ready yourselves. We will camp here an extra day, and everyone who is able should scout. The children as well. Gather as much wood and water and food as you can find.

We will need every bit of it to survive the next" —she glanced at the Teller and hoped his guess was right— "twelve days."

The crowd had gone completely quiet. Some people sat down as though overcome with their burdens. Others put their faces in their hands. "Couldn't we go around it?" someone called.

Cloud glanced at the Teller and he shook his head. "Unfortunately, no," she answered back. It was hard to keep the weariness from her own voice. "Some have tried. There are no tales of anyone succeeding. To the north, the Stone Wastes end in a deep gorge that they say is impossible to climb down. And to the south… well, I don't think any of us are ready to risk the forest."

At that, some turned away, muttering in low voices. She raised her own louder to get their attention. "Please. Remember. All the food and water and supplies you can find. The more we have, the better the chances everyone makes it through without… without serious discomfort. And those of you with no shoes—the ground is sharp and can cut your feet. Get help from the leatherworkers and collect extra bark to wrap. Everyone should carry spares. The coming days are going to be difficult, but I—" She looked around in dismay. Most were not even listening to her anymore. "But I know we can make it. We are the People of the Savanna. We are strong. Remember those who are relying on us back home."

"Wish *we* were back home," came a voice from the middle of the crowd.

"Who said that?" Cloud demanded, but the Teller put a hand on her shoulder. She looked back at him and he shook his head.

She sighed, nodded, and he helped her down from the boulder. "I don't think that went very well," she told him when they were out of earshot of the crowd. "I should have asked you to talk to them. You're so much better with speeches."

"You're the leader. You have to do it. But next time, maybe start with the bad news and leave the good for the end, to bring their spirits up. Now everyone is stuck thinking on the hard times."

"Well, they should be thinking about it. They need to know that the road ahead is treacherous."

"They'll see it as soon as they head over that hill," he said. "Let's give them some time, and then I'll talk to them. We'll give them a little excitement and energy. Tell them it's not so bad."

Cloud pressed her lips together firmly. "Basket, I appreciate your advice, but I know these people. You see them at their best, when they're sitting around the bonfire, full of food and wine, happy and dancing and excited to hear your stories. I was their healer. When they came to me, it was when things had turned bad. When they were sick, or hurt, or dying. I see them during adversity. Fear and difficulty turn people stupid and mean. They will turn on you. You have to keep them focused."

"You might be right," the Teller said, rubbing at his chin and tugging the plump folds beneath it. "You have certainly had a difficult time in the village between the last rains. I must respect the things you learned from that. I guess I caught myself thinking of the Tale of the Two Healers."

Cloud glanced at him in surprise. "You know that one?"

He answered only with a patient smile, and she wanted to pinch herself. Of course he knew it—he was the Teller, after all. But the Two Healers was a story passed down from healer to healer as part of their training. She'd told it to Yellow Bug, and Cloud's mother had taught it to her. The story of the Two Healers was considered as important as knowing which medicines became poison in too high a dose, which should not be administered with wine, or which were best for children. But its relevance here…

"It isn't the same," she said. "These people, they complain, they accuse each other, they—"

"They chose to follow you," the Teller said. "Every one of them. They left their families behind because they believed in you. Cloud, I know they hurt you. But I know too that you love them. And I know you believe in them or you wouldn't have agreed to come out here and lead them across the wilderness. You made that choice, Cloud. Why? I know it is because you have faith in them."

His words caught at her tongue. With all her snappishness and weariness and pain, how could he find something that generous inside her? She didn't have the heart to tell him he was wrong.

~

There was no bonfire, of course, but they did make a small circle out of a few torches. Remembering Basket's advice, Cloud made no fuss about them burning the extra wood. If the people could have one good night before all the bad, maybe it would give them the strength to press on through the Stone Wastes.

And the Teller did what he was best at: he reminded the people who they were. Cloud had thought he might tell tales of journeys, but instead he told old tales of home, and others of Bogana. These tales were strange, and broke, to Cloud's ear, the rules of storytelling, but that was common with tales from another people. And the Teller laced those stories with mystery, asking people what they thought the homes looked like there, or what the food tasted like, or how it felt to stand on the cliff of the great water and look out into the endless domain of Mpo, and know that you were tiny in the eyes of the gods.

He talked about their journey as though it were a great quest to save not just the People of the Savanna, but all the peoples of the world, and maybe to save the gods themselves. He asked everyone to do their best so that there would be new stories that their grandchildren and great-grandchildren would tell of them while they shone in the heavens with their ancestors. And when he spoke of their venture in this way, Cloud found herself believing it, too.

It was easy to become absorbed in the daily hardships, the pains and privations of travel. It was easy to miss home, to grieve for those lost, and to fear what might lie over the next horizon. The circumstances that had set them on this journey were extraordinary. And the Teller spoke of this journey not in isolation, but as though it were the final verse of a larger song that had begun the night many rains ago when the fires came across the savanna and drove the People from their homes.

But Cloud remembered back farther still. She remembered why her family had left Bogana in the first place, and why she dreaded returning. It was Bogana's influence that had shaped Two Broken Hands, her son Knife Strap, and his son Mirage. And Mirage had killed Left Rabbit in front of the whole village, shocking the people into choosing exile and following Cloud. Story followed story followed story, and now they were returning to that city, where, Cloud supposed, new tales would find their beginnings.

Now they were in the middle of their own, one that she hoped would be told to their children. They had fled demons and angry gods. They would brave the Stone Wastes and the Unclean City. They would try to save all the peoples of the world.

"But why?" Someone had stood up in the group of people, hunched over on her stick. Her hoop earrings glinted in the torchlight. Okra Bush, one of the youngest council members. The people turned to look at her. "Why do we think Bogana will help us? Won't they say, 'Sorry, but we have our own troubles?' We are coming all this way for a very faint hope. Will they lend us hunters to fight our own people? Or spells to convince them?"

The Teller made a sweeping gesture with his hand toward Cloud. "We have our own one-time resident of that city guiding us back. Elder Cloud, will you tell us what you hope to find?"

She got to her feet and shuffled over to his side. She didn't need her stick as much these days. The journey had strengthened her. "When I was a young girl in Bogana, I remember that the people there did not hunt much for meat. There were animals to hunt, but much of our food was fish from the great water."

She paused to let people talk and explain—not everyone would be familiar with fish. They had encountered it occasionally in lakes, though as elusive creatures, not as a food source. "Now there is a river in the forest called Asubonten—you remember it from the stories—and the great crocodile goddess who it is named after. The Asubonten catches all the rain that falls in the forest and carries it west until it reaches the great water, right near Bogana.

"But now that our sons and daughters are burning the forest, the rains will catch ash and smoke. The river will be choked with it. It will carry all this to the great water and poison the fish. When this happens, Bogana will suffer. The people will have no food. Even if they were willing to offer us no help at all, it would be right to warn them of this danger.

"We will take whatever assistance they can offer, whether it is strong young men and women who can help us peacefully convince our people to stop burning the forest" —she stressed the word peacefully— "or wisdom that can help us to understand what the thing is that has consumed our prince and given him such terrible power, and how it may be stopped."

She glanced at the Teller. "But there may be deeper wisdom to be found. Bogana long had a reputation for songs that held the secrets of the gods. Songs without singing."

"What kind of song is that?" someone from the crowd wanted to know.

"I was only a girl then, and I do not know. But I have heard the tales. They say the other peoples of the world used to journey to Bogana to learn and take this wisdom back to their people. And so they helped all the people of the world. If that wisdom is there, it may help us, too."

"It's not a lot to hope for," Okra Bush said, shaking her head. "Perhaps we ought to discuss this in a council meeting."

Anger surged in Cloud like a sudden storm, building out of nowhere. Of course Okra wanted a council meeting. Because she was tired, and her feet hurt, and the journey was growing difficult. And if it came down to a vote between people who were sore and tired and wanted to stop and those who had the courage and discipline to keep going, well… tired people would take the short view over the long. Of course, as chief elder, Cloud could override any vote, but for Okra Bush to question her leadership here, now, in front of everyone, only made her job harder.

She resisted the urge to suggest Okra Bush was simply undisciplined. And then she resisted the urge to chastise her in front of the people. And then resisted the urge to argue about whether convening the council was necessary. If they started fighting each other now, their journey would be over when they were halfway there. People would lose spirit.

*There once was a city with a great sickness. So many were sick that the King hired a second healer from a faraway people to help keep everyone well…*

She was tired. She hadn't wanted to be a leader of these people. She'd done it because she had to. The physical weariness and the privation were one thing, but the negativity of her own people? It was like traveling in the season of high wind, always blowing her back, making each step harder.

*The King's healer did not like the faraway healer. Her knowledge was different, but good, and her treatments were capable. But the faraway healer coddled her patients. She lied to them.*

The journey ahead would be the most difficult part of their trip. The people would need all their strength, all their resolve, to make it through the Stone Wastes.

*The King's healer knew that for her patients to survive, they had to be strong. They had to know the disease they were facing, the injuries they had to overcome. They needed to be prepared. And so when she visited her patients, she told them: you are weakening. You must be more careful. You will be dead in five days if you do not take your medicine. You must change this dressing every day, or you will lose your leg.*

*But the faraway healer told her patients: you are getting better! Well done! You look so strong today—you must be taking your medicine. Look at how you are moving about. Good job changing your dressing. She told them these lies even when the patients were doing poorly. Even when they worsened. Even when they were dying.*

Cloud looked over the group of people, examining their faces in the firelight. The Teller's words had cheered them and given them heart, but beneath that she saw the lines of all the grief and worry and despair she felt herself. Even if you had the strength to put one foot in front of the other, or the energy to continue with little food into a place of shadow and death, why do it? Where did the will come from?

*The King's healer went to the King with her concern. She said: this healer you found is dangerous. She is careless with the facts and careless with her patients' lives. Many will die because of her methods.*

*But the King was angry at being confronted over one of his decisions. He told her: I followed my advisors and the guidance of my priests. I hired the best healer in all the lands. You will work with her and be quiet about it. And so the King's healer had no choice but to continue back to the sick houses and continue her work. Her patients depended on her.*

Everyone was watching Cloud, waiting for a response. The night had gone quiet but for the crackle of torches and the singing of insects.

She took a breath. "You are wise, Okra Bush, but in this, I believe you are incorrect." Even as the other elder puffed up, toad-like, Cloud continued. "It *is* a lot to hope for. A chance to save our people and the world? A chance is all we need. A chance is worth traveling any distance for, worth braving any hardship."

"Even if it kills us all?" Okra Bush growled, waving her arm at the crowd around her.

*The King's healer went to the healer from faraway and told her: you are hurting your patients. You had one two days from death and you told her she was getting better. Now her bed is empty. You lied to her. To her family and friends. You gave them false hope. Now where is she?*

*But healer, said the faraway healer, she's at home. She is well again.*

"We will not die," Cloud said. "We are the People of the Savanna. We journey to save our friends and family. You have courage, all of you, or you would not be here with me today. You are strong, and your strength has grown with this journey. I've seen you encourage others and help others. I've seen you take time to laugh and enjoy the journey, despite all the hardships. It means so much. It helps me to go forward. All of you, here with me… it is you who give me strength."

The words when she spoke them were a lie, but as they fell from her lips and she saw the faces of her people, they transformed into truth. As her words touched them, their backs straightened. Their shoulders squared. She saw the strength in them that she had not seen before. They looked toward each other with kindness and renewed determination. And now she wondered at the Teller's power with his stories. How many of his words were true only because he spoke them? They were like seeds planted in the People of the Savanna, sprouting virtues.

*The King's healer said: that is impossible. I know this disease. Your patient had worsening symptoms the same as my own. We used the same treatment, and mine was younger, stronger. What did you do that was different?*

*The faraway healer smiled. She said: I did nothing different. I only told her she would live.*

~

The scouts still had not returned. Cloud cast a worried look toward the eastern horizon, but her vision wasn't as clear as it had once been. If Beetle, Long Neck, and Firefly were out there, sharper eyes than hers would have to find them.

"Do you think they'll be able to track us through the Stone Wastes?" Basket asked her.

"Of course," Cloud said, with more confidence than she felt. "They're trained hunters. And you could walk a group this size through the clouds and they'd leave a trail. They'll find us." Her people bustled behind her, most of them packed and ready to go. They'd roused themselves with more energy and enthusiasm than in previous days, though perhaps she thought so only because of her own lifted spirits.

"You did well last night," Basket said. "I always told you you'd be a wonderful leader."

Cloud grunted as she shouldered her pack. "My goodness, an 'I told you so.' And you only had to wait forty rains for that one."

His face creased with a grin. "There is a very special pleasure in being right."

"I see your plan to get through the Stone Wastes is to float across it on a cloud of your own smugness."

Basket shrugged. "Better than walking."

Cloud set out down the hill, trying to look straight and energetic so that the people would have a good example. She leaned on her stick, but only a little, and the people followed behind her. After a short time, a child piped up with a song, and it spread throughout the crowd until nearly all were carrying it.

This was a good day, Cloud thought. Better than she'd expected heading into the Stone Wastes. She wondered how long the high spirits would last.

As they traveled, the grass thinned, and the earth turned to sand. Shards of flat, plated rock jutted up through it at sharp angles, and Cloud found herself slowing to pick her steps more carefully. Soon there was no more earth at all, and the ground was entirely stone. There was no more place to put her feet without knifelike edges of stone cutting into them, so she called a short break and pulled out the shoes she had had made: soft, flexible baobab bark wrapped in hardened eland leather.

She'd worn them several times before, to soften them and shape them to her feet, as well as to allow her skin to adjust to the leather cords tying them in place. It would be no good having them rub her flesh raw and bleeding a day or two in. She only hoped the shoes would last all the way through the wastes. But she was small and slight and wouldn't wear them out too quickly. Basket was another case altogether. On her advice, he'd had two extra pairs of shoes made.

They continued on. The shoes weren't pleasant to wear. They made her feet feel thick, heavy, and clumsy; and she missed the stabilizing feeling of the earth beneath her toes. But they were a song and a prayer better than trying to walk over the serrated terrain of the Stone Wastes.

Their travels finally took them among the stone columns, and up close, these proved not just to resemble trees—they *were* trees, denuded pillars of wood transformed to stone. Up close, one could see the grain of the once-wood, with cracked whorls of rock that had been knots or the bases of branches. On most of the trees, the bark had split and cracked away, lying around the roots in weathered piles, but on some it clung still. From the gnarled bark and the shape of the roots, these must once have been muyovu trees, which explained their tremendous height. Cloud found herself staring up toward their dizzying tops in wonder, although to do so risked a painful stub or cut on her toes.

"What do you suppose turned them to stone?" she asked Basket.

"The stories say that Mother Fam came through this land once, and was hungry, but it offered her no food, and in anger she cursed it, turning it to stone."

"That doesn't sound much like Mother Fam," Cloud objected.

"I agree, which is why I don't tell that story."

Cloud frowned at him. "I don't know if I like your deciding who the gods are and are not."

Basket shrugged. "That's not what I'm deciding. The gods can be whoever they like. But it's up to us to decide who the People of the Savanna are and are not, and we do that by choosing which stories we listen to."

"And what will you tell the People of the Savanna if they ask who turned these trees to stone?"

He smiled. "Who knows? Maybe I'll tell them that no one knows for certain. Life is better with some mysteries, don't you think?"

"I prefer facts," Cloud said.

Basket smiled at that and did not answer. They continued on until all the world around them was grey-pitted stone. Here and there, shrubs and grass poked up heroic little thatches around the petrified ground, but there was very little greenery. In the late morning, they found a stream running through the middle of the wastes, and people eagerly refilled their water skins and drank. The water tasted strange, like broken eggshells.

When they were stopped for a rest and after Cloud had attended to people's questions and concerns, as well as more than a few scrapes and cuts, Basket took her aside. "Cloud, what do you think we will find in Bogana?" he asked, and this time he met her gaze directly. His face was serious. "I know you're worried—"

"Yes, of course. You know of the things done in that city. The sacrifices they made to the gods once. Not only food and animals, but people. You know the cruelty Two Broken Hands learned there."

He puffed out his cheeks. "I don't like thinking of any people as all cruel or kind. It makes the stories boring. Besides, Bogana gave us you, so how terrible can it be?"

"If you think all that honey on your lips will get me to taste them again…"

"But there is something else, isn't there? Something more that you're afraid of." Basket gave her a searching look. "What don't I know, Cloud?"

Heat stiffened her cheeks. "It's not something I'm proud to speak of."

"You're our leader, though. You have enough burdens. Don't carry anything on your own that you don't have to." He put his hand, damp and cool with sweat, on her shoulder. "You know that you can trust me."

She should tell him. She wanted to. But when she reached down inside herself for the words, she wasn't a wearied and experienced elder leading her people. She was small and terrified. She tried to shape her mouth around the confession but found only the buzzing of flies crawling on her tongue. She shuddered in horror and wrenched her mind away from the memory.

And then she felt his hand on her shoulder. He was there with her. He was patient. He kept her steady. She looked up into his calm, brown eyes. She took a breath. She said, "I was only a small girl when I lived in Bogana with my parents."

Hurried footsteps came from behind them. "Elder Cloud! Elder Cloud!"

She turned to see one of the children rushing up with the seriousness of a child who knows he has been given an important mission. "Yes, what is it?"

"They said that—that I was supposed to come and tell you that—that the scouts are back. And they found somebody. It's him. The bad man!"

"The bad man? Do you mean Prince Laughing Dog?"

"No, the other one. You're supposed to come and see! Come on!"

The child scurried off.

Cloud gave Basket an apologetic glance and hurried after him, as fast as she could across the sharp stones. When she reached the middle of the group, she heard the loud noise of people shouting and hooting, a large number of them clustered together. In their midst she could make out the tall figure of Beetle, his spear planted firmly in the ground in front of him, as well as the yellow and purple haft-feathers of Firefly's and Long Neck's spears.

"Well?" she snapped as she reached the group of people, pushing at their sides. "Here I am. Let me through!"

The group parted to reveal the three scouts, all of them looking unharmed, thankfully, and between them, hanging their heads, their arms bound behind them, were the subdued figures of Mirage and Knife Strap. They had no shoes, and their feet were already bloodied from the brutal terrain.

Cloud strode up to them, past the angry cries of "murderer," and lifted up Mirage's chin with one hand. His nose was swollen, round as a tortoise. He wore a sullen scowl and would not meet her gaze.

"Well, boy," she said. "You just can't stop making mistakes, can you?"

~

Ant With a Leaf thrust her finger under Cloud's nose. Her face was more grey and terrible than the Stone Wastes. "You cannot believe we will take him with us. He's a *murderer*, Cloud."

Cloud stared through the jagged pillars at Mirage, standing bound to one of them a little distance away. He stood with his head proud and his jaw set, but his broad shoulders were slumped, and even from here she could see his tremble. "He's a boy."

"Laughing Dog was a boy, too."

"Yes," Cloud answered wearily. "He was. But he became something else. And you and I both know it."

"And Mirage is his tool!" Ant threw up her hands. "How can you think it is right to take him with us, to offer him our precious food and water and bark for shoes. He should be punished, not aided!"

"Look around you, Ant. Look at what remains of our people." Cloud spread her own hands wide. In the dying light of the day, people huddled here and there. There were a few scarce fires, and very little food being cooked, to be shared by many. Backs were hunched, shoulders stooped beneath grey or balding heads. "Most of us are old. Many will see ten rains, twenty, but we will have no more children. Even if we succeed in our quest, it cannot be merely to save ourselves, or our people will die out. It is not enough to keep our truth, if no new Tellers repeat it when we are gone. We must hope that the young hear our voices."

"So, what, you honestly believe you can change his mind? *Him?* He would never listen to you. And even if he did, the People would never accept him."

Cloud leaned against a pillar, ignoring the way the sharp edges dug into her shoulder. "I remember when I believed I knew what the People would never do. And look at what has happened."

"What that should tell you is that people can be more treacherous than you believe them capable of. That boy must be exiled. He followed us out here, he can find his own way back. Give him knots he can work out of in a day and leave him there. We must never let him back among us."

An old shadow fell across Cloud's heart. "That is a mistake I will not make again."

"Again?" Ant asked suspiciously. "What do you mean?"

Cloud shook her head and for a long time could not bring herself to speak, but stared toward the east, toward home. Her voice broke when finally she said, "It was I who advised King First Claw to exile Laughing Dog."

"It was the right decision."

"Was it? He was a boy, Ant. A boy who had made a mistake, and I robbed him of his family and his people. I sent him out into the wilderness and he came back with fire inside him. I think about it every day. If I had only drawn him closer instead of sending him away… from the people who could have guided him with love, shown him by example how to live a good life. I took away everything he could have used to save himself and left him with nothing. He had no one to listen to but a demon. And then he came back and did such terrible things. If it were not for me, Left Rabbit would still be alive. If not for my choices, Mirage would be innocent yet. So his guilt is mine. Of course I do not bear it alone, and of course he must learn. But I have to believe that he can. It must be the first step to setting all this right."

The tall woman puffed out her cheeks and turned away. "Well, I think you are a fool."

"We are all fools. But Mirage is a young fool. The story of the People of the Savanna will be his one day. I must believe he can tell it well."

# 13 The Fist

They had given Mirage shoes so that he would not slow them down. He walked in defeated silence through the strange terrain, imitating the high steps of those around him that they claimed would keep the rocky ground from abrading his shoes too quickly. The gait was unnatural and tiring.

No matter how still he tried to hold his arms, the cords around his wrists rubbed the raw spots deeper. The bindings were not to keep him from running away—he wouldn't make it very far through the Stone Wastes. Elder Cloud had even argued for leaving him unbound, but Ant With a Leaf pointed out that for all they knew, Laughing Dog had sent him here to assassinate Cloud or someone else. She strode next to him, keeping at least one baleful eye fixed on him at all times. She stood more than a head taller than him, an imposing figure, and everyone knew she'd attacked Laughing Dog once. Every time he glanced in her direction, her hard stare made him look down at his feet. He didn't dare speak to her, not even to ask where his father was.

Soon after they'd been brought to the camp, Knife Strap had been led to a different group. "We'll want to ask them questions," Ant With a Leaf had declared, "and we'll want to be sure they don't agree on their answers together."

That arrangement suited Mirage fine; he'd rather his father be kept as far away from him as possible, and he had no intention of lying to anyone. There was no reason to. He'd already been caught spying, and King Laughing Dog hadn't given him orders to do anything more. He had resolved not to tell anyone that the King could hear them through the flames—if that was even true. If it *was*, then the King knew about his plight already. The scouts who had captured them had torches, and all their conversation would have been easily audible to the King.

The more Mirage considered it, though, the less likely it seemed that the King could hear them at all. His father's mockery had planted seeds of uncertainty in his heart. Mirage had seen Laughing Dog wield the power of fire—the whole village had. But throwing fire, and listening through it, days and days journey across the savanna, was another thing. Did the King listen through every spark and every flame cast, all across the world? Did he hear, constantly, the roar of the sun, and the screams of animals dying in savanna fires far away?

Mirage chided himself for being faithless. He only questioned his King now because he was distant from him, alone with his thoughts, swayed by his father's jibes. What reason had the King given him to doubt?

The people traveling around him didn't look like woebegone exiles. The journey was difficult, true, and they were sparing with food and water, but there were smiles and conversation. They helped each other. Some of them sent scowls or suspicious stares his way, but not all. A number of the elders gave him kindly glances. A couple even put a hand on his shoulder as they passed, as though to reassure him. He shrugged these off angrily. He did not need their forgiveness or their pity.

A few even tried to speak to him, but Ant With a Leaf shooed them away. Her voice was kinder when she spoke to them. To him, she only issued curt orders. She puzzled him. She was strong and capable, known among the people for being both a fast runner and a skilled hunter. And at one point, she had been promised to Laughing Dog, but had broken that engagement.

"Why are you here?" he finally asked her, after the silence had grown too tedious to bear.

"Be silent," she snapped at him. Then she turned a curious eye his way. "What do you mean?"

"You're not like these others. You don't just sit back and let others hurt you."

"People like Laughing Dog? Or your father?"

He flushed. "Like the gods! Why didn't you join us in fighting back? You're strong, and you don't let people push you around. You could have been the wife of the King. You could have helped us all to stop Kwaee's tyranny."

The interest fled her eyes like a torch going out. "Oh, I see. You boys. As if being mighty in the arm is the only way to be strong."

"I'm not a boy!" he snapped.

"Yes," Ant With a Leaf said, "you are. You think the only thing that matters is who wins. One person left standing on a smoking hill, that would be enough for you, right? These people around me, all of them? *They* matter. The kinds of lives they live matter."

"If their lives matter, why didn't you do something?" Mirage said. "Why didn't you fight Kwaee? Why didn't you stop Cloud when she was poisoning—"

"Cloud didn't poison anyone. Your precious King did. And he's a monster. I saw it."

"You're envious," Mirage said with a burst of realization. "You saw his power and you wanted it for yourself. *You* wanted to lead the people—you and Cloud together. And you didn't care how many people died—"

Ant With a Leaf whirled on him, her bow gripped in both hands as though she intended to strike him with it. "*You* don't get to talk about people dying. Ever."

She stepped in front of him, bending down to speak face to face. She bared her teeth like a threatening lioness. "Someone is dead because of you. Not because of some mysterious plague. Not vines from the forest. Not an angry god. *You*. You may not believe what we've told you about Laughing Dog, but you know what you did. There is no forgiveness for that. You think you're an outcast now? Wait until you die. I promise you this: your ancestors are ashamed of you. You will spend all eternity alone. There will be no light or peace for you. No place among the stars. And you will have no descendants to look after or call to you. That is what you have made of yourself. But you can sit by yourself alone in the endless night of stars and tell yourself that you were strong."

She stood, and the anger drained from her face, leaving behind only pitiless contempt. "Now get moving, and keep your mouth shut. Save your voice for nightfall. We are going to have a lot of questions for you."

Mirage gave a snort of defiance he did not feel and followed. The pillars of the stone trees rose all around him, fingers pointing toward the sky where Father Wem and all Mirage's ancestors sat waiting.

Ant With a Leaf was wrong about one thing. One of his ancestors, at least, would approve of him: Two Broken Hands. Even if all others abandoned him, his grandmother would be at his side. So, too, he thought, would his father. He would be with them, and them alone, forever.

His breath stuck in his chest and would not come free.

"I don't like that we have to keep you tied up." Cloud stood over Mirage, leaning on her stick.

Mirage said nothing. They'd sat him up against one of the stone trees. It wasn't very comfortable. Everything his body touched was sharp stone, still hot from the afternoon sun. He scowled up at her. Of course she didn't like it. She and the other elders had never liked responding to threats instead of ignoring them.

"How's your face? It looks painful."

He didn't answer that, either. It was a constant throb. His nostrils were swollen shut, his sinuses full and heavy. He had to breathe through his mouth.

"I wish I could give you something for the pain, but we have nothing. It's not broken, I think. Nothing to do but wait for it to heal." She crouched down next to him. The sun was gone, and a half moon barely lit her features. "Do you want to tell me what you and your father were doing following us?"

"You can't make me."

"No. I can't." Her voice sounded tired. "You must be hungry."

His gut was a gnawing, hollow shell, but he didn't intend to show her that weakness. "And I suppose I can have food if I talk?"

Even in the darkness, he could see her eyebrows raise at that. "If you talk? Who do you think we are, boy?" Then she called over one of the exiles and asked him to bring Mirage some food. Soon, he found himself unbound with a handful of roasted breadfruit seeds and a little dried venison. It wasn't much, but he had to fight off a wave of gratitude.

Cloud sat in front of him, watching him eat.

"Could we get a little light?" he asked, trying to sound nonchalant. If King Laughing Dog was listening, maybe their talk would prove informative to him.

"We have to conserve our wood," Cloud said. "None of it in the Wastes. And we'll be in the thick of them for several days at least. So no torches."

He finished his handful of food and the swallows of water that were offered, and someone came by and bound his hands again. Cloud continued to sit near him, saying nothing. Her presence quickly became frustrating. How long was she just going to sit there?

He gritted his teeth and ignored her.

She hummed a song quietly to herself. Fine. This was a mind game. He could ignore her.

After a while she yawned loudly. "It's late."

"Then you should go to bed. You're an old lady. You need your rest."

"I do," she agreed. But she didn't go. She began tapping her stick against the ground. "This journey has been hard," she said, after more time had passed, "but not as hard as I'd feared. Everyone has been so dedicated. We worry about everyone back in the village. We saw the smoke. It was very bad the first few days. Is everyone all right?"

"How would I know?" Mirage snapped at her. "I left not long after you did."

"Did you, now?"

He cursed himself for saying anything to her at all. But still, it wasn't like he'd given anything important away. He was just angry that she'd tricked him into speaking after he'd sworn not to. Well, fine. Maybe if he gave her what she already knew, she'd leave him alone.

"King Laughing Dog isn't stupid, you know."

"What makes you say that?" Her question was casual but curious.

"Because he knows when to fight back. All you elders ever knew how to do is run away. Run away from the savanna fires. Run away from the attacking forest. And now you're running away from your own people."

"But you think we should fight our own people," she suggested.

He felt the heat of frustration in his face. "That isn't what I meant."

"But isn't it what you did? When you killed Left Rabbit?"

This again. She was just here to judge him, to throw that death in his face. He clenched his jaw. Let her feel superior, then.

"Mirage, I am asking because I want to know. Whatever you believe about Laughing Dog, he and I had a disagreement about how our people should be led, a disagreement that no amount of discussion could resolve. Do you think we should have fought him, with fists and spears and bows?"

"Of course not! You—you elders, the old King, all of you, you had the chance to try your way. You… tried to placate the gods, even when they were killing us. It didn't work! You should have stood aside and let someone else try. You should have let those of us who were willing fight!"

"I see. But that sounds like you're not angry with us for backing down. You're angry because we stood up for the course we thought was right."

"You were disloyal," Mirage said. "You fought us instead of the enemy. You should have joined us in turning our spears and bows against the forest that you *knew* was killing us."

"Disloyal?" Cloud spoke the word with surprise. "All of us? Two Kings, the council of elders, the Teller, the guidance of our ancestors, all of us, disloyal to one prince who wanted to fight the gods?"

"You're not going to convince me that what I did was wrong. I was tired of feeling weak and helpless. We all were."

"Mirage, I'm not trying to convince you. I'm trying to understand you. I want to know how we failed you."

There was pity in her voice now, and he loathed it. "You failed all the People of the Savanna. Not just me."

"You're right about that," she said. "We let two of our young men grow up to become killers. With Laughing Dog… I fear it is too late for him. Whatever evil is inside him has nearly consumed him. I've seen it. Others have, too. But you, Mirage… there is no evil in you."

"I thought I was a murderer."

"Yes." She sighed. "That is a pain and a darkness you will carry inside you forever. It won't go away. But you can atone. You can use your life to make others' better. Take away a thousand times the hurt you caused." Cloud's knees and back popped as she pushed herself to her feet.

"You don't get to feel good about yourself anymore, Mirage. No matter how much you do, your spirit will always be in debt for the life you took. But there are more important things than feeling like a good man. *Being* a good man, that is more important."

She turned and began to walk away from him.

"You're leaving? I thought you wanted to know what I was doing out here."

"Oh, no," she said. "I already know. Your father, he told us everything. Goodnight, Mirage."

She left him there, sitting in the dark, guarded by a sentry already sagging with drowsiness. Mirage scowled after her. He didn't need her pity or her supposed understanding. If she thought a little lecture was going to convince him to change his allegiance and side with the exiles, then age had granted her very little wisdom indeed.

Maybe things were more complicated than they'd felt when he was running with the fire hunters, striking back at the forest god and providing food for their people. For a while they'd strode through the village like they were little gods themselves, celebrated for providing feasts after rains and rains of long privation. He'd felt a righteous certainty then. Their world had made a kind of sense. Now that sense flickered dimly, and the passions he had kindled in the fires of his conviction now barely glimmered among its ashes.

But what he'd done was not wrong. Fighting the gods, fighting for the People of the Savanna's right to live with shelter, to eat and drink from the forest without fear of divine wrath, all that had been right. No one would convince him otherwise.

He felt weary after the events of the last two days—dealing with the arrival of his father and their subsequent capture had exhausted him in ways mere physical exertion could not. And there would be more questioning or scolding tomorrow, surely. He'd hold up better under it if he got some rest. But he could not sleep. It wasn't just the sharp edges of the ground digging into his backside; his mind was too active, turning over and over and refusing to settle.

He looked out over the campsite but could see little under the half moon. There were a few yellow glows of fires or torches, but not many. He wondered if his father sat near one, and what secrets or lies he might be telling Cloud even now. Knife Strap wasn't a habitual liar, but neither was he above it when he thought it might grant him an edge. He could have claimed Mirage was up to any number of things.

Mirage would have to try to feel things out tomorrow. And the next chance he got, speak into a flame and hope that King Laughing Dog really was listening. He'd have to explain that yes, he'd been captured, but none of it was his fault—it was Knife Strap's, who King Laughing Dog had *promised* to watch. That rankled. His whole mission had been compromised by circumstances out of his control. It had been the King's failure, not his. But he couldn't frame it that way—Laughing Dog was not well-known for accepting blame graciously. He was a good King, just…

Just, out here in the dark, finding his admiration for his King felt like trying to catch smoke. It was sitting out here with the exiles, it was talking to his mother and father, all of them whittling away at his reasons for following Laughing Dog. He needed to be back with the others to feel it again. He needed not to be sitting in the dark, alone—

A hand clamped over his mouth, along with a barely audible, "Sssss!" to shush him. His heart slammed against his chest and he bucked against the stone tree in shock. The fingers across his mouth were slender and short.

A woman's hand. He pulled his head away but kept silent, watching the guard assigned to him. The man's chin was on his chest.

Mirage slowed his breathing and turned, trying to get a glimpse of who had touched him. His mother's shaved head leaned into view. Her hand sliced across her lips in a "silence" gesture. Trying to still the alarm still pumping through his blood, he nodded. A tug at his wrists. She was cutting through the cords that bound him.

He had assumed that she'd abandoned him. He tried to reconcile the woman who had crept into an enemy camp to save him with the one who had, over and over, cringed away from his father's abuses. For now, he was just grateful to see her. The pressure snaked away from his arms. He shifted quietly into a crouch, keeping one wary eye on the guard and rubbing at his raw wrists.

His mother clasped his shoulder once, then beckoned, creeping away on all fours. He followed in kind, recognizing that the posture not only made them less visible, but less likely to kick a stone or crush noisy rubble, and with his hands he could feel out the treacherous terrain in the dark. The stars told him they were not moving the direction they'd come, but north.

For quite some time he followed his mother as she prowled through the Stone Wastes like a stalking cat. When they finally could no longer hear the voices of the people in the distance nor see the glow of their fires, she turned to him. "Are you all right?"

"You came." And finally speaking the words sent relief flooding through him.

"Of course I came." She said it as though there were no question about it, as though she hadn't cowered and failed over and over, all his life. As though she hadn't run off and left him with his father. Any other day, he'd have been angry, but right now, he was just grateful to have the company of someone who didn't hate him.

~

They traveled northwest but didn't cover much distance that night. With little light, the terrain was too hazardous to traverse quickly, and Mirage's mother pointed out that scouts would expect them to return east, the way they had come. Besides, she reasoned, if they intended to continue following the exiles, they ought to move ahead, not lose ground.

Mirage didn't ask if they were going back for his father, but his mother addressed it anyway. "Knife Strap will be much safer with the exiles than he would be with us."

He wasn't sure what she meant by that. Would she actually attack his father? Or did she expect him to? He didn't want to ask. He was too exhausted to challenge her. She pushed on much farther than he would have on his own, continually insisting that they hadn't traveled far enough, that they weren't safe yet. When finally she let him rest, he practically collapsed to the ground. He didn't care about the discomfort; he sprawled out, face down.

He awoke sometime later with a stream of drool against his cheek. He moved to change positions and felt little wedges of tenderness where the petrified earth had dug into his skin. His mother's hand slipped from his head as he shifted, and he rolled to look at her through gummy eyes. She looked peaceful, her face relaxed in sleep. He knew she'd been stroking at his braids like she had when he was younger.

For a moment, he wished he were that boy again. His father's abuses would still be ahead of him, but… so would everything else. He'd been innocent, once, or at least as innocent as an energetic young boy could be. And that, at least, would be nice to go back to. Back before he'd—

But that was just the exhaustion and isolation and Cloud's smug lecture rattling around in his mind. His anger toward her surged in his thoughts and he welcomed it. It shoved away his melancholy and reminded him why he'd fought.

Cloud. So righteous, and yet so useless. What had all her purported wisdom brought her? A split people, exiled, wandering around a cursed land for… what? If she was going to Bogana, then it could only be that she hoped to find warriors to help her take control of the village again, to wrest it away from Laughing Dog's control. And what reason for all of this? None Mirage could discern. She and the elders were ashamed of being wrong, of counseling inaction. And now King Laughing Dog and the fire hunters had made them all look foolish.

Cloud was an elder, perhaps, but she was one who had spent her whole life hiding in her tent with her herbs and incenses. She knew nothing of what it meant to fight back against your enemies, the rush of joy and relief at standing up and putting a fist in his accursed eye. She didn't know how right it felt to finally do something, anything, instead of lying back and waiting for another blow, another murder, another cruelty.

Who was she to lecture him? What he'd done was justified, even righteous. He had felt proud to stand up for his people. Everything he'd done was…

He hovered in the moment, his bowstring drawn. *You don't get to feel good about yourself anymore.* Cloud's words were a poison, weakening his confidence.

He pushed that moment from his memory, but it always came back: that instant and terrible decision. He still didn't know why he'd done it. It had been something in that moment, some magic. They had been triumphant. The forest had attacked them, and they were fighting back. They were going to win, and then Cloud had turned to Left Rabbit. "Tell everyone the truth," she'd said.

That nagged at him. What truth? If it had been from Cloud, he'd have expected some lie, but from Left Rabbit? What was he about to say?

"Kill him," Laughing Dog had ordered Mirage.

Mirage had been so proud to be the King's chosen champion. At his right hand, leading the fight against the evils that had besieged his people. But what evil could have come from Left Rabbit's lips? Left Rabbit had been his friend, once. He wasn't a liar. He had been annoying, sometimes, but too earnest and simple to lie.

It wasn't the forest gods that Mirage had turned his bow against. It wasn't the monster that had killed his grandmother or their King. It wasn't even Cloud, or one of the others who had held them back from the fight. It was his friend, who had been about to say something Laughing Dog didn't want anyone else to hear. What was it?

And then Mirage knew it didn't matter. Because of all those times sitting at meals or maintaining tools or just lying in his tent when Knife Strap had come in, drunk or tired or just plain mean. And he'd insulted them or complained or needled. He'd pushed and pushed and pushed until someone had spoken up, fought back, shouted, argued. And then Knife Strap had used his fist. He'd used it to punish them, to shut them up. He'd used it to silence them.

Just like Laughing Dog had used Mirage.

That was what he was now. Not a villager, not a hunter, not a son. He was the fist.

He lay back against the stone tree and felt it dig into his back. He ignored it.

He stood atop Gamewatch Rise. The other fire hunters were at his side. The people were gathered below.

"Kill him," Laughing Dog ordered.

Mirage turned his bow toward Left Rabbit in an instant. The bowstring cut into his fingers, he had pulled it so tight. He hovered in the moment, hesitating, determined to stay in that moment as long as he could, to live as long as he could in that fraction of a second before he let go, before he became a killer and ended Left Rabbit's life and his own in the same instant.

But the moment was a lie.

"You didn't even hesitate," Broken Stump had said.

It was true. He hadn't. He'd loosed the string the moment Laughing Dog spoke the words.

His arrow flew.

Left Rabbit fell.

Left Rabbit fell.

Left Rabbit fell.

# 11 Unclean

At last, the Stone Wastes were behind them, and they had all come through all right. Cloud was proud of her people. Of course, they had all known privation and undergone rationing before, but this time there had been so few complaints, and in times when one family had come up short, others had gladly shared. Even so, their supplies had run treacherously low, especially the shoes, and the last day had been a torturously slow shuffle as those with protection for their feet tried to help along others with none. The Wastes had sprouted a sparse pattern of bloody toeprints along its western edge.

Now, with fresh grass beneath their toes and game for their hunters to catch, it felt as though they were through the worst of it. She feared, though, that this was not so. It would not be long until their first glimpses of the great water. The people moved with renewed vigor and enthusiasm, and she walked behind them. No need to stride on ahead; the directions were simple. Follow the sun.

The Teller was up ahead with his daughter, Baobab, but he fell back to speak with her. Baobab did not follow. Cloud suspected the young girl was not entirely pleased with her father's dalliances with her.

"Still no sign of Mirage?" the Teller asked.

"No. He's clever enough to hide from our scouts. And I doubt he'll be back for his father any time soon."

"Any idea who cut him free?"

Cloud shook her head. "Not anyone from our group. No one here would forgive him for what he did. Not that easily. Which means someone outside. If I had to guess, I'd say possibly Dry Grass."

The Teller's eyebrows rose. "His mother? You think she came all the way out here?"

"A mother looking for her boy with a cruel man following? Isn't that a story you know?"

"I suppose it is. I just didn't realize it was her story. Are you going to keep looking for Mirage?"

Cloud sighed. "I'll have the scouts keep an eye out, just in case he's up to no good, but I don't think we have to worry about him. We already know why he's here, and it doesn't seem he can do much harm. And his mother can probably reach him better than we can, if she's inclined to. Showing up to Bogana with two prisoners wasn't going to look that good anyway. One is enough."

"Not planning to let him go too, then."

"Knife Strap? He's volatile. Unpredictable. I want him where I can keep an eye on him. We'll just have to explain when we get to Bogana."

"Mm."

After a while, The Teller's silence began to needle at Cloud. "Well?" she finally asked, a little peevishly. "You didn't come back here just to ask about Mirage."

"I do enjoy your company, you know," he said with a smile. "But you're right. I was hoping that you might be interested in continuing the conversation from the other day. Sometime before we arrived at Bogana. Something there worries you, and it might be a good idea to talk through it before you return."

She let out her breath in a long sigh. "You're probably right. It's not something I like thinking about. But you should know. Maybe others should, as well, but… I don't want to frighten everyone without reason."

"Sensible. But you will not frighten me. I promise."

"Probably not. I'm probably just being silly. But places on the great water have their own troubles. They're different."

"I can only imagine," the Teller said.

"So can I, for the most part. I had only seen a few rains—four or five—when my parents left. I don't remember much of the city. I remember the great water, spreading out endlessly before us, like the sky had fallen to the ground and covered it. I remember the homes—round, and stacked, with dark, narrow windows like eyes. Stone streets and dogs wandering around. I remember the boats and the smell of fish. A boat, it… it's like a tree that travels across the water."

"I know what a boat is," the Teller said, smiling again.

She slapped herself mentally. Of course he did. He'd told stories of boats, even if he'd never seen one.

"I didn't know when it happened. I just remember our mother and father acting angry or frightened for no reason. They would shout at my sister and me if we tried to go out. And there were… flies. There had always been flies, but these made my mother very frightened. She would hang strips of… some kind of plant, I don't remember… from the ceiling, coated with honey to catch the flies. She would scream and try to crush them if she saw them flying free. She put something over the windows so that the flies couldn't get in. Woven palm fronds, maybe. I can't remember.

"One day a man came to our door and tried to get in. He was gibbering, incomprehensible, and was covered in sweat. He waved his arms at me and my mother, and there were welts, bite marks, on them and on his face. It was very frightening. My mother shouted at him and hit him with a pot hook until he left. Then she put the pot hook in the fire and kept turning it until it burned.

"That night, my father came to me and my sister and sat us down. He told us that a boat had come to the city and it had a very bad kind of fly on it, and the flies were biting people and making them sick. He said that we had to go so that we would be safe. I remember crying and shouting because I didn't want to go. They packed up everything they could and wrapped me and my sister up with pelts and we left."

"You spoke of a plague before. You said it was spread by breath or by touch."

"That was at first," Cloud said. "And all healers know of those sicknesses. But as long as you stayed away from others, you could protect yourself. When the flies came… how could you avoid those? Then the plague became a terror. It spread everywhere."

Cloud was quiet for a while after that, finding the rest of the story inside her. Basket walked patiently by her side, waiting for her to continue.

"My aunt Reeno, came with us." She chuckled, remembering, but her laugh was rueful. "My sister and I hated her. She was always complaining about everything. Pfeh pfeh, this food tastes like dung. Oh oh, this bed is too hard for sleeping. We didn't understand why she was so miserable all the time. I think she was used to a better life than us. When she came for meals, she would always take the best parts of the dishes for herself. If she cared for us while our parents were out, she would slap us and pinch our arms. We didn't want her to come with us, but I think we understood that she couldn't stay.

"She was in a panic the night we left. Talking about men with sores, women acting crazy, infants falling asleep and not waking up. She kept talking louder and louder and then my mother would put an arm around her and speak gently to her. Shush her as though she were an infant herself."

Cloud suppressed a shudder. "I remember looking back as we left. The city was covered in flies, a black swarm of them, so thick you could barely see the houses. It can't be a true memory—there can't have been that many, or they would have bitten everyone. But that's how I remembered it, later."

"Sometimes we remember things truer than they were," Basket said.

Cloud shrugged, not entirely understanding what he meant. "I don't remember much of our journey. We followed the trade paths north. I assume we were looking for the People of the Savanna. I was small and tired and couldn't keep up. My father carried me when he could. Aunt Reeno hated it. If she had to walk, everyone had to walk. I think my mother and father were tiring of her. I would hear them arguing with her late at night, very angrily. But it didn't help anything. The next morning she would be complaining again.

"But after a while, she began complaining less and less. Instead of sniping at us or chattering at my mother, she would just stare at her feet, at the road. When she did talk, it was as though she were sleepy or had drunk too much palm wine. My mother searched her and found a bite here." She touched a finger behind her left ear, deep in the crevice. "None of us had seen it. But she knew. She had to have known."

Cloud sighed. "I didn't even think of it until now. But if she knew… then when she complained about the walking, it might have been the sickness wearing her out. When she wanted to go back, begged and pleaded and shouted at my parents… she knew she was going to die. She didn't want her last days to be ones of hardship. Her last meals to be what we could scavenge on the journey."

Basket's firm, warm hand gripped her shoulder, and she was grateful for its solidity. "I wonder why she didn't tell your parents she was bitten."

"I'll never know. Maybe she was afraid she would be left behind. But once my parents found out, they looked for a spot to stay and made a small camp. My mother stayed with Aunt Reeno. I remember her crying constantly. My father looked grim and distant. And now Aunt Reeno got all the best food, the most comfort. In those days, our parents almost forgot us, caring for her. I don't know if she realized what they were doing for her."

She didn't need to explain. Basket, at least, would understand. To stay in one place in the wilderness for that long, caring for someone sick. They were risking the lives of their children. Other people might have left Reeno behind. She was going to die anyway, so why risk their children to forestay it? But they did.

"Aunt Reeno started sleeping all day, but then she would be awake all night. She would have long, listless conversations that we could barely understand, her words were slurred so badly. She stopped eating. She would demand, sometimes, to know where she was. Where her sister was. She didn't recognize us anymore. And one day she went to sleep and never woke up again."

She stopped, the finality of the memory overwhelming her. Basket's arm folded around her shoulders. He pulled her heavily into his soft side. He was damp with sweat.

"I don't know how long it took her to die after she went to sleep. A few days at least. We stayed until she was gone." Bitterly, she recalled, "I was glad she slept. There was more food for me and my sister. Children are selfish.

"I suppose they must have had a funeral for her, but I don't remember it. Isn't that odd? I recall being happy she wasn't eating, but I don't remember the pyre. Strange the things the memory chooses to keep. The next thing I can recall is resting in a trader's camp. Having a good meal for once. And eventually we found our way to the People of the Savanna."

She let out a heavy sigh. "And now I'm going back. To the city of black flies."

Basket's voice cracked when he spoke. "This story is precious to me, Cloud. It is the storm that watered the seed of you."

She gave him a questioning look.

"Your fear of flies," he explained. "And what made you a healer. You saw your parents caring for your aunt when she suffered. That care was more important to them than anything, even the safety of their children. And that has always been in you. This. This is your story of yourself. I will treasure it."

Cloud felt something deep within her shudder and crack open, and she knew again that she loved Basket, and she had always loved him. "Then you should know my name. The people of Bogana don't name themselves like we do. They have names from an old language. One I don't remember."

He held her at arms' length, his eyes searching her face. "Your name isn't truly Cloud?"

She smiled up at him. "My parents renamed me Cloud to help me be one of the People of the Savanna," she told him. "They named me Kalu."

He folded her in an embrace as though he would never let her go.

~

Many days after leaving the Stone Wastes, the People of the Savanna saw the great water for the first time. The scouts reported it first, hurrying back with dazzled eyes. Breathless, they spoke of a vast plain, like the savanna itself, but blue as the sky. Impossible, they murmured in wonder. Impossible that there could be that much water in the world. Cloud asked if they had approached it, and they both shook their heads wide-eyed. No telling what creatures might live in it, or whether it might carry them off.

Their stories stirred a deep longing in Cloud. She had not seen the great water since she was a young girl, and that memory was no longer true, but the memory of a recollection of an image, faded and flattened to stillness with time. She called the people and they hurried ahead. The great water revealed itself first as a glinting ribbon against the horizon, over which mountainous clouds hovered. The journey across the plains traveled steadily downward, and the plant life changed and thickened, the grasses spikier, thatching around broad, palmy spreads of fleshy-leafed plants.

Then Cloud caught the smell of it, briny and raw and stormy. Her lips flecked with salt. And she was a little girl again, running along its shores. She recalled perfectly the feeling of wet sand under her toes, the way the tide kissed her feet, the way it pulled the sand away around them, leaving her balancing on little balls of mud. Not the great water, a mystery to inland people, described by traders or refugees. The ocean. It had been swelling and falling inside her heart all this time.

The memory restored a vigor to her limbs, and she hurried ahead, stumbling over the ruts of the trade route moving north along the coast. Soon she could see it properly, her eyes drinking in its unending blue plain. Its waves puffed white as they rolled in to meet her. The sand was hot and crunched at her feet as though a crust had baked on it. She ran through the patches of feather-fingered grasses and down into the tidelands, and everywhere were littered the broken white and pink shapes of shells—she had forgotten shells. She ran down the shore into the lapping waves, and the cool water kissed away the aches and weariness of her feet, and before her spread the endless, breathing sea. She fell to her knees and let the waves stampede up into her lap and splash her wet and cool.

She looked back and laughed out loud. Her people had lined themselves along the water. Some stared at her as though she were mad. Others dipped experimental toes, jumping back in alarm when the waves approached. Few dared stare out into it, and many shielded their eyes with their hands. Basket was one of these. He approached her with his gaze pointed fixedly downward, a grimace on his face like he was nauseous.

She stood, water streaming down her body, clumps of sand clinging to her knees. "What's wrong, Basket?" she asked, laughing. "It's not going to hurt you."

"It makes me dizzy," he explained with a weak smile. "It's hard to look right at it. It feels as though the world has tilted."

"It might take a while, but don't worry."

"I didn't know. I didn't know what it could be like. I didn't expect it to move like that. Stories are one thing, but to see it—" He dared a glimpse outward at the horizon, then tottered and fell toward her in the sand.

She caught him as best as she could, though he was far too heavy for her, and laughed and kissed his neck. "I missed it so much," she told him, and she slung her arms around his middle and sat with him as, bit by bit, he dared to look longer and longer out into the great water.

"It's beautiful," he said finally. "But is that a storm?"

"What?" She sat up to look where he pointed. She had been so overjoyed at seeing the ocean again, she hadn't noticed that out over the water, far to the southwest, a great circular wall of clouds swirled. Beneath them, there was only darkness.

~

The city of Bogana clung to the cliffs like a wasp nest, its clay-grey buildings protruding between crags and jostling each other for space and elevation. The cliffs sat high above sea level, and homes or buildings for other purposes jutted out bravely above the water, looking at any moment ready to tear free and collapse down the cliffs into the waves.

The massive, white building on the hill at the very edge of the city, with its high stone pillars, resided in only the faintest parts of Cloud's memories—a temple, she thought, remembering the Teller's stories of places devoted to worship of the gods. The forbidding-looking stone walls surrounding Bogana, however, were utterly unfamiliar.

"Smaller than you remember?" Basket asked, strolling up next to her.

"Bigger," she said. "But more crowded." In her memory, the city had been open and sprawling, not crammed inside close walls. Her eyes lit on the boats lining the rocky shoals below the cliffs, and now she saw the path winding downward from the city proper, steep but well-trodden, hewn with stairs for fisherman and sea-traders. "If it weren't for the boat-shoals, I'd think it was a different city entirely."

Cloud's vision was too blurry to make out much of the city's features, but as they drew closer, some of the sharp-eyed scouts were able to make out signs of habitation: people traveling up and down the paths to the shoals and boats moving out on the water, a sight which astonished them greatly. Most of the city paths were hidden behind the walls, but some of those near the rise of the temple could be seen, and there, people bustled about.

Now that they were this close, relief mingled with apprehension in her breast. They had made the journey to the west with no loss of life and little severe hardship. Compared to the days after the death of King First Claw, filled with monster attacks and starvation, tyranny and plague, the journey had seemed almost an age of plenty for the people. She wondered how the others were faring under Laughing Dog's rule. And how much of the great forest they had already burned.

She led her people along the trader's route toward the city. The ocean wind was uncomfortably cool, making her skin clammy and her bones ache, but walking helped. Other exiles shuddered and pulled pelts tightly about their shoulders. Some still shielded their eyes so as not to be dizzied by the liquid horizon.

The travel-beaten path led to a high, broad opening in the walls, which, though plainly built of stone, appeared seamless. Even carefully worked rock should have gaps between the stones. She supposed they must be daubed with mud or clay. The Boganans had the knowledge of rope-making, and the entrance here was barred with a gate of tall, heavy tree trunks lashed together by massive coils. She had no idea how they opened. The trade route swerved toward the gate and then continued on past the city to the south, but there the road broadened, churned and pitted with the signs of heavy travel, scarred with hoofprints and wheel ruts, and littered with animal droppings. Faintly, she thought she recalled fields to the south dedicated to farming, pasture for goats, pottery digs, and further away still, tanning yards.

Someone moved behind the top of the gate, and a man's voice called out words she did not recognize. She gave Basket a querying look, but he shook his head. He had some knowledge of the tongues of other peoples, but not this one, it seemed.

The group of people behind Cloud had spread out. Some gathered up behind her in curiosity, but others were beginning to unpack their things and set up camp. She supposed there was no point in stopping them; they wouldn't all be able to find accommodation in the city, and only now it occurred to her that barging in with sixty tired, hot, and stinking people and all their possessions might test the limits of hospitality.

She waited, expecting to see the great gate open, but after a moment, a smaller part of it swung outward, wide enough for two men to walk through. They were shaved bald and thickly muscled. Their chests and bellies were protected by some sort of thick, hard leather, their faces and ears pierced by colorful rings and bars that gave them a fearsome countenance. Each carried heavy-looking spears with shafts painted blood-red, their tips carved smoother than any Cloud had ever seen. Had she not been so intimidated by their appearance, she might have laughed. All this display over their little group of weary travelers.

From behind them a smaller man stepped. He was middle-aged, perhaps forty rains, but stooped and plump, thin-limbed like a much older man, and dressed in a dazzling green robe that made Cloud's old dress seem faded rags by compare. His fleshy face sagged, and his gaze was at once bored and insolent. He scanned the group of people once and, making some kind of decision, stepped up to Basket. "*Jala*?"

Cloud did not recognize the word, any memory of her childhood language long faded in her memory, but she was the leader of these people, not Basket. She pushed her way toward the man and stood tall, gripping her stick with tight knuckles and meeting his gaze directly. "Hello," she said firmly. "I am Cloud, chief elder of the People of the Savanna."

He stared at her as though she were something unpleasant he had stepped in. "Ah. You are plainsfolk then. *Cevash*."

Again, a word she did not recognize, but it did not sound flattering. "We have come a very long way to speak to the elders of your city on a matter of urgent importance." She had no illusions that this man might be an elder. He was far too dismissive. An elder needed to be alert, to listen without prejudgment. No, this man was no elder.

"You have no trade goods?" he asked. His accent was thick, spiced with melody, and though she could see his naked disinterest in his eyes, could not decipher it from his voice. "You are not seeking shelter? Asylum?"

"Asylum from what?" she asked before she could stop herself. She cursed herself for revealing ignorance before this functionary. "No, we are not seeking asylum. We have come a long way and can shelter ourselves. Though guidance toward food and water would be appreciated."

The man's face folded in on itself, his eyes sinking deeper. "These people cannot stay here. The city is only for residents. They cannot camp like a pack of vagabonds."

"But we are outside the city."

"The city includes all the surrounding areas as well!"

"Then what are the walls for?"

The man's cheeks wobbled. "That is beside the point. They cannot stay here."

Cloud was getting angry with this petty little man. His refusal spat in the eye of all recognized laws of hospitality. She forced herself to remain calm and pleasant. Men who believed themselves important were more susceptible to flattery than defiance. She pointedly cast a withering look toward his two stern bodyguards, and then gazed up and down at his attire. "I can see that you have been granted a position of esteem. You must be very skilled at your job."

Sparks of grudging pride lit his eyes. "Yes. I am the Chief Gatekeeper. And there are rules about vagabonds camping outside the city. Rules about cleanliness."

"Rules that you yourself wrote," Cloud said, nodding.

That suggestion skipped his mental gait slightly. "Yes. Well. No, the rules have been in place for a very long time. But it is my duty to see they are strictly enforced."

"Ah, I see," Cloud said appreciatively. "And you, the Chief Gatekeeper, decide how those rules are enforced."

"I… yes, that's right."

"Then it is fortunate that we have the chance to speak to you, the decision-maker, and not one of your charges who would have turned us away without a second thought. For we urgently need to speak to your elders. We have come from many days' journey away, at the edge of the forest. Something terrible has awoken, and we are all in danger."

"I see." Boredom reentered his face. "And what is this terrible thing that has awoken? A demon, perhaps? An outbreak of witchcraft? Monsters stealing away children in the night?"

Cloud hesitated. The truth was virtually unbelievable, and if he turned her down, she would never get through the gates. On the other hand, lying your way into a city was a poor start to diplomacy. She let her composure fall. Let the weariness show in her face. She fixed his eyes with hers, willing him to see the truth in them. "It was a god. The god of the forest attacked us. The god of fire… took one of our own. We think he means to—to…"

She trailed off. The officious man's wobbly jaw had gone slack. Narrow-eyed interest had slipped the sneer from his face. "You are not lying about this? You had better not."

"Why would I travel all this way, with so many people, to lie about something like that?"

"No. No, of course. You must speak to the Matron at once. Select two of your people to join you. The rest must wait outside."

Cloud conferred briefly with her elders about who to bring. She considered a strong hunter in case the Boganans were hostile, but what good could one hunter do in a city full of strangers? They needed to show the elders and this Matron their strength, and that was not in sinew, but in wisdom. From her elders, she selected Bad Water, who grinned a toothless, excited grin at being chosen, and Basket. The latter choice was not strictly favoritism. The Teller, having learned many stories of many people, would surely be best suited to understanding and communicating with a council of cultural strangers.

"This is it, then?" the Chief Gatekeeper asked, looking at the two other elders with an expression of chiseled skepticism. "Very well. I am Petrel, Chief Gatekeeper of Bogana, and I will be admitting you to see the Matron."

At the introduction, Cloud reached out her hand to clasp his forearm in a show of trust and friendship, but he yanked his arm backward as though he had been stung. "Don't!" he snapped. "Don't… touch me. You are not from Bogana. You are not… not clean. Follow me."

He turned, his hands clasped behind his back, and strode toward the large city gate. The guards stood behind, giving the three elders impassive stares.

Cloud raised an eyebrow to Basket and followed Petrel, stepping through the opening in the wooden gates. Beyond them, the noise of the city was much louder, the sound of uncountable people talking over each other and the bleat of goats and the shrill tones of children shouting, their voices echoing around the corners of streets and from behind stone and clay homes, though she could see none of them. The smell of the city was strong as well: old fish and manure and fresh vegetables and earth and standing water.

"Few in Bogana will speak your language," Petrel said, not looking back as he strode ahead. "I will serve as your interpreter."

From behind them, a loud *clunk*—one of the guards had lowered a heavy-looking bar across the door. Cloud was acutely aware of how vulnerable they were now. Her people were on the other side. She was a stranger in her own birthland.

"You will have to wait while the Matron is alerted to your presence. She will decide whether she wishes to speak with you or have someone else take your report. Accommodations will be made. But first you must wash."

Cloud could appreciate that. Her hands and face were dusty from the journey. It would be good to scrub the dirt from them, especially if food and drink were to be offered them, as the rules of hospitality encouraged.

The streets themselves were wide and formed of many curious, rounded stones. Cloud had seen similar stones along the ocean shore and suspected that these had been collected there. They felt pleasant and smooth under her feet. Basket looked everywhere, craning his neck, no doubt trying to find the narrative behind the placement of each stone, the origin of each high building.

These were rounded, with dark openings. They looked like giant, empty gourd shells and towered above the streets, stacked atop each other haphazardly. The effect was disorienting, and Cloud felt uneasy when she looked up, as though the whole jauntily arranged pile of stone might collapse on her.

They didn't have much time to look around: Petrel took them only a short way down the street before stopping next to a dim and somewhat forbidding looking doorway into one of those gourd shells. "You will wait here for your inspection."

"What inspection?" Cloud asked.

Petrel's back stiffened with pride. "Bogana is a *clean* city. A healthy city. We do not permit the spread of contagion or sickness."

"Then you are fortunate to have admitted me. I am a healer with many rains of experience. I can assure you, none in our group are afflicted with any illness."

Petrel stared at her as though she were a squashed cockroach. "In Bogana, we do not trouble ourselves with bush medicine. Here we have advanced knowledge of sickness and disease. It is necessary. We are a port city. We must protect ourselves from the corruption of the savage world."

The assertion was arrogant, but possibly correct, Cloud decided. And if lucky and diplomatic, she might find an opportunity to learn some of this advanced knowledge herself. Better to keep quiet and ignore any slights. She let her annoyance drain, nodded respectfully, and entered the doorway.

The room inside didn't smell homey—no scents of human life or the warmth of pelts or the sour aroma of a well-used bed or fresh straw. It smelled earthy and stale, like standing water. Wooden benches had been placed around the walls, and there were windows to let in light. Cloud had never been in a building like this—well, at least not since she was a young girl—but it was a little like being in a very large tent, like the king's tent or her sick-tent, or like huddling inside the giant, hollowed trunk of a baobab.

Basket and Bad Water entered behind her, looking around with expressions of discomfort. Petrel stood in the doorway, his hands still clasped behind his back. "The healer will be here soon to look you over," he said. "You can save him some time by removing your clothing and personal effects and placing them in that basket there. Clean clothing will be provided for you, and your articles returned upon your departure from Bogana."

"Undress?" Cloud asked in mild shock. What possible purpose could such a request have other than to humiliate guests, stripping them of their signs of social status and culture?

"If you please. Clothing can carry contagion as well as parasites. This request may seem excessive to you, but an infestation of fleas or bed mites can be devastating to a city like Bogana. Trust me when I say that we are asking nothing of you that we do not ask of any other guest, whether noble or common, arriving by land or sea. We understand that some do not wish to comply and will cheerfully escort those who do not from the city."

The speech sounded rehearsed, at least in content if not in dialect. Petrel gave them all questioning looks, as though hoping that each of them would decide that the stipulation was too demeaning. Well, Cloud had no problem disappointing him. She'd learned no vanity working with the sick and dying. Taking the lead, she stripped away her beaded garment and her leathers, dropping them in the basket.

The Boganan man looked aside with an expression of distaste, one that did not escape her. The People of the Savanna wore coverings in public, but cared little about nudity beyond that, clothing serving both utilitarian and cosmetic purposes, but there were tales of other peoples that looked down on it as shameful. She hadn't expected the Boganans to be one of those. Or perhaps he just didn't like the look of her.

Basket followed in kind, removing his faded and dusty purple robe. As he dropped it into the basket, he murmured to her, "These are not the actions of trustworthy people."

"Not trusting people, anyway," Cloud answered. "But what choice do we have?"

When they all stood naked before Petrel, he gave a brief nod, still carefully keeping his gaze above their shoulders, and strode out. A young boy, no more than nine or ten rains and clad in cloth about his waist, scurried in after him. He gave all three of them an appraising stare, then picked up the basket and left with it.

"The healer will be here momentarily," Petrel said from outside. "The guards do not speak plainstongue, but they will be outside if you require anything. Do not attempt to leave this room." And with that he closed the door.

Cloud and the others had little time for conversation before they were visited by the healer, a nervous little peafowl of a man clad all in white cloth. Unlike Petrel and the two guards, he had no compunctions about seeing the three of them unclad. Also, he had no piercings or jewelry, and his clothing would have been extremely simple were it not so unblemished. Cloud couldn't understand how the man could go through his day, much less the messy work of healing, without spotting and staining his garments. Did he never sit or kneel? Or did these people know some miracle of purging stains from their clothes?

She wasn't going to get an answer from him on those questions, however, for he spoke no words comprehensible to her. "Jado," he said when he entered. She shook her head, and he repeated the word insistently and pushed his hands toward them, palms upward. He wanted them to back up and make room, she supposed.

As she and the elders retreated, four broad-shouldered men entered the room in pairs, staggering with the weight of large wooden basins, each filled nearly to the brim with water that smelled neither of brine nor of stagnation. The men set these two tubs in the middle of the room.

"Lovra tu," the healer told them. Cloud had already begun to think of him as Jado. When they did not respond, he pointed to the tubs. "Lovra *tu*." He lifted one foot high, then the other, miming the act of stepping into the tubs, and then cried out in dismay when he saw Bad Water on his knees, drinking deeply from one.

"No! No! No!" he shouted—a word that either was the same in their language or one of the few of theirs he knew. "No golad. *Lovra tu.*" He reached his hands down about his knees, lifting up imaginary palmfuls of water and splashing them across his chest, his armpits, his groin. "Miz? Lovra tu."

Cloud stared at him in astonishment. If she understood him, this would be a shocking waste of drinking water.

She looked at Bad Water. He shrugged. "Tastes like flowers."

With periodic glances toward the healer to reassure herself that she wasn't committing some unspeakable insult, she slowly eased herself into the basin. It felt criminally wasteful, but she reminded herself that rainwater would not be as rare here. Perhaps this was even considered a generosity to guests. She crouched in the water, wetting herself thoroughly, mimicking the gestures the healer had made and splashing all parts of her.

Looking uncertain, Basket followed her lead, stepping into the tub and dousing himself, and as he did so, the healer brought an orange clay pot that was full of odd-smelling, dark-colored sand. He picked up a little bit between his fingers and rubbed it vigorously on the flesh of his neck, then on the inside of his arm. He held the pot out to Cloud.

The stuff was coarse and pungent, though the scent was not unpleasant, smelling slightly of ash, but the scouring of it against Cloud's skin felt almost pleasant as she scrubbed. The sand dissolved quickly, but plenty more was offered. She worked it all over her skin, even her scalp. When she clambered out of the tub, oil was proffered, with the healer indicating that she should rub it through her hair. Doing so allowed the many tangles to pull free and left her hair heavier, brushing loosely against her shoulders instead of hovering above her ears.

Basket, too, stepped free of the tub, and Cloud thought his skin looked both darker and more youthful than it had in as long as she could remember. Such luxuries they had in Bogana!

She glanced at Bad Water, who had not yet had an opportunity to bathe himself, and found him doubled over with tears of laughter in his eyes. He had prepared to climb into the tub, only to discover that the water left over from Basket's bath was dark brown, almost black—and her own bathwater was not much better.

"Bad water for Bad Water!" the old man crowed through his laughter. He was about to climb in anyway, but the healer snapped something to the men outside, and they came back in, removed the basins, and replaced them with a fresh one, into which Bad Water cheerfully climbed.

He insisted on singing loudly to himself while washing, which made the healer scowl the whole time. While Cloud and Basket stood wet and dripping, the healer came up to Cloud and studied her, starting with her hands. He scanned her fingernails and palms, and moved up her forearms and shoulders, inspecting every inch of skin and paying special attention to insect bites. She thought she had some idea why.

He had her open her mouth and peered suspiciously at her tongue and teeth, and he combed through her hair carefully, flattening it between his fingers to scrutinize her scalp. She did not feel any particular violation in this inspection; she herself had had to screen her own patients with similar meticulous care. In this, at least, she felt a kinship with the healer.

Apparently satisfied with her condition, the healer moved on to Basket, and finally Bad Water, and then the three of them were provided with garments of a dazzling white color, which the healer had to help them to put on—they contained odd openings for their arms and included a long strip of fabric that looped around their waists and was tied in a loose knot.

Cloud found the clothing both coarse and uncomfortably restricting—it rubbed against her shoulders and her hips in a way that was constantly distracting—but it would help none of them to insult their hosts by rejecting their hospitality now.

The healer spoke a few incomprehensible words to all of them and left, leaving them to sit and wait for quite some time, during which Bad Water attempted no fewer than four times to remove his clothing, only to be scolded by both Cloud and Basket. Cloud wanted very much to confer with Basket on everything they had seen, but she couldn't be certain that the men standing outside could not understand plainstongue. It was best to assume that all they said and did would be reported to their hosts. She hoped their people waiting outside the city gates were not busy making diplomacy more difficult.

When Petrel returned, his wide face was creased with a smile far more welcoming than before. "Excellent news. The healer has confirmed that all of you are healthy and can be welcomed into the city."

"When can we see the Matron?" Cloud asked.

The smile remained fixed. "Ah. Well, of course she is very busy caring for our city and preparing for our worship, so I'm afraid she will not be able to welcome you all properly today. But rooms and beds have been prepared for all three of you, and you are to be afforded every comfort. Tomorrow is the earliest that she would be able to receive you."

Cloud glanced to Basket and Bad Water. The latter was busy scratching and tugging at his garment. Basket gave her a grimace, then a short nod. He didn't like this, but it was best to go along for now.

"Our people will worry," she told Petrel. "It would be best if we could return to them for the evening."

He blanched. "But we would have to provide baths and inspections all over again!"

She didn't like that implication. The heavy traffic on the path outside the city suggested that many people and animals traveled in and out regularly, and she doubted they all subjected themselves to the same treatment every time. Which meant, she supposed, that Petrel or the city's leadership looked upon outsiders as intrinsic carriers of blight or disease. She took a slow breath and kept the anger out of her eyes. "Very well. But a messenger who speaks our language must be sent to our people so that they understand what has happened."

"I will have it done," Petrel said. "But for now, may I show you our city?"

He led them out into the streets. Cloud was glad to be out of the building—the walls were too close, too confining. Here in the streets, the buildings might look as though they would topple on all of them, but at least they'd have the chance to run, to see threats before they arrived.

A wind from the great water had arisen and now it gusted through the roads, tugging and flapping at their clothing. It smelled of storms, but Petrel seemed unbothered, leading them down the road toward the sounds of many voices. Behind them, the guards marched, using their spears as walking sticks.

Where the streets crossed, Cloud saw the statues. They flanked the corners, each standing twice the height of a person, shaped in the fashion of god-masks, but hewn out of stone instead of wood, and unpainted. Cloud could not fathom the amount of work and dedication it must have taken to chip away at a boulder until a face had been fashioned out of it. And these faces were terrifying. They did not resemble anything human, possessing broad, triangular snouts with blank eyes, carved with neither brow nor pupil, spaced wide between earless temples. The head resembled that of a fish, were it not for the strange fan of plumes that sprouted from its forehead, curling backward as though bent by wind. And Cloud had never seen a fish with such an unnaturally stretched grin of a mouth, especially one filled with uncountable, triangular teeth. Other than the heads, the bodies of the statues appeared human, though the torsos were smooth and featureless. No breasts, no navel, and below the waist, the carving ended in uncarved stone, a pillar that widened toward the base of the sculpture. Each grinning statue held one hand aloft, its fingers clenched in a fist. And meticulously carved around the fingers of each fist were dozens of large, crawling flies.

Cloud shuddered and could not bring herself to look more closely. She could not tell whether the figure's fist was meant to be crushing the flies or if the insects were swarming out of it. Either way, she did not like it. She cast an uneasy glance toward Basket and caught a disquieted grimace creasing his face. That didn't make her feel any better.

"I wouldn't ask," he murmured, drawing near and keeping his voice low so as not to be overheard by Petrel or the guard. "Anyone who would hew an image out of the very stone may be insulted by others not recognizing it. How much time must this have taken? And there are two of them."

Following Petrel, they rounded a corner and saw that there were, in fact, a great deal more than two. The road into the city opened into a wide square filled with people milling about, shouting, children running. There were more people than Cloud had ever seen in one place at a time. The open space—if it could be called open when crammed with this big a crowd—was lined with various stalls made of stone or wood and stocked with things for trade: various roots, grains, and vegetables; fish of a wide range of shapes and sizes; colorful beads, earrings, and other jewelry; great swaths of bright fabric colored blue, red, green, and white; an array of knives and odd, pronged spears.

Cloud was dizzied by the sheer commotion and business of the crowd, and stumbled back against Basket, who caught her arms. His hands, clammy, left smears of sweat on her arms that chilled in the air. He was looking up, and she followed his gaze. Ringing the area, carved out of the sides of buildings or perched atop them like watchful birds, were dozens of the statues, their half-moon mouths stretching downward to reveal their fangs, their fists, filled with flies, clutched toward the heavens as if in defiance of Wem himself.

Petrel had moved some distance ahead, and the guards, looking impatient, struck the butts of their spears on the ground and jabbed their chins at the three of them. "I think they want us to keep moving," Bad Water said.

They shuffled obediently through the crowd, but as they moved forward, people almost fell over themselves to get out of their way. Curious, Cloud reached out as if to grasp at the arm of one of them. The woman made a gasping little shriek and jerked away, squeezing herself into the crowd. "They don't want us touching them," she murmured to Basket. The thought was distressing. She moved forward again, and the crowd melted away from them. And yet as soon as they were immediately out of reach, no one paid them any attention.

Basket, two heads taller than either of them, scanned the crowd. "We're the only ones wearing white."

He was right. The people wore many bright colors: reds and greens and purples and deep blues, and some of them wore clothing that shimmered with light like heat on the horizon, in shining yellow and grey hues. Others were mostly unclad, with little more than a cloth wrapped around their waists. Many of them were adorned with jewelry like Petrel and their guards wore, bright colors and glittering stones at their ears and noses and fingers, around wrists and toes and ankles, or woven intricately into their hair, on children and adults alike. But none wore white.

None, that is, except for a few of the merchants operating stalls around the edges of the squares, selling hooks, carved wooden dolls, pottery, or baskets. None of them, Cloud noticed, were selling food.

Petrel came pushing his way back through the crowd, his thin nose crinkled in irritation. "Will you hurry? Hey. Hey, you," he called to Bad Water, who was wandering further into the crowd, staring up at the walls with a rapt expression. "Come on. We need to move through the square before—"

Bad Water's long, skinny arm lifted high, and he pointed a stubby finger at the top of one of the buildings. A man stood up there, so high up it made Cloud's stomach drop. He reached down and pulled up from someplace concealed in the building a wide, round drum. Its sides were painted a deep blue-green, and the hide stretched across it was almost white.

"Filth and fester," Petrel snarled. "It's too late. All right, everyone—"

He was cut off by the sound of three rapid beats from the drum. *TuntunTUN!*

The crowd grew silent and began to withdraw from the stalls, gathering in the square in rows, each standing about arms' length from the other. All of them turned to face the west, where the sun had already begun to dip. Where the waves of the ocean whispered their infinite secrets.

The man atop the building raised two sticks and struck the beat again. *TuntunTUN!*

This time, whether because new drummers had only just joined in or because the crowd had quieted enough, Cloud could hear the beats answered, almost in unison, from elsewhere in Bogana. The whole city had gone still and dark, as though a cloud had passed in front of the sun.

"We're going to pray now," Petrel told them. "Don't make a fuss. Just follow along, and you'll be fine."

*TuntunTUN!*

A rustle moved through the crowd as, like a wave, they knelt.

A man sung, his voice low, resonant, finding answer in the walls of the buildings around him. "Mpo." He hung onto the last vowel, turning it into a hum, into a call.

*TuntunTUN!*

The Boganans dropped to the ground, pressing their palms down, their gaze fixed on the stones beneath them. "Mpo," another sang, joining the first, and then another and another joined in, voices blending together in the pitch, adult and child alike, all calling out the name of the goddess of the sea.

Petrel, already stooped, hissed back at them, "On your knees, *now!*"

"This is not how we worship," Bad Water said.

Behind him, a guard raised his spear and, before Cloud could shout a warning, struck Bad Water across his back with the haft, eliciting a yelp of shock and pain. He aimed another blow with the butt of the spear at the back of Bad Water's leg, driving the old man to his knees.

"When you are in Bogana," Petrel growled, "You worship as the Boganans do."

Fury dimmed Cloud's vision. "You can't—" she began, but then Basket put his arm around her shoulders and gripped it firmly.

"We're not at home." His voice was tight with fear. "There is no home anymore." She looked back, and the guards were the only two not kneeling.

But even they were droning the name of Mpo. Their eyes flashed with warning, their spears held ready for another blow.

And so, while Bad Water moaned in pain, writhing on the stones of Bogana, Cloud and Basket both knelt in the square. They faced the west. They pressed their hands to the stone. And they, too, sent their voices into the chant, calling the name of Mpo.

What had Cloud led her people into? She'd escaped the fanatics of fire, only to find themselves surrounded by fanatics of the sea. Their voices surrounded her, drowning her out, drowning everything out but the name of Mpo, repeated over and over, until even the consonants slipped beneath the surface of the long, assonant drone of her endless O.

Cloud dared a look up, and the man on the roof was kneeling too, his back to them, facing the west. The only figures not facing the sea stared down at them, a ring of statues, their eyes bulging, grins wide and fanged, hands upraised to crush the insects of the world.

# 15 Shadow of the Storm

Three days by the great water and Mirage still did not like staring directly at it. It looked inherently *wrong*, a blue and boundless plain chewing into the edge of the land, as though an enormous piece of the sky had fallen and crashed into the savanna, grinding its edges to dust. Sometimes thin white clouds appeared to drift through it, blowing in to the land before evaporating. The sight of it made Mirage's stomach lurch when he looked at it. But none of this was why he disliked it.

No, what was most upsetting was that it was a boundary. In most places people lived, there were no boundaries. Savanna, forest, sahil, or desert, if a threat appeared, you could run any direction away from it. If you saw something interesting, you could pursue it. But the great water was an edge Mirage could not cross. Like Kwaee's hostile forest, it was a limit that bisected his world. He could travel north along the coast, or south, and he could return to the east, the way he had come, but to the west, there was nothing but water.

Wem's world was meant to be endless, but Mirage had found its end. He had flirted with that boundary when they first arrived. He and his mother had found a ridge far enough up the coastline that they would not be overseen by the exiles, but from which he could monitor their movements discreetly. And then he had confronted the great water.

It had seemed a living thing, rising and falling under its own power. It tugged at his feet and ankles, pulling him out into it, and he fought a low but steady panic, recalling the way Kwaee's vines would, if you strayed too close to his boundaries, drag people into the forest never to be seen again. Mirage found himself able to resist it, though the further he traveled into it, the stronger its tug grew, until finally a rise of the water lifted him off his own feet, and he shouted in terror and floundered his way back up onto the shore. From then on, he distrusted it and kept a wary eye on it.

He lay on top of the ridge, fingering unconsciously through his Priest's Procession as he did so. The sea grasses here were tough and coarse, suitable for weaving. Far to the south, the city of Bogana crouched on its cliff. Mirage could make out the clusters of buildings that sprouted from its center like mushrooms from a dead tree. Below the city, the camp of the exiles spread out, a herd of oxen around a dangerous waterhole, none daring to approach, all too thirsty to leave.

He wasn't sure what had happened—they'd been gathered there already when he and his mother finally arrived—but he suspected that Cloud and some of the elders were already inside and had been for several days. The gates of the city opened exactly twice a day: once at dawn, and once at dusk, and with each opening, a great crowd of people moved in and out, traveling with animals, tools, and carts empty for filling or laden with goods. Each time the gates opened, a few people from the camps would approach those entering and exiting, but each time, they were sent away again.

The beach grass rustled behind him. "Any change today?" His mother lay down next to him, leaning on her elbows to gaze down the coast at the encamped exiles.

"No. Same as the last two days. When are they going to do something? Are they just going to wait out there forever?"

"You could ask the same of us. Here." She dropped three sandgrouse eggs into his palm. "Not cooked this time."

Grateful, he took an egg and poked a hole in each end with a shard of the pottery-like shells they'd found on the beach, then sucked out the contents. "I'm really hungry," he admitted.

"I am too. There's less food here. Or at least, if there is food, we'd be better off asking the Boganans how to find it. All the plants are pulp. Lots of birds, but I've no idea how to catch them. There are crawling things down near the water if we want to try those."

"This is what I've been wondering," Mirage said. "Why would the Boganans choose to live here, on the edge of all this nothingness? There's so much water, but none of it is good for drinking, so what's the point of it? Why didn't they all leave long ago and move someplace where they're not trapped against"—he waved his arm toward the great water— "all of that?"

His mother sat up, crossing her legs, and gazed out over the ocean. "Well, there's the view." Her voice was distant.

"I can't even look at it. I don't know how you can."

"You don't think it's beautiful?"

"I think it's dangerous." It irritated him that the great water bothered him so. He was a Boganan, by blood if not by upbringing. He should feel at home here, should understand these people. And yet this place unsettled him, whereas his mother found a kind of quiet peace along the shores. Perhaps all the sensible denizens of the city, like his grandmother, had left to find good homes living on the savanna, and the only ones who had remained were mad or foolish.

His mother gave a long sigh, and when he looked up at her, saw she was still transfixed by the great water. "How long do you plan to stay here?" she asked. "Your King told you to find out where the people were going and report back."

"Where they were going *and* what they were doing," Mirage said, aggravated by the question. Not because it was a bad question, but because he didn't really know why he was staying either.

"Well, they seem to be waiting. Maybe they want to join the city."

"Maybe." Mirage grimaced down at the camps. Everything still looked very temporary. No one was putting up more permanent tents. No one had formed scouting parties—luckily for him, as traveling north up the coast would be logical for scouts, and he didn't relish the idea of wandering back east to look for another vantage point.

"So yesterday nothing happened, and today nothing has happened yet," his mother said. "And if tomorrow nothing? Or the next day? How long do we wait?"

He sighed. The point was well-taken. Food was scarce, and every day they waited here meant a greater chance of discovery. "Tomorrow I will travel out as far as I can and tell King Laughing Dog what has happened. I will tell him that we've waited for a runner from him and heard nothing. Then we will head home."

Home. Where they called him a murderer. Where even his fellow fire hunters regarded him with suspicion. But at least he would have his tent. At least he would be able to talk to others again. At least he would not be, himself, another exile, banished from his people and his home, wandering the wilderness in search of a purpose that slipped through his fingers like sand.

~

There was a great feast. Everyone else had hands full of fried caterpillars and boiled eggs and sizzled boar fat, but he could not find where they were getting the food. Everyone he asked shrugged their arms helplessly and covered their mouths with their hands, too full to speak. Or perhaps too uncaring. They were all happy, all celebrating, flush with wine and dancing, but when they looked at him, their eyes saw past him.

"Mirage!" the voice whispered on the wind. He turned to look for it and it was the voice of the ocean hissing over the sand. The smell of salt stung his nostrils. "Mirage," the voice hissed again. "Wake up!"

He blinked his eyes open. "What? What's happening? Where are we?"

"Mirage, look." His mother gripped his shoulder with one hand, tugging. She pointed toward the ocean.

"I know, I know, it's the great water," he groaned.

"No," she said again, and she pulled him upright.

The air was uncomfortable. It tugged at his hair and pulled the heat from his skin, making him shiver. "What?" He blinked in the direction she was pointing, but his eyes were gummy with sleep and lack of fresh water.

"*Look!*" His mother jabbed one finger toward the sea. The moon hung over it, half full, its light reflected off the water as though someone had clumsily spilled it. To the left of the moon, there was a place where the stars went dark. A cloud, a big one. This was no revelation—the southern skies had been shadowed over the water for the past two days by enormous, billowing thunderheads, light and fluffy on top, but dark on the bottom. Unlike clouds over the savanna, though, those dark clouds over the great water didn't move. They hung in place as though affixed there by Father Wem, his personal landmarks, unmoving and solid.

"It's just the storm," Mirage said, his eyelids drooping. "It was there yesterday, and it will be there tomorrow. Go back to sleep, mother."

"No, wait. Look."

She sounded afraid. Maybe it was just a nightmare, or maybe she'd seen something. He rubbed the sleep from his eyes and blinked out over the water again.

Lightning glowed in a cloud, illuminating its silhouette and then its milky depths. It branched out over the water. Where something *moved.* Something terribly big. Bigger than the city that clung to the cliffs, bigger than many of the clouds in the sky.

Another bolt of lightning licked the storm, and Mirage got another glimpse of whatever was out over the water. It was shaped like a person, but *wrong*. Deformed. Its head, what he'd been able to see of it, was horribly misshapen, its back angular and twisted.

The growl of thunder poured over him. His skin was tight, prickling.

"What is it?" his mother whispered.

"I don't know. Some beast of the great water, maybe." Another flash, this one farther away. Only water beneath the forbidding clouds now. "I think we're safe where we are. And it's disappeared."

"It disappeared last night too. I didn't wake you."

"You didn't tell me?"

"I thought I must have imagined it. And last night, it was…" She stopped and shook her head.

"Last night it was what?"

"Last night," she said, "It was so much farther away."

~

The next morning, Mirage awoke to a sickly yellow dawn and the taste of lightning on the air. A heavy wind hissed through the beach grasses and sent waves roaring up the coast. The countless keening birds that usually careened through the air or strutted up and down the wet sand were nowhere to be seen.

He licked the taste of salt from his lips. At home, salt in a meal was a rare treat, but here it was as common as sand. His mother sat on a dune, hugging her arms about her. She'd shaved her head again and was now staring out at the wild water as though entranced.

"Well," Mirage said, climbing up the dune to sit by her, "there'll be no lighting fires today. Not in this weather."

"Do you think it can reach this high? The water?"

"No, of course not," Mirage said. Though the moving hills of the great water were taller in height than he. "It would have to rain a great deal to make the water rise that high."

"It's raining out there." His mother pointed. The storm over the great water had drawn much closer, and a dark shadow outlined the slanting torrent of its rain. "Do you think it gets higher every time it rains?"

"Maybe. No. It must run off somewhere, like a river."

"Where?"

"Who knows?" Mirage shrugged. "Edge of the world, maybe."

"I thought that's where we were." She dug her thin fingers into the sand. They'd grown stronger. Hardened by the journey. "I could stay here, I think. If there were people to talk to. I could learn the land, the food and types of wood. Catch seabirds and carve pretty things out of the shells."

"Not me. The way the great water moves makes my stomach ill."

"I like it. It's powerful. Angry, but calm most of the time. It knows when to show it."

"All right," said Mirage, bemused. "I don't know how you know it's angry."

She gave him a long stare. "No," she said. "You never did."

~

Around midmorning, someone dressed in rich green colors exited the city, his clothes flapping around him like a giant attacking parrot, baring his skinny brown legs. He held his hands over his face and, flanked by two large guards holding staffs or spears, approached a small delegation from the exiles.

Mirage wished he were closer and had some idea what the man was saying. The wind blew in a constant, fine spray from the great water, soaking his hair and misting his skin. He kept having to wipe trickles of it from his eyes.

Whatever they were talking about seemed to be exciting or angering for the exiles—it was impossible to tell. The men and women in the delegation gesticulated wildly and stamped their feet, and then they went back to talk to the rest of the exiles.

News spread through the camps, and people began to pack up their belongings and gather near the gates. More guards emerged. There was some sort of disagreement about their belongings, and after a few of the guards struck at packs and drag-carts with their staffs, it became clear: the people were being permitted entry, but without their things.

Everyone gathered around, clustering together, and there was what appeared to be a long argument, exciting for those near the front but boring for those in the back, who shifted from foot to foot or squatted to wait. Some at the fore of the group appeared to be shouting.

"What's happening?" His mother came to the top of the dune and shielded her eyes from the wind.

"They're taking people inside, I think. People look pretty upset. They're not letting them take their stuff."

"So they're capturing them."

"No, it looks like people are going willingly."

"Doesn't mean they're not captured," his mother said archly. "They've got Cloud in that city, we think, and at least two others."

"The Teller, probably. He's pretty easy to recognize from a distance, and I haven't seen him."

"If they have Cloud and the Teller, then they have the head and the heart of the exiles. The rest will do whatever the Boganans say."

"And risk *everyone's* lives?" Mirage snorted. "That's not very smart." He ignored the hooded stare from his mother.

The light of the day was growing worse, not better, as the sun rose and washed everything in an ethereal amber. The air was thick, humid and heavy, and prickled with the promise of lightning. "It might be the storm," he said, looking westward. Most of the great water was shadowed now. The massive thunderheads hovering over the great water had grown and spread to cover the horizon, and the glimmer of lightning limned their bloated bellies. "I've never seen one like this."

It was not the rainy season, at least not on the savanna, though they had all learned that weather could differ dramatically in different regions. The forest had a rainy season just as the savanna did, when the rains came for days upon endless days, but there was no dry season there. Perhaps storms were a common thing by the great water. Perhaps this one would last for days or even moons. And if the rains raised the height of the great water, or rushed in great, knee-deep floods across these beaches the way they could across the savanna, the exiles would be in trouble.

"You might be right," his mother said. "They might be bringing the people in for their own safety. If so…"

"If so, we're in peril out here." Mirage scanned up and down the coastline. There were hills, of course—little rises and falls, but no place that resembled shelter. The most elevated point was the city on the cliffs above the sea, and presumably the Boganans would have built their city in the safest location they could find. A flood even knee-deep could sweep a grown man from his feet and carry him away. Mirage shuddered at the prospect of being dragged by flooding rains into the endless expanse of the great water.

What would happen if the rains lasted longer than a day or two? There would be no food, no shelter, perhaps no place to sleep. Rains would make tracking game impossible. It would wash away snares. And there would be no lighting any fires to report back to Laughing Dog.

He peered back over the dune. The debate below appeared to have ended. The People of the Savanna were filing into the city, several small groups at a time. Some of them had slumped shoulders. Children clutched at their parents' legs. People huddled against each other, leaning against the wind as they disappeared into the city.

Mirage gnawed at his fingernails. What were they doing in there? What if they didn't come out? He could hardly go back to Laughing Dog and say he left all the exiles inside the city of Bogana without some report of what reason they'd entered or what they'd done inside. Suppose the exiles came back with a fully armed hunting party from Bogana, or new magic or tricks that would help them to take the village back?

Soon the campsite was just a large empty field, the grasses trampled, the sand churned up. Pelts and carts, gourds and baskets lay everywhere. They wouldn't leave all their treasures behind, not without being forced to. Mirage waited, half expecting scavengers to scurry out of the city and begin picking through the exiles' belongings, but no one emerged.

He waited. His mother went to gather as much food and wood as she could before the coming storm, but when she finally returned, her arms laden, he was still lying atop the dune, waiting. The sun was lost behind the impending storm, and the twilight had turned the land from gold to a bilious green. By now, the gates should have opened to permit the entrance and exit of merchants and farmers, traders and goatherds, but they stayed shut. The city, which had always looked still from this distance, now appeared lifeless.

"You're going down there, aren't you?" his mother asked.

Mirage felt for his knife at his waist and remembered that it had been taken by the exiles. Maybe it was down in the camp somewhere. "Either they're up to something, or they're in trouble. I can't wait. If they're planning something, I might miss what it is, and if they're in trouble, I might get there too late to help."

His mother folded her arms and turned into the wind. "I don't think you should go, son. You know the savanna and our people. You do not know this place. Whatever the lives of the people in that city, they are foreign to us. There will be dangers that we cannot even imagine."

"And I suppose you would have me do nothing. Leave our people to face those dangers on their own."

"We could return to the village. Let Laughing Dog and the others know what has happened. They could come to help."

Mirage rolled his eyes. "It would take months! And King Laughing Dog is busy fighting Kwaee—he isn't going to come out here to rescue a bunch of…" He trailed off as he realized what he had admitted. "He—he would need to know more first. Before risking all our people to go chasing after exiles who made their own decisions and may not even be in trouble. You know that he would help if—if there were a real danger to—to any of our people."

He picked at grains of sand, feeling his face growing hot. "Look, he's doing something. Maybe it's right and maybe it's not, but he's trying. He's not just sitting around waiting for the next attack, the—the next death."

*His arrow loosed. Left Rabbit fell.*

"And I'm not going to sit around either, waiting on this stupid hillside for however long it takes for our people to make some terrible plan against the rest of us. Or for them to face some terrible fate inside. I don't know what the right answer is here, but it's not 'nothing.' And it's not spending moons traveling back for help that might never come. I have to do something, mother. I have to. So I'm going inside."

She was quiet for a while, her eyes unreadable as they flicked back and forth over the horizon. "All right," she said. "Then I am coming with you."

~

They picked their way through the beach where the exiles had camped. Belongings lay everywhere—not castoffs and detritus, but valuables and sentimental treasures. Fine pottery and colorful painted baskets, freshly hewn knives—Mirage pocketed one of these—a rare lion pelt, and carved toys and dolls. Jewelry. Clothes. Water skins. No one would willingly leave these behind.

"I don't see anyone watching us," Dry Grass said, peering up at the city. "But they might be concealed. Maybe we should try to approach closer to the water."

Mirage didn't care for that idea at all—the constant motion of the sea made the ground feel unsteady beneath him, but he could find no flaw in her reasoning, and so followed her down to the shore.

"We should walk in the water," she said, "so that we don't leave footprints." She strode down the beach to the dark line where the sand was wet and then made her way toward the city, letting the water wash over her toes. He had to hold his hand to the side of his face to block his view of the swimming horizon.

Closer to Bogana, the smooth, submerged land was increasingly interrupted by dark brown rocks from which a slippery green grass grew and hung in the water like fine hair. Soon there was little sand to stand upon, and Mirage and his mother were forced to clamber over boulders and seek purchase for their toes between the slick stones. Mirage tried stepping on their surfaces twice and nearly fell each time. It would have been far easier to walk on the sand.

Among the boulders, they searched for a path toward the bottom of the city that was neither too exposed for them to be noticed by potential lookouts, and yet not too far out into the sea to be dangerous. The waves of the great water were powerful and capricious and often surged toward Mirage just as his hip was near a jabbing outcropping, or right as he'd placed his toes in prime stubbing position for an underwater boulder. Making their way through even thigh-deep water was surprisingly exhausting.

And there were *things* in the pools: drifting, gelatinous tendrils; plants or creatures that looked like palms with wide-spread fingers; square little many-legged things with scorpion pincers and eyes that jutted upward unnaturally. None of them were particularly threatening, and most darted away from his path, but he disliked them all the same. He wondered if a Boganan meal involved feasting on these creatures and felt nearly hungry enough to sample one.

The sun was low in the sky by the time they approached the city. Mirage was panting and sweating with exhaustion and his fingers had gone swollen and wrinkled. He was fairly certain the sharp rocks had cut up his legs and toes as well. But the city hung above them, clutching the tops of the cliffs. Below them and not too far away were alcoves with boats dragged up on the shore. Even though he had witnessed it many times over the previous days, he found the idea that anyone would dare sit in one of those precarious things and ride it out into the great water incredible. Surely making such a venture would be to welcome death.

He clambered up onto the pebbly beach after his mother, grateful to be out of the water. The stones here were worn smooth like those in a river bed, good throwing ammunition. Above the beach, a well-traveled path cut into the cliffs, climbing the hillside toward Bogana. This, then, would be their path into the city.

Neither he nor his mother said a word. They knew that the chance of being overheard and captured was very high here, and the rocks and cliffs could carry sound more easily. At least they had the roar of the waves to cover the sound of their movements, but there would no doubt be scouts or guards watching the trail up from the water. They would have to wait until the edge of twilight to ascend, when the light would be too dim for them to be seen easily, but hopefully not so dark that they could not find their way. The path was well-beaten, but steep, and the rocks below would not treat a stumble gently.

When the sun had descended below the edge of the sea and Mirage judged the light dim enough for them to risk it, he motioned to his mother,

and together they clambered up the path to the city. It was steep, but the path was wide, and steps long-since worn into rounded ledges had been hewn into the grey rock. Heavy ruts had been ground into them in pairs, suggesting many carts had been pulled up and lowered down the hill, perhaps by ropes or buffalo. It would have taken many weighty carts many seasons to erode tracks this deep into the stone pathway.

All this suggested a high rate of traffic over a long period of time, which puzzled Mirage. Watching the city over the past few days, he'd seen farmers and merchants move in and out of the city gate, but very little movement up and down the paths to the rocky beach, and the boats that they had seen resting there were small and could not have carried many goods. The ruts in the road were not freshly cut, and old dirt had collected in them. The sea-road must have been busy once, but it was no longer in popular use. Did traders and merchants no longer visit Bogana?

The climb took much longer than expected. Up close, the cliffs of Bogana stretched much higher than they seemed from afar. He paused, wiping the sweat from his brow and catching his breath. They were nearly into the city now, and though the steep incline continued, there were little paths crossing it, leading to small buildings that clung to the outskirts of the city, looking about to fall into the sea. The Boganans couldn't build past the walls, so they built buildings one on top of the other and out over the cliffs. It seemed terribly dangerous. One even squatted partway above the canyon of the path, clinging to the side like a frog on a rock, built into the building next to it and bolstered by wooden stilts wedged into the stones, its small dark openings peering down at him like empty eyes.

He shuddered and continued climbing, but just as he did, something small darted across the path, a white tail flashing. He stopped, puzzled. A hare, here? He peered after it through the gloom, and then the voices reached him. Someone was coming. If he'd walked further, he'd have stepped right into their path. He nearly tumbled all the way back down the hill in his haste to scurry into a niche in the wall, panting in mingled panic and relief. His mother had already flattened herself against the opposite bank.

Above them, two women walked across, traveling along some other road. They didn't glance down the sea-road at all, but were engaged in animated conversation with words unfamiliar, in accents that reminded him immediately of his grandmother. She'd spoken to him in Boganan much of his life, and he'd listened with fascination, the words a secret language that she and he shared, that even his father had forgotten. As he'd grown older, he'd listened less, and the meanings of the words slipped away from his understanding.

But he recognized some of them still—the women spoke of "people" and "earth" or "dirt," and "trapped." Surely everyone would be talking about the sixty-odd people who had been summoned into the city this morning. Were they trapped somewhere? Imprisoned, perhaps, in some kind of earthy place? Or was he simply assuming that any conversation he overheard had to be about them?

When the women's voices receded, he crept out of the shadows, and he and his mother moved up to the path. Only now did he realize how challenging their task would be. The streets stretched crookedly in every direction, winding between uncountable buildings of varying widths and heights. Many windows glowed with firelight, and smoke drifted upward from openings in their rooftops. The people could be concealed in any or all of these, and Mirage could hardly go sticking his head in each one to try to find them.

He'd imagined that the city would have a large, open area, for council fires and work and food preparation, and he would be able to find at least some of their people there. But this place made little sense. Where did people go during the day to be with each other? Where did they share their work and their meals? Where did they dance and tell stories? The walls here were too close together, the spaces too narrow. Perhaps, Mirage surmised, they built their homes like this to protect themselves from the unsettlingly empty sight of the sea at their gates.

Casting about, he spotted an out-of-the-way niche behind one of the buildings, and he quickly crept over and darted into it, motioning to his mother to follow.

"How will you find them?" she asked, once they were safely out of sight.

He winced. The corridors between the buildings amplified even hushed tones and carry them up and down the streets. "I don't know. It isn't what I expected."

"Well, they can't be in any of these buildings. They're too small."

"Maybe they split up the group? One exile housed with each family?"

She shook her head. "There would be too many arguments and complaints. Everyone would have their own ideas about how to treat them. The city elders must have everyone in one place. We just need to find it."

"But the light's going. We'll never search all of these pathways before it's too dark."

His mother surveyed the building in front of them with a thoughtful expression. "Maybe we don't have to," she said. She studied the wall a moment longer and then astonished Mirage by clambering, lizard-like, up the sheer wall of the building, her fingers and toes finding crevices and tiny handholds that had been invisible to him.

He tried to follow, but whatever purchase she'd managed to find eluded him, and he ended up only scrabbling at the side of the building and sliding down again. So he was left waiting at the bottom, staring up after her as she disappeared over the top.

After a long while, her head poked over the roof. She waved at him and then clambered down as easily as she'd climbed up. He stared at her in amazement. "I didn't know you could do that."

She gave him a pleased smile. "I used to climb all the time when I was a girl. I guess you never really forget how. Anyhow, I looked all around. There are lots of lights in the windows, so the paths aren't too hard to see. I didn't see many people out, although there are some walking about with torches. Everything looks pretty crowded, but over near the gates, there are some bigger open areas. There could be people there. And there are some larger buildings to the south. There were no lights in most of them, and they looked more open than these, and made of wood, not… dirt or clay or whatever these are. And there's that very large building we could see from the beach, far to the south, and that's all lit up with many fires and people around it. My guess would be that our people are somewhere over there."

"Of course," Mirage agreed ruefully. "The place where there will be plenty of people to see us and lots of light to see us with. I don't like it, but you're right. That's where they would be."

"I tried to memorize the way over there. I looked for paths that were darker."

He gave her a look of grudging admiration. "All right, then. Let's go."

〰

Mirage huddled with his mother in the darkness of an alley near the enormous white building. Up close, it loomed even larger than it had appeared from outside the city, taller than most trees and, Mirage imagined, expansive enough to hold all the people of the world inside it at one time. The massive structure was composed of pale, white stone, brilliant even in the darkness, the light of the moon and the torches glimmering off the lustrous material.

Unlike the jumble of misshapen homes below, this building was formed of smooth, straight lines describing a perfect geometry that unsettled Mirage. Nothing in creation had a shape so unmarred, so exact and smooth. Instead of blending into its surrounds and conforming to them, it cut into the rock and sky, an unnatural rectangular edifice both more and less real than its environs. Its façade was inscribed with images that Mirage could not make out in the firelight and shadow, and its high roof was supported by fluted columns, each like a gigantic bundle of reeds. Arranged in neat rows, the pillars extended far back into the darkness of the building, as though some divine hand had taken the Stone Wastes and forced them into an artificial and exacting order.

The structure perched at the very edge of the city, up against the southern wall and apparently on the edge of the cliff, as from here Mirage could hear the great water dashing itself against the rocks below like a huge beast breathing and wheezing just outside. Spreading down and away from the entry were an endless series of steps and terraces, and it was here that the torches burned and men and women carrying bows and spears stood guard, some of them never moving, others wandering back and forth and engaging each other in conversation.

Most unsettling of all were the statues, like those of the fish-headed monster women all throughout the city, but these each were taller than five men and carved from unblemished alabaster stone, flanking the steps in pairs atop every terrace, with two even larger guarding the entryway, each with one arm raised, their clawed hands crushing masses of crawling flies.

"Well," Dry Grass said with a grim expression, "this is where all the guards are. And the light. If our people are prisoners, they're almost certainly in there somewhere."

He hated to admit it, but she was right. "But we'll never get in there without being seen. And there's no telling what's inside."

His mother held up a hand to block the glaring light of the fires from her vision and peered into the darkness. "Maybe we don't have to enter from this side," she said. "There are paths around the building. We might be able to find a way in from behind."

With no better ideas, Mirage nodded, and they crept along the pathways, keeping out of the light as much as they could, pressing into the shadows. The structure sat on a broad terrace—in the front, this could be ascended using the wide steps that fanned out from the entrance, but beyond the steps, there was only a wall dropping down from the level above, so straight and sheer that it might have been part of the building itself, and this looked unguarded. Now far enough from the torchlight that they had to strain to see, Mirage and his mother followed the wall, keeping it on their right as they traced it to the walls of the city itself.

Here, the sounds of the wind and the great water below masked their footsteps and their hushed whispers. Just as Mirage had hoped, there was a passageway behind the huge building and the wall of the city, and steps led downward into an encompassing darkness. He could not see his mother's face. "Should we go down?" he asked. He knew the answer—they had entered the city for this purpose, and the longer they dawdled, the greater their chance of being discovered—but he desperately wished to avoid a descent into that yawning black. What if the statues were warnings? What if somewhere in that empty darkness, the creature they depicted scuttled about, its eyes wide and vacant, its mouth full of fangs, flies pouring out from between its fingers? What would they even be able to discover down there in that pitch black?

"I will lead the way," his mother whispered. She moved silently down the steps into the darkness. Heart pounding, he followed after.

He hadn't gone more than a few steps before he could see nothing at all, so he sat, putting one hand on the wall and feeling out each step with his toes before moving. It would do no good to be under-cautious, blindly miss a step, and crack his head open on the stone below.

"I'm at the bottom," came his mother's voice just ahead. "There's a hallway. I can see light at the end of it."

He could make out none of this, but after a moment his toes discovered the smooth stone floor. He stood and, keeping his hands against the wall, scooted forward until he found a corner, and beyond that was a long passage with the yellow glow of firelight at the end of it. Grateful for the light, but still wary of shadows, he followed his mother's silhouette down the hallway.

The rock of the passage had been ground smooth, amplifying sound the sound of every breath, every footstep, like the walls of a narrow canyon. He tried not to think about how much heavy stone was above his head, nor wonder what kept it from falling and crushing him. The whole city felt wrong, but this place felt more wrong than the rest of it.

His mother paused at the end of the hall and leaned around the corner in the direction of the torch-glow. Whispers and low-toned voices echoed off the stones—he recognized fragments of words, the rich round tones of his people's speech. He had never been so glad to hear it. He hurried after his mother.

Around the corner, the corridor led out into open sky and a flat, empty area surrounded by high walls. The light came not from torches, but from two pedestals holding wide bowls filled with burning embers, and from their light he could make out the expanse of the open room. Statues of the monster creature lined the walls, and but for these details, the room was empty. The floor, however, was pitted with gaping dark holes, tens of them, spaced evenly across the room. Each of the pits was wide enough that Mirage could barely have reached across their breadth lying flat. Unlike the neat lines of the temple, the edges of the holes were rough and ragged, as though giant beetle larvae had chewed into the solid stone.

The voices and whispering were even louder here, and this puzzled Mirage until he saw his mother creep up to the nearest hole and peer over the edge. She flinched back, one hand to her mouth, and then beckoned him over.

At her side, he leaned over the edge of the hole. The pit went down, down, deep, its sides sloping outward like the inside of a calabash. At the bottom, huddled in the darkness, were his people, eight of them. There was not enough light to see who they were, but he could make out their figures, a child huddled into the side of an old man, a woman squatting and weeping into her hands, a boy lying face down on the floor of the pit, unconscious or dead.

Mirage's skin tightened into prickles of fear. Who could take other human beings and drop them into a hole in the ground as though they were beasts in a trapfall? And what could he and his mother do against a whole city of people willing to do such a thing? A foul odor lingered about the pits, sour and bilious at once. The smell of death. Of rot.

"Hello," his mother whispered into the pit. "It's me. It's Dry Grass. Please don't make any noise."

The people in the hole looked up, all of them, except the boy on the ground. "Dry Grass?"

Mirage recognized that voice. Firefly, one of the scouts who had captured him outside the Stone Wastes.

"Yes, we followed you in here," Dry Grass whispered. "What happened?"

"They told us we had to come inside the city. They said Cloud had called for us."

"Where is Cloud?" Mirage asked.

"Mirage? You're here too? Thank Wem. We don't know where Cloud is. They brought us here and forced us down into the pits with ladders. Those of us who didn't climb down were pushed. She's wasn't with us."

By this point, other people must have heard them, as they began to call out, their voices much less subdued. "Who is that?" "Has someone come to rescue us?" "Get us out of here!" "You have to get us out!"

"Quiet!" Mirage hissed at the room, but his words were inaudible under the rising calls for help from the pits all across the room.

"*Je taar!*" A man's accented voice, alarmed, came from outside the room. The voices in the pits went quiet, but it was too late. His cry was answered by that of another man, a little further away, and then running footsteps approached the room.

Mirage couldn't move. His breath was as rapid as a hare's. The darkness seemed to recede from the room. There was no place to hide. Not unless they wanted to climb into the pits themselves. In that moment he was a boy again, instinctively looking to his mother for direction. Her eyes were wide, vacant.

*"Han! Han deej!"* Two men had come into the room, tall and powerful-looking, dressed in red and gold, both armed with bows. When they saw Mirage and his mother standing there, they both nocked arrows and drew the strings, barking orders at them in unrecognizable words.

Mirage shook his head, raising his arms to show he didn't understand, but this only provoked the men more. They shouted at him, repeating the words, *"Hala ben tojo! Hala ben tojo!"* and motioning with their drawn bows toward the pit. That was clear, then—they wanted him to jump into the pit.

His heart was a clenching fist of terror. He didn't know what he was going to do, but he definitely was not going to drop into that pit. He looked to his mother again.

He knew the look in her eyes. He'd seen it uncountable times before. It was the flat, accepting acceptance of imminent brutality, the dazed exhaustion of a hare caught in a hunting snare. She would give in. She would give up, as she had every time before. And, he realized, he couldn't hate her for it. There was nothing for them to do, nowhere for them to go. They had no choice.

*"Hala ben tojo!"* the guard shouted again.

"All right, all right!" his mother called back. Her voice was heavy with despair. "We understand. We'll do what you say."

And then she gripped Mirage's arm. Her thin fingers were hard and unyielding. She stepped into his side, her head near his shoulder. "Run," she said. "Down the corridor we came. Find a place to hide until it's safe. You have to save us. You have to."

And then, before he could even understand the gravity of her words, she turned back toward the guards. "Which one?" she shouted. She pointed at a pit closer to them. "This one?" She walked toward it steadily. Mirage stared after her in astonishment.

*"Eh, eh! Hala ben* jama *tojo!"* The guards were clearly alarmed now. They swung their bows back toward the pit near Mirage.

His mother looked at him over her shoulder, her eyes full of desperate urgency. "Run now!" she hissed at him, and then she charged at the guards, raising her arms over her head, wailing like a woman waking from a bad dream, like a jackal crying in the night.

Something instinctive propelled Mirage. As though of their own will, his feet launched him toward the corridor, the slick stone sliding under his toes, the furious pace of his heart grateful to have a tempo it could beat to, his lungs suddenly filling with deep breaths of air as he fled. Away from his mother.

Shame peeped quietly in a forgotten corner of his terrified mind, but he could not hear it, not even as the guards loosed their arrows. Not even when his mother called out—not a scream, not a cry of pain, but an "Unh!" as though surprised, as though someone had hit her in the stomach. Over one shoulder he saw her twist and fall, headfirst, skidding on her face across the stone, her legs over her head. There was the snap of wood as an arrow broke.

And even though that quiet peeping shame grew and grew in Mirage's head to a roar, it still could not drown out his terror. It could not stop his feet from pushing him faster and faster toward the corridor, even as another arrow flew by him, its flight so slow he could see the wobbling of the shaft in the air. It could not even make him turn around to see if his mother was dead or alive.

He ran.

# 16 A Lonely Magic

"Perhaps it is time to consider whether Mother Fam truly wants us to visit her." Doto's flat, human teeth chattered as he spoke. With an expression of irritation, he pulled the fur tighter around him. It was a leopard pelt he wore, its contours lumpy and ill-fitting around him.

Clay had one similar, against his strenuous objections. He'd worn clothes made of animal hide before, of course, but to wear fur from the animal resembling his divine form felt macabre and deeply wrong. Not to mention itchy. This wasn't proper clothing, cleaned and weathered and tanned so it would not rot. Stray fibers itched at his back. It was unpleasant, but not unpleasant enough for him to want to remove it. Night was coming, and the air grew impossibly colder. He wondered how deep a cold was even possible.

They'd been prepared to face the discomfort of the chill on leaving the forest, but soon both their bodies were shaking as though gripped by terror. An aching pain gnawed its way into their joints, and eventually they were huddled against each other, trying to leach the warmth from each other's bodies. It had not taken long before Doto had firmly declared they were returning to the forest.

Leopard fur kept him warm as a god, he'd declared, and so it would keep him warm as a fire bearer as well. He'd summoned several leopards—which had taken no short amount of time arriving—and then calmly killed each of them. Clay hadn't been able to watch that part. Then, much as Doto had once used his power to shape the wood of a tree to form a prosthetic foot for Clay, he'd warped and twisted the leopard skins, fashioning them into wearable pelts that, while disgusting and unpleasant to wear, did serve to keep away most of the chill once out of the forest.

Clay was surprised to find Doto so willing to use animal skins for such a purpose. Long ago, he'd reacted with horror to the idea of drums—stretching animal skins across wooden frames to create "the Cry of the Dead," as he called it. But when Clay asked him about it, he'd only shrugged and said they were cold, and there was little difference between using an animal for food and using it for warmth.

Clay had also explained about shoes to protect their feet, and Doto had shaped two pair of these as well, but those had proven less successful. Both Clay and Doto's feet were as tender as that of newborns, and after walking a very short distance, both were limping from chafing and blisters.

"Why would Mother Fam hide herself in such an unpleasant place if she truly wants company?" Doto wanted to know.

Clay shrugged. "It's not for us to know why the gods—" He barely stopped himself before finishing that sentence, but Doto gave him a brown-eyed glare anyway. Clay shrugged. "I suppose they—*we*—are all temperamental in our own ways. Maybe she's hurt."

"Hurt? By what? In her own realm?"

"Not physically. Her feelings. I mean, you said that she practically raised you when you were a… kitten. But you never went looking for her, did you?"

"You know Kwaee forbade me to leave the forest."

"Yeah, but you did it anyway. For me," Clay added hastily. "And I'm glad. But… if she was important to you, why didn't you go looking for her?"

"I almost do not remember her," Doto confessed. "And for a very long time, I was much like my father. It was you that changed me. Before you, I never even thought of leaving the forest. I suppose you may be right about her being sad."

"When you see her, you can ask her!"

"*If* we see her," Doto said. "These mountains are only getting higher and colder. And I am tired and no longer certain whether we are even heading in the right direction."

Clay glanced at Doto—he could practically see the lowered ears and drooping tail. Even in his fire bearer form, Doto was very catlike. "We could stop for the night," he suggested, and was relieved when Doto nodded.

"You will dance up a forest circle. Then we can eat and sleep as ourselves and not be cold and exhausted."

"All right. Let's find a good spot." Clay took the lead, the promise of rest and food giving his legs a burst of energy as he surmounted the ridge they had been climbing. The terrain here was littered with squarish rocks and boulders, light grey like a rainy sky. Few trees grew anywhere, and the thick, knee-high grasses between the boulders looked fluffy, but had coarse blades and irritated the skin.

At the top of the ridge, jagged, dark grey rock bluffs jutted over a slight incline. He traced the long row of crags from north to south. They'd need either to find a way around or risk climbing them, and Clay little cared for the thought of risking his tender soles to the scabrous surfaces of those bluffs. And if he fell… well, he wouldn't die, but the prospect of returning to his temple and having to make the trek all the way back to this point was a disheartening one. But there was no hint of any alternate route to the mountains in either direction.

He frowned at the obstacle, thinking. "Let's head up to the cliffs. I have an idea."

"You should just tell me the idea instead of making me wait," Doto complained, but he followed after Clay with exaggerated weariness.

As they approached the bluffs, Clay scanned their uneven surfaces for a section where the upper ledges overhung the ground below and led Doto there. "Now just sit here. This is where we'll make camp. See? When I dance the forest circle, we can grow a tree and just climb it to the top of the cliffs."

"That is very clever," Doto said appreciatively. "It must be your fire bearer side coming out again. They are very good at making use of the world around them. When they are not burning it up."

Clay shoved aside a flash of discomfort and revulsion at the memory of his people. He couldn't think about that now. He breathed in deeply, remembering the song and the dance that he had invented for Doto. It had been a long time now since he had sung it, and he found that he missed it. There was something simple and freeing about worship—the release of your desires and fears to something greater than you. They no longer had to be yours to worry about. You acknowledged them and set them free.

But now that he himself was part god? What happened to all those desires and fears? Did they just come back to him? He sighed. Another line of thought he could ill afford. He didn't need doubt right now. He just needed faith. He stripped away the stinking, itchy clothing he'd been forced to wear, a nod to Doto indicating he should do the same. The mountain wind prickled his skin with goosebumps. The shock of the chill cut through his weariness, woke him a little. He found his focus, lifted one foot, and danced.

His toes described the circle of forest around Doto, raising a shimmery border between woods and mountain that bisected his body. With the summoning, he began to shift, the bones in his feet lengthening, his teeth sharpening against his tongue. His tailbone ached and twitched as it stretched partway, his skin prickling as rosettes mottled it, but fur grew only in places—up his forearms from his fingertips, up his calves from his toes. His ears tugged and pricked, trying to move toward sound but without the mobility required. The sensation was jarring, sending his dance and song into off-kilter tempos. His senses buzzed, blurring between the vibrancy of a god's world and the flat dullness of human senses.

Finally he stopped, allowing himself to drop to all fours inside the forest circle, in his leopard form. It wasn't much of a forest. Sprigs of saplings sprouted here and there, and limp bushes sprawled on their sides. In the midst of it sat Doto, looking grumpy, twitching the tip of his tail.

"This is even worse than that time in the savanna when you were very tired," he complained.

"I couldn't do it properly when I was changing the whole time. It felt odd. Uncomfortable."

"Try again, with a little bit smaller circle inside the one you already made," Doto suggested. "That way you'll be your god-self the whole time."

"All right." Clay was glad at least to be inside the circle, fully himself again. He breathed the rich, comforting scents of forest air and renewed his dance, careful to keep his fingertips and swaying tail inside the outline of forest he'd created before. But still something was wrong. There was an energy that ought to have moved through him, calling the forest, filling him with worship and sending that praise out with every reverent note, every beat of his toes against the loamy earth. It was there, but faint: the echo of a song, a dance in dreaming. And there too, a faint reminder of the burn, a prickle of numbness moving through his body.

He left off his praise. The forest circle had not responded to him. It still was as sparse and patchy and limp as ever.

"You should not be tired now," Doto observed. "Not inside the forest. My weariness has left me, though I still desire sleep."

He was right. Clay felt full of energy and strength again, as he always felt within the walls of the forest. "I'm not tired. It just doesn't work like it used to. Not that I feel any less devotion to you," he added hastily, noticing the disappointment in Doto's eyes. "But maybe it's because I'm part god now. Maybe gods can't really… praise themselves this way. Otherwise they could just trample all over the world, making every place they touched their own."

Doto's ears lowered. "That is a sensible explanation. I suppose we should be glad you can do it at all. And inside the circle, we can still make this a proper forest."

He pressed his fingers to the ground, closing his eyes. Clay felt the power radiating from him like ripples in the water of an oasis. The tiny patch of forest stretched upward, fed by the power of its god. Limp bushes filled out, their stems thickening, their branches extending. Saplings stretched, stems broadening into trunks, leaves spreading like opening fingers. One acacia sapling bent and arched toward the cliff face, its branches gripping at the cracks and outcroppings, trunk growing thicker and winding upward like a giant serpent uncoiling and slithering toward the top.

The forest around Clay was now so thick he would not have been able to move through it, had it not been inclined to give way and bend before his passing.

"Now that," said Doto, "is how you grow a forest." And he climbed up into the branches of the acacia to curl up and sleep.

Smiling fondly to himself, Clay followed, and after a long and difficult day, slept in comfort and peace.

~

Doto woke slowly. Clay lay slumped halfway across his back, still fast asleep, and for a time Doto was content to let him lie there, the two of them balanced on the broad branch of the acacia.

It amused him to see Clay sprawled there so comfortably. His old fire bearer self could not even have clung reliably to the branch without falling off, much less dozed off on it. Doto really had given him a miraculous gift. What creature in the history of the world had ever given more, he wondered? Surely no one, ever, which in Doto's estimation made him the supreme mate and lover in all of history.

But soon they would have to leave the safety and sanctuary of their tiny forest circle and adopt their fragile fire bearer forms. He loathed his own, with its frailty and awkwardness. Every step in that apelike body felt as though he were teetering and about to fall. Clay moved much more naturally in his because he'd had a lifetime of experience walking around in it. Though, Doto thought, even in fire bearer shape, Clay looked and moved a little differently now. More graceful, more catlike. He prided himself on that as well—his magic had made everything about Clay's life better.

He yawned lazily, stretching out his arms, his claws extending.

Clay groaned and shifted against him, wrapping both arms tightly around his waist. "No, let's just stay here." He yawned too, his pink tongue curling between his fangs and prompting thoughts about other things that tongue might curl around.

"It is tempting. But the sooner we find Mother Fam, the sooner we can return to our temple." Reluctantly, Doto extricated himself from beneath his mate and stood up on the acacia branch, balancing on his toes. "Good job sleeping," he said, feeling a positive comment was called for. He looked to the east, where the sun was still rising, a brilliant white circle casting long shadows across the mountainous terrain. The cliff bottom below him was still in shadow.

Clay sat up on the branch, his legs and tail dangling. "How far do we have to go?"

"Sense it for yourself. You know what it feels like when a god is near. Can you feel it?"

Clay nodded.

"And can you tell which is me, and which is Kwaee?"

"I think so." Clay's brow furrowed, his gaze going distant. "It's like when you can feel a storm blowing in. There are… crackles of it coming from all directions. But I recognize yours. It feels kind of… green and musky. Kwaee's too, but it's sharper. Stronger, but farther away."

"What else can you feel?"

"Something to the north. I can feel where north is, like something's pulling my whiskers slightly in that direction. But there's something there. Yellow, woody. Hungry and peaceful all at once."

"Yes. That is Sarmu."

Clay's expression soured. "I can feel Ogya too. Beneath my feet. Far beneath, but I know it's him. Ashy. Starved. It burns my… not my nose, my… I have no word for it. And the feeling in my chest, where he—"

"Don't pay attention to that. Feel for Mother Fam. Where is she?"

Clay's eyes flicked back and forth as though scanning the horizon. "I think there's something," he said. "Something close. To the east. It's rich and loamy. Rotting, I think, but not unpleasant. Earth. Decay. It—it should disgust me, but it's full of life, isn't it? And it's deep. Stone-deep, sea-deep. I don't know what that means."

"That is her," said Doto, pleased. Clay had been able to find her so quickly, with such innate facility.

Clay's eyes sparkled. "She's close, then! I think we might be able to find her today!" He sprang along the branch of the tree toward the top of the cliff, stopping short at the shimmering wall of the forest. "I don't really want to go out there again, though."

"Nor I," Doto agreed. "But unless you have found a new trick that lets you carry the forest with you, we must. And you should go and retrieve your skin and shoes from below. The air smells very cold this morning."

~

"I'm sorry that the forest circle was so poor," Clay said. They were clambering through a narrow gully between two knobbled peaks of stone. The travel was not easy—in the latest leg, they'd had to help each other up large, round boulders twice their height. Their hands, feet, knees, and shins had long since been scraped bloody by the rough surfaces, but at least the exertion was keeping them both warm.

"You should not be apologizing," Doto informed him. "You did the best that you could, and anyway, a god has no reason to apologize."

Clay stopped and turned around. "You really think that?"

Doto frowned. Upon consideration, that assertion could be rather easily challenged.

"I used to believe it," Clay said, struggling to pull himself up another immense boulder. Doto came up behind him and placed his fire bearer hands, with its spindly fingers and flat, useless claws, on Clay's backside, boosting him up. "But after meeting the gods and seeing what they've done to the world… I think if anyone owes the world an apology" —he grunted, pulling himself up— "they do."

"That may be," Doto granted, taking Clay's hand and allowing himself to be hoisted up the boulder, "but I would not mention that in their presence. Or anyplace they could hear you. Which is, I suppose, nearly anywhere."

Clay looked about as though hearing a predator. "Mother Fam? Can she hear me now?"

"Certainly. But she might not be listening. When Kwaee sits on his throne, he can see and hear all the forest. But when you can see and hear everything, it is difficult to pay attention to any one thing in particular. Look back there." Doto pointed the way they had come. "You can see every blade of grass, or nearly. But you would not notice the movements of any one of them unless you were looking at that particular one with interest. Ogya sees and hears through every flame. The echoes of every sound travel across the savanna. Mother Fam feels the tremor of every stone, every footstep in the earth. But does she listen to every single one? No god could."

"Not even the Sky Father? Doesn't he see everything?"

The question gave Doto pause. There was no point in feigning omniscience around Clay any longer. Clay had been witness as his understanding of the world and his place in it had crumbled. Together they were learning truths about the gods that neither of them had ever suspected.

Kwaee had always told him that Wem saw everything, that not a blade of grass withered in the forest, nor a mosquito egg hatch in a pond, but Wem knew of it. But if Father Wem saw everything, then he was only a pair of eyes in the sky, a sun and stars watching through day and night, but changing nothing.

Doto tried to fold his ears back, but the inadequate flesh circles he had in lieu of proper ears would not comply. He tried for a snarl instead. "I do not believe even Wem pays attention to everything at once. If he saw what was happening now, surely he would change it. He would not let Ogya burn his creation."

"So you think he cares?"

"Why make everything if you don't care about it? Why do anything at all?" Doto sighed. "He must care. He must."

They continued in silence for a time. Their path led them into a deep canyon that cut a stony ribbon through a valley of green grass, ringed on all sides by mountains. Doto didn't wish to travel downhill if they were only going to have to climb up another one of those mountains, but they could only follow the pulse of Mother Fam's power. Their going seemed so slow, and each time they settled for rest, the burn of the fire bearers had crept ever closer to his heart. In the forest, they could have reached their destination before the sun had crept a beetle's width across the sky. Here they could not even run the distance, among the steep inclines, boulders, and terrain littered with sharp stones. These fresh mortal bodies wounded so easily, tired so quickly.

"What does it feel like?" Clay asked suddenly.

"What does what feel like?"

"Sorry. The dance, I mean. When I dance for you, it does something to you. The first time, it grew that feather, remember?"

Doto unconsciously reached up toward his forehead to stroke his feather, but it was not there in his human shape. "I remember."

"When a fire bearer—when a worshiper gives you praise, as a god, what does that feel like? You seem to like it."

"It is—" Doto searched for the words. "It feels like you are answering your purpose. Your worshiper calls the power of the world around you, and it flows through you, and you change it. You make it yours—or maybe it takes something from you, but something that you were made to give. The first time you ever danced for me, that was the first time I truly ever felt like a god. But not… not in a proud or haughty way," he hastened to add, hearing for a moment the touch of his father's arrogance in his voice. "I only mean that when you sing for me, it feels as though I have a *reason* to be a god."

He faltered, various explanations coming to his lips but all of them inadequate. How could he explain the strange feeling that all of nature, all the rules that governed stone and tree, bird and beast, existed for his worshiper? That in the dance, he felt adored, yes, and loved, but also out of control, all his power a tool for the fire bearer? That the song of adoration praised but also commanded, that the tempo of Clay's dancing feet pulled the forest through him?

"I love it," he said simply.

"It sounds wonderful. Do you think that maybe someday someone might… for me?"

"I doubt that very much." Doto strode past him. "You would need a song of your own and someone to sing it. And I do not think any of your people are very interested in praising you." He realized his mistake immediately. Reminding Clay of his people only reminded him what they had done to him. He didn't look back to see the stricken expression.

"No, I suppose you are right," Clay said after a moment, hurrying up behind him. "But you know, *I* wrote a song for *you*."

"A very good one. You sang it only last night. Did you think I had forgotten it?"

"No, I only thought that maybe you might…" He faltered.

"Might what?"

Clay sighed. "I just want to know what it's like, is all. To know your purpose. I felt it a long time ago, as a hunter running across the savanna. I felt joy, that—that I was doing what I was meant for. Like my feet were falling in the footsteps of… something greater than me. But since everything that's happened, it's not the same. And I thought maybe the dance, the way you describe it… it sounds… I just wanted to feel it too. If I can do it for you, and I'm part god, and you are *also* part god…"

"Yes?" Doto asked, uneasy.

"Maybe you could make a song for me. Dance for me sometime. Only once. Just so I could know what it's like."

"That would not be appropriate."

Clay gave a little nod as though the answer was expected. "Oh. I see. Only—only why isn't it?"

"All the divinity in you comes from me," Doto said. "It would not be right for me to praise or worship myself, would it? If I dance around singing the praises of Clay, god of the forest, and how great he is, I am truly singing the praises of Doto. And that would be prideful."

"I guess that makes sense."

He sounded so dejected that Doto looked back over one shoulder. "But… you are right. As a god you should experience this. Perhaps when we return, we can capture a fire bearer and make him sing and dance for you so that you can know."

"I don't think it works that way, Doto. You can't make someone love you." He sighed. "You don't think that you could try it, just for me? If it felt inappropriate, you could stop. And no one else would have to know."

Doto almost asked why he wanted it so badly, but the question wasn't an honest one. Of course Clay wanted to feel that worship; anyone would. But to do that… worship was his—it was something due a god. A true god, not one converted by the side effects of healing magic. Clay might be divine now, but it was Doto's divinity. It was something he had lost. Something he missed. Something that, if he could, he would take back. He did not regret healing Clay from his wounds. Not for a heartbeat. But he could not celebrate that Clay had that power now and he did not. He was walking a stony landscape with torn and bleeding human feet, no pelt to protect him from the cold, weak eyes that could not see at night, a nose and ears that kept the world around him muffled. He was hungry and exhausted, and Clay wanted him to dance and sing about it? How could his mate be so callous as to ask such a thing?

But of course Clay would not see it that way, and if Doto explained it, it would only make him feel bad, so he thought of an excuse that also happened to be true. "Inventing songs and dances is a fire bearer skill. I doubt any god is able to do such a thing on their own. Perhaps if you were to show me how to dance and then write a song to yourself," he added, feeling sly at the suggestion.

"I couldn't write a song to myself," Clay protested.

"No, you are right. That would be inappropriate." He tried to suppress a smirk at having proved his point, but human faces were bad at concealing emotion. He hurried ahead so Clay would not see it.

After a short time, noticing that Clay had been particularly quiet, he turned around and saw his little fire bearer sitting down on a rock a good distance back, hugging himself with his arms. Doto must have said something wrong. He hurried back over.

"I'm sorry," Clay said. "I'll get up in a minute. I was just feeling..."

"You are feeling sad," Doto said, rather proud of his deduction. Emotions were much more difficult to read without a nose that could detect the many scents bodies emitted to make them evident, but expressions and body language were turning out to provide many valuable clues.

"Not exactly," Clay said. Well, body language wasn't perfect. "It's just that I don't know who I am supposed to be now."

"I do not understand this dilemma. Are you certain this is a real problem?"

"I'm not a fire bearer anymore. I mean, I know I look like one now, but being a fire bearer means being with your people. Sharing your life with them. Knowing that when you die, you'll join your ancestors." He sighed. "My people are afraid of me. They try to kill me. And when I die, I don't join my ancestors. I just come back. Over and over again. There is so much about being a fire bear—a *human*—that I don't get to have anymore."

"You want to *die?*" Doto asked, baffled. Every time he felt close to understanding Clay, the fire bearer would say something that showed him just how far away he was.

"No! Yes. I mean... no, I don't want to die, I just want to know—to *feel*—that I belong somewhere. And I'm not a fire bearer anymore. I think—I think that's the real reason I kept going back, after everything that they did to me. I had to know they were still my people."

"But they are bad!" Doto flung his arms wide in frustration. "They are doing terrible things. You are so much better than them now. And you *know* where you belong. You belong with me."

Clay gave him a faint, sad smile. "But I'm not a god either, am I? Not really. I have a little bit of power, and it's awesome and scary. And fun. But no one will ever worship me like they do Kwaee or Mpo. And that's fine," he added hurriedly. "I can't be a big divine power controlling the forces of the world. I wouldn't know what to do.I think I would feel bad. Undeserving. Because I'm not really a god. I'm… I'm Clay. But if I'm not a god and I'm not a fire bearer, what am I? I don't know what that is or what I am supposed to be doing."

"You are supposed to be saving the world with me," Doto said, still somewhat puzzled. "Which is what was happening until you sat down on that rock and felt sad. I don't know what it is like to have a people, so I cannot know why you want to be with them. I suspect that they all know that you are the best of the fire bearers and are envious, or maybe want to kill you so that they can be the best instead. It is the way apes behave much of the time."

"They're not apes!"

"Oh yes, they are," Doto declared. "I have seen more than enough apes to know. Fire bearers squabble and screech just like them. But I do not understand why these questions bother you. You belong in the forest. You can tell because that is where you are powerful."

"But I'm not a real forest god. There is Kwaee already. And you. Where do I fit in?"

Doto sighed. "Clay, you must stop asking yourself those kinds of questions. You fit in where you decide to, and you always have. Do you think when I stole you from your nest it was because I intended for you to change me as you have? You made my life different. You changed Kwaee's mind, something I could not do in a thousand years. You won Asubonten's respect and Ogya's enmity. Everything and everyone around you changes. You do not fit in. You make the world fit you."

He crouched before Clay, taking his mate's hands in his. "Do not ask who you *should* be and where you *belong*. These questions do not matter to you. You are who you decide to be. And no one can tell you where you belong when you make up your mind."

"You just said I belong in the forest," Clay pointed out, but he was smiling, and his eyes were wet.

"And yet here we are out in the middle of a wretchedly cold mountain pass. Do you think that was my decision?"

Clay giggled. "No. No, I guess it wasn't."

Doto showed him his teeth in the manner of a happy fire bearer. "Well then stop feeling sad about deciding what everyone else is going to do. It makes me very grumpy."

He leaned forward and pressed a kiss on Clay's mouth. The feeling was strange without a muzzle, their lips soft and fleshy and flexible, and their noses pressed together in a way he found off-putting, but it was not unpleasant. This close, he could smell Clay easily even with his human nose, beneath the odor of the pelts they wore, the sweat and the dirt. Clay's scent changed with his form, but it was still unmistakably him.

Doto pulled back, confident he had reassured Clay, but Clay clasped his head with both hands, fingers sliding into the thick black hair above his neck, thumbs at his ears, and pulled him back into a kiss again, his flat teeth nipping at Doto's bottom lip.

Doto tried not to show his surprise. Clay liked him even like this, in this feeble human shape? Then he dismissed his surprise. Of course Clay would know how to find other fire bearers attractive—he used to be one. Beneath the leopard pelts, Doto's erection rose. It was foolish to think that they could mate here, in the harsh stonelands and the cold, but he found himself kissing Clay more fervently, sliding his tongue into the warmth of his lover's mouth, his fingers fumbling as they slid under the rough protection of the pelts. Clay's waist was warm and smooth beneath, and Doto gripped it firmly. The smooth skin there felt different under the touch of uncalloused fingertips, and when he slid his hands around his mate's back, Clay shivered and kissed hungrily at his mouth again.

He smoothed his fingers down to the swell of Clay's rump, pleased at the way his breath caught in his throat. "We can't do this here," Clay breathed, but then he kissed Doto again more fiercely. Doto lifted him—his fire bearer arms were not as strong as the leopard's, but more than adequate to the task, and as he hefted, he felt the nudge of Clay's erection against his belly.

His excitement rising, he leaned Clay back against a boulder, trusting the pelt to protect him from scratches. His skin was flushed so warm that he barely felt the chill of the wind as he pulled open his pelts and bared his arousal. Clay leaned up on his elbows to peer at it.

"You've seen it already," Doto pointed out.

Clay curled his fingers around it. "Not like this." He gave Doto's length a tug that made him gasp.

"You like it—*me*—like this?"

Clay gave a breathy laugh. "Of course I do. You're very handsome. Besides, I know it's you in there. You're who I love, Doto."

Doto leaned forward, his shaft rubbing against Clay's, the sensation strange with smooth skin and very little fur, and kissed him again, everything else—the cold, their frail bodies, the rough terrain and their exhaustion—melting away in the height of his passion.

It didn't stay melted away. The knobby surface of the rock made Clay increasingly uncomfortable; the pelts kept itching; and they had nothing slippery to coat Doto's shaft with for proper mating—he licked his fingers and slicked it up but it was still not slippery enough for Clay, who couldn't manage to take the girth of Doto's shaft without lubrication. Doto was more than ready; his erection ached with a need that overwhelmed and surprised him.

"You could dance, and we could use nectar as our leopard selves," he suggested.

"No, please, I want you like this." Clay kissed him again, and then planted kisses down his chest, taking Doto's erection into his mouth. Doto panted, his fingers gripping at Clay's shoulders, no worry about hurting him without his divine strength or feline claws. Clay had licked him to climax many times, but the fire bearer tongue was slicker and gentler than a leopard's, and it took little time for Doto's excitement to crest and consume his body, his back arching and hips jerking as he painted his mate's mouth with seed.

Clay slumped back, panting, and began to pull his pelts around him again, but Doto put one hand on his chest, stopping him, and leaned down to reciprocate. He had expected to find the task a mere duty, but a lick up Clay's shaft made his mate moan and twist in a delightful way, and soon he found that he enjoyed eliciting these paroxysms of pleasure from Clay. What had changed? Why had he never been so interested before?

Perhaps it was the power, the ability to affect Clay so intimately. But he had always had that—Clay responded to everything he said and did with passion. Then what? Doto could not find the answer, and decided to let it remain a mystery for now. For now, he was content to drag his tongue up the dark skin of Clay's shaft and feel it strain harder against his lick, to kiss the pink tip and taste the slippery salt of readiness, to press it deep into his throat and watch Clay's lithe stomach tense and ripple with his happy groans of pleasure.

Afterward they lay together, panting, their pelts wrapped around both of them to protect them from the chill wind, forming a cocoon in which they rested, skin against skin, sharing heat, sharing each other in a way they had not, even when sharing minds. Here their intimacy formed a bulwark against the rest of the world. Here they needed each other.

It was uncomfortable. The pelts stank and were itchy. They didn't cover their whole bodies so the wind was always chilling some part or another. And fire bearer bodies were not put together as well as leopard forms, so knees and elbows were always bumping together, and the ground was supremely uncomfortable.

They wrapped their arms around each other and hid away from it all. It was the happiest Doto had ever been.

~

The cave mouth was at the bottom of a deep gully. Clay did not like the look of it. It yawned dark and threatening, wide enough easily for twenty people to walk side by side into its abyssal gape. Stones hung like teeth from its ceiling, pointed and menacing.

"Are you certain she is in there?" he asked.

Doto nodded. "She is goddess of the earth. That cave goes into the earth. And the pulse of divinity came from this direction."

"It looks dark. Neither of us can see in the dark like this."

"Can you not make fire to light our way?"

"And risk Ogya seeing us? Besides, I would need sap or oil to make a torch. And tools to light the fire. There's nothing around here to use."

"For a fire bearer, you are very poor at bearing fire," Doto said, sounding grumpy. "But you are right. We should not risk Ogya learning our movements." He paused and stared into the mouth of the cave.

Clay suspected he knew what Doto was thinking. The last time they'd gone into a hole in a mountain, it had been a prison of Ogya's making. Then they'd had little choice, and there had been the light of fire from within. Here there was only a forbidding darkness. It felt wrong to wander into a hole in the earth, but he could think of no alternative other than turning back. They'd stayed in a forest circle the previous night, and the thrum of divine power—of *Fam's* power—had drawn them unmistakably in this direction, down into the canyon they'd seen from the ridge above. That pulse had felt deep. Not forward, but beneath them.

He gazed again at the opening in the earth. It seemed to spread wider, a giant maw. "Well," he said, "this is what we came for. There's no point in turning around now." He wrapped his pelts more tightly around himself, some anxious part of his mind expecting the hole in the earth to be colder, and picked his way down the slope of the canyon.

Stepping into the cave reminded him of passing through the forest wall, though he felt no similar change in his awareness. It was a boundary; he was crossing over into another god's domain. Inside, the rock took strange and eerie shapes, like nameless creatures hunching in the darkness. He picked his way between the stones, but the terrain here was softer, smoother. His bark shoes slipped and slid on wet stone and mud, so he stripped them off, rubbing a little of the cool mud onto his chafed heels and ankles. A few experimental steps further found his bare feet glad of the gentler surface. He gave a nod to Doto, who crouched to remove his own shoes.

Still, he wasn't sure how they would make their way without any light. The depths of the cave were cloaked in darkness. He missed his night vision. He tried to tell himself that it wasn't that he'd become dependent on his new gifts; it was simply that he had no way to be a proper fire bearer out here. He needed the calluses on his hands and feet to protect them. He needed tools—his knife, if nothing else. All the same, he looked forward to each night in the forest circle, his feline body curled around Doto's, immersed in the life and vibrancy of his domain.

He blinked into the dimness. Beyond this path, the formations of rock grew odd and unnatural. The very surface of the stones looked melted, as though formed out of wax left in the sun. Their outlines shimmered, wet, but the spaces behind them held only darkness.

They would never find their way any deeper. If the cave grew any darker, they'd have to grope their way forward, and one wrong turn in the dark… he dreaded to think how lost they might become.

*Reeget!*

A high-pitched chirp came from a rock nearby. He glanced toward it and then rubbed at his eyes. He thought he'd seen a point of light.

"What was that sound?" Doto asked, coming up behind him. "It sounded like a frog."

*Reeget!*

It *was* a frog, perched atop a nearby hump of glistening stone, no bigger than Clay's thumb. Its shiny skin was mottled black and pale blue, but impossibly, the blue parts were glowing, lit like pale moonlight. The frog swiveled its head to the side as though it hadn't quite caught what Doto was asking. A questioning bubble appeared at its throat.

*Reeget!*

This time, the chirp was answered—*Reeget!*—by another frog, and—*Reeget!*—then another—*Reeget!*—and—*Reeget! Reeget! Reeget! Reeget! Reeget! Reeget! Reeget! Reeget! Reeget! Reeget!*

The cavern was full of them, their cries echoing throughout its stone tunnels, so many of them calling at once that they sounded like birds. Doto stared upward, and Clay followed his gaze. Little points of light were flickering into view: the walls and the ceiling of the cave were speckled with them. They glimmered like stars at twilight, their tiny glowing bodies shifting and twinkling as they crawled or hopped around. The light of their glow flickered on and off as well, though if there were patterns to the flicker, Clay could not discern them.

"Have you ever seen anything like this?" he breathed to Doto. Trying to follow any one speck of light was dizzying.

"Of course I… have not," Doto said, swerving toward humble honesty halfway through his sentence. "There are no creatures like this in the forest."

The frog on the stone in front of Clay gave one final *Reeget!* And then sprang from its spot with an impudent little kick of its black-toed feet. It landed on a rock a couple paces away, fixed both of them with a boggle-eyed stare, and hopped again, a little further.

"They're showing us the way," Clay said in delight. "Mother Fam must have sent them. I told you she wanted to see you."

"She could have chosen a more convenient meeting spot," Doto grumbled, but there was a glimmer of enthusiasm in his eyes.

Clay followed the frog as it hopped deeper into the cave, but soon lost it among the myriad others. "What do they eat in here?" he wondered aloud.

"I don't know, but I am sure there are other living things in here."

The thought of other creatures huddling somewhere in that darkness sent Clay backing up to walk next to Doto.

It soon became obvious that the frogs were leading them in a specific direction, as the cave paths narrowed and became labyrinthine, branching and winding off in countless other directions. Only one path was lit by the frogs, however; the rest were swallowed up by darkness, and Clay had little desire to go exploring.

The frogs took them through difficult passages, including a gap so narrow that Clay and Doto had to wriggle through it on their bellies, and around a wide pit that led straight down into unending darkness. Clay tossed a rock into it, and a great deal of time passed before they heard its faint clatter below. “Probably a lot of dead things at the bottom of that pit,” Doto said in an oddly appreciative tone, and a shiver went up Clay’s spine as he considered what would have happened if they’d tried to blindly grope their way down toward Mother Wem.

They traveled for so long that Clay began to wonder if it was getting late. There was no sun or moon, no way to tell how long they had been traveling other than the gradual increase of their weariness. Only the darkness of the stone depths and the glittering light and shrill song of the frogs.

“Do you think forest would appear down here if I danced?” Clay asked after a while. They might need to try if they grew too hungry or exhausted.

“I would not care to risk it,” Doto answered. “I do not know what happens to a cave when it… stops being a cave. Perhaps it is only the power of Fam that keeps the whole mountain from collapsing atop our heads.”

Clay wished he hadn’t asked. The thought of all that stone above his head was unnatural. Living in the forest had itself been an adjustment. As a fire bearer he had relied on the sky and the open horizon to tell time, gauge distance, and look out for game or predators. In many places in the forest, the foliage was so thick that he could not see the sky. That had taken a while to grow accustomed to. This was something else altogether. The stone all around him, in every direction, made his pulse pound. Without the light and guidance of the frogs, he and Doto would be trapped. Their only escape would be to fling themselves down one of those gaping pits and hope to awaken in their temple, leaving two more human corpses to lie among the bones and slowly moulder.

Clay shuddered and wrested his thoughts away from that image. He didn’t look at the walls, at the stone that jutted up and down like fangs, dripping as they closed around the two of them…

He focused on the frogs. They would show the way. He had faith in them, faith in Mother Fam. When things looked bleakest, you needed the gods. You needed something to focus on, keep you moving forward, keep you from panicking at the terrible and endless darkness.

The frogs led them downward now, winding a corkscrew path into a deep abyss. When Clay dared to look over the edge of the spiral, he grew dizzy—it was as though he lost the ability to tell down from sideways. He looked away.

At the bottom of the pit, the mud was thick, so much so that walking through it proved almost impossible. Each step sank in halfway to the knee, and pulling that foot out for the next step was difficult: the mud sucked at their feet, releasing them only with a nasty squelching sound. It caked thickly around their legs and feet and between their toes.

"This is a bad place," Doto declared. "I do not care for this one bit. It is wrong of Fam to make us come this way when she could much more simply come to us. Or at least give us an easier path."

"Easy?" The voice was a woman's, a rich, amused timbre that echoed all around them through the cavern. Clay looked around in mild alarm, but saw nothing but darkness, mud, and glowing frogs. "Why should it be easy? But as you wish, my dear little Doto. Let me give you a path."

The mud before Clay bubbled, and he nearly fell backward in alarm—only the grip of the earth around his feet prevented it. Before him, out of the mud, rose a broad, flat stone, easily large enough to stand on. Beyond that, another surfaced, and still more, forming a footpath through the muck.

Gratefully, he clambered up onto the rock and did his best to squeeze the thick coating of mud—it's clay, he realized with amusement—from his legs and feet, though the stuff was sticky and clung to his fingers just as readily. Doto made a disgusted face, scraping the stuff away from his limbs on a platform.

The footpath before them led into a broad, open chamber. Clay took a few shaky steps toward it, and as he did, the room filled with light so bright that he put his hands to his eyes, dazzled.

"Come in, children," the voice said, and now he recognized it—not just from the tent on the night before his execution. He recognized it as surely as he knew the voice of his own mother. It was a voice that some part of him had always known.

"Come back to me, finally. Rest in my arms. I will tell you everything, and there will be no more secrets."

# 17 Extinguished

The ants had killed Half Moon. The hunters set his body—what was left of it—on a pyre and sent it to Father Wem. The whole time Ogya cackled in Laughing Dog's mind. He boasted that every body they burned was his, not Wem's. That the dead resided eternally in his undying flame. Laughing Dog wasn't sure whether to believe him.

There hadn't been much of Half Moon left after the ants had been at him. What flesh remained hung from his skeleton in unrecognizable strings and clumps. The other fire hunters said the insects had swarmed his body, covering him in his own beaded black carapace. They'd gone for his eyes first. He screamed in pain and then they crawled into his throat. He'd choked and flailed. When Laughing Dog asked the other hunters why they hadn't helped him, they said they were terrified of the ants.

Their wounds made him inclined to believe them—none of his hunters had escaped the savagery of the insects. If Laughing Dog had not destroyed Atatea when he did, all his hunters might have perished. They were covered with bite marks—slashes in the skin where the ants had dug in their hook-like mandibles. Many of them still had ants clinging to their skin; even in death the creatures would not let go. They had to be cut or burned away and the pincers carefully removed.

Yellow Bug had encountered nothing in her apprenticeship to prepare her for this kind of attack. She used flint needles to try to extract the pincers lest some piece remain in the skin to fester and rubbed the bite marks with a poultice of sage, which the hunters claimed relieved some of the pain and itching.

But the real damage was not the loss of Half Moon, his council member, nor the injuries to his hunters. The men were spooked. Atetea's tiny army could have killed every one of them, and they knew it. It was only the ant god's forbearance that had left any of them alive. Laughing Dog was glad he'd sizzled that monstrosity in its shell when he'd had the chance.

He'd lost two hunters in one moon—one to the ants, another to the flaming manifestation of Ogya. And with Mirage gone, he was down to nine. Nine men against the god of all the forest. He'd have to recruit more from the village, he supposed, but that would be more difficult now. Questions of his leadership would be spreading.

He watched the flames of the pyre devouring Half Moon's carcass. How long until he, too, lay in the flames, his body consumed, the smoke rising to Wem? An ugly memory resurfaced: that of Sedjet, the man in the desert with a hyena in the back of his head. He'd knocked Sedjet into the flames and later found only a massive diamond. It had sunk into his flesh when he'd grasped it, and that was when he first heard the voice of Ogya. On his pyre, would a diamond fall from his burning corpse? Who would pick it up and inherit that curse?

A memory of Ogya's threat echoed through his mind: *I will burn myself out of your body. Just as I did your friend Sedjet.* Had Sedjet been just a man as well, one carrying the curse of Ogya?

And now a more horrible thought occurred to Laughing Dog: did he, too, wander around at night, tottering backward like a demon, a hyena face sprouting from the back of his skull? How had he never considered this before? That moment in the desert had fled his thoughts, more nightmare or fever-dream than a true memory. But it was real. It had happened. He had seen that monster. And he had trusted the power the gem granted him—why? Because it promised him the chance to save his people, of course. And it had wasted and parched him until he had no choice if he wanted to survive. And then he'd drunk deeply of water and drowned the voice, weakened it.

Yes, water was the way to fight Ogya. Laughing Dog needed to remember that. He didn't have to remain cowering in the back of his skull while Ogya took control. The god was cleverer than Laughing Dog had given him credit for, confusing him in turns by punishing and then seducing him, whispering paranoias and then shouting commands. And Laughing Dog had been weak. He'd been devastated by the losses of his family, his people. He'd caved under the pressure of trying to keep his people alive and thriving when everything was going wrong. That had fractured his control of Ogya. He needed to get it back.

He became aware that someone had been speaking to him. "Sorry, yes?" He turned his attention outward. It was Burning Star, the largest and strongest of his hunters. Burning Star had lost an eye to the ants. What good was strength against such an enemy?

"Are we still going to keep going? After everything that's happened?" Burning Star hid his feelings behind a gruff bravado, but Laughing Dog could tell the man was frightened. He wouldn't meet his King's eyes, for one thing.

"Of course we are. Kwaee's cruelty toward us doesn't end with our own losses. This will be a long battle, Burning Star."

The large man nodded and rubbed at his shaved head. "Only, if little insects could hurt us so badly, how can we fight an entire forest?"

"One tree at a time, Burning Star. And you do not need to fear the ants again. I burned their god to death in his skin."

*And how delicious he tasted.* The words echoed so deep inside him. Were they his thoughts? Or Ogya's voice?

"Of course, my King. We're all… proud of the vengeance you took for Half Moon and his family. But what if there is a god of wasps? Or of eagles? Or lions? Some other terrible thing that wants us dead for what we've done?"

Laughing Dog hesitated. It was a question that had not occurred to him, and one that frightened him to consider. *But lesser gods are fickle and subject to the laws of nature. Animals do not attack fire bearers unless directly threatened, and thus, neither can their gods.*

He was as sure of this truth as he was uncertain as to how he'd known it. So. The lesser gods would not attack unless threatened. But surely Atatea was not the only lesser god who lived in the forest. Eventually they would have to encounter others. *But not all animals have lesser gods ascribed to them—they are not common, and many live outside the forest. Atetea was an irritating but rare inconvenience.*

Again, knowledge for which he had no source—no source, that is, but Ogya. A low panic rose in his belly, but he was stirred from it by Burning Star's worried gaze. "My King?"

He set his jaw and met his fire hunter's eyes. "I was considering your concern. It's troubling, but I don't think we need to worry about further attacks."

*There is no god of wasps.*

"There is no god of wasps."

*And the god of lions roams far east, in the savanna.*

"And the god of lions roams far east, in the savanna." He spoke the words almost as they occurred to him.

*The lesser gods cannot attack us unless we confront them directly. And by the time that happens, I will have grown far too powerful for them to stop.*

"The lesser gods cannot attack us unless we confront them directly. And by the time that happens, I—" He frowned. Those words were surely not his. Why would he speak them to his men? They sounded like madness. "I will have found another way to defeat them," he finished weakly. "We can only reckon with the challenges we face today. No use wrestling with those we can't yet see, Burning Star."

The large man nodded but did not look entirely mollified. "As you say, my King."

*I should burn him alive for his cowardice.*

Even as the thought entered his mind, he felt the song to summon Ogya's power warm his tongue, his feet brace for the dance. No, no. He didn't want to burn his men. These thoughts were not his. They were Ogya's. His panic rose again. Always there had been a boundary in his mind between the god's words and his own. Always he had heard Ogya as a voice around him. This was something new.

"What have you done, Ogya?" he murmured under his breath. "What are you doing to me?"

*You do not resist me anymore. My thoughts guide yours, as my words have always done.*

Fear seized him. He backed away from the pyre, trying to tear his eyes from the entrancing flicker of the flames that devoured his hunter's body. Ogya had to be lying. But with what purpose? Why would the fire god make him believe he had no control? No, far simpler would be to… to make him believe he had been in control all along.

*Hahahaha.* The laughter crackled throughout his mind. He tried to pull his thoughts away from it, but just as Ogya's voice surrounded him in the air, so his presence echoed in every dark crevice of his thoughts.

*You cannot run from your own mind, little king. You accepted me. You welcomed my power. Now you and I are one.*

"No!" he cried out loud, faintly aware of the other hunters turning to stare at him. Panic gripped at him. Threats were on every side: the suspicion of his men, the disillusionment of his subjects, the threats from the forest, and within him, within his own thoughts, the possession of a mad god whom he did not control—whom, he now feared, he had *never* controlled.

He turned and fled, running away from the pyre and their campsite, across the savanna. Let his men think what they want. He was beyond their judgment now. Beyond their help.

*What do you think you can do now?* he asked himself, but no, that was not his thought. Ogya.

"You don't control my feet. You don't control my body."

*You control them. And you are we.*

He thought about slowing down, then. About heading back to his men, claiming it was only grief and remorse for the loss of Half Moon that had made him flee. He could gather them together, motivate them. The right mixture of inspiration and fear was all he needed. There was a trick to it. You spoke in a loud voice and a quiet voice, and they would reject the loud and unthinkingly obey the quiet…

Not his thoughts. They were not his thoughts. But his feet had slowed all the same. He had turned to run back to his men.

"No!" he roared in his loudest voice. "No, I will not be your slave, Ogya!"

He forced himself to focus, forced away the hungry parts of his mind, the parts that thought of devouring, of taking, of controlling. There was a pond nearby, a small one. It was full of rain runoff and not so muddy with ash as other water sources. He ran for it.

*I know where you are going.*

He ignored the thought. It was not his, and Ogya did not need to know his reaction.

*But I can hear your thoughts so easily. You do not need to speak to me. The walls of your mind's secrets shrivel before me like a flower wilting in the heat of a flame.*

His feet beat against the savanna. His toes smashed against a rock as he ran; he didn't care. He set his foot down on a thorny vine that pierced his sole. He hobbled onward, favoring the edge of his foot. "I will stop you," he panted. He used to be better at running, back before he had grown fat and heavy with muscle. "I will stop you."

*Go ahead.* His thought—*Ogya's* thought—was sneering and confident.

There. There was the little pond. He stumbled as he ran for it and fell onto his elbows and knees, skinning them badly, the painful jar of a bruise shooting up his right upper arm, making his fingers numb. He ignored it. "I will stop you."

On hands and knees, he crawled for the pool. It was a slim chance, and he knew it. He'd guzzled water before to silence the voice of Ogya, and it had only served to mute the god for a while. But it was his only chance. His fingers dug into the earth as he pulled himself forward to the pool. The water was ashy and bitter, but he sucked it down as though it were sweet. Water extinguished any fire. Water was the key. He swallowed, nearly gagging on the foul taste. His stomach bloated with it. He choked and could drink no more. He lay belly down in the pool, water running down his nose and chin, soaking his chest. Then his stomach rebelled, and he vomited, spewing up a grey flood of bile and ash water.

Ogya's laughter echoed in his mind and his voice in the world around him. "You still thought it would work. You thought I, god of fire, could be defeated by a pond."

"It worked before," Laughing Dog cried. Despair and terror seized him. He was a prisoner then. A captive of this evil god. And his people were captives too. He'd doomed himself. He'd doomed them all.

"It never worked, you foolish boy. I let you believe it. You wanted to believe it. That you had control. Control over *me*, a god."

Laughing Dog slumped into the dirt in utter despair. It was over, then. He was lost. There was no hope. "I didn't want this," he moaned. "I only wanted to help everyone."

"But you did," his own voice mocked him. "You wanted power. And I gave it to you. I gave you everything you wanted. You could never, ever give it up."

"I'd give it up now," Laughing Dog sobbed into the dirt. "I would give it all up, if only you would go."

*What?* The thought was his, yes, but also Ogya's. And it was true.

"I don't want your power anymore. I don't want to be King. I don't want to hurt people. I wish you would go away. I pray it. Ogya, please, please. No—I demand it! Take your power and leave me alone."

*You—you fool!*

Something burned sharply in his right arm, a terrible lancing pain deep in the forearm. He screamed and clutched at it with his other hand. The pain moved up his forearm, a jagged, blazing ember crawling through his flesh and bone. If he'd had a knife, he would have dug it into his skin to try to free whatever caused the pain. All around him, the voice of Ogya roared in inchoate fury, and the sound echoed in his mind. The rage and hatred were his own.

And then they weren't. Then the voice was discrete. Separate. Alien and hostile. The bones of his wrist cracked and crackled as the pain moved upward through it and into his palm. It felt as though his skin were being torn open, and he clawed at his palm with the nails of his other hand, trying to rip the pain away.

In the center of his palm, a translucent point emerged, and grew, squeezing out of him.

His body shuddered and slithered around him as though made of snakes. He writhed on the sand.

Then something solid dropped from his palm, and the pain was gone. In the mud and vomit, a diamond glinted.

He felt small, frail, and terribly weak. In a fit of revulsion, he shoved the diamond away from him with both hands, pushing the sand and careful not to touch the rock itself. It slipped into the pond and vanished below the murky surface.

Shaking, Laughing Dog pushed himself to his feet. He was feeble and emaciated. His skin hung from him like old pelts slung over branches.

But there was no voice in the air. No strange thoughts in his mind. Ogya was gone.

He was free. Free.

# 18
# The First Story

Doto ought to have been frightened by the huge, muddy arm that swooped down on him as soon as he entered the larger cavern. He ought to have bristled and hissed as he was lifted suddenly into the air and then clasped to a voluminous bosom that smelled of new grass and old leaves, of mushrooms and flowering figs, of milk and childbirth and sex and death all at once.

But he was not afraid, not even as earthy fingers as big around as his waist squeezed him close, as his face pressed into soil and stone. He finally pushed free and stared up at a face as wide as the moon, the face of a fire bearer, but all in shades of brown and grey and red. Her brows were craggy shale; her lips glittering mica; and around her great head her hair grew in waves of golden savanna grass, radiating all directions like shafts of daylight escaping a cloud.

"My Doto," Mother Fam said, and her voice came from a long-ago childhood. It spoke out of his own memories; it rang with love he'd forgotten he'd ever felt. His fears and worries spilled out of him, chased away like distant dreams. How could he have accepted her banishment? How could he have resisted seeking her out? She would make everything right. He clung to her, wishing only to remain there in her arms. He could trust her completely, and she would keep him safe forever.

"And is this my Clay?" Doto's world tilted as Mother Fam leaned down to pick up his mate, and he clung more tightly to her breast, even though her arm kept him clasped safe. Then Clay was near him, held in her other arm, his skin and pelts smeared with brown mud, his eyes staring up at her in wonder.

"How you two have changed! How you've changed each other! I am so proud of you both." Her arm squeezed Doto tightly once more, and then he was lowered back to the cavern floor, mud and dirt falling from him.

For a moment, he panicked at being put down—to be out of her arms was to be lost, abandoned. The world they'd come through to find her was hostile and cruel, and neither he nor Clay were equipped to handle it on their own. He fought the urge to weep, to lift up his hands and beg to be

held by her again, to be pulled inside her where he never need fear again. Instead, he straightened his back and gazed up at her.

She stood tall, taller even than his father, and her frame was round and plump, her limbs thick, appearing both soft and powerful at once, her hips wide, her belly heavy and abundant, supporting the fullness of her breasts that spilled across it. Her body looked entirely mud and rock, though when she moved, he saw hints of other materials within her: bark and bones, crystal and moss. She was both familiar and unfamiliar—he could not remember seeing anyone like her when he was a cub, but he *knew* her, every movement and gesture, the shape of her the shape of all life, from which every being took inspiration.

"I'm glad I'm here. I've missed you," he said. They were not the words he had intended. He had intended to ask her why she'd wanted to see him, why she'd stayed away, why she'd made it so hard to find her, and what were they going to do about Ogya? But he looked at her wide, smiling face, and it filled him with love so complete that it emptied every other thought from his mind.

"I know you have, dear boy," she said, and he thought he might melt. "I have missed you, too. More than you could know. I miss all of my children."

Doto looked at Clay, expecting to see him prostrating himself before her in his usual somewhat embarrassing way, but Clay just stood and stared up at her, his eyes wet. "You sound so much like her," he said. "Or… she… sounds like you? I don't know."

Mother Fam took a few steps backward and settled into the embrace of her temple—if this was indeed her temple. It felt like one to Doto. It resonated with intimate power, prickling at his senses even with no forest beneath his toes. But, other than the size of the cavern itself and the throngs of glowing frogs, it was unremarkable for a temple. A god's temple showed the beauty and power of that god. Kwaee's was an enormous arboreal bower filled with mighty trees, ever-shifting shafts of daylight, and a dreamy pond at the foot of his moabi throne. Clay and Doto shared an ever-changing garden sequestered in the niche of a waterfall—nothing so grand and majestic as Kwaee's temple, but more comfortable and beautiful. Mother Fam's temple was only a hole in the ground, a damp, earthy place filled with mud and the glow of uncountable anuran lights. But as she spread her arms wide and lay back against the cave wall, it merged with her, the earth and rock melding with her own body. And Doto wondered if this cave was truly her temple, or whether this was part of Mother Fam herself. Perhaps she cradled them inside her.

"I sent for you boys a long, long time ago now," Mother Fam said with a smile. "No—no, Clay, don't look so dismayed. You had every reason not to remember, after your death and resurrection. Of course I understand. I'm glad you are both here now. I have such secrets to lay bare. The world must be done with secrets now."

"Father made you leave," Doto said. "You cared for me when I was a kitten, and he made you—made you abandon me."

She smiled at him, but her eyes grew sad. "He did. It is all right to be angry with him, Doto. There are many things I would have taught you if I stayed. But your father feared for you. He feared that my words would harm you, that teaching you compassion would make you vulnerable as he is vulnerable, and lead to pain such as he feels and cannot escape from. So he bade me go, and gods must heed the wishes of other gods when in their domains."

Clay reached for her, arms upstretched like a child's. "Can you come with us and help us to stop Ogya? Come see my people and tell them to stop fighting. They would listen to you. Everyone would listen to you. You could make the whole world better."

Mother Fam's great, round shoulders shifted, and her fingers twitched as though to reach out to Clay. But then she sighed a long sigh, her breath green wood and young blood. "You tempt me, Clay, and you do not know how cruel that temptation is." Seeing the dismay fall across his face, she added, "But of course you were right to ask me. How could you see the all the suffering you have seen, come all this way, and then *not* ask me? But no, Clay. I must not speak with your people."

He put his arms down, visibly disappointed.

"It's forbidden, I suppose," Doto offered.

"Forbidden? No, nothing is truly forbidden the gods. There's only what we can do and what we should not."

"My father said healing magic is forbidden." He found a perverse pleasure in reporting this to her, as though expecting her to be angry. But she only gazed back at him with a quiet smile for a moment, and he shrank back in himself with embarrassment.

"It is not that speaking with the humans is forbidden. And you are right, Clay. They would listen. They would follow me without question. That is what children do. But a mother does not suckle her children forever.

She helps them to be strong. She allows them to grow up and sends them out into the world to be independent and capable and kind. To keep them by my side would be wrong. I would be forcing them to remain children forever."

"But Ogya is doing it now," Clay protested. "He's talking to my brother. Making him—making him do things. He's cheating. And now the forest is burning."

Mother Fam drew up higher, rising up the stone wall as though floating. She took one step forward and the earth shook beneath Doto's feet. When she spoke again, her voice was hard and terrible. It was all Doto could do not to cringe beneath its righteous anger. "And what would you have me do, child? Do battle with the other gods for the right to command the people of the earth? Should we divide our worshipers up and go to war with each other?"

Clay dropped to the floor, weeping uncontrollably at her anger, his hands covering his face. Mother Fam gave Doto a flick of her opal eyes and he understood, running to Clay's side and taking him in his arms. Clay buried his face in Doto's neck, shaking with fear and remorse.

When Mother Fam spoke again, her voice was once more gentle and kind. "Even now you feel it, Clay. When gods speak, our children listen too well. Our words brand themselves onto their hearts so that they can hear nothing else. I pity your brother for the evil Ogya has wrought against him. I pity all those who have heard the voices of the gods. Every word a god speaks to a mortal echoes down over generations. It rings through lifetimes. It is repeated in stories told by grandmother to father to son to grandchild, on and on."

Doto's limbs felt suddenly stiff and cold. "Are you saying that with Clay, I… and my father… could have…?"

"No, Doto. Not every soul is harmed by a god's words. And you gave Clay what he needed to protect himself."

"Some of my divinity," Doto said, nodding.

"No. Doubt. You showed him that the gods could be wrong. That they are fallible. He suspected it the moment you didn't know what his spear was called. By the time he met Kwaee, he knew you. He loved you already. But what the two of you have done together…" She smiled. "Already the stories are changing. There will be new legends. There are people who know of who you are, Clay, and what happened. They will tell others. You are part of the stories of the gods now, whether you like it or not."

Clay looked up from Doto's arms. "Mother Fam, you said the gods can be wrong. How can that be? Why are so many of them so… unhappy?"

"Ah." Mother Fam leaned back, crossing her stony arms behind her head. "That is the question I hoped you would ask. Its answer is a story—the *first* story, and it is one that no human knows, and few gods will ever admit. And like every true story, it starts—"

Mother Fam paused then, leaning back farther and farther into the wall, until Doto could not see her arms or face at all. Her legs stretched across the room, thicker and wider, and then they sank into the floor and were gone. There was only her belly, huge and brown and round, and that began to swell larger and larger, taking up more of the room. Doto clutched at Clay now more out of confusion than a desire to comfort. Mother Fam's belly swelled and expanded, and the floor rose up to join it, a rising moon of earth that lifted Doto and Clay with it.

The room had grown impossibly large—or perhaps he and Clay had shrunk—and they now sat holding each other atop Mother Fam's belly, which had become a hill, and as the dim light of the cave increased and brightened, Doto saw that there were many other hills around them. With a tickle and a gust of wind, grass sprouted beneath them, furring the hill and radiating outward to the others.

They stood outside, somehow, atop a great, round-topped rise, looking out at an endless field of rich green grass, spreading to every horizon. And in the green grass were white flowers, and above them was a blue sky, and the blue sky was reflected in crystalline lakes and rivers that shimmered in the endless plains.

Mother Fam's voice came from all around them. It thrummed through the earth beneath their bodies. "With me."

Doto stood, shading his weak fire bearer eyes from the sudden daylight. Clay stood next to him, sliding an arm around his waist and clinging to him, visibly overwhelmed. "What is happening?" he whispered. "How did we get outside?"

Doto tried to twitch a tail he did not currently possess. "Mother Fam is goddess of all earth. She can take us anywhere in the world she wishes. She can shape it to her will."

"With the consent of the gods who reign there," Mother Fam's voice came from all around them. The air hummed with her smile. "They were all my children. Kwaee, Little Sarmu, Mpo, Atekye, even Ogya. Gods you've never met—of deserts and lakes and prairies and mountains and glaciers. A god of dark caverns in the heart of the sea, a god of clouds, a god of frost. In the beginning, there was only Wem and Fam, sky and earth. I shaped this world, but it needed guidance beyond what one mother could give. So I birthed the gods to care for the creatures of the world, and to govern all life and death within their dominion."

With the sound of her voice, trees rose across the hills in waves, blanketing the land in forests and glens, sprouting up along the rivers. Astonishment prickled Doto's skin—was all of this real? Or some kind of divine illusion? The hilltop on which they stood remained open and unforested, and he longed to take Clay's hand and dart into the safety of the woods, to see if his power and proper form returned.

"This was the Firelands, once, before Ogya took it." A trace of sadness tinged Mother Fam's voice. "And here Kwaee reigned over my forests, and Firaw in my lakes, and little Sare in the meadowlands. There is Kwaee now, look!"

From beneath the cover of the forest strode an enormous leopard, but aside from the tilt of the jaw and the shape of the eyes, it looked nothing like Doto's father. It strode on all fours—it did not walk upright like a god but crawled like a beast. Nor did it have Kwaee's spread of colorful plumage atop its brow. It sat on the edge of its forest and looked out over the landscape spread before them, its expression tranquil.

"That doesn't look much like the Kwaee we know," Clay said to Doto in a low voice. "For one thing, he's not throwing anybody."

"The gods in those days were not as they are now," Fam's voice said. "They lived as beasts, and their lives were untroubled. Within their domains, all was subject to their power. Your father, Doto, was the forest, and the forest was him, without anger or sadness or any emotion at all."

"Sounds preferable," Doto muttered.

"It was my humans, my fire bearers, who changed everything."

Something stirred in the valley below, and then fire bearers, wild-haired and naked, crept out of the undergrowth, pausing by a river to crouch and drink. There were few of them—just a family, not a whole group like in Clay's village, and they had cubs with them, pudgy little things scurrying around their legs. They did not see the leopard god sitting up on the hill, watching them with interest.

The cubs ran into the water, splashing and shrieking with laughter and their parents laughed and dashed after them, teasing them in an incomprehensible language.

The leopard that Kwaee had once been tilted his head.

"It was the humans who showed the gods joy, which they had never seen and never experienced. In them they saw much they could not understand: relief, pity, comfort, anger, grief, elation, friendship. For how could a god understand any of these things when his power grants him everything? There can be no relief when there is no suffering, no pleasure when there is no discomfort, no joy when all desires are instantly satisfied. The gods saw that although nothing in all the world was barred to them, they could never be part of it. They saw that of all creatures in existence, humans experienced the fullest measure of life, and this they coveted dearly.

"We gods found it intolerable that any experience of the world we ruled be beyond us, that any knowledge remain forever outside our understanding. How could we rule the creatures of the world without knowing what they experienced? How could we judge them without knowing what they felt? And so the grand bargain was forged."

The hill on which Clay and Doto sat turned, the ground rotating around them dizzyingly. Doto tried to turn to follow the scene before them, but everything had changed. Now their hill sat near the churning waves of the sea—on seeing this, Clay's eyes widened and he clamped his arms more tightly around Doto. Below their hill, along the shoreline, was a great plain of sand and grasses, and filling it, an uncountable number of fire bearers. Doto had not imagined there to be so many in all the world, but he found himself staring across a veritable forest of unfurred brown skin and bobbing, black and grey-haired heads. The people were gathered in an enormous circle around one hill even higher than theirs.

Atop that hill stood the gods, not as Doto knew them, but in the form of giant beasts. There was Kwaee, and the huge crocodile Asubonten, and the hippopotamus Atekye. He could make out some of the animal gods, as well: Gyata, god of lions; Sohari of the ostriches; Aponkakan of the giraffes; Akadea of the eagles. And there were many, many gods he did not recognize at all, in the shapes of beasts he had never seen. They occupied the water as well, paddling shapes of creatures beyond imagination, with long arms like vines or wide mouths full of fangs or massive bodies longer than trees. Were these gods who no longer existed, or was the world that much wider and more full of strangeness than he had imagined? He pitied them, being so far from their temples and the safety and power of their domains.

Amidst the gods on the hill stood Mother Fam—a great, shifting mound of earth. She did not have the shape of a fire bearer, nor of any creature at all, unless, perhaps, a beetle for a moment, or a mushroom the next, or for a second or two an enormous tortoise. All shapes lived within her, none more truly her own than any other. She shambled down the hill on two legs, then six, then on a serpentine belly, until she stood before the fire bearers.

Among them, one elderly woman, shaking and bent with age, came forward. Mother Fam loomed over her, a hill with eyes one moment, then muddy feathers the next, and extended a tendril of mud. The old woman reached out one shaking hand and pressed it to the mud firmly.

"The gods agreed," the voice of Mother Fam boomed from all around them, "to share their power, a little from each, with the humans. In exchange, they would take some of the humans' vulnerability. They would become weaker."

"Well, that is idiotic," Doto muttered. "Why would they want to be weak? No god would make such a bargain!"

"Such quick and judgmental words you speak, Doto. But you accuse yourself, for have you not made this bargain twice for Clay? That is the bargain of love: to make yourself vulnerable so that you might feel joy." Mother Fam's voice hummed with gentle reproach, and Doto hunched his shoulders, ashamed at his words.

"It is a bargain every living god made—all but Wem, who has remained unchanging. The accord was forged and could not be unmade."

A powerful wind rose, whipping at the grass and sand and water. It moved in circles around the humans and the gods assembled there. The gods were speaking: in unison, they chanted the words: *Out, out. Into mortal blood and flesh, into the soul of humankind, into life and death, into spirit and body. Take what is mine. Take what is mine. Take what is mine.*

They chanted the four words over and over, and as they spoke them, the wind circled harder, lifting earth and water into the air, pulling the clouds into its vortex, until the sky was darkened. Doto gripped at Clay's shoulders, holding him close, half-fearing that the terrible wind and power might somehow carry them apart. It tore their crudely-fashioned pelts away, leaving them naked, holding each other.

Clay's eyes were wide with wonder, the gusts pulling tears from them, but he neither shook in Doto's embrace nor hid his face. His arm clasped tight around Doto's waist, but he leaned into the storm, shielding his eyes with his free arm. It was a storm like he had seen before: when Doto had healed his foot. And a similar one had risen at his resurrection. Had he been aware of that, as well, with his spirit wandering through the mysteries beyond death?

This storm was like that, but far, far larger and stronger. The roar of the wind grew so loud that Doto could hear nothing else, and the air so full of water and flying earth that he could see nothing either, nothing but the sudden jagged branches of lightning that struck all around them. And then, in the direction of the gods, there was light—at first yellow through the sand and rain, but then brightening to pale white, going so bright that Doto could not bear to look at it, and closed his eyes, but even then the light shone through. He dropped to his knees, clamping his fingers over his lids, but the brightness seared through those as well. All was light. It poured through him. It burned away every dark place inside him; it scoured away his resistance, his clarity of thought, and even the pain he felt at its intensity. There was nothing left of him but the brilliance.

And then he was huddled on the ground, face-down, panting, and the light and the storm were gone. As his vision slowly returned, Doto could again make out the shapes of the gods on the hill.

"The gods awoke from their magic," Mother Fam said, "And found that they had indeed, changed. They had become more like the humans they bargained with. Now the gods walked upright."

From amidst the gods, a leopard stood up, standing tall on two legs. It was Kwaee, as Doto had always known him, though without the brilliant crown of feathers that sprouted from his brow. And around him, other gods stood, shakily at first, testing out long, humanlike legs they had never used before, stretching out arms, hands, fingers, reaching toward the sky in their new shapes.

"Impossible," Doto breathed. "The fire bearers… they—they walk like we do. They stand like we do. We are not like *them!*"

"Every god is part human," Mother Fam's voice rang over them. "And every human contains divinity. From the gods they gained the ability to shape their world, to fashion earth and forest into spear and bow, the hides of animals to make clothing and drums and tents. From the sea they learned to ride across it. When we gave the humans part of ourselves, we gave them tools. We gave them stories. We gave them fire."

The hill rotated again, the world spinning around them, and as it turned, night folded over the sky. Stars glittered above them, and a sheltered valley opened below, with a small group of fire bearers lighting a great bonfire and gathering around. They shared food and chatter. They blew into wood to make a sound like birdsong and beat the Cry of the Dead from their drums. They sang songs to each other and danced about the flames.

"The humans had gained other powers from the gifts of the gods as well." Mother Fam's voice rained down on them from the stars. "Now they could speak to the gods and the world around them through prayer. They called to the gods using the gods' own power. How could we fail to hear our own voices? How could we resist our own will, even wielded by another? The humans prayed to us, and when those prayers were true, and resonated with our own nature, we could not fail to answer.

"They learned how to call our nature truly in our songs and our dances. They learned how to take and yield power to shape the world. They had become children of all of us. When they danced, the part of them that was Sarmu could give way. Sarmu could surrender his savanna. And then the part of them that was Kwaee could grow his forests."

The fire bearers danced and sang around the crackling bonfire, and as they did, vines and shoots sprouted from the savanna. Saplings sprung up, thickening into trees, stretching taller and taller, extending heavy limbs that unfolded into branches and twigs, that feathered with broadening leaves to soak up the starlight.

The forest spread throughout the valley and up the slopes until it covered the hill on which Clay and Doto sat. It rose around them. Doto breathed in with sudden shock as his power flowed through him again. Hunger and weariness left his body as his limbs grew fur and strength. Clay grew in his embrace, becoming taller and stronger. He tilted back his head and took a slow, happy breath as the magic filled him.

Doto wondered again at the power of Fam. Could she truly shift the world so easily? Could she grow back the forest that Ogya had burned, or fell it all to prairie at a whim? She had said every god had dominion in their own realm, and she could not defy that. But she had birthed the gods and their temples and the lands they ruled over. Her power, he supposed, and its limitations, were beyond his comprehension. He was glad, for now, just to have his divine form back—though it was apparently less divine than he had always supposed. He sought out Clay's tail with his own and let them twine around each other.

"And we called the humans many new names. We called them fire bearers. We called them god-kin. We called them the children of a thousand. We called them world dancers. And they grew stronger and more numerous than we ever thought possible. They reshaped the world in their images—and that of our own. We feared their new power.

"But now the humans knew us as well. They knew that they existed because we gave them life. They knew that the world was shaped by our fingers. They knew that both catastrophe and abundance were ours to wield. They learned that they would live for but a flurry of heartbeats and die, while we would go on forever, eternal and unchanging. Lost in the mysteries of day and night, wind and stone, they found truth in our voices. They jealously guarded every word we gave them. They could live their lives devoted to a single declaration from a god."

The sun rose like a bird taking to the sky. Kwaee strode to the edge of the trees, and fire bearers gathered around, prostrating themselves flat against the ground as Clay had done before each of the gods he'd met—though not, Doto recalled, Mother Fam. He'd run up to meet her, arms outstretched, with no thought of reverence. Not like these fire bearers pressing their faces into the soil. Even from here, Doto could hear their chants and songs of adoration, and as Kwaee stood before them, basking in their worship, feathers sprouted from his forehead—first only one, and then more, until a wide fan of red and blue plumage crowned his imperious brow.

"But that was a power even we had not understood. A single word could have a devastating impact on them."

Kwaee spread his arms, speaking. The fire bearers rose from their worship to listen, and then turned toward each other. They engaged in conversation that quickly became acrimonious. Men shouted and stamped their feet. Women scowled and clapped their hands together. Children cried. Then, without warning, one man, his face puffy with anger, struck another. A woman attacked him. Another woman drew a knife from her belt and stuck it into the first woman's throat. She screamed and fell, clutching her neck, and died. Another man struck the attacking woman with a large club, knocking her down, and then someone thrust a spear through his side. Within moments, they were all killing each other.

Doto recoiled in horror at the senseless violence—what creatures killed each other over a sentence? But Clay, he noticed, was watching with a cool and detached fascination, his head tilted and ears perked as though to catch the sound better.

It was not long before all the humans were dead—all but one: a man who, stained with blood, held up the viscera of his kindred to Kwaee as though in offering, grinning with fanatical ecstasy. And Kwaee bowed his head and glided back into the darkness beneath the trees.

Mother Fam's voice cracked with an ancient grief. "We learned to stay hidden from the world of the god-kin, to show ourselves only in disguise, if at all. But the bargain we struck with the humans was more terrible than any of us could have known. We had learned to feel the emotions we craved: relief, comfort, joy, and even love. But with them came feelings more difficult to accept: suffering, grief, craving, fury, and fear. A mortal child, helpless in a dispassionate world, must learn to tolerate and accept these feelings. But a god, all-powerful in his domain, does not.

"We all felt the pangs of humanity in different ways. Sarmu, even as a little god of fields and meadows, became indolent and passive, refusing to wield his power even to help himself." In the distance, a shadow rose against the horizon: the forbidding silhouette of Ogya-Bepow, the volcano that Doto and Clay knew only too well.

Then, far out over the horizon, a great, dark figure stood up against the sky, a storm swirling over its triangular head, lightning forking around it, the brief illumination revealing a monstrous visage. "The goddess Mpo learned wrath, and she wielded it against all in her path with terrible cruelty." The figure raised both her arms and slammed them downward. The ground shook beneath Doto's paws, and Clay trembled at the sight.

"And Doto, you know your father's weakness, I'm certain."

Doto frowned. His mind was already whirling with incredulity at the tale Mother Fam had told them, but the suggestion that his father was fallible? That was not difficult to accept at all—he found himself having difficulty choosing only one flaw—Kwaee's inability to accept loss? His stubbornness? His cruelty? His single-minded—

"His pride," Clay said. "I know he hurts over losing… losing your mother, Doto, but it's his pride that keeps him from letting anything go. It makes him arrogant and fragile."

"Just so," Mother Fam's voice thrummed with sad agreement. "But it was Ogya who was changed the most. The mortal spirit afflicted him with a terrible hunger. It is like a deep wound in his belly, never satisfied, always propelling him to consume more. It has made him a glutton—for land, for the taste of the world incinerating on his tongue, and for power. Only the limitation of a god's power slows him down. It forces him to chew up only what the steady spread of fire and the scorch of burning winds can grant him. But this merely hinders, not halts him. He devours the world and will not stop."

As she spoke, the spectre of an enormous, fiery scorpion rose over the hills to the north. Ogya swept his titan pincers and seared countless trees from the ground. He leaned down his massive, segmented body and gobbled up the grassland with clicking mandibles. An inferno spread out from him in all directions, swallowing up trees and shrubs in red fire. Black smoke blotted out the sun.

"Doto," Clay said in rising panic. "Doto, the fire is coming toward us. We have to run!"

Doto put his arms around Clay and held him close to his chest. "It's all right. The fire isn't real. Mother Fam would not hurt us."

But the heat of the fire felt real enough. It roared toward him in a blazing wind, faster than any flames could move. The tips of the inferno rose higher than the forest, so high they would scorch the clouds, and as the conflagration rushed up to envelop him, he could not fight his panic—he gripped Clay tightly and dropped to a crouch, holding both their heads down as the fire engulfed them both. Beneath his knees, the earth collapsed and turned gritty. The heat was all about them.

And then they were in their fire bearer forms again, their itchy pelts wrapped around them. The heat was gone, but so were the acuteness of his senses and the strength of his power. He looked up and gasped. The forest had vanished. The trees. The bushes. The grass. Nothing about them lived. The lakes and rivers they had seen below them had evaporated into nothingness. There was only sand and stones now, hills of endless desert.

"The Firelands." Clay's voice was a horrified whisper.

Their hill turned again beneath them, and as it turned, night fell like a pelt of darkness being pulled across the sky. Doto blinked, his feeble fire bearer eyes all but useless. He stared upward until the brightness of the stars returned—only the smell of the air had changed. It was no longer fresh and arboreal, but deep and wet and earthy. And the stars weren't stars at all; they were countless, tiny glowing frogs clinging to the wet stone of cavern walls.

With the sound of grinding stone, the hill on which Doto stood with Clay lowered and settled back into the floor. Amid the lights of the frogs on the wall a silhouette appeared—that of a large, human-shaped woman. She stepped forward and sat down before Clay and Doto. Even seated, she towered over them. Her lower half merged with the cavern floor, indistinct mounds of earth and rock roughly in the shape of legs. She rested plump hands on boulder knees.

"Yes, that was the birth of the Firelands. Not all at once, as I showed you, but over time. Ever since the grand bargain, hunger has gnawed relentlessly at Ogya. As he has gnawed relentlessly at my creation, never satisfied, always growing and extending his reach. Without the help of the fire bearers, the expansion of his domain is slow but steady. When they help, his fire spreads wildly, for they can send his flames beyond the edges of his natural domain."

"Yes, but we know all this already," Doto said. "Not… not the parts where you claimed that all the gods are… corrupted by human weakness, but we know of Ogya's hunger and his desire to spread. We've been fighting him all this time. He demanded me as a meal from Kwaee in exchange for a thousand years of peace."

"And Kwaee refused?" Genuine surprise rung in Mother Fam's voice. When Doto nodded, she smiled, and at the sight of it, a wave of trust and absolute happiness washed through him again. "Then he has changed after all. I had not thought it possible. A thousand years of peace would have been an enormous temptation. There would have been time. He could have prepared, set traps for Ogya, built his defenses. He could have wooed the humans to his side, set them to fighting Ogya. My child. My boy has grown."

"Don't get too excited," Doto advised her. "He's not changed that much."

"He threw me across about half the forest," Clay said solemnly.

"Not that much of it," Doto said.

"It *felt* like that much of it."

Mother Fam chuckled, and the echoes of her voice throughout the cavern sounded as though there were a score or more of her, the ground itself bubbling with fondness. "I know my own children. The Kwaee I made had little feeling for anything other than himself. He loved your mother, though, Doto. She called to what was human in him. Just as Clay does with you."

She sighed. "But it is fortunate for us that he did not take that bargain. A thousand years of restraint from Ogya might give us time, but with the power he would have consumed from you, Doto, he could be unstoppable. With the power of a forest god, even a small one, he might be able move through Kwaee's domain without detection, without the forest even seeing him as a threat."

When Mother Fam had suggested that his father might have changed, Doto had felt a moment of hope. Kwaee was still surly and obstinate, but he had been different lately. His edges had been softer. And Doto had hoped, fervently, that his father's casual cruelty might be at an end. That they might even be friendly with each other. Sometimes, when his thoughts were wandering, they would settle on that moment, when Ogya had demanded him as sacrifice—when Doto and Clay had both stood before Kwaee, utterly at his mercy, prepared to be served as a peace offering to an insatiable fire god… and then Kwaee, his father, god of the forest, had stood up to the demon god Ogya, and said no. But now Mother Fam's words crushed all those hopes.

"Then that explains it," Doto said. "That's why he said no. Not to protect me, but because it would have made Ogya more powerful."

Mother Fam laughed abruptly at that, rolling back into the stone, the whole cavern shaking with peals of mirth. "Oh, Doto. You have nothing to fear. Your father loves you, and here is my proof. Ever since the grand bargain, Kwaee has been a creature of passion. He lusts, he covets, he fears. Even before the bargain, he was never a strategist. He does not think five steps ahead as Ogya does—no, he feels and acts. When Ogya made his offer, Kwaee rejected it because he was thinking of what he felt most strongly. I was not there. I cannot tell you what he felt. But you know what he chose, dear Doto."

Doto let out a long sigh. Arguments rose to his tongue, but he could not give them voice. He believed her. She knew Kwaee better than anyone. And her voice was full of certainty and joy. Which meant Kwaee loved him. His father loved him. Of all the strange truths he had learned today, he folded up that one and placed it deep inside of himself, a seed of trust.

"But what of Ogya?" Clay asked. "We've seen what he means to do, and how terrible he is, and this… this incredible story you have told us explains how it happened. But you still haven't told us what to do. How do we stop Ogya from burning the world? How can we defeat him?"

Mother Fam's laughter faded, as did the smile from her face. Sadness weighted her eyes, the sparkle going from them, flattening them into dull mica. "Oh, dear Clay," she said. She reached out her arms to embrace him. "I'm so terribly sorry. But there is nothing you or anyone else can do to defeat Ogya. His power is too great, and his temple is unreachable. Even if you could find it, how would you destroy the endless fire at the heart of the world? To do so would kill the world itself. No, dear Clay, with this no one can help you. Ogya is too strong. He cannot be defeated. Not by me, not by Father Wem, and not by you. I'm so terribly sorry, you brave and kind little human. But your struggle is in vain."

# 19
# An Empty Man

Laughing Dog sat on his pallet and stared at nothing. People came to speak to him. His fire hunters sat before him and pleaded to know what had happened. Yellow Bug queried him endlessly, checking his eyes and mouth in vain for symptoms of a malady she did not recognize. She pulled at the loose skin that hung from his arms and midsection. He largely ignored her. He could not summon up the words to answer her questions or to explain what had happened to him. Villagers came by with gifts and food. His gaze went past them. He would not open his lips when people attempted to feed him.

He had not known he could feel this empty. He was not hungry—Ogya's cravings had left his body and he felt as though he never wished to eat again. Memories of what he had consumed through divine fire turned his stomach. The stink of char almost made him retch. And now he missed the hunger, a pang that reminded him he was alive. The power and bulk of Ogya was gone from his body now, and his flesh felt empty. His *bones* felt empty.

But worst was the space in his mind, the haunting, voiceless void. How long had Ogya been boasting, sneering, conspiring in his thoughts? How long had Laughing Dog had to fight to keep that domineering roar of flame from drowning out all his other thoughts? And now it was gone, the inside of his head hollow and dark. The loud voice was not all that was missing—only now, in their absence, could Laughing Dog sense that there had been other voices too. They had been quiet, whispering to him beneath the imperious roar of Ogya's commands and sneering.

Those quiet voices had been nudging him, manipulating him, stroking his vanity and guiding his thoughts. He had relied on them, leaned on them without even realizing they were there. The quiet voices had made him a murderer. They had whispered to him to kill Abram and Sarai by the oasis in the desert. They had turned him against his brothers. They had twisted his yearning to defend his people from the abuses of the gods into a lust for power and destruction. He thought that he would surely hate them if he could feel anything at all.

But Ogya's presence had been like a riverbed in his mind, the nudge of those quiet voices guiding the many droplets of his thoughts into a single stream, flowing in a direction. Without the riverbed, his thoughts drained away in a thousand directions, without focus. Without purpose.

And so he sat on his pallet and watched the days pass him by. He drank water when it was offered to him but ate nothing. He felt his growing hunger, but it was insignificant—nothing compared to the insatiable starvation of Ogya's presence. When people spoke to him, he forgot the beginnings of their sentences before they'd reached the end. Single words he could follow: sleep, fight, Ogya, fire, hungry, King. He knew all these and could nod yes or no to them. But more complicated concepts fell through the grasp of his mind like water through his fingers.

It was defiance that first reminded him how to control his own thoughts again. Wasp came to see him, his lean face pinched with worry. He crouched before Laughing Dog and made words about "food" and "survive" and "need you." And then he and two other fire hunters held Laughing Dog down and forced the lip of a gourd between his teeth, pouring what tasted like ogbono soup down his throat. He choked and coughed, spraying them with the soup, but ended up drinking a good portion of it before they allowed him up and let him be.

His stomach felt full and empty at the same time. The heaviness of the soup was painful, as though the sides of his stomach had stuck together and now were peeling apart. He resented them for doing this to him against his will, and he held their names in his mind, reminding himself over and over of what they had done. Wasp, it had been. Wasp, his council member, with two other fire hunters: Mother's Tree and Caterpillar. Wasp, Mother's Tree, Caterpillar.

Wasp was his council member, he recalled. His most trusted now that Half Moon was dead. Ants. The ants had eaten Half Moon. Which left Wasp in charge. Wasp, Mother's Tree, Caterpillar. They'd made him eat when he didn't want to. They'd made him. Why would they do that?

Survival. They wanted him to survive. He was King. They were fighting the gods. Fighting Kwaee. They'd had Ogya's help before. Ogya was gone. He clutched at his temples, exhausted at the work required to assemble concepts into thoughts, thoughts into understanding. He fell back and went to sleep. His dreams were full of distant screaming as he sat in a void of endless blackness. When he woke, he managed a word— "water" —but could not follow the series of excited questions and chatter that surrounded him after he'd drunk.

The days passed, and he gradually learned to guide and direct his own thoughts again without the ever-present influence of Ogya. Soon he was able to have short conversations with his fire hunters.

—Who had done this to him? Ogya.

—Why would Ogya do this? The gods are unjust. And evil.

—What would they do now? Keep burning. Fight the gods.

—Would the power return to him? No. He didn't think so.

Whenever they asked him about this last point, disappointment showed on their faces. They drew aside for hushed, sober conversations with each other. All of them looked to Wasp for guidance and leadership. Laughing Dog might still be their King in name, but no one looked at a King with such pitying expressions, with grimacing mouths and slow shakes of their heads.

It was Ogya who had made him King, and Ogya had taken it away. He had taken everything away. When his hunters and the healer left him alone, he stood in his tent and held up his arms. The skin hung from them like pelts over poles, his flesh too large for his frame. He looked like an unwell, elderly man. No one came to visit him in the evenings. No one saw him huddle down in the heap of his own skin and weep. But he comforted himself with the certainty that what he had done was right. He suffered, but he and everyone around him was safer with Ogya's power gone from him for good. Nothing could change his mind about that.

~

He woke one morning and was tired of lying about his tent. Yellow Bug's patient advice be damned—if he was to recover, he needed to be moving about, strengthening his limbs and his mind again. His thoughts were no longer spread thin and unfocused, but he needed a task. And he needed to show his people he could be their King again. He sorted through his pelts and robes, looking for something not ostentatious, but that would conceal as much as possible the extent of his wasting. He settled on a white, hooded robe his father had bought from an eastern trader, meant for shielding one's head during travel across the Firelands, where the sun burnt too hot for exposed skin.

The village was quiet. His legs shook as he looked around—he felt at once both lighter and heavier than before. He had lost a great deal of weight, but much of that was powerful muscle. Holding his body upright was exhausting. But he could not let his people see him frail. He pulled his shoulders back and tried to keep his feet from dragging as he walked.

None of his fire hunters were around. Perhaps they were all back at the burn site, carrying out his work? But no, the sky was clear. Even upwind, he should be able to see the haze of smoke in the air. The morning sun should glare through it, red and murky. So, they were not burning, then, and had not done so for days, just as he had feared. But where were they, then?

He roamed the village, seeking out his hunters. He tried to avoid the gaze of the people, lowering his hooded head and steering away from groups, but several sought him out. It was good to see him up and walking, they said. They hoped he was doing well. Some clasped his hand warmly and sought out his gaze, leaning down to meet his eyes. He did not know what they wanted from him.

He found his fire hunters eventually—three of them, anyhow. They were gathered with others in the circle of council—*his* council—in the shade of a large tree a little distance outside the village, sitting and, he supposed, discussing problems and making decisions. Without him. Without their King. Fury stilled him for a moment. He knew for certain where the decision to stop the burn had come from.

They were weak, every one of them. Traitors. They had turned against him the moment he'd fallen ill. But he could hardly charge into the middle of the circle and demand their obedience. They knew that whatever power he'd had was gone, and with it, his sway over the people. Strange, how his blood still burned, how quickly his fury rose. How, in relearning how to focus his thoughts, he so readily focused them down the paths Ogya had seared into his mind. That was not him. That was not Laughing Dog. That was the trick. He needed to remind himself of that, of who he was. He let his anger go.

Then he walked up to the circle, keeping his head lowered, and took a seat on a log.

"King Laughing Dog," said one of the elders, recognizing him. "We didn't expect to see you back so soon."

He pushed back the hood of his robe. "No, it seems you did not." He let his gaze travel across the circle.

An apologetic smile creased White Sand's round face. "King Laughing Dog, it was thought that I should join the council to replace Half Moon—just until you were feeling better and could appoint your own replacement."

"I see." He let his gaze travel to Caterpillar, who looked embarrassed. And sweaty.

Caterpillar rubbed at his head and cheeks with both hands. "I, ah… I ah…"

"Caterpillar was sitting in for you," Wasp volunteered. "Just until you returned."

"Well. I'm back now, aren't I?" Laughing Dog met Caterpillar's gaze, letting his stare linger long enough that the man began to rise, abashed, and then said, "No, no, don't get up. Council members, I chose all of these fire hunters myself. It does me honor to know that you included them on vital decisions while I was… unable to weigh in."

"You weren't saying nothing, King Laughing Dog," Caterpillar blurted out. "And we didn't know if you were gonna be normal again or not."

The entire council circle squirmed. Wasp stared with wild eyes at the ground, clearly wishing he were anywhere else.

"Of course not," Laughing Dog said, allowing Caterpillar a gentle smile. "I know that important matters don't stop happening just because a King is unwell. I'm pleased you all have been looking out for our people. It gladdens me to know that my trust in all of you has been so well placed."

People around the circle visibly relaxed. "We're grateful to hear you say that, King Laughing Dog. Of course, as you say, we've only been trying to take care of the things that need it."

He let his smile turn downright benevolent. "Of course. And you have my thanks. All of you." After the chorus of you're-welcomes and well-wishing had died down, he asked, "So where are the rest of my fire hunters, then? Attending the burn?"

Glances traveled between the council members like sparrows flitting back and forth between tree branches. "Er, they're actually out hunting right now, King Laughing Dog. The six that are to spare."

"So no one is burning the forest right now. Well—"

"We—didn't know where to burn," White Sand stammered. "When you were there, we had your… special help. But without it—"

*You burn the forest*, Laughing Dog wanted to snap. *How difficult is that?* But this was why they needed him. To provide direction. Motivation. "I understand." He considered his shaky, weakened legs. "It might be a few days until I can make it out there myself, but I can at least tell you where to—"

Wasp cut in. "We were thinking, King Laughing Dog, that perhaps this would be a good time to… take a break."

"A break?" He forgot his composure, spluttering the words. "A *break?* Tell me, has Kwaee taken a break from murdering our people?"

"Well, no one's died since Half Moon was eaten by the ants." Another council member, her expression apologetic. "Maybe if we stopped now and offered prayers to Lord Kwaee, he would forgive us."

"Forgive us? You would have us beg forgiveness after, unprovoked, he set the forest against us and killed our brethren? How many have died now because of his cruelty? Would you have me forget my father? My brother? Your own friends and family?"

White Sand raised his hands as if in supplication. "What other choice do we have? This dream of burning the whole forest—it's madness. The forest is endless, and we are only a few. With the help of another god, perhaps we could have done it, but all on our own? It's impossible. Even if we could burn it all, then what? Are we to sit among the ashes and beat our chests at our victory?" He meekly looked about the council. "I don't think any of us understand anymore what we are trying to achieve." Nods moved around the circle.

"And we are doing well enough, are we not? We have water. Food is scarce, but we can find it. There have been no more animal attacks from the trees. Maybe Lord Kwaee heard us. Maybe we could live in peace. And have clean air again. Clean water."

"And that is worth the price of your safety?" Laughing Dog snapped. "Would you live in fear? Fear that another of us will be eaten in the night, or beaten by monsters? That one of our children will wander too close to the forest and be torn apart by the very trees?"

"We live with it anyway," Wasp interjected. "We fear all those things now, but also we fear Ogya and his flames. The smoke chokes us and keeps game away. The flames took Broken Stump and now you are shrunk and weakened. We thought we had lost you as well. It is time to accept the truth, Laughing Dog. We are only people. We cannot fight gods. There are forces in the world more powerful than us, and we can't destroy them all. Would you wage war on famine next? On storms? These are things we must acknowledge and live with. Unless you can tell us how, specifically, we might prevail. There is no point in us wasting valuable time on burning a little bit more of the forest every day, when we might spend it hunting, rebuilding the village, or finding our lost people. My King," he added, as though in afterthought.

His equivocations and rationalizations were, at first, infuriating. Laughing Dog wanted to roar and rage at him, to accuse him of treason, to burn the traitorous thoughts out of his head. But that was the riverbed again. He tried to remember his old self, before he'd been exiled into the wilderness. He'd been irreverent and willful, certainly, but not this full of rage. It was good that Ogya was gone. A relief, surely.

And the more he considered Wasp's words, the more sense they made. He had started—so long ago now, it seemed—just wanting to free his people from the absurd rules and rituals that they labored under to serve the gods. Where had it turned into a plan to burn the entire forest? Had that been his plan at all? Or was it entirely the influence of Ogya in his mind? Now free of Ogya's whispers, he could not recall, nor even see the sense of it. And if he could not see it, how could his people? How could he convince them? Why should he?

He realized that everyone was staring at him, waiting for his response, some with folded arms and stubborn expressions, others anxious.

"We could—we could live well enough, King Laughing Dog," White Sand ventured. "And we wouldn't have to stop forever. Just long enough to see if perhaps Kwaee will not attack us anymore. And there has been nothing for a while. Even your brother has not…" He broke off, looking abruptly alarmed. Several council members winced.

"My brother? What about him?" Laughing Dog demanded. "Which brother?" The council members looked at each other. White Sand bit down hard on his lip. "Well? Speak up! Or am I truly no longer your King?"

"Well, it's just that he hasn't shown up lately."

What madness was this? "My brothers are dead."

Wasp gave a sigh of resignation. "Yes, my King. Perhaps you were… distracted, but… a little while after the death of Great Ram and the attack on the village, something that looked like Clay came out of the forest, wishing to talk to us. We didn't know whether it was a ghost, or a demon, or some trick of Kwaee. We… killed it and burned the body. But it came back, over and over. We must have killed it twenty times before it finally stopped coming."

"And no one told me? No one thought to inform your King that the ghost of his brother was coming out of the forest?"

"But we did tell you, King Laughing Dog. Do you not remember? It made you so angry."

Images teased the edges of his memories. The figure of Clay, moving with eerie agility, striding toward their village from the edge of the forest. But he hadn't truly seen it, had he? Hadn't it been simply another dark dream from Ogya?

"It wasn't right away we told you. None of us knew at first," Wasp said. "We were all at the burn camp, and your br—the ghost came to the main village. It was several days before we found out, and then you came to see it, and told us it was all just a trick of Kwaee and to burn it with fire every time we saw it. You—you watched us burn it." His face looked almost panicked. "You truly don't remember? Were we wrong to burn him?"

Laughing Dog tried to assemble memories from the splinters in his mind and could find nothing. He must have been far gone by then, huddled deep in the shelter of his psyche and barely watching through the distant openings of his eyes. What could the apparition have been? Some new trick of Kwaee's? But surely Ogya would have delighted in using that to taunt him. Why would Ogya have hidden this from him?

Prickles ran up his arms and legs. What if it had truly been Clay? What if, just as Laughing Dog had found a shard of Ogya in the desert, Clay had found a shard of Kwaee?

It was foolish to think. Impossible. And yet the chance that he might have been deceived so greatly twisted his stomach. He ducked his head to hide the tears welling in his eyes. "Please… please excuse me."

Ignoring their comments, he pushed himself to his feet and shuffled away from the council circle, walking aimlessly. It could not truly have been Clay. Impossible. It must have been a spirit of some kind. Or some sort of golem created by Kwaee to taunt him. He felt toyed with, buffeted about by divine forces beyond his comprehension, and all his anger and defiance rose to the surface of his mind again. Humans were nothing to the gods, were they? Just playthings to be tormented or milked of worship and praise.

And it had been Clay, hadn't it, who had been the first casualty of the forest? Long before Laughing Dog had met Ogya or declared war against Kwaee, a beast had come out of the forest and taken his brother. And for what? No, Laughing Dog had not started this war. It was Kwaee, the murderer. The tyrant.

He shuffled through the grass of the savanna, turning his memories over and over in his head. Those of his days with Ogya roaring in his mind were obscured by smoke, a remembered dream more than a true recollection, but there were truths that were undeniable. A beast had taken Clay into the forest. A beast had devoured their father. More had attacked their people and killed one of them, injuring others. Everyone had seen it. All these things the forest had done.

And then a thing resembling his brother had returned, but it had not been Clay. No, it could not have been. It was a creature disguised as him—cleverly, convincingly, perhaps, but not human. That had been the cruelest trick of the gods: using his own brother's face against him. He had wanted so badly to believe it was Clay. But Laughing Dog had not been deceived for long. And in the end, neither had Great Ram. They had executed the Clay-thing in front of a divine beast of the forest, a great leopard, an emissary of Kwaee. The forest had raged against them then, attacked the village with ferocity. They'd destroyed the forest's deception.

But apparently it had sent another, and another, all of them wearing Clay's face. Why? Surely Kwaee could not expect them to be deceived again. What use was there in creating more? Why so many times? And then what finally made the forest stop?

He found himself up against its borders, wandering dangerously close to the line of stones that marked safe territory from lethal. He wanted to flirt with it, to taunt the edges with his toes and see if the woods still writhed in hatred of humans. But the last time he'd done so, he'd nearly been dragged into the forest by vines and killed. Ogya's power that had saved him then, burning the grasping tendrils away and giving him a chance to escape. He dared not approach it.

The woods were placid. Birds sung from the trees. Patches of sunlight drifted across the ground. Of course it was peaceful now. It was not being burned. It had won. Kwaee had won.

"I hate you!" Laughing Dog's voice sounded small and feeble, even in the still of the day. There was no wind. "I hate you!" he shouted again. "You took everything from me! Everything! My father, my brothers, my people, my home!"

Silence, but for birdsong.

"Why should anyone follow you? What do you deserve of praise or worship? Everything my people did they did without you. They built lives and had families and left legacies. There were no gods helping them. There were no miracles. We clawed our food out of the ground. We fled famine. When lions came after our people, no gods smote them down." He struck at his chest. "We did. By our own strength, with spears that we constructed and bows we built. We did not pluck these things from the ground, fully formed. We labored for them. We worked our fingers bloody. No god guided our missiles through the air to strike our quarries. We had to build strength in our arms. We had to learn how to shoot, how to throw, how to protect ourselves from charging game, how to stalk, how to lie in ambush."

He clenched his fists at his sides. "Our lives are our own, Kwaee!" he shouted into the forest. "Kwaee and Sarmu and Fam and Wem! We built them ourselves! And what do we get in return for our worship of you? You send storms and fires and droughts. You plague us with disease and deadly serpents and monsters. You wound and murder us." He let his gaze stray back into the depths of the forest, half-fearing he would see the visage of Clay again, a trap wearing the face of family.

"And after you've done it… you mock us for it," he spat. "You mock us with our own faces." It was only through Ogya's guidance that he had seen through the deception at all. Without the fire god revealing the truth, the people might have had a demon in their midst the whole time without realizing it.

"And why my brother's face?" he shouted at the forest. "Why him, when you might have used any one of… us…"

All the thoughts fled from his head, and a prickle crawled over his scalp and down his arms and legs. Any one of them. Supposing the forest hadn't stopped with Clay? Supposing it had just… *learned.* If it could imitate the guise of Clay over and over, it could imitate anyone. Kwaee could have his demons among the people even now. He could have sent a beast into the village to capture someone just the way Clay had been taken. Then all he would need to do is send in an imitation, someone who could move among them, kill the people, influence and manipulate them, or simply replace them, one by one.

His stomach clenching, he tried to run back to the village, but his weakened body quickly left him gasping for breath and shaking. He checked the council circle first, but they no longer sat in discussion, so he made his way back to the village proper, pushing his way past the gate lookout.

He had to talk to Wasp. He strode through the village, clutching his robe about him, uneasily meeting the gazes of the people around him. Who among them might already be a demon? How far were they infiltrated? It could be any of them. Only Ogya had known.

He finally found Wasp talking with a couple leatherworkers and, still gasping for breath, pulled him aside, demanding to talk to him.

"What's this about?" Wasp asked with a frown, once Laughing Dog had him in a secluded spot where they wouldn't be overheard.

"Kwaee," Laughing Dog managed. "It's Kwaee. Listen to me, Wasp. If he can send in a demon that looks like *Clay*…" He trailed off, letting the implication speak for itself.

Wasp frowned, shaking his head.

"He could send in demons that look like any of us, Wasp. Any one of us."

Wasp's expression fell. "That's… that's a terrible thing to think, Laughing Dog. But—but surely we would notice."

"We barely noticed with Clay. Think about it. Kwaee knows that we can destroy him with force, so he's attempting subterfuge. He could have killed and replaced anyone by now."

His friend took a deep breath and rubbed at his face. "We can't talk about this with people, Laughing Dog. Everyone's fragile. It's too much."

"But—"

Wasp put a heavy hand on his shoulder. "I know. It's… almost too big to consider. But we should keep what we know to ourselves for now. Look out for people behaving suspiciously. We can't have anyone panicking. Turning against each other. That would only help Kwaee, wouldn't it?"

Laughing Dog peered at him. "I suppose… but listen, Wasp, we can figure this out, can't we? Think. Who was it who first brought up stopping the burn? Was it… was it one of the other council members? Or was it one of us? Was it White Sand?"

An uneven, nervous laugh escaped Wasp. "You can't—you can't suspect your own fire hunters."

"Why not? Wouldn't it be easiest for the forest to take or replace one of us? We spend much of our time nearly inside it, but far away from the rest of the people. Then there's the time we spend traveling between the burn and the village… and then White Sand. You saw at the council circle how strongly he spoke against continuing. It could be him. It could be. If we took him to the forest, we'd know, just like with Clay. Some part of him would change—"

"Or the forest might tear him apart, as it has so many others. No, my King. This line of thinking will only lead to chaos. We have to trust each other. We have to."

"But White Sand—"

"I was the one who recommended stopping the burn," Wasp said with sudden fierceness. "It was me, all right? This suspicion of yours is treacherous."

Laughing Dog stumbled a step backward. Could Wasp, too, be a demon sent by Kwaee? Laughing Dog searched his face for signs of unfamiliarity. The thing wearing Clay's face had looked exactly like Clay—though it had moved slightly inhumanly. It had possessed a smooth, agile grace and an easy self-confidence that Clay had never demonstrated. Something about it had seemed more… or less… than human. Its gaze had been different, too: steady, focused, remaining fixed even when its head turned or when it moved across the village. Laughing Dog had not noticed any of that in Wasp.

Wasp narrowed his eyes. "Now don't you go making out like I'm some demon, too. I can see you thinking it."

"You don't—you don't tell your King what to do," Laughing Dog stammered, backing away from him. "You haven't treated me with respect since I—" *Since I threw away Ogya's power*. "Since I recovered."

"You're still not entirely well. Why don't you come with me, and we'll go see Yellow Bug." Wasp reached for his shoulder again.

"I don't want to see Yellow Bug," Laughing Dog shouted, twisting away. "I want to save our people."

"Look, Laugh—my King, so do I. I swear it. But—"

Laughing Dog turned and stumbled away from him, knowing that he couldn't run, but sure Wasp—or the thing masquerading as Wasp—wouldn't dare attack him in front of everyone. He pushed his way past tents and out into the main area of the village. People sat at their workstations, honing knives, preparing food, carving wood.

"People! My people!" he shouted at them.

Heads turned toward him. He tried to track all of their movements, suddenly overwhelmed. Did any of them move with unnatural agility? As they'd turned, had their gaze locked on him with the inerrant attention of a predator? Who among them watched with hostility, cunning, or mistrust? Alarmed, he realized he could not tell. It might have been any of them. It might have been all. They all fixed him with expectant stares.

"I—I'm feeling much better," he managed. "And I have a new plan, something that will save all of us. I will… carve out the sickness from within us. Your King is well again. He will lead you faithfully."

He tried to ignore their stares, their chatter between each other, their questions, striding as quickly as he could past them and out of the village.

~

The pond was still there. It was less clogged with ash and muck now, its water clearer. There was no sign of the gem he'd pushed into it. What if someone else had come by and taken it? Supposing an enemy now had that power—that curse? An animal might even have happened by and swallowed it while drinking from the pool. The absurd image of an eland gallivanting across the savanna wielding summoned gouts of flame provided a moment of dark amusement.

All he would have to do was run his fingers through the mud to find out if it was still there. But surely this was a mistake. His time with Ogya in his head had been a nightmare, one in which he had lost more and more control. He dreaded the thought of having those voices in his head again, pushing his thoughts around, bellowing at him, torturing him… deceiving him. It had been terrible. A torment. Getting free had been a victory.

And now, free, he had nothing. No family, no friends, no power, no people he could trust. A village full of potential enemies. He would live the rest of his life never knowing who was real and who was a guised demon from the forest. He would he lie awake waiting for one of the beasts to devour him in the night as they had his father.

And then there was the flame. It had done something to him, hollowed him out, left empty spaces through which his raw thoughts echoed and rattled like seeds in a calabash. There was no hunger in him anymore at all except hunger for the flame, hunger for *hunger*. The surge of power at his fingertips, pouring out of him, devouring everything he pointed at, feeding him its essence, boiling water out of the trees, charring earth and blood, flooding his senses with it.

He knelt, letting his fingers trail across the surface of the water. Expelling Ogya from himself had been the most difficult thing he'd ever had to do. But if you wanted to survive in this world, you needed power, and power always came at a cost. He'd promised his people that they could use the power of the gods to save themselves. He'd sworn it. Was he a liar, or had he just grown weak? Had he deceived himself, all of them? Or was the power of men truly great enough to challenge the gods?

Every child plays with fire and gets burned. They do not learn never to go near fire again. They learn that fire must be handled with caution, with respect, but it is still a tool, a necessary one. And when was it more necessary than now, now when all the people were threatened by the forest god, and when any among them might be a deadly spy? When *all* of them might be?

Had Laughing Dog been frightened before, when he had expelled Ogya from his body? Of course, he had been terrified, but then, he hadn't known he could break free of the god. He hadn't been sure he had control. Now he knew for certain, painful or not, that he could. Either this was defeat, here and now, or it was not. He had rid himself of Ogya once. He could do it again. And these were desperate, dangerous times.

Closing his eyes, he plunged both hands into the pond, raking his fingers across the muddy bottom. At first, he found nothing but mud. Then something hard—a stone. Something stabbed at his finger—a bit of thornwood. He dug through the mud, churning up the surface of the water, going deeper and deeper, crawling into the pond, and still he could not find it. Gone. The gem was gone, he thought to himself with a sense of relief. Something hard and pointed jabbed at his knee.

He felt for it, and his fingers closed around the diamond. He held it up in the sunlight, rising to his feet and waiting for it to sink into his flesh, waiting for the voice of Ogya to mock him once again, to hiss and crackle in his thoughts, to punish him or suffuse his body with power. But nothing happened.

Maybe the water had somehow quenched Ogya—he dried the gem and his hand with his hair. Nothing.

"Ogya?" he said aloud. He waited. The wind rustled around his ears. Cicadas sawed their high-pitched songs from the trees. He listened for the crackle of fire, the hiss of flame.

"So," the voice from everywhere said. "You finally see how much you need me. I have watched you, Laughing Dog. I knew you would not take long."

"Yes. I cannot do this without you. I will take you back… into my body. Into my mind."

"Will you, now?" Ogya chuckled. "But, frail little human king, I will not take you."

Laughing Dog had expected this response. He knew Ogya would be furious about being rejected and expelled. "Then how will you continue your war against Kwaee? How will you consume the forest? You need me, Ogya."

"Do I." The voice did not sound convinced. "Toss this tiny fraction of my power, this mote of my being, back into the water if you will. You simple fool. Do you think you are the only one I can possess, control? Someone else will find it. And if not, I can make a thousand gems more. I can litter the Firelands with them. I will imbue uncountable little kings with sparks of my eternal fire and they will raze the forest for me."

"Then why aren't you doing that already? That does sound like a better plan. You're right. You don't need me. Except I see a lot of forest growing and spreading in the rains and nobody out there stopping it."

Silence.

"So I can let you wait in that pond while you summon your army of fire bearers, however long that takes. Or we can work together to finally defeat Kwaee."

"NO." The voice became a roar, so loud that Laughing Dog fell to his knees. He dropped the gem, cupping his hands over his ringing ears. Surely someone from the village would have heard such a bellow, like thunder, like… But as soon as he let go of the gem, the roar ceased as though it had never been. He could not let Ogya go again. Clumsily, he fumbled in the sand for the gemstone.

"How dare you, *pataku*? You, work with me? We are not allies. We are not equals. I am a divine and immortal god. I am the belly of the world, the scorch of the sun, the warmth in your bones. Without me, your bodies falter. Your life winks out like an extinguished flame. Without my heat, the world turns to white and biting stone where none may live and nothing can grow. I have culled humankind before for its insolence. I can do so again.

"You are useful to me, as a knife is useful to you. But a tool with a will of its own is unreliable. If I take you up again, I will not assist you. I will wield you. Your body and will must be mine. There will be no further arguments about tactics, no more sparing the feelings of your fellow humans. They will serve the god Ogya or suffer his wrath. And in exchange, I will allow you to taste my glory."

Laughing Dog waited, silently, letting the fire god simmer.

"Well?" Ogya finally demanded.

"I don't accept your terms. Humans will not be slaves to the gods. The only reason we fight is to be free of your tyranny. Burn us if you must. Abandon us if you wish. As bad as things may be now, I will not throw off the tyranny of one god only to accept that of another. If that's unacceptable to you, then go off and find one of those other kings you talked about." Now the thrill of his own boldness raced through his veins, the thrill of the hunt, the rush of a daring leap he wasn't quite certain he could land. "If you want my help, this time, you must agree: I will be in control. You will lend your power to me whenever I wish. You will not appear in front of my people without my approval. You will be silent when I need to think. You may be a god, but the time of the gods is ending. Men will be in control of their own fates now."

He half-flinched in anticipation of Ogya's rage. And indeed, a roar of fury bellowed through his mind. The diamond in his hand blazed with orange fire, then blue, then white, so bright he could not stand to look at it. But there was no pain. His flesh did not burn.

Ogya roared curses, screamed at him, threatened to murder all his people in one final blaze of fury. In response, Laughing Dog lowered his hand and let the gem hiss and fizz under the surface of the pond. Great bubbles formed on the surface and burst in sulfurous gasps. He waited patiently until the blaze of light dwindled and the roaring stopped. It was good to feel in control again.

"Well?" he said finally.

"You are an insolent whelp, *pataku*. You make demands no mortal should ever make of a god. It is an offense to all of us, to earth and sky."

"The world is changing."

Ogya's voice crackled. "Perhaps it is," he admitted. "Perhaps we have gone on as we have done for too long."

"Then work *with* me. Let us help each other. It can be a way forward for gods and men."

Another long, sizzling silence. Ogya sounded reluctant when he spoke again. "My power at your bidding would consume you. Before now I have only wielded it through you, channeling it through your fingertips, letting you taste it but not own it. If it is truly to be yours, to wield as you wish, you would need to admit it into your mind as well as your flesh. It would be too much for you. You would lose yourself."

"I am stronger than you think," Laughing Dog said. "All humans are stronger than the gods think."

"Then… I agree," Ogya said. "I will grant you my power. Tell me that you accept it, and take it deep within you. Not within your hand or your arm, but into your mind. It will be yours to control. Do you accept?"

Laughing Dog squeezed his eyes closed, his mind dancing over the risks. Supposing Ogya was right, and the power was too much for his mortal mind? What if it burned him from the inside out? What if he lost himself? What if Ogya changed his mind and decided to fight him from the inside again? That, at least, was less concerning, for he had already shown that he could expel the fire god if he became too feisty. And amid all the whirling admonitions and fears in the darkness of his mind, one point was clear and bright and undeniable: it was Kwaee who had taken everything from him: his father, his brothers, his people, his village, his bride, his birthright. Because of Kwaee, he was nothing. And Kwaee deserved to pay. And if Laughing Dog truly wished to make that happen, if the forest god were to be dispatched and the People of the Savanna raised on high, he would need power. Oh, that power. The mad joy of consuming everything, of tasting everything, of having the world break before him. The gods would tremble before humankind.

He squeezed the gem so tightly the edges cut into his palm. "I accept." He relaxed, opening his mind to accept Ogya's divine gift.

A scorching heat enveloped his hand as the diamond within it melted into his skin. He was screaming. The fire traveled up his arm and into his head. It boiled behind his eyes; it lit up rivers and channels throughout his mind. He could see nothing, could not even raise his eyelids. Insects of searing flame skittered across the inside of his skull, pulling threads of blazing oil around his mind. He tried to clutch at his head but could not find his arms—the sensations from them were distant now. He could hear his screaming still, but it was far away, coming from outside his head rather than in it. And then his mouth closed of its own and the screaming stopped.

The voice was back in his head now, drowning out his own thoughts, roaring with malicious laughter. *Fool. Pitiful little fool. I lied.*

Laughing Dog had made a terrible mistake. Ogya's avarice roared through his mind. He would destroy the forest. He would destroy Kwaee. And in his ambitions, the entire world was food. He sank fiery mandibles into stone and gorged on it, devoured it, and regurgitated it again, chewing his way across a dead and smoke-choked world. Nothing would remain.

But Laughing Dog could do nothing. He could feel his skin, feel the muscles move around him, but his mind was disconnected. He could not even try to move. He could not remember how, could not recall how one went from wishing to outstretch an arm to actually lifting it. His eyes opened, but once again the world was remote, as though viewed from a great height or from within a darkened tent.

"Perfect." It was his voice but not his tone, not his thoughts.

And the threads of flame around his mind cinched tighter and tighter, burning him endlessly, squeezing him into a smaller and smaller space within his own skull. He searched within him for his safest, most immalleable thoughts: the rough touch of his father's hand on his shoulder; the taste of fried caterpillars; the sparkle of a full moon on the dunes; his mother's lullaby; the cool of the first rain on his face; Clay teaching him to bind his first spear. He took these memories of the things he loved and used them as barricades, surrounding himself them even as Ogya, roaring, attempted to beat down these walls with flaming fury. Ogya's blasts of fire could not penetrate them, though. Laughing Dog held onto them. They were all that was left of him. His only truths. He would not surrender them. The threads of fire cinched tight around the memory walls, trying to buckle them, crumple, them, but they held firm.

Now it would come. Ogya's punishment. The fire god would burn him from the inside. He would die in agony, but it would stop, for a while at least, the terrible god from destroying everything. He waited, expectantly, surrounded by his memories, his shields, for the final inferno.

It never came. Ogya ignored him.

Laughing Dog was trapped in his own mind. Ogya had his body and was King of the People of the Savanna. And he would devour them all.

# 20 What the Sea Demands

Cloud awoke to the sound of someone rapping at the door of the little building they'd placed her in. Wobbling, she managed to extricate herself from her odd sleeping surface—a bit of woven material stretched between two walls. It swung and pitched whenever she tried to climb out of it, which she could barely manage without having an accident. Besides which, it sagged dreadfully in the middle and left her stiff and aching in the mornings. She'd crawled out of it the first night of her stay and slept on the floor, but this seemed to appall and offend her hosts. So she'd resigned herself to discomfort in the interests of good relations.

Before she'd had a moment to clear the rheum from her eyes and collect her thoughts, the door opened and Petrel swept through it, today bedecked in brilliant garments of red and orange, blood and fire. "Elder Cloud," he said. "Please take this opportunity to eat well and cleanse yourself. The Matron has heard your petition and has elected to meet with you today. She would like to… show you her city."

Finally, Cloud thought in relief. This had been the third night she'd spent alone. The door to her domicile was always barred and, she suspected, guarded. Meals of bland, spice-less fish and vegetables had been delivered to her door regularly, but she had not been allowed to leave since arriving, not even to make water. This function was apparently done in a pot that was emptied by the attendants who delivered her food and fresh clothing every day. She found it peculiar that people in a place so fixated on cleanliness made a habit of making waste indoors, and not outside the city like a civilized people. And that they apparently had such an abundance of clothes that they could afford a clean change of them every day, though she supposed all the water they had available might have something to do with that.

Each day, Basket and Bad Water had been brought to her from housing similar to her own. Neither had seen the rumored Matron or even anyone else who could speak their language, other than Petrel. They were not prisoners, he had assured them, and could leave the city at any time, but would not be granted readmittance, and so they had little choice but to remain shut away in their buildings in hopes that they would have a chance to speak to the Matron or to the council of elders.

But none of the three had been thriving, shut up in the stuffy air of the city, with no glimpse of the sky beyond the slivers gleaming through the narrow windows. No chance to visit with other people. No satisfactory sleep or palatable food or daily exercise. One more day, she'd promised them. Then we'll tell them either we share this vital information with their leader or we will go. It did no one any good for them to sit around waiting endlessly while their home burned. How could this Matron be so busy that she could not afford a brief audience with a visiting elder? It was bad hospitality, they'd agreed, and reflected poorly on the Boganans.

Privately, though, Cloud knew they had few other places they could turn. Bogana was the only permanent settlement anyone knew of that was close enough. To be sure, there were other peoples in the savanna, but they were migratory and impossible to find, and the only other known city was far to the northeast and required months—perhaps years—of travel, especially if you didn't want to risk traversing the lethal Firelands. And they had traveled so far already, far from their village, across the savanna, through the Stone Wastes, and down the coast, all to find some hope, some answer of what to do about their misled people, only to end up here, held in civil hostage by a foreign power.

But the difficult choice of what to do next had at last been removed: the Matron would see them. Cloud thanked Petrel, dressed, and cleaned herself with the basin of water that had been provided every morning. She even ran her fingers through her hair, pulling out the tangles and snags. She liked the way it had felt since the bath—lighter and airier, floating around her head like it had when she was young.

Petrel nodded approvingly at her ablutions. "It is good that you so quickly adopt the true ways. Not all plainsfolk show such… willingness to learn."

"I don't know how necessary all this washing is. Where we live, water can be hard to get. Better to use it for drinking and cooking. What use is it to wash the dirt from your shoulders in the morning when it will have returned by nightfall?"

Petrel's mouth stretched in a smile that the rest of his face seemed unaware of. "But you are a healer, are you not? You must know that cleanliness prevents disease."

Cloud knew of the importance of washing out a cut or burn before treating it, but she had never heard of regular immersion warding off illness. She wondered whether it was true or simply another expression of the Boganans' peculiar obsession. "I remember the plagues of your city from long ago," she answered, guarded. "You must have had to learn many techniques to prevent such a terror from returning. The People of the Savanna, happily, have never been similarly afflicted."

Petrel smiled more genuinely now and spread his hands wide. "Ah, but that is true, forgive me. I had forgotten that you were once a child of our city. Perhaps that is why you take so favorably to our rules."

"Or perhaps," Cloud said in an even tone, "it is because the People of the Savanna know how to be good guests and to answer hospitality with courtesy."

"Ah, yes. Good guests. Yes, you have been that. Very good guests, indeed." He seemed to find this sentiment funny. "Very well. If you are prepared, I will take you to see the Matron now."

"My fellow elders—when will they join us?"

"This meeting is for you alone. To confer with the Matron is a special honor that is not shown to many."

This statement made little sense to Cloud. How could a leader be effective if she didn't meet with her people? If she didn't live among them, work with them, take meals with them? What kind of a person was this Matron? She supposed she would soon find out. She only wished that, at the very least, Basket could join her. She did not care to be in this strange place alone, city of her birth or not.

Petrel led her out of the building and down the city streets. He didn't walk so much as waft, his brightly-colored robes fluttering like a flower caught in a breeze. He was much taller, and she had to hurry to keep up, ahead of the two guards who followed behind, matching their paces to each other, clicking the hafts of their spears on the stones of the street with every other step. Did they really need two severe-looking guards for a little old woman, Cloud wondered?

They did not pass through the crowded square she'd seen three days before, but the streets were busy enough, filled with people hurrying up and down, carrying bundles and baskets, leading animals, scolding children running back and forth. There were so many, they could have filled ten villages. How on earth did they feed them all? How could there be enough game, enough fruit and roots to sustain them? How did they have enough wood for spears and bows and the little stools she saw them sitting on in the entries to their homes? Where did their waste go? Who settled disputes and made sure the men were behaving? The task of managing all these affairs seemed impossible, and Cloud found herself developing a new respect for this Matron. Anyone who could keep this many people fed, healthy, and happy must be very clever and very hard-working.

They wound through the streets, passing buildings that were plainly homes, some rather old-looking and crumbling, others finely made and grand and daubed in bright colors, with cloth fluttering in openings in the walls. She realized that the little buildings they'd kept her and the others in were extremely plain and small—some of these appeared large enough to get lost in.

As they made their way through the streets, she saw other buildings that were not homes—from some of them, heat and the smell of cooking food drifted through the open doors, and people wandered in and out, many of them emerging with wrapped bundles. Cloud supposed that these must be work areas for food preparation or crafting. She couldn't smell the stink of butchery or leather tanning, however, and supposed that these tasks must be performed outside of the city.

Down several of the wider roads, she caught glimpses of the great, white building that dominated so much of Bogana, and she had initially assumed that the Matron would be found there, but none of the turns led them in that direction. Instead, they moved toward the western part of the city, and as they progressed, the jumbled rows of houses gave way to something more orderly. Crooked streets straightened. The buildings here were not round and squat, but square, lined up flush with each other, their openings spaced with an unnatural geometry that unsettled Cloud.

And everything was so *clean*. Even the stones of the street. Did they scrub them every night, on hands and knees? There was no litter, no detritus, nothing to let you know that people lived here. While the previous streets had been busy with people bustling about, paying little mind except to dart away when Cloud drew close, here people walked in orderly lines, their heads down, as though contemplating some abiding mystery, or filled with great sadness.

She saw few children here, and those behaved with the same seriousness and placidity as the adults. Any that dared run out into the street or raise their voices were swiftly chastened by their guardians. There was fear on their faces. Cloud knew it well—she had inspired it herself in enough unruly children—but these children did not misbehave. They had simply, for a moment, behaved like children.

"What is wrong? Excuse me, but what is happening here?" She tugged at Petrel's robe to get his attention. "Has someone died? Everyone looks so unhappy."

Petrel pulled away from her, distaste flashing across his features. "They are not unhappy. They are..." He frowned as he did when searching for a word in plainstongue. "They walk in awe of our Lady. They are respectful."

"You mean Mpo."

Petrel dipped his head.

"But why so somber? The gods ask us to celebrate. To sing and dance and shout their stories."

"I promise you, Bogana knows exactly how to worship its Lady. You and your people could learn something here." He gave her a smile that knew it was patient. She kept calm by imagining how it would look slapped around to the other side of his head.

The streets widened as they neared the city wall, the buildings larger and spaced farther apart. But here they were not painted the bright and appealing colors of the rest of the city; the stone was white and unblemished. The sky was cloudy, the day dim, but for a moment the clouds parted, and the midday sun shone through. Reflecting off the white stone, it was almost blinding, and Cloud shielded her eyes.

A man in black robes walking along the side of the street noticed her and approached her rapidly. She drew back, wary of this unexpected attention, but he only raised one arm high over his head with his fist clenched in imitation of the statue of Mpo and declared something forcefully in Boganan. He glanced at the two guards as if seeking approval and then walked off.

"What was that? What did he say?"

Petrel glanced back at her. "It is a religious phrase of ours. He said, 'You wash away the filth of the foreigners and drown the black fly.' "

Cloud sniffed. "Unkind. And does Lady Mpo now discourage hospitality?"

"He does not know how… courteous you have been. You must understand. Foreigners have a reputation in this city. Not all of them have been as tractable as you." She was still considering how to respond to that when he extended one arm toward a large and imposing-looking building. "The home of the Matron."

It was not a fancy building. There were no colors painted over it—not even the white of the other buildings in the city quarter. And the other homes she had seen had stone in their floors and in some parts of the walls, but they involved wood and clay and daubing in their construction. This was heavy, solid slabs of unpainted grey and white stone, squatting on the edge of the city with ponderous importance.

The cloud cover had thickened overhead, and even through the briny burn of the ocean air, Cloud smelled rain. It would be good to get indoors. She climbed the high steps to the Matron's house. Her hip bothered her greatly, and she wished she had been allowed to keep her walking stick. When she reached the top of the steps, one of the guards rapped the tip of his spear against a little wooden box, making a hollow knocking sound that was surprisingly loud. Effective, but Cloud wondered why people just didn't call out their arrival like at home.

A woman came to the door. She was nearly as short as Cloud and clad similarly, in plain white garments so spotless that Cloud felt the self-conscious urge to check her own for stains. She was lean, her black hair pulled straight back, so tightly that it must have been painful, tied behind her head where it spread out into a small poof. There were lines of grey in her hair, but she still appeared younger than Cloud by perhaps fifteen or twenty rains, her face lined more with severity than with age. But her gaze was steady, calm, and attentive, and she met Cloud's own readily.

"You must be Elder Cloud." Her voice was gentle and quiet, and she spoke the language of the People with only a mild accent. Though she did not reach out to clasp arms, she put her hand to her breast and made a shallow bow, a clear gesture of respect that surprised Cloud. "Please forgive the delay we have shown in welcoming you. It is inexcusable to have treated a respected visitor in such a way."

She lifted her chin to look at Petrel, who, Cloud noticed, appeared confused. "You may go now, Petrel."

He puffed out his cheeks. "But—but Matron, don't you think it would be best if—"

"Thank you, Petrel. I will be fine."

Still puffing, Petrel reluctantly allowed himself to be ushered from the room. Cloud was not sorry to see him go.

"There. Now we can speak freely, leader to leader." The Matron folded her hands and moved serenely back into the room. She was collected and gracious, but there was something in her eyes that unsettled Cloud—a spark of some passion she didn't recognize.

A measure of modesty would be wise here. "We may both be leaders, but it is hardly the same. I sit on a council with a fraction of our full people. You govern this city, full of more people than I knew the world even held."

The Matron made a dismissive sound. "Leading is leading. It's seeing past the emotion of the moment to what needs to be done to care for everyone. It requires patience, wisdom, and clarity. Let us agree that we can respect that in each other." She walked across the room, the scuff of her feet on the floor echoing in the empty space. "Please. Are you hungry? Thirsty?"

"No."

"Then let me show you where I go to think."

Cloud followed her into the room, marveling at the size of it. The place was spacious but just as austere as the outside, with few ornaments or decorations. There were stools and a bit of thick woven fabric on the floor, too thin to be a sleeping pallet. She could see no tools, no jewelry, no clothes—not even sentimental objects. Had her mother and father given her no gifts she wished to keep? Did she not trade items of value or beauty with friends? Perhaps all of these were in another room—openings in the walls led in all directions.

Privately, Cloud thought that despite the simplicity of the room, it was just as ostentatious as Petrel's robes. To have all this space in a city in which buildings and people were crammed up against each other to avoid being pushed over the cliffs into the sea, and to use it for nothing? In a way, it was worse than being showy, because it was extravagance masquerading as humility and asceticism.

The stone of the floor was cool and damp under Cloud's feet, and a humid wind moved continually through the building. When she followed the Matron into the next room, she understood why. The Matron's house was broken by an enormous, wide window, cut or shaped right through the western wall of the city. Through it was a view of the sea, looking angrier and more dangerous than it had in all their time along the coast. It churned and roiled far below the cliffs of the city, waves dark and frothing.

Cloud had seen storms roll across the savanna before—not the season of rains, which could last for many moons, but sudden, terrible, dark things, charging across the sky like angry rhinos, lightning jabbing at the ground, the spear-thrusts of a violent Father Wem. You had little warning. When the storm came, you did what you could to pull your tents flat so that the wind would not take them, you huddled down, and waited it out. It blew over you, pounded you to the ground with rain and tore at you with wind, and then in the same day, it was gone.

The storm growing outside the Matron's house was not one of these. It enveloped the whole sky. Monstrous. Dark as night. Patient. Thunderheads rolled over and over, showing white bellies and then black arms, flickering and glowing with captured lightning. Cloud dizzied at the sight of it. Outside the wall of the Matron's house, everything moved. There was no land. No stability. No safety.

"You've never seen the skies like this before," the Matron observed coolly.

Cloud found a wall and leaned against it, wishing again for the comforting support of her stick. "Are we safe?"

The Matron gave a laugh, not unfriendly. "We are never safe. But the city sees storms like this several times a year, and none of them have scrubbed us from these cliffs so far."

Uncomfortable, Cloud turned from the window.

The Matron moved to one side and pulled on a length of rope, and a heavy wooden plank lowered over the opening, cutting off the roar of the wind and waves. "Do forgive me. I forget how disorienting this sight can be. And the rain is growing heavy too. I keep my window open when I can to remind me of what is important."

Interesting, Cloud thought, that your window faces out to the sea and not toward the city and your people. "I try always to keep that in mind as well."

"But forgive me—you are a child of Bogana! Is it strange returning after so many years?"

"I remember only a little. The smell of cooking fish. The sky between the tops of buildings."

The Matron crossed her hands behind her back. "Much has changed in the seasons since you must have left. I suppose it was during the plague?"

"Yes."

"It was the foreigners who brought it. On their boats, carrying disease and pestilence from their homelands to infect and kill us. An irony. Our city grew and thrived from trade. It was the sailors who brought us cloth and the trick of weaving it. They showed us new methods of working wood and stone. But the very people who made us nearly destroyed us. The scourge that drove you from our home was not the first, and surely not the last. But since then we have learned to protect ourselves. Under the laws of Mpo, no disease has touched this city in more than twenty rains."

Cloud raised her brows. "Impressive."

"Sadly, this means we must treat our visitors in ways they are not accustomed to. We must clean them, check them for pestilence, and isolate them for a time to be sure that they carry nothing that might cause others harm."

"You might have saved us some worry and tension if someone had explained this to us when we arrived."

The Matron sagged slightly as though weary. "Petrel. He does not have a gentle way with guests. But he is one of the few in the city who speak your tongue."

"I notice you are quite comfortable with it."

"I try to learn most of the local languages. A man who can speak without your understanding has a power over you. I prefer not to let him keep it. It is not only contagion that men from foreign ports bring with them. They bring heresies—lies about false gods—and a lust for conquest. Bogana is a bastion. A rampart against the corruption of mankind. Here we fight to preserve our world and to serve the divine."

"I'm pleased to hear you say that." Cloud tried to put sincerity into the words, but she did not feel it, for a flinty certainty shone in the Matron's eyes. There was something manic about it, as though the Matron did not see this world at all, but through it to some private vision Cloud could not share. She felt as though she were back in the village talking to Laughing Dog, every word fraught with danger. She spoke carefully. "The People of the Savanna have faced a new heresy. There is a terrible peril that may threaten us all. This is why I have come to you."

"But you did not come alone," the Matron said in a thoughtful tone. "You brought all you could with you. But not your whole tribe. There are few among you of fighting age. Where are they, I wonder? Back at home? But why would they not accompany the elders of the tribe? Your infirm, your very young, they are with you. But no hunters. No warriors. Perhaps they wait now in hiding places outside of the city while you and your scouts learn of our strengths and defenses. Perhaps they seek the treasures of Bogana for themselves."

"We are not a warrior people."

"Starvation has a way of changing that. There have been droughts in the savanna, I am told."

"Your reports are accurate. Our people have chased the rains south for many seasons now, but we have found a home on the edge of the forest where the rain falls reliably. Every day, it seems, waiting for no season."

"And when did you first come to this place?" the Matron asked.

"The rainy season had come and gone just when we arrived there," Cloud answered. "And now has done so again."

"I see. Please. Come with me. Let us sit down. We are not so young as to use our stamina injudiciously, hm?" With a smile, the Matron led Cloud back into the previous room. From a wooden ledge that jutted from the wall, she took a clay vessel and poured water from it into two stone cups. She handed one of these to Cloud and went to sit on one of the stools.

Cloud sat across from her, sipped from the cup, and was surprised to find the water slightly sweet, with a pleasant, herbal odor and flavor.

"So," the Matron said. She leaned forward with her elbows on her knees, holding her cup in both hands. "Perhaps fifteen moons ago. And it was not long after that that the forest turned against the people of the world. We lost perhaps a dozen to its savagery. I don't suppose I would have your people to thank for that?"

"Our people were surprised by it, too. You speak truly, that it was soon after we arrived that the woods turned hostile. But none of us understand the reason. We believe it to be a war between gods."

"A war," the Matron repeated. Her tone had gone very, very still. "Between *gods*."

"Yes. And our own have become embroiled in it as well. Our People—those of us who are here—are here because we do not wish to serve one over the other. We are not champions or legends of old to become involved in their affairs. We wish only to live our lives in devoted service to all of them."

As she spoke, the lines on the Matron's face were growing harder and harder, as though she suspected Cloud of speaking some grave falsehood. Whatever the offense might be, Cloud could only continue. "But some of our people, our younger men and women, have become involved despite our counsel and efforts. They have taken to burning the forest, first with oil and arrows to avoid the attacks from the forest god, and then with pitch and carefully set torches." Cloud took a deep breath. "I do not know if it can be done, but they mean to burn the whole thing, to punish Lord Kwaee for his attacks on our people."

The Matron's face was still hard, but one eye twitched at this revelation.

"Of course, if they manage it, all people will suffer. The rivers will be filled with ash. The skies will be clogged with smoke. I believe it may be enough even to poison the great water."

"I understand why you have come to me," the Matron said in a tight voice. "But this is your concern, not ours."

"But to burn the entire forest to ash—"

"Is impossible. No doubt your people consider the savanna great, but I assure you that the forest is greater still. It is vaster than you can imagine. We have taken boats across the great water to lands you have never heard of. We have traveled to the great river city in the northeast, around the Firelands and all the savanna. But as far south as we have traveled, we have never seen the end of the forest. All your people and all their children, and all their children's children, going down into countless generations, could never burn all of it."

"Not on our own, perhaps." Cloud took a deep breath. "But one of us has assistance that we did not expect."

"What kind of assistance?"

"A prince of our people—young, arrogant. He was sent into the savanna, banished from the village for blasphemy. And when he returned, he did not come back alone. There was something inside him. Few believed at first, and those of us who noticed it thought he carried a demon within him."

"Demons are a fantasy. They do not exist."

"It may be true," Cloud admitted. "But our prince came back with a touch of the divine. He carried within him the voice and flames of the god Ogya. And he—"

The Matron rose to her feet, her eyes blazing. "That is enough."

"Matron?" Cloud said in bewilderment. The woman's jaw bulged with a clench. Her shoulders were drawn back as though pinched together.

"I know you are from a primitive people. Confounded by savage lies and heresies. I have been willing to overlook your minor sacrileges. Allowances must be made. But I will not have you profane our city with the names of false gods."

Cloud stared at her. "What in earth and sky can you mean by that? What false gods? Do you mean—"

"All of them!" The Matron's face shook as she shouted the words. "They are lies, fabrications invented by humans to scorn the one, true Goddess."

"Mpo." Cloud barely breathed the name. Her skin prickled as now, suddenly, she saw the shape of the city: the strange statues everywhere, the cleansing rituals, the guards, the gates, the abandoned countryside and docks.

"You say her name with reverence, but you pollute it. She is divine among the divine, goddess above all other gods."

"But if there are no other gods—" Cloud began.

"I will not listen to blasphemies spat from the mouth of a heathen. Our Lady Mpo is great beyond greatness, more wondrous and more powerful than you and your people can imagine." The Matron turned her face upward toward a grey ceiling. "It was the scourge of the Goddess that cleansed our cities of the filth of the invaders. It was her storm that purged us of our illness and our iniquity and made us whole again."

"I understand," Cloud said carefully. She knew now that she had found herself in a very dangerous place with a very dangerous woman. It should not be me here, she thought. It should be the Teller. An orator. An entertainer gifted with words, or an advisor skilled at persuasion. Not a woman verbally clumsy, a woman who spent her life avoiding everyone. What of Bad Water and Basket? Were they back in their houses? Were they safe? Or could her words here doom them?

"I know what you understand. I can see your fear. You are not the first people to come to Bogana seeking succor or alliances or trade. I have seen that expression on the faces of many men and women. You fear your situation, but you do not yet fear Mpo. You do not worship her. You do not glorify her name. Because you do not understand. But you will." She turned toward the west, where her shuttered window banged and thumped against the fury of a storm wind. She spoke her words in reverent recital. "Create in us clean souls, Mpo, and purify us of evil in your sight. Purge us with your storm, and wash away our iniquity, as you have engulfed our enemies, as you have flooded the black fly."

The Matron looked back to Cloud. Fervent tears streaked her cheeks.

5

The streets were empty but for Cloud, the Matron, and her retinue. They walked in slow, deliberate steps, moving south along the western wall of the city, toward the temple, whose alabaster luster was now dimmed by the storm. The entire city huddled in a midday darkness—an eerie, shadowless twilight.

Behind and in front her marched the guards, still bejeweled and brightly clad, but to either side of her were men and women dressed all in white, their garments like Cloud's and the Matron's—immaculately clean, but simple compared to the elaborate garments of the others in the city. They walked with their heads down, hair and scalp covered in white hoods. They spoke no words. Cloud wondered who they could be. Other elders from the city council, perhaps? But why this silence? It was not just those around her. The entire city was quiet, except for the constant wind and the roar of the sea crashing against the cliffs below like the breath of some slumbering leviathan.

Where was everyone? Cloud's questions had been ignored. She'd turned to the hooded men and women walking next to them, pleaded with them for help, but they gave no answers. When she tried to stop, the guards shoved her forward roughly.

She knew she was in grave trouble. She prayed to Wem that Basket and Bad Water were safe. There was no point making that prayer on her own behalf. She knew she was not. Why had she not prepared her people for this possibility? Made plans for what they would do if she was taken from them?

They marched up the great, white steps to the temple. No one spoke. To either side towered monster-headed statues, teeth bulging from downward crescent mouths, white eyes staring blindly toward either side. When the wind shifted, it must have blown through the jutting grimaces, because the statues howled with wailing voices into the storm. Cloud couldn't bear to look at them. The wind beat her rough clothing against her legs.

They passed through a wide, white stone hallway whose floor was pitted and worn with the passage of many, many feet over time, still scrubbed clean. And then before them, dark and churning beneath a black sky, lay the great water. The rear of the temple was completely open. No walls separated them from the yawning abyss of the ocean. Their path led directly to a precipice above the sea. Cloud fought a surge of vertigo and looked away.

Only then did she see the galleys to either side of them, curling out toward the ocean in the shape of a semicircle, open to the sky. They were tiered, with level after level steeply descending the city's cliffs. They were not on a precipice at all, but on the top row of an enormous amphitheatre. She had not seen the lower levels at first because the decline was so steep, each row of galleys barely cutting into the vertical cliff face, accessible by flights of precariously steep stairs. The rows were populated by the people of the city, some dressed in bright colors, others in grey or black. No one in white but Cloud, the Matron, and the hooded Boganans walking with them. No one reacted to their entrance; some stood against the rough cliff walls and some sat on narrow benches, but all were transfixed, watching the stormy sea as though entranced.

From the bottom of the amphitheatre jutted a square column, like a finger pointing toward the sky, and at its top was a flat platform. Notches had been cut in the side for hand and footholds, and Cloud shuddered, hoping she would not be forced to climb it. She had never liked heights in the best of conditions, and with the wind, the stinging rain, and the arthritis in her fingers and hip, she knew she would never make it.

But this was not to be her fate: the group moved down the steep steps toward the base of the tower, allowing her time to scoot downward on her backside so as not to risk falling. At the base of the amphitheatre, the sea looked close enough to rise up with one mighty wave and dash them all senseless against the cliff, but when Cloud leaned to peer over the precipice, she saw rocky shoals far, far below. A guard grasped her arm firmly when she did, and she clung to the reassurance in that moment. They did not want her to die, then. Not right away, anyway. Or not like that.

The Matron touched Cloud's arm and nodded at her. Her eyes were shining with fervor, wet with the rain. Then she turned and began the climb up the column, moving slowly but methodically, placing inerrant hands and feet in the holds. She had done this many times. At the top, she clambered up onto the platform. Her clothes were soaked through, clinging to her limbs, and yet somehow undirtied by the climb up the stone. She stood upright, leaning into the wind, the white fabric flapping behind her like a bird struggling against a gale. She raised one arm to the sky, fist clenched.

The hooded people who had traveled alongside her spread out, assembling along the edge of the cliff with a daring that Cloud was not sure she could have mustered. Boganan words passed between the guards, and then most of them left together, sidling carefully along the ledges to the right, moving past the assembled crowds, all the way to the edge of the cliff, where they disappeared into a shadow in the rock.

Only two remained with Cloud, their spears crossed behind her. Were she a younger woman, escape might have been possible. She might have darted to one side, found another passage in the cliffs, or scrambled up between the crowds of people and made her way back through the temple and city. But she had no hope against young, strong warriors in their own home. She nestled back against the spears, as far as they would let her, and waited to learn her fate.

Above her, the Matron shouted Boganan words toward the sky, in the practiced cadence of ritual. Cloud expected a call and response, the people behind her to echo her words or give an expected answer, but they remained silent, and that was worse, somehow. It was as though they had become something else—statues more silent than those that howled before the temple.

The Matron's words cut through the roar of wind and sea. Cloud wished she could understand them, as though words could somehow instill sense into what was happening, but then the guards returned, filing along the narrow ledge. Others were being guided among them, but at first Cloud could not see who they were between the large, decorated men.

There were three of them, shivering, naked, their skin slick with the spray from wind and sea. Her heart sank. The first turned out to be Bad Water, his toothless mouth stretched wide in terror, the puffy white hair across his chest and stomach sagging with rainwater. The whites showed all around his eyes, and he could barely move—the guards had to force him forward each step. He gaped when he saw Cloud. "Why are they doing this?" he begged her. "What's happening?"

She tried to step toward him, to give him some answer or comfort, but one of the guards angled a spear in front of her. They pushed Bad Water a little past her. His hands were bound behind him. One guard gripped him by the cord around his wrists and held him standing against the edge of the cliff, his skinny, naked legs shaking with error.

Behind the next guard shuffled a tall man with a heavy build, and Cloud's heart refused to beat. *Not Basket. Please, anyone but Basket.* The prayer shamed her, but she could not stop it. But then the guard stepped out of the way, and the man was not Basket, but Buffalo Tail, their best cook. Cloud sagged with traitorous relief. Then her knees nearly gave way as she realized: Buffalo Tail had not come with them to the city. They would have had to go out into the camp of the People to find him. None of them were safe. Some of them had been captured—perhaps all. She had led her people into the arms of an enemy.

Buffalo Tail shuffled up to the edge of the cliff with a dazed expression, as though he did not know where he was. He did not notice Cloud. Behind him strode another guard, and behind that guard was Firefly.

"No!" Cloud tried to reach forward again and was rewarded by the crack of a spear haft across the back of her head. She stumbled, her vision blurring, the pain spreading over her skull like hot water. She tried to ask how many were captured, how many escaped, but she couldn't manage the words through the pain, and when she attempted it, a guard clamped his hand over her mouth. "*Kota*," he warned her.

The Matron never turned around, never broke from her chanting, never turned from the sea even as rainwater streamed down her face, even as the wind whipped her wet garments against each other with slapping noises, threatened to tear her away from her precarious perch and dash her against the rough stone of the amphitheatre. She cried louder and with greater fervor, her skinny arms spread wide as if to embrace the coming storm.

Cloud wished she could understand the words but knew she did not need to. Fanaticism was the same in every language. The Matron reached a crescendo, holding one fist up toward the sky again, crying, "Mpo!" And for the first time in the ceremony, the crowd answered her: "Mpo!"

Twice more she called the sea goddess's name, and twice more she was answered by all the people of Bogana in one unified, thundering call. The last part she shouted in Cloud's language. "We offer you the sacrifice of these foreigners that you may cleanse them of their filth! Purge us with your storm and wash away the stain of our iniquity!"

"No," Cloud shouted again, past the pain still throbbing in her head. "Please, no! They are innocent! Please!" She pushed forward, past the spear haft still blocking her way, as though alone she could stop this, as though she could gather up her captured people in her arms and drag them away from the abyss.

Instead, a guard grabbed her roughly by the back of her garment; the coarse fabric pulled tight around her neck, half-choking her, but she struggled forward all the same, gagging, reaching out with both hands.

"*Ahaba sa magae*," the Matron shouted. "The wave is the way."

Bad Water half-dropped to his knees; Buffalo Tail stood as though dazed; Firefly looked back at her over one shoulder, looked at her as he had the day she told him his son would die of the poison. He had been loyal to her and she had failed him. She had failed his son. She had failed his wife, No Rocks. She saw it all in that look.

The guards gave each man a shove. Bad Water, Buffalo Tail, and Firefly vanished over the side, soundlessly, like falling stars going out. Cloud cried out again, no words this time, and pulled free of the guard—or perhaps he let her go. She scrambled to the edge of the cliff on all fours.

Far below, their bodies lay broken on the rocks. Tiny. Like discarded toys. The dark black of a wave slid over them and swallowed them up, mouthing at the cliff with the white-foamed lips of a rabid beast. When it receded, they were gone, as though they had never been.

There would be no funeral rites. No sending their bodies to Wem so they could join their ancestors. The great water had swallowed them up. Cloud bit hard at her fist so she could swallow that pain instead.

But the Boganans had begun to chant: "Mpo. Mpo. Mpo." They chanted in unison, along with the Matron, who did not deign to look down at the horror she had wrought but stretched both arms toward the storming sky.

"Mpo. Mpo. Mpo."

Louder and louder they called. Cloud wanted to shut it all away; she covered her ears with both hands, but still there was the endless roaring of the wind and the cry of the crowd.

Then, out in the storm, the sea bulged. It was so strange that Cloud forgot herself and stared in astonishment.

Something terrible and enormous rose up out of the great water.

# 21 The Prison of God

The shape of the goddess Mpo towered over everything. Her pointed, grey head pierced the clouds. Her flat, black eyes stared from horizon to horizon. She raised her impossible arms amidst a maelstrom that swirled endlessly around her as though the very sky spun on the tip of her head.

Cloud flattened herself down against the rock floor of the cliffs as her mind gibbered in terror, unable to hold onto any thought, any attempt to grasp the events before her skidding against the surface of her sanity.

Her people were imprisoned, three of them sacrificed to the divine titan looming above them all. This was no world for her. She was a small, frail, and insignificant human, only trying to save her people from the whims of angry and unjust gods. But Cloud saw now that there was no saving them. Whatever the gods did was just, and all humans were dust before them. The monstrous goddess of the sea could fell them all with one blow of her webbed hand.

She boomed out words to the people of the city—words Cloud did not understand, but which sounded Boganan, if that language could be spoken by a roll of thunder. From all around came the murmurs of the gathered people, speaking the words in concert with the rumble of the goddess's voice, not a call and answer, but a chant, a recitation of sacred words spoken in unsinging chorus with the divine.

Fear blared through Cloud's mind… but she was lying face-down on the edge of a cliff, and rocks were jabbing into her knees and elbows, and rain had soaked through her garment and was dripping from her skin, running off her breasts and stomach and down her legs. Her hair was heavy with the water. The little, insistent sensations of being alive were content to wait as fear and panic ebbed. Her breath was hot in her face. It panted against the rock below her and spattered droplets of rainwater against her nose. The guards had prostrated themselves near her, and one of them, in the middle of his chant to Mpo, emitted a small belch.

That was enough to break the grip of Cloud's fear completely.

The gods might be all-powerful, terrifying, and completely in control, but humans still needed to breathe and stay dry and eat and shit and belch. And escape danger when they could.

Cloud dared to tilt her head upward and steal a glimpse of Mpo. Seemingly unaware, the goddess waved her long arms. She pointed a clawed finger at the sea and at the city, thundering more incomprehensible words. The smooth, flat lines of her legs intersected and blended with the sea as though she extended from it; the waves did not break around her nor part for her towering frame. They flowed into her, their dark, choppy crests mottling the surface of her flesh, halfway up her smooth trunk of a torso.

She was not just goddess of the sea. She was part of the sea. And I bet, thought Cloud, she can't leave it. But there aren't many people on the great water. So she has to come here, to the coast, to a border. That's a limitation.

But not much of one. Cloud and all her people were trapped here, and she now suspected that the stories of the goddess washing the city clean were not metaphor. Just one of those enormous, liquid hands splashing down could drown all of Bogana.

Mpo continued booming incomprehensible words and waving her arms. What was she doing? Why would a goddess even try to communicate with mortals? Her stretched, grey face was alien and towered far above them, and Cloud could not read the emotions on it. But this goddess sounded passionate. Angry. Her eyes bulged as she shouted. Her lips stretched wide around her words.

She wants something, Cloud thought. She communicates because she cares about what we do. She wants to terrify the people in the city. We can do something she wants. Or, she considered, there's something we can do that she won't like at all. And that means she can be fought.

Her thoughts fled as one huge, clawed finger moved to point directly at her with a spray of seawater that drenched her again. That thick talon was white as the belly of a dead fish. Muck caked the goddess's skin and fell away; plants from the bottom of the great water hung between her fingers; small, insect-like creatures with large claws skittered across her flesh and disappeared into pale holes in the mud, crawling into the skin of her fingers and arms.

She boomed Boganan words again, and Cloud quaked in primal terror. The great head of Mpo dipped down, down, and Cloud stared into a maw that could swallow her whole village and everyone in it, past gums and rows and rows of arrowhead teeth and into the blackness beyond. Then Mpo turned her head and regarded her with one flat, lidless eye—a black and weeping moon.

Cloud flattened herself against the rocks and held still, listening to breath like waves. She waited to die.

But death did not come. With a rush of wind and a crash of ocean waves, the presence of Mpo receded. The storm winds died. And when Cloud finally dared to look up at the sea, she saw only empty waves sawing back and forth as though searching for the missing goddess. Around her, the people of Bogana trembled, knelt, or prostrated themselves in the throes of religious ecstasy.

And on her pedestal, the Matron stood, arms outstretched toward the sea like a child forgotten by her mother.

~

The guards escorted Cloud away from the temple's sacrificial cliffs. Their eyes were unfocused and they spoke little. As for Cloud, once the rush of terror had finally ebbed, she sagged and began to shiver. She could barely walk at all, and they half-hoisted her, half-shoved her along. Her mind, which floated a few feet behind her own head, recognized this state as common after a life-threatening event, and prescribed rest and hot tea, but she doubted she would be afforded either of these.

She was not led to the home she had stayed in before, and was at first grateful for this, as she was not sure she could have made the trip in her condition. Instead, the guards led her around, down a side hallway of the temple and through a dark passage whose walls had burned soot-black by torches. The rest of the temple was so clean and white, but vigilance could scrub away only so much smoke. Ogya had left his mark even here, in the temple of Mpo.

Near the end of the passage came the sounds of people talking. The sounds echoed enough that she could not make out the words, but she recognized the intonations and inflections of the People of the Savanna, and both relief and dread gripped her heart. At least they had not all been sacrificed.

The passage opened into an open area of flat stone floors broken up by many round, regular openings, and it was from these holes that the sound of chatter echoed. They had shoved her people into pits as though they were nothing more than captured beasts. The stench was terrible: human waste primarily, but also blood, and underneath it all, the sickly-sweet, noxious odor of death.

"What have you done?" she murmured to herself. "What have you done?"

Ignoring her, the guards looped rope around her arms and legs and led her to one of the holes. The rope dug into her skin as they hoisted her off the ground and then, hand by hand, lowered her into the pit.

*Please*, she prayed to Wem. *Please let there be someone there with me. Don't make me spend this night thinking of the horrors alone.* It was too dark to see very much, especially with her eyesight, but she could make out no one. Her feet touched wet stone, and then her hands. There was no one there. The guards tugged sharply on the rope, but she didn't think she had the strength to extricate herself from it. She pushed herself to her feet, trying to pull the bonds from where they had cinched into her hips and armpits. Her knees buckled with weariness.

Then a voice from behind her: "Cloud? Oh, thank the tears of Fam, Cloud!"

She almost collapsed in relief as Basket pulled her into his soft, warm arms.

~

Basket held her close until she was able to stop shaking. Where was Bad Water, he wanted to know, but she only shook her head and wept. Bad Water. Firefly. Buffalo Tail. All three gone forever, and no funeral, no pyre to send them to the stars with their ancestors. She hoped that Father Wem found a way to bring them home anyway. She hoped that little Whistling Thorn would not be waiting among those stars for a father that never came.

When she could, she told Basket everything that had happened: her encounter with the Matron, the ritual on the cliffs, and the terrifying and incomprehensible appearance of Mpo. He listened with chagrin and eventual disbelief when she told him of the goddess.

"It cannot be," he said. "They drugged you. Gave you iboga to make you see the spirit world."

"I would know the taste of iboga. And its effect is medicinal, not supernatural. This was *real*, Basket." She looked up at the small window of sky the top of the pit afforded her. "I never knew a living thing could be so enormous. I suppose you couldn't have seen from here. But even if not, you must have heard her voice. So loud. So terrifying."

"We did hear a terrible booming, but we couldn't recognize it. We thought it some trick of the thunder, or the roaring of some terrible giant beast in the great water."

"She *was* a beast. A monster like I've never seen, all teeth and dead eyes. She leaned down. She looked right at me, up close. I've never been so terrified. I felt less than an insect. But then I wondered: why do all this? Why speak to us? The only reason we speak to insects is to thank their spirits before we fry them." She shuddered. "I wish I could have understood her when she spoke."

Basket's arms tightened around her. "Maybe it's better you couldn't. Surely the people in this city have been twisted by her words."

"Perhaps so." Cloud sighed and leaned back against Basket's soft belly. "But the Boganans have shared dark stories for a long time. This is not their first sacrifice. And you do not know the fear of the plague."

"There was plenty of fear of the sickness in the village. It made people suspicious. Desperate."

"Not like this," Cloud said. "That was just a few. Imagine if everyone was dying. Just… falling asleep and dying. And if the Matron speaks the truth, it was Mpo that saved them from it. Gave them… gave them a lasting fear. It threads through every part of their lives now."

"The statues."

"Even their words. Cleanse. Scourge. The black fly. The foreigner. Basket, we should never have come here. These people can't help us."

He gave a long sigh and was quiet. She had learned by now to recognize his thinking sighs. She lay back against him and let exhaustion flood through her.

When he spoke again, she started, rising from the shallows of a deepening sleep. "I do not like having only a single story for a people. Surely they cannot all share the same tale."

She sat up a little. "But Basket, you didn't see them. All those people, all in thrall. They adore her and fear her. How could any of them deny her? They believe she saved their city and protects them. And any of them who are unfaithful might be sacrificed, just as…" No point thinking about that again. "They gave human sacrifices before, and now they've started again. It's in their blood."

"And yet, for a time, they stopped. Someone made that happen. Someone decided: no more sacrifices. What happened to that story?"

"I don't think this Matron allows other stories to be told anymore. Maybe they all forgot it."

"Did she tell you what she intends to do with us?"

"No. And none of my guesses are happy ones. I think she is mad, Basket."

"Then we will have to wait and pay attention and pray to the gods that they remember us."

Cloud remembered the glossy black eye of Mpo staring into her. "Perhaps we'd all be safer if they just forgot us."

Basket sighed. "It's hard for me to understand. I keep trying to place these events in the stories of the gods that we know, but they don't fit. The gods are known to be capricious and fickle, but always to punish people for some wrong. Has something changed? Have the peoples of the world committed some terrible crime? Or is this cruelty part of some lost, older truth? Or one we never knew?"

"Perhaps they have decided we were a mistake. Like your stories of the first peoples, who came out wrong, and so the gods destroyed them. Maybe they have decided to destroy us, too." Cloud closed her eyes. "Maybe it's not something we've done, but what we are. Maybe this is the end for all peoples."

~

"Hfft!" The hissing sound filtered into Cloud's dreams. She tried to ignore it, because sleep had not come easy to her, and she wished to cling to it as long as possible. Waking meant the pit, and the mad city, and the wrathful goddess. But the sound repeated. "Hfft! Hffffffft!"

And it brought with it other distractions: the stink of the pit; the clamminess of water against her skin; the rough stone and gravel digging into her legs; the gentle snoring of Basket. Cloud floundered in the shallows of sleep for a moment longer and then reluctantly opened her eyes.

The night was still dark, the opening above her only a bit lighter. Dawn was still distant. But interrupting that circle of sky was a shadow: a head covered in a hood.

"Who is there?" Cloud asked. Her tongue felt thick and dry in her mouth.

"Quiet. The guards are not watching now but they could overhear us. Are you the leader of this people?" The voice was a young woman's, her Boganan accent thick, but the tones strangely familiar.

Had Cloud heard her voice before? She pushed herself upright, immediately alert. "How do you know that?"

"They like to put leaders in this pit. Farther from the others so you can't talk to them."

"Who are you? How do you speak our language?"

"It's safer for me if you don't know. We can't—I can't let myself get caught."

So there was a *we*. "Can you help us get out?" She did not allow herself to hope for a yes, but neither could she let the question remain unasked. Basket stirred beneath her, and she felt his breathing quicken.

"I am working on it," the woman above said. "It will not be easy. There are so many of you. But listen. For now, you must be calm. Do whatever the Matron says."

"We have been! She killed three of us. Sacrificed them to Mpo."

"And she means to do so again, until all of your people worship Mpo."

"But we have always remembered her in our songs and stories," Cloud protested.

"It is not enough. She will wish you to worship only Mpo. She will order you to name all other gods false. And you must do so, or more will die."

"What?" Basket's voice was hoarse and thick with sleep. "But—but that is sinful. It would anger the gods and shame our ancestors."

"Your ancestors can tell you personally of their shame in a day or two if you do not heed. You are the…" The voice above hesitated. "The priest of this people?"

"I am the Teller and Keeper of stories," Basket said.

"Then listen. The Matron will be interested in you most of all. She will ask you for all your stories. If you do not answer, you will be beaten. If you speak heresy, you will be beaten."

"Then it seems I am to be beaten," Basket said wryly. "What can I do?"

"She will wish to know if your people can be set on the path of true faith. There were people who came before you to this city. Those who held onto their beliefs were killed or given to Mpo in—in offering. But some still live. They now worship only Mpo."

"They live here, in the city?" Cloud asked, wondering if she'd seen them—and more, wondering how a people could trust a subjugated enemy. Surely the temptation to seek vengeance or to flee would be strong.

"No. She sends them out in boats, across the… the great water, you call it. To distant lands, to spread word of Mpo. Lady Mpo believes all should worship her and only her. So the Matron sends out people with this teaching. Most do not return."

"So our choices are to be thrown into the great water to die or sent across it to die?" Basket asked. "Why choose one over the other?"

"To live as long as you can. It may be that— that I can find some way to free you. But for now, you must not give the Matron any reason to sacrifice more of you. Tell your stories of the other gods, but seem to doubt them. Be ready to listen to her words. But not too quickly, or she will suspect you. You must seem…" She paused. "Sturdy? No, stubborn. But afraid. You saw the goddess. You must show them that your fear will lead you to worship her."

"When did Mpo become like this? What has changed?" Cloud asked. "I was very young when I was last here, but Bogana was not like this before, and we have heard nothing of it from traders."

The figure at the top of the pit was quiet.

"Was it recent? Perhaps less than a rains ago?"

"I do not know 'a rains.' But a few moons ago, Lady Mpo grew more angry. She shouts to us about the filth from false gods staining her pure waters. She is greatly angry about Asubonten and her 'shit-water.' "

The mud-flows from the fires, Cloud thought. Could the burn have spread so far that the rains carried its ash all the way to the Asubonten?

"Then before that, the city was peaceful?" she asked.

"Oh, no. Lady Mpo has visited our city for as long as I have been alive. Some elders say that she goes away for a very long time, so long that the grandparents of grandparents do not remember, but she always comes back again. There were stories that she takes offense to the boats on her skin and always follows them back to Bogana, but nobody really remembers them. We are not supposed to speak tales to each other. Not unless Lady Mpo commands it."

"You're not allowed to keep your own stories?" Basket asked, appalled. "But then how do you keep your family histories? Your wisdom? How do you remember the bonds you have to each other? You forsake your ancestors!"

"All living in Bogana have forsaken their ancestors, then." The figure's voice was sad. A little more hopefully she added, "But some of us remember them as well as we can, in secret." She turned her head to glance up at the sky. "Dawn comes. I have to go."

"Wait," Basket called to her. "One of our own is still free, I think. He may be hurt. A boy named Mirage. Do you know anything?"

Cloud looked up sharply at that. Mirage was here? But how? And why? Had he rejoined the people only to be captured with them? No, she surmised, he must have followed them in, probably hoping to report to Laughing Dog on their fate. If he were free, he was probably running back to the village now. No one there would come to help them, nor could they do much against such a powerful city.

And now she wondered if Basket were wise to trust this Boganan woman who claimed to be helping them. This could all be a ruse, a plan of the Matron's to further press them into pliability or to trick them into giving up information. But they had little choice. If there were any hope for the People's survival, she would cling to it.

"A tall man? Young? Strong-looking and lean? Face round, like a moon?"

"Yes! That is him!" Basket said. "Has he been found, then?"

"Not yet. The guards search for him. They tell his description to everyone. He was seen here, by the pits, but he ran away. There are many places to hide in the city, if you are clever. Is this boy clever?"

Basket bobbed his head from side to side, making a non-committal noise. "Ennnh."

"I see. Well, I will try to find him before the guards or priests do."

"Wem bless your ancestors and keep you safe," Basket said.

"I must go!" The woman's head disappeared and the sound of running feet faded across the courtyard above them.

Cloud leaned against Basket's side. "Well, it's not much of a hope. But it's something to hold onto. How did Mirage return?"

"I'm not certain. He and Dry Grass found the pits somehow, but the guards surprised them. She was hit by an arrow. He escaped."

"Her wound, is it serious?" She wondered what she could possibly do to aid her from here.

"I don't know. But the people here are not fond of injury or illness. She received some treatment. I could get few details. We can talk to each other a little, but there are many echoes, and it's hard to hear, and after a while the guards come and threaten us."

Cloud slumped down against him. She wrapped her arms around his belly. "I've failed our people. We were better off back in the village."

He put a soft, heavy arm across her back. "I try not to decide the ending of a story in the middle. Especially not in the parts when the night is darkest, and the monsters have come."

"It's been a very long night, Basket. The droughts, the journeys, the deaths, the beasts, the angry gods… I'm beginning to forget what daylight looks like."

"I'll tell you what it looks like for me. It's you and me on a hillside, looking down into the Stone Wastes. And we are afraid, but we find each other's arms. It's waiting a lifetime for you, and finally having you near me. Even here, Cloud. Even afraid and tired and sad, you are a sunbeam, reminding me that no night lasts forever."

Cloud marveled. That he could be in this terrible place, with no way out, and all the forces in the world opposing them, and she responsible for leading him there, and yet still he found strength in her. Even when she could no longer find it in herself. She tightened her arms around his belly and found comfort there, too. Why had she waited so long to go to him? Why had she hidden from everyone? She thought of her husband, who had died, and how she had blamed herself. She had been with Basket when Wind needed her. When he'd died. And so she'd hidden inside her shame, and it had kept her safe, but it had kept her small.

So late, she thought. So late in life to learn that other people could bring you joy. That loneliness was a prison and its walls were built of fear.

She tried not to weep onto his skin. She embraced him wordlessly. She held onto him as tightly as she could, until Petrel and the guards came and dragged him away.

# 22 The Breakwaters

It was hard, crouched where he was, for Mirage not to long for the village he had left so far away. He had left the daylight, the open spaccs, the play of sun across the wide grass, the embrace of the afternoon rains. He had lost his people, the guidance of his king, back in their adopted homeland. He had lost his father in the Stone Wastes, and his mother in the prison pits of the city, and now he was horribly, wretchedly alone. To have journeyed so far, and to have learned so much of the world, and now he was huddled like a rat under a log. He did not know what to do next. There was nothing *to* do. He couldn't save his mother. He couldn't escape to his people. He could not even find a flame to call for a king who, the heaviness in his heart told him, would never answer.

The spaces beneath the structures of Bogana were dark, rank, and wet. They were also not very roomy, and Mirage was forced to lie nearly flat, crawling on belly, elbows, and knees across the ragged stone. His hands and feet had gone pale and puffy from the constant damp. Some buildings were raised higher off the rock than others, but he did not trust these, because more than once a wandering child had ventured underneath and spotted him.

He had decided the animals would know which hiding spaces were safely and when he noticed a brown fuzzy mammal or two scurrying into the shadows, he'd followed, finding sheltered spaces where no Boganan eye could notice him.

During the bright of the day, he remained hidden beneath the crawlways, avoiding the sight of the Boganans, who he suspected were actively hunting for him. From a distance he'd seen people dressed like the city guards moving together down streets and through squares, checking alleys and looking under the buildings. He nestled in the dark shadows where they could not see him and tried to sleep.

Sleep, however, did not come easily to him. Besides the damp, the fear of being captured, and the unending commotion of an alien city, he was not alone in the underbuildings. He shared his cramped accommodations with rats that scurried around him, unafraid, and had more than once awoken him with an experimental nip that had made him shout and kick at them, only to panic and lie bleeding, heart hammering, terrified that someone had heard him. Besides the rats, there were insects: crawling roaches, flies that clustered in tizzing masses over sundry rotting bonanzas, and strange, pale insects that crawled in puddles and hopped out with great, springing leaps. These he suspected were responsible for the small, itchy welts that covered his body and that were impossible not to scratch.

Besides the insects, the crawlways were populated by strange, black creatures with many legs and broad, flat shells. They had pincered arms that they waved in alarm whenever Mirage moved near them and were capable of nasty nips if he wasn't careful. They scuttled sideways beneath the buildings, like him, and he began to feel a kinship with them, but not so much that he wouldn't crush the larger ones with a stone to slurp their soupy innards out of cracks in their broken shells.

The days were the most miserable, but it was a misery he deserved. He had run. His mother had fallen to an arrow and instead of saving her or fighting her attackers, he had fled. His shame at the memory burned in his face and knotted his empty stomach. He could not hate her anymore. He could not even judge her.

It seemed to him that he had inherited the worst part of both his parents. From his father, he had learned violence, and had murdered Left Rabbit. He had rejected the tyranny of Knife Strap and then bowed eagerly under Laughing Dog's rule. He had respected strength, but he had never stood against it, always with it, and that made him weak. It made him even weaker than his mother, who might not have fought to oppose violence, but was silent in its face, and fled from it even when it harmed her own son. He had run. He had left her, at best, to be shoved, wounded, into one of those horrible prison pits.

At worst… the first night and day, he had not allowed himself to think about the worst. But by the second night, the images had clambered into his imagination: his mother, an arrow through her chest, coughing on her own blood, her life fading, the last thing in her darkening vision her beloved son running away and abandoning her.

He could not call himself a son. He could not call himself a man. He deserved these dark and cramped spaces. He deserved the stinging, bleeding scrapes on his chest, knees, elbows, hands, and feet. He deserved the welts and the rat bites and the hunger. And he remembered Cloud telling him what he had done. That he would need to spend his whole life atoning.

More than anything, he wanted that chance now. He wanted everything to be all right, for his people to be back safe in their village, and the discord to end. He wanted to serve them. He wanted to spend his entire waking day making things better, making things right, putting some good into the world again.

In the night, he felt safer in some of the more open crawlspaces. He could creep out into the markets and squares and forage for fallen scraps of food. These were rare, as, in the mornings and evenings, Boganans dressed all in black would move through and obsessively sweep and scrub every inch of the open streets, accompanied by the chants and songs of the city folk. Food was not left to moulder; it was gathered up into buckets and carried away. And whatever morsels the cleaners didn't find, Mirage had to compete for with the rats and seabirds. By the second night he was so hungry, he considered attempting to eat *them*.

Water too was scarce, and his throat had parched and chapped. There were puddles here and there beneath the buildings, but these smelled fetid and brackish and had *things* living in them. Buckets for cleaning hung about the city on little pegs, and Mirage managed to secure one of those and leave it out for the rain. It wasn't a lot, and rationing it required more self-control than he could muster. Strange to be surrounded by so much water and to be so thirsty.

The second night, he prowled the darkened streets, keeping aware always for the approaching glow of torches and careful to stay away from the illumined strips of city streets lit by open windows. They burned and flickered, the eyes of Ogya, watching him. Accusing him.

He was searching in the darkness for some solution for his people. They would all be relying on him—to his knowledge, none but he had escaped. How could he free them? If he could find rope and avoid the guards, he might be able to spirit away a few, but not all. A troop of sixty foreigners creeping through the city in search of an exit would be impossible to conceal. And yet he had to try something. He couldn't leave them there to face death or whatever other horrible fate the Boganans planned for them.

It was no good trying to creep back into the temple, either. The entrance he'd used before was manned by two guards, and both had the eerie ability to fix their eyes on whichever of the shadows Mirage happened to be crouching in. He'd fled before the muffled pounding of his heart or the growling of his stomach betrayed him to attentive ears.

He spent another miserable day trying to sleep in the baking heat amid the constant searches from guards and the bites of the rats and the hopping bugs. His head began to feel loose and slippery, as though his mind were not attached but could swim away, drain out his nose, or slide down his neck.

That was the day of the storm. He didn't know how late it happened—time was almost impossible to measure amid the endless waiting, the sleeping in fits and starts. But the city darkened almost to night, and a cool but sturdy wind blasted through, howling like a pack of wild dogs as it curled and twisted around the edges of the buildings and gusted beneath them as though hunting him.

The rats vanished into buildings and crags in the rock. The scuttling shelled creatures retreated into the water. Above, he could hear clatters and slams as the windows were boarded up. Then the rain rattled into the city, fierce and violent. It pounded down on the streets and splashed up in clear, wet flowers. He dared to poke his head out from beneath the building and swallow as much as he could. The sky was shadow-dark and roiling as though furious. And for a moment, he thought he could see, in the distance, something enormous *moving*. Then running footsteps approached and he quickly retreated under the building.

He'd thought himself safe and relatively dry in his hiding place, but even there, the powerful wind and driving rain found him, spattering his skin and soaking his hair, leaving him shivering and rubbing it out of his face and eyes. The day turned darker and darker, and then the voice came, impossibly deep, impossibly loud, feminine and furious, making boulder-shaking demands in words he could not comprehend. To his terror, the voice reminded him of nothing so much of his grandmother in her moments of fury, when she would mete out punishment or scorn to her son, his wife, their child. The voice was pitched the same, the accent summoning memories both nostalgic and terrifying.

He was grateful when the booming ended, but it left him with an itching sense of guilt. His past was tied up with the Boganans; his ancestors were their ancestors, and their crimes and evils, whatever they were, made up his past, shaped his parentage, made the world that made him. In his mind, his grandmother's gravelly voice snarled, sneered, or trembled in religious fervor as she remembered the good old days of sacrifice. Was there no part of him that was truly good?

By the fourth day, he felt madness tugging at his thoughts. How much longer would he lie here, tormented and claustrophobic, slowly starving? Wisest would be to leave, to run as quickly as he could back to the village, and report what had happened. He had little faith that the words he'd murmured into firelight had reached Laughing Dog's ears. And he doubted that anyone would bother to mount a rescue for the imprisoned exiles, anyway. He could hear Laughing Dog now, telling him imperiously that the exiles had chosen their fate, and they would have to rely on their own gods to save them. What could a few fire hunters do against the entire city of Bogana, much less the angry goddess who ruled it?

Besides, he couldn't leave. Not when there was any chance he might be able to do something. Not while his mother might yet live. He couldn't keep lying here waiting for… what? Someone to save them? They were all imprisoned.

As soon as the streets were dark and empty enough, he made his way back toward the temple again. The trip was arduous, crawling blindly across the rough rock in the black space beneath buildings where his hands and feet were cut by rock or pinched by scuttlers, but he had nothing else to do, so he made his way there and sought out the side entrance that he had explored before. Finding a good vantage point beneath what smelled like a fish shop, he settled down and watched the guards carefully.

He was less concerned about those who moved about in the raised area at the top of the steps, or those who patrolled, two by two, around their base and the main street. He kept his gaze fixed on the two who stood by the main entrance.

When others were nearby, they stood to attention and remained quiet, but left alone, they were less attentive and would lean against the wall or strike up conversation with each other, though of course Mirage couldn't understand them. They weren't very concerned about watching the shadows, however.

As the side streets were dark and no passersby traveled this way at night, Mirage felt safe creeping out from beneath the buildings to stand upright. Gratefully, he worked the stiffness out of his knees and ankles. He noted with dismay that his toes and shins were dark and crusty with dried blood. With the patience of a hunter, he waited for something to change—for the guards to begin dozing or change shifts with their replacements. But nothing happened. They chattered in low tones, and twice replaced a guttering torch with a fresh one from a nearby basket. But otherwise they didn't move.

Mirage had no way to check the time—clouds prevented reading the stars, but he guessed the torches, if they were like those from his own village, soaked with pitch and palm oil, would last about four to a night. The night crawled, and Mirage was exhausted. He wished he still had his twine to play with. Something to keep his fingers busy.

He watched the guards, the flames, and the floating spots the light left hovering in his vision like the things drifting in the puddles beneath the buildings.

His head sagged and he jerked it upright. Had he been asleep? For how long? He looked around, but there was only darkness. The guards by the side passage were gone, and they had taken the torches with them.

Something moved in the shadows—something small and furry. A rat, he thought, but it was larger. It stood up on its hind legs and he saw two long ears pointing upward. It was a hare. It sat in the middle of the street, rubbing its paws together, and then it licked them and began to wash its face. He stared at it. What could it be doing here? Then it turned its head toward him, lifted a paw, and waved. His skin prickled. It was *that* hare. With a flash of white tail visible even in the dim light, it bolted, scampering toward the passage in the wall and disappearing down it.

Not quite understanding why, he started after it. It would be better to have patience and wait. Who knew where the guards had gone? But a creature behaving like that… it had to be a sign, didn't it? He crept across the stone streets of the temple plaza up the steps to the side door. It was still dark. No torches lit the passageway—the only light came from a sliver of moon and the fires above, near the main entrance.

He paused, holding his breath. No footsteps. No voices. He would dare to enter, and then… then he would decide what to do next. Even if it was only to find his mother and join her in her prison. Anything would be better than another day under the houses. He stepped into the passage.

And then someone slammed into him from behind, knocking him to the ground. He managed about half a yelp before a hand clamped over his mouth.

A warm body straddled his. Alarmed breath, ragged with fear or excitement, panted into his face. "Are you mad?" a voice whispered in his ear. The syllables were Boganan accented, but the language was his own. "Are you trying to get captured? Or killed?"

He turned to stare up through a cascade of black braids into the shadowed face of a young woman. "Come on," she whispered. "We have to get you out of here and some place safe. Mirage, is it?"

He nodded wordlessly.

She extended one hand. "Then let's go! Quick, the guards are coming!"

Baffled, he rolled to his feet and followed.

~

He awoke in darkness so complete that he could not tell that he'd opened his eyes. He felt the thick torpor following a long sleep, but why was it still night? Even in his tent, he should see—but no, he wasn't in his tent, was he?

His bleary mind recalled in jumbled order the events of the past months. Following the exiles. The torment of hiding in the heat in a hostile and strange city. His mother. The capture of the exiles by the Boganans. The horrific voice from the storm-lashed sea. The woman. He scrubbed his mind for the name she'd give him. Orupetra. Oru.

He rolled onto his side, searching for some light. The pallet beneath him was soft, but damp. It smelled of mildew. The sound of the waves of the great water, magnified and repeated by echoes, filled his ears.

And now he remembered the woman in the temple plaza, her palm flat over her mouth to warn him to silence. She'd led him through darkened streets and darker alleys, turning and doubling back so many times that he was completely lost. They'd gone down stone steps, and then followed a rocky trail into the crags of the cliffs. Only when they were swathed in complete darkness had she spoken to him again, bidding him follow her voice and feel with his hands and feet for the path.

He'd crept behind her, following the sound of her feet on the rough stone trail, the sound of her hand sliding against one wall. "Don't lean too far left," she had warned him, and he did not have to ask why. Far below echoed the sound of water dripping. They traveled a long time, sliding step by careful, sliding step along the path. Sometimes she took his hand and led him right or left, choosing her route in the darkness, he supposed, by sheer memory. After a few stubs of his already bloodied toes, he learned to move his feet more slowly. Once, he stepped rather than slid his foot and put it down on nothing at all. He lurched in the darkness, gave a yelp of terror, and flattened himself against the reassuringly solid rock wall. He wondered how many others had taken a wrong step before him. He wondered if there were bones down there in the darkness. Corpses staring up into nothing with hollowed eyes, scuttlers crawling in and out of their sockets.

They traveled on and on. Mirage had been almost too exhausted to stand by the time he saw the light: a flame left burning atop a thin, brown pillar of something oily-looking in a small clay pot.

The little flame illuminated the shining, wet surfaces of a cave whose reaches stretched into darkness. The uneven cavern floor was lined with several musty-smelling pallets, and he could make out the silhouettes of supplies stacked beyond: baskets and pots and bundles of cloth.

"You can sleep here," Oru had told him. "You will be safe as long as you do not walk in your sleep. Here." She passed him a pot full of water, which he drank eagerly, and two packets wrapped in some kind of soft leaf. One was sweet and rich with honey, and he could not stop himself from cramming it into his mouth immediately. He regretted it, though, because the thing was far too sticky to chew easily, and his mouth was too full to answer when she asked if he needed anything. He shook his head and wiped saliva from his chin. When he finally managed to swallow, his stomach sucked at the sustenance like dry sand drawing away a first rainfall.

"I will return for you tomorrow," she said. "And we can discuss your future. Do not go wandering if you wish ever to be found again." And then she had departed, leaving, to his great relief, the flame burning in its little pot.

The other packet had turned out to contain a large chunk of some unidentified, flaky meat with an odd flavor and a worse smell. He wouldn't have cared for the taste on any other day, but he was so hungry, he barely noticed it, and finished it as quickly as the sticky sweet. After that, he supposed, he must have found the pallet and fallen asleep, but he couldn't remember any of that.

Now he was awake, rested, and not starving, though his stomach had begun to complain again. But he was stuck where he sat, in the dark. He strained his eyes for any sign of light, but there was nothing. In the pitch black, his vision played tricks on him, making blobby streaks of color when he moved his arms or head.

How much time had passed? What was happening above, in the city? Was it day or night? He had no idea.

He waited for an interminable amount of time. After a while, he began plucking long strands of somewhat damp straw from his pallet and twisting them into twine as best as he could, trying to amuse himself with the patterns of Priest's Procession, but they only fell apart.

More time passed. Oru still had not returned for him. What if this were a trick? Or another prison? What if she intended just to leave him down here in the dark?

When he first saw the glimmer of light on one far wall, he thought his eyes were deceiving him again, but soon he heard footsteps and the sound of hushed voices speaking Boganan. His first panicked thought was that the Boganan guards had finally come to kill him, and he cast about for a place to hide. There was not enough light for him to see, though, and he feared tumbling over a precipice and lying somewhere in the dark, bones broken, starving to death.

He forced himself to breathe slow, deep breaths, reminding himself that Oru had led him here because it was safe, and that if anyone had come down here, they must be friendly to her. So he knelt on his pallet with his hands raised.

A group of seven emerged from a bend in the passage, carrying torches. Oru was among them, and the others consisted of two elders—a man and a woman—and two men and two women about the age of Mirage's parents. They exclaimed and pointed when they saw him.

Oru said something to calm them and moved briskly to his side. "I am pleased to see you did not decide to go wandering," she said in her soft, accented voice. "I came earlier, but you were still sleeping." She passed him a long calabash full of water and a leaf-packet of more of that odiferous meat. "The people behind me are my friends. They can be trusted. Edaala here will see to your injuries."

She beckoned, and one of the younger men came up. He had a wide, friendly smile, and made unintelligible but amiable conversation as he cleaned the blood from Mirage's feet and chest with a wet cloth.

"Who are all of you?" Mirage asked. "Why are you helping me?"

Oru tilted her head back and took a deep breath. For the first time, her features were revealed by the torchlight. She was young, as young as he at least, with rounded, plump features. Her hair was not tightly curled like that of the People of the Savanna but hung in loose ringlets around her shoulders. Her eyes were close-set and the flesh under them was baggy, suggesting a weariness. Then again, Mirage considered, she *had* been up all night.

"Most in Bogana follow Mpo blindly," she said, settling down cross-legged on the pallet next to his. "They accept her laws and her punishments because she is a goddess and commands it. Because she saved our city from the sickness. Some of us do not. I am too young to remember, but others recall the time before, when we were free to live our lives. When we would travel the… the great water and go outside our city walls without fear. When we did not kill others. So we meet down here, in the places the city guard have forgot and where Mpo cannot hear us. We resist Mpo and fight her cruelty. We try to save those we can. We call ourselves…" She frowned as she searched for the term. "The Break…waters."

Mirage looked at her with new appreciation. It was hard not feel a sense of kinship. After all, was that not what he had been doing as well? Taking up arms to fight the injustices of a tyrannical god? "These others remember a better time," he said. "But you don't. You can't remember the freedom the others fight for. What makes you fight?"

Her face tightened a little. "You do not need a reason to oppose cruelty and murder," she said. "No decent person does. More would surely join us, but we do not know who we can trust. Anyone might betray us to the Matron. And then what lives could we save? There would be no one left to help those who need it."

The kinship he felt began to ebb, replaced by an uncomfortable realization. She was part of a small resistance, opposing her leaders, standing in the way of power. And that… his mind paced around the growing thorn tree in the middle of it… that wasn't exactly what he'd been doing in his village, was it? Of course, they'd been fighting the oppression of an angry god, but…

But they'd been the ones in charge, hadn't they? It had been the King and the fire hunters controlling everything. And they'd killed to do it. *He* had killed. Because his King had ordered him to. He hadn't fought power. He'd *been* the power.

A prickle stole across his flesh, tightening his scalp, his forearms, his thighs. Had Cloud and her followers had met in secret just like this? Had they struggled to understand what to do next? Made plans for resistance?

Perhaps they had. Perhaps they had been afraid of their King, of the fire hunters, but stood up to them all the same. And one of them had been killed for it. They had all been banished. And he, Mirage, son of Knife Strap and Dry Grass, grandson of Two Broken Hands of Bogana, had been part of it.

He didn't deserve to be here, in these caves, sleeping on the beds and eating the food of the Breakwaters. Still, if allying with the group held any hope of rescuing his mother, he had to do so. With a pang of guilt, he realized that he had forgotten to ask about her. "My mother," he said quickly. "Do you know of her? If she is all right?"

"She is the one you were caught with? The one shot by an arrow?"

"Yes! Do you know anything?"

Oru shook her head. "The guards say that a woman was hurt. But not killed. She would have been put with the others. Are there healers among your group?"

"One."

"Then they may put her with your healer to be looked after. They do not like people to die in the pits."

So now Cloud, whom he had hated and scorned, was now his only hope for his mother's life. He could not understand how the whole world had turned beneath him. He breathed a silent prayer to Father Wem. *Save her, and I will spend my entire life making up for it.*

"Can we find her? Maybe give her bandages or medicine?" The hope was a faint one, but he had to ask.

"Not without making the guards suspicious. They cannot know someone is helping your people. It could risk everything. All of our lives." Regret creased her kind face.

"Then let me go and find her! At least talk to her," he pleaded.

"Take you into the most heavily protected area of the city, where everyone is looking for you? It is too great a risk. If you were captured, they would make you tell them where you have been hiding. They would make you tell them about us."

"I wouldn't," he swore fervently.

"You would. They would hurt you until you would tell them anything. Or they would hurt *her* until you would."

He sat back, stunned. "So what do you plan to do, then? Why did you bring me here?"

"We plan to fight back."

He shook his head. "We tried that, in my village. You can't fight a god. Our King is burning down the forest trying, but… it's just made everything awful."

She gave him a hard, humorless smile. "But you haven't tried what we are planning."

"And what is that?"

"Not for you to know. How can we trust you, grasslander?"

Mirage looked up, acutely aware now that the others in the group were staring at him, some with intent suspicion. The echoes of other voices filled the cavern, and soon more people filed in, all coming from the same direction, dressed in the bright colors of the city. All stared at him. He was plainly the focus of conversation as they entered. He could understand none of the words, but their expressions looked none too friendly.

"What possible reason could I have to be untrustworthy?" he asked. "I'm depending on you to help me and my people."

"And we hope to help them, young man." A man's cracked, quavering voice, thick with accent, spoke over the small crowd. An elder hobbled forward, leaning heavily on two walking sticks. He was the oldest-looking man Mirage had ever seen, so heavily stooped that his back was a hunch. Mirage marveled that he had apparently traversed the steep and winding paths of the cavern.

"Elder Tobosu," Oru greeted him, bowing her head low. "This is Mirage, the plains boy I told you of."

He made a noncommittal grunt at her and, with a ponderous show of aching and creaking and leaning on his sticks, lowered himself to one of the pallets. "I don't like it down here," he said, apparently to no one.

"It makes his bones hurt," Oru explained to Mirage.

"It makes my bones hurt!" Elder Tobosu scowled at her and shoved one finger in an ear so full of hair it looked as though it had swallowed all but the end of a buffalo. "Now, what was I…" He removed the finger and pressed his thin lips together in thought. "Yes. Yes, we hope to help your people. But we hope to help all the people of Bogana. Even—yes, even the ones who don't wish to be helped. And there is nothing you can do to aid us, boy. There are secrets that belong to Bogana. And we… we have forgotten them. Do you remember them, boy?" He fixed Mirage with a gaze that consisted of one rheumy eye and one squeezed closed. "Do you?"

Mirage just stared at him mutely.

"No, I thought not. So you sit here and you wait. We will try to recover the secrets of our past. And if we can save your people, all the better."

Mirage puzzled through this. "But… you must have lived such a long time. If even you don't remember the secrets, then there must be a Teller or a keeper of stories who remembers them. Yes?"

The old man puffed up a little when Mirage complimented his age and then gave a dry, mothy laugh at the question. "No one living remembers, but—"

"Elder Tobosu," Oru said in a strained voice, gently taking his arm.

He swatted at her with a gnarled hand. "Oh, what can he do? Who can he tell? Did you plan to let him out before we'd won?"

Oru looked away, her gaze downcast.

Mirage tried to hide his sudden alarm. He'd known, logically, that he couldn't go back up into the city, but it hadn't sunk in that he was a prisoner here. And that there might be worse things than crawling around under buildings slowly dying of thirst and exposure. Things like being shut away forever in an empty, sunless cave where your mind played tricks on you when the light was gone, and the only measure of time was the endless, maddening drip, drip, drip of water falling into an echoing abyss.

He must have failed to hide his shock, because Tobosu leaned toward him and grinned. "Don't look like that, boy. You won't be down here forever. We will find our lost secrets."

"But what secrets are they?" he blurted out. "And how can they possibly help now? What can they do against a god? And how can you even find them if no one alive remembers them? And what's to stop the guards from marching down here and capturing everyone, if these secrets are so dangerous?"

"The Matron—not our ruler now, but one long ago—had these caverns sealed off to stop anyone from finding them," Oru said, pushing her hair out of her eyes. "My father said Mpo herself had ordered it. We know there is something down here she doesn't want us to find."

"They didn't do a very good job of it," Mirage observed.

"There are ways in, if you know them. The cliffs are full of passages," Elder Tobosu said. "One of them happens to be underneath my own house. Very convenient, wouldn't you say?"

"The question is, what secrets could be so terrible that Mpo would fear them?" Oru said. "It must be something that could stop her."

Elder Tobosu fumbled with another of the little wax pillars on a clay dish and irritably waved at one of the crowd until a man with a torch came over and lit it. He gazed into the flame, and Mirage wondered uncomfortably if Ogya were listening through it. Or Laughing Dog. When the elders turned back to Mirage, the shadows and flame stretched and exaggerated his features into a god mask. "The old names of the gods. That's the secret. The ones with power. They're buried beneath us. All others have forgotten, but I remember the stories my grandmother used to tell us in darkened rooms, when no one else was listening. Call a god by their true name, and you have power over them. If we can learn those names, we need not fear Mpo. We can banish her, should we choose."

Control the gods? Banish them? Hope stirred in Mirage. Then they could not only free Bogana from Mpo—they could stand up against Kwaee. Free their people! How King Laughing Dog would welcome this news! Mirage would be a hero. He would accomplish what Laughing Dog and all his fire hunters had failed to do! And if Ogya dared stand against them, why, he could banish Ogya, too. But only if this were all true, and not the fancies of a mad old man.

"But you said these secrets were lost," he said. "How can you possibly find them now?"

"Ahhhh." Tobosu gave him a wide, toothless grin. "We cannot ask the living. So we mean to ask the dead."

~

The discussion among the Boganans had turned into outright arguing, with much waving of hands and pointing of fingers, sometimes at Mirage. They had been at it for some time, and without any understanding of their words, the debate had melded into a bubbling, meaningless roar, as indecipherable as the sound of the great water through the caverns.

After a while, Oru stumped back over to him, frowning. She flopped on the pallet nearby. "Wem save us from men who know everything." She didn't say it directly to Mirage, but she'd said it in plainstongue, so he supposed he'd been meant to hear it.

"What are they arguing about? Is it about this… journey to question the dead?"

"I guess." She flopped backward onto the pallet, then grimaced and fished a few wet pieces of straw from down the back of her garment. "Not talking to the dead, though. Elder Tobosu uses those words because he likes to be… *kasa rotun…* a storyteller." She shook her voice and waved her hands in front of her face dramatically. "But in truth it is only legends of divine beasts somewhere in the caves beneath the city. They are all dead. No one knows what truth they can speak to us, but Elder Tobosu is convinced that they have wisdom."

She sighed. "It maybe sounds more stupid in your language than mine because I am not good at saying yours. Not much—" She frowned again. "*Kasa rotun, kasa rotun*—Not much time speaking yours. Am I very bad at it?"

"No, you are quite good," Mirage answered truthfully. "How did you learn it?"

"My father made me learn. He is Chief Gateskeeper and sends me to do little works for him whenever we have captured people or when they come back from... job-journeys?"

"Missions," Mirage suggested.

"Yes. Missions. When we send them out on the boats. Most do not come back. The things we do to other peoples are terrible. Anyone can see that. But most do nothing. Even though they see it. Even though everyone knows. They say others should be punished for worshiping wrongly. For being unclean. So they do nothing. Only the Breakwaters fight back. When they are not arguing like this, ugh!"

Mirage glanced over at the group. Elder Tobosu jabbed a finger into the darkness of the cave and then smacked the back of one hand into the palm of the other to punctuate his words. "So why are they arguing?" Mirage asked. "Why has no one made this trip to see the divine beasts before?" These beasts seemed even more interesting than speaking to the dead, which was something you did every time you prayed to your ancestors.

"Oh, we have," Oru said, rolling over and propping up her head with one elbow. "But the people who go do not come back. There are many holes in the rock. Not safe."

"What happens to them?"

"How would we know? They do not come back."

"I don't know." Mirage felt uncomfortable now. "I thought maybe you could hear a scream and someone falling or something."

"They do not come back. That is all. And then their families must cry and wonder what happened to them forever, and never have the peace of knowing. We cannot tell them without being discovered. And we cannot send their bodies to Wem. It is very sad, and very difficult."

"I'm sorry."

"And that is why they are arguing. No one wants to be the next one to disappear into the caves and never come back. Some of them are calling

Elder Tobosu a confused old man. They are saying that there are no divine beasts and that these are just stories his mother told him, or nightmares he had as a boy. They think we should just use these caves to hide and make some other plan." She heaved an exaggerated sigh at the ceiling. "And they can't agree on what other plan to use. None of them are good, and I should not tell you them in any case."

She leaned toward him and added in a conspiratorial whisper. "One of them involves *poison*. And the *Matron*."

"Orupetra, what are you telling our guest over there?" Elder Tobosu wandered back in their direction. His voice was firm, but his eyes twinkled.

Oru picked with sudden interest at the straw of her pallet. "Just about the caves and how they are certain death."

"Ah. Well. We must not be so hopeless about it. Certainly those we have sent on have not returned. But we know there must be a way through. It was a sacred journey made by our *hala*—the men who serve the temple—at least once a moon, perhaps more. There are many tunnels through the rock. Some of them must be safe to travel. I have looked for signs of their passing—the black from the smoke on the cave ceiling, or the slipperiness of stone smoothed by the passage of many feet. But it is no good. In some places, many of the tunnels have traces. In others, none of them do. And every wrong turn risks a traveler being lost forever in the darkness, or slipping off the path to his death."

Oru flopped backward again. "And now no one will go. Elder Tobosu doesn't even want to let them."

"I could not risk losing another," the old man said, and his voice trembled and broke. "I would go myself, but if I fell, who would commune with the divine beasts? None others remember their secrets. None who would assist us, that is." The firelight grew lower and made the old man's features appear craggier, wearier. "But we must. We must."

"I told you that I would go, Elder Tobosu," Oru said.

"If you went missing, your father would tear apart the city looking for you. All of us would be found out. Anyway, you are too young. A fine leader I'd be if I let one of our youth suffer for the folly of their elders. I would spend the remainder of my life atoning, and it would not be enough."

Mirage made a sound like a grasshopper was caught in his throat. They both looked at him curiously.

"Are you all right, boy?" Tobosu asked.

"Yes. Yes," he said, coughing a little. He took a few deep breaths when he was able. He clenched his fists until his nails bit into his palms. He tried to keep his gaze from wandering toward the interminable void of the caves beyond them. "I… I…" he began. He squeezed his eyes shut. "I will go."

Elder Tobosu's eyebrows jumped up like two startled, bushy caterpillars. "What did you say? Go? Go where?"

"Go… into the tunnels. To try to find the secret paths."

The old man and the young woman exchanged glances. "You are young as well," Tobosu said, finally. "And these are not your caverns. Can you even—I think there is no word for it in your language. Stay atop deep water, and not go under? Or move through it like a fish?"

"Swim. No," Mirage admitted. "But those are my people up there, not yours. If there's something that can help them down there in the dark, well, I think you should let me try to find it. If you don't let me, I'll only go alone," he added hurriedly, seeing doubt settle across the elder's face. "But I reckon I'd be more likely to survive if you… if you helped me."

The elder came before him and, emitting an impressive series of pops and cracks, made an effort at crouching down in front of Mirage, before finally giving up and settling back on Oru's pallet with a little groan. "It's a very brave thing you propose. Braver perhaps than you know, sitting here in the firelight, surrounded by others. Your choice may feel rather different to you when you are alone in the dark, with only the dripping of water and the whispers of the spirits of the fallen to keep you company."

Mirage squeezed his eyes shut. "I know. But I have to try. I have to."

"Why?" Tobosu asked, leaning closer and peering intently. "Suppose another goes instead. Would you stay behind?"

Mirage shook his head wordlessly.

"No. It is something more than courage, isn't it?"

"I killed a man." The words escaped Mirage's mouth almost unbidden, as though they were bile, as though he had needed to vomit them out. They left a foul taste behind, but it felt good to be rid of them. "Not a man. A boy. Someone my age."

He became aware that Oru had sat bolt-upright on her pallet and was staring at him, her eyes wide. He tried not to look at her. "Our King—my King—ordered me to. And I did it. I don't—" He rubbed angrily at tears forming in the corners of his eyes, ashamed of them. "I don't even know if I wanted to do it. It just… happened."

Aware that he sounded now as though he were letting himself out of his own snare, he added, "Only I must have wanted to. Because I did it. And I… I boasted of it after. I thought it was brave. I thought it was right. That's why I… no. That's not why I did it. I did it… just because. There was a big crowd, and we were finally standing face to face with… with the people we thought were our enemies. The whole world was hot. It was hot inside me, like a dance. It felt joyous and angry at the same time, and I held my bowstring, and the bowstring was my whole body, and the King told me to let it go, and I did, I let it go, and for a moment I was glad. I was *glad*. And then he fell. He was my friend. And I couldn't pull the bowstring back again." He hid his face so they couldn't see the tears. They ran hot down his arms and cool when they dripped onto his legs.

"So I have to go. It's what you said. I could spend the rest of my life trying to make it right, and it wouldn't be enough. I know even if I go, and the gods are with me, and I find what you're looking for, I won't be done. But if I don't… if I don't try now, when everyone up there is depending on me… I *really* will never be done. Do you see?"

He finally dared to look up at them, trying somehow to surreptitiously wipe the tears away on his arms. To his dismay, he saw that Oru looked shocked, her mouth open, and the kindness had gone from Elder Tobosu's eyes. There was no malice there. No anger. The old man's gaze was calm and steady, his expression neutral.

"I understand," he said. "I do see. Yes. I think it is right for you to go. Come with me." The old man pushed himself to his feet again and moved back toward the small group of people, raising his hands for attention.

Mirage wearily stood too, suddenly aware that his puffy nose and red eyes would not fool anyone even in torchlight. On the pallet beside him, Oru backed away, hugging her knees and watching him with wary eyes. He suspected she would never treat him kindly again. He could not fault her. His right to live among the gentle people of the world had flown away on an arrow.

~

The cavern beyond the meeting room with the pallets was smaller and darker, and the pathway on one side dropped away into a frightening darkness. The sound of water trickling came from far, far below. Mirage waved his torch toward it, but still could see nothing.

"Keep away from the edge if you want to be seen again," Elder Tobosu warned. He lifted his own torch to illuminate the room. Two passages other than the one through which they'd entered led away from it, one winding steeply downhill, the rush of water coming from it, and another climbing upward, its footholds craggy and slanted.

"We know the first few paths to take," the old man said. "We think, anyway. Each time, we lost someone. There, the mark on the passageway. You take this bit of whitestone."

Mirage took the triangular chunk of stone from him, a little bigger than his thumb. It felt soft and crumbly and left dust on his fingers.

"You make one mark across when you attempt a passage. If you make it through to the next branch in the caves, you mark the way you came from with two slashes, like this. Then you return to the previous room and cross your first mark with a second. That way those who come after know the way is safe. You see?"

Mirage nodded. "But what are those marks up there?" He pointed at the cave wall above his head. Between the two passages, someone had meticulously carved a design that looked like many lines moving together—in some places, one line crossed over another. One ended. A new one began.

"Some symbol from an older time, perhaps. No one really knows." Elder Tobosu looked over his shoulder. "I know what you are thinking. A map. We thought so, too. But there is no relation between the marks and the passageways. Many lines, see? Only three routes out. One route ends—for our scout never returned—but how does it match the line on the mark? It does not, so far as we can tell. Come now. If we who have studied it for many rains cannot find it, then a boy from the plains has no hope of it."

He led Mirage through the left passageway, and they climbed up and up in the darkness, so high that Mirage thought they must have reentered the city somewhere, and indeed, they passed by one wall that must have been a passageway into Bogana, but it had been blocked up with boulders too heavy for five strong men to move. There was another carving on the wall here, like the one before, but not quite the same—the lines were in a different configuration, one line passing over three at once. But there was only one path to be taken. Elder Tobosu was right: there seemed no correlation between the mark and the passages through the tunnels.

Mirage followed on. A few of the Breakwater men had followed behind at a safe distance, carrying torches of their own and chattering to each other in Boganan, somehow still managing to convey their contempt for him in tone if not in words he could comprehend. The passage moved through a tunnel with low ceilings, and these bore the signs of tool work.

Someone had widened the tunnel to make travel easier, so surely this route was correct. Mirage wondered at the skill of Boganan craftsmen, who had the ability to work stone not just into simple knives or spearheads, but into masks and figures of the gods. A civilization that could bore tunnels through solid rock was formidable indeed.

"This choice cost us dearly," Elder Tobosu said as they reached the next junction. This one branched into five different corridors. Three of the tunnels had single, horizontal lines next to them. One had no markings. One was crossed. Mirage did not need the markings explained to him. Three scouts had gone missing before the fourth had found the safe passage.

Again, the carved marking was on the wall, again with its confusing row of lines crossing and twisting. He stared at it, puzzling for a moment. There was something about it that tugged at his thoughts. What was it? They'd gone left, and passed a sealed off passage, and now they were taking the second passage. It was like a long-forgotten childhood song, the words almost familiar, but just out of reach of his memory.

They took the second route through a tunnel so tight that the Teller could not have passed through it. Mirage was lean and wiry enough to have no trouble, but Elder Tobosu had to suck in his stomach and straighten his hunched stance to squeeze by.

Thin shafts of sunlight speared the next room, shining through cracks in another sealed-up exit to the outside world. The cliff was so honeycombed with passages that it was a wonder the whole city didn't go collapsing through the rock and into the great water.

"And this is where I stop," Elder Tobosu said. He waved his torch about, but after the darkness of the previous rooms, the faint sunlight made it unnecessary. Three possible exits led from the room. All three exits had single lines beside them.

"But there is no path forward," Mirage protested. "All of them have been tried."

"Two of them were dead ends," Tobosu said. "And the scouts returned. From one of them, no one ever came back."

"But then what am I to do? Perhaps the exit collapsed? Or perhaps he never returned because he went on ahead? Or slipped and fell?"

"Perhaps." The old man shrugged his hunched shoulders. "It is your choice, now. We know there used to be a way. I remember, as a boy, watching the *hala* gather in their brown robes, singing their praises to the moon, who is sister to the sea, and one by one disappearing into the rock to send prayers and offerings to the gods."

"Maybe they only dropped the offerings into a hole."

Elder Tobosu scowled. "No, boy. There were temples that rang with their song. Valuables stored as signs of reverence to the gods. Priests would remain for days in prayer and supplication. They gave their songs to the divine beasts. They would not have lied to us about this. There is a way."

Mirage sighed and sat down on a large, round boulder, staring at the room. Three passageways, all false. Or perhaps the untested passage back in the other room was the true route. Or perhaps that, too, led to death. Perhaps one of the previous routes from which no one had ever returned was correct, and someone had merely slipped and fallen on their way to return and mark the passage. There were too many variables.

You could spend your whole life wandering these caves and never find your way through. He wondered at the lives it must have cost to explore them in the early days. Perhaps the gods had guided them. Or perhaps they'd simply sacrificed uncountable citizens.

He peered into the darkness of the tunnels and down one of the passages, he swore he saw something move in the darkness, something small and roundish in shape. The shape in the murky shadows looked like a hare. It lifted a stubby paw and gave him a wave. He rubbed at his eyes. There was no way it could have followed him down here. Torchlight and shifting shadows, that was all.

His gaze slid up the wall, and there he saw, again, the mark. Again it was changed, again it was indecipherable, with five lines, when there were only four tunnels. He scowled at it. What was the point of a mark on the wall to show the way if it was too complex to understand? It ought to be something simple. Something easy, so that even a child could—

He stared at it again. He worked his fingers, tracing their path. They'd gone left, and then right, and then left again…

Left, right, left…

He stared up at the mark on the wall.

"I see it," he said.

"What's that?" Elder Tobosu eyed him skeptically. "You think you know the next path?"

"Not just the next path," Mirage said. "All of it. I know how to get to the temple."

# 23 Tenets of a Young God

Clay gazed up at the massive figure of Mother Fam, filling her cavern of light, smiling with love and sadness down at him. He searched her expression for some reason to hope, but he knew that she had spoken the truth. Ogya was too powerful. His temple was unreachable, in the belly of the world, and at a moment's notice, he could move it anyplace with sufficient flame, ash, or where heat had baked the life out of the land. Her story of the history of the gods had ended in a terrible, flat fact: Ogya could not be defeated. He had lost everything—his home, his people, his very body—and it was all for nothing. Even in his human form, he felt, in his chest, that terrible line of emptiness creeping toward his heart. But that couldn't be *it*. They couldn't be out of hope.

Why would Wem design a world that could be so easily unbalanced? He had learned at least that much during his time as a god: everything in creation existed in balance. Death and life gave way to each other. Predators thinned the numbers of prey and kept them from starving. Plant and animal depended on each other for life. All the world required balance. So how could Wem have created one force that could destroy all others without a counter of its own?

Mother Fam's radiant smile was that of his own mother—of *all* mothers. He felt safe, warm, and loved in her presence. She was the mother of all gods. The creator of all life. And so what he did next was the bravest thing he'd ever done.

He stepped back and folded his arms. "No," he said. "I don't accept it."

He waited for her to be angry, for her to boom with divine fury, to command him from her presence forever, and he knew that command would devastate him. But she only laughed. "Dear Clay. I saw this in you when you were only an infant. I knew then how strong you would grow up to be, here." Her huge finger touched his chest, sending him stumbling backward, a smear of primal earth-mud caking his skin. "Barely divine, and yet you would challenge us all to save the world. But I spoke the truth. Ogya cannot be defeated."

"Well, why are we only talking about defeating him? Perhaps we could change his mind?"

Doto snorted. "You couldn't change the minds of your own people, Clay. Ogya is cruel, evil, and driven by endless hunger. You'll never talk him out of it."

Dismayed, Clay hunched down a little. "I didn't mean me. I thought perhaps if the other gods spoke to him, persuaded him to back down… Fire doesn't like water. Perhaps if Mpo and Asubonten and Atekye spoke to him?"

Mother Fam's great head swayed from side to side. "He would not listen. He has not since the bargain that inflicted him with hunger was first struck. And no god would trust him, not after he imprisoned Sarmu."

"But then… if we can't defeat him, and we can't persuade him, maybe *we* could imprison *him*?"

The goddess leaned back into the wall of her cavern, the stone melding with her earthen flesh. She tilted her head back, seemingly lost in thought.

"Even Sarmu is not truly bound," Doto reminded them. "His spirit would return to his temple if he dared to touch the fire below him and destroy his own avatar."

Clay had not thought of that. Sarmu remained in his prison out of laziness or ennui, or perhaps fear of the pain of his avatar's destruction. Presumably Ogya would have no such compunction. "But then why does Sarmu's body not starve to death or die of thirst?" he asked. "You and I grow hungry when we travel outside the forest."

Doto shrugged. "Sarmu is the god of fat and famine. Perhaps he cannot."

"And if Ogya is a god of hunger, then he is the same?"

"It could work." Mother Fam unrolled herself from the cavern wall with a rumbling of earth. "It could fail terribly, but it could work. Every god's avatar is different. You two and Kwaee, my little forest gods, you are not simply gods of the forest. You are gods of life. Your avatars are governed by life's laws. When not sustained by the forest, you must eat, drink, sleep, and breathe. But Sarmu does not. Nor does Mpo, nor Asubonten, nor Ogya. Even outside his temple, where he seldom travels, Ogya has a body of flame. It consumes and breathes but will never starve or suffocate."

"I've tended a few fires," Clay said, objecting, "and they go out without fuel or if you cover them from the air."

"Fire has many ways to burn," Mother Fam said gently. "Beneath my depths of stone and earth, Ogya's realm of fire blazes without air or fuel. It is endlessly burning stone. Ogya's body can live imprisoned in stone."

"Like we have seen in Ogya-Bepow," Doto said. "But suppose we build a prison of stone? What will keep him from simply melting it and escaping?"

"Water!" Clay shouted, excited. "If Mother Fam could fashion a prison out of stone and earth and then we place it underwater, Ogya could never escape!"

"Or he could try, and drown himself. Or perhaps there are fires that burn underwater, too."

"There are," Mother Fam said slowly. "But fire fears water nonetheless. Ogya would not dare risk his body being quenched by a flood. It would be against his own nature. You are a clever creature, Clay."

He blushed, awed and delighted by the praise.

"But Mpo has her own troubles. She would never agree to house a prison containing Ogya, and the sea is turbulent and in constant motion. We could not risk a prison there. Perhaps in the swamps. Atekye could help, perhaps, though she will not grant her assistance lightly."

"And—and you would help us with this, Mother Fam? You could make a prison that could hold Ogya?"

She reached down with both arms, cool mud pressing about him as she lifted him up and pressed him fondly to her bosom. "Of course I will help, dear Clay. I do not wish to see all the world burned." She touched his face with one pillar of a finger. "But you are weeping, child."

He felt the hot tears. "It's just… you're the first person in all the world we've met who was willing to help. I thought maybe there was no one left. That all the gods were—were…"

"You thought that you were alone."

"Yes."

"Clay. You never were. You never are. All of life is with you. All around you. We are all part of the same thing. Some of us struggling, some of us failing, some of us at peace. But this is life. The spark that fuels you fuels everyone you've ever known. Even Ogya."

"But we're still going to imprison him?"

"I think I can construct a prison. A room with layers of water and stone that can hold him—there is stone in my body too strong even for Ogya to burn away. But we will need to capture him, somehow. We will need to be swift, to cut him off from his temple and prevent him from returning to it. We must hit him with something fast and powerful."

"Like a river!" Clay was growing excited now. "If—if we could get Asubonten to change her course, we could surprise Ogya. Sweep him off his feet and into the prison."

Doto caught the excitement. "But Asubonten always follows the shortest course. She told us that herself. So we'd have to change it. For that we would need Mother Fam to move the earth."

"And Kwaee to grant permission, since it would be through his forest," Clay said. "Mother Fam, you said you cannot act in a god's terrain without him allowing it?"

She smiled. "Yes. The god of the forest must permit me to enter. I must work in concert with him to change his territory. And, of course, we must secure Asubonten's cooperation as well. But how will you summon Ogya's avatar? If we are to trap him, we will need a lure."

Clay faltered. "I'm not sure. He wants to burn the entire forest. What could we have that would pull him to one place?"

Doto stepped forward. "We know what he wants. He told us. Well, he told my father. And my father refused him."

The blood drained from Clay's face. *Give me your son, forest god. Open a path to his temple. Let me taste the sweet flesh of divinity.* The numbness crept ever toward his heart. Toward Doto's heart. "Doto—Doto, no, we can't do this!"

"What other choice do we have? I know you are afraid for me, Clay, but if this is truly our chance to stop Ogya, then we must take it." He looked up at Mother Fam, gold-green eyes searching her glittering mica discs. "*Is* this truly our chance?"

She was quiet for a long time. "I do not have a better answer," she said finally. "I am certain that Ogya cannot be defeated. It may be that this plan will not suffice to contain him. But it is better than no plan. It will be difficult. You will have to convince your father to go along with it, which will not be easy. He is a stubborn god."

Doto laughed dryly.

"And then you will need to persuade Atekye and Asubonten as well. Remind them that Ogya threatens their domains, too. The river has already tasted his foul sludge. The swamps will clog and dry up. They must listen."

Doto shuffled his bare feet in the mud. He curled his toes, and Clay knew he missed the flex of tendons, the comforting extension of his claws. Clay missed them, too. "But will it work?" Doto insisted. "It would not be only my life at stake if we fail. My temple and Clay's… we are one. If Ogya consumes it, we will both die."

"This is the burden of being gods," Fam answered. "There is no one to reassure you and guide you. You must choose your own path. I cannot promise you that this plan will work. But Ogya has troubled my surface for a very long time, and among all the gods, you two are the only ones who have dared to try to stop him. I will do everything in my power to help you succeed."

Clay thought then of their confrontation with Ogya by the edge of the forest—the terrible heat, the choking smoke, the burning rocks piercing his body. That torment had been awful. So, too, the many deaths he'd suffered at the hands of his own people, those he was trying so desperately to save. But he knew that those agonies would be gentle compared to the fires of Ogya raging through his and Doto's temple. All other injuries and deaths had been to his avatar. The temple was made up of their merged souls. He would not only perish in torment, he would watch his love suffer beside him.

But the risk was surely worth it. Was this not already the end that awaited them, once Ogya had carved out the forest and found them? And if Clay was truly a god, even a small one, wasn't this his responsibility? Wasn't this his forest to save?

"Mother Fam, you say that when you're a god, there is no one to reassure you and guide you, but… when I was just a… just a human, it was the same. The gods never spoke to us. We believed they were out there. We believed they were helping us. But they weren't, were they? Not like we thought, anyway. We had many stories, and as far as I can tell, few of them were true. We were alone. We thought the gods were guiding us and saving us, but they weren't. Sarmu would do nothing for us. Kwaee and Ogya hated us. And Father Wem only watches and doesn't help."

He sighed. "My people will suffer if we do nothing. They will die. I do not—" He broke off. There was something hard and sharp inside him, as though a knife had been planted in his heart, and when he thought of his people, it cut deeper and more painfully. They had beaten him. Lacerated him. Burned him. Murdered him over and over. His own brothers. Those he'd grown to love and trust.

"Clay?" Doto's voice broke his thoughts, and he realized his teeth were bared, his nostrils flared. "You… snarled."

He felt the heat of his blood in his cheeks and forehead. Gingerly, he felt for that part of himself that thought about his old life and about who he used to be. And then he shut it away. It was too painful to touch. "I do not care what happens to them. They are too foolish. Too selfish. If they would kill each other and—and burn their own homes to the ground, then let them. I cannot fight for them anymore. But the forest is innocent. If I am truly to be a god, then I must fight for *it* and protect it. Not just so that Doto and I can live. But because I love it."

He gazed up at Mother Fam, adoring her, grateful for how she made him feel safe and loved, grateful for the world she had birthed. But there was sadness in her expression. She knelt down like the setting of the moon. "Of course, then, I will help. Together we will stop Ogya. You will go to Kwaee and Asubonten and Atekye and secure their assistance, and we will set a trap for Ogya he could never expect. And remember: breathe no word of your plan near dry ash or flame. If he overhears, we will never be able to deceive him."

Clay looked back at Doto. "We'll take this chance together?"

Doto put his hand on his shoulder. "Of course we will."

"Then we will do it. One last chance to stop Ogya and save the forest."

Mother Fam put thick arms around Clay, drawing him close to her muddy body. In the embrace she said quietly into his ear, "I am proud of you Clay. But please, be careful. Your humanity is a gift—the gods do not know how to use it, but you were born with it. It is the most valuable part of you. Do not lose yourself in your determination to become one of us. This is a struggle to the end. None of us can afford to abandon any of our strengths now."

She let him go then and reached out for Doto who, wide-eyed, lifted his arms for her and let himself be pulled into her hug. If she whispered something to him, too, Clay could not hear it. Then she stood and stepped back, sinking into the cavern wall, her great body submerging into the stone like it was mud, her arms and legs losing form, her breasts and belly disappearing, until only her craggy face remained, a convincing formation of stone. "Goodbye, dear children. See Kwaee first. Urge him to allow me back to the forest. I will be watching as closely as I am permitted. Have strength. Have heart. I am proud of you."

And then her face, too, disappeared, and they were left deep below the earth, with only the chirping songs of a million glowing frogs to remind them they were not alone.

~

Doto thought the journey back to the forest swifter than their trip to Fam, though the days numbered the same. He was eager to return to the safety of his domain and feel its full power running through him once again. He yearned to bask with Clay in their temple and forget the mud and the cold and the hunger. But would have a heavy task lay before them. He wondered if that was what kept Clay so quiet—his mate forged ahead across the barren landscape with a determined step but a distant expression.

He considered asking, but the explanation might be an unpleasant fire bearer thing, full of emotions and flawed assumptions and difficult to understand. Or possibly Clay was annoyed with him for some reason, and he did not particularly want to learn about that. So he kept silent and reasoned that if Clay had anything he wanted to talk about, he would mention it. And besides, it was only fair, since Clay had not asked what was bothering Doto.

In the middle of the second day of their journey, they were both proceeding down a steep slope when the rocks slid under Clay's feet. He grunted in annoyance, his arms wheeling for balance, and fell to his side but only continued sliding, and then hit a larger rock with one foot and went head over heels down the mountain.

Doto felt a very stupid moment of panic, worrying that his little fire bearer would be killed, and then chided himself for his idiocy and hurried after Clay, trying his best not to tumble as well.

He found the rough tracks of Clay's slide, extending nearly to the bottom of the slope, where Clay sat holding one ankle and muttering to himself. He was disheveled, his hair matted into clumps and his skin almost as muddy as after one of Mother Fam's embraces. Even with his weak human nose Doto caught the scent of blood. "Are you hurt?" he asked with some concern.

"A little scraped up, I guess." Clay didn't look up, inspecting his foot. "I think I hurt my ankle when I hit the rock, though. It's throbbing."

"You really do not care for that foot," Doto observed. "Every time I catch up with you, you're trying to get rid of it."

Clay peered up at him. "Was that an actual *joke?*"

He sounded half amused and half annoyed. Doto decided to play it safe. "Perhaps."

With a groan, Clay pushed himself to his feet, taking Doto's proffered hand. "Ugh. No, I can't put any weight on it right now. This is… this is stupid."

"What is?"

"Spending all this time trekking back to the forest." He slumped. "If we just *died*, we'd wake up back at home."

"But that is not going to happen."

"No." Clay sounded emphatic. "Not if I can help it. But I can't walk on this ankle all the way. I can't. I don't want to go any further like this."

"But what other choice have we?" Doto did not enjoy this weak fire bearer body, but he had found that he liked being with Clay outside the forest; it reminded him of the days when they'd first met. Even if in those days Clay had been suffering continually and Doto had been taking him to his doom. He loved Clay's bush of a mane and his wide, brown eyes and his round cheeks. And though he greatly approved of Clay's new, more noble feline form, it didn't remind him of those early days. It had been growing more difficult to see the fire bearer he fell in love with in the avatar of a forest god ascendant. "A little bit of our domain would make all of this so much easier. You could do a little dance, perhaps? Just enough?"

"I'm not going to be dancing up a forest for us like this!"

Doto crouched to inspect the injured ankle. "It does not look so bad. Besides, just a few steps of dancing and it will heal, and then you can finish."

"I can't put any weight on it without pain. I can't make the forest circle. You are going to have to try it."

He fought down a surge of anxiety. "Clay, I have explained this before. I do not know how to do the song or how to make the dance, and you do not even have a song for me to sing and I do not know how to invent one."

"Well, you're going to have to dance for me or carry me back, so make up your accursed mind!" Clay gave Doto what was probably meant to be a shove, but only sent himself sprawling back into the grass.

Doto's ears tried to flatten, but of course, these round fleshy circles didn't move that way at all. Fire bearer bodies were so expressionless. Puzzled, he reached down to try to help Clay up, but Clay ignored his hand and sat, hugging his knees.

"What is wrong, Clay? Your ankle will get better. We will find a way." There was no answer, and Doto paced in an anxious little circle. "Are you afraid of the gods? Or is this about Ogya?"

Still no answer.

He scratched at his chest, thinking. "Is this about your people killing you many, many times?"

Clay's eyes were red and wet when he looked back up at Doto. "Yes. Yes, of course. It's about all that and everything else. It's… it's that I've lost my whole family and suddenly I have these powers and I lose my mind and I go from thinking the gods are far away and perfect to finding out they're all around me and they're flawed and kind of awful, and now the whole world is going to be destroyed and my people, my *friends*, are afraid of me and tortured and murdered me over and over and meanwhile I'm the only one who can save the world and you're not helping me, Doto. You're the only one I have left, and you can't do this one thing that would help me to get better and feel safe and loved. And I'm just so tired. And cold. And hungry. And… tired."

Doto flinched back from the tirade, stung. He had never heard Clay speak this way before. There had been some very impolitic things said about gods being awful in the middle of it, but it was probably best to ignore that for now. "I healed your foot before," he said.

"I know."

"And I brought you back to life."

"Yes."

"Even though it cost me my own divinity."

"I couldn't forget. You keep reminding me."

"Well, good," said Doto, though the way Clay had said it, it didn't sound like it was good. He wished he had a tail to switch. It helped him think. Instead he dropped down into a crouch and put his hand on Clay's shoulder. "I know these things are hard and you want help, but this is part of being a god. You have to learn to be strong."

"I'm tired of being strong!" Clay half-shouted the words. "Don't you understand, Doto? I miss being me. I miss knowing my role, who I was. I miss having people take care of me when I'm feeling weak. I miss believing that the gods were looking out for me, that when things in the world were going very wrong, somebody was going to make it right. The gods were supposed to keep us safe. But it turns out that they're just as damaged and rotten as the rest of us, and when things are going really, really bad, they're not saving us. They're *causing* it. So now…" He rubbed at tears wetting his face. "So now suddenly I'm a god, the world is going to end, and I have to save it."

"All this was going to happen anyway, whether you became a god or not," Doto said gently. "The only difference is that now you have a chance to stop it."

"I know." Clay rubbed his eyes clear again. "I know. I just wish someone else would do it for once."

Doto looked fondly over his confused and sad little fire bearer and picked a few bits of dried leaf out of his hair. "What was it Mother Fam said to you back underground? These fire bearer ears are very inferior, and I could not hear her."

Clay gave a long sigh. "She said I should hold on to my humanity. That—that it was important somehow. I'm not sure what she meant."

Doto considered this. "Maybe fire bearers can do something gods can't," he suggested. "Although I can only think of one thing."

Clay groaned. "All *right*," he said. "All right. If only so my ankle will stop hurting."

He pushed himself to his feet and, gritting his teeth, began to limp in a wide circle. "Oh, he is Doto the Mighty…"

5

They were not long back in the forest when they heard the screeching of a baboon. If they had been rushing at high speed back to Kwaee, they might never have heard it, but Doto had suggested they rest and allow their moods to be rejuvenated within the forest, and to his relief, Clay had agreed. Even after healing in the scraggly forest circle he'd danced up—which could barely be called forest at all—he still acted angry and tired. He needed to rest and let his mind drift away from all the troubles. Doto had *hoped* for a few days spent lovemaking in their temple, but Clay didn't seem very much in the mood for that, and Doto had not pressed the issue.

So they walked back at a somewhat leisurely pace, enjoying being neither hungry nor cold, smelling the rich scent of their dominion, surrounded by the birdsong and the whir of insect wings and the rumbling of plant roots furrowing ever deeper into the soil. The forest was so thick here that midday was as dark as dusk, but they were its gods, and underbrush parted to let them pass; roots flattened so as not to trip them; rain guttering through the folds of broad leaves sieved through their fur without dampening it. Clay seemed to be relaxing. The tension was gone from his shoulders and neck and he didn't smell as stressed as before.

Then the cry of a baboon came, one of an animal in pain. Clay's ears perked toward the sound and he paused, sniffing the air. "That's—"

"Just an injured beast. Like the kind that Kwaee sent after you to kill you. A baboon. They cannot harm you now, you know," Doto added in reassurance.

"Come on," Clay called, and then he was gone with a rush of air, the forest leaves whipping around in his wake.

Puzzled, Doto followed at a somewhat slower pace. He found Clay in a small clearing in the forest. One baboon lay sprawled out on the ground and another crouched close by him, brushing at his shoulder with the backs of her knuckles, clearly distressed. Both regarded Clay and Doto with guarded expressions.

A few sniffs of the air told the story: raw, green wood from a stripped branch that smelled of baboon; torn leaves in the tree and on the ground below; the scent of green wood and leaves on the paw of the fallen baboon; blood, on a jagged rock beneath the tree and on the back of the baboon's head. The scent of a larger troop of baboons hung in the air. Many had passed this way, one had fallen, and most had left him, but one had lingered by his side. Perhaps a friend, or a recent mate.

Clay approached slowly, step by step. He probably thought he looked non-threatening, but a leopard creeping closer like that just looked like it was hunting.

The female baboon screeched at him, baring her fangs. *Get back, Forest Lord! He is not yours!* No beast dared show disrespect to a god, but baboons often flirted with the idea.

"It's all right. It's okay." The low, gentle tone of voice was familiar to Doto. Clay often used it on him when he was feeling irascible. "I'm not going to hurt you. I just want to help."

Doto was at his side in an instant, prompting another screech of alarm from the baboon. Both creatures reeked of fear. Doto gripped Clay's forearm tightly and leaned in close. "You *cannot* help this creature," he growled low. "You know that. You know what will happen."

His face and muzzle flared with remembered pain: his father slashing it open in punishment, in his most starkly remembered lesson. The genet cub, the one with its back legs crushed, the one he had tried to heal so long ago, when he was just learning to be a god. His heart had ached for it. He'd longed to heal it. But a god did not interfere in that way. And the cost of that magic—who knew it better than he and Clay?

"Would you give this creature the power I gave you? Would you make my mate part baboon as well? I forbid it!"

Clay shook his head as though weary. "I'm not going to use my power to heal it, Doto. I'm just going to *help* it."

He knelt near the fallen baboon. The female screamed at him. *Stay back!* She moved to stand over her companion in defiance, then scrambled a few steps away, her courage shaken. The fallen baboon struggled, trying feebly to push himself away. Waves of fear rolled off both of them.

"Be easy," Clay cooed. He put his paw to the injured creature's body, and it thrashed in terror. "Be *still.*" His voice was heavy with divine command—something Doto had never seen him do before—and both baboons froze, unmoving, watching him with a guarded expression. Impressive. Doto had never managed to persuade baboons to behave. But then these were alone and away from their pack. Their hearts scampered, their breaths short and terrified.

Carefully, Clay inspected the wound, brushing dirt out of it. After a moment he raised a paw and the tree branches above bent, a current of rainwater funneling through the leaves and pouring down in a stream that he used to wash and clean the injury.

Doto paced in frustration. This was wrong. This was against the rules. His father's old admonitions came to his tongue. "This isn't the way of the forest, Clay. We're not here to try to take away all pain. We only—we only move it. To another place. To the prey this beast will devour later, or to the suffering it will feel when it dies another way. We are here to preserve the laws of nature. The balance. That is all."

Clay looked up at him with ears back. "The *balance*, Doto? What balance? The forest is dying under Ogya's onslaught. Your father uses beasts as his weapons. We know from Mother Fam that all the gods are… out of balance. That the whole world is. Balance is a lie. It always has been."

"But the laws of nature—"

"To ash with the laws of nature! I think they are something your father invented to excuse himself, his inaction. Are we not gods of the forest?"

Doto gaped at him. "You—you're not sounding like yourself. This is wrong, Clay."

"I don't think it's wrong. I think it's wrong if you can help and you do nothing." Clay frowned, his brow furrowing. "What were the plants that Cloud used for pain…?"

He put one paw to the ground and closed his eyes. Divine power rolled around him in waves, calling the forest to him. Then the forest floor around him shifted, fallen leaves nudged aside by rising stems. Green shoots rose up between his fingers, climbing his arm.

The baboons, still quiet, cowered but did not move as Clay went from plant to plant, plucking leaves, squeezing out sap, or tearing away roots that helpfully unearthed themselves for his convenience. "I don't really remember what all of these are, but… I can feel they're right." He gave Doto a searching look. "I think I can, anyway. These roots, I think, help with pain. These leaves and these" –he put them into his mouth, chewing them up, and then spat out a green wad of mulch— "will stop bleeding. Here."

He lifted the injured baboon's head carefully. "Still dirty. Don't want you getting infected." He leaned down and cleaned the wound with a few slow drags of his tongue, taking care not to let the rasping spines wound it further. The creature went very, very still. Probably it thought it was being eaten. Its companion frantically paced back and forth a few feet away. Baboons were a favorite food of leopards.

"This isn't a good idea, Clay," Doto warned him, but Clay gave no indication he'd heard him. Instead, he pressed the pulpy mass of plant material to the back of the baboon's head. He secured it there with a broad leaf and two long vines that he tied in that clever way of fire bearers.

Once satisfied, he then chewed up other bits of plant and fed them to the creature, patiently coaxing it until it finally accepted and swallowed the medicine. No doubt sensing how his presence distressed the two, he got to his feet and came back to Doto's side. "Maybe he'll be all right and maybe he won't," Clay said. "But I tried."

"He's not going to survive just lying there anyway. Something will come by and eat him. Probably a leopard." Doto folded his arms across his chest. "Baboons *are* delicious, you know."

Clay wrinkled his face like he was tasting the air. "Why do you have to be like that?" He curled his toes into the earth and in a moment a small thicket of brambles sprouted and grew around the two animals, concealing and protecting them. "But thank you for the advice."

The scent of fear had begun to ebb from the area, as had the stink of pain. The heartbeats of the two creatures were slowing, and after a little while, the male drifted into sleep. Doto waited to hear if its heart would stop, but instead it settled into a low, steady rhythm. "Maybe—*maybe*—you helped this time," Doto conceded. "But it's not the way of the forest."

"Well, it is now. Or at least some small part of the forest. My part. I'm not trying to change the balance. I know all your arguments for why we shouldn't do it. I know it's not been the way of the gods. But Doto, the way of the gods isn't working."

Clay turned to him and put both paws on his shoulders. And for the first time in many days, the fear and hurt and anger were gone from his eyes. For the first time since his very first death, Clay looked at peace. "I think I understand what Mother Fam meant. We can't just keep doing things the gods' way. That's how we got here. That's why the world is in danger. We have to be better, my love. We have to change everything."

# 24 A River of Ash

Finally back in the forest, and recuperated, Clay and Doto raced to find Kwaee and tell him their plan, but he was not in his temple. Together, they followed the ripples of his presence through the forest and found him near the perimeter of the fire, one that burned far higher and hotter than when they had left. It raged above the treetops, clouds of yellow smoke filtering the sunlight and bathing the midday forest in a baleful, blood-red hue. The blaze was so hot and high now that even the afternoon rains could not quench it. Whatever tricks the fire bearers had learned while Clay and Doto had been away had proven effective in spreading the inferno.

When Clay let his senses open beyond his own skin, the pain of the forest nearly overwhelmed him—and left more of him numb and unresponsive, like a limb he had slept on and crushed the feeling out of. An enormous portion of the forest was missing now, cut off from his senses. How could the humans have killed so much of it so quickly?

"You took too long!" Kwaee shouted as they approached. He stood with his arms outstretched, calling the forest to respond to him. From the ash-powdered earth, saplings twisted upward in a line that extended in both directions. The finger-thin trunks thickened and bulged, groaning in low, unnatural voices as their wooden hearts swelled faster than their natures willed. They shuddered as thick, thorny branches split from their sides and intertwined with those of their brethren.

Letting his senses explore, Clay became aware of a vast network of roots spreading out beneath them, braiding together, fingering outward to find every hidden pocket of moist soil, every grain of rare stone they hungered for. The ground bulged beneath them with the spread of the roots, and the atmosphere itself grew clearer, the cool, hard edge of fresh air cutting through the greasy staleness of the smoke. Above them branches crowded for every spare mote of fire-filtered sunlight.

Kwaee's new trees grew together, their bark flowing like liquid as they swelled into and merged with each other, and their wood was shiny and dense as stone. Clay knew that they would not burn easily. Kwaee had grown a tall, wooden wall, bristling with thorns, tall as the tallest trees, too thick to be hewn down by the sharpest fire bearer weapons, but he had done so at a great cost. The rapid growth and absolute cover of the trees had sapped the soil. Within a few seasonal cycles, the giants would weaken, and then they would die. Nothing near them would ever grow, not until they decayed and gave back to the soil what they had taken.

Kwaee turned to them, his feather crown flared with triumph. "The fire bearers will find that a setback. And if they should break through, I have worse surprises for them. Trees whose pollen rends the lungs, whose sap boils the skin. Mushrooms whose spores will sicken them, and should they press on, my death-apple trees, whose smoke, if burned, will turn their lungs to blood."

"What has happened here?" Doto asked, with a look of dismay. "The forest extended far north of here. I thought the fire bearers' burn was slow. Is it all lost?"

"They have new tricks now. They cut up the forest into large pieces they can burn faster than I thought possible." Kwaee's voice cracked with grief. "There were small deer that lived there. White and tiny, no larger than a dik-dik. They live no more. None remain. Ogya has cut out a part of me that will never regrow. And the blaze grows larger every day, burns more quickly. The fire bearers head toward something southeast. I suspect Ogya follows the pulse of your temple. He hungers for you still."

Kwaee stared down the length of his muzzle at Clay. "Will you protest now? Condemn me? Plead for the miserable lives of your people?"

Clay bared his fangs. "They are not my people."

"Well, well. How quickly we ascend. And now that you have transcended your bestial origins, there is no need to bow before gods?"

Obediently, Clay prostrated himself before Kwaee, and beside him, Doto did the same. Beneath the sour reek of ash, the earth smelled empty and barren. Everything in it had been drained away to fuel Kwaee's defenses.

The forest god gave a low rumble that might have been pleasure. He curled his toes and around his feet, spreading in a thicket as high as a fire bearer, snarls of blackvine grew, curling in dark loops, their gnarled stems jutting thorns as thick as Clay's claws, and far sharper. No barb touched Clay, though; the vines bent away from him in deference.

Doto lifted himself from his deep bow. "The journey was difficult. There were complications."

"What sort of complications?" Kwaee said.

Doto exchanged a glance with Clay, who immediately understood. With his deep loathing for fire bearers, Kwaee would surely not care for the news that Doto now slipped into human form outside the forest.

"Our powers don't work out there," Clay said hastily as he, too, rose. "And the journey was long and arduous. And… cold. We had to journey far underground." He saw Kwaee curl a lip in distaste. The forest god likely had no more love for caverns than he did.

"Mother Fam told us *everything*," Doto said. An edge hardened his voice.

Looking uneasy, Kwaee stepped backward, the blackvine clattering as it parted for him. "Everything. I don't know what that means, everything."

"About the fire bearers. And us. You. Why you stand upright instead of walking on all fours like a beast. What you got and what you… gave up."

"Ah." Kwaee looked everywhere but into his son's stare and apparently decided that fixing Clay with a murderous glare was the safest bet. Clay didn't know what he'd done to earn it or how all this could in any way be his fault.

"Why did you keep it a secret, Father? Why did you not tell me? Why hide everything and banish Mother Fam?"

"You were stubborn and recalcitrant enough already! Why should I tell you of every god's greatest mistake? We do not speak of this even to each other! Do you wish me to bare all my secret shames to you?"

"Of course not," Clay answered in what he hoped was a soothing tone.

Doto folded his arms. "But this knowledge does not affect only you. The bargain was made with all the gods. It's where Ogya got his hunger to begin with!"

"And what will you do with that knowledge?" Kwaee said. "How does it help you to know the source of his rapaciousness? Can you dismiss it? Take it back? No. He hungers all the same, and nothing can sate it. Did Mother Earth offer any way to combat him amidst all these informative stories? Or have you returned to your lair with no prey and your stomachs empty?"

"There may be a way," Clay said, forging forward. He cast an uneasy eye toward the flames, wondering if they were far enough away that their god could not hear him. He lowered his voice just in case. "Ogya has imprisoned Sarmu in the savanna."

"Sarmu is a fool," Kwaee declared.

"Er. Yes, all right, but Mother Fam thinks it may be possible to imprison Ogya the same way. There are stones that even the god of fire cannot burn."

"Imprison the god of fire?" Kwaee narrowed his eyes in thought. "It would be a difficult trick. And how would you accomplish such a feat?"

Trying to be respectful and to ignore Kwaee's regular, impatient interruption, Clay and Doto explained the plan they had laid out with Mother Fam. At the end they stopped, watching Kwaee and waiting for his reaction. He strode with his paws behind his back, staring at the ground and muttering to himself, the thorn bushes parting before him like grass bending in the wind.

"So your plan involves allowing Mother Fam back into my forest, allowing her to reshape *my* land? Is that right?" He gave each of them a challenging glare, his claws clutching at the word "my" as though he could clasp the entire forest to his chest.

Clay looked at Doto. Neither of them answered.

"And then you propose to send Asubonten, willful as she is, crashing through my trees on a new course? Will she be two rivers, then? Will she usurp even more of my domain?" He bared his fangs. "And of course, I must risk my son and his temple to lure the fire god into a trap that may not succeed. You could die. You both could."

Doto lowered his head, but his tail switched in defiance. "We know that. It is worth the risk."

"And then this prison containing Ogya? It is to be housed in the heart of my forest? And for this, there will be new swamp that we will, of course, simply *give* to Atekye." Kwaee stopped pacing and folded his arms across his chest, his crest of feathers raised and bristling. "It is an awful lot of giving I am expected to do, is it not? I must grant Fam free permission to shape my skin to her will. I must sacrifice countless reaches of my belly to Asubonten for her new river. I must surrender some precious valley to Atekye so that she can have her new swamp in the middle of my heart. And to ensure that this hastily conceived and dangerous plan works, I must risk my only son, who only recently have I—have I—" His voice broke, and he looked away as though he had caught some distant sound in the forest.

"No," he said hoarsely. "It is too much. I will not agree to this plan."

Clay felt the words like blows. To have gone so far with so little hope, only to finally find a chance. "But Lord Kwaee, if we do nothing, Ogya will not be stopped, and the cost is so very—"

Kwaee surged toward him, a blur of golden fur.

Clay wanted to jump back, or perhaps to cower, and then his fighting instinct surged in him for a hiss, a twist away into a crouch. He did none of these things. Instead he stood unmoving, his gaze refusing to focus. Kwaee stood over him, almost twice his height, his paw at the back of Clay's head, his fingers gripping Clay's scruff tightly, pulling it upward.

The pull on the loose pelt at Clay's nape suspended his mind and all his thoughts with it. It was not that he could not move. He could not remember *how to* move. His jaws ached with an inexplicable urge to yawn.

"Do not speak to me of *costs*," Kwaee growled low into Clay's ear. His voice tickled the tufted fur, but Clay could not even twitch it. "Your life is a blink of an eye. You could surrender the whole thing and it would be nothing. I must last for eons. My forests must grow until the stars go out and the moon falls from the sky. And a thousand years before you were a mote of light in a sea of souls, I fought Ogya. I surrendered a full fifth of my body to defeat him. The plains on which your people crawl like fleas are the corpse of my last sacrifice. Would you give a fifth of your body to defeat him?"

Kwaee lowered a paw and Clay felt the slow drag of a thick, curved claw scrape against the flesh of his legs, drawing a line across his thighs. "Everything from here down. Would you give that to stop Ogya?"

Clay dropped to the thorny floor of the forest, his scruff suddenly released. For a moment, he felt neither fear nor anger, but a lingering complacency as his mind recalled to him how to twitch fingers and toes. "If I could, I would," he told Kwaee with conviction.

"Hm. Well, you would not do it twice," Kwaee said. "Not once you had given that much only to see the fiend on your thresholds a second time. You would swear never to surrender yourself to a hostile power again."

"I don't think my life meant less to me because it was short." Clay struggled to keep his voice from shaking. "It meant more to me. Every day mattered."

"But now you are a god, and you must think of every life. Does the life of a fire bearer matter more to you than that of a gorilla? Of a parrot? An ant? A tree? Will you favor one over the other? You ask me to fell thousands of my trees for this plan of yours. Why should I value their lives less than those of any other creature?"

Doto came between them, his fur bristling. "You are already losing them, Kwaee. How many have fallen to the flames? Would you forfeit all of them because you were unwilling to surrender a few?"

"I will not give Ogya another inch of this forest!" Kwaee roared. "He will have to fight me for it! For every life, every tree, every mote of dust in my dominion! I will surrender none of it willingly! None!"

Understanding broke across Doto's face. "Oh, I see. This isn't about what you lose, is it? It's about what you give." He sighed. "Kwaee. *Father*. Every paw's breadth of forest Ogya takes now, he takes with his own power. But that which you give him, *you* control."

Kwaee peered at him. "So what? What is that supposed to mean?"

"It means that as long as you fight him like this, you are letting him win on his terms. His rules. Why not play by your own rules, Father? Throw him off-balance. Try something he will not expect. Then you control the battle."

The god of the forest stood silent, his arms folded. "Perhaps you are right. I have allowed Ogya to define the conflict for too long. But I do not consent to surrender any more of my forest to this ill-conceived plan. Nor, I think, will you find the water goddesses any more inclined to support it. However, I will give you the chance. If you and your… mate… can succeed at convincing both Asubonten and Atekye to lend their aid, then perhaps—*perhaps*," he repeated, "I will agree to this plan. It would be better to choose how and where our battles are fought."

He bared fangs bigger than Clay's fingers. "And good to see a surprised look on that greedy fool's face for once." The forest god's arms bunched at his sides, knife-like claws extending from his fingertips. "I hunger to be the predator once more. It is in our blood!" He paused. A roar had crept into his voice.

He dropped his eyes as though only now noticing Clay and Doto, as though remembering himself and where he was. He relaxed his shoulders and stilled the lash of his tail. He ran his paw over his head, smoothing back the feathers at his brow. "But you must convince the goddesses to aid you."

Clay bowed low, trying to hide his excitement and hope. "Of course, Lord Kwaee. We will not fail."

The forest god's eyes glinted green. "Your confidence had better be well-rooted. If you are not successful, then I will make you prove your allegiance to the forest and to me. You will lead me and my son to your people's nesting grounds. I do not require divine powers to kill a few apes. Together, we will slaughter them under cover of darkness, when they cannot see. We will fell them all and end this curse of fire."

~

They ran for the Asubonten, their senses leading them unerringly to the locus of the river goddess's power. Doto could scarcely believe their fortune. He had expected his father to remain sulky and stubborn, fixated on the past he had lost and refusing to acknowledge a future he could not avoid. But Kwaee had changed. He had emerged from his temple. He was combating the fire in new and powerful ways that had never occurred to Doto. The fight was back in his blood again, his anger no longer sullen and unchecked, but controlled, focused.

Doto had never seen his father like this, but it was an improvement. And it was all due to Clay. His little fire bearer had been like a new stream creeping through a barren land, transforming everything around him.

Clay ran at his side now, matching him in speed, but looking around at their surroundings as they passed with wide eyes, ears twitching toward errant sounds. If Kwaee's admonition worried him, he did not show it. Doto wondered if Clay were truly ready to kill those he had once called his own people. He wondered if he *wanted* Clay to be. A god carried no physical scars, but they could bear other wounds for far longer. Kwaee himself was proof of that. Who would Clay be when his life as a fire bearer was a distant memory, and the wonder of new divinity had worn off? Would Doto still love him?

A ridiculous question, he decided. He would always love Clay. Nothing could change that. But Clay's love for him had begun—had been rooted—in worship. What happened to that love when the awe faded and the roots died?

He resolved not to let worry take hold now. There was hope. They had a plan to deal with Ogya, Kwaee had improved, and Clay loved him. For now, that was all he needed. And perhaps when all this was over, and Clay was no longer troubled, things could go back to something like the way they were, the way their love had started. He held onto that. He held onto every hope, every good moment. Like now, with Clay running at his side, each of them making a game out of darting between the shafts of sunlight piercing the canopy.

The acrid scent of old smoke caught his nostrils, and he put a paw on Clay's shoulder, slowing them to a stop.

"What is it?"

Doto curled his upper lip, tasting the air. "There shouldn't be ash this deep into the forest. The fire bearers cannot have burned close by."

Clay sniffed. "It doesn't smell new. And I smell water. A river, here?"

"The Asubonten," Doto said, staring at Clay. Had he forgotten where they were going already?

"But that's impossible. We can't be at the Asubonten already. The last time, it took us days to—" He broke off, his tail swaying erratically as it did when he was thinking, and then he put his paw to his forehead. "We're faster now. Right. Every time I think I've grown used to this…"

Together, they passed between the trees until arriving at the lip of a steep bank, and at its base, the broad, churning mass of the Asubonten. The river was narrower here than the broad, lazy channel where they'd last met the goddess, but not as quick and spirited as the one that passed beneath the shadow of the ruined city, Abansin.

But both of those rivers had been green and alive. This one looked grey and dead. The water ran thick and viscous, like the spittle of a dying beast. Bubbles and brownish froth drifted along the banks. It stank, sour and ashy, and its surface was broken by the dark spots of dead fish, carried by the current toward the great water.

"Oh no," Clay breathed. "How could it have gotten this bad this quickly?" He sprang down the bank to the water's edge in a few easy bounds.

Doto followed a little more cautiously. The goddess Asubonten was near. A sudden anxiety about slipping on some stones and landing face-first in the river right in front of her proved difficult to banish.

"Where is she?" Clay wondered aloud.

"She's here. Feel her presence?" Doto called out over the water. "Sister Asubonten, we have come to speak with you. Will you come up?"

They waited. The water churned down the river but gave no signs of any enormous creature rising from its depths.

"Lady Asubonten," Clay began, but Doto put a firm paw on his shoulder.

"No. Not Lady. Sister."

"But she isn't—"

"You are a god now, just as she." He leaned closer and whispered, "No point in stoking her pride any greater than it is."

"O-okay." Clay's ears folded. "Sis-sister Asubonten, we come to speak with you about the… the ravages of Lord—of Ogya. It seems that you suffer from his abuses, too. We have a plan to stop him, but we need your assistance."

Again they stood together and awaited the river goddess's response. A couple of wide, fat bubbles rose to the surface of the water and rode downstream a little distance before bursting wetly. There was no other answer.

"What do we do if she won't even listen to us?" Clay asked. "Maybe Kwaee was right about this."

Doto paced along the banks of the river. He had a nasty feeling that if he were to wade out deep enough into the water, he would transform into his fire bearer shape, just as he did outside the forest. Asubonten barely respected him as it was. She would never let him forget that. "Asubonten is prideful," he mused aloud. "Call to her, plead with her, and she may ignore us, but she is fiercely protective of her dominion. We may have to provoke her."

Clay hunched into grass, his pupils dilating. "Anger a goddess?"

Doto sighed. He was growing tired of reminding Clay of his status. "Remember the last time we met her? What I did?" He knelt down by the riverbank and put his paw on the ground. "Send your senses out. Do you feel the river?"

Clay pressed his fingers to the muddy bank and closed his eyes. "I feel... *where* it is. But nothing in it."

"The river is her terrain, and your power ends with it. Now feel below. Find stones, big ones, big enough to reach the surface of the river. Use the earth around them. Use the roots of trees. Lift the stones, push them upward, let them find the edge where your senses end, and push them through." He acted as he spoke, finding an enormous boulder already jutting up into the riverbed. He channeled the earth as though it were water, as fluid as the river itself, flowing beneath and around the rock and hefting it upward, inch by inch levering it up into the stream.

Clay managed with a little less finesse: he gave a yowl of surprise as a boulder the size of an antelope suddenly broke the surface of the water with a terrific splash, arced into the air, hung there for one glittering, water-flinging moment as though hovering, and then crashed down into the water with a terrific splash that sent drops raining down on them both.

"That works too." Doto said.

Their combined efforts must have had some effect, for the patterns of flow on the surface of the river shifted, side-currents twisting into wild eddies, the water level rising up the banks. Doto was halfway through warning Clay to stand back when the river bulged in the middle.

The great, crocodilian head of Asubonten revealed itself—not so large here as when Clay and Doto had met her before, as she grew or shrank to fit whatever stretch of her river she occupied. She was still enormous, though, her snout long and broad enough to snap either of them up as easily as they might swallow a forest mouse. Runnels streamed from her jaws and around her scales as she rose, leaning toward them and then towering over them, splatted first one and then the other hand in the mud of her mucky banks.

Doto looked to one side just in time to see Clay already diving for a belly-flat bow; he caught Clay's arm in one paw and hoisted him upright again. "To Kwaee and Fam," he growled out of the side of his muzzle. "Not to her."

Asubonten swayed over them, water pouring down her scales. A black serpent twisted and jerked across the top of her snout and then braved the plunge through open air into the safety of the currents below. She regarded the two of them with one rheumy eye. She did not, Doto observed, look very well. Her hide appeared too loose for her body, skin sagging, sliding along the movement of muscle and bone. The scales of her neck and underbelly had turned a sickly, pallid yellow, the black of her back a slimy green. She listed from side to as though the weight of her head had grown too heavy.

"Godling," she rumbled to Doto, and a torrent of muddy water and dead fish was disgorged from her maw. Long streamers of riverweed dangled from her teeth. "I should have known only you would dare encroach on my waters. It has been some time since you skipped across them. I am—" She lurched, her heavy head dipping sideways toward the bank. "I am not at my best. The foul Ogya has poisoned my river."

It was unlike Asubonten to admit vulnerability. Doto had braced for a confrontation, but now he felt only concern. "But Sister Asubonten, the fires are far from your domain."

Her eyes rolled backward in her great head. "And what would you know of the quests of water, little forest creature? Of how it falls from Wem and strikes the earth in an explosion of joy, how it takes in all it touches and carries it to me? Ogya falls from the sky in flakes of ash, his smoke clogs the air, his filth coats the ground. And the water brings it here. I was… I was unprepared. It poisoned my temple. Had I not been clever enough to move my heart upstream, into the joyous and craggy reaches of my fingertips, it might have murdered me.

"But I am not so easy to kill, am I? The great Asubonten, mightiest of all the world's rivers, cannot be so easily blighted. I will persevere." Her yellow tongue slid crudely across her fangs, and she pushed herself up shakily on both arms. "I will live on."

She lurched in her regard toward Clay, fixing him with a bewildered stare. "But I cannot be so poisoned that my vision fails me. You have another with you, godling. Have your father's profligacies extended farther than I knew?"

Heat flared in Doto's cheeks and ears. That she could think Clay his brother! He started to protest, but a stammer corralled the words on his tongue and before he could free them, Clay stepped forward, smiling up at the enormous river goddess. He seemed calm and breezy, but from behind, Doto could see the anxious prickle of fur down his spine.

"I am Doté, of the forest, Sister Asubonten. Like Doto, I share dominion over the forest, but I am not sired by… by Lord Kwaee. I am not Doto's sibling, but his mate."

"His mate?" Asubonten reared upward with a steamy snort of surprise, and the birds that had casually settled along her back scattered upward, twittering and cawing in annoyance. She peered down her long snout, her slitted yellow eyes darting between the two leopards. "Well. Gods may do as they please. You have your father's ways about you, after all, Doto."

She leaned down toward Clay again, taking deep whiffs of the air through her nostrils, her fanged jaws agape. His toes curled into the mud of the riverbank and his tail froze, but he did not run.

"But why does your mate smell of fear, godling?" She rubbed at her jaw, eyes narrowing in suspicion. "And something else. Something familiar…"

"Lady—" Clay faltered, clearly flustered. "Sister Asubonten, we come to you on an urgent mission. It is about Ogya."

Asubonten lashed her tail, showering the far bank of the river with her waters. "That fiend! That nuisance! You see what he has done to me? It is a violation! He and his filthy fire bearers foul my waters with his poison, with his ash and lye." She groaned then, her great head listing to one side, eyes rolling backward before, with some struggle, she pushed herself upright again. "Of all our kind, only he has dared attack the rest of us. Even your father shows respect, Doto. He knows his rule ends in my waters. But Ogya—he has always hated the river goddesses, for the rain is our mother, and she quenches all his ambitions." Her jaws lolled open. "If we could, we would drown him in his home."

Doto sent a hopeful glance in Clay's direction. "Then you will be pleased to hear of our reason for visiting. We agree that Ogya must be stopped."

"No change in the forest gods' opinions, then. Did you come all this way simply to inform me that wood hates fire?"

"We came to tell you that we have a plan. That we intend to remove Ogya's avatar from this earth once and for all. And it will not be only the forest to fight him this time. Mother Fam has sworn to lend her power to defeating him."

"Fam!" Asubonten sat up taller. "These are strange days if Mother Earth herself takes sides in this battle."

"Not merely strange," said Clay. "Pivotal. If we do not stop Ogya now, we may never have another chance. He may grow too strong to be checked ever again."

"And why should I listen to you, new godling I have never seen or heard of before?"

"Has Ogya ever poisoned you like this before?"

"Not this badly," Asubonten admitted. Her yellow tongue stubbed at her teeth. "I tasted the lye when it seeped into my banks but thought myself strong enough to resist it. I ignored it, and it seeped into my temple, weakening me. Hurting my eyes. My stomach. My head. It makes me feel thick and slow, like mud. Sleepy."

Clay nodded. "You don't have to listen to *me*, then. Listen to your own words. Ogya weakens us all, bit by bit, until we are too diminished to fight him. You must know what he is like. What he has become since the—the grand bargain. You must know he will not stop."

"The grand bargain?" She blinked her beady eyes, a transparent film sliding over their lenses, and turned her attention back to Doto. "So that old stream finally found the sea, hm? Your father hated for anyone to speak of it."

"And so that's why you never mentioned it to me, is it?"

"I never mentioned it to you, godling, because I didn't care. Because you meant nothing at all to me beyond an occasional annoyance sliding across my surface like a water bug. I had no reason to dredge up old memories from long ago. The gods do not much care for each other, if you have not noticed."

"Mother Fam cares," Clay declared. "And so do I."

"Yes," Asubonten answered, suspicion creeping into her voice. "You do."

"And perhaps we must all care if we wish to save ourselves from Ogya. This plan of ours—we need your help."

The crocodile goddess lifted herself up out of the water, tilting her head back to bellow her booming laughter. Birds rose from the trees and banks of the river, crying in alarm. "Of course, of course. That is why you come to me so politely. That is why you care. You need something from me. Now, when I am sickened, and weak, you come soliciting favors."

Doto put both paws up, trying to calm her. "But this could help you as well. Will you not at least listen to what—"

"Listen? Who listens to Asubonten? Have you heard my song? My song…" Her heavy head swayed. "It has been so long since I heard it. I almost cannot recall…" For a moment she stared beyond them, leaving the words hanging in the air, but then her eyes focused. "Now you come to me demanding that I listen."

"Do you not wish vengeance against the god that sickens you? We can tell you how—"

"Ah, an education. Young godlings running to me to teach me things. To instruct me how to quench my poisoner. But what do you know of the river? Perhaps you wish me to overflow my banks and quench Ogya's flames. It cannot be. The river takes the shortest path, and though Ogya may have intruded into your domain, it will be long before he reaches my curves and courses. I can do nothing."

Doto bit his lip. Frustration and anger were mounting in him and like all human emotions, he struggled to reckon with them.

"Can do nothing? Or *will* do nothing?"

Slitted eyes narrowed. "Careful, little leopard."

He snorted. "Of what? Will you do anything to stop me? You are the *mighty Asubonten,* but you cannot even crawl out of your bed to save yourself." Clay put one paw on his shoulder, but he shrugged it off, seething with annoyance. "I told you, we have a plan. We believe Ogya can be stopped. And you will not even hear us? Your pride makes you weak."

Her jaws slackened. "Weak?" she bellowed. "You dare? I am the river that cuts through your forest! Your father yields to me, wherever my waters turn! Make no mistake about my strength. Nothing stands in the way of the river. These jaws cut through stone. My tail slices mountains in half. You and your forest are nothing. Your father is nothing. Your mate is nothing.

And poison or no, my river cannot be stopped. Even when you and all that you love is burning, it will still run to the—to the—" Her deep voice cracked and turned hoarse mid-sentence, and she turned her head downward and coughed harsh, rasping coughs. From her wide mouth, muck and rotten fish erupted, splattering against the ground.

"You see?" Doto said, stepping toward her again. "You are ill. This will only worsen, until your river is choked with mud, and then what will you be goddess of?"

She spat at him. He was so shocked it took a moment for him to realize what had happened; he was suddenly drenched with cold, viscous river water and sludge soaking through his fur and pouring from him in long, mucilaginous ropes of slime. His nose burned with the stenches of rotting vegetable matter, dead fish, and sour ash.

He trembled for a moment in shock and revulsion, and then anger burned through him, overwhelming. He leapt at her face, claws bared, ready to fight.

It wasn't the right thing to do, he realized mid-leap. There was no way that slashing the face of a goddess or attempting to claw out her miserable eyes as the heat of his blood was suggesting could possibly help him win her over. This was not diplomacy. He could imagine the look of chagrin on Clay's face even now. Not the right thing to do.

But more importantly, it was not the *smart* thing to do. Even more rapidly than he leapt, the goddess turned and opened her pale, yellow maw. He tried to scramble out of the way in mid-air, but, as he was not a god of gravity, he descended toward that wide-open mouth and her jaws snapped closed around his legs. Her teeth dug into his flesh and muscle as he struggled, but she could not hurt him like this—not above-water, anyway.

It was a fact she well knew, and she began to slither backward into the river. She would pull him underwater, drown, and devour him. It was not the ill treatment of his avatar that worried him. A drowning would be an unpleasant torment, but he would awaken in his temple and could return swiftly. But the river was her domain, not the forest. He would change into his fire bearer form, and she would know immediately. She would taste his human flesh on her tongue, smell the ape-reek of his body. Then, even before it had begun, their plan would be ended. Asubonten would never trust him or work with a fire bearer, not after they had contaminated her domain and poisoned her body.

He struggled in her jaws, trying to force them upward with both arms, but however great his physical strength might be in his domain, she was far larger and far stronger. As long as she kept her feet planted in the river, he could not overcome her. He roared again and flailed, clawing savagely at the side of her snout, and was pleased to feel fine scales tear away. He smelled her hot, mineral blood as it soaked into his fur and spattered his vision. She gave a guttural roar around him in response, her slick tongue sliding across his back, but her unyielding jaws would not release him. He tried to pull his legs free to rake at the roof of her mouth, but they were gripped too firmly; he could not do so without peeling muscle away from bone.

His efforts only urged her back into the river more swiftly. Her long, dark back sunk beneath the surface, murky water churning around the ridges down her spine. One yellow eye gleamed in satisfaction as she pulled her head downward. His paws dipped into the water first; she intended to savor his drowning. He felt them tingle and then twist as they dipped past the wall of the forest's magic and into the river, thick leopard toes reshaping themselves into narrow human ones, bones shifting as a fifth toe sprouted on each foot.

The pain of the wounds in his avatar had been muted—recognizable as injury, but a merely informative sensation. As he shifted toward human, it sharpened into agony and then beyond, a blinding pain that made him yowl in torment, made him twist to get away from her, even if it did tear the muscle from his bones. There was nothing in his mind but the pain.

"Lady Asubonten!" It was Clay's voice. It rang with the timbre of a god's command, but held a pleading, desperate note. Through the pain, Doto turned to see him stretched out on the bank of the river, prostrated and prone. No god should lie with his face in the mud like that. Especially not his Clay.

But Asubonten paused. The one eye Doto could see gave a slow, curious blink. She lifted her head from the water, and the pain in Doto's legs, all he had been able to focus on, eased back to mere information, a sensation he could process and ignore.

"Yooo blaaaaal trm—" she began, and then then paused, clambered upright onto the bank again, and spat Doto into the muck. He hissed at her, scampered a little distance away, and compelled the mud to abandon his fur in a magic-propelled shower.

"You bow to me?" Asubonten repeated to Clay in tones of surprise. "And you call yourself a god? But wait. I have seen a bow like that before. A young boy. A fire bearer. With an injured foot." She lowered her face toward him and whuffled, her throat spreading wide and contracting in rhythmic patterns, her method of sniffing the air. Doto didn't need a reminder of what that breath smelled like. His fur still reeked of it.

Clay drew himself upright to meet Asubonten's gaze squarely. Doto wished he could implore him not to speak. As well beg the sun not to rise. "I am Clay, and we have met before. Please forgive the deception. We were worried you would not—"

Her eyes flashed like sun on the waves. "A fire bearer!" she roared. "It was you who poisoned my river!" Her accusation was scarcely spoken before she was clambering up out of the river after him, moving with astonishing speed, her heavy, sinuous body trampling reeds and brush. Clay scampered backward, barely out of her reach.

The old fool. In her impulsive anger, she had left her domain behind. Her dark-scaled back snaked from right to left as she pounded after Clay, long jaws snapping at his toes. Her limbs were longer than a crocodile's, proportioned like a fire bearer's, and she could walk upright if she chose to. Now, crawling after Clay on all fours, she had an eerie, spider-like gait. River mud squelched out between her fingers.

Clay scrambled low through a thicket, taking advantage of his feline flexibility to keep close to the ground, but her fangs clamped around the weeds and wrenched them free, flinging away great clods of earth. He tried darting between her arms where her jaws could not reach, but she leaned to one side and swatted him into the air with a hand that could palm his whole body.

Doto winced as his mate smashed into the top of the tree. More than anything he wanted to come and save him, but his pierced body was still healing its wounds. Asubonten had only one foot in her river now; she had nearly abandoned the source of her power to attack another god in the seat of his own.

Clay clung to the branches of the tree, dazed only momentarily.

She belched a terrible, croaking roar, and with one tremendous bite, smashed the trunk of the tree to splinters and tossed it aside like a stick. Its branches bounced as it crashed into the underbrush, but Clay had already leapt to another branch. She snapped at that, too, but this time he was ready for her, and the branch curled like an oxtail and then lashed out, opening up a stripe of pink flesh across her cheek. She bellowed in pain and lunged after him, pulling herself upright to reach as he danced across the branches, leaping higher and higher into the treetops with unerring grace, each branch snapping at her jaws, her hands, her eyes, until her face and arms bled from a score of cuts—cuts that were no longer closing up. She had left her river.

Doto would have enjoyed seeing Clay defeat her, but he wasn't sure Clay would appreciate being left alone in this fight. She was so fixed on her attack that she didn't notice until too late the vines snaking around her tail, the thick hardwood trunks sprouting up her legs. She snapped again and again at Clay, but now he stood poised at the very top of one of the tallest riverbank trees, his toes perched atop the thinnest twigs and leaflets at its crown, capable of holding him aloft only because he willed it so.

But Doto had a different plan for the local foliage, and now that Asubonten was rooted to the spot, he selected two of the heaviest nearby trees and instructed them to fall, sending his will into their roots and releasing them from the soil. The great, shaggy crowns of the trees nodded in the wind, pulled back as though determined to hold onto their commanding position in the skyline even as the sturdy trunks that bore them toppled sideways.

Asubonten's head turned to one side; she'd caught the sound of cracking and splintering branches, and now she saw the great, mossy trunks tilting toward her. Her jaws gaped in surprise, and she tugged at her feet—but she was trapped. Even now, the vines and trunks of Doto's forest twined higher up her body, reaching out grasping tendrils for her arms. In panic, she tried to pull away, but Doto had done his work well; the latticework of roots below her stretched its web deep. She would have to lift the whole clearing to pull herself free.

The slow fall of the first tree clubbed her over the head and rolled down her back, spinning its limbs like a dancer out of control. It knocked her easily to the ground, her limbs splayed, and before she could recover, roots had already sent fingers up out of the soil to grasp her own, pulling them down to the earth, binding her there just in time for the second tree to land atop her neck. It pinned her to the ground, its branches bouncing.

Doto grinned up at Clay. He had done it! He had felled the mighty Asubonten! Let her call him godling now! She might call him weak, but he had beaten her. He was a little disappointed to see Clay with an aghast expression, one paw over his muzzle. He'd wanted to talk it out, no doubt. Well, now was the time for that.

Doto strolled around to face Asubonten's pinned-down snout. "And that is our plan for Ogya, as well," he said in a conversational tone.

"Release me at once," snarled the crocodile through vine-clenched teeth. Doto's work was quickly turning her into a mound of vegetation. As an afterthought, he sprouted a little crown of colorful flowers atop her head and was rewarded, as he'd hoped, by a feline giggle high above him.

"You left your seat of power," he observed. "Put yourself in a position of weakness. And we were able to surprise and imprison you."

Her yellow eyes rolled backward. "You would not have been able to capture me were I at my full strength. The fire bearer leopard thing. Its people poisoned me. And now you are allied with it. And them. And Ogya. This is all a trick. What do you want with me?"

"Only your assistance, Sister," Doto said pleasantly. "And we are enemies of Ogya as we have always been."

Clay dropped to the ground beside him. "I am no longer a friend to the fire bearers," he told her. "Not after they—after what they…" He looked away. "I can't be."

"I hear pain in your voice. I believe that more than your words. But how have you come to be this way? Why are you like *him?*" She was barely able to move her head, but she managed to glare in Doto's direction anyway. "How could he have this power? Like yours, but… weak. And yours… weaker now, too." Then her eyes went wide. "No! You… healed him?"

Doto inclined his head.

"He brought me back from death," Clay said. "When I awoke, I was like this."

Asubonten narrowed her eyes again. "Then you cannot be trusted. Not if you would sacrifice your own divinity to save a fire bearer. What else would you sacrifice? How could we ever trust you not to work with Ogya?"

Doto gave an exhausted sigh and sat down in front of her. "Why by Wem's breath would I do that? All Ogya wants is to burn the world, and he's starting with my home. He wants my temple. He begged my father for a taste of me. No. I want him dead. And since that is impossible, imprisoned forever."

"As you think you have imprisoned me?" She said the words caustically, but there were notes of worry in her voice. "I am not so easily captured. The river will flood, and—"

"I have no intention of keeping you bound. Even though you chewed on me so rudely. And," he added in a less friendly tone, "even though you tried to devour my mate."

Clay sat down cross-legged next to Doto, exuding exaggerated calm, though his still unsettled fur betrayed him. "We need your help if we're going to stop him, Sister Asubonten. We must surprise Ogya. Carry him off of his feet using something he cannot burn. Mother Fam will encase him in a prison of stone too hard for him to melt."

Clay pressed one paw against the ground, never taking his gaze from Asubonten's eyes. The vines binding her loosened, allowing her to raise her head and send the heavy tree trunks rolling away from her with great crashes.

She worked her jaw back and forth with a sullen expression but did not attack. "Your plan will not work. A river does not leave its course."

"You left the river just now," Doto pointed out. "Because you were angry enough. Would you let your anger drive you to attack a little god of the forest, but cower beneath the advance of the god who poisons you?" He found the flash of anger in her eyes enjoyable.

Clay placed a paw on his arm, which meant: easy. Be calm a moment. "We would not ask you to go against your nature, Sister Asubonten. But we have help. Mother Fam will change the shape of the ground. Your river will change course because she will bend beneath you." He loosened her bonds further, freeing her arms and legs, allowing her to sit up.

Doto half-expected Asubonten to snap at him again, but instead she began to creep slowly back toward the riverbed, like raindrops seeking the stream. "It would be good to see new vistas," she murmured in a voice that shook stone. "A river changes, but only over great time. The bends of our body slow us. We drop earth where we slow, and scrape it away where we quicken, until a shallow curve bends into a deep one. We bend more and more, until back touches back, until we eat our own tail, and then the course quickens once more, and those old deep curves are abandoned, little lost strips of ourselves, hatchlings sprawled in reaches of the forest that we have forgotten. We must abandon them to find the sea, where we end, where Mpo invades and swallows us.

"The forest and swamps our coursings eat through are known to us and unchanging. It would be a fine thing to set our eyes on hills and to shape our body into new bends. I would taste fresh soil, gift frogs to new banks, and lure new fishers to the life within me."

She watched Clay and Doto with cautious eyes as she set first one foot, then the other, into her waters. Neither moved to stop her, and she shivered all down her long back as her waves lapped over her scales once more. "It feels good, even with the grease of Ogya's ruin sloughing through it." More fiercely, she added, "You would not have beaten me were I not sickened and lazed by his ash."

"Will you be all right? Will you recover?" Clay asked.

Bemusement at the concern in his voice spread across her face. "I have removed my temple beyond his reach for now. This lethargy will pass, but my domain will take much longer to recover." She breathed in deeply through her nostrils and closed her eyes. "Very well, then. You have won my attention. And it is true that Ogya must be stopped. Tell me your plan."

They explained at length, interrupted by many challenges and questions from the river goddess, just how they hoped to entrap Ogya. She seemed impressed that they had secured the agreement of both Fam and Kwaee to work together to stop the threat, and shocked at the bait they would use to lure him.

"And how long do you think you will be able to imprison him?" she asked.

"Mother Fam claims she holds within her bones stone that will not burn, too hard for any force to break," Doto answered.

Asubonten blinked a filmy white blink. "Unbreakable? Perhaps. But there are forces no stone can resist. With time, I cut through the hardest of it. I shape craggy boulders into smooth pebbles and spit them into the skin of Mpo. No walls will hold forever, little godlings. And no prison, either."

"Perhaps not," Clay said, with a note of uncertainty, "but it should give us time to think of something else. Perhaps in another ten or fifteen years—"

He was cut off by her sharp, booming laugh, one that made an array of teeth scissor up and down. "Ten or fifteen? I think we can do better than that. Ten thousand, perhaps. Twenty thousand. A thousand thousand years. Enough time to think of a new plan. Or," she added coyly, "enough time for all those little fire bearers to die out. And then who will Ogya get to do his bidding? Perhaps he will be helpless, and we gods without worshipers once again. Perhaps we will swim through the raw, wild world as we did before the great bargain.

"Oh, don't look so crestfallen, little godling. They are not your pack now. You do not nest in their trees. And creatures die out all the time, when they grow too strong and greedy, or when they make the burrow of their lives in the skin of a god who needs to shed. It is the way of things. You will learn, as you persist."

She settled backward into her river, the polluted water bubbling around her black scales. "Your plan is almost certain to fail. You must know this. Ogya is powerful and crafty, and he will not allow himself to be imprisoned easily. But there is a chance. And I would not have it said that the world was saved without Asubonten. No, I will be part of this story. I will see new bends in my river, and I will take great pleasure in extinguishing the flame of that mad scorpion. When you call on me, I will come."

Clay dipped his head low. "We thank you for your promise, Sister Asubonten. Defeating Ogya will be a great good for the world."

"We must hope so. And now I grant you passage across my surface, for your journey does not stop here." She shuffled aside in her river, making huge waves that washed up against her banks, her tail swaying slowly as she swam in place.

Then Doto showed Clay how to dance across the water, moving too rapidly to sink, never daring to slow lest they lose their connection to the forest magic and drop beneath it. Clay skimmed over the water like a thrown stone and stood astonished with Doto on the other side. "We can run across water? This will save so much time! I thought we would have to head up and cross at Abansin."

"Of course not. I only passed that way last time because I had you with me, and you could not have crossed."

"Couldn't you have carried me?"

"I could have, but the speed would have broken your neck. And then I would have had to heal that, too."

Clay's eyes widened. "Then I'm glad we took the detour. Goodbye, Sister Asubonten! It was an honor to meet you again."

And defeat you, Doto thought with no small amount of personal satisfaction.

Asubonten opened her long mouth. Small, white birds had already settled there to pick at her teeth. "Farewell, godlings," she called back. "And good luck with my sister Atekye. She will not be so easily reached! No," she added in a near-mutter, as much as a creature with a mouth that could snap up a grown elephant *could* mutter. "No, there will be no persuading the so-called Queen of Reeds."

Then she sank beneath the water of her river and was gone, not even a dark shadow beneath the filmy current.

# 25 Mired

Doto gasped for breath as he pushed himself up out of the water, slimy grasses and long strands of something Clay could not identify clinging to his curly hair. He wiped swamp muck from his eyes with both hands and spat. "This is the worst place that we have ever been."

Clay was inclined to agree. His skin was a mass of welts from uncountable bites from mosquitos and horrid, monstrous black flies, and it was all he could do not to scratch ceaselessly. His feet were caked in muck and bleeding from the cuts of stones and stems beneath the surface of the water. "I thought you had been here before."

Doto clambered through the knee-deep water to what appeared to be a solid mound of earth, tried to sit down on it, and immediately disappeared beneath the surface of the water again when it turned out to be nothing more than a floating heap of moss and algae. Clay waited, sinking slowly in the mud, while the flailing, furious human managed to flounder back to his feet again.

"I *have*," Doto finally managed, "but not this far into the swamp. And then I was able to avoid the water by jumping through the treetops. And the insects knew cursed-well-enough to leave me alone!" He slapped vehemently at his shoulders, his teeth bared. Then he spat again. "Do they *want* to be eaten?"

He had tried leaping through the trees anyway, against Clay's firmly worded advice, and despite his lack of divine strength, sharp claws, or feline agility. It was only with a lot of struggle and shouting that he'd managed to climb the first tree. He'd balanced out on one limb, eyed the next tree he wanted to jump to, gauged the distance carefully, crouched low, bunching his thighs, and then one foot had slipped off the branch and he'd fallen sideways, landing flat on his back in the water with a *whap* that had knocked the breath out of him.

Astonishingly, even after all that, he'd made a second try. That time it went much better. That time he'd managed to jump before falling.

"I think," Clay said in answer to his question, "they want to eat you."

Doto flailed his paws at the little cyclone of midges orbiting his body. "Nasty things. When I am back in the forest, I will kill every last one of them."

Clay sighed. "Do you want me to dance us up a forest circle so we can take a break?"

"It's too early still. We'd better keep going."

They marched on. Moving through the fen was exhausting—the most tiring travel he had ever attempted. He would rather be shivering on the wind-blasted side of Mother Fam's mountains, trudge through the harsh and burning desert, pick his way up the treacherous side of Ogya-Bepow, than travel one more day through this swamp. Even the journey through the forest on a missing foot, now literal lifetimes ago, had been easier than this.

The swamp sucked at his feet, trying to pull him down. When the water was ankle deep, or on those rare occasions when they found solid ground to walk across, it wasn't so bad, but wading through standing water that was knee or waist-deep made every step an exhausting struggle. Even treks across solid-looking ground were unsafe; what appeared to be forest floor could be merely a carpet of leaves floating atop standing pools. Clay had splashed into more than one of these and come up with a slimy, jellied substance covering his arms and shoulders—he had half-tried to claw his skin off when Doto had informed him they were insect eggs.

Something in them had *wriggled.*

But the wetlands were teeming with all manner of life, not just insects. Monkeys howled and screeched at them from the treetops as they passed; the opportunistic orbs of crocodile eyes regarded them from the pools; a family of gorillas gave them wary stares; and uncountable birds sang in branches, dove and snapped for insect lunches, or stalked long-legged through the fens.

Clay scrambled backward, sloshing through the water to avoid the sinuous curves made by an aquatic snake whose bright colors suggested it was quite venomous. "If something nasty out here kills me," he called to Doto, "and I'd have to come all the way back from our temple, I'm not going to. It's too much. Even Ogya wouldn't bother trying to burn his way through here."

“If you hadn’t taken all my godhood,” Doto growled, clinging to a tree trunk for a panting moment of rest, “I could have leapt through the trees and carried you.”

Clay imagined bouncing up and down jerkily in Doto’s arms for a few hundred thousand leaps through trees and decided that maybe the swamp was slightly preferable. He floundered forward through a thatch of woody reeds and dropped into another pool, this one far over his head.

Wheeling his arms frantically, he tried to find the solid ground he’d just stepped off but only moved further away from it. Few times in his life had he ever had to worry about this much water. The savanna rains could be fierce, forming floods that could sweep you from your feet, but seldom were they deep enough to go over your head. Clay splashed in terrified desperation, managed to seize one deep, soggy breath of water, and slipped beneath the surface. He hung in place, surprised at the sudden way his body and limbs weighed nothing at all, and opened his eyes.

The world below was like nothing he had even seen: blue, green, and brown pierced by white, angular sunbeams that rolled and twisted in the water, folding it around them as their bright spots searched the swamp floor for drowned secrets. Things moved in the murky blur of the bottom: many-legged creatures half-crawling, half-swimming; fish zipping in quick darts through the protection of submerged reeds. There were larger things, too, sleeping down in the mud or curving through the water in swift, sinuous movements.

Clay watched, too astonished for a moment to remember his panic, and then some new instinct seized his limbs. He gave a few quick frog-kicks with his feet and found his head suddenly in the air again, his hair heavy and sagging with the weight of water. He stayed in place, legs kicking slowly, arms moving as though smoothing out a hide.

“There you are,” Doto said with a note of irritation. “What were you doing down there?”

“I…” Clay had no good answer.

“You are a very good swimmer for a land ape,” Doto observed. “You said you couldn’t do it.”

“I can’t!” Clay’s protest lacked a bit of conviction in the face of the obvious evidence. “Well, I’ve never tried, anyway.”

“Since you can, we can try swimming across some of the deeper pools to save some time. But try not to be eaten by anything.”

"Uh. All right." Clay thought of the shapes he'd seen lurking beneath him and felt uneasy. Then he considered just how much space there was beneath him, and floating in a pool began to feel very wrong. He paddled to the bank closest to Doto until his toes found—not exactly *solid* ground, but enough that he could stand upright.

"I don't think we should swim across. There could be crocodiles."

"Do not worry. I know how to watch for them. I will not ask you to swim across a pool with crocodiles in it. Or venomous snakes. Or leeches, if we can help it."

"What are leeches?" Clay asked, dreading the answer already. When Doto told him, he decided he hadn't been dreading it vigorously enough.

"Swamps are the worst places in the world," he told Doto as they mucked through a massive, slowly moving mud field. Every time he pulled up a foot, the other sank deeper, so they had to crawl across on all fours to keep from getting stuck. There had probably been a nice meadow, he thought to himself, before the swamp got to it and turned it into slime. "I'm glad it was a god of the forest who found me in my village and not a god of swamps."

"Every god loves his territory," Doto said between grunts of effort. "Atekye moves through here easily, because it is her domain. Think how much you love the forest."

And, Clay realized, he did love the forest. He loved it deeper than his village, deeper than the joy of running, deeper than his reverence for the other gods, deeper even than his love for his family, all so far gone now. It had taken root in the secret heart of him, and he loved it as he loved Doto. It was part of him. It *was* him.

"That is how much Atekye loves her own domain. My father says Atekye is closest of all the gods to Fam, because Fam gave birth to all life, and there is no more life anywhere than in the swamp."

Clay glanced at his shoulders, which were furred black with mosquitos taking advantage of a helpless bag of blood stuck in the mud. "I can believe that," he said. He dragged himself up onto the thankfully solid bank on the far side of the mud and, with some thoughtful consideration, slathered the rest of what he could of his exposed skin in handfuls of caking mud. The mosquitos keened in impotent protest and began inspecting other body parts for exposed skin.

"It is very lucky you knew how to swim," Doto said as he, too, began covering up with mud.

"Yes, I still don't understand how."

"All animals can do it." Doto flattened his ears. "Except for apes. You put a chimpanzee in the water and it will go face-down to the bottom. Gorillas drown even faster if you get them in water deep enough. You were an ape, too. But you swim very fast and very well."

"It was like I remembered how." An uneasy thought tickled the back of his mind. "Not… not everything goes away when I leave the forest. I still understand the words you speak in god-tongue."

"Because you are still a god, even if you cannot carry enough of the forest's magic to hold your divine form outside of it. Of course you would understand god-tongue. And all other tongues you learn. I had to acquire yours before capturing you." Doto sounded a bit proud at this point. "It took nearly three days."

"That's… that's very good," Clay said, impressed. He wondered if he could do that now—if the strange, twisted dialects of the other grass kingdoms would sound natural to him after learning them. It seemed impossible. But then, he had learned the languages of the animals and birds, had he not? Inside the forest, he could understand them perfectly, rude and basic as much of their talk was. But even here…

He tilted an ear toward a stork, which, eyeing a curving ripple in the pools, sent up a hollow, beak-clattering call to its neighbors: "Snake! Snake in the water!"

He shouldn't know what that meant. And, now that it occurred to him, he shouldn't have been able to tilt an ear. It hadn't moved much, but it *had* tilted slightly—and entirely by instinct. Just as he had been able to swim.

"You're right," he said to Doto as, reluctantly, they made their way down a little slope and back into the slow, slogging march through the water. "I'm still… not a fire bearer—not *human*—even when I leave the forest. I've been acting like I'm the same, but I'm not."

"I told you that." Doto's attempt at a knowing expression was ruined somewhat by his struggle to clamber through a thick clump of papyrus stalks. Their round heads bobbed above as he disappeared beneath them. "Before," he said, when Clay caught up to him, "you walked around like an ape. Like—" and he demonstrated, hunching his shoulders and tottering around with clumsy footsteps and exaggerated arm swings. "But now you walk better. More like a leopard. It is quieter. More controlled. Better for pouncing."

Clay chewed on this, feeling uncomfortable. He'd known for a while that he couldn't simply go back to live in his village. When he thought of it, the memories of torments and murders gnawed into his bones. On the rare occasion he allowed himself to dwell on it, he could feel himself sliding back into the memories, as though they had slippery edges and he could find no clawhold in reality. And then the pain and terror would come back, nearly as sharp in recollection as in the moment.

He tugged his concentration away from thoughts of burning, flaying, piercing, his lungs on fire, the forest curling past his dying eyes, wild green sprouting from his spreading blood. What would he do, anyway? How could he go back to them? What would his life look like? Doto would not want to live in the human village. And Clay was not one of them now.

Perhaps there was a way that he could give it away—give all the godhood he had received from Doto back to him. But that would surely be fatal. Godhood was all that was keeping him alive now. He had died. Not once, but over and over again, and each time he had gone back. Death was always hard to accept. Clay had never really let go of his mother. Not all the way. She had been gone a long time, but there were memories of her that still felt new: the way her laugh made her teeth look enormous; the way she tilted her head back in the rain. Even after rains and rains had passed, she was still sometimes there, looking out of someone's eyes, hiding in the silhouettes of trees, the familiar movement of another woman's walk.

And the losses of his father and brother were incomprehensible to him. He had not seen their bodies or attended their funerals. Their deaths were only words, holes in a world he no longer inhabited. He had gone before they died. He remembered the last time he'd seen his father, tears in his eyes, pleading to the gods to return his stolen son—a prayer they had answered too late. When Clay finally returned, the village had been so changed, his people so frightened, that it hardly seemed the same place he had left. You could not feel the absence of someone in a stranger's home.

Clay was the one who had died. There was no future for him in that village, but he hadn't seen it. He had gone back over and over, a haunting spirit. And they'd answered by banishing him, killing him, each time, trying to get him to understand, each time calling him… "I *am* a demon," he said in slow realization.

Doto turned. "Did you say that you are a demon? Because if you did say that, perhaps you should rest. And have something to eat."

"Demons are—"

"Imaginary," Doto said. "And you are not."

He thought of elaborating. Demons are creatures that wear the faces of your dead loved ones. They come into your house and try to soak up the love you have for those you lost. Then, of course, they usually kill you, so it wasn't a perfect comparison, which is why it probably wasn't worth explaining to Doto. Doto didn't have much patience for allegorical nuance. "Never mind."

He slogged along, ruminating, feeling too tired to talk to Doto anymore. Too tired to explain normal human emotion, to beg for comfort, to find the right words to relate to someone who ought to understand him better. The trees looked the same, the ponds with their floating scum and flat-leafed plants the same as the last half-day of travel. Were they even getting anywhere?

The hazy blob of the sun crept across the sky, filtering in between breaks in the canopy. In every sunbeam, insects swarmed in a mad storm of frenetic breeding, but the rest of the swamp felt lazy. Indolent. Endless.

Like his life. Like being a god. If he could not return home, what would his future be? His temple with Doto was a paradise, but paradise, even with someone you deeply loved, someone who was literally a part of you, could be lonely. He was a homesick ghost. And he had no one else to be. Surely not the small, unnecessary echo of a forest god in a burning forest.

He followed the sound of Doto's splashing, his feet feeling heavier and heavier. He knew that his gloomy thoughts came from exhaustion weighing down his mind, but it didn't make them any less true. He might never die, now, and even if he did, would he be greeted by his ancestors? Or would he enter the wild and dark hollows of fallen gods? Would he ever see his mother again? His father or brother?

He lurched in the water and splashed, half-falling into a broad, open pool. Cool, enveloping mud engulfed his foot and one knee. He tried to stand upright and, alarmingly, felt his toes sink deeper, as though the swamp bottom were a soft, dead mouth sucking him down. "Doto!" He spluttered the word weakly through a mouthful of fetid water, splashing backwards and using the swimming motions he had learned to right himself.

A little way ahead, Doto stopped and looked back. "What is the matter? Swim over."

Clay floundered in the chest-high water, splashing. He hoped the noise wasn't attracting crocodiles. "I can't! My feet are stuck!"

He tried to pull one foot out of the mud, but the sucking force was too strong, and trying to pull his right foot out only pushed the left one deeper. Panic flooded him, rising as high as the water.

"Well, stop splashing around," Doto said. He sounded tired. "Just be still. I'll pull you out." He stumped over to the edge of the pool.

"No, wait, don't come in here! You'll get stuck, too!"

"Gods do not get stuck," Doto declared.

Clay stared at him.

Doto folded his arms and stared back. Eventually he slumped. "What do you want me to do, then?"

"Get a vine or something? Something to pull me out?"

"Very well. Be still and try not to sink any deeper." Doto disappeared into the underbrush.

Clay wiggled his toes and ankles, trying to loosen the mud enough that he could pull free, but it didn't help. He paddled with both arms as though swimming upward through the chest-deep water. The mud slid between his toes, and for a moment, he thought he was making progress, but when he finally stilled, the water level was a little higher, nearly reaching his neck. "Doto!" he called again, trying to quell his alarm. "Hurry!"

"I am trying!" Doto's voice came from a short distance away. The sound of thrashing leaves was punctuated by grunts. "But these ridiculous vines do not want to come free. If we were in the forest, this would be easy."

*If we were in the forest, we wouldn't be in this trouble*, Clay thought to himself. Something soft curled around his knee and made him jerk in panic, pushing his right foot down. Swamp water lapped over his shoulder.

"Here!" Doto shouted, appearing among the rushes. He tossed a thick, grubby liana toward Clay. It splashed down nearby.

Clay grabbed the vine with both hands, holding tight. "I got it," he called and Doto pulled. Slickened with algae and muck, the vine slid right through his waterlogged fingers, tearing his thumb open in a gash. Great. If blood in the water wouldn't attract the crocodiles, nothing would.

"It's not working!" he called. "I can't hold on!"

"Maybe tie it around your middle and I can pull you out."

Lianas weren't rope or twine, and they tended not to bend so easily. This one, though, had apparently been wet long enough to be pliable, and he was able to loop it around his torso, under his arms, and wedge the end of it into a makeshift knot. He took a few deep breaths. Don't focus on what might go wrong. Don't think about crocodiles or drowning. Just hold onto the vine. Get your feet free. Get out of the pool. He gripped with both hands, hoping the loop around his chest wouldn't slip free. "I'm ready."

The vine went tight, pulling Clay forward, but his feet were still stuck, and so it pulled him *downward* as well. His head plunged beneath the water, leaving barely a moment to grab a lungful of air.

He struggled. The surface was a shifting, distorted blob of light just above his head. His lungs tickled with inhaled water, but he couldn't cough, or he'd lose the only air he had. The liana sawed into his sides as it pulled, but his feet would not come free. He kicked with one leg, then then the other. Neither would budge. The mud was going to pull him down. It was going to kill him.

He needed air. Little red spots pulsed in his vision. He tugged at his feet again and again.

The vine felt as though it was going to tear him in half.

His lungs ached with a desperate saw of hunger for air.

He pulled at the vine with all his strength, terror making his fingers claw hard at the woody pulp.

Pain tore into his left hand as a fingernail pulled free.

His chest gave a convulsive buck as it threatened to force a breath. No use for it. He had to untie himself.

With both hands, he pushed at the end of the knot, trying to prise it open so that he could reach for the surface again. It wouldn't budge.

The edges of his vision began to narrow.

He pushed again, desperately, in terror, and finally the end of the knotted liana slipped free. The wooden coil scraped around his back and sides as it pulled loose.

He clawed, flailed for the surface of the water, not quite reaching it before inhaling a lungful of swamp.

Then his head broke free into the open air and he was thrashing, convulsing as his lungs heaved up water. At first all he could do was flounder, pushing at the water with both hands. His feet had shifted in the mud, tilting him forward, and it was difficult to stay upright. His lungs wracked with violent coughs, and he tilted his head back to keep from accidentally inhaling more of it.

Doto was shouting something.

"It didn't work!" he croaked back between coughs. His heart was still racing with lingering terror. With broad sweeps of his arms, he managed to swim backward enough to stand upright again, pushing water and wet hair out of his eyes as his breathing slowed. Blood from both hands ran down his forearms.

Doto pushed through the reeds, looking annoyed. "Why did you let go?"

"It—it pulled me under. I nearly drowned!"

Scowling, Doto prowled around the edge of the pool, poking at the water with a stick. It turned out to be a little basin; Doto could make his way all the way around it, but from no edge could he reach Clay. At least there didn't seem any way for crocodiles to get him easily. "Well, what do we do now?"

"I don't know. Maybe if we could get a huge branch or a tree to lay across, I could climb out? Or you could crawl across and pull me out?"

Doto folded his arms across his chest, looking around. "I do not see anything like that. And I do not know why you think this frail fire bearer body would be capable of dragging a tree over to you."

Clay coughed. His finger with the torn nail was throbbing. "No, I suppose not."

"Fire bearers are so fragile. I cannot think how your species has managed to survive for so long."

"Well, for starters, we don't go into swamps. This much water is unhealthy."

Doto stalked around the edges of the pool again. He shook his head. "Clay, I do not think I can get you out of here."

"Well… well, you *have* to. I can't stay here! We have a mission!"

"What would you have me do?" He raised both his hands in the air in frustration. "I cannot come to you, or I will be stuck. I cannot pull you out without drowning you. I looked for trees above you so that I could pull you from above, but there are none, and even if there were, this ape body has no claws for climbing." He grimaced. "If there is another way, I will be glad to hear it, but I cannot see one. I do not care for it, but I think you may have to drown."

"What?" Clay spluttered. The words felt like a blow. "Doto, no! No, you can't let that happen! You can't!"

He nodded slowly. "I know it is not ideal, but you will wake up in our temple and can find me from there. I will only be a day's journey ahead."

Clay bared his teeth at him. "It's not about the time or having to push my way back through this miserable swamp alone again. Doto, I don't want to die. Ever again. Everyone else in my life has either killed me, wanted me dead, or left me to die. It's not…" He trailed off. He couldn't tell if tears were streaming down his face or only swamp water. "It's not only the pain. Not only how terrifying it is. And it gets worse every time, Doto. Every time. I'm so—so afraid of it happening again. I need you to treat my life like it's still important. I need one person left who isn't going to let me die. I need to feel *safe* with you, Doto."

"You *are* safe," he said, looking mystified. "You are a god now. You are always safe."

"But I need to *feel* safe. You're my mate. That's your job." He was sinking deeper into the mud and had to tilt his head far back to keep the water away from his mouth now. "And you can't keep telling me I'm a god every time I feel something human. I'm a fire bearer, too. That *matters*."

"You are very bossy for a fire bearer," Doto said sternly. "But you are… very often right." He shook his head. "I do not know what else I can do, then. I will come in and try to pull you out. Maybe I will find solider ground than you. Maybe I will be better at not getting my feet stuck. If not, then we will drown together."

He stepped into the pool.

"No!" Clay shouted. "No, not yet, please. It feels too much like giving up." More foul-tasting swamp water splashed into his mouth. He huffed air frantically through his nose.

"Then what?"

"I don't know! Something. Anything!"

Doto scratched his fingers through his thick, curly mane. He looked around with a miserable expression.

Clay slapped at the water, trying to keep afloat, but he was tiring.

Then Doto nodded, as if to himself, and turned to one side. "I am very sorry for this," he said to Clay. "I am not going to do a good job. This is not how it should have happened." He lifted one foot.

"What—urp—are you talking about?" Clay gasped between breaths.

But Doto ignored him. He paused for one moment, one foot held in the air, and then stepped forward. And he sang.

*Out of grass and fire comes the blessing*
*Of Doté the renewer.*

*You calm the wrathful and shame the unjust.*
*You are the god who joins and merges.*
*You are the god who does not fight but embraces*
*And in your arms the lost recall their true selves.*

The air crackled around Clay. "What—what are you doing?" he gasped, but he knew. Something powerful was flowing into him. Something wondrous. He felt the forest again, and his connection to it, but also something deeper. Something beyond the forest. When in the forest, when he opened his divine senses, he could sense all its life—every beast and bird, every insect, every plant, and the uncountable, teeming, invisible lives that clustered around and within everything.

But this was something else, something outside the forest. Other lives, beating hearts, some strong, some feeble, sparks in a darkness that spread beyond the borders of the world.

His body changed, his hands twisting into paws, the lost claw regrowing. His spine lengthened with his feline height and his fur-bearded chin rose from the water. He took a deep, grateful breath of forest air.

Doto continued to dance, his changing body granting his limbs new agility; now the reeds and rushes parted for him; the water drained away beneath his steps.

*All may love you, but none can own you.*
*Where you walk the world changes*
*and old laws die and are forgotten.*
*You are Doté the compassionate.*
*You give voice to the people the gods forgot*
*joy to those who have never felt it*
*life to hearts that had tired of beating*
*In every realm your footstep is welcomed.*

The ground firmed around Clay's feet and rose, lifting him up as swamp water rushed away, leaving a thick field of mud that quickly furred over with moss, sprouting saplings, bushes, and flowers. All of Clay's weariness was gone now. The despondent malaise that had overtaken his mind fled, and he saw that his dark thoughts had not truly been his, but seeds finding purchase in his exhaustion, hunger, and misery. There were still insects everywhere, but they now avoided him respectfully, no longer crawling into his ears and nose, and he no longer wanted to claw his skin off scratching at their welts.

He crouched, panting, in the sudden circle of forest. His shortness of breath was not from exhaustion, which he did not feel in his divine avatar, but from wonder. He could still feel those sparks flickering out there in the darkness of the world beyond the forest. In a smooth motion, he stood upright and saw Doto standing in leopard form just inside the circle, holding his paws close to his chest.

"Was that—was that all right?" Doto asked. "I wasn't sure what words to use, but I thought of you and—and words came."

"Doto." Clay rushed to his side and clasped his face in both paws, planting kisses across his muzzle and cheeks and nose. "Doto, you saved me. You *danced* for me!"

"Yes." Doto leaned back, looking bewildered. "You seem… very pleased." His ears gave a hopeful lift. "You are not disappointed?"

"Of course not! How could I be disappointed?"

The leopard prince stepped back. He met Clay's gaze only in quick, darting glances, as though afraid what he'd see when he looked in his eyes.

"Maybe you do not see me as so much of a god now. Now that I have danced for you like a fire bearer. Like a mortal. Maybe you will not be impressed with me… as much."

"Oh, Doto." Clay pressed both his paws to his chest. "Doto, do you think that that's why I love you? Because you are a god?"

"You love all the gods," Doto said uneasily. "And you hate the fire bearers now. I won you because I was powerful. Because I could command the forest. And because my form pleased you."

"Doto." Clay smiled. "I was impressed with you, certainly. It was wondrous to me to have a god speaking to me, to have the tales of the Teller come alive before my eyes. For a while, I felt as though I were becoming part of the tales themselves. But that's not why I fell in love with you. I fell in love with what I saw beneath the god. The way you were afraid I would see you didn't know everything. Your wonder at experiencing the world after you healed me. The way you cared for me. The way you stood up to your father, to all the gods, to keep me safe."

Doto's head was tilted, his brow wrinkled. "You do not… love the part of me that is god?"

"I do," Clay said. "Now. But I fell in love with the part of you that was gentle and worried, the part of you that wanted to grow. That learned compassion and wonder. The part that got embarrassed when you tripped. I fell in love when I saw you changing."

"Changing," Doto repeated, almost to himself. "Yes. And I did not care for you at first. I thought you weak and irritating and helpless. Ready to bow for anyone. Undeserving of the attentions of a mighty god. But then you found ways to be strong. You challenged the gods. You challenged me. You made yourself better. And then—and then you made *me* better."

Clay smiled. "Thank you for dancing for me, Doto. It was wonderful."

"You liked it?"

"Would you do it again?"

Doto tilted his head, paused a moment, and then spun back into the dance, and this time he moved through the whirls and leaps with feline grace, moving through handsprings and gyrations while his deep voice sung the song of Doté in naked jubilation.

And as he sang, those sparks in the darkness beyond the forest brightened again, and Clay almost knew them. He could almost hear their voices. They were fire bearers out there, stars glittering in a distant sky. And one of them was very close, singing his praises, dancing for him. The praise—it was a bond, a connection between him and the singer. The singer resonated with all fire bearers, sharing their devotion, their beliefs, their stories with him.

Yes, the fire bearers had stories. Above all else, above tools, above the flames, above hatred and love and revenge, above crops and hunting and children and ancestors and gods, they had stories. They were story-bearers—that was their truest name. Their priests, their magicians, were Tellers, communing with the gods, translating their relationship with the past and their world into tales that they planted like seeds in their hearts.

The story-bearers shared many stories. Some only in their own hearts, some with families, some with tribes, some with countrymen, some across the world. And one story that many of them shared was that gods should have crowns. Brilliant crowns of glittering black stone, or headdresses of crystalline water, or tiaras of flowers. Or feathers.

The gods worshiped by the humans had crowns.

Something solid rooted deep in the skin of Clay's forehead, between his brows. It did not itch as it grew, but he felt it extend upward all the same, rising to catch the slow, still breeze of the swamp. It tugged at his flesh. He brushed at it with his fingertips. "Is it?"

"A feather," Doto breathed. "Like mine. Like the one you danced for me. But yours is red. Like blood."

Clay brushed it with his fingers. "I could feel the change. Did you feel it too, when yours—"

He stopped. Something buzzed at his senses: a tug, a ripple of power. It was intense. And close.

"Doto…" he began.

And then the waters of the swamp bulged as though pregnant. Something brown and pink and massive erupted from the surface, with a face as wide as a cave, sawing yellow teeth, and a yawning throat that could swallow either of them whole.

"Insolent spawn of Kwaee," the creature roared. "You dare break our old pact? I will send you back to him as a heap of entrails!"

Atekye, a mountain of round, furious power, charged.

# 26 Queen of the Reeds

Doto's fur stood on end as the massive, brown and pink form of Atekye barreled out of the swamps toward them. With one outstretched paw, he urged saplings to sprout in rows from the ground, angled toward the charging goddess, their bodies hardwood, their tips sharpened to deadly points. He reached back with his other, attempting to guard Clay from Atekye's charge, but Clay stepped aside, lifting his own arms.

A network of vines whipped between the trees, interlaced between branches at the right height to catch Atekye around the arms and head. Through his alarm, Doto felt a flash of pride at Clay's quick thinking—he was getting much better at using his abilities instinctively.

But there was no time now for praise; the goddess lumbered toward the two of them in their little circle of forest. She was slower now that she had risen from the water, but not by much. She was not a giant like Asubonten, but still imposing and enormous, half again as tall as Kwaee, and her body was thick with fat and powerful muscle. With sweeps of her trunk-like arms, she snapped the hanging vines away, leaving the treetops shaking. She stamped down one hoof-toed foot and splintered the rows of saplings.

"Intruders!" her voice thundered, and she smashed her way toward them, shouldering trees aside as though they were swamp reeds. "Interlopers! Oathbreakers!" She punctuated every accusation with another stamp of a foot large enough to crack either of their bodies beneath it and send their souls back to their temple.

Doto backed with Clay to the edge of the forest circle, but there was nowhere to run. They were surrounded by swamp on all sides, swamp that was slow to slog through even when it *wasn't* sucking them down. And besides, the swamp was *her* territory. Lacking any other option, Doto sprang up into the trees, using his claws for purchase until he landed on a branch high above Atekye's head. Clay moved up at the same time, scrambling and pouncing between branches to crouch beside Doto.

Atekye pounded toward the trunk, and Doto realized she could easily push it over and send the two of them plummeting into the swamp. He hissed at her, his tail lashing.

The hippo goddess stopped and stared up at him. Her small ears wiggled. Then her broad, round snout cracked into a grin. "Ha. Ha ha! Ha ha ha ha!" She tilted her head back and bellowed a deep, booming laughter.

Doto passed a bewildered glance to Clay, who shrugged. Below their branch, the goddess leaned back, holding her belly as she guffawed. Her mouth was somehow wider than her entire body. If either of them dropped now, they'd fall right between those fleshy, yellow-toothed jaws.

"Oh great Atekye," Clay began, rising to no doubt attempt a bow while balanced on a treetop.

Doto interrupted. "What is happening? Why are you acting like this?"

The goddess leaned against a tree, shaking with mirth, pounding it with one fist as tears of laughter streamed from her eyes. Doto grimaced as the tree leaned, creaking its complaints. He wondered if he ought to use his power to strengthen it to hold her or let go its roots and dump her into the water.

"You… should have seen… your faces," Atekye gasped between laughs. "Your fur poofed out—*pfff!* And then you popped up into the tree like damned birds! And then, '*Sssssss!*' Was that supposed to frighten me?"

"It is a natural reaction," Doto said, trying to pat his fur down. "Times are not safe, even for gods."

"Well certainly not for cute little kitten boys like you." Atekye chuckled again and rubbed at her eyes. "You can come down out of the tree now, if you like. I won't hurt you."

"We can see you better from up here," Doto pointed out.

The grin dropped from Atekye's face, and her voice, while still mellow and pleasant, developed a hard edge. "Well, if you want to be *rude* to the Queen of Reeds…"

Doto cast about for some dignified retort, but Clay had already stepped off the tree branch to land in a crouch before Atekye's feet. He was probably about to grovel, Doto thought, but instead he merely dipped his head low.

"It is a great honor to meet you, Lady—"

"Queen." Her voice was firm.

"Queen Atekye."

"That's better. The little humans used to call me that, when they lived nearby. Atekye, Queen of Reeds. I liked it." She settled her massive bulk down before him, leaning on one elbow and kicking a few trees into splinters with her short legs.

Doto sighed and dropped down to the ground next to Clay. The round shape of Atekye filled his vision. Well, at least she wasn't trying to kill them. Even if he didn't much appreciate her sense of humor.

She leaned her mountainous head down to peer at both of them with her small, brown eyes, and her ears wiggled again. "You look like Kwaee's boys, but I thought he only had the one. That cat's been dumping a lot of his shit in my swamp. Burned shit. Ashes. You think I like that?" She poked a stubby, hoofed finger into Clay's chest, sending him stumbling backward.

Doto opened his mouth to protest, but she cut him off. "Oh, I know where it comes from. Me and Asubonten had words. Well, it's not like I don't see her all the damned time. Rivers and swamps come together. Where Asubonten spills into the sea, that's where swamps are born. Where they grow. That's where I become mighty. And when she slithers her way through my body, we talk, at least when I can stand that puffed-up old lizard. Well? What do you want anyway? Come down here just to stand there catching flies? Close your mouth, kitten, or speak up."

"Queen Atekye—" Clay began.

"Now, which one are you? Doto?"

"Oh, no, Lady—Queen Atekye, I'm not—"

"*I* am Doto," Doto said stiffly. "Son of Lord Kwaee, prince of the forest."

"Prince now, are you?" Atekye grinned broadly, her huge, yellow tusks jutting. "Did you ever call yourself that *before* you heard me call myself Queen of the Reeds?"

Doto felt his ears go flat. Clay grinned at him.

"That's what I thought."

"If you can call yourself Queen of the Reeds—"

"Humans called me that. And I liked it. What do the humans call you, Doto, son of Kwaee?"

"Well, this one calls me mate," he said, and felt no small measure of pride at that. "And the fire bearers called him Clay, prince of the People of the Savanna."

The goddess peered at Clay, her ears fanning like dragonfly wings. "This one is no fire bearer." She ran one finger along the feather sprouting from his brow. "He even has a little crown like your papa. And last I heard, fire bearers couldn't be—"

Her small, brown eyes widened. "No!"

Clay nodded. "Doto saved me after my own people killed me. And some call me Doté." He sent a shy smile to Doto. "The Renewer."

Atekye pushed herself upright, leaning back. "You brought this boy back from the dead?" She stared at Doto in a mixture of admiration and horror. "Do you know what that cost you?"

"I know," Doto answered.

"Half your power!" she bellowed. "Half! And word was you were already a halfling to begin with."

He fought to keep the twitch from his tail. "That's true."

A powerful shudder moved across Atekye's body, as though she were shaking off flies. "Well, I couldn't have done it. Wouldn't have. No pretty little worshiper is worth that."

Clay stepped forward, his head tilted, ears perked. "But surely you have already done so, Queen Atekye."

She folded her arms across the top of her belly. "And how's that?"

"Mother Fam told us. The great bargain. You gave up your power too, didn't you? To know what we—what the fire bearers felt?"

"She told you about that?" Atekye turned her gaze back to Doto. "She told *you* about that? But Kwaee had told everyone—"

"I found her. We found her. And sought out the truth."

"Well, well. Yes, Clay, prince of the People of the Savanna, I gave up a little of my power. Not *half*."

"And Doto gave up a little more. For me. To save me."

Atekye fixed Doto with a squinty stare. "And never regretted it? Not once?"

"I often wish I had my power back," Doto confessed. "But if Clay were gone, it wouldn't be worth it. I do feel things more strongly now. Joy. Love. Peace. But also sadness and weakness and fear. Those are part of having something you never want to lose. I am glad every day that Clay is here, and to me the cost is nothing. You would know that if you truly knew my father, who also had the chance to pay it, and refused."

"Well, well, well," said Atekye. "You heard about that too? Then I guess you *do* know everything. So. You came seeking out old Auntie Atekye, hmm? Not a pleasant trip for the two of you, I bet. Old Featherhead hated coming into my realm, even though we share."

"You share?" Clay blurted out. "With *him*?"

Doto readied himself for anger, but Atekye only dissolved into bubbles of laughter. "Well, not like either of us had much say in it, boy. The line between forest and swamp moves constantly with rains and floods, and sometimes it overlaps, and the two of us share. Not that either of us enjoy it, but nature is what it is, and what it is is sloppy sometimes. Still, he never liked it and never came this way. Old Atekye had to rely on Asubonten and the animal gods for conversation. And sometimes Mpo, but whew! She got weird. Started talking to her followers too much. Started believing what they were saying. It's not good for a god to do that. Makes you a little crazy, if you want to know."

Atekye waggled her finger at the two of them. "You pay attention to that, you hear? Don't spend too much time around your worshipers. It starts out okay, but eventually, it's just a bad time for everyone."

"I don't think you have to worry about that," Clay muttered. "I don't even have any. Except Doto, and that's a kind of mutual thing now, I suppose. That's why we're here. The fire bearers don't exactly like us. Or Kwaee."

"Oh, but they like Ogya fine, don't they?" Atekye's voice went as sweet as honey. "So that's what you want? Come to see if Auntie will bring up her waters and flood them out?"

Doto blinked. "Could you do that?"

"What? Put out all the fires in the world? Do you hear yourself? Ogya would still burn in his temple in Fam's belly, and not even Mpo has enough water to drown that fire. But even if I could, why would I?"

Clay and Doto glanced at each other. "You don't care if the forest dies? And what's to stop Ogya when he's done with Kwaee?" Doto demanded.

Atekye stared at him. "You mean other than the endless fields of swamp water that we were just talking about me using to put out Ogya's fires?"

"I—I—" Doto stammered.

"Ogya can't burn down a damned *swamp.* I don't care how many fire bearers he's got with torches and arrows and oil. The two of you could barely make it in on your own. You think you could have done it carrying a flame? You think fire would make a difference to me, here? You think even big bad Ogya could stop the rain?"

"But the ash. The mud. Asubonten said it poisoned her river."

Atekye rolled her broad shoulders and leaned back, spreading her arms as though reaching for the sides of the horizon. "She's just a river. Powerful, quick, but slim. There is too much Atekye for Ogya to do anything about. If he gives the swamp mud, the swamp will use it. Ash will fertilize my roots. And his flame will not spread far here. He cannot destroy me—no, he only can only help me grow. If Kwaee falls, then I get back the land he stole."

Doto's lips curled in a defensive snarl. "Stole? My father stole nothing from you!"

The hippo goddess gave him a weary, sidelong glance. "And what would you know of it? You didn't even know we shared. That there was overlap."

"How could he steal from you? A god cannot rob another of territory!"

"But the territory moves. When the rains are gone. When flooding ends. And when the land goes to Kwaee, Kwaee makes sure it doesn't go back. The roots of his trees heap earth high and stop it moving. Fallen leaves and branches dam the flow of water. And what would be flat and flooded one season stays forest the next." Atekye's eyes glittered with anticipation. "But if Ogya burns the trees, they don't hold the earth in place. The mud runs into me, and toward the sea. The land goes flat, and where it is flat, the swamp spreads. Hear me, child, if Kwaee dies, Ogya will have nothing left on the surface to burn. And my waters will spread far and wide. I will be not a Queen of the Reeds, but queen of the whole world. Pretty good bargain for Auntie Atekye, don't you think? Do nothing and rule the world?"

The longer she spoke, the hotter the fury built in Doto. His forearms tensed, sliding his claws from their sheaths. Gods were infuriating—so selfish, so blind, so stupid. And now the smirk on her face. She knew she was enraging him and she didn't care, cared nothing for the world. Unbidden, a low, menacing growl spilled from his muzzle. "How can you be so—so heartless?" he demanded.

Atekye turned an unimpressed gaze toward his predatory crouch, his moon-curved claws. "That was always the trouble with you forest gods. All heart and no head."

"An easy judgment from one who does not worry if she will survive." Doto's muscles strained as his body fought to leap at her in fury.

Clay's paw on his chest stilled him, sending peace through Doto's body as only his touch could. "I am disappointed to hear these words from you, Queen of Reeds," Clay said.

Atekye turned her regard toward him, and he met her gaze unwaveringly. "You speak impudently for a fresh little quarter-god."

"I speak not as a god now, but as a fire bearer, as the greater part of me. We always believed the gods loved us. Or at least cared about us. But over and over I have seen that they do not, or that their care and love means little. I had hoped you might be different."

Atekye's smile held, but too still, like a hare that had spotted a predator. "And why should what a few apes think matter to me?"

"Didn't you say they called you Queen of Reeds? It seemed to matter then."

"I don't know that I like your little friend, Doto," she said.

"But you should care anyway. Because you made a bargain, Queen of Reeds." Clay somehow made the title sound shameful, embarrassing instead of impressive. "Didn't you?"

The grin had fallen away from her face completely now. Doto didn't know what Clay was doing, but from the way the powerful muscles were tensing under her thick hide, he suspected they were both about to be sent back to their temple via a very uncomfortable shortcut. "And what bargain would this be?"

Clay blinked and tilted his head. "The grand bargain that you and all the other gods made. With the fire bearers. You gave us some of your power, didn't you? Didn't you get anything in return?"

And Atekye, giant hippo goddess of the swamp, pushed herself backward several paces. "That is hardly your concern."

"At times it only feels like weakness, doesn't it? Like you're vulnerable? Like you might not be strong enough, like you might fail? Like you might end up alone and afraid? Like there's an emptiness in you and nothing can make it heal?"

She drew herself up. She probably intended her smile to look lazy, but even to Doto's eyes it was forced—hammered across her face. "Of course I—"

"All fire bearers feel like that, a little, all the time," Clay said. "But there's a good side, too. All the hard things make us grateful for the good things. Like a good meal when you're really hungry, or cool water when your throat is dry and sore." He smiled toward Doto. "Or the warmth of coming in out of the cold. Or someone to hold you when you're lonely or afraid. It's better, isn't it? Better than never feeling hungry or cold in the first place."

Doto nodded, surprised to find that he agreed.

Apparently fearless, Clay stepped closer to Atekye, his tail still, his ears focused on her. He almost looked as though he were hunting. He tilted his head. "And then there's everything else besides. Feeling joy when we accomplish something hard, or when we're free of our troubles for a while. Reaching out to someone you love and making them feel better. It's all wonderful. Life would be nothing for me without it. Did you get none of that? No joy? No love? No relief? What did you get from the bargain?"

Eyeing him as though he might be poisonous, Atekye pushed herself another few steps back, sliding partway into the water.

"I don't mean to make you uncomfortable. But that is why Doto asks how you can be so heartless. Surely you got something from the bargain that changed you. You must care a little."

Atekye straightened herself a little. "And why aren't you asking these questions of the great god, Ogya, hmm? He made the bargain too. Why don't you ask what he feels, whether or not he cares?"

"Ogya murdered my family and turned my brother into a monster. I couldn't know how to reach him even if I wanted to." Clay looked up at her. "But you're not Ogya. You're Atekye, Queen of the Reeds, and you don't make bad bargains. You're proud of the name the fire bearers gave you and proud of your swamp."

"It is the strongest land in the world. All the powers of earth and water together. His father has trees? I have trees. I have mud. I have stone. I have swarms of insects and countless birds. All elements of the world are part of my dominion, here."

"All but fire," Clay said.

"Even fire burns within me, but it cannot stop me. I can suffocate it as easily as rolling atop it."

"Then help us stop Ogya. Help us save the forest and the savanna and all the creatures and the fire bearers too. Help us save all your birds and insects who will choke to death on his smoke even if you don't."

"And just how do two little forest godlings plan to stop the Blazing God? You know what he is. You know what fire burns. You two are *made of* his food."

"We have a plan to stop him. We're going to capture him in a prison of unburnable stone in a field of water. We have Mother Fam on our side, and Asubonten. And Kwaee, of course. But we need you, Queen of the Reeds. We can't do it without you."

"Probably," Doto interjected. He'd seen what Clay was trying to do, but it wasn't going to work. Atekye was proud, and pride needed to be stung, not stroked. Besides, there was something she was missing. Something she wanted. Something she craved.

"What do you mean, probably? How can you accomplish this without me?" The hippo goddess shook her broad shoulders, and water sprayed everywhere. A swarm of insects took flight, buzzing around in annoyed circles before settling again.

Doto flicked his tail lazily. "Well, we do have Asubonten helping us. Her waters might be enough. If you have no wish to be part of our grand plan against Ogya, it is understandable. Your swamp looks… comfortable. If you choose to wait in it during the battle of the gods and see how things end up, no one can blame you. You can wait. Do nothing, as you said. And maybe we will be fortunate. Maybe we will be strong enough without you. And one of us will be sure to hurry back to you as soon as we can and say, we have succeeded alone; such a thing has never been done before, and the great Atekye, Queen of the Reeds, was not even needed."

Atekye's face had been growing darker and darker the whole time Doto had been talking. He could smell her rising indignation, her blood pounding close below the surface of her pink-brown skin. "If you seek to anger me, spawn of Kwaee—"

"Or perhaps we will lose," Doto said. "And the temple Clay and I share will burn, and we will die. And Kwaee's temple will burn, and he will die. And Asubonten's river will turn to poisonous sludge, and she will die. And all the animal gods who have their temples in the forest will die too. None of us will be able to come back to tell you of our loss, though. If you never hear from any of us again, you'll know we didn't win. Although I suppose the birds can tell you when they fly here fleeing Ogya's smoke."

"No one would tell me…"

"But you can tell Mpo," Doto added brightly. "The next time you see her. If she's in a listening mood."

"Her? Listen? Hmph. All she does is go on and on about purity and cleansing and how all the other gods are nothing compared to her."

"The gods should talk to each other more. Not just thumping our chests like gorillas and boasting of our strength but talking about our lives. Kwaee should have come to you the moment Ogya showed up on the borders of the forest. He should have introduced you to me. Auntie Atekye. I would have liked to have known you. I was lonely in that forest, my father shut away, never speaking to anyone, sulking on his moabi."

Atekye snorted. "He forbade me or any of us talking to you. Fam, Asubonten, any of us. About anything that mattered. He holed himself up in that temple of his like a wounded animal."

"He didn't want me finding out," Doto said. "About my mother, about what he'd done, about the bargain with the fire bearers. It all looked like weakness to him. But now I know everything, I think. And that means I can come back and see you again."

"You could?"

"We could?" Clay looked as surprised as Atekye. "I mean, of course we could, it's just that—"

"Just that we would probably have to find an easier way of getting here," Doto admitted. "Neither of us are very suited to moving through your domain."

"I saw." Atekye grinned. "Nasty little problem you've got there, but if you gave part of yourself to your mate, then that explains it. Does your father know?"

Doto shook his head.

"Best he don't find out, huh?"

"I don't know, but I'm tired of not talking. If we get through all this, I'll tell him. And I'll go to visit Mother Fam again. And Sarmu in his mountain prison. I'll go and find the other gods, ones whose names the fire bearers have forgotten, ones who they've never even seen. And I'll come see you, Atekye." Doto sighed. "The fire bearers—they all live together. They talk all the time, chattering. They're a herd animal. I think they need each other. Herd animals aren't good alone. You've seen it. They suffer. They die. If they're young, they don't grow up right. They go mad."

He looked back at Clay and took a deep breath. "Maybe that's what's really wrong with us. Maybe we're not supposed to be alone either, but here we are, huddling behind the walls of our domains, slowly going mad, too. And we try things, like finding creatures to worship us, or kidnapping fire bearers from their nests while they sleep, or—or just trying to eat up everything so it can all be inside us. But I think the grand bargain made us need each other. Like the fire bearers. And if we live through this? I promise you'll have one more god to talk to."

"Two," Clay said.

Atekye tongued at her tusks in thought, her ears fanning. "It would be a terrible shame to miss such a meeting. Kwaee, Asubonten, Fam, and Ogya, all together."

Doto added, "If you were there, it would be an even greater meeting. One any god would be sorry to miss. The day that the gods of earth and water united to bring down the god of fire forever."

"Forever, ha!" Atekye scoffed, but intrigue still curled her voice. "Well, where is this meeting of the bold supposed to happen? Your Auntie isn't looking forward to a long trek through a dry forest with a lot of trees close together. Not without her power. Too tiring. Not enough water. And you get hungry outside your own territory. It's awful. You boys know."

Clay and Doto glanced at each other. "Yes. We know," they said in unison.

Doto cleared his throat. "It would need to be close to the swamp," he said. "As close as we can get without arousing Ogya's suspicion." He explained the plan to her in brief, concluding with, "So once Ogya is trapped in the prison, Kwaee will surrender part of his forest to you, so that you can turn it back into swamp and…" He hesitated. This was the part she wasn't going to like. "And keep Ogya prisoner there. Forever, if you can."

He squeezed his eyes closed at that part, not daring to look at Atekye's expression. Asking her to play warden to an angry god for eternity was risky. Perhaps fatal to their plan. But he heard no snorts of anger. She didn't get up and storm off. There no protests or shouts of outrage. Instead, she laughed, a high-pitched, bubbly chortle. It was almost a cackle. He cautiously opened his eyes.

"Hold on," she said. "You mean Lord High Treecat is going to *give back* some of the forest he stole from me? Of his own accord? And all I have to do is show up?"

*Well, and then guard a power-mad god of hunger for all eternity inside your realm*, Doto didn't say.

"Boy, you should have led with that. We all could have saved ourselves a lot of yakking. Not," she added in a more gentle tone, "that I minded the conversation."

~

The journey back to the forest was swift and easy compared to their previous slog through the swamp. When they asked for assistance returning to the forest, Atekye closed her eyes and, amid trembling of the ground, a lot of bubbles, and more than a few farty noises, a long, serpentine path rose from the swamp muck.

The path was stable, if not strictly solid, and Clay and Doto were easily able to sprint along its soft-mossed surface all the way to the edge of the forest, reaching in a short period of light running what had taken them nearly a full day of miserable thrashing before. Even the mosquitos left them alone.

Still, it was a relief to Clay when they finally reached the forest wall. He was hungry, scratched, bruised, bitten, itching, and exhausted, but when he stumbled through the border of his territory, all that disappeared. Energy and strength rolled through his body as he tumbled forward onto feline paws and was himself again.

He sprawled lazily across the moon-dappled forest floor, his eyes opening to take in the night. He watched Doto stagger through the forest wall moments later, his leopard shape rippling over him. Doto started a little when his gold-green eyes lit on Clay, and Clay realized he had unconsciously sunk into camouflage and gone invisible to Doto's human eyes.

"It feels so good to be back," he purred to Doto, and swiped lazily in his mate's direction, ready to lie with him here, amid the forest insects and frogs singing their love-songs.

"It does," Doto agreed, and from the lingering look he gave Clay, it was clear he was tempted. "But we should go and inform my father immediately."

It was the last thing Clay wanted—another conversation with an insufferable deity. He wanted to lie with Doto in his arms and chew on his shoulder. "Ugh. I suppose." He rolled to his feet. "But after that, you're mine alone for a while."

"If there is time," Doto agreed.

They set out at a run for Kwaee's temple, twin streaks of pale gold winding between the trees, sometimes vaulting up an angled trunk to dance across the canopy, sometimes crouching for soaring leaps over thicket too dense to part quickly with their magic, at least not without harming it.

Clay watched the forest speed by beneath him and thought, I am almost used to this now. Once, running was all that gave me joy, and I dreamed of the gods speaking to me. Now I am faster than any fire bearer and I am running to speak to the god of the forest, and I didn't even want to do it. When I came back into the forest, I was so relieved to be rid of my human shape and all its weaknesses. So glad to be home. And I dread the idea of leaving the forest, of going to see fire bearers again.

What remains of who I was? Perhaps Clay really is gone, now. Perhaps I truly am Doté.

On his forehead, he felt the tug of the large, red feather that had sprouted there.

~

Kwaee narrowed his eyes when he saw it. "An eventful journey, I see."

"Father, what happened here?" Doto trod through Kwaee's temple, his footsteps tentative, toes lifting as his feet crushed the desiccated husks of fallen insects. He stepped with caution around the stiff carcasses of fallen birds.

Clay followed after him, uneasy, his ears folded back. Something *had* happened. The temple at first glance appeared the same, carpeted with moss and ferns and high grasses, and sheltered from direct sunlight by the thick canopy. But beneath the green was a thick layer of fallen leaves, branches, and tree trunks. "Did Ogya attack somehow?"

"Does anything look burned to you?" Kwaee snapped. "Then how could it be an attack from the fire god? No. I simply… had a moment of distraction."

Doto waved a paw at Clay and slunk close to his father. He murmured words in very low tones, but Clay, his ears perked, could easily make them out. "Was this like before, Father? Like with Abansin? Were you thinking about… her?"

Kwaee stalked back to sprawl in his moabi again. Clay would have sworn he was *trying* to look sullen. "I was not, and how dare you question me in front of…" He looked at Clay and cleared his throat. In a louder voice, he said, "My moods are none of your concern. You've returned from Asubonten and Atekye. Did you manage to speak to them at all while you were gone? Or were you too busy" —his gaze flicked dismissively toward Clay's forehead— "doing whatever it is you were doing out there?"

Doto puffed out his chest. "We did speak to them. And they have both agreed to help us."

The god of the forest tilted his head slightly, blinking. "I—you said that you—you talked to *both* of them?"

"Yes, Father."

"And they both agreed. To *help*."

"We were very persuasive. Doté knew what to say to Asubonten, and I worked out how to persuade Atekye."

Kwaee let out a strange, forced exhale. A breeze wafted through the temple, and all the flowers closed their petals. "And—and what conditions did they have? Surely they made demands on you. The goddesses would not do anything without exacting a cost."

"Well, Asubonten already suffered from Ogya's ash. It was necessary only to persuade a little. And, of course," Doto added in casual tones, "best her in physical combat. It was nothing that Clay and I could not manage. Atekye calls herself Queen of Reeds, now. And you are right. She did have demands."

"Ah!" Kwaee's eyes glittered.

"But nothing that you had not already agreed to. She will assist upon the return of her lost swampland." Doto ran his tongue over his teeth. "She says you shored it up during dry seasons. Took it."

"And you believed her. Of course she said nothing about doing the same during flooding! The same old Atekye, she—"

"She just wanted a little company. Doté and I promised to visit her from time to time, if this all works out. And that was all."

The forest god shook his great, feathered head, still staring in apparent disbelief. "Then we are truly about to embark on this… foolhardy venture."

"Foolhardy?" Clay and Doto said together.

"To attempt to deceive and entrap one of the strongest gods in the world? Even you cannot be so naïve. If we are successful, it will forever change the balance of power in this world. It may even change what it means to be a god. If one god can be imprisoned, why not another? Nothing will be the same."

Clay shrugged. "And what's so good about the way things are now? Things *should* change."

"You grow more arrogant by the day. You think yourself a full-fledged god now? Where did you even get that feather? Who under Wem did you persuade to dance at your feet and worship you?"

"I gave it to him," Doto said, smiling at Clay.

"You?" Kwaee blinked at him. "*You?*" He shook his head. "I truly do not understand this world anymore. Perhaps it already changes faster than I can follow. Then what else? Ha ha!" The laugh boomed out of him, amazed and humorless. "Why not? Surrender yourself to Atekye and Asubonten and Mpo. Put your fate in the hands of your own children."

Clay gave Doto an uneasy glance. Hadn't this all been decided on? Supposing they couldn't count on Kwaee?

Doto nodded at the look and said to Kwaee, "That was the plan, was it not? You agreed to it."

"I said perhaps. I said *if* you persuaded the water goddesses…" The forest god trailed off into a growl.

Clay spoke up. "You didn't think we would succeed."

"No."

"And you don't think we will be successful in our plan with Ogya."

"No. I will carve out another piece of myself, pay another price, and for nothing."

Clay flung his paws upward. "Asubonten nearly ate Doto. The swamp near drowned me. We were miserable the whole time! Why even send us at all, if you didn't intend to help us?"

"So you could fail!" Kwaee roared. Every tree in the temple vibrated with the timbre of his voice.

He stood panting a moment, flexing his fingers, his claws sliding in and out. "So you could fail in a harmless way," he said, more evenly. "In a way that did not involve inviting the god of fire into the heart of my forest and endangering my son."

"In a way that did not involve you losing more of your territory, you mean!" Doto snapped. He stepped back, took a deep breath, and then sighed. "No. I see now. Come on, Clay." He stepped down from the moabi's hill, taking Clay's paw as he went by.

"And where are you going now?" asked Kwaee. "Another hopeless plan? Gone to beg Sarmu for help? Or Mpo?"

Doto shook his head. "I'm tired of you, Kwaee. When I saw how you fought for the forest, I thought you had learned something. But you haven't. You only repeat yourself, over and over. You cannot change."

"The forest *is* unchanging!"

"No, it is not! It burns, even now! One day there will be nothing left. And while it burns you will sit here and torment yourself over my mother. That is what you were doing—do not lie to me. I have seen how you get. Your whole temple must have died, and you didn't even clean it." Doto's nose wrinkled. "You just grew over it. Like it didn't happen. And all of this so you can make the same mistakes once again. Refusing to give. Refusing to bend."

Kwaee was trembling in fury as Doto spoke, his fur lifting along his back, his teeth baring, and now he surged forward, a blur of speed, his claws bared, his arm raised for a vicious swipe. But when he stopped, Doto was not there; he had stepped neatly to one side. Kwaee whirled on him in confusion and rage.

"You see? The same mistakes. Do what you like. You cannot stop me now."

"Stop you from doing what?" The words were growled between clenched teeth.

"We will enact Mother Fam's plan. Without you. We will save your precious forest, since you are too cowardly to do it yourself."

The forest god's gold-green eyes were narrowed into suspicious slits. "You cannot. You have no land to give to Atekye."

Doto blinked at him impassively. "We have a little. With a stream." His eyes met Clay's, and they were full of meaning; Clay sent his mind out, into the forest, where it found Doto's.

*Our temple?*

*I'm sorry. I should have asked you first. But it is the only way. Is it all right?*

Clay thought of all that he had gained since Doto had saved him, and all that he had lost. And all there was yet to lose. Perhaps there would be a way out of it. They would have to surrender their temple to Atekye to catch Ogya. They would have had to risk it anyway, to lure Ogya in, but only temporarily, in space granted to them by Kwaee. With no place to retreat, their temple would be utterly subsumed by swamp. What would happen to them then? Would Atekye grant them some space of her own to escape to? Or would they disappear? Or become a part of her?

It was, ultimately, an easy decision. Risk themselves to keep the world from ruin? What else was divine power for? And what sense trying to continue in a world of ash?

*Of course it is.* He gazed at Doto proudly. How changed he was from the demanding, puffed up forest god who had dragged Clay from his village so long ago.

Kwaee's expression, though, was not so proud. He looked bewildered, the whites showing around his eyes. "How could you do such a thing?"

Doto swiveled his ears backward. "Because it is the only way I can think of to stop all this."

"No." Kwaee frowned. "I mean, how do you surrender yourself over and over, knowing the cost? How do you make yourself do it? I cannot… I cannot find the way."

Doto stepped back toward Clay and slid an arm around his waist. He was warm and comforting and strong. "Father, if you had asked me three moons ago my deepest fear, I would have said that I was too much like you. Now I look at you and I do not even understand you. It is like you are squeezing thorns in your paws, and you are pained all the time, and blood runs down your arms. And then you ask me how I let go. I do not know what to say, because I do not understand why you grip your pain so tightly. Just… let go. Let go."

There was a long silence. The wind drifted through the temple, scattering dead leaves through the new grass. Kwaee's fingers opened and closed. He turned his gold-green eyes to meet his son's. "I'll fall," he whispered.

~

Near the agreed-upon meeting place, Clay and Doto made themselves a comfortable little hollow, carpeting it with thick, plush moss and filling it with colorful, sweet-smelling flowers. They lay in each other's arms, Doto's head resting against Clay's chest. "Are you afraid?" he murmured.

"Of course I am. A little. But I have an idea. If Kwaee won't give us enough of the forest, perhaps we could take it from him."

Doto leaned up. "How do you mean?"

"You and I… we could dance it to each other. Like we did in the savanna, the mountains, the swamp. Even here in the forest. All those little spots where I danced before. I can feel that they're there, can't you?"

"Yes, but none of them are big enough for our temple. Not even close."

"No," Clay agreed. "But if you and I danced several circles… it would take a while, but—"

"But they would be our territory. And then we could move the temple there long enough to tempt Ogya. Clay, that's brilliant! And we're the only gods who could even do something like this, because—"

"Because we're the only ones who are part fire bearer. Only they can dance the forest." Clay paused. "Kwaee would be furious, though. After all our talk about letting go, to take his territory and use it for this."

"If it works, then Ogya's imprisoned and he has to thank us for saving his entire forest. And if it doesn't, we're all dead anyway."

"I suppose. It still feels wrong."

Doto sighed, his breath ruffling Clay's chest fur. "Wrong is letting your son go to his doom when you could stop it."

"He stood up to Ogya before, not long after you had saved me. He loves you. I think he will remember that. I think he will come."

"I don't want to think about that right now. Not with the short time we have until we call Ogya." Doto leaned up to gaze into Clay's eyes. "Now I just want to be with you."

Clay bit off the end of that last word with a kiss, firm and hungry. He took Doto's head in his paws, running his fingers through the soft fur of his cheeks. And then Doto was kissing him back, tail swaying above him, pouring a growl down his throat.

Clay let his mind go out into the forest for a moment, his arousal spreading into the flowers and trees around him, sending throes of lust into the nearby wildlife. Before he had even meant to, he was spurring rut out of season, sending the insects swarming, propelling birds into desperate courtship dances. His mind searched for Doto's so that he could share the sensations of holding and being held, to braid their twin excitements together into a spiral of desire.

But no, this was not how he wanted it to be, not this time. He wanted something simpler. Grounded. He wanted to remember being human as well as divine. He caught a fleeting impression of the puzzlement in Doto's mind as he touched awareness and then withdrew, and then he was back in his own body, and he kissed Doto again, lifting his legs to hook them around his lover's back.

Any uncertainty Doto may have felt was dispelled; he tugged gently at Clay's tongue with his teeth and then kissed down his jaw, his neck, and chest, rasping at the fur with his tongue. He leaned up, his hips moving to probe with the tip of his arousal, already stiff, already ready. He found Clay's entrance with the ease of experience and paused there.

His eyes were hungry; he looked down at Clay as though they had been apart for an eternity, not quite meeting his gaze, but staring slightly above. At the feather. It still felt strange to Clay, the solidity of the quill embedded in his skin; the way it tugged at his forehead in the wind; the way it could rise or lower with his expressions. Being reminded of it now made him feel stranger. Doto gazed at it for a while, keeping the tip of his arousal achingly close, a casual movement away from promised pleasure.

"Doté," he breathed, as though tasting the word for the first time. "Doté the compassionate. The renewer."

"Clay," Clay begged him. He could not reject the new name; it was part of him now, like the feather, like his fur, like the power of the forest that flowed through him. Like the loss of his family and village, like bargains with gods and dark fears and death after death at the hands of his people. But there would be time enough for that. Now, he wanted to be Clay—simple, unassuming, devoted. In the arms of the god who loved him.

And without their minds meeting, without sharing thoughts or sensations, Doto looked into his eyes and understood. "Clay," he said, and the name was music on his tongue. And as he said it, he slid into Clay and filled him with pleasure.

~

The meeting spot was not far from the swamp, but not so close as to arouse Ogya's suspicion. A gentle incline led toward shaggy green hills; somewhere up above, a good distance away, the mighty Asubonten hit a boulder and forked southwest where she might have turned northwest. A little change in the hills' topography could send her careening down a much different path.

Clay and Doto strolled into the glen, leaning on each other. They were incapable of tiring themselves out within the forest, but they had given it their best attempt, and though they had not shared their recreation with the forest, it had responded nonetheless. Errant wisps of pollen floated behind them.

Mother Fam was already there, her great, round body shaggy with moss and sprouting mushrooms all over. She beamed widely upon seeing them, spreading her arms wide to embrace each of them in turn. "I knew you would be able to do it," she said. "Well done, both of you. I am so very proud."

Clay shook the mud from his fur and gazed up at her, again feeling like a small child in her presence. "I only hope it works," he said. "If it doesn't—"

Mother Fam put a heavy hand on his shoulder. "Sweet Clay, your mind doesn't need those fears right now. Let them go."

He found, to his surprise, that he was able to.

"I see you have found your own private worshiper," she said with a genuine smile, flicking Clay's feather with a fingertip. "Doto. You have grown so much."

"Thank you. It—I worry sometimes that I have become less." Doto looked surprised to have blurted out the confession so openly.

"That worry deceives you. You are more, Doto. More than you were. More than your father ever was. Loving more never makes you less."

Through the thrumming of the power of Mother Fam, they hardly felt Atekye approach, the ripples of her power like whispers in a windstorm, but they heard her, crashing through the underbrush and muttering curses in god-tongue. She finally arrived, pushing her bulk through the trees, looking weary and uncomfortable without the support of her terrain. "Whew! I thought you said this was going to be close to the swamp, not a long prickly hike!" She leaned against a tree, wheezing, and lifted one flat broad-toed foot to rub at it. "I need a nap. And a snack."

"Atekye, it is a pleasure to see you."

Mother Fam turned to Atekye, her arms opened wide for another embrace, but the hippo goddess held up one wide, flat palm, the other braced on her knee to catch her breath. "No no. We don't have that kind of relationship, Fam."

Clay thought he saw a trace of sadness on Mother Fam's face, but she lowered her arms. "Of course."

He wondered how anyone could say no to that presence, how you could refuse the embrace, but Mother Fam had spent a long time underground, he supposed. Kwaee had banned her from the forest, but surely she could have moved among the other gods. They all had their own troubles, it seemed. But Fam had withdrawn so easily. Was it possible, perhaps, to be too considerate, too gentle? To give way so easily that you didn't fight for the people you cared about?

All the gods but Wem had made their bargains with the fire bearers. They had taken weakness and human failings in exchange for emotion. Even Fam. *We're all flawed, all of us. Gods and fire bearers alike. Maybe none of us really knows how any of this is supposed to go.*

"Asubonten is upriver," Atekye reported. She had caught her breath but was now vigorously scratching her back against the tree behind her, which groaned its complaints as it bent. Clay quietly sent some power to strengthen it and grow its bark out sharper to make for a better scratch. Atekye looked toward him and Doto with one brow raised and then smiled.

"Will she be able to find the place?" Clay asked.

"This place? This place is glowing with power like the moon at midnight. She couldn't miss it."

"But then surely Ogya will know you're all here, too," Doto said. "Won't he suspect?"

"He will not notice our power," Mother Fam said. "Not when your temple is here. The heart of that power will blind him to all else."

Atekye said, "Excuse me, but speaking of power, aren't we missing our grand high Lord Kwaee? He's the reason for all of this in the first place."

Clay looked at Doto. There was a long pause.

Doto flicked his tail and grimaced. He took a deep breath. "Kwaee—"

He was interrupted by a sudden gust of wind and a golden blur. Kwaee stood before them in a vortex of leaves blown up by his arrival. "I am here," he said. He put his paw on Doto's shoulder and squeezed it once, then a second time, as if convincing himself.

The god of the forest straightened his shoulders and stood tall. His plumage rose, a red and blue crown. "Now. Let us stop the god of fire once and for all."

# 27 A Reign of Fear

Cloud huddled in her pit as the morning crept on. She tried not to think of what they might be doing to Basket. The young woman who had whispered to them in the middle of the night suggested he would be beaten, and there was no one else in her hole to distract her from her worries. Basket was no longer a young man. A beating could do more than injure him. It could stop his heart.

She felt too heavy and afraid to weep, so she sat against the inward-sloping wall of her prison and gave her mind other things to focus on throughout the night. She recited her lineage as far back as she could remember it. She listed the names of medicinal plants and their uses. She tried to recall the names of every living member of the People of the Savanna, but she faltered when she recalled Firefly and Bad Water and Buffalo Tail, who all had died because she had led them here.

The scuffling of feet around the opening of her cell woke her from an uneasy slumber. Her neck and back ached. The morning sun was still low in the sky. She creaked to her feet, squinting in the pale twilight to see if they were returning Basket to her, but instead, the figure of a woman was awkwardly lowered over the edge of the pit, rope looped under her arms. It was Dry Grass. She hung limply, arms swinging, and her waist was encircled by a tight loop of white cloth. It bore a dark brown stain against her lower back.

Cloud reached up to take her ankles and ease her to the floor as the rope lowered. With some difficulty, she managed to work Dry Grass's arms free so that the rope could be retracted by the guards above. A face appeared—not Petrel's, but some other Boganan who spoke words that sounded as though they had been rehearsed, not learned. "Yoo hee ler. Yoo tek carrof her."

"I need hot water and clean cloth!" she snapped at the head breaking the circle of sky above her. "And—" She had intended to demand medicines, but she realized it would be of no use. The man clearly did not understand her.

She leaned Dry Grass carefully against the wall. The woman's skin was cool. Good. Fever had not taken her, so perhaps the wound had been cleaned properly. "Dry Grass?"

"Mmm." Her eyelids fluttered. She was conscious, or close to.

"What happened?" Trying not to move her too much, Cloud inspected the bandaged part of her lower back. The cloth was white and clean, except for the dark brown stains that adhered the material to her lower back. Beneath the mineral sting of blood, it smelled of salt and herbs. A professional healer had attended it, then.

"Arrow," Dry Grass mumbled. "Is Mirage…?"

"Escaped," Cloud told her, firmly. Not strictly true, but true enough. *There were two healers.*

Dry Grass slumped backward, and Cloud held her in her lap and let her sleep. And soon Cloud slept as well.

~

The heat of the midday sun finally woke Cloud again. Her eyes blinked open to see Dry Grass standing, with evident discomfort, at the opposite side of the pit, staring up at the bright circle of sky. Basket was still not with them. All Cloud could do was pray to the gods that he was alive and well. She did not include Mpo in her prayers.

The pit stank of standing water and human waste. The guards lowered pottery twice a day so that their prisoners could relieve themselves, but the bottle shape of the pit kept the air's moisture and odors trapped. Even through the stink, Cloud's stomach was raw with hunger; she supposed she had dozed through the morning's ration of fish and salted greens.

Her bones ached, and her muscles were stiff. Imprisonment had not been kind to them. Dry Grass must have heard her moving, for she turned and shuffled over to help her up. "No, no," Cloud said, waving a skinny arm at her. "You're injured. You must be—" She grunted as she managed to push herself upright. "You must be careful not to open the wound again if you are to heal."

"Then you think we will get out of here?"

"One way or another," Cloud answered grimly. "When we do, it would be better to be whole than broken."

"What are they to do with us? Why have they captured us like animals?"

"It's the goddess." Cloud moved through stretches, trying to work the blood through her limbs again. She considered that had she not been strengthened and toughened by days of journey, she would surely be in far greater discomfort. "I saw her. Impossible. Terrifying. I think her voice has driven these people mad."

Astonishment shone in Dry Grass's eyes. "You saw a goddess? What do you mean? Which goddess?"

"It was—" Cloud hesitated with the name still on her lips. Surely a goddess would hear her name spoken. She was already angered enough without hearing blasphemy. "The sea goddess," she said. "Head of a demon, teeth of a monitor lizard. Taller than a hundred trees, her head in the clouds."

"I—I thought I saw her too. Wandering the sea beneath the storm, far away."

"She wasn't far off when I saw her. She came. They… the Boganans, they pushed three of our men off the cliffs. Not Knife Strap," she said hastily, noting a sudden spark in Dry Grass's eye. "Firefly. Buffalo Tail. And Bad Water. The sea took them."

Dry Grass nodded slowly.

"I should never have brought us here," Cloud said. "I'm so sorry. I thought we could find help, but I was wrong. I led our people astray. I don't know what they'll do to us. Kill us, perhaps. Sacrifice us to the goddess, like… like the other three. Or, if we're lucky, force us onto boats and send us to foreign shores to try to proselytize M—the sea goddess. I'm so sorry, Dry Grass. I'm sorry for what happened to you and to your son. And I'm sorry that we ended up here."

Annoyance flashed across Dry Grass's face. "Sorry, pah! It is not your place to be sorry." Cloud stared at her in surprise, but Dry Grass said nothing else for a time. A stony, confused silence hovered between them. Eventually, she added in a more solicitous tone, "Last night, I thought I heard you say Mirage escaped."

"Well, they were looking for a young man who ran." Cloud watched Dry Grass's expression carefully. "He ran from you, didn't he?"

Dry Grass set her jaw. "Yes. And I am glad he did."

"Because he escaped?"

"Because he will learn."

"Come here. Turn around." Cloud inspected Dry Grass's wound in daylight. The skin was neither puffy nor inflamed. "This is two days old?"

"I think so."

She prodded gently, and then more firmly at the flesh around the wound, eliciting a low grunt of pain from Dry Grass, but not more. "How deep does it feel? Is it stabbing? Or is there a deeper ache?"

"Not deeper, I think."

"Mmm. Good. This wound may not kill you. But you must be careful not to tear it. Bleeding outside is bad. Bleeding inside is worse. I wish I had herbs for you."

"The healer here used some."

"I see the stains in your cloth. I can smell some of what she used, and it's good, but it should be fresh. Your cloth should be fresh too. Try to keep it clean and dry. Do not get water on it. The water may not be clean."

Tending to the injured made her feel better, more like herself, like she was donning her old green robe which was now rags distributed among many. It was a comfort, when she'd failed so terribly at leading her people, when she was helpless.

She patted Dry Grass on the shoulder, turning her. "I never knew you well, back in the village, or before. I remember—" *Injuries. Beatings. An edict from the King that you were not to be touched again.* "—you came to see me several times. But you are different now. Not the woman I remember."

Dry Grass gave her a calm, measured look. "Yes. I had things to learn, too."

"And what were those?"

The woman sighed. "For one, what fear really is. Knife Strap always tried to make me afraid, but it was not the pain that frightened me. 'I will strike you'—that never frightened me. I could take his fists all right. Pain is but a moment and you deal with it in that moment. But 'No one will ever love you?' That kind of fear makes you hurt yourself. And he knew how to use it.

"I felt such shame, Cloud. Fear ruled me, and in the wrong moments, it rules me still. And it made me feel weak and ashamed, and that made me further afraid. But I know it was not my failure. The failure was in the one who made me fear. The one who took all the ways he was broken and made them my fault. I will not own that weakness anymore."

She glanced at Cloud. "And neither should you."

"You don't understand. It's different for a leader."

Dry Grass gave a bitter laugh. "Different than for a mother?"

Cloud could say nothing to that.

"I will not live among the ghosts of the choices I did not make. And I will not strengthen my fear with shame any longer."

Shame. Cloud knew it well, and she thought she had rid herself of it. It was shame over her husband's death that had sent her back to the healer's tent for decades when she could have been a leader. And when the abuses of Laughing Dog had finally grown too great, she had finally taken the staff of leadership and brought her people here, but had it been shame even then that motivated her? And now that they were imprisoned and imperiled, was not shame her closest cellmate? Shame that she'd made the wrong choice, that she'd trusted the Boganans, that she'd doomed them all.

She'd taken the wrongheadedness of Laughing Dog and the pious cruelty of the Matron and the mad abuse of the sea goddess and made them her own. *I let it come*, Cloud thought. *I welcomed the shame. I let it tell me I was a failure, that I did not have to act. And that was easier. It let me hide away in my tent while others made the mistakes. And I welcome it now, because at least if I lie back against the wall of this pit and blame myself, no one fights me. Because I am so tired, and it is easy.*

And then she laughed, because she felt shame over her own shame, like a lion devouring itself. Dry Grass gave a her a suspicious look. "You judge me for my attitude. You think I should feel regret."

"No." Cloud put her hand on the woman's arm. "No."

She tightened her other hand into a fist. She would not let shame stop her again. She would—

Footsteps came from above. A low, weak moan.

Basket was shoved over the side of the pit, swinging from the rope looped under his arms. He had been beaten. His face was a field of bruises and welts, both eyes swollen shut. Blood dripped from his broken lips. His forearms were thick, with dark marks around each, a sure sign of internal bleeding.

"By all the gods," Cloud murmured, and she rushed to help him as he was roughly lowered into the pit. He shook against her, his spittle thick and hot where it spattered across her shoulder. She took him in her arms, and he screamed, a raw, hoarse, yawp of pain.

She had felt the bones move in his arms, grinding beneath the swollen flesh. Both his arms were broken.

"Oh, Basket," she cried into his beaten ear as he stumbled against her, as Dry Grass pulled the looped rope free from his arms. "Oh, no. This is all my fault. All my fault." The lion took another bite.

"I'm sorry," he wept, his words so slurred she could barely understand them. He was missing teeth, and blood spattered the ground when he spoke. "I shouldn't have told them—I shouldn't—"

"Come on," said an accented voice from above. Petrel. "You next, Cloud. The Matron wants to see you."

The words barely penetrated. "You can't take me now," she cried upward. "He needs care. He needs healing, or he could—"

"Ah. I see. You are refusing to come. I should tell her that? Perhaps I should bring some of your people to explain to the Matron why their leader refuses to follow the commands of the true Goddess."

"What?" Cloud turned her head in dim confusion to peer at the blur of Petrel's face outlined in the circle of sky above.

"Come along now or more of your people will be beaten." There was grim distaste in his voice, she thought, and she wondered if he were hostage to the goddess, too. Perhaps the Matron was. Perhaps they all were. Frozen in fear and shame. So glad that it was someone else being beaten, someone else being sacrificed.

"I'll come."

She stepped into the loop of rope and hooked it under her arms.

As she was hoisted to the top of the pit, she looked past her swaying feet at the diminishing figure of Basket, lying curled and heaving in the small circle of daylight.

~

Shaking in terror, Cloud stumbled out onto the broad, flat roof of the Matron's home. The surface was not white, not scrubbed stone. Up here, where the people of the city could not see, the material was grey, and softer under her feet. Perhaps the secrets of stone buildings could not account for the regular fall of rain, or perhaps the goddess allowed special dispensation for uncleanliness where others could seldom see it.

The guards had ushered her up the ladder and left her there. The Matron sat in a small seat made of wood and straw, staring out over the great water. Cloud wondered if she had the strength to grab the woman and hurl her from the roof. She wondered what Mpo would do to them then. Surely the guards would kill all the People of the Savanna.

"The sea is large," the Matron said, without looking around. The breeze muted her words. "Much larger than you plainsfolk know. You think you can travel for moons, even rains, on land, and that means it is all there is. The sea is much, much greater. It has a hundred savannas drowned beneath it, encircles whole lands that are deserts as great as the Firelands. Beneath it are mountains, lost cities. Beasts that could swallow everyone in Bogana in one bite."

Cloud said nothing, her mind racing for words.

"There is only Mpo. She is the only goddess, because she is greater than the others. She is greater than Wem, because she fills the skies with her waters. I have seen them rising from the surface, clouds lifting from the sea to the sky. She births the rains that give life to all the lands you know. The rivers come from her. The forests spring from the earth due to her rains. All life sprouts from her water. We did not emerge from Fam's soil or stones. The whole world exists because of Mpo."

The Matron turned in her chair to look at Cloud. The streaks of tears shone on her cheeks. "Do you understand why I am telling you all this?"

"I think so." Cloud wondered if she was going to be beaten like Basket, but there were no guards here. "You need to convince me that Mpo is the only god, because you fear her."

"I need *you all* to fear her. It is not for my sake. It is for yours. I could commit you all to the sea today, and Mpo would not be angry." She reached out her hands to Cloud as though pleading. "But I am not a cruel woman. I care. I do not want your people to die. I simply need you all to understand."

"You say you are not a cruel woman," Cloud said through teeth clicking in fright, "but I saw what you did to Basket."

"It was for the benefit of your people," the Matron said severely. "They will listen to him. They *need* to listen to him, and he needs to tell them the truths that will save their lives. You saw her. You know what she can do. She could flood this whole city with a wave of her hand. She could dash us lifeless against the stones as quick as thinking."

Then why doesn't she? Cloud left the words unsaid. No point in further unseating someone as deranged as the Matron.

"Surely you, at least, fear her, having seen her," the Matron prompted when Cloud made no response.

"I do."

"Then you must persuade your people. Persuade your priest." The Matron settled back into her chair. "He is full of stories. I have broken his kind before. They are all full of stories. Mere words, words that dishonor the Goddess. That dishonor all of us. His stories are lies, you know. He admits it to me. Can you believe that?" Her knuckles clenched at the edge of her seat. "He confesses that he preaches lies to his people. That you repeat them, even! He willingly admits that he has led you astray."

"We don't see it that way," Cloud said, feeling she needed to defend him. "The Teller says that there is truth and lie in every story, and if you hear only one, you have stopped listening. Sometimes a lie is only another way to see a larger truth."

"Do you even hear your own words?" The Matron's voice could have etched stone. "Justifying heresy, blasphemy. Small wonder your people have been led so far astray. Your priest's mouth will no longer give voice to stories that are not approved. Stories must be lessons. They must contain only truth, the truth of the Goddess Mpo. He would not listen to me. He repeated his lies even when beaten."

She snarled the last words as if to the open sea, but when she turned back to Cloud, her face was calm, her eyes flinty and empty. "But he told us truths, all the same. Stories of his people. What you love. What you fear. He could not help himself, I think. We could not still his tongue. But you …" She smiled. "You like the taste of it, I understand."

Cloud blinked at her in confusion.

"So heartwarming to find love at such an age. I urge you to use it. Convince him to set aside his old tales and tell only those he is given. When your people see he is swayed, they too will follow. This is how these things go. When the priest is compliant, the people listen, and the people join the great civilization of Bogana. When the priest is not…" She shook her head, lowering her eyes. "There is much more death. So If you love your Teller, this Basket, you will convince him. His tongue will speak only the glories of Mpo."

She added, in the same tone of voice that she might dismiss a meal that had gone rotten, "Or it will be cut out. Do you understand?"

"I—I do, but please, Matron, if you would but hear me for one moment."

To her surprise, the Matron swiveled on her seat and turned fixed attention on Cloud. The stony certainty was gone from her eyes. "Of course. A wise ruler always listens. It is why I learn as many tongues as I can. Only a fool shuts her ears to truth. Please, speak openly. Only," she added, extending a slender finger, "no blasphemous talk of other gods. There is only the Goddess. Can we agree on that?"

"Y—yes," Cloud said, privately telling herself she had only agreed not to talk of them; not that they didn't exist. She took a breath. "Perhaps Lady Mpo is angry because—because of the rest of my people. They have been burning the forest because of… because of their beliefs. When we traveled away from them, we suffered from the smoke for many days. We fear they will burn more and more of the forest."

The Matron raised a hand. "But you have told me all of this before. And I assured you that what they attempt is impossible. These are concerns for your people, not for us, not for the Goddess."

Cloud took a deep breath and rallied. "But if all the world is the Goddess's as you said, doesn't it concern her? If the forests she grew of the rains in her body burn, might that not anger her? And if the ash poisons the rivers filled with her rains, and it washes back down to the great water, wouldn't she be angry still? Wouldn't she be angry about men worshiping fire instead of her greatness?"

As she spoke, uncertainty creased the Matron's face, and she frowned, her eyes darting back toward the sea several times. "It is true that the Goddess's ire has been… more roused, lately. Our boats come in with reports of men building huge fires in every city they visit. Chanting the name of… a false god. It must enrage her. Everywhere our scouts and traders visit, men are going mad. Burning each other on pyres. Torching their cities. Perhaps your own village is nothing special."

Cloud thought about the things she had seen in the past moons: the madness of Laughing Dog; the alteration of Clay; the great tree flung from the furious forest that destroyed their village. Could their little tribe be the center of something shaking the entire world? How far did Ogya's influence reach? Were others as affected as Laughing Dog? No, she did not believe it could be so. The coincidence would be too great. But Ogya had followers. He could speak from the flames. He could convince them. And if the words of a god sent people mad…

She sought for words that could reach the Matron, different approaches leaping to her tongue, but in each there was forbidden knowledge: a tale she must not tell; a god she must not confess to knowing.

Cloud looked out over the sea, where the Matron's gaze strayed constantly. On the horizon, the hint of dark clouds gathering once more. "Will

Lady Mpo come again?" she asked with as much respect as she could give the words.

"She always comes," the Matron answered. Her voice was calm, but now Cloud could hear the tension straining it.

"It must be difficult to wait. To know that she will come again."

"We wait in joyous expectation of the Goddess's return. It is our duty, as her subjects, who obey her. Who fear her and love her." Her lips were pressed together, and when she looked at Cloud again, fervent, deliberate piety shone in her eyes. But those eyes strayed back to the ocean. Back to that dark spot on the horizon. And her fingers clenched again.

Cloud said, "But we both know how difficult it is to lead, to have all that responsibility. I have only a few, as you've seen, and it wears on me. I couldn't imagine what it must be like to have all these people, this whole city, relying on you to—" *To keep them safe*, she tried to say, but that was stretching the truth too far. "To tell them how to worship. How to please her."

The Matron's forehead lined with suspicion. "The goddess tells us herself."

"Yes, but you are her instrument, aren't you? You're the one they look to. You choose the sacrifices. It can't be easy."

A long, slow sigh rose from the Matron. Her shoulders, always held rigid and straight, began to relax. "No, of course—"

And then she stopped. She tilted her head as though trying to hear a tiny voice carried on the wind. The lines smoothed from her face. Her back straightened. "Of course it is easy. The Goddess makes it easy for us, for all of us. You backwards plainsfolk with your primitive rituals—you fumble in ignorance for ways to honor your false gods. But Mpo is kind. She does not let us flounder in doubt and uncertainty. She tells us exactly what she wants and how to worship. All that she requires from us is obedience."

The Matron stood, crossing her arms behind her back and called for her guard.

"I don't understand," Cloud stammered. "Have I said something wrong? I'm trying to understand your worship, your love of the Goddess. How can I communicate to my people if I don't understand?"

"That's the trouble—you *don't* understand. We waste our time with words, because words are a barrier. They communicate, but it is not true understanding. You must know, as we do, what it is to fear the Goddess so completely that you obey without thinking. You think to lead your spirit with your head. When you truly worship the gods, your spirit leads, and your head follows. You obey deep down, instantly, as a babe cries for its mother or a bird follows its flock. You will learn this, and you will teach it to your people."

She nodded to the guard. "Take her back. Put her in the special place we have prepared." The Matron stepped forward and took Cloud's forearm in her hands. They were rough, chapped by salt and scrubbing stone. "You do not see how filthy you are. You don't understand it. But I swear it, before the Goddess returns, you will beg to be clean."

Cloud wrenched her arm away in a panic, but found her shoulders gripped forcefully by the heavy hands of the guard behind her. "What do you mean? What are you doing?"

"It is a lesson. All tales must have lessons. Yours comes now. And you will cry out for the Goddess. You will cry out to be purged of the filth of the foreigner. *Ahaba sa magae*. The wave is the way."

"*Ahaba sa magae*," the guard repeated, and he led Cloud down the steps of the house.

~

She feared she was to be sacrificed, but the guard led her back to the temple, back into the terrible stone field full of holes. She didn't know what they had planned for her, or what this "special place" was, but she looked forward to seeing Basket again, even if only for a little while. She could use his softness and Dry Grass's strength now.

But the guard led her past her pit, and past others, from which she heard low moans, whispered conversations, and sometimes quiet sobbing. She wished she had words to console them or give them hope, but she had none for herself.

There was no fighting this mad goddess or the people held in her thrall. There could be only escape. They needed to flee as far away from the great water as they could, farther than that terrible figure could ever reach even with her long arms. Cloud wondered if she could ever feel the rains again without seeing the sharp-toothed leer of Mpo in every droplet.

There was another pit, a greater distance from the others. So. That was where they were taking her. The hairs on her arms and legs rose. *What was in the pit?*

It stank. The closer they drew, the more the foulness in the air intensified. Cloud knew the smell from every gangrenous wound, from every corpse she rubbed with perfumed oils to prepare for cremation. It was the retching-sour stink of rotting flesh. And where there was old meat…

Cloud's vision had blurred with age, but she was certain something moved in the air over the pit. The lip of it was impossibly black as they drew close, as though no sunlight could penetrate it. It seemed to shimmer.

*Flies.*

Her stomach knotted in terror. "No!" Her cry rang hoarse in her ears. "No, you can't put me in there!"

She turned and beat at the guard's stomach with her skinny arms. "You can't put me in there! Please! Please don't put me in there!"

When he ignored her, she twisted to one side and tried to scurry out of his reach, but he put out one implacable hand and seized her arm. His fingers were as immoveable as stone.

*Don't scream, don't make a fuss. Your people will hear you and fear. They need you to be strong now.* The thought rattled around in her head, trying to find her will, trying to be obeyed, but she was already screaming. She dropped to the ground, but the guard dragged her as easily as if she were a child. She scrabbled at the stone with her free hand but could not find purchase on the smoothly-polished surface.

There was no rope nearby to lower her in.

The guard bent down and gripped her waist with both hands. The flies were already crawling on her arms and she beat at them. They crawled on him. Their shining, round, honeycomb eyes. The black tufts of hair poking out between. They rubbed their filthy legs together as though planning. They fanned their spitbubble wings.

The guard lifted her up above the pit. It wasn't dark inside at all—the daylight shone straight down where it could heat the rotting meat. Empty white eyes of beasts—goats and antelope—stared up at her. Fish carcasses lay in a putrefying mound. The whole heap wriggled with white worms. Maggots, born of rotting meat. Maggots, which split open to release the black flies, flies which would crawl over you, which would swarm, which would bite, and then you would slowly go mad and confused, like Aunt Reeno. And then you would die. Just from one bite, behind the ear, or on the eyelid, or the elbow. And no healer could save you.

She felt the tickle of flies on her arms, her legs. They were on her neck. They crawled into her hair. She couldn't breathe. Her lungs couldn't take the air in; as soon as she tried, it was all squeezed out of her again, like someone was sitting on her chest.

Then the guard dropped her.

The landing was like falling into thick mud, except where something—a bone, perhaps; a tooth—stuck into her arm, where it could let the rot in. And except for the way everything *moved* beneath her.

She floundered in the muck, the reek of it making her eyes stream. And then the swarm covered her.

She wanted to scream. But she couldn't scream. They would crawl into her mouth.

# 28 A Tomb of Tales

The paths into the caves below Bogana were dark and deep, winding and twisting in ways that would have confounded even the most reliable navigator. Mirage wondered how anyone had explored their depths. It must have taken unimaginable dedication and caution. Then again, they could have put the resources of the whole city behind it; they could have filled the rooms with light and used ropes for safety against whatever hazards lay down the wrong tunnels. And probably those who traveled them had not had to fear the treachery of the sea the way Boganans now feared it. Were there traps down the wrong tunnels? Slippery slopes? Or an angry Mpo who did not wish anyone to find the cave's secrets?

Still, the tunnels must have been well-traveled in their day. Here and there the flickering torchlight revealed signs of passage: an enigmatic picture carved on a wall, a step worn noticeably smooth, a discarded wooden sculpture or tool half-rotted into soil.

Behind him, the Breakwater men and women followed at an uneasy distance. Oru was among them but had not spoken to Mirage since their last conversation, and when he glanced in her direction, she looked away. He understood, but she had been a friend, had saved him, and he felt dearly, desperately grateful. Still, he didn't regret telling her what he'd done. It was better to be loathed for who you were than to be loved for who you were not. All he could do was carry on.

He followed the wet, uneven stone paths. Rarely now, the tunnel split, but when it did, Mirage knew which way to turn. "There won't be too many more splits in the path now," he said. "Either we are nearly there, or I have run out of information to choose the next pathways."

Elder Tobosu scuttled at his side, peering up at him. "And you say this knowledge comes from a toy? A game?"

"Priest's Procession," Mirage said. "My grandmother was from here, and she taught me. You weave grass together, or palm fibers. Stalks wind around each other. Some end or loop back, but one goes all the way through. And that's the path we're on. The one that goes all the way through."

"Fascinating. Ancient Boganans must have taught it to children to help them learn to find the temple."

"But you don't remember anything about it?"

"Perhaps they were already forgetting it when I was young. That you, a plainsman, could know it now, here, after living so far away? It must be providence. The" –he looked around uneasily before saying the word—"The gods must have sent you."

"Not any god I know of," muttered Mirage, and then he thought of a flash of a white tail and a small animal disappearing in the twilight.

Behind him, the Breakwaters followed, murmuring to each other in low voices. They sounded uneasy.

"These divine beasts," Mirage said to Tobosu. "How do you plan to speak to them?"

The old man shrugged bony shoulders. "I don't know. The secrets may be lost forever. But if they are, then why did the gods send us someone who knows how to find them?"

"If the gods wanted you to find the secrets, then why wait until now, when everyone is suffering and miserable and so many have died? Why not send someone long ago, when it could have mattered more?"

"Perhaps they did. And we weren't listening. Perhaps they're speaking to us all the time. I can think of no reason why of all the people in the world, it would be you, the one who knew the secret of the tunnels, who would find himself among the Breakwaters."

"Maybe it was Mpo who sent me," Mirage suggested nastily, "to find all the rebels and destroy them at once."

Tobosu gave Mirage a narrow squint. "Your mouth gets you in a lot of trouble, doesn't it?"

"Well, this is it," Mirage said, glad to change the subject. "The last choice."

They had strolled out into a large, flat area that was half-submerged. The cavern was wide enough that the torches couldn't light the other side. Nearly dividing the room was a large pool, churning with seawater, the current frothing spume against the rocks. The sound of the sea had crescendoed as they descended, and here it surrounded them, echoing off the cavern walls and ceiling, as if the ocean itself was above them, thundering on the roof of the cavern, pounding its way in.

Mirage sidled up to the edge of the water, trying to avoid getting his feet wet as the Boganans behind him made their way down the narrow ramp to the floor of the cave. They spread out, torches raised, lighting as much of the room as they could.

"*Holfa!*" one man shouted in alarm. *"Holfa!"* He waved his torch low to the ground. Grey-black bones littered the rocks, almost unidentifiable if not for the distinct shape of ribs, of skulls. Tatters of brownish clothing lay strung among them like cobwebs. Many people had died here. Mirage felt a prickle up his thighs and back. Those who were not sent to Wem in the smoke might not be able to join their ancestors. Their spirits might remain here. He fought a rising panic.

Oru was shouting something excitedly; she came stumbling across the rocks, sloshing through the shallow end of the pool.

"She's found something," Tobosu told Mirage. "A boat? But no, that cannot be, not in here."

But it was. They followed Oru to the other side of the pool, where torchlight revealed the remains of not one, but three large boats. They lay on their sides, two of them bent and broken as though struck by a mighty fist. The little shelled creatures Mirage had seen on the beach crawled over them, and over the scattered bones that littered the wooden husks.

"Could these be the divine beasts you were thinking of?" Mirage asked.

Elder Tobosu frowned. "What do you mean? The skeletons? The *okoto*? Or the boats? No, no, what I cannot understand is how the boats got in here. It's impossible that they might have been carried down through the tunnels. Look at the timber, the huge pieces of wood. They're too long and straight for those winding paths."

"Maybe one of the other paths leads out?"

"Perhaps," Tobosu said. He held his torch high and carried it to the far side of the cave. "Ah. As I thought. Look here: this cavern was once open to the sea, you see?"

Mirage peered through the gloom. Most of the cave walls were smooth, but the deepest part of the pool was bounded not by a worn cave wall, but by heaps of enormous boulders.

Tobosu nodded in satisfaction. "The tunnels were the back way. Boganans took boats from the sea into this cavern. They would have moored them here at *dopo*—the time when the waters are deeper—to reach the temples. Until… until they could not."

"Someone must have collapsed the side of cavern," Mirage said. "Or… or the cliff face."

"Not someone," Tobosu said darkly. "Mpo. She didn't want us finding what was here. We are in the right place, my boy."

Mirage peered around the dark cavern. Its roof was engulfed in night, torches making flickering halos around their bearers who explored the walls. He shivered. "It doesn't feel right." Forbidden by gods. Full of dead ancestors—perhaps even *his* ancestors. One of the old boats creaked as it leaned, and the sound echoed around the cave, the groan of a giant skeleton.

"Well, it isn't quite. The beasts aren't here, that I can see. You said there is one more path to take."

"Yes." Mirage stumbled on the uneven rocks, tracing a path back along the cavern walls. There was only one obvious tunnel leading from the room, which made sense. At the last stage of Priest's Procession, only one thread could make it to the end. The other passageways were clear dead-ends, and he supposed the exit to the sea might once have counted.

The final passageway, though, was partially submerged in seawater. Mirage stared at it distrustfully. "I don't think we can go this way."

Elder Tobosu only chuckled and called the other Breakwaters over. One tall woman, carrying a torch, sloshed her way through the water to the far side. The water only reached her waist at the deepest part, and she was soon motioning for the others to cross.

Perhaps sensing his unease, Tobosu took Mirage by the elbow and gently guided him into the water. It was dark and sucked the warmth from his feet and legs, and the rock surface below was irregular and slimy. He walked close to Tobosu and tried not to think about things beneath the water: horrible sea things with grasping claws, or the clutching arm of a great-great-great-uncle. He squeezed back at Tobosu's skinny shoulder. The man didn't laugh or shake his head, but only gripped Mirage more firmly, his bony fingers surprisingly strong.

Sudden gratitude flowed through Mirage: that he didn't have to lead for once; that he could rely on someone else, someone who knew what he had done but didn't hate him, who hadn't let him down, who didn't expect him to be a monster. Someone who could find the way for *him* for once. In the middle of the passage, he nearly wept, and, mistaking his half-sob for fear, Elder Tobosu squeezed with his fingers and told him, "We're nearly there," and that was almost too much for him. Down here in the dark, in deep water under a mountain, far from his people and even farther from his land, something heavy inside him lifted. He leaned gratefully on the old man's shoulder until the water was ankle deep again.

The passage opened into another large cavern, dark and yawning, its ceiling so high that they could not see it even when raising the torches. There was a stale, sooty smell to the air, mingled with the odors of old wood and buried stone. A continual tick-ticking sound echoed throughout the room. Mirage wondered at its source, like a light rain hitting palm fronds, but all around them, far from rain. Drops of water?

Then his foot came down on something hard and smooth, something that was not stone, something that *wriggled.* He would have yelped in terror had fear not stuck his breath in his lungs. The best he managed was a panicked "Uhhh—hhhh!"

One of the Breakwater men grinned at him through his beard and swung his torch low. Dozens of small shapes scuttled away from the light, waving tiny claws upright. The tick-ticking sound was thousands of tiny, hard feet moving over the rock. It was more of the shelled creatures that had crawled along the beach and below the buildings of Bogana. They were everywhere. Mirage decided he hated them.

"This is the place," Tobosu declared. He spoke to the others in the group and then translated for Mirage: "I can feel it. Almost remember it. Perhaps I came here once before, as a boy. We should move together, as a group."

"Do you think it's dangerous?" Mirage asked.

"I couldn't say. Perhaps. But I'm more worried about one of our group stumbling over and perhaps destroying whatever we were meant to find."

"The divine beasts?" Mirage thought of long-dead things waiting for them in the darkness. Things with hollow eyes and gaping mouths and forbidden secrets.

"It might be. I suppose we will know what we are looking for when we see it. Come. We will follow the right wall and that way we will not get lost in the darkness."

He called over one of the taller Breakwater men, who held his torch high, illuminating a larger circle around the group as they moved forward. Though everyone had been ready to explore in the large cavern with the boat, here no one was eager to stray too far from the circle of light. Mirage ended up getting shuffled toward the back, which was fine with him until he thought of *things* following behind them in the dark, and somewhat urgently wriggled his way back into the middle of the group.

The sour stink of rot wafted through the air as they followed along the cave wall, and soon after noticing it, several of the group cried out in dismay.

"What is it?" Mirage asked, but his query was lost in sudden chatter as the people hurried forward, crowding around something on the ground.

A young woman circled around the group to meet him. It was Oru. "A body. It is one of our own. Lanathu, who went searching the tunnels a few months ago. It seems he found this place after all. He is not pretty to look at now."

"Did something kill him?"

The woman shrugged. "He had no torch. He was probably lost down here in the dark until he died of thirst or fear."

Mirage shuddered. There were worse places to die than sprawled on the rocks beneath the houses of Bogana. Yes. Getting lost down here where there was no sun and no sky was worse.

The group moved on, making a detour away from the wall to avoid the body lying there. Mirage caught a glimpse of it: a grey bundle lying against the wall, its head still thick with hair, its arms and legs picked clean of flesh. The shelled creatures clambered awkwardly over the body, still looking, he supposed, for morsels of meat.

Oru kept her face turned from the sight. "Elder Tobosu says we will come back with cloth and carry him out so he may be buried. But perhaps his spirit will show us the way."

"If he couldn't find his way when he was alive, I wouldn't bet on him doing it now," Mirage muttered under his breath.

"What was that?"

"Nothing. But I'm… glad you decided to talk to me again."

Oru tilted back her head, giving her braids a disdainful toss. "You are still a killer," she said stiffly. "But you did find this place. Perhaps the gods did send you to us." The sound of waves crashing against stone seemed to grow louder and fill the cavern. "Though not all of them."

"No, not all of them," Mirage agreed, eyeing the flare and flicker of the torches all round. Could Ogya hear them now? Was he listening through the flames?

"I do not think Mpo can hear us here, though," Oru added soothingly, mistaking the source of his unease. "She is goddess of open sea. She needs broad skies and big waves. Not salt water lost in caves."

Not long after moving past the corpse, shapes loomed in the darkness—high, regular, *crafted* shapes, like the worked stone of the statues and buildings of Bogana. The shapes loomed beyond the reach of the torchlight, fire glimmering against curves and high walls. It was some kind of building, erected deep in the heart of the cavern.

The Breakwaters chattered excitedly and moved around the small building, and then there was the sound of fire catching once, and then again, and then a brighter glow filled that small area of the cavern. Mirage pushed his way through the group, eager to see.

Low fires burned in two basins set at chest height—a black rock or charred wood had been lit and now burned with a hot, yellow flame. Mirage was astonished that anything down here could still burn, especially after all this time. The fire illuminated circular walls that were built low in the front but rose twice the height of a man in the back, surrounding what proved to be a small shrine. At its far wall loomed a statue, its features contorted by shadows. Mirage did not like the look of whatever the statue depicted—it had many arms and insectoid features locked in an endless grimace.

The men and women spoke in fearful tones seeing that, and Mirage caught the name "Ogya" more than a few times. Several, shaking, dropped to their knees and bowed before the statue. Was this meant to be the fire god? Mirage had always imagined a man wreathed in flame, his head a tall point, with blazing white eyes and teeth of embers. He preferred his version to whatever this thing was.

The floor of the temple was strange, a smooth surface, black and so glossy it looked wet. The fires blazed in dark reflection beneath its surface. Mirage reached down and rubbed the black stone, finding it slippery and unyielding, polished to a shine. He asked Oru and Elder Tobosu if they knew what it was, but they had never seen anything like it. Nor did the material seem to exist anywhere outside the surface of the temple.

From here, the firelight revealed the outline of another shape squatting in the cavern, some small distance away and, gathering up those who still prostrated themselves before the figure of Ogya, they moved toward it.

This proved to be another shrine with another pair of braziers in front of it, but this had none of the black rocks to burn, so a couple of men ran to retrieve some from the temple to Ogya. When ignited, the flames lit up a figure of Mpo, like those placed throughout the city, but this one had no upraised arm clutching a mass of flies. She stood with her head lowered, her crown of water plumes pointing upward, her mouth of daggers barely open.

Murmurs moved throughout the group at the sight of her. "What are they saying?" Mirage asked Oru in a hush. He didn't know why he was whispering; the place commanded silence, somehow.

"The image of Mpo—it is sacrilege. She has ordered how she should be shaped from stone. We must see her defiance, her fury, and how she has saved us. Whoever made this statue… they did not know the Mpo we do."

"Or they did, and didn't care. She can't see down here, can she?"

Oru furrowed her brow. "I don't know. Look at the floor."

Unlike the floor of Ogya's temple, this was a circle of water. It teemed with the scuttlers, but these had pure white shells and no eyestalks at all. There were odd shapes in the water that reminded Mirage of his exploration of the rocky beaches with his mother—strange, long-limbed stars, and stony circles with double rims. "I thought you said Mpo needed open air and a wide horizon to hear us," he said.

"I did. But I think this is her space. Don't you?"

They moved on to the next shrine, this one with a leopard god standing tall, a crown of feathers carved onto his stony head, and in the midst of his circle, the rotten remains of what had once been trees and leaves.

Another shrine had a circle of murky, stinking water with a statue of Atekye, the hippo goddess. Another was hollowed deep into the cavern floor, its statue an image of a creature half man, half rhinoceros, leering and holding his gut with both thick-fingered hands. In a fifth shrine, they could barely make out the statue of a curly-horned aoudad behind the cone of stone that jutted up from the center.

These last two gods, if they were gods indeed, Mirage had no name for. Perhaps they had been forgotten in the tales and songs of the people. He wondered if they were angry, if those who ascended to Wem would be punished for letting them slip from memory.

They passed other temples, lighting their braziers as they went, and soon the whole cavern was flickering with ancient fire from wall to wall. Now that there was light, the Breakwaters milled around, moving among the various temples and bowing or chanting at each of them. And yet they had not found what they were looking for—the place was deserted, with no beasts living or dead, which filled Mirage with both disappointment and mild relief.

He searched through the people until he finally found Elder Tobosu staring up at the statue of Mpo with a puzzled expression. "How could she have done this to us?" he said in Mirage's language. "And why? How could we have forgotten something so important to our people?"

Mirage thought of his own people, laboring under the direction of Laughing Dog and Ogya to stop attacks out of the forest. Here in Bogana, it had been disease. What would his people owe to Ogya when everything was over? He had a sudden image of the fire hunters marching through the village, enforcing worship of Ogya and erecting great wooden carvings of the snarling, multi-armed scorpion beast everywhere.

He thought of his grandmother, Two Broken Hands, muttering with grim nostalgia, "In the old days in Bogana, we understood how to serve the gods. We knew the meaning of sacrifice."

And he thought of Left Rabbit, poor, innocent, honest Left Rabbit, speaking up in a crowd of people to challenge orthodoxy, to decry the Official Story. And he knew what had happened. "They sacrificed them. All the people who knew and wouldn't keep quiet about it."

Recognition broke across the old man's face, the lines of age deepening with sadness. "I fear you are right. Many have been sent to the stones over my lifetime, by this Matron and those who preceded her. Any who knew of it and remain may have considered it wisest to forget." He looked around, forehead still etched with dismay. "And yet, wondrous as this place is, I still see no sign of what we came to discover."

"What did you expect to find? Bones? Spirits that would speak to you?"

Elder Tobosu shook his head. "I am not sure. I know only that they told me when I was young that the elders sang their songs to divine beasts that lived in the tunnels beneath the city, and that the beasts would sing them back upon command, even after death."

"But how can the dead speak? They are gone. Is it some sort of magic?"

"I think, yes, magic, of a kind. But how to summon it I do not know."

"Are you certain the stories are true?"

The old man set his jaw. "Yes. The priests who told me would not have lied about this. Not in their last hours. Not before being sent to the stones. There must be some answer in these temples or statues. How strange they are! How did our ancestors craft them? The pool for Mpo might be natural, but the rock in Ogya's temple is joined to the cave floor as if it had always been there. And there is no sign of how to call the beasts."

Mirage didn't know how to help. They moved from shrine to shrine, studying each. Tobosu named the rhinoceros god Obonka, god of canyons, but didn't recognize the aoudad. Studying each they found signs of people who had come before, perhaps in worship: fruit pips, scraps of cloth or leather, carved bits of stone toys or fetishes. But whatever ceremonies or rituals had been performed here must have been lost to the ages.

Tobosu spoke aloud to the statues in Boganan, calling to them for aid or wisdom. He cried to the empty air for the spirits of the ancestors to guide him, his voice thrown back to him by the far cavern walls. There was no other answer. He prostrated himself before an open temple, this one with no statue or unusual floor, but above it the cavern roof glinted and glimmered as though embedded with flecks of stars. A temple to Wem, he suggested to Mirage, and offered up prayers for guidance.

He was interrupted by a woman who hurried up to him, calling his name. She chattered something to him in excited tones, and his face brightened.

"What is it?" Mirage asked.

"They've found something. Come!"

They were led beyond the cluster of little shrines to a far wall of the cavern, barely visible beyond the firelight of the temple braziers. Here a small structure had been erected, made of thick, rotting beams of wood that had probably come from the boat in the other room. The hut was covered with some kind of pitch-sealed cloth, not much taller than a person and about the size of three village tents, a single door leading into its shadowed depths.

Keeping torches held low to avoid igniting the musty roof of the building, Breakwaters crept in. The small room was filled with large, round bundles, each about the size of a person curled up, bound up in dried reeds. Elder Tobosu shouted something, and a couple of men edged out with one of the bundles and with slow care set it on the ground. Everyone clustered around, torches held high.

The reeds encasing the bundle had been sealed in a brownish, tarry pitch or sap, and prying them apart proved impossible—one man jumped back, sucking at fingers sliced open by sharp edges. Eventually several people produced knives and, with Tobosu snapping at them the whole time, sawed through the reeds and pulled them apart.

They all stared at what was inside, exclaiming to each other in astonished tones. It was a hollow dome, comprised of fist-sized segments joined together, with a flat bottom and two large openings at each end.

"It's a tortoise shell!" Mirage breathed in surprise, but he had never seen a tortoise even half the size of this one. "Those are the divine beasts?"

"A water tortoise, I think," Elder Tobosu said. "Surely this is what we are looking for."

"But how can they speak to us? All that remains is the shell."

"Look closer, boy." The elder beckoned him, lowering his torch to the huge, hollowed dome. "See?"

Mirage peered. Someone had decorated the shell with uncountable tiny, odd carvings, but whoever had done it hadn't been very good at it. There were no intricate designs, no working with the structure of the shell, no sense of aesthetics. Just long, neat rows of crude little etchings, many of them repeated over and over, as though someone had been practicing designs. He frowned, almost ready to dismiss it, but then he remembered the symbols over each of the passages on the way down, the ones that had been representations of each of the steps of Priest's Procession. "Do they mean something?"

Elder Tobosu was shaking with excitement. "Mean something? Do you have any idea what this is, what we've found?"

"What is it? Sacred art?"

"More than that, boy. More than that. These are the secrets of Bogana. I thought all of it had been lost or destroyed. The Matrons called it sacrilege and ordered it so. *This* is the wisdom of our ancestors!"

Mirage tilted his head, trying to see it. "Are they… are they pictures?"

"Of a sort. Our ancestors had a way of sealing speech in stone." The old man's hands trembled as he traced the carvings with his fingers. "These are *words*. Left for us by our ancestors." He looked back toward the building. "And there are so many more of them. So many more. Mirage, we've found it. Every story and song of our ancestors. They're here." He grinned wildly. "And I can listen to them."

~

Elder Tobosu's interpretation of the shells seemed to go on for days. Down in the darkness of the cavern, there was no way to mark the passage of time, which made Mirage increasingly uneasy. The elder paused to sleep at least once, and Mirage himself nodded off—he didn't know for how long. They were brought food twice—more leaf-wrapped packets of fish and baked fruit eaten in flickering firelight, and not much of that. Most of the people with torches had left, and the braziers around the other shrines were extinguished to preserve fuel.

Initially, they carried the shells to the floor of Ogya's shrine, where the light burned the brightest and the floor was smoothest and allowed Elder Tobosu to crouch and spread out, but Mirage panicked, thinking of Ogya staring out at them through those flames, and so, after some insistent urging, the Breakwaters agreed to move the shells to the sandy expanse of Esayra So, who Tobosu named as a minor desert god.

As he translated the symbols on the shells, he grew increasingly excited, exclaiming to himself in Boganan and multiple times sending the Breakwaters back to the little hut to retrieve more of the shells, which were apparently stored in some sort of ordered system that Mirage could not discern. The old sage dragged them around, arranging them in lines, some of them branching off in different directions. Some of the shells had fewer symbols on them, the series of carvings etched in patterns like spirals or circles, and these Elder Tobosu had ordered moved near specific shrines—perhaps they were words pertaining to those specific gods.

Mirage passed the time by taking a torch and exploring the dark cavern, investigating the remnants of worship and honor to an ancient pantheon. Eventually, bored and driven to distraction, he sought out the sage and found him slumped against one of the old shells, fast asleep, the braziers on either side guttering as they spent their fuel.

"Ah! Mirage!" the old man murmured as he rose through the fog of sleep. "I… rested my eyes for a moment. But—but what we've found here, it changes everything. No wonder the gods wanted it forgotten."

"What do you mean?" Mirage asked, sitting down beside him. "You think all the gods wanted this place lost? Not just Mpo?"

"I would not be surprised. The secrets we have found here, if they are true… it could be seen as the deepest blasphemy. Everything we have been told about our relationship with the gods is wrong."

"How do you mean?"

"I mean that we have always been taught that the gods had absolute power over us. That they commanded, and we obeyed. That we prayed to them but were at their mercy. But if this is right" –he spread his arms wide, gesturing toward the shells around him— "if the words here are true, then we were not so helpless after all. We were not simply mortals who had to obey and follow and yield when gods commanded. Our relationship was more…" he struggled for a word in Mirage's language and finally gave up. "More two-way."

"I don't understand. You're saying that we—" Mirage glanced at the firelight and lowered his voice to an uneasy whisper. "You're saying that we had some kind of power over the gods? Or some way to resist them?"

Elder Tobosu gripped his shoulder with strong, skinny fingers. "More than that. If these words are right, then we *are* gods, Mirage. All of us, a little bit."

Mirage pulled away from him uncomfortably. "I don't understand. What do you mean, we are gods. You mean Boganans?"

"All people, not only Boganans. The tales stored here tell of an agreement with the gods—one in which they gave all humans a little of their divinity. So you, Mirage, have a tiny speck of Mpo's power in you. And some of Sarmu's, and Kwaee's, and even Esayra So's and Obonka's."

Sleep had left the old man now; his eyes were wild with excitement. "And it gave us power. When we pray, we pray with the will of the gods. They answer us because it is *their own will* calling out to them. And there were songs. Songs and dances, all of them written and described on the shells, one for each of the gods. But they're not only songs. They are spells, each one an act of surrender of… I'm not sure. Space, or… homes, or territory… something. The shells speak of great magic when they are sung. Of a change."

"What kind of a change?"

"I cannot be sure until we try it, but if I understand these words, the spells call on the divine will of each of the gods inside us and urge them to surrender their claim on a space. And one god gets it all. So if we gathered the people together and had them sing and dance a spell to Atekye, then the land itself would change in some way. It would belong to her."

"Wait." Mirage frowned, his mind racing with possibility. "You're telling me that people can *work magic against the gods?*"

"No, no, not against them. With their own cooperation. We urge all other gods to give away their territory to Atekye, and they cannot *resist* cooperating—it is their own nature willing the change!"

"But—but that means that we could go down to the sea and use one of these spells, and—"

"And take the sea away from Mpo. Yes. But I am only guessing now. We must try it. We have to know if it will work. If it does… if it does, we can fight the Matron. We can show Mpo we will not be ruled by tyranny, and we can do it using her own power."

Mirage stared around the darkened cavern, the shapes of the closest shrines barely visible, each of them with strange circular floors of rock, sand, water. Could people have really wielded this kind of power? All his life he had been taught that they must bow before the gods, subject themselves, obey them. And the gods had been cruel or careless and had let the people suffer. And then Laughing Dog had found a new way—he had fought back, had encouraged others to fight. And that had been terrible in a new way. Lie down or fight. Those had been their only choices. Take the beating or become the fist. Each path led to suffering, each was laced with cruelty.

But the Boganans of old had found a third way, neither subjugating themselves nor defying the gods. They had redirected the gods' power, used worship as wile. What if he brought these spells back to the People of the Savanna? What if instead of burning the forest and giving themselves over to Ogya, they could take it via spells? What if they could decide for themselves which gods were worthy of praise?

"You're right," he said. "We have to know that this will work. How can we test it? Can we do it now?"

The old man grinned at him. "I think we must! But it will take time to prepare, and we will need the others. Go, boy! Run back up the paths and find the others in the upper chambers. Bring them back as quickly as you can. I must try to learn the spell so that I can teach them!"

Mirage nodded and grabbed a torch, so excited now that he did not even fear wading back through the dark water at the cavern entrance. He ran as quickly as he dared in the darkness toward the tunnel.

"Wait, boy!" The old man's cry echoed through the cavern.

Reluctantly, Mirage returned. "What is it?"

"Without you we might never have found these secrets. So I leave it up to you. Which of the gods should we sing to? Atekye, perhaps? Sarmu, for the land of your people?"

Ogya. That was what he should have said. That was his mission. If he called the power of Ogya now, he would fulfill his charge from Laughing Dog. It was the order from his King. He could ask for aid. He could speak through the flame, beg the fire god's assistance in freeing their people. Surely Ogya and Laughing Dog would hear him through a summoning of fire that powerful, that called out to him through the will of the divine itself.

He opened his mouth to say it. He tried to say it. But he choked on the name. Was not Ogya as great a terror as Mpo? Fire and water, inferno and flood. Those were the old way.

And he thought of the miracle of a forest growing far underground, of returning to his people with a new path, neither subservience nor defiance. Of growing life out of dead and barren stone. And of showing a forest god who had been their enemy who he was dealing with now.

"Kwaee," he said, clenching his hands into fists. "I want to sing to Kwaee."

# 29 A People of Many

Little pinches here and there. The flies were biting Cloud. They were infecting her with their pestilence. Her brain would rot like Aunt Reeno's. She would turn dull and stupid. She would become sluggish and then go to sleep and die here in this pit full of decay.

Tiny, tickling feet crept over the flesh of her arms, her legs, her hands, her neck, her cheeks, her eyelids, her lips. They wriggled under her clothes. Their wings buzzed in her hair.

The carcasses beneath her were hot and slippery. Tiny things squirmed there, too. The little bodies of flies she had crushed beneath her. Maggots crawling through the foul meat. Unclean. Diseased.

Cloud's heart hammered, but she couldn't hear it over the interminable buzzing. Her chest felt as though an elephant had sat on her. She hissed desperate, spittle-flecked breaths through her teeth, not daring to open her mouth, not daring to draw in breath through her nostrils. The foul, tickling touch of the flies was there already, investigating the heat of her. A tickle in one nostril as one wriggled its way in. Another crawled into her ear.

She wanted to slap at them, she wanted to scream, but an elephant sat on her, and she could not move, could not get breath. All she could do was shake and suck air between her teeth and spit at the hard, bristly bodies that wormed their ways between her lips to taste of her.

The pit reeled in the hot sun, swaying side to side and even looping upside down. Cloud's stomach knotted and pitched, and her gorge rose, but she feared opening her mouth even to vomit. The flies would get in. They would pour down her throat. They would fill her and crawl around her brain, behind her eyes, under her fingernails.

So instead, she dropped away, going down, down inside herself, to a place where there was no light and very little air, and now the tickling was far away, so far that she could scarcely feel it. It might be a mere tingling on her flesh, in her fingers and toes. A numbness.

She knew this place. It was fear, a fear so deep and paralyzing that it was almost death. It was the fear of an animal caught between the teeth of a predator. It was a mercy from the gods, a terror that wrapped itself around your brain and your arms and legs and held you still and quiet so that when you died it almost looked like peace.

She'd not felt it in a long time, not since she was a child cowering the dark, listening to large creatures moving in the brush at night. When you grew older, it was replaced with other fears, slower fears. You feared losing those you loved. You feared letting people down. You feared failing when it was important. You feared the recurrence of old pains. The slow fears kept you a prisoner for a long time. They made you bite your tongue instead of speaking. They made you hold yourself apart and alone rather than risk love. They trapped you in lives you didn't want but that were still better than the lives you feared. The slow fears were long fears. They lived with you. They shaped you. They warped your bones.

The childhood fears, the ones that usually faded with adulthood—those were quick fears, a flash of panic and lightning in your blood. A little quick fear here and there would make you run, make you fight, or make you hide, trembling. And a lot of quick fear would stake you to the ground. But the hot, electric world of a quick fear could not last for long. Quick fears faded.

And so, too, Cloud's terror dwindled. The flies crawled over her, pinched and tickled and probed at every opening into her body. And she still floated in some deep darkness lit only by a distant red glow that was the sunlight blooming through her eyelids, even though she was squeezing them shut so tightly that pale green spots drifted in twitchy circles across her vision.

The flies had done their work. If they were infected with the plague that took Bogana before, then she was already diseased. One bite was all it took, and that? That would be a long fear, she knew—a constant reassessing of her thoughts to see if they were still as quick and steady, or if she was slowing and dulling like her aunt. What, then, was left for the quick fears once the terror faded? Only the crawling of flies. Insects easily crushed.

And as the quick fear ebbed, Cloud's rational mind floated up from the darkness to take control again. *The Boganans are obsessed with cleanliness.*

*It is the heart of their faith. They would never allow disease back into their city. This is simply a cruel torment.*

Her heart was slower now. The elephant had gone. She let her mouth relax, let her breaths come more steadily and easily through her faraway lips. Just flies. Little insects, the kind you saw every day. Not disease. Not death. Just flies.

And then she knew that the Matron had made a mistake. Because the quick fears were only good for a little while. A moment of terror to make someone obey. To rule someone, you needed the slow fears, the long fears, the fears that would trick someone into putting themselves into a prison of their own making for moons, rains, for their whole lives. It was the slow fears that controlled you. That was what Dry Grass had been trying to say.

Cloud had many slow fears, all tangled up with shame. That her negligence had led to her husband's death. That she had led her people astray, and they would all die because of her. And before that, before any of it, that none of them would ever love her, that she would never be part of them, never be connected to any of them, because she was strange, uncomfortable, different. And that fear was buried deep, deep within her, from childhood, from the days when she'd arrived a stranger from Bogana, when she hadn't known the songs and stories everyone else did, when she hadn't even known the language. When the other children made fun of the way she spoke, the way she played. It was as deep as the death of her Aunt Reeno, as deep as her terror of the flies. And yet no more real.

That was the mistake that the Matron had made. A quick fear was easily broken. And once you learned how to break one fear, you learned how to break them all. The flies were only flies. Her fear was only fear. She could see through it now, see how she had kept herself apart. How she had been afraid to speak to others because she didn't know the right words. Because she was afraid they wouldn't welcome her, wouldn't love her. She had hidden in her healer's tent, away from her shame, away from her guilt, away from Basket and the council and the life she might have had.

The long fears made you imprison yourself. And Cloud was done with prison.

She came back to herself. The slimy heat of the carcasses was slick against her back. The flies swarmed over her, crawled on her, tasting, biting, tickling.

She closed the fingers of her right hand around a mass of flies, crushing them to lifelessness. She raised her fist toward the sky.

~

The brush of coarse rope nudged against Cloud's face, sending flies into angry buzzing. Two men shouted incoherently. Cloud waved the flies away from her face and opened her eyes to see that the orange cool of evening had settled across the pit yard. Two men had come to let her out.

She pushed herself wearily to her feet and hooked the rope under her arms, allowing the men to hoist her out of the pit. Neither of them would approach her, but they led her to a small room adjacent to the courtyard where they allowed her to dispose of her clothes and wash herself. She thought she saw discomfort in their eyes—even pity. The rope they used to hoist her out of the pit was tossed into a fire. She was allowed a small portion of steamed vegetables and meat and then led back to the pit yard, where they lowered her into the hole with Basket and Dry Grass.

Relief shone on their faces when they saw her, and both stood to help her down, though each moved slowly due to their own wounds. They held her close, and she assured them that she was all right; that they had not hurt her. She didn't tell them what had been done to her, only that she had been kept apart to frighten her. She did tell them about her meeting with the Matron.

And then she checked and tended their wounds. Dry Grass needed a fresh bandage, and Basket had cuts and bruises that needed cleaning, to say nothing of bones that had yet to be splinted so they would not set wrong. He moved, for the first time since she'd known him, like an old man. His smile was broken.

A voice rang across the pit yard. "Is that Cloud?"

"Yes," she called back, and then several voices cried out to her, asking if she was all right.

*They care*, she thought, and then she chided herself. *Of course they care. They sided with you against their King. They followed you across the savanna to this terrible place, all because they trust you. Because they believe in you. You are not apart from them. You are part of them.*

"I'm all right," she called back to them.

There was a murmur. "We thought they might have hurt you."

"They couldn't even frighten me!" she called back, and then the guards came around, shouting at them in Boganan and jabbing their spears toward them in a vaguely threatening manner.

Cloud met their eyes steadily, unblinking, until they looked away. Caution might be necessary, but she was not afraid of them anymore. Not them. Not the flies. Not the Matron. Not the towering figure of Mpo. She thought she might not be afraid of anything.

~

The night came soon. As the light faded, she found Basket and rested in his arms, though it was hard to find a place to lie against him that hadn't been bruised or injured.

Sometime in the night, she awoke to the sound of his snoring. A shaft of moonlight lit their pit. Dry Grass sat opposite her, watching, and so Cloud slowly extricated herself from beneath his soft, heavy arm and crept over to the woman's side.

"You should sleep," she said, pressing her back against the stone wall to pop out the kinks in it.

"Why is that?"

"Because sooner or later, there will be the chance for us to escape, and I will need you strong and rested. You must be prepared to help others."

Dry Grass gave her a sidelong, appraising look. "Something happened to you while you were gone. What has changed?"

There was no way to explain, to put into words how her most terrible fear had surrounded her, and she'd survived it. She could give the details, but her experiences were her own. No one else would understand how that fear had gripped her, nor why it had weakened and lost its hold. Her palm tickled with the memory of crushed flies, and she absently wiped it on her robe.

"I listened to your advice," she said. "It helped. Thank you."

"Do you know if they have found my son?"

Cloud considered what she knew of the Matron. "I think if they had, they would have boasted about it. To dishearten us."

"The Boganans don't intend to release us, do they?"

"Not until they're sure they've broken us, I reckon."

"*Will* they break us?"

Cloud set her jaw. "They haven't yet, and they've already had to resort to murder. They've shown us who they are. What they believe in. How they live. Anyone swayed by that world would have stayed behind with Laughing Dog."

"They might kill us all, then."

"If they have to, that wouldn't make their goddess look very impressive, would it?"

"More impressive than a pile of dead people," Dry Grass said, but she was smiling. She put her arm around Cloud's shoulders and together they spoke fondly of home while they watched the edge of moonlight creep up the wall of the pit.

~

A noise came from the pit yard, the sound of something hard striking something soft. Something fell to the ground, and the light of a distant torch flickered. Cloud had half-nodded off, but Dry Grass rolled immediately into a crouch, watching the sky.

"What is it?" Cloud murmured blearily. A man's cry cut her off, wordless but still somehow accented Boganan. There was another loud thump and the sound of someone falling to the ground.

"Someone is coming," Dry Grass said. "And I don't think they get along with our captors. Wake the Teller. Quietly."

Footsteps shuffled across the stones above. Could this be rescue? Cloud shook the cobwebs from her mind, pushed herself to her feet, and crept over to pat Basket awake. She held a hand over his mouth to stifle his befuddled grunts.

There were more than one set of footsteps; in fact, it sounded like dozens of them. Whoever was up there, there were a lot of them. Torchlight tinted the edges of the pit orange as people approached. The echoes of many hushed whispers filled the air.

A face appeared over the edge of the pit, and Dry Grass's hand flew to her mouth as though to catch the faint cry escaping. Cloud peered upward, trying to make out features against the too-bright blaze of the torch. Impossible. It was Mirage.

He waved the torch down into the pit, nearly setting his hair on fire in the process. "There you are!" he whispered. "Mother, I've come back. And I've brought friends. We're getting everyone out tonight. Can you walk? I heard the arrow hit you and I thought…"

"I am all right," Dry Grass said. "Cloud tended me."

The figure shifted its torch, peering into the pit. "Cloud! So you're here, too. Thank you! Thank you for… for doing what I couldn't."

"We'll talk later," Cloud promised him. "You're going to free us?"

"Yes, we're leaving Bogana now. I have brought friends."

His face disappeared, and then a man and woman shifted into view, holding a wooden ladder which they maneuvered into the pit, struggling with its weight as they tried to avoid any scraping sounds.

Cloud stared at it, almost unable to believe it was real after days of fear and despair. She stepped aside, motioning for Dry Grass and Basket to climb, but Dry Grass shook her head.

"You are our leader," Basket whispered to her. "The people will need your guidance as they're freed. They need to see you."

*Freed.* She closed her fingers around the knobby rungs of the ladder and ascended from the pit. At the top, two strangers took her arms and helped her find her footing. She thanked them in a whisper, but they gave blank nods and beckoned the others to climb.

Their saviors numbered between ten and twenty; it was difficult to make out in the dim light. They had only two torches between them, probably to be less noticeable, and those moved through the pit yard casting light for the other rescuers lowering ropes and ladders into the holes. Across the yard, near the main entrance, the bodies of two men lay against the wall. Cloud didn't know if they were unconscious or dead. They looked dead.

Their rescuers continued to work, pulling more people out of the pit, and she worried that someone would talk or cry out in surprise or confusion, giving them away, but even without that, the hiss of whispers echoed through the yard like rain in high grass. People climbed or were hoisted by rope out of their prisons. They rubbed sore limbs and joints, stretched out their backs, and then quickly moved through the pit yard, aiding their rescuers and seeking their friends and family.

"Mirage," Cloud began, meaning to ask him how he had managed all this, who these people were, and what was their plan for escaping the city. She found him locked in embrace with his mother, weeping silently. "I'm… sorry," she muttered, turning away to let him have his moment, but his words came to her ears all the same.

"I ran," he said through shaking sobs. "I left you. I'm so sorry."

"You did the smart thing," Dry Grass answered him. "You had to. You see? You brought people here to rescue us all. If you had not run, we would all still be in those holes."

"But I—the arrow. You were shot. I left you and you could have died."

"I had Cloud to care for me. Sometimes running is the only thing you can do."

The crowd of those rescued was milling in their general direction, and the hiss of their whispers was rising into a low hum.

Cloud hated to ruin their reunion, but they were in enemy territory. She stepped toward them. "Voices down. Dry Grass, can you help the others and get them ready to go?"

The woman nodded once.

"Good. Mirage, we will have to have a long talk about how you managed this, but now, we need to get everyone out of the city and as far away as possible. I do not think the Matron will let us go willingly. Do you have a plan to get us out of the city?"

"These people do. They're a resistance, fighting back against the Matron and the laws of Mpo. They have… they found…" Even in the darkness his eyes shone with wonder. "There's no way to explain right now. The main gate will be guarded, but there's another path, through the city and down the cliffs. My mother and I came in that way. There will be patrols. It will be risky, but—"

"But it's the only way."

He nodded.

"Then we try." She glanced up at the eastern sky. Back that way lay their village. The forest. The savanna. The rest of their people. Back that way lay home and all the troubles they had still failed to solve. They would be slinking home with nothing—with less than nothing, for they had lost Firefly, Bad Water, and Buffalo Tail. But now, at least, the problems of home seemed approachable. Laughing Dog might be deranged, and the gods might meddle with their lives, but at least they didn't openly attack. At least they didn't demand sacrifice. At least you could speak to your opponents and they would understand you.

Back that way was home, but that way also was the impending sunrise, pale dawn already limning the temple walls. They would have to hurry.

The crowd was quieting now that the separated had found each other and as they urged others not to speak. Frightened energy crackled among them like sparks—they were ready to run. They were ready to fight if they had to.

A tall, broad-shouldered man demonstrated hand gestures he would use to motion people through the city. Hand up, stop. Both hands palm down, quiet, be still. Palms pushing toward them, go back. He led them toward a corridor that presumably led out of the pit yard, away from the guards.

Cloud moved up to the front of the group, ready to be seen, to follow their rescuers and guide her people to freedom, but she was interrupted by someone's hand on her shoulder. "There is a problem."

She couldn't make out the speaker in the dark. "What is it?"

"This way." He led her back across the pit yard. Most people were out of the holes now, with only the farthest cells still being emptied, the remaining few people untying the ropes from around their chests or clambering.

Dry Grass stood near a hole against the far wall. Her arms were folded. "No," she said, in a voice loud enough to risk discovery. She pushed away one of their rescuers who motioned again with the rope. "No."

"She won't let us rescue him," the man who had brought Cloud complained. "She refuses."

*Ah*. Cloud walked up to Dry Grass's side. "Knife Strap?"

"We will not take him with us," Dry Grass muttered through her teeth. "We will not. He should have been exiled for what he did. He will never leave us alone."

"You can't leave me here." Knife Strap's voice floated up out of the pit, taut with fear.

Cloud searched Dry Grass's face, but her eyes were too dim, and the morning was still too dark. "These people will surely kill him if we leave him here."

"They may not. He has always been… adaptable. Perhaps he will fit in here."

"If they do, his death will be on your conscience."

Dry Grass set her jaw. "No. It will be on the consciences of those who kill him. I have accepted the burdens of other people's wickedness for long enough."

"You could live with abandoning him here?"

Dry Grass looked away and did not answer.

A hoarse voice came from the bottom of the pit. "You—you can't leave me to die with these heathens. Dry Grass… wife… let me out. You have to let me out." The sound of weeping floated upward again. "I can't bear not seeing you again. Not seeing my son again. Please… please, have mercy."

"Be quiet! Do you want to have the guards down on us?" Cloud hissed into the pit.

"Please!" the conspicuously loud voice sobbed. "Please don't leave me here!"

Dry Grass turned back to Cloud, her eyes flinty. "I don't know if I can live with leaving him here. But I know I cannot live with him following. He stays."

Cloud cracked her knuckles, thinking. The people were already filing out of the pit yard. She needed to be with them. "These are my people. They chose me to lead. I cannot leave one of them behind."

"He is not yours to lead. He stayed behind with Laughing Dog."

"So did you." Cloud knew it was a cheap answer. Dry Grass had stayed behind because Mirage had stayed. Because Mirage had become a murderer and there would be no succor for him from the People of the Savanna. But she could not reconcile leaving a single person behind in the clutches of this merciless city.

"Yes. So did I." Dry Grass's voice was calm. "So you have no claim on the obedience of either of us. This man will not be set free."

A low moan of misery rose from the pit. Cloud didn't know that she had many other options. She wasn't strong enough on her own to free the man, and she wasn't even sure she wanted to. If he kept making noise like that, he'd risk them all. She looked across the crowd of people quietly milling toward the exit. None of them were paying her much mind except Mirage, who stood against a nearby wall, watching intently. This was a family matter, and she was trapped in the middle of it. "Let's discuss it over there in the light," she said. "You down there, stay quiet until we get back." She took Dry Grass's elbow and led her across the pit yard toward the group shuffling into the corridor. And didn't stop when she reached them.

"What did you want to say?" Dry Grass asked.

"Nothing. Let's go."

And then, employing a few jabs of elbows and mutters of "excuse me," she pushed her way to the front of the group again. Mirage and Dry Grass followed without another word.

The passageway was all darkness and shuffling. There was no way to know who was there and who was not. The people stank from days in the pits, and they limped from stiff joints, weakness, and weariness. They were also shaking in fear. Not a one of them spoke or gasped or grunted, but the sound of that many feet moving on the ground was noticeable. Their guides had discarded the torches so they wouldn't be seen on their trek through the city, and only moonlight and the dim yellow of distant firelight illuminated the tall man making hand signals.

They moved out of the narrow corridor and into a somewhat wider alley that traveled between the steep slope of the temple walls and the buildings on the opposite side. The guide raised his hand in the signal for stop, and the people up front obeyed, and everyone behind clumsily stumbled into each other. Cloud clenched her teeth; it was impossible that they wouldn't be heard. Wriggling her way up to the very front, she spotted the reason for their pause: the wide-open courtyard and temple steps lay to their left. Torches burned brightly, lighting up the whole courtyard and the surrounding walls, and two guards walked in their direction.

They paused at the edge of the temple terrace, staring out into the city, directly over the people. There was enough moonlight here to make out the crowd. Surely they would be seen. The moment hung like stars in the sky. And the two guards turned and walked back toward the temple and the bright firelight there. That was why the group hadn't been seen, Cloud reasoned. The men's vision hadn't adjusted to the darkness; the brightness of the flames had blinded them.

The group continued, spreading out into the wider street. There, it was easier for everyone to move quietly since they weren't jostling and bumping into each other and skidding feet. Their guide took them on a circuitous path, moving out of the wider roads whenever possible, taking them behind buildings and through a section of the city that looked abandoned, the structures in disrepair, sagging or flaking, doors hanging open.

Several times they had to wait in an alley, bunched up and trembling, while someone wandered their way through the dark streets on some early morning errand. The trip was taking too long. The labyrinth of the city was unending, and the eastern sky was growing paler. By Cloud's estimation, their guides were leading them roughly north and west, and if her sense of direction was reliable, that took them closer to the Matron's home than she would have liked. They were certainly entering a more active part of the city—lights flickered in a few windows, and the sounds of sleepy conversation and the smells of cooking breakfasts floated down into the alleys. She bit at her thumb anxiously. Even if they made it out of the city, how could they get away if the guards came to round them up?

Well. Surely some of them could, if not all. They could fan out. Those who *could* run could scatter, making pursual more difficult. If even a few could escape, they all stood a better chance of surviving.

This section of the city sloped downward to the north, and the group followed the descent. Someone put a hand on her shoulder, and she looked up to see Mirage walking at her side. It was strange to feel grateful at seeing a fire hunter, one of Laughing Dog's loyal, and a murderer on top of everything else, but these were strange times.

They traveled behind another cluster of homes to the end of an alley and paused again, waiting for their guide, who stood pressed against the building with his hand up. Opposite the alley sat enormous stone boulders, a path leading down between them. They waited there for a very long time, enough that that the group turned restless and uncomfortable, shuffling about. And then, finally, two guards sauntered casually up the slope between the stones and headed past them into the city. The guide waited until he deemed them out of earshot and then motioned everyone forward again.

Mirage cheered up as the group made its way down the slope. The path narrowed and grew much steeper, with ruts worn into the stone, and then they left the buildings behind. Now, in the pale pre-dawn light, Cloud could make out the blue of the great water below.

Even their guide's shoulders relaxed, and he no longer moved with the precise stealth that had ushered them through the silent city. They were almost out. Down the hill to the sea, and then back up along the coast into the grasslands beyond, and from there… well, they could decide that later on. She cast one last look over her shoulder at the massive, shadowy city of Bogana, and shuddered, glad to be free of it, but uncomfortable having it behind her, like a predator up on a rock.

And then, in front of them, two guards stepped out from behind the slopes flanking the path. Cloud nearly fell in surprise, fear knotting in her stomach. Behind her, the People of the Savanna gasped and stumbled to a stop, those far behind bumping into the others in confusion.

They had been caught.

The guards lowered their spears. A plump man in bright orange and green robes stepped out and stood between them. Petra. The smirk on his face was triumphant: a cat who had caught a bird. "Sneaking out in the middle of the night? How terribly rude."

Cloud thought, *If we rush them now, most of us might escape. They can't spear all of us.* But then from further down the slope came the sound of footsteps, and more guards trooped up behind, spanning the narrow road. The only way around them would be to tumble down the cliffs.

Cries of dismay rose from the crowd behind her; she turned to see the people shuffling aside at spearpoint as another contingent of guards marched through their midst. In the middle, her face calm and unreadable, strode the Matron, dressed all in white. And at her heels slunk Knife Strap, his wrists bound, a guard's spear tip pressed into his back. Cloud cursed under her breath. She knew it had been a mistake to leave him behind.

"You forgot someone," the Matron said in light, airy tones. "He was so dismayed at being abandoned that he couldn't stop calling for help." With disbelieving cries, the people nearest shrunk back from Knife Strap as though he was diseased. He kept his head lowered and would not look at any of their faces. Ignoring all this, the Matron stopped in front of Cloud and Mirage. "So this is the unity and loyalty of the People of the Savanna. I am unimpressed."

"It looks like your own city has a little disloyalty too," Cloud said. She started toward the Matron, but the firm grip of the guards clamped onto her shoulders and held her back, pushing down so heavily that her knees buckled.

"Yes." The Matron gave a sidelong look at the crowd over her shoulder, picking out the faces of the men and women who had helped them escape. "They will be dealt with. This city will be purged of iniquity."

She raised her voice. "Do not misunderstand me. Those who aided our guests in escape will share their fate. The rot in this city must be dug out and cleansed."

Cloud's heart sank. The thought of these brave souls being put to death for trying to help them was almost too much to bear.

The Matron turned back to her. "Come. This place is not suitable for talking." She strode past Cloud, her bony hands clasped behind her back. "It seems you all wished to go down to the—what was the quaint term you had for it? The great water. Well. Let us all go down and remind ourselves how great it is. We will call on Mpo."

Numbly, Cloud stumbled down the steep path, following the Matron, her people close behind. Her thoughts twisted toward despair, but she wrested them away again. She would not be afraid any longer, not even now. She would accept responsibility, but not guilt. She would not burden herself with lamenting past choices and what she might have done differently. What mattered was now. And now her people needed a strong leader. Even if they were about to die. Especially if they were about to die.

But on her lips, silent but spoken, were prayers—to Wem, to Fam, to Sarmu: do not let us die this day. We have endeavored in everything to be faithful. Kwaee, for whatever crimes you hate us, we repent. Ogya, if we have dishonored you, we are sorry. Mpo, for every way we have failed to show you reverence, forgive us. We are mortal. We are weak. And the words of the gods twist us and confuse us. We cannot see how to behave in the world you occupy. But we are honest, and we are true. We have sought to honor you all in the best way we can. All gods we know, please hear us and do not let us die this day. All gods we have forgotten, lend us your strength now so that we might once again learn your names. Do not let us die. Save us. Save us from this madness. Let us return home and learn anew to be a part of your world.

She let the shape of her words hang in the morning air as she went. White birds with yellow beaks perched atop rocks and pilings along the path, watching them with intent yellow eyes. The road downward was steep and winding, pitted with ruts and holes, and not as clean as the city above, littered with sand, the old bones of tiny creatures, and scraps of weed. Though it was uneven the Matron glided down it as though her feet barely touched the ground. On either side, the guards marched, their jaws set, their eyes grim, spears at the ready.

The People of the Savanna followed behind, whispering, weeping, stumbling after their imprisonment. Intermingled with them were those Boganans who had risked helping them, now caught by their own, guided down to whatever fate the Matron had in store. Amidst and behind them came the guards, some of them making comments in their own language, their voices haughty, their words peppered with smug laughter. And behind all of them, the people of the city filled the narrow pathway, following in huge numbers, a massive crowd shoving and pushing its way down the slope, perhaps propelled by curiosity as to the fate of the foreign visitors, or perhaps eager for the spectacle they already expected.

The Matron led them down beyond the end of the path, past the husks of boats hunched on the shore like cicadas, past the piles of wooden boxes and reed baskets and odd cages. She took them north, out of the shadow of the city, and along the shore. To the People of the Savanna, the sea still looked unnatural, disorienting, and now they knew that it contained terrible and malevolent things. They sheltered their eyes with their hands.

Cloud did not hide her own eyes. There were dark clouds over the sea, as though it was waiting for the Matron to call it. As though it *knew*. The sky glowered with the burning red of the sunrise, and the dark waters below the clouds were tinged with the hues of blood. Wind rustled and whispered in Cloud's ears.

The Matron stopped a little further up the beach. The wind tugged at her white robes. Cloud stopped in front of her, and behind, the People of the Savanna gathered in an anxious circle, holding each other. A ring of guards surrounded them, spears canted inward, others with bows ready to nock should someone take a chance and try to flee across the sand. And beyond them, the people of Bogana gathered around, thronging four or five deep, clustering behind the guards and watching the prisoners like jackals circling their prey.

The Matron spoke so calmly that the wind stole her words. Cloud gave her a puzzled look, and she said, louder, "We are not an unjust people in Bogana. Our Lady Mpo desires worshipers more than sacrifices. Save yourself and your people, Cloud. Tell them now the truth. Tell them that there is but one goddess, Lady Mpo. Tell them to forget their old stories now. Let us teach you how to praise and adore her. Tell them now. For once, lead them down the right path. Save them, Cloud."

Cloud stared for a moment at the woman standing in front of her. She was old, like Cloud, but she had not had a life like Cloud's. Cloud's life had been full of mistakes and missteps. Cloud had doubts and uncertainties. Cloud had fled her home very young and had followed the People of the Savanna on a trek across the world, sometimes never staying to see the rains twice in one spot. The Matron had lived her entire life in one place. She had never had to take everything she could carry and flee a fire. She had never had to find a new home. She worshiped the goddess of the great water, but her home was stone, immoveable, solid. Unchanging. Satisfaction gleamed in her eyes now, because to the Matron, there was one way this was supposed to go.

One way. One city. One leader. One goddess, one way to worship, one goal for the people. Only one outcome if they did not obey. One story.

Cloud turned toward her people, who clutched at each other in the wind. There, at the front of the crowd, was Basket, his body bruised, one eye swollen, but he smiled at her. His eyes were fixed on hers, unwavering even though the wind whipped tears from them. And there was Ant With a Leaf, standing tall, defiant, her hands clenched into fists. Dry Grass was there too, looking calm and unafraid.

The whole crowd watched her, waiting to see what she would tell them—whether she would urge them into a life of subservience to Bogana or commit them to whatever terrible fate the Matron had in store for them. It shouldn't be her choice, not for all of them. She should not have to choose.

So once again, she sought for words. What could she tell them, when they had followed her here? When her choices had led them to imprisonment and sacrifice, and now, no matter what happened, they would lose themselves? They were afraid and despairing, and she could not help them because she was the same. *She was the same.*

And there, she found her words.

"I'm glad that you're all with me right now," she said, raising her voice to pitch it above the wind. "Not glad that we might not live to see another day, not glad about this terrible fate that has befallen us. But glad not to face it alone. You're with me. You give me strength and hope. You remind me who we are.

"The Matron of this city wants me to tell you to forget the stories you grew up with, the stories of Fam and Wem, of Kwaee and Sarmu, of Atetea and Adanko and Makobe. She wants me to tell you that we must all worship Mpo, and only Mpo. And if you do this, that there will be a chance you all will live. And perhaps you will be allowed to live here in Bogana, or perhaps you will be sent out on boats to tell other people in faraway lands about Mpo and how to worship her. The Matron wants me to tell you to forget every story, every song, every dance but for those for Mpo."

She cast a glance over her shoulder at the Matron, whose eyes had narrowed in suspicious expectation. She wondered how many times this ritual had been carried out, how many groups of people had stood shuddering on this grey coast under a blood-red sky. How many had surrendered? How many had been sacrificed?

"The Matron asks me to do this because I am your leader, and because in Bogana, the leader decides everything. The leader decides who people will worship and how. The leader chooses who will live and who must die." She took a deep breath, trying to phrase her words so that she would be allowed to keep speaking as long as possible. "The People of the Savanna have not done things this way. We have never had one god. We have had many gods, and we worship them each according to our place in the world. We do not have a single story; we have many, and they contradict and disagree and make for good arguments, yes?

"And we may have one King, but our King never gave us orders like this, and never alone. He had a council who gave him advice, a group that he listened to. We have never been a people of one. One god, one story, one way to live. We have always been a people of many."

She could hear the Matron growing restless behind her; in her peripheral vision, the guards came toward her. She spoke faster, calling out, "So if you wish to follow the Matron's advice and join the Boganans, then do so. You broke away from King Laughing Dog of your own choice. You followed me here of your own choice. And this choice? I cannot make it for you. I cannot tell you to do what the Matron says, because we are all the same. We all choose. We are not a people following one leader or one god! We are a people of m—"

Her teeth clattered together, and her chin hit her chest. She was on the ground, sand digging into her knees, her arm, her cheek. A balloon of hot pain grew bigger and bigger in the back of her head. She twisted where she lay to look upward, and in her floating, blurred vision, a guard hefted his spear. Something dark dripped from the haft.

The Matron strode into view. Cloud grunted as something bony dug into her side. It was the Matron's foot. There was a crazed, furious edge to her voice as she shouted to the crowd. "Your leader has failed you!" she crowed. "She has led you only to blasphemy and ruin! See now the terrible power of Mpo! *Ahaba sa magae!* The wave is the way!"

*Ahaba sa magae,* the crowd of Boganans repeated in the circle. *Ahaba sa magae. Ahaba sa magae.*

The wind rose, blowing so fiercely that Cloud could not hear the words the Matron shouted, but she suspected she had heard them before, down on the cliffs, below the temple, where Firefly, Bad Water, and Buffalo Tail had been sacrificed. And though it was dawn, the sky was darkening.

Her head aching, a throbbing behind her eyes, Cloud tried to crawl out from under the foot of the Matron, but her fingers dug uselessly into the sand. The Matron leaned down toward her, thin lips pulled back from her teeth. Her eyes were wild, manic. "Watch!" she shouted at Cloud. "Watch as the doom of your people approaches."

And she shoved Cloud firmly with her foot. When Cloud didn't move, she kicked her once, again, a third time, until Cloud, groaning, rolled onto her side. All around her now the Boganans chanted "Mpo. Mpo. Mpo."

And from the water, taller than the entire city of Bogana and the cliffs that supported it, water streaming from her head and shoulders in misty cataracts, her fanged, curved mouth gaped in an inhuman grimace, rose the great grey form of Mpo.

# 30 Firetrap

Clay seldom felt true discomfort in the forest, but the wooden grip around his wrists, ankles, neck, and tail came close. Kwaee had sprouted the tree around him, the wood surging up out of the earth, flowing like water into the shape of a thick, dark brown trunk that grew around him, spreading his arms and legs wide, bait for something terrible. The narrow branches of his arboreal prison waved in his vision. Their leaves were small and half-formed, the trunk beneath him swollen, gnarled. It was an aberration, a twisted thing made by Kwaee only to ensnare him, not to live and grow as part of the forest.

He pulled at his arms and legs, testing his strength against it. He had some idea that his feline body was physically powerful, though he had never sought its limits, but even straining with all his might, he could barely budge the wooden grip holding him. Curiously, he sent his mind out into the forest to see if he could urge the tree to release him and set him free, but in some way Kwaee had rendered the forest impervious to his power. He could feel the outlines of the wood around him, could feel the forest floor and the wind moving through it, but he could not send his mind into it any more than he could push his hand into solid stone. After existing so long as part of the forest, inside it in every way, it felt strange to be bound by it, as though he had fallen asleep in the wrong position and woke to a stranger's numb arm beneath him.

He sent his thoughts to Doto, who lay across from him, his arms and legs stretched wide, pinned to another squat and solid tree trunk. *You realize Kwaee could give us up now, if he wanted to. He could let Ogya eat us. We couldn't get away.*

Doto's gaze was steady and untroubled. *If Kwaee truly wanted to serve us up he would have done it moons ago. Anyway, you know he hates giving up anything that is his.*

*Are we his?*

*He did call you Doté. And he stopped throwing you. That's as cuddly as Kwaee gets.*

"Stop it, the both of you." Kwaee stalked into view, his crest of red, blue, and gold raised so high it looked like it wanted to rise off his head.

"You can hear us?" Clay asked in surprise.

The forest lord bared his fangs. "No, but even a mortal would sense the power moving between you two. Ogya must not suspect that anything is out of the ordinary. You are food to be served to him, nothing more. No magic, no sending yourselves out. If he sniffs out our plan, it will be ruined forever. He will not trust a second offer.

"Asubonten is waiting up the mountain, Atekye and Fam stand nearby, ready. The trap is set and baited. Nearly." Kwaee took a deep breath and held it for a moment, his ears folding back. "Very well. Doto, Doté, I…" He spoke the next words from between clenched teeth. "I surrender this circle of forest to you. I give it up. It is your territory now. Rule it through your own power."

A strange rush of energy surged through Clay. It flowed through his chest, through his arms and legs, filling him with exuberance, with strength. He felt as though he'd had a meal after days of starving, that weakness he hadn't even been aware of was fleeing his body. His senses attuned anew to the forest around him. He felt larger, somehow; a greater part of the world. Was this what Ogya felt when he ate? And Clay had only gained a small amount of power just now. What must it be like to consume an entire forest and add it to yourself? What must it be like to take more and more?

He caught Doto's expression and saw that he, too, was amazed and enthralled by the sensation. It was new to him as well. His whole life here in this forest, and Kwaee had never given him anything, not one piece of territory beyond the copse that formed his temple. And then he saw Kwaee slump, shoulders sagging. What must it be like in reverse, then? To give it up, as Kwaee had done, to suddenly feel weaker, smaller, diminished. Hungrier.

And Kwaee had surrendered a fifth of his forest to stop Ogya. Clay could not imagine doing such a thing. He could not imagine carving out a fifth of himself to fend off an attacker. He felt so much more real now, so much more solid. What must Kwaee have felt after his surrender? Like a weary shadow, perhaps. A ghost. A mist. And it had all been for nothing, because Ogya had come back.

"It is time," Kwaee said. "I've given you the land. Now call your temple here."

Clay blinked at him, puzzled. He looked over at Doto, who lay with his eyes closed, his breathing slow.

"Well?" Kwaee demanded. "What is stopping you?"

"I—I don't know how," Clay admitted. His ears folded back, burning. "How do you make it move?"

Kwaee snorted. "You are a miserable excuse for a god. Doto?"

Doto opened one gold-green eye. "I do not know how to do it either."

"By all the—"

"Well, when would I have ever done it?"

The forest lord pinched at the bridge of his muzzle. "Very well. All this time, when you have moved about the world, it has been only your avatars that travel. Your true selves are the temple, and while you travel, that remains."

"Like when you sleep, but dream of traveling," Clay suggested.

Kwaee gave him an irritated stare. "I do not sleep."

"Sorry."

"My son has demonstrated how to move your power out into the world around you to change and affect it. You focus on sending it out and into branch and root, into soil and stone, yes? But you are only using the power contained within your avatar, drawn from the forest around you. To move your temple, you must send the power that is your true self out of the land that holds it. Go within. Feel your true self. Do you feel it?"

Clay had no difficulty returning his concentration to his temple. After days of travel both in human and feline form, in both the shelter of the temple and across the harsh terrain of the world outside, he yearned for its embrace again, to lie with Doto in the soft and secret place of their shared soul. And he was there again. He had never truly left. He enjoyed the gentle movement of his branches in the wind, the splash of the fish in his stream, the reassurance that Doto was there, with him and part of him, and always would be.

Kwaee's voice came from a long distance away, heard by a pair of ears Clay had sent out into the world, on a distant, little leopard body. "Now send that self out, out of the soil and stone that holds it, out of the land and into another place. There is only one place it can go."

He didn't want to leave. This place was sacred. It was special. It was home. Safety. But part of him, the part that was Doto, was already moving, and they could not leave each other behind. Their sanctuary was a place of light, and beyond was a darkness they would surge into. Doto's eagerness mingled with Clay's reluctance and pulled him forward, made him feel as though it was his own urgency, and they flowed out of their place of safety and into the darkness. They could not hover; they could not exist without land. Their power would wink out like a candle flame being extinguished.

Here and there in the darkness were spots of solidity, little circles spread across the world. They were places where Clay and Doto had danced for each other, where they had gifted themselves tiny pieces of forest, but each were too small to contain them. There was only one space large enough, and in an instant they streamed toward it, the only place they could go.

An infant god took its first step.

The forest shuddered. Clay opened his eyes. Before him, beyond the trees that bound both himself and Doto, their temple nestled into the forest circle, illuminated in golden sunlight. It had transformed the forest, the squat, gnarled trees that had filled the circle now graceful, arching, with long, gentle leaves. Flowers nodded in the breeze. There was their mossy meadow, and there their treetop perches. They had no cliffside to provide a waterfall and stream, but a series of clear pools shimmered in the afternoon light, fish drifting through them. Bees hummed lazily among the flowers. Where it all had come from, and what had happened to the forest that had been there before, Clay had no idea. Nor what remained where their old temple had once stood. Barren rock and soil? Perhaps the two circles of forest had simply switched places.

Clay longed to pull himself free and slink back into his temple; it was so close. He tugged urgently at the tree that bound him and noticed Doto doing the same, the leopard's thick muscles bulging as he strained against his bonds.

"I could not allow the circle to enclose you," Kwaee said calmly. "In your temple, the trees that hold you would have vanished. You would free yourselves without even thinking, and Ogya would not be fooled. Well. I have done my part. It is time to summon the fire god." He strode past Clay and Doto into a small clearing in the forest. His crown of feathers lifted higher. He closed his eyes.

"Wait!" Clay shouted. Panic had risen in him. He felt terribly vulnerable here, pinned spread-eagle next to Doto, to a tree from which he could not escape, the delicate jewel of their temple just behind them.

Kwaee opened one eye.

"Will we be safe?"

Scorn curled Kwaee's lips. "No. If you were safe this would not work." He lifted one paw and material drifted down from the trees: leaves suddenly dead and dry; thin twigs, raw bark with thin, fuzzy backing; bits of flower fluff and dead petals. They floated down in circles and accumulated in a soft heap at the forest god's toes. "That should be enough to sustain a little fire," he said, his voice heavy with distaste.

Then, from the ground around the heap of kindling, four serpentine roots thrust upward like long, pointed fingers. They bent and curled around each other in a braid. "And now, heat."

He clenched his fingers into a fist, and the interwoven roots began to seethe and writhe, knotting around each other, twisting, sliding in and out of the mass obscenely, with a sound of scraping, rasping, splintering. In only a few moments, thin grey wisps rose from them, and Clay's sensitive nose instantly caught the scent of wood smoke. Then the flare of light, and then the kindling was burning with a rapidly rising flame.

Clay was impressed; building a fire among the people was a project that could take a long time, especially at their village's current site, where the rains fell every day. But Kwaee had done it in mere moments. Clay had expected to have more time to prepare. He held his breath.

Kwaee stepped back as the flames burned higher. "Ogya!" he roared. "You win! I agree to your proposal. Come into my forest and take your damned prize. Come and… and devour my son." His voice broke in that final sentence, the words dripping with regret.

Clay caught Doto's gaze—he didn't dare send his thoughts to him now, but Doto's eyes were wide. Could this sacrifice be real? Instinctively, he searched out into the darkness of the world for that circle of solidity. It was still there. They could send their temple away. They were not trapped, he told himself.

The fire popped and crackled, and then it rose higher and higher, burning brighter, swelling outward, long tendrils of flame curling and hissing in the forest air. The thin ropes of fire whirred and twisted, thickening into columns and then developing into limbs of living flame. Blazing scorpion claws spread wide and then slammed into the ground, charring the soil and sending smoke rising; Kwaee flinched as his forest floor was seared so close to him. Then, with the roar of an inferno, the air warping with the fury of the heat, the massive bulk of Ogya clambered out of the ground.

His many eyes were blazing circles in a face of flame; saw-toothed chelicerae flickered around the spiny hole of his mouth. His many arms clutched and scrabbled at the soil as he pulled himself out of the fire and earth. He stood upright on two armored legs, towering over even Kwaee. With a chittering hiss and crackle, he wrenched his tail free of the earth; the segmented appendage arched up over his back, barbed tip swaying above his head and dripping molten flame.

"Kwaee." His voice was the death of wind. "You would not think to deceive me, now, would you?"

"No deception," the forest god said. His voice was hoarse. "See for yourself. My son and his mate together. Their temple, for your consumption. But I want two thousand years, not one."

Ogya hissed. His small eyes did not move, fixed in his face and down his blunt neck; Clay could not tell where he was looking. It was unsettling. "Not the arrangement."

"Two gods, two thousand years. It is fair."

"I think not. Two bodies, but only one god between them."

Kwaee scowled. "Still twice the eating. Two thousand. Or I send them away."

The enormous scorpion took a step toward the two of them, sparks whirling upward from his chitinous foot. His chelicerae twitched and stroked at his face, toothy tongues licking a hungry mouth. "Very well. I am well-known for my patience. Two thousand years you will have for these little… morsels."

He took another step and paused, holding his four arms close to his body. He tilted his wide, domed head, leaning closer to Clay and Doto. "They do not scream," he said in suspicion. "They do not beg for their lives."

"There has been plenty of that already," Kwaee said with a snort. "Be thankful you were not here to witness it."

Ogya lumbered right up to the two of them; Clay shrunk back in horror now. The heat from the god's body was painful, blistering. His vision was filled with a massive torso and shifting, elongated arms, each two-fingered, scraping and clawing reflexively at the creature's thorax. Terror wracked his body; he wrenched uselessly at his arms and legs, his back arching, tail lashing as he tried to flee in panic.

The fire god chuckled. "That's better." His head swung from Clay to Doto and back, mouthparts glistening with blue flame, twitching greedily. "I think I'll start with this one," he rumbled. He was looking at Doto.

This wasn't how this was supposed to happen. "You—you can't!" Clay blurted out before he could stop himself. Ogya turned a suspicious gaze toward him. "Pleading is over, is it? This one seems surprised."

Kwaee sneered at him. "You old fool. These bodies are only their avatars, bound here so they don't try any tricks to move their temple. The temple is over there." He pointed beyond Clay and Doto, toward their peaceful haven. "Surely you must feel its power. That is your meal."

Ogya's finger-claws drummed a tattoo up his body. "You think to lecture me about consumption? I know well where my dinner is, stick-god." And then he reached down with the massive claws of both upper arms and crunched away the wooden branches binding Doto's arms, neck, legs and tail. "But I like to whet my appetite."

He seized Doto, claws about his chest and belly, and wrenched him away from the tree, hoisting him into the air. Doto screamed. Clay had never heard him scream before. It was awful: raw and terrified. Smoke rose from his fur where Ogya gripped him. He flailed, beating and kicking at the fiery beast that held him even as flames caught in his fur.

"Let him go!" Clay screamed. "Let him go let him go let him go you damned monster!"

But Ogya ignored him. He lifted Doto to his face, his mouthparts spreading wide. For a moment he paused, his chelicerae opening to stroke Doto's face, burning away his whiskers. Then he shoved the screaming Doto head and shoulders into his mouth. There was a terrible crunch. Doto's legs and tail swung limp.

A kind of madness reddened Clay's vision; he couldn't look at this, couldn't watch his mate being devoured. He whipped his head right and left, as though he could shake the image out of it, and he caught sight of their temple. It was still there. It was all right, and if it was all right, Doto was too. He knew this. He'd been killed before. He knew how this worked. Doto was all right. Doto was fine. He stared into their temple, trying to ignore the hissing, visceral slurping and crunching right next to him. Then there was silence, except for the roar of the heat.

"Ah," rumbled Ogya. "Delicious godflesh. But I am never satisfied, am I? And now the other. My palate has not tasted enough blood."

Clay kept his gaze on the temple as the heat drew near him. He hoped it would not hurt too much when Ogya ate him. But it had sounded like it hurt. Enormous, toothed claws reached toward him. He braced for the pain.

Something moved in the grass of their temple, and Doto sat up. Clay couldn't help it—he gasped in relief at seeing him.

"What is that?" Ogya paused and then drew back. He had caught Clay's gaze. "But of course. You little godlings make your avatars over and over." He laughed, a kind of chittering giggle. "Why stop at devouring your forms once when I can eat you again and again and again before moving on to the… main course?"

He lumbered toward Doto with all four arms outstretched, his arched tail with its fat barb swaying just over Clay's head. Droplets of liquid fire spattered outward, sizzling and smoking in the earth around him. He didn't pause at the edge of their temple, but Clay felt it the instant he crossed the boundary; there was ugliness suddenly inside him, a force of hatred, murder, and greed moving through his core like a worm in his heart. He convulsed in his prison, a wave of nausea and revulsion rolling through him.

And then Ogya's foot touched the soil of their temple.

Clay had had molten rock embedded in his body. He had been trampled, nearly died of blood poisoning, and then killed over and over in every way imaginable. Nothing he had ever felt could have prepared him for the touch of the fire god in his soul. A low, quick flame moved out from Ogya's footstep, burning a radius of tender, young grass and flowers to black and embers in an instant. Burning a hole in their temple. In them.

Clay had burned to death by fire. It had been agony. Unbearable. But he would have welcomed that flame now—*that* only destroyed his body. The touch of Ogya in his temple burned away what made him Clay; it consumed what remained when the body was gone. He remembered then the moments after death, when the world had been composed of light, when *he* was light, all those brilliant colors of magic, of nature, of *existence* making him up. And he knew—he could feel—that those lights were flaring, bursting, and going out.

He heard screaming: wild, hoarse, uncontrolled shrieks of agony. It was not only his voice. Doto was matching his screams in unison. One touch from Ogya and they were not simply dying; they were being *destroyed*. There would be no afterlife, no ancestors, no world of floating stars for them.

A lesser pain, physical pain, stabbed into his gut. A hole had formed there, its edges blackened and charred, the insides still burning. It felt like it went all the way through. He had to hold on. This was where Ogya needed to be. But where was Mother Fam? Where was Atekye? Why was she not summoning the flood?

Ogya was not all the way inside the temple. All of this agony had been over the space of half a breath. He took his second step, reaching for the writhing Doto.

Another spear of agony, of unmaking, lanced through Clay, burning a hole through his chest. He clutched at it instinctively, only distantly realizing that in his convulsions he'd broken the wood that encased his right wrist. The light of the entire world before him flickered, like torchlight about to go out. He would have retreated into unconsciousness, perhaps, but that was no refuge. Unconsciousness was a protection from physical pain. And the physical pain was nothing next to the flames of nothingness that scorched his being.

He couldn't help it. Something primal and automatic took over; his inner self recoiled in agony and terror and then retreated. There was a sound like someone dumping out a basket of sand, and their temple was gone. Clay could feel it, far away, back up on their mountainside, huddled in pain and terror. But it was not burning anymore, and Ogya couldn't get it.

The fire god stood in the middle of the forest clearing, blinking down at Doto with an expression of confusion and anger. "What is this?" he demanded turning to Kwaee. "A trick?" His claws clicked rapidly.

"No trick. Not by me. They must have found some way to move their temple." Kwaee strode toward Clay, fury in his eyes. "Where did you send it? Tell me, you pitiful excuse for a godling!"

Why wasn't he calling to Mother Fam or Atekye? What had happened to the plan? Where were the waters to trap Ogya? Clay clawed frantically at the wood around his neck. They had been betrayed. He had to break free. He had to escape with Doto before they were both sacrificed to this madness. The holes in his body flared when he moved, but the pain hardly registered. He didn't think after today anything else would hurt again. "I don't know what you—you—" he stammered. "Why haven't you—?" There was no way to finish the sentence.

"Why haven't you what?" Ogya roared, turning. He took one menacing step toward Kwaee.

Kwaee clamped his paw around Clay's wrist, holding it down. "Don't waste time, I've got this one! Catch my son, you fool, before he escapes!"

Ogya glanced over one shoulder at Doto, who, slumped against the support of one arm, was trying to crawl away from the enormous scorpion.

Two deep holes had been burned through his body—one in his arm and another in one thigh. His ears were pinned back, his eyes wide in terror. Wounded, he was no challenge for Ogya. The scorpion lunged toward him, claws outspread, and snatched Doto about the chest in one enormous pincer.

"How could you?" Clay wept through his own pain. "Your son. Your own son."

Kwaee bared his fangs at Clay; this close, his mouth looked large enough to snap Clay's head off in one bite. "You insolent little whelp," he growled. He moved his fingers and the wood flowed back around Clay's freed wrist, encasing it again. "What did you think would happen? There is no place to run from this. No place you can hide. I know where you moved your temple. You and my son are insignificant. Nothing. You have only two spots of territory. Up on that mountain, and here. That's all the power you have in this whole world. What did you hope would happen? That someone would come rushing in to save you? Fool. You and Doto will die, and no one can help you. The only thing you have left is to surrender." He grasped Clay's muzzle in his paw. "Do you understand me?"

"I won't let you kill him," Clay gasped in Kwaee's grip. "I can't."

"Do not think about that." Kwaee leaned closer, and his expression softened, his crest of feathers flattening backward. And deep, deep in his eyes was an expression of desperation. "Just *surrender*. That is all you have to do."

Surrender surrender surrender. The word rattled around in Clay's head like seeds in a gourd. Something was going on here, something he was supposed to know, something he'd forgotten. Surrender to the will of the gods, to the edicts of the King, to his own fate, to Doto, to love, to death, all that he was, all that he had hoped to be, everything he had gotten, to Ogya, to Kwaee, to Sarmu, to Fam, to Atekye, to—*to Atekye.*

The land, the forest in which Ogya was standing, where their temple had stood. They had sent the temple away, but the land still belonged to them, it was Clay and Doto's, and no other god had dominion there. Atekye couldn't move in because they needed to give her the territory.

Clay had no time to think about it. No time to work out how to do it, no time to be taught, no time to feel anxious or worry. He thought about his power, the new power that he had been given from Kwaee, and the circle of the forest. Send it out, out, away into the world, to another god, to—

He felt their presences there, deep in the ground. Atekye hiding in an underground cavern with Mother Fam, pulsing power as bright as the sun. He sent his own power to Atekye, and felt, distantly, Doto with him, doing the same. Her power grasped it, sucked it in hungrily, taking the land from him, and as before he had felt expanded, strengthened by Kwaee's gift, now he was diminished again, weakened.

Ogya stood taller, looking around, the arm that gripped Doto lowering. "Stop. Wait. Something is wrong here. The temple is gone. So where is that coming from, that power—"

There was a hissing sound. The ground beneath Doto's dangling toes made a pop, a puff of dirt erupting in the air. A little hole had formed there, and a long, expectorant noise came from it. Another hole appeared, with a spitting sound, and then another. They were opening up all around Ogya. A rumbling sound came from a long way off.

He dropped Doto. "It *is* a trick! I knew it. Kwaee, you have made a terrible error today. I will never show you mercy or trust again." He drew himself up, the fires surrounding him flaring brighter, blazing as he prepared his departure… and then they guttered and went out.

Without them, he was still terrifying—a monstrous scorpion creature with deadly claws, a nightmarish face, and a swaying, evil-looking tail. But his body looked weaker and softer, his chitinous armor the pale, damp grey of old embers. He looked ancient. Burned out. Bewildered, he swung his domed head about, his chelicerae chittering, and then he looked down and saw the swamp waters rising around his feet. The water had severed his connection to his fiery domain and extinguished his power.

Abruptly, the wooden bonds imprisoning Clay released, and he dropped to the ground. He pushed himself to his feet. The pain was not so terrible now, but he could feel that part of him was missing, an empty space inside him where there should be body and soul. Across the forest clearing, Doto had risen and was limping toward him, away from the ash-grey monster. His fur was scorched black across his chest and leg, but it was healing.

The rumbling sound was getting louder. Ogya clacked his pincers rapidly, looking from side to side for the source of the treachery. He hunched, raising his claws before his face, waving them outward as though to ward off a giant, unseen foe. Then he ran. Though his body was enormous and terrifying, it was not made for speed. His tail, threatening when he was approaching, proved to be ungainly and poorly balanced. It swung wildly to one side, nearly pulling him from his feet. His top-heavy body wobbled and lurched, each of his arms moving after his feet, some residual reflex of the days when he had scurried on eight legs through the primeval fires of the world.

His escape was made even more difficult by the growing swamp. The ground beneath his two-clawed feet had gone soft, and each step sunk deeper and deeper into thick, slimy, brown mud. Reeds and swamp moss were sprouting everywhere, gripping at his legs. The air was suddenly filled with a symphony of deep croaks and shrill chirps, the voices of thousands of frogs.

Shaking his head and pulling himself free of grasping grasses, Ogya finally managed to synchronize the movements and balance of his body and start to run, but that was right when he hit the wall. It shot out of the ground fast as a striking serpent, a monolith of solid rock that jutted abruptly into the air, tall as he was. He scrabbled at it disbelievingly. "What is this?"

The great, round shape of Mother Fam rose out of the earth outside the pool of swamp water, the moon bulging up out of the horizon. She spread her muddy arms wide as if to embrace Ogya, but her face was sad. "Oh, my child. I'm sorry for this. But you have to be stopped. You're out of control."

"None can control me!" Ogya roared, but his voice without the flame was thinner, hollower. It seemed to Clay for a moment as though the fire god was shrinking, but then he saw the bubbles rising up around his legs; he was already knee deep in swamp water. Dark green tendrils encased his limbs, holding them in place. He struggled, tugging at one and then the other. The rumbling sound was now a distant and approaching thunder, so forceful that it sent the trees shaking. The breeze lifted suddenly, turning into a powerful wind gusting in from the east. Birds rose up out of the forest, calling in alarm; others flew in colorful streaks past the gods, fleeing for their lives.

Ogya wrenched at his feet; with the snapping of vines and reeds he pulled one leg free. "You cannot stop me!" he bellowed. He took another step forward and his foot sank deeper than before, leaving him hunched forward in the muck. "No!"

The wind rose, and the rumbling was now so loud that the earth was vibrating beneath Clay's toes. Kwaee's massive paw gripped Clay's shoulder. "Quick, Doté, that way. Run!" He shoved Clay away from the scene and dashed toward Doto, who was still limping toward them, clutching his wounded leg with one paw.

Clay started to run and then froze when he saw what was coming from the east. A massive, white wall of water roared toward him, growing larger and larger as it approached. Trees bent, snapped, and were pulled up by the roots before disappearing in its wake. It came straight for them, not curving to move with the boundaries of the land, not stopping for even the mightiest trees or the proudest of boulders. It stormed through them as though they were nothing but mirages. The Asubonten had changed course. And amid it all, the crocodile goddess herself rode, surfing atop her wave of destruction, a great, black, unstoppable monster, laughing madly through the mist and spray as she roared down the hillside directly for the trapped form of Ogya.

Kwaee scooped up Doto under one arm, pivoted on his toes, roots from the forest sprouting up beneath it to give him leverage, and dashed back toward Clay.

"You cannot kill me!" Ogya roared. "My temple is infinite and unquenchable! I will return over and over! And no prison can hold me! No bonds are strong enough! I will escape! I will return and devour y—"

The wall of water slammed into him and swallowed his words. Clay got a glimpse of a claw flailing frantically, clutching at the trees from the roiling, white spume, and then he was gone. From far to the west, the rumbling continued as Asubonten wound her merry way down, down on her new course toward the sea.

Kwaee set Doto down next to Clay and stood back. He looked weary. Not slumping or out of breath, but his usual sense of poise and grace was gone.

"Did—did we do it?" Doto panted. He staggered over to Clay and collapsed against him. Clay held him in both arms, ignoring the bolts of pain that lanced through the missing spaces where Ogya had consumed him.

Kwaee looked distant for a moment. "I sense so, but I will not be satisfied until I see with my own eyes. It is too large a moment to be believed. I will go and look. You two, return to your temple. Rest. Heal it and heal yourselves. I… You…" He faltered, his brow furrowed. He stared at the ground.

"Father?" Doto reached toward him.

Kwaee set his ears back, his crest lowered. "Your plan was… good. I think that you may have saved us. Saved… me. All of us. I am…" He took several breaths, then sighed. He met first Doto's gaze, then Clay's. "You are not godlings or whelps or children. You are worthy. You are my sons. And I will never again forget it."

Clay worked his jaws for a moment as about ten different ill-considered replies tried to work their way out at the same time. Kwaee caught his gaze. "Although you took *far* too long with your part," he added sharply. "Next time, do not hesitate."

"Next time?" Clay managed.

Kwaee shrugged. "You are gods. Do you think this is the only difficult thing you will ever have to do? Now go and heal yourselves. I will see to our captive."

Clay and Doto exchanged a glance. "We can heal later," Doto told him. "We need to see too. It has been too long. Too much. We will not be able to rest until we know."

The forest god nodded. "Then come."

~

The going was slower than they would have liked. Both Clay and Doto were badly wounded and couldn't move at the wind-blur speeds of their uninjured selves. The other injuries of the day healed themselves quickly, but the holes that Ogya had burned into their bodies did not recover, and every movement was a little stab of pain and a frightening sense of emptiness, of something missing. Kwaee eventually lost patience and ran on ahead.

Finally, following the new path of Asubonten, they came upon the swamp. Neither of them relished the idea of venturing into the mire; they both agreed that the last thing they wanted, so soon after Kwaee had offered them his respect, was to show him their naked human bodies floundering through the muck.

But even from the edge of the forest, they could see the prison that held Ogya. The swamp basin itself had been constructed by Fam and Atekye, a massive stone bowl filled with pools and mud and trees and above all, water. And in the center of it, an enormous dome of stone and earth, gripped about and secured by trees. From within the dome came the furious roars of Ogya. Openings around it occasionally revealed the wave of a grey claw or the bob of an enormous head, small black eyes squinting out into the world beyond.

Kwaee came to their sides, standing with his paws on his hips. "He is secure. He will not escape."

"Will it really hold him?" Doto asked.

"It would take the will of multiple gods to let him go. The swamp water keeps his fire out. The prison is layered with shell after shell of mud, water, and stone too strong for even fire to burn through. The trees are mine, and I will sense it if even one root snaps." He bared his teeth. "No. Ogya will never get out again. We will not let him. We have done it, my sons. The forest is saved."

At his side, Clay and Doto leaned on each other and stared down at the end of their troubles.

And in his prison, Ogya slammed his body over and over against the unyielding walls of rock and mud, sloshing through the water, bellowing. "Please! I need to eat! I need it! I am so hungry! So hungry!"

It began to rain.

# 31 Godrise

The world had gone wrong. A primal terror jolted through Mirage's veins. The morning sky was black with clouds, a terrible wind blasted in from out of the sea, hurling stinging sand against everyone's skin, and some *thing* had come up out of the sea, a thing like a monstrous woman, towering into the clouds above the great water. And Mirage, along with many of those around him, flung himself to the beach.

The creature stood—or perhaps floated—waist-deep in the water. Her streamlined torso glistened with scales. Her angular mouth was a crescent filled with uncountable fangs. Open slits flared in her neck as she leaned toward them, her alien face twisted with rage. She raised one greenish-black arm, lined with fins, and spread webbed, clawed fingers. With her hand, the dark ocean itself surged, rising upward in a wall of water painted blood-red by the dawn. She shouted at them, her deep, wet voice booming out over the land in words he could not comprehend. By the look of the Boganans, *they* could.

All of this was his fault, he knew. The Breakwaters had planned a slow and steady rebellion, teaching those they could trust their newly gained knowledge over time, but Mirage had pleaded with them to help his people escape before they were sacrificed—or worse—to the Matron's designs. And when they remained reluctant, he had reminded them that all that they had gained, all their new knowledge, was because of him and because his people had brought him here. That those people were now suffering due to Boganan inhospitality. And did not the gods have laws about hospitality? Even in Bogana? Perhaps, he had argued, their newfound magics would fail if they did not truly honor the gods.

Reluctantly, the Breakwaters had agreed to help him, though the risk was high and their chances of success low. One thing he was going to do if they survived this, he decided, was hold down his father and cram his loud mouth full of sand.

But they were not going to survive this. A goddess wished them to die, and that was what was going to happen. Mpo, Kwaee, Ogya. It made

no difference which of them, did it? Humans were lives to be toyed with or taken.

Waves roared up the sandy slope of the beach. Above the sound of the wind and water rang the voice of the Matron, clear and firm, cutting through the chaos with surety. Mirage had no idea what she was saying, but many of the Boganans moaned and wailed at her words.

There was movement around him. Fighting his clutching fear, he risked raising his head. There was the dark sky, there the titan, her hands raised to the heavens, behind her a wall of water poised, ready to rush in and obliterate all of them. But the Boganans were leaving—most of them. They were backing away from the trapped group of Mirage's people. Those that had weapons kept spears raised and bows nocked. Those with no weapons moved behind them, but they looked no less threatening, their hands clasped at their chests, gazes focused on the sea goddess. In some eyes, an eager viciousness glinted. In others, rapt adoration.

The Breakwaters, however, were not permitted to follow. They had been left behind with the People of the Savanna. There was Orupetra, there was Elder Tobosu. One man tried to rejoin the Boganans, pleading with them in his language, his arms outstretched. A guard, his face twisted in contempt, aimed a kick at him, shoving him back with the captives.

The Matron pointed at the crowd of Boganans, calling out something to them. A movement and bustle went through the group, with much shoving and shouting, and then several more people were pushed out. Mirage recognized several of them as other Breakwaters, those who had not joined the rescue attempt. He wondered how they had been caught. Leaving the caves, perhaps, or fingered by suspicious neighbors—perhaps people who had been out all night, or people who smelled a little too strongly of burning torches for this early in the morning. So he had doomed not only his own people, but the Boganan rebellion, too.

The Boganans backed further and further up the beach. The Matron's voice continued to cry out in her language, but now she was turned with her arms upraised, calling out to the sea. The only word Mirage recognized was "Mpo."

"Curse this and damn it!" a voice swore. A man got to his feet. Mirage cringed. His father. "I'll not stand here and be sacrificed with a bunch of exiles. I've done nothing wrong!" He pushed away from the crowd and tried to stamp up the beach toward the Boganans, but the sand was deep and awkward, and he stumbled.

The tips of many weapons swiveled toward him. He raised his arms. "These aren't my people!" he shouted up to them. "They're exiles. Traitors! I'm not a part of them! I just came after my son! But he's chosen his path, so let me choose mine. I want to stay with you. I'm one of you! Boganan by blood and ancestry! You want me to worship Mpo, I'll worship her. Show me how! I… I claim my heritage."

Not a weapon lowered. Every arrow and spear was trained on him.

He reached both hands toward the Matron. "Lady Matron, I beg of you. These are not my people. They never have been. I am Knife Strap, the son of Two Broken Hands—*Se Twala Jaht*—and I am Boganan. I serve Mpo."

The Matron regarded him with calm brown eyes. "But Mpo is the sea. Constant. Reliable. She demands unwavering service, not merely when it is convenient. And you are no Boganan. Listen to your clumsy accent. Look at your filthy skin and clothes. You cannot even understand our language."

Knife Strap dropped to his knees in the sand. "No. I can learn. I can clean myself."

"*Mpo* cleans all of their filth and sin. We cannot clean ourselves. And she has no use for the disloyal. Nor for cowards. Go and join the rest."

"But Matron—"

Bows creaked as they tightened. Arms holding spears tensed.

Trembling, Knife Strap returned to the group of people huddled on the beach.

The Matron raised her voice. "Anyone who tries to flee will be shot immediately. Do not think to test the skill of my archers."

Mirage stared at the group of men standing around her with bows drawn, ready to murder anyone who only wanted to leave, or to stand up for their truth, for their gods, and for a moment, he stood among them, his own bow drawn. It was the same group of people—the very same, standing before another tyrant who wanted to dictate the rules of worship. Who wanted only one story for everyone.

But there had been other stories.

His father came stumbling back, pushed to the outside of the group he had just denied being a part of. Mirage ignored him.

Other stories, other songs, he thought. This is how we survive, how we thrive: we make the world bigger. We need more stories. More voices. Because all gods are flawed, every one of them cruel in her own way, oblivious in his, unkind, short-sighted, vain, wrathful, arrogant, or jealous. We need to be able to choose the stories, the songs that help us. The gods do not choose us. We choose them.

We choose now.

Mirage shuffled through the crowd until he found Oru. "I'm sorry you're here," he murmured in her ear. "I'm sorry I got you into this."

She bared her teeth in what might have been a grin. "I'm not sorry. I'm glad to be in the fight. Did you see my father's face when he saw I was one of the rebels? Even if we don't survive this, he must know he is in big, big trouble."

"*Can* we survive? What are they going to do?"

"I have seen this before, with a people that would not surrender or yield to the Matron. She calls Mpo. The people will go up the hill and leave us here. Mpo will send a wave that will crush or suffocate all of us, but only wet the feet of the others. Some few of us may survive if they are strong at… staying atop the water… and if they are lucky not to be washed into trees or stones. But nearly all will die, every time. There will be nowhere to run. The wave will cover the whole beach, as far as you can go. And if you try to go up the hill, the archers will shoot you."

Mirage frowned, thinking. "We may have a chance yet. I think I know what we need. Bew. Do you understand? Bew."

Oru set her jaw. "I understand." And she began to push through the crowd, moving toward the other Breakwaters to spread the word.

Mirage shoved his way past frightened, crying people until he found Cloud. She stood near the seaward edge of the group, her eyes fixed on the leviathan, who stood with her arms raised the sea churning behind her, waiting for her sacrifice to be ready, booming words like thunder in her angry and incomprehensible language. The Teller was there at Cloud's side, his heavy arm around her, his forehead pressed into the frizzy tangle of her hair. The way he held her, Mirage wondered if perhaps he had been missing something about the two of them all these years. This was not the time for that, though.

"Cloud."

She turned her head at his voice. "Mirage. You risked yourself to save all of us, didn't you?"

"It doesn't atone for what I did."

"No," said Cloud. "But it's a start. I wish I could grant you a finish, but…" She waved her hand toward the wave offshore. It looked tall enough now to reach the highest cliffs of Bogana.

"There may still be a chance. I can't explain, but we found… prayers. Songs. Can you tell everyone to listen to my words and follow?"

"What are you planning, boy?" Her forehead wrinkled in suspicion. Now? She was going to be stubborn *now?*

"You came here looking for secrets, right? Something that could help us fight the gods?"

"You and your King wanted to fight the gods! We want—"

"Something else, yes, I know. Just… please trust me. Get everyone else to sing, too."

She looked back toward the towering figure of Mpo and that wall of water. Then she pressed her lips together and gave a curt nod. She moved toward Ant With a Leaf and leaned up to call something to her. Ant cast a narrow-eyed scowl in Mirage's direction, but nodded, and the two of them headed off in opposite directions in the crowd.

Mirage wasn't sure how much time he had, but the people would listen to their elder and warrior before a murderer and spy, so he didn't try to persuade anyone else. Instead, he searched through the crowd until he found his mother. He found her standing on the outside of the group, facing the sea, staring up at the titan Mpo, who boomed words over the water in incomprehensible syllables.

"I feel I almost understand her," Dry Grass said over the wind.

"The goddess? How?"

"I don't know. The anger. I… sometimes you wish you could wash everything away, don't you? Like it never was."

"I think she's more like Knife Strap."

"Well, anger takes different forms, I guess. I wonder what she wants?"

Mirage shrugged. "Does it matter? To be worshipped exclusively, maybe. Maybe she hates the other gods and doesn't want *them* to be worshipped. Or maybe she's naturally angry."

"Anger is only fear turned outward. Does she fear being alone? Unloved? Unworthy?" The massive wave rose higher. Its tops were white, its walls now a pale green. "What can it mean if you can be an all-powerful, undying goddess and still feel those things?"

"I don't know. But I hope today we can give her something new to be afraid of."

"What do you mean?" Dry Grass asked.

He squeezed her shoulder. "You'll see. I hope." The Boganans had moved far up the beach, now. The Matron still stood out in front of them, shouting to Mpo, but from here, he could not make out the words. The guards were now so far off that Mirage didn't think they could successfully attack any of the People, but it didn't matter anymore. Where could they run? Mpo's wave stretched to the horizons, and surely she could simply reach out an arm and crush any of them like flies.

The Matron lowered her hands. The goddess took a single step toward them, and the wave followed behind her like a cloak of water. The sea before her bulged and surged forward in a miniature of the wall behind. The grey surf turned white as it flowed up the beach toward them, surging around the ankles of the frightened crowd. People shouted in alarm and clutched at each other.

They had to act now or die. The Breakwaters who had been captured with them had filtered through the group; they watched Elder Tobosu with expectant faces.

The old man lifted his head and sang.

His words were lost in the wind, but he kept singing. He lifted a foot and danced a step to the right. Other Boganans in the crowd caught the song and joined their voices to it, and now it was loud enough to hear: an unusual, foreboding tune whose pitch went up when Mirage would expect it to dip, its cadence halting and slow.

The wind died.

All was still on the beach except for the rushing of water. Mpo no longer boomed her incomprehensible imprecations. She peered toward them, her alien brow furrowed, her flat black eyes fixed on them. Up the shore, the Boganans shuffled around uneasily. The Matron did not shout or chant but stood watching. Even from here, Mirage could see her jaw was set, her eyes narrowed.

The Breakwaters did not stop singing. The words were Boganan, but Mirage had learned the translation, and now as the whole group began to dance, moving in a circle through the crowd, he joined in, singing the song of praise in the words of the People of the Savanna.

*Bew, Sky-Scratcher and Bulwark of the Ancients*
*Oh Watcher of Wem*
*Cloud-headed and hoary*

*Mightiest of mountains*
*You are our path to the heavens*
*Unmoving, unshaking, all must move around you,*
*River and moon change their paths*
*Your nose pierces the night*
*And your shadow lengthens it.*
*Taller than dawn and wider than midday*
*Your girth shelters us*
*Your strength guards us*
*You stand steadfast against the changing world*
*And when all else would alter or fade*
*You endless endure.*

The cadence was wrong for a song of praise, and Bew was a god unknown to Mirage, so singing a song about his eternal nature felt dishonest, but he tried to forget that and focus on imbuing the words with sincere praise. As he moved through the dance, others began to follow and pick up the song. The People of the Savanna could memorize a tale or song after hearing it only once or twice, and now, haltingly, they joined in, singing with him as best they could.

The air was still eerily silent, but now a rumble shook the ground beneath them. The sand on the beach began to shift strangely as it shook, forming little mounds and depressions in response to the ground's vibrations. People in the crowd cried out in surprise.

"What's happening?"

"It's the attack!"

"No, keep singing, remember what Cloud told us! Follow the song!"

More and more people picked up the music now, following Mirage, moving in the circular dance, their voices beginning to drown out those of the Boganan singers.

Out of the water, Mpo leaned closer, her black eyes stretching wider and wider. Her crescent chasm of a mouth opened, building sized teeth parting. Her mouth inside was pale. The teeth jutted from ragged white gums, rows and rows of them. Her white tongue shifted. "How dare you sing praise to false gods in front of me?" Her voice echoed across the land, so loud it made Mirage's ears ring and he could no longer hear the words to his song. He kept singing nonetheless. So, you knew our language the whole time, he thought. She'd never spoken it before now. But they'd pushed her. She didn't like what was happening. He sang louder.

And now the ground beneath the people was no longer merely shaking; it was rising. People stumbled in the middle of their dances and Mirage nearly fell himself but caught his footing and moved on. The sand beneath the crowd began sifting away beneath their feet as the ground rose higher and higher, lifting the people up off the beach.

Mpo roared in fury, again deafening Mirage. "Cease this false praise at once!"

Up the beach, the Matron shouted something at the Boganans around her, and several of them loosed arrows, but they were too far back, and the shafts thudded harmlessly into the sand some distance away.

Louder. They had to sing louder. Mirage waved his arms in encouragement and moved through the dance more vigorously, struggling to keep his footing as the sand flowed away beneath him. Below it was earth, hard and packed, but that too was breaking apart. What emerged from the crumbling loam was hard, solid stone, a little cone of it thrusting up from the sand at the center of their group.

They had called a god, one they had all forgotten. Bew, god of mountains and strength, unknown to any of them in tales or songs. But he was real. And he was answering. Already they stood on a rising plateau of stone thrice the height of a man, its sloped sides spreading out across the beach, rumbling with moving rock and hissing as the sand poured away on all sides.

From Mpo rose an inchoate bellow of fury. She clenched her fists, slammed her arms down to her sides and released her wave. It crept toward them with deceptive slowness, but its approach darkened the sky with mist and spray. Seabirds squawked panicked cries as they winged their way inland, trying to escape the surge. Beneath the rising hill, the water drained away, sucked back out to sea, leaving solid ground behind, the naked sand streaked with sea plants now lying flat, tasting the dry air for the first time. Fish lay on their sides, struggling beneath the sky amidst stranger creatures that waved pincers or lay in sodden heaps on the exposed seabed.

The wave neared, and with it came the rumble and rush of water. It was dark-walled now, and taller than it had appeared from the shore. Her face twisted in hatred, Mpo raised her arms, palms upward, and the wave surged higher. Again she lifted her arms upward, and again the wave rose. It was impossibly tall and still rising; as it sped toward them, birds vanished into its darkness and were gone. Their little mountain was not high enough; the water would easily engulf them. So, too, would it have no trouble reaching the Boganans who had retreated up the hill. A few of them recognized this—they jabbed their fingers at the rising wave. Others turned and ran, scrambling on all fours further up the slope in their haste to get away. The Matron shouted something at them, but whatever it was only made the group panic further, and others fled.

"Filth!" bellowed Mpo. "All of you are filth, and I shall scour the land clean of you!"

But if before the Breakwaters and the People of the Savanna had sung haltingly, stumbling over the words, now they found new passion for the song. Desperation drove their steps as they danced in a shifting arc, those near the center moving in tight circles; those at the outside slower but trying to press their way inward to escape the remnants of the sand still sifting down the sides of the young mountain. Their voices rang out anew; their tongues found the words to their liking and sung them with greater surety; they had called Bew and he had answered. But they were not yet saved.

They sang, and the mountain rose beneath them, higher and higher, answering the song. Its foot stretched out across the beach, sand piling up in heaps around it, extending out past the waterline and sending beached sea creatures rolling downward or buried under heaps of sodden sand.

The wave would still obliterate them; they were not high enough. *Keep singing!* Mirage wanted to shout to everyone, but the only way to do that would be to stop singing himself, and the exhortation was unnecessary—all those around him had become sudden, devoted disciples of Bew. Past him spun Ant With a Leaf, singing, "mightiest of mountains." The Teller danced closer to the center, words of Bew's endurance on his tongue. There was his mother, raising her hands to the sky as she sang—and even his father, not meeting anyone's gaze, but singing the praise of Bew all the same.

And their mountain rose. Its sides were bare and stony, with no vegetation. It grew into the hill that led down to the shore, starting a small rockslide. Higher and higher it elevated, lifted by the songs of the people and the power of a forgotten god, until it met the water. Stones crashed into the shallows with little splashes.

Mpo roared and raised her arms again, but her wave would go no higher. It met the base of the mountain before it touched the shore. Black-green water turned loamy as it swallowed up the earth, the white foam churning into dark brown. The wave broke around the new mountain, streaming to either side and flowing up the slope and still its peak had not hit them. Mirage was not sure even now that their mountain was high enough, even though they stood even with the city of Bogana on the cliffs to the south.

The wave crashed against that precipice, shooting a fan of water wider than the city high into the air. A moment later they heard the sound—an earth-shattering boom, a roar of water like a rainstorm, and then a loud, final-sounding crack, as though an enormous boulder had split in two. Against the wave, the seaward side of Bogana trembled.

The bulk of the wave still approached them, and now Mirage could not hear his own singing over the thunder of it. The whole mountain beneath their feet shook, and as a group, the people fell, grasping at the arms, legs, and waists of those on the outside to keep them from sliding down the bare slopes.

The water had broken entirely around the mountain now, flowing past, though it had hit the slope with enough speed that even here, at the peak, the brine surged over the tip, flowing around ankles or fallen bodies with deceptive force. They clung to each other more tightly, gripping rocks to avoid being swept down the far side.

Behind them, the Boganans up on the hill were all fleeing, slipping and skidding as they tried to scramble up the slope to escape the wrath of Mpo. All but the Matron. She stood facing the wave, her face stretched in a terrible rictus, teeth bared, but whether in ecstasy, fury, or terror, Mirage could not tell. She held her arms outstretched as if to embrace the approaching wall of water. She vanished beneath it.

The remaining Boganans had managed to get above the crest of the wave, but it was not far enough. The water poured up the slope, a roiling brown flood, churning with earth and stone as it rose past them. All were swept off their feet in an instant and disappeared beneath the surface, flailing to catch themselves as the force of the wave took them inland. Then they were gone.

Dripping, excitement and fear warring in his veins, Mirage struggled back to his feet, offering a hand to those nearest him.

As one group the People of the Savanna stood atop the mountain Bew had raised. Water surged around it on all sides, its slopes extending far out into the great water. They faced Mpo.

She stared back at them, her arms lowered, her mouth hanging open.

Someone bumped against Mirage's side. He looked down to see Oru standing next to him, her eyes shining. "We did it!" she said to him. "We actually did it! We found the secrets! We fought back! We can be free!"

The wondering crowd parted for Elder Tobosu, who pushed his way into the center and stood at the very peak of their new mountain so that he could stand head and shoulders over the rest of them. He lifted one fist to the sky—looking much like the statues of Mpo throughout the city. And then he called out to her in Boganan.

"What is he saying?" Mirage asked Oru.

"He says there will be no more talk of one goddess. That Bogana will be free to worship all gods and… and bring back our… ways. The ways of our people that we were made to forget. He says we will worship Mpo but never bow only to her. That there will be no more killings and no more punishments, or we will take the sea from her, mountain by mountain, until there is no place left for her on this planet."

A prickle went up Mirage's back. How close this sounded to Laughing Dog's defiance of Kwaee, his threat to burn down the forest tree by tree until nothing was left. And perhaps it was not fighting the gods as Laughing Dog did, but did it not make them beholden to another power? Was depending upon the might of Bew any different than subjugating themselves to Ogya? But perhaps Elder Tobosu would be wiser than Laughing Dog. Mirage hoped he would be.

And the prayers had worked; the waters had already begun to flow back, brown with earth, receding into the sea from which they came. And, looking stricken, her mouth still open, the goddess Mpo led them, walking backwards, her arms at her sides, receding lower and lower until only her face with those dagger teeth and staring black eyes was visible. And then that, too, sank beneath the waves.

They had won.

A smattering of cheers moved through the dizzied, disbelieving group. And as they turned to embrace each other or slap each other on the back, another loud crack echoed across the mountain side.

They turned.

The seaward side of Bogana had shifted; it looked lower than the inland side. There were large puffs of dust rising into the air from within it, and little tumbles of stone and dirt rolling down the cliffs. Even from here, even above the rush of receding water, Mirage could hear a chorus of shrill screams.

Then the entire cliffside went sliding downward toward the water and, its buildings breaking apart or toppling over, the edge of Bogana followed.

# 32 Containment

Kwaee sat on the slope that led down to the basin holding Ogya's prison. It had not been swamp yesterday, but now it belonged to Atekye. And Asubonten cut a new scar through the forest. Kwaee was convinced that she'd deliberately found the most circuitous, winding path possible, taking as much of his forest as she could.

Still, he felt glad to have surrendered it this time. It had cost him so little. His conflict with the fire bearers had been far more ruinous. They had blazed a scar into his northern rim that would take many rains to recover. It was a glowing edge of pain, a bite out of his forest that nagged at him continually. He had lost power from it. His forest was smaller, his size diminished, perhaps irreparably so. The fire bearers had wanted to prove they could hurt him, and they had.

But with Ogya now separated from his temple and the source of his power, the intensity of their fires had waned. Many of them had been fueled by divine power, driven to unnatural heights and heat, but now they flickered and dwindled. The fire bearers who set them had lost direction. Their flames still spread, here and there, but Kwaee was easily able to snuff them by moving earth or sprouting barriers. The burned areas were no longer growing significantly. And from the ashes, new green would sprout.

They had won. They had *won*. And not like last time, not with Kwaee greatly diminished in power and Ogya simply delayed. Now Ogya was imprisoned, and he would never, ever go free. Without embers to warm his toes or ash to ground him, he was separated from his domain. His fires were out. And his prison was layered—water, mud, root, and mineral that would neither break nor bend by the strength of any creature.

Not that Ogya hadn't tried. He had roared and cursed and pounded on the walls of the half-buried orb that contained him. But it had been well-constructed; he could not budge a single stone, crack a single wall, sever with his pincers a single root. When four gods wanted you to stay put, you weren't moving.

The only thing that could possibly free him would be if his avatar were killed, and that would not happen. As a god of hunger and flame, he might suffer, but would never die of lack of food or water. He had tried drowning himself in the mud and pools at first, but Fam and Atekye would not let that happen. They formed a lattice of stone and root in the floor that kept his feet wet but denied the monstrous creature enough water to drown himself. He beat his head against the wall, but his carapace was sturdy and would not crack.

No fire bearer would ever reach him. Not here. The prison was well-made. It would hold Ogya until the end of the earth. And he knew it, too. Soon enough his flailing and pounding had ceased. He no longer roared his fury and curses; he simply lay on his side and moaned for food, always for food, bewailing his endless hunger.

Kwaee did not tire of this. He thought he might move his temple closer so he could watch Ogya for a while. It had been thousands of years, but finally his enemy was defeated. After all this endless conflict, it was difficult to know what to do next. Perhaps he would work on the forest again. Invent new fungi. Create a labyrinth of strangler figs. Redesign his temple.

The sound of rushing air came from behind him, along with twin pulses of divine power. "Doto. Doté," he greeted them without turning.

"How is Ogya?" His son walked up to his side.

"Calmer now. He knows he will not escape."

A long, low moan rolled up from the valley. "Feed me. Please feed me."

"Can we give him food? Ease his suffering?" *That* question could only have come from Doté.

"It will not help. His hunger is unslakeable. His prison did not inflict this on him; he is as hungry out of it as in, and consumption will make no difference. It is not a need. It is a drive." He turned, finally, regarding the two. "I see your wounds have healed."

Doto folded his ears back. He looked almost shy. "We danced for each other. In our temple. The burned spots grew back."

"Thank goodness." Doté shuddered. "I never felt anything so horrible."

"So you are the only gods who can heal themselves." The world kept changing, Kwaee mused. Perhaps it was still young. Perhaps the rules were still being set. Perhaps they were all moving toward some new equilibrium that no one could anticipate.

Doto flicked his ears and looked up at him. "We do not heal ourselves. We heal each other."

A snarl rose unbidden in Kwaee's chest, and he puzzled at it and fought it down. He settled his fur, using the touch of the wind to smooth it again. "That… distinction may be more important than I had thought," he admitted. "For so long I stayed shut away in my forest, in my temple, never looking out, never talking to others. I ordered everyone away who I thought might corrupt you, turn you against me. Or deceive you as I believed the fire bearers had done to me. But if you had not spoken to them, you would still be… alone. And the fire bearers would still be burning my forest even now. Doté, Fam, Atekye, Asubonten… we needed them all. I will not isolate them any longer." He smiled ruefully. "I cannot. We require their help to keep this prison secure."

Doté stepped forward, holding his paws close to his chest. "Lord Kwaee, does this mean that you will end your campaign against the fire bearers? That the forest will no longer harm them?"

That thought rankled. Distrusting them, hating them, that was easy. It was familiar. He noticed Doté cringing back and realized that he'd unconsciously bared his fangs at the boy. Ruinous old habits. He allowed himself to relax again. "Their fires have not stopped burning."

"But supposing they stopped. If someone w… If we were to go out to them and t… If…" His son's mate was unable to get the words out. His ears folded back and he hunched down, clutching at his sides. His tail lay limp across the ground.

"What is this? A sudden weakness? Are you affected by something? Is your temple being harmed?"

Doté shook his head wordlessly.

Doto's fingers rested on Kwaee's arm. "It is hard for him, Father. He tried to persuade them to stop many times. They killed him for it." He moved past Kwaee and crouched next to Doté, putting his arm across Doté's shoulders. "It is all right. They are not here. You are safe. You are with me."

"Killed him, what do you mean, they killed him?" A low growl came from Kwaee's throat. "You mean they killed his avatar?" It was almost unthinkable. The animal gods sometimes, due to misfortune or a predator that got the better of them, were killed. They described it as agony. Kwaee had felt pain, of course, but his avatar had never perished. That the fire bearers had dared to do something so blasphemous to a god renewed a little of his distaste for them.

Doté put his face into Doto's chest and slowed his breathing.

"Yes," Doto said. "Many, many times. It is difficult for him. Something is scarred inside him because of it. Something I cannot heal."

"But how could they have killed him many times? Surely he would be reborn in his temple."

"He was. He went back. Over and over he went back, and each time they killed him."

Kwaee stared down at them in disbelief. "Why would he go back after they did this?"

Doto looked up at him, his expression puzzled. "To get them to stop burning you. To persuade them to put their fires out."

"But—but that is..." Kwaee fished for words and came up with only water. He didn't know what strength was, it seemed. The fire bearers had hurt him once and he'd shut them away forever. They'd hurt this boy as deeply as anyone could be hurt many, many times, and he had never stopped trying to save them. Even now, he was still pleading on their behalf.

He'd always thought the grand bargain a terrible mistake—that he and the other gods had granted their strength to the humans and received only injury and weakness in return. They had, he thought, received too much humanity in exchange. But maybe this whole time it hadn't been enough. What was this power, where you could accept the pain and struggle of life and yet not be ruined by it?

He absently reached up and combed his multicolored feathers through his fingers. "They prayed to me, again. In a sacred place. I heard their voices as though they were there, in front of me. I know it was one of your ilk, Doté. It has been long since I heard the old song sung. It called me. My magic. They reached out to me. They called to me first."

The forest lord took a deep breath. "I will not let their cry go unanswered. I will not fight the fire bearers again," he said. "And I will fill my forest, where I can, with food and good wood for their shelters. Instead of sending beasts out to attack them, I will send game for hunting. I will give them a reason to protect my forest, not burn it."

And it was that easy. What if he had done this years ago? "But it would be nice if someone could go and talk to them again. From a safe distance," he added. "I could send beasts to protect you."

Doté stood, finally, looking a little more composed. "I will… need to see—need to *make* myself see them, one more time. There are those who might still listen, now that Ogya does not influence them. They were traveling somewhere, you told us. To the west? There is a city there. Maybe we could find them."

"The west?" Kwaee frowned. "I have seen strange things that way from the eyes of my birds. Mpo is raging again. Her waves dashed against my western side and flooded it. She uprooted many trees. It has been long since I have seen her so furious. The fire bearers there must have provoked her again. Foolish for sea dwellers."

"Sea dwellers!" Doté's eyes widened in alarm. "But that must be Bogana! That is where they went! Doto, we must go and help them at once!"

And with another rush of wind, he was gone, racing through the forest at high speed.

Doto looked up at Kwaee and shrugged. "I had better go," he said apologetically, and then he, too, raced off.

Kwaee stared after them for a moment. Strange times. The world was changing, and finally he, too, was changing with it. He gave the prison a long, last look, and then returned to his temple.

He stepped up into his moabi and leaned back. His temple was still and quiet. Gnats hummed in the air. Damselflies hovered over the surface of his pool. The trees grew taller, stretched their branches wider. Life and death hummed in balance all around him.

And his heart knew no pain or resentment or fear or anger. He was at peace. He opened his eyes to the forest. His sigh rustled every leaf in the world.

# 33 The Way of the Wave

Atop the mountain that had risen beneath her, Cloud stood staring in disbelief. Ruins of Bogana's western precipice lay in a landslide at the bottom of the cliff. Where they had seen moored boats, now there was only a slope of rubble, broken stones crushed under fragments of houses. The Matron's own home must be among them, she thought. Where it sat, facing the sea, it would have been the first to fall. The buildings there had not been colorful—they had been white and grey, all hard, severe angles. Now the grey sea lapped against their hard angles and poured into their broken windows. Other buildings teetered on the edge, and every now and then, another would fall over, bouncing and folding and flattening before crashing into the remains below. If bodies lay among the ruins, Cloud's eyes were too weak to make them out.

The people who had brought them down here to see them sacrificed to Mpo were gone, washed away by the wave surging up the hill. She had meant to go after them, had started descending the new mountain, but Ant With a Leaf and Dry Grass had both held her back. "They will need healers!" she had protested. "And scouts!" But they had warned her that leaving immediately was impossible, pointing to the heavy flow of mud and water surging around the mountain.

Though the god-flung wave had sped toward them with terrible speed, it was taking its time leaving. A nonstop torrent of dark brown water painted the shoreline as far as they could see, gushing back into the great water. A brown smear spread curls and plumes out into the expanse. Mpo would not like that either, Cloud supposed. But Ant and Dry Grass were right; if Cloud set foot in that flood she would be as lost as the rest of the Boganans. There was nothing she could do to help them now.

The others from Bogana, the ones who had helped them, were stricken. Some could not stop talking; others stared at their ruined city and scarcely moved; and many wept, openly and loudly.

Mirage came by and sat beside Cloud. "You'd think they'd be happy. They were nearly killed a few hours ago. But they won. They overthrew the Matron. They're free!"

"People died, Mirage."

"Yes, the Matron and her guards, but they were—they were villains! They were going to kill us all!"

Cloud peered at him. "They're still *people.* And besides, who knows how many were killed up in that city? Who knows how many who came down here with her were forced to? Or were simply curious? Have you learned nothing?"

Anger flashed across his face, but he calmed himself. "I'm sorry. You're right. And I—I *have* learned things, but it's hard. I know that you were right. I know that I must spend my life atoning for the things that I did, but… doesn't this count at all? I helped liberate a city and stop a cruel god. It feels like… it feels like people should be happy."

Cloud sighed. Why would anyone ever wish to be young again? "Mirage, I'm very grateful for what you did. You came after us when it was risky. You set us free when you could have run. You found secrets that we can take with us, back home, and perhaps change the world. But this moment now is not about you. Their tears are not about what you did. Their tears are for their home. That city. Which is ruined, now. For their families, who live in that city, and their friends. They don't even know if they're still alive. Victories are never clean. They are never pretty. They're just the change from one kind of fight to another."

He grimaced. "I hoped it would feel… better… to win. When does it feel good?"

"When it does. Not right after a lot of people have died." She found his look of dismay reassuring.

Though she was anxious to do something, anything, for now they were all trapped by the water, so she moved among her people, answering their questions as best as she could. Most wished to know what they intended to do now that they had been freed: whether were they heading home, and when, and if they had what they needed to persuade the rest of the village to support them—yes, she didn't know, but not immediately, and she thought so.

Mirage became a center of attention when he spoke to the group of what he'd found beneath the city: spells for all the gods, even forgotten ones like Bew. With the right song for a god, you could raise a forest, or sink a lake into the savanna, or cut a canyon through solid stone. There were songs for all the major gods.

Basket was particularly excited about the description of the cavern full of shrines, and the way that the spells had been somehow etched into the shells of tortoises. His questions for Mirage were unending.

Eventually, the water pouring down the slope subsided enough that the scouts deemed it safe to leave, and the people climbed down a mountain that no one had ever climbed up. They were already calling it Fist-of-Bew.

Scouts went out to search for the missing Boganans who had been washed up shore by the wave. Cloud wanted to enter Bogana to help the wounded, but an old man from the city, Elder Tobosu, stopped her once again. "I fear the People of the Savanna will not be welcomed there," he told her. "Not now. Perhaps with time. We have our own healers. We will tend to our own wounded." And so she had little to do but field questions from her people and wait.

Bodies came back first. She recognized none of them until she spied the brightly colored robes of Petra. His head was half-crushed, probably by a rock. When he was brought back, a wail of despair came from Oru, the young woman who had spoken to Cloud in her cell what seemed a lifetime ago. She ran to her father's side and beat on his chest and wept. Mirage followed her and held her, and she did not push him away. Perhaps there was hope for the boy.

The bodies were laid out along the top of the flood-ravaged hillside—first only a few. Then five. Then twenty. Many of them were guards. Then there were the survivors—some priests, some guards, some civilians, with injuries ranging from scratches and bruises to broken legs and arms or perforations from branches. Some were shaking with shock, others had inhaled debris and water and could not stop coughing. Many were unable to walk and had to be carried back on cots formed of borrowed robes and spear hafts.

Cloud set to work on those that would let her. Some would not let the hands of a heretic touch their flesh, and they were escorted by scouts to the city walls. For others, she bandaged wounds and bound breaks. She cast about vainly for her herbs and medicines, and realized she had none of them. They had all been taken from her when she entered the city—those that had not been left behind in the camp.

The camp. The thought hadn't even occurred to her until now; she was so taken aback by the miracle of the rising mountain, so grateful to have escaped certain death with all her people unharmed. But everything they owned—everything they had carried with them during the moons-long journey across the savanna—all of it would be gone. Food, water skins, knives, leathers, clothes, tools, jewelry, mementos of ancestors and lost family. All gone. Mpo might have washed away their enemies, but she had also washed away their lives. The journey back to their village would be arduous and painstaking.

Cloud would have to think about that later, though. For now, she healed the wounded Boganans as best as she could, and scouts helped them back to the city. Cloud hoped they still had healers and supplies able to tend to them. She hoped that few of them lived in the western side of the city, near the priests and wealthy, but she had an uneasy feeling many had perished in the crumbling of the cliffs. Even now an occasional loud cracking sound would come from a falling boulder or piece of a building dropping down into the great water.

"Cloud. You must come quickly."

She looked up from the Boganan whose shoulder she had just finished binding in a seaweed sling. Ant With a Leaf stood over her, looking uncomfortable. "What is it? Who is hurt?"

"It's not that. They… found the Matron."

"Alive?"

"Unhurt."

Cloud didn't know how to feel about that. She didn't want any more death or injury, but she also didn't want to see a zealot given further evidence her goddess protected her. "Take me to her."

The Matron stood, stiff-backed and stone-faced, under the shelter of a palm that had somehow managed to withstand the force of the wave. She watched with a cool contempt the people who surrounded her now. They had no weapons, of course, other than stones and broken bits of wood, but these they held at the ready as though they expected the Matron to personally lunge at them with nail and tooth.

"It's all right," Cloud said, motioning for them to lower their arms. She didn't think the Matron could be much trouble now, and besides,

Ant With a Leaf was at her side. She stepped closer to the leader of the Boganans. "Are you hurt?"

The Matron drew herself up taller, giving Cloud a calm stare. Her hair, usually pulled tight and straight, had come untied and now hung heavy and matted on her head in clumped ringlets. Her clothes were torn and ragged, the once-white cloth stained brown and dirty green. "I am fine." She kept her gaze unwavering, even when Cloud looked down at her scraped skin, the toenails missing from her feet. "What do you intend to do now?"

"What should I do?"

"Let me return to my people. They need their leader."

"As you let me return to mine?"

"You are with them, are you not?"

Cloud took a deep breath and unclenched her jaw. "You tried to kill all of us."

"I left your fate in the hands of the goddess. I am not to blame for her actions nor her edicts. Would you argue with a god?"

"We did argue with one!" Cloud snapped. "Rather successfully, don't you think?" She pointed to the mountain behind her, the one that towered over the land. "What do you think that is?"

The Matron's eyes glanced in that direction, and for a moment, unease flickered across her face. "The—the will of Mpo."

"Mpo. The *goddess of the sea* raised a mountain to stop herself from killing us."

"It is not for us to question the will of the goddess."

"She destroyed your city!" Cloud shouted.

"Then we must have deserved it."

"With all those laws? All those sculptures of stone? The temples and the prayers and the chanting and the—the sacrifices? And still you deserved it?"

Stony certainty had found its home in the Matron's composure again. "And what should we then do? Beat our chests? Curse Mpo? Defy her? Should we name ourselves stronger than a goddess who can destroy our home and kill all of us on a whim? We are not gods. You are a little person from a little people. You must know even in your heretical beliefs that when a god commands, you bury that command in your heart. You make it part of you. Part of the blood that moves through your veins. You work obedience into every movement, and prayer into every word. What other choice do we have? We are nothing compared to them."

"No." The voice came from behind Cloud.

"Quiet," said Ant With a Leaf, pulling Mirage back by one shoulder.

Cloud shook her head. "Let him talk."

Ant's eyes narrowed, but she let him go.

Mirage stepped forward. Tall, he loomed over both Cloud and the Matron, but the Boganan would not turn her gaze up to his face. "We're not nothing. We have… divinity in us."

"More heresy."

"The early Boganans didn't think so. They stored their truths about the gods below your city, carefully, in… ways I don't entirely understand, but they thought it was important! They have songs that can call to all the gods, bring their power here by—by reaching out with the part of them that's in us. In all of us! You understand? You have part of Mpo, a very little bit, inside you. And part of Ogya, and part of Sarmu. All of them. That's the secret they thought it was so important to protect. We're all a little bit divine."

She still would not look at his face, but her lip curled in disgust. "The worst kind of blasphemy."

Cloud sighed. "You love that word. I don't even know what it means."

"No, I can see that you do not. You do not realize the fate that heresy will lead you to, even though you have fled here plagued by fires and famine, seeking the help of true worshipers. How arrogant of the wretched to pass judgment on those they depend upon! Your so-called gods have failed you, and you come here to our shining city to beg succor, but still you will not hear the truth, because blasphemy has polluted your minds."

"And what is blasphemy? Why should the gods care what we think and say unless they are afraid of it?"

"You were not here during the bad years. It was Mpo who freed us, who purged us of the filth and disease of the blasphemers. She saved us and gave us edicts so that we would not be harmed again."

Cloud stared at her and then gestured wordlessly with both arms toward the crumbling city on the cliffs. As if to punctuate her point, a house hanging on the edge shifted and then, with large grey puffs of dust, collapsed inward, folding like a tent.

The Matron barely glanced in that direction. "We will rebuild it. Would I be the leader who guided her people into heresy? No. I would not shame our ancestors so. I will not usher my people back into the days of plague and disease. We will make Bogana even stronger and more beautiful.

We will work our adoration of Mpo into every wall and every street. Her laws will be carved into every doorway, every cobble. We will ink it into our own flesh if need be. She will see our renewed devotion and bless us in ways no people have been blessed before."

Cloud sighed. It was like trying to argue with the great water itself. "Do what you must. But if you're rebuilding the city anyway, you might try putting it somewhere higher up. Where Mpo's waves can't touch you. If you're looking for a spot, say, a mountain, well, we raised one for you."

She stalked off, fuming, the heat of her anger melting the exhaustion out of her bones. People were the same everywhere, weren't they? Laughing Dog, the Matron, just two people so lost in their fanciful view of the world that they couldn't see past it, couldn't change even when it hurt them, even when it turned them into monsters, even when it destroyed the people they were supposed to care about and protect. They only dug deeper, clung even harder to their own certainty.

Gods made you mad because you couldn't question them. Doubt, curiosity, questions, those were what made you whole, made you balanced. It was certainty that made you mad. That's why they needed many gods, many stories, many different ways to view the world. Even if they contradicted. Especially if they contradicted.

She was so angry, she didn't even consider where she was going until she found herself atop the ridge above the shore, not far from where the trees thickened into forest. A scout was running toward her at high speed.

"Cloud! What are you doing here? But—but oh, you need to come with me! You have to come right away!"

"Why?" she asked uneasily, wearily. The anger was beginning to burn off. She would sleep well tonight, she was sure of it.

"There's… someone you need to see." The scout's face was drawn and slack, and his eyes were wide.

"Who?"

He could barely stammer the words. "You—you won't believe me. You have to come right away. Wait. Not right away. We should have the others. Wait here."

And so she waited until he'd run off and come back with Ant With a Leaf and Basket and several of the other hunters and elders. All of them looked mystified.

The scout ran ahead, leading them toward the edge of the forest. Someone was standing there, outside the tree line, but her eyes were old and couldn't make out the features. The figure was poised strangely, as though it were not truly standing on the ground but had landed there, perched as if on a branch.

As they drew nearer, others in the group gasped, and some cried out or offered up prayers to Wem. Cloud demanded to know what it was, but people were speechless or simply shook their heads. A few turned around and headed back the way they had come.

The figure standing outside the trees came closer. It was a man, she could tell—a tall one, and athletically built, and he moved with an eerie, unnatural grace, gliding over the ground more than walking. He was hesitant though, like a rabbit venturing out of tall grass, ready to turn and run in an instant. He was naked, unadorned, his hair bushy and unbound.

The group with her had stopped, unwilling to move forward. Only Ant With a Leaf and Basket walked with her, both of them staring, their mouths open. They both looked afraid.

And finally the man drew near enough for her vision. She blinked, distrusting her own eyes, even after all the events of the day. It couldn't be. It was impossible. He was dead.

"Hello, Cloud," said Clay. "I'm so glad it's you."

# 31 Among the Embers

The bonds of fire around Laughing Dog's mind blazed one moment, and dissipated into ash the next. Ogya's hold over him was suddenly gone. The control over his body vanished, and he felt himself collapse to the earth. He could see and hear the world outside, but as though from a great distance, as though peering at it through the gaps of a darkened tent. Half of his vision was the ashen ground, and the other the burning forest. He watched the fires fueled by Ogya's divine magic dwindle and flicker. Trees that had been like giant torches a moment before, blazing with heat and light, now guttered, still on fire but with low, idle flames.

Faraway cries of alarm told him his fire hunters had seen him fall. They gathered around his prone body, calling his name, prodding him. He tried to answer but could not remember how. An animal caged for too long will not come out even if you open the door. It cannot recall how to live uncaged. Laughing Dog's body was there. He could feel his limbs and the sensations of burning embers scorching his skin, but could not recall how to respond, how to move his arms, how merely by willing it someone could tighten their vocal cords, move air through their throat, past their lips, form words, make sounds.

He felt a distant relief as his fire hunters hefted him by his limbs and lifted the weight of his body up off the pain of the embers. They called to him over and over as they carried him, swinging between them, down the hill. No, not him. They were calling to Ogya. *Ogya is gone,* he thought fiercely at them. He found a way to move his lips. "Mmm," he managed. "Mmmmah." They didn't hear him, didn't see the movement. It was all he could manage. He drifted into sleep.

When he woke, he felt that a great length of time had passed. The roof of his tent pattered with the sound of rain. His body was heavy and settled into his pallet, stiff and aching in the way bodies ache when they haven't moved in a long time. His lips were dry and chapped. He could move now, a little. His fingers twitched at his sides. His toes curled. He tried to open his mouth, but his lips were painfully stuck together. There was no hurry, he told himself. Someone must have been coming to give him water every day. He had waited this long. He could wait again.

So he lay and, honing his resolve, ventured outside that cage door in his mind. When Ogya had gone the first time, when Laughing Dog had willed—*compelled*—him out, there had been a terrible, haunting emptiness. No such emptiness now. Instead of feeling hollow and abandoned, he felt freed, able to explore, in his own time and space, the smoke-filled chambers of his psyche. Many had been ignored by Ogya. Ogya had never laughed. Never told a joke. Never embraced a fellow, never made idle chat, never slowed down to enjoy a drink, never danced, never sung, never become entranced by a good tale, never wrestled a companion for the thrill of it, never lusted, never admired another. Never wept. Never stopped to watch the sun set. All these human faculties lay dusty and unused in Laughing Dog's mind.

He missed them. He missed the way things used to be. He missed his tribe, his brothers, the routine of day to day. He did not miss Ogya.

*Because I am not gone*, hissed a voice in his mind.

No. He'd known it the whole time. Ogya was diminished, but not disappeared.

"What happened to you?" he croaked. The stuck skin of his lips tore as he spoke.

*Betrayal. Lies. Dishonor. Your brother is behind it.*

Clay? Clay was dead. So was Great Ram.

*Dead and not dead. Your brother lives. Kwaee uses him as his pawn to defeat us. I am trapped. Imprisoned. Our campaign is nearly lost.*

Laughing Dog did not respond. *He* had lost long ago, could scarcely remember why he had begun this battle against the forest god. What had set him so hard against the forest? What had made him commit body, mind, and soul, and that of his whole village, in this undertaking? Clay had been taken by the forest. Yes. That had been the first of it. And then the forest had begun attacking them, had killed his people. And then his father. Kwaee had deserved to die.

But, Laughing Dog knew, he deserved to die too. He had killed those two people in the Sahil, Abram and Sara. He had led his village to ruin. He had ordered the death of Left Rabbit, exiled all the elders, and thrown his own people's lives onto the bonfire of his own hatred. He had used his people as kindling for the wrath of Ogya. He had believed that he was strong, that his people were strong, that *humanity* was strong enough to fight the gods. He had believed it so strongly. They didn't have to be helpless, subservient, obeying every ridiculous rule and ritual invented. They could be their own people. They could fight back. They could rule themselves.

*It was a pretty dream,* Ogya hissed through his thoughts. *But a lie.*

And Laughing Dog, broken, hollowed-out, ruined, admitted finally that it was so. Compared to the power and knowledge of the gods, humans were nothing. Their lives, their wills, were not their own. They could not fight. They could not challenge. They could only obey. His defense of humanity, his determination that they could choose their own course, had been pure hubris.

*Finally you understand.*

"Yes. I see now. I… we… are nothing."

*Then you will obey.*

"I… will obey."

*Then get up.*

Under the fire god's command, Laughing Dog found he was able to move. His limbs, heavy and torpid, shifted on his pallet. He breathed deep and tasted the dank, human scent of his tent, mingled with smoke. Once it had been filled with bones and garbage from his insatiable hunger. Now, that hunger was gone, and the tent had been cleaned. Had Ogya done it? Or his fire hunters? He wasn't sure. His belongings were collected in a little pile: some braided palm fiber rope, clean leathers, his knife, his spear propped against the side of the tent, some finer garments suitable for a King. And something else, something that had belonged to Clay, once, lying in a heap.

*That is important to us now. Take it.*

He picked it up: a small, carved—or shaped, really, since it showed no knife strokes—wooden leopard on a thin loop of vine. He had taken it from Clay just before… just before Great Ram had killed him.

*Put it on.*

Obediently, he put it around his neck, and as he did so, saw his body for the first time since waking. It was unrecognizable. Pink burn scars mottled his skin. He had been healthy and fat once, but now the extra weight was gone, and his skin hung loose and wrinkled. His skinny legs trembled as he stood.

He pushed his way out of the tent and squinted in the grey afternoon light. The raindrops on his skin were cool and soothing. He turned his head up to the sky to let it run down his face. He caught raindrops on his tongue and could not remember the last time he had done so.

The village was empty. Of course, this was the old village, and most of the people had moved further west, but even so, he might have expected to see his hunters gathered around, scraping hides or sharpening spears or arrowheads or preparing meals. There was no one present. Even the tents of most of his fire hunters were gone.

So. They had abandoned him as soon as he was incapacitated. They had probably moved west with the rest of the village. Now, all that remained of their home was a mudslide. The walls were slanted and fallen, half-buried in liquid earth. The work pits were overgrown with weeds. A number of tents belonging to the exiles still remained, but without maintenance and care these had slumped and sagged like old carcasses.

He looked to the southeast, but there was no smoke of a burning forest there. All the fires had gone out.

Laughing Dog stood on the top of the hill in the pouring rain and stared down at the remains of his ruined village. His people were gone, scattered into the west. His family, all of them dead. His promised fled in hatred of him. The traditions of his people lost. His home half-drowned in toxic mud. His body scarred and ruined. He had nothing left. Nothing except the spark of a defeated god still smoking in his mind.

"King Laughing Dog," he said aloud. "King of nothing." His voice was a deep rasp. He laughed, and then the dryness of his heat-scarred throat sent him into a coughing fit. He squatted on the muddy hillside, heaving with the cough.

A hand pushed aside the flap of a nearby tent. The face of Mother's Tree appeared in the gloom within. "My King?" The big man unfolded himself from the entry of the tent, ignoring the rain that spattered his bald head. "You are awake!"

"Where—" Laughing Dog began, and another fit of coughing interrupted him again. The heat of the fires had permanently destroyed his throat, he suspected. "Where is everyone?" he rasped. "Have they given up?"

"Given up?" Mother's Tree blinked. "No, my King! But—surely you already know?"

"Know what?" Laughing Dog asked irritably. "I've been unconscious, how could I know anything?"

"But it is your great victory, we thought—we thought that was why… when you collapsed…"

Laughing Dog sighed. "The… the power of the god Ogya consumed all my attention. Assume I know of nothing that has happened since the last time we started burning again."

The big man's brows knitted in confusion, or perhaps worry, but he nodded. "We all suspected something had changed after the last time. You didn't act like yourself. You barely spoke to us except to give orders or to demand food. You… encouraged us all to work… continuously. More than many of us could manage." Somewhat timidly, he ventured, "Do you remember that?"

Laughing Dog shook his head.

"Hill in High Wind was too weary and refused you. So you… you burned him. With the fire from your hands. Only his bones were left."

Within his mind he heard a hissing, slathering sound from Ogya, like fire licking around a wet log.

"After that no one complained anymore, but Caterpillar ran off in the night. No one knows where he went. And then you were calmer and worked us not as hard. But there were only eight of us left, including you, and some of us had to hunt for food and supplies. It was a hard time, my King. And then, three days ago, you were burning a ways to the southeast. The great fire beast was with you, larger than we had ever seen it before, cutting trees with pincers, breathing flames across the canopy, and of course we all stayed away, but then suddenly it crawled back into the ground and was gone. And then, not long after that, all the fires dimmed like a flame under a pot. And you fell to the ground, my King, and could not be wakened. Your body, it… shriveled, as though cursed. You had been working so tirelessly to defeat our enemy, we all thought you were just exhausted. But then we learned the truth. You won, King Laughing Dog! You defeated the forest god!"

Laughing Dog looked toward the forest, so much of it still so near. The heads of trees bobbed in the wind and rain, though they were grey with ash and soot. "The forest still stands, I see."

"But it doesn't attack us anymore! People can go in and out with no trouble. We gathered food, wood, herbs, even hunted game, and it never moved against us. You did it, King Laughing Dog! You made Lord Kwaee back down."

*This simple man! He thinks a few months of fire could stop the god of the forest? No. Kwaee stopped attacking only because he thinks he has won. He believes he has beaten me! But we are not destroyed yet. Not while this part of me still remains uncaged. No. I can never be defeated. My hunger will never end. And you will help me feed it again, my little servant!*

Laughing Dog nodded miserably. "Yes, Lord Ogya," he said.

*Get up.*

Mother's Tree blinked at him, nonplussed. "I'm sorry, King Laughing Dog? I don't understand."

Laughing Dog ignored him and rose.

"You must come back to the village! The other fire hunters and all our people are waiting for you there! Only we didn't want to move you while you were unwell! But there is a great celebration planned now that you are recovered!"

*Out of the village and into the forest. It will not attack you. It cannot even see you.*

Obediently, Laughing Dog walked down the slope of the village, half-skidding in the mud. He went past the barren work area and the sodden field of circles where the people's tents used to sit, toward the entrance.

Mother's Tree lumbered after him anxiously. "Now? You want to leave now? But you've only just woken up! You haven't drunk or eaten anything." His voice took on a cajoling tone. "Wouldn't you like a nice meal? There is fresh boar meat."

Even the thought of food did not appeal to Laughing Dog now. The hunger of Ogya was still there, but distant, an itch that vanished when he stopped thinking about it.

*Southeast. Follow the burn.*

Laughing Dog walked out the gaping village gate—the fence was so poorly maintained that an exit was scarcely necessary—and headed for the forest.

"But King Laughing Dog, the village is back the other way. The people will want to see you." Mother's Tree slipped in the mud and fell with a grunt. He scrambled to his feet again. "My King, the burn is completed. There's no more need to… my King? Where are you going?"

"Wherever the gods tell me," Laughing Dog answered finally, to shut him up.

"But… you obey the gods now? But the People of the Savanna have no gods. We are masters of our own destiny. You taught us that."

"I taught you wrong." Laughing Dog stepped over the stone-lined edge of the forest. Though his legs were shaking, it was with weakness, not fear. No grasping branches reached for him. No vines laced around his ankles. No toxic spores exploded in his face. No thorns lashed at his skin. The forest was silent and still. "The gods are more wise and powerful than we could ever be. We are nothing compared to them. My father was right. The Teller was right. All we can do is listen and obey."

Mother's Tree caught up and grabbed his shoulder, a strong grip spinning him around. "You can't mean that, King Laughing Dog. This is… this is the dark fears of some nightmare, some terrible fever dream from your illness."

Laughing Dog twisted away and kept walking.

"But—but everyone is waiting for you back at the village. What should I tell them?"

Laughing Dog stopped. He turned and looked into the eyes of one of his people for the last time. "Tell them I'm sorry. That I led them astray. That I was wrong. Tell them to worship the gods with all their hearts. To obey. To bow down. To—"

…Clay, crouched in the savanna, so long ago, before the big eland hunt, before everything had gone wrong…

Laughing Dog choked on his grief and turned his head so that Mother's Tree would not see his tears. "To bless their spears. Goodbye, my friend."

And he walked on into the forest, leaving his fire hunter standing bewildered by the edge of their ruined village. He walked through the ash and mud coating the forest floor, walked until night fell and he could no longer see, and then he slept in a sooty hollow near the base of a pearwood. When he woke, he kept walking, ignoring the pangs of hunger and the weariness in his emaciated body. He walked into the scar they had burned through the forest and followed it, a wide, muddy grey road of death and ruin that ate its way into the green life of the forest. How could he ever have believed this was a good for his people, for the world? He wished he could take it all back now.

But there was nowhere left to go but forward, nothing left but to follow the final command of the divinity that had taken up savage residence in his soul. A god commands. You must obey.

He reached the end of the burn, the road that chewed its way toward some mystifying destination in the southeast, toward some great meal that Ogya hungered for greatly but had never divulged.

"Where now?" he asked, looking into the silent forest.

*I know the way. I saw it. The traitor imprisoned me, but not before I got a taste. I know what godflesh tastes like now. I burned the little whelps' temple. You should have heard their delicious screams. They sent it away from me, but it was still burning.*

*That was their terrible mistake. Through my flames I saw. I know where they sent it. And when we reach it, I promise you, little fire bearer, that I will finally set you free.*

"Reach what? What is it you've found?"

*A delectable meal. Something that will ease my hunger for a while. A shady little garden nestled on the side of a mountaintop, full of fruit and flowers. And a waterfall. And a stream with fish. And the hearts of two naïve little godlings who have nowhere else to run.*

# 35 Prescripture

Clay had lingered at the edge of the forest for some time, unwilling to show himself to the fire bearer wandering along the edge. Clay recognized him immediately, of course—one of the People of the Savanna, so far from home and, thankfully, not in any noticeable danger. Something terrible had certainly happened here, though—the forest was full of saltwater, a briny sting in his nose. The foliage was half-drowned, half-crushed by the impact of a now-ebbed wave, and dead fish lay among the tree trunks. Clay had never seen anything like it.

He wanted to ask the scout what had happened, and whether the people were all right, and what had become of Cloud and the others, but every time he thought about approaching the man, his chest squeezed and his skin tightened, making his fur bush out. His claws scythed out from his fingertips. There would be stones thrown. The slash of knives. The searing impact of arrows. The agony of torches put to his skin. He could not fight it. He could not force himself to step out of the forest and be vulnerable again before this human.

The man wandered up to the edge of the forest and gazed into it for a moment, his eyes searching the shade, passing right over Clay and Doto, whose camouflage concealed them even though they stood barely an arm's length away.

Doto put a paw on Clay's shoulder and sent his thoughts to him. *You do not have to go and see them. Not after what they did to you. It is all right to move on. They are not your people anymore.*

*Yes, they are,* Clay answered, giving Doto's paw a grateful squeeze. *They're where I come from. Remember what Mother Fam said. This is where my* strength *comes from. I wouldn't be who I am without them. And neither would you.*

He let his mind settle, finding his place in the forest around him, in the stillness that was there, in the throb and pulse of life that teemed all through it. He let the trees root him in the earth; he let the birds carry him on the air. He could do this. He was in control. If the people were afraid or hostile, he could flee back into the forest. And nothing they did to him now could be as terrible as the feeling of unmaking, the dreadful violation of Ogya's footstep inside his temple.

He would not become Kwaee. He would not hide away in the forest forever to nurse his pain and grief. He had seen where that path led.

The man was already leaving.

Clay stepped out of the forest, stumbling a little as his strong feline form fell away, his divine senses muted as though he'd been wrapped up in thick pelts, and then he stood in his new-skinned human form at the edge of the forest. His body trembled and he could not stop it.

"Wait," he said to the man, who nearly fell over in surprise.

~

"No," Cloud said, peering up at him. "You're not Clay, are you? You *look* like him, but you're… something imitating him. What are you?"

"Cloud, I swear to you, it's me. Ask me anything."

"Clay is dead. We all saw it."

Clay nodded. "I was killed, yes. But Doto brought me back." He extended an arm toward the forest behind him, and Doto let his camouflage fall away, eliciting gasps from the People. "This is Doto, god of the forest, and my… husband." The word tasted strange to him, but more relatable for his people than "mate" and more complete than "lover."

Several of the group had already dropped to their knees; others bowed their heads. The Teller was there too, Clay noticed, staring and murmuring silently.

"Yes," Doto said, standing as tall and regally as he could manage. "I saved Clay by giving him some of my power. And he saved me by giving me some of his. He is a god now, like me, and none of you must harm him or kill him or the forest will be very angry with you."

"You're a *god?*" Cloud said. Clay hadn't been aware that someone could roll their eyes using only their voice, but Cloud had managed it. In answer, he simply stepped backward beyond the forest wall and let his feline form assert itself again. A single step, and he felt so much safer, so much stronger, so much more at home.

More gasps came from the group, along with startled cries, and those who had got to their feet began to bow down again.

But Ant With a Leaf only snorted. "Of *course* this would happen to *you*. You were a sanctimonious little twit before, and now you're going to be absolutely insufferable."

And just like that, the reverence and tension snapped. Everyone looked aghast at Ant With a Leaf, but Clay had to hide a smile. If Ant could be her old self around him, then everything was going to be all right. With more ease this time, he stepped out of the forest, and this time Doto followed him, scowling at the discomfort of being human, squinting in the light outside the forest.

Clay had to fight a surge of panic when, this time, the people came closer, clustering around him, their human hands reaching toward him. His fur bristled, and his claws came out. His stomach lurched, and he turned to dive for the forest. No knives, he told himself. No spears. No fire. They won't hurt you. They won't hurt you. He tried to make himself believe it, but the fear surged over his thoughts, drowning his control. And then Cloud put her arms around him and embraced him, and he knew her touch, knew it from before everything else that had happened. Hers had been the first hand ever to touch his body, taking him from his mother. Her wrinkled, rough fingers pushed under the layers of fear and panic to find the man beneath. They brushed away memories of pain. They reminded him who he was. He was Clay, of the People of the Savanna. He was with his people, and they loved him.

And when Cloud's bony arms were around his shoulders and her head right next to hers, she whispered into his ear, "You do know you're both very naked, don't you?"

~

They sat near the forest for some time as Clay told his people of everything that had happened since his execution at Great Ram's hands. The people stared with wonder as he spoke of meeting ancient gods, traveling into the bowels of the earth to find Mother Fam, and sealing Ogya inside his prison. The Teller was especially rapt, barely able to contain himself with excitement, and he peppered Clay with questions the whole time. After a while, Doto relaxed around the people enough to feel comfortable correcting Clay about certain details or adding a boast or sardonic observation of his own.

As he answered questions and continued his recounting of events, though, Clay began to feel uncomfortable. The Teller's expression was so avid. When they'd talked before, he'd been jocular and evasive, his tales leading down unexpected side trails, his questions meant to lure you into questioning yourself. But now all his queries were direct—what did Mother Fam look like? Was Atekye cheerful? How big was Asubonten? He wanted details he didn't intend to question.

And Clay thought back to all the council fires. "My people," the Teller would cry, "would you hear the tale of the broken crocodile teeth?" Or, "Would you hear of the oven of the gods?" Or, "Would you hear of the day the moon rose into the heavens?" And the people would call back, "We would hear it."

But now, Clay knew with uncomfortable certainty, there would be a new council fire, and the Teller would call out, "My people, would you hear the tale of the gods and the great bargain?" Or worse, "Would you hear of the forest gods Clay and Doto and how they imprisoned the god of fire?" And the people would call back, "We would hear it."

And then the tales he was telling now, only half-considered, ill-rehearsed, would be spoken, every word familiar to those who listened. The people would move their lips to the words and call out their favorite parts; the Teller would leave out an important but favorite bit to make the children protest. The children. They would learn the stories by heart, they would make them part of their spirit, and they would grow up and teach their children those stories too. And generations would remember them. They would become the stories of their ancestors, sacred tales of the old world and the gods.

Once even the old stories Clay had learned as a child had been new, and those were not true either. At best they were a version of the truth, but they had led people astray. Laughing Dog had seen through them, seen the inherent lies that everyone believed, and felt so angry and betrayed by them that he had turned against the gods themselves and rekindled an ancient conflict.

And some young person in the future would hear a version of the story of Clay and Doto, some imperfect, unhelpful account of events long past, and call them lies, and turn against their own people. Gods, faith, religion, it was all a cycle, a moving beacon of truth that was only helpful for a while.

The sun rose and set, and overhead, it lit things clearly, but in the evening it stretched shadows and tricked the eyes, and then night would fall. Truth and the sunlight, rising and setting, illuminating the world, warping it, leaving it in darkness.

What was it the Teller used to say? *The story of ourselves is always a lie and always true. Only when we know both the truth and the lie can we be happy.*

But it was a cycle that Clay did not know how to break. What could he say now that would do it? "Don't believe everything I say?" But then nothing he said would be truly helpful. The People needed to know the truth as best as he could see it. They needed to understand that the gods were flawed and dangerous. They needed to understand what they had inside them that made them, in their own way, greater than the gods. He couldn't hide it. Not the deceptions or hunger of Ogya. Not the jealousy and insecurity of Kwaee. Not the delicate balances of power that ruled the gods, nor the great bargain they had made with the people. To hide it would only make that sun set earlier and make the night of bad religion last longer.

All he could do was speak his truth as clearly as he understood it and trust the People to figure things out on their own.

"So the forest is safe for us again?" Ant With a Leaf asked when he had finished his story.

"Yes. Kwaee has agreed that he will not attack fire bearers anymore. It should be safe to return to the village, if you wish."

Cloud scowled. "Little good that will do us if our people are still set on burning everything to the ground."

"We don't think they are," Clay said. "When Ogya was safely imprisoned, we… we felt most of the fires go out. They haven't set new ones."

"You *felt* them go out?" Cloud asked in an amazed voice.

Doto stared down at her. "We are forest gods. Do you find that difficult to understand?" He leaned toward Clay and muttered in god-tongue, "I don't remember you being this stupid when you were a mortal."

Clay answered in the same language, "She is not stupid. She is the wisest person I know, excepting perhaps the Teller. But she knows me as Clay. It may be a difficult adjustment for her. It was for me, if you recall."

Doto rolled his eyes. "Oh, I recall." He retreated behind the forest wall so that he could lurk there in cat form.

Clay noticed that everyone was staring at him. He smiled, abashed. "Sorry. I was explaining to Doto, in—never mind. Yes, we can feel what happens in the forest. Sometimes too much. But if my brother is still King, I don't think he is leading the fire hunters anymore. At least not to burn the forest. If you wanted to go back—"

"We cannot return anyway," Ant With a Leaf said, folding her arms. "All of our food and supplies are gone. We would never survive the trip."

"But of course, you haven't told me what happened to all of you. What happened in Bogana? Kwaee told us that Mpo was very piqued. He said the forest here was flooded, and we can smell the brine. Is everyone all right?"

"No," Cloud said, shortly. "Our visit to Bogana was terrible. We lost Firefly. Bad Water and Buffalo Tail, too. Murdered by the ruler of that city."

Clay bared his teeth in an unconscious snarl and then realized what he was doing. "You must tell me everything," he said.

And so he listened, by degrees fascinated, worried, furious, fearful, and amazed as Cloud related the events that had befallen them in their journey from the village to the city of Bogana, their meeting with the Matron, the sacrifice to Mpo, their captivity, release, and final encounter in which they called up the mountain of the forgotten god, Bew, whom Doto claimed to have heard of, long ago.

"But this is incredible!" Clay said. "These must be the same rituals used by early fire bearers after the great bargain with the gods. Just as Mother Fam showed us. Fire bearers used to be able to call up a forest or sing down a swamp by performing the right dances. I suppose all of that knowledge was lost long ago."

"I wonder why," mused the Teller. "How could any people lose knowledge of such power?"

"Likely the gods had something to do with that," Doto said darkly from the forest edge. "Gods do not enjoy having their territory taken away from them. If fire bearers tried to do that to me, I would find a way to make them forget how."

The Teller looked very interested at this comment. Clay wondered how that little detail would feature into future stories. Perhaps some warning that this new power must not be used indiscriminately lest it anger the gods.

"So you have your own part of the forest too, Doto?" Cloud asked. "And—and that must mean that Clay does as well?"

"Yes, of course—" Doto began, but Clay interrupted.

"Only a little. Enough for our temple. It's deep in the forest."

"And you are not allowed to see it," Doto added sternly. "It is very private."

Clay sighed. "Kwaee has given us only enough of the forest to keep our temple. All the rest belongs to him, except for little spots here and there that Doto and I danced to each other."

"Wait a moment," said the Teller. "You both have dances, too? So… we could sing a song of praise to—to *Clay?* And then change the land to become *his* forest?"

Ant With a Leaf put her head in her hands. "No. No, by all that is sacred, we are *not* going to sing a song praising *Clay*."

Doto was warming to Ant With a Leaf. He gave her an approving nod. "That is what I said too, but it was necessary. And now I am glad I did it. Although of course you would need to praise his divine name, which is Doté."

The Teller repeated all this to himself under his breath. He seemed enthralled, but Ant looked as though she was going to be physically ill. Clay fought the urge to giggle.

"Anyway," he added, "you shouldn't go around using those songs. We only just got Kwaee on our side again, and if we go around taking bits of his forest away so soon, it will only antagonize him."

"You must teach them to us anyway," the Teller said. "We need to know the songs of all the gods, and we must find ways not to forget them again. All the tragedy that might have been avoided if we had used these songs! So this knowledge must be preserved forever this time."

"Of course, for the major gods," Clay said, feeling a little uncomfortable. "But Doto and I don't need—"

"*All* the gods," the Teller repeated. "It is not for you to decide what we need to know about the gods. You see? Already you want a little of the knowledge to be lost. You want us not to carry it forward. And you wonder how it could have been forgotten before. These stories and songs must be ours, Doté. They belong to humans."

Clay flinched at the use of his other name—the one that made him different, separate. "But—but all right, when I go into the forest I change, but out here, look at me, I'm human."

The Teller's gaze was steady and calm. "You think you look human to us?"

"Of course!" Clay looked down at his arms, his body. It was all fire bearer, all the way to the baby-soft soles of his feet. Sure, it might be unscarred and unweathered, but every part of him was fire bearer. If you cut him, he would bleed like any other.

And then plant life would sprout from the drops of blood. Vines and berry bushes and red-capped mushrooms from each droplet. And if he bled enough, he would not die, no, he would return again and again.

He looked up to see the shifting, uncomfortable eyes of the People of the Savanna. No one would meet his gaze directly.

"You wear humanity about you like a costume," the Teller said in a gentle voice. "But it's all poise and imitation. Humans move about more than you do. They sag and slouch. They lean. They blink. Their movements are easy, lazy, practiced. You… don't do these things."

Clay *felt* human. He certainly could grow hungry or tired. He didn't have his divine senses nor the incredible strength and speed his forest form possessed. And even here the roughness of the ground outside the forest pained his uncalloused feet. But he didn't favor the sore spots or step gingerly; he ignored the pain. And now that he thought of it, everyone among the people stood shorter than he recalled. Ant With a Leaf had been taller than him once, hadn't she?

No wonder, then, that the other villagers had killed him over and over. He had resembled his own self, had thought he looked the same, but he had been *something else*, some unknown thing that had come out of the forest wearing a dead man's skin. Something that had known how to seem human but only on a superficial level. Something that stood and walked and moved in uncanny description. Something that sprouted the standards of the enemy from its blood.

And they *had* cut him. They had bled him. They had burned him. Not these particular fire bearers, but others, and no matter how much he tried to find the peace inside him, it still mattered. More than godhood, that had changed him. Human eyes looked alien to him—not filled with hatred and cruelty at the moment, but so capable of adopting their shapes. Even now, among his people, he felt wary, ready to bush out his fur, scratch, flee.

"I'm still a fire bearer where it counts," he said, and realized then that he hadn't said "human."

Cloud came closer, smiling gently. She took his hand and squeezed it. Her fingers were gnarled and bony, the skin rough with life. Again Clay almost wept at the contact. The last fire bearer to touch him had been his brother, just before slitting his throat. "I believe you are, Clay. But your change could mean a lot to us. More than a lost prince, the People of the Savanna could use a god on their side. Could you and your—could you and Doto remain in your… other forms and perhaps conceal yourself for a while? There is someone I want to meet you."

Clay agreed, relieved to remain in his realm again for a time.

Doto stretched lazily, watching the People of the Savanna leave. "I can see that made you uncomfortable. I do not blame you. They did not kill you this time, and I am very glad of that. But they were not respectful or worshipful at all when meeting gods."

"No, and *I'm* glad of *that*," Clay answered. "It would have felt terrible if they were falling all over themselves. But they still treated me different."

"You *are* different."

"I wish it could be the same. I wish that… I don't know, that we could go and live with them, at least for a while, and I could show you what it's like to be a fire bearer."

"I would not care for it," Doto declared. "They are very smelly. And I would not like to live outside the forest for very long. We could dance a circle to each other in the village, perhaps, and—"

"No, that would be missing the whole point." Clay sighed. "I want to get up before dawn for a hunt with my limbs stiff and the sleep sand in my eyes. I want to stay up late around the fire until I stink of smoke and my head aches from too much palm wine. I want to feel how soft and welcoming my pallet is after a day of hard work, and to remember how much better food tastes when I'm hungry. I want cool rain on my face in the middle of a hot day. I want to spend a week making a gift for a friend. I want to blush from embarrassment and—and say something stupid and feel guilty about it later. I want to cry because I haven't in a long time and it feels good. I want to need things again. I want to sit among a group of friends and not have them all staring at me like I descended from the stars, but just be one of them. Belong."

"Well, I am sorry about that," Doto said, sounding a little bemused. "But you have to be a god instead."

After some time, their ears perked toward the sound of the fire bearers returning, and so they faded into the forest to wait. There were many more of them—nearly a third of the village. So many faces that Clay recognized, with the ache of nostalgia. And among them, other people, dressed in strange clothing. He supposed they must be Boganans.

At the head of the group was Cloud, marching with authority, her head held high, and guiding at her side another woman, this one not so old as Cloud but possessed of as much natural bearing. Her face was expressionless but for the creases of a long and very stern life. She did not look around but kept her gaze steady and distant, like someone who knows the future is out of her hands and who does not expect it to be pleasant.

Still, she slowed a bit as Cloud led her toward the forest, pressing back against the firm pressure of Ant With a Leaf's hand on her shoulder. "You intend to push me in there?" she said. "You will sacrifice me to your so-called forest god, then?"

"Oh, stop being so dramatic," Cloud said, and stepped beyond the boundary of the forest.

The other woman had no opportunity to protest as Ant propelled her after Cloud with a decisive push. She cringed as though awaiting attack, but of course, none came. Clay thought he could feel, far away, the eyes of Kwaee on his throne, watching the scene with interest.

"Matron of Bogana," Cloud said in a formal tone of voice, "I introduce you to Doto and Doté, gods of the forest."

Clay and Doto stood before the Matron and let their camouflage fall away. The woman let out a half-yelp and stumbled backward, and would have fallen over, but Clay quickly bent tendrils of nearby plants to catch her, coiling them around her waist, back, and legs and setting her upright again. She swatted at them in a vague panic, as she might have tried to brush away fire ants.

Other startled cries came from the new people in the group, who had not known what to expect. Murmurs passed between them, some in plainstongue, and others in a language that Clay did not recognize or understand. But the sounds were *almost* familiar, like the name of a person or place he had forgotten but was still buried in his memory somewhere. He twitched his ears toward the foreign words, and as he listened, they twisted in his understanding until they almost made sense.

The Boganan woman recovered her composure, though fear still glimmered in her eyes. "Lady Mpo says there are no other gods," she muttered in accented plainstongue, staring fiercely at the ground.

Clay stepped toward her, his tail swaying, and crouched down to meet her gaze. "Well, you can't believe everything a god says," he told her. "Some of them are terrible liars."

A giggle came from somewhere in the group of people. He thought he saw, for a moment, a pair of large, furry ear tips moving among them, but no, there was only the crowd.

"You speak blasphemy," the woman said in a strained voice.

"Well, maybe," Clay agreed. "But just because something's blasphemy doesn't mean it's not true." He enjoyed seeing the Teller start at that comment. Again the mutters went through the crowd; someone was translating his words to the Boganans in the group, and as they did so, he saw the sense behind them, the natural order of their language. Of course *this* word in plainstongue would mean *that* word in Boganan. All the inscrutable meanings of their language fell into place.

He tried their language on his tongue and liked the taste of it. "My friend Cloud tells me that you have been very unkind to my people," he said in Boganan. *My people.* The phrase meant something else now, didn't it? "They tell me that you killed Firefly and Bad Water and Buffalo Tail. That you murdered them. And you would have sacrificed them all to Mpo."

The Matron cringed, but she lifted her gaze, flinty defiance in her brown eyes. "I can't be sorry for what I've done," she said.

Doto's ears perked in curiosity. "Why can't you? What has happened?"

"She means she won't," Clay muttered.

"I cannot," the Matron repeated stubbornly. "My actions were decreed by Mpo. It was she who ruled how the city should be run. She gave us laws and demanded sacrifices. We cannot disobey the commands of our gods."

"Of course you can," Doto said, frowning. "You fire bearers do it all the time."

Clay added, "You just didn't choose to disobey when it came to things like murdering people."

"I have never disobeyed a command from a god," the Matron said. She still sounded defiant, but a tremble shook through her. "Not one clearly given."

Clay gave Doto a sidelong look, sending him a silent thought. "Well… *we* are gods," he said. "Remain standing."

And at the same time, Doto commanded, "Kneel before us."

The Matron jerked as though someone had bumped into her from behind, lowering as though she intended to kneel, but pausing halfway.

"Ah, so she prefers obeying me to you," Clay said to Doto.

Doto bared his fangs in feigned ferocity. "You have made a powerful enemy this day."

The Matron's face darkened. She was still staring at the ground. "You seek to mock me."

Clay sighed. "I only want to give example. You heard conflicting orders from the gods, and you *chose*. And that means the choice was always yours. The gods… I know a few of them. They're not perfect. They make bad decisions. Bad commands. They contradict each other all the time."

"And yet we are nothing before Mp—before them," the Matron said in the pious tones of someone reciting words of faith. "Who are we to question their wisdom and judgment? We are as gnats before—"

Clay interrupted. "You're fire bearers; you're *humans*. You're godkin. You have a divine spark in you. All these other Boganans with you, they chose to fight back. They chose to reject orders that were cruel and evil. You had that same choice and you didn't take it. You took that spark and lit something terrible with it, because you wanted to, because some mad goddess gave you permission to. So you *could* be sorry for what you've done; you just won't."

She lifted her face to them finally, staring into their eyes each by turn. A tempest stirred the expressions on her face. Then the dull glint of fervor returned to her eyes. "You are not true gods," she sneered. "You are demons sent to test my faith. But you will not find it wanting. I have seen true power. True divinity. And compared to it, you two are mere beasts crawling in the dirt. I have seen the face of the One True Goddess, and I will not forget it. Do what you want with me. She will not find my devotion lacking."

Clay sighed. "You know, I am getting really tired of everyone assuming we're demons. Where did everyone get the idea of demons to begin with? They aren't even real."

One of the other Boganans came forward, an elderly man with a large, bushy beard. "What do you wish us to do with her, Lord Doté, Lord Doto?"

Clay shuddered. *Don't call me Lord,* he thought. But if he said it, would that become some element of further dogma down the road? Maybe this whole encounter would be the source of arguing scholars, or even a battle between two tribes of people who disagreed about what the gods *really* meant by all that, and shouldn't we prioritize the words of Lord Doto over those of Doté, who had claimed not to be a Lord?

Every word, every action, could have repercussions that would impact these people's lives for generations. He didn't want this responsibility.

But he had it anyway, and he needed to speak up now because Doto was opening his mouth and doubtless about to say something imperious and damaging.

"You have to decide for yourselves," he said. "The gods can't—well, they *shouldn't* do that for you." And then, realizing that he did have a chance to do some small good, added, "But no killing."

Doto nodded. "Killing greatly displeases Lord Doté, trust me. And if Lord Doté is displeased, then… it feels bad."

The Boganans looked among each other, bewildered. "What feels bad, Lord Doto?"

"It. Me. Us. The forest."

Clay cringed, already imagining the lines in the story. Do not displease Doté or the forest will grow unhappy with you. One way or another, the stories would happen.

"And how do we know what displeases Lord Doté, Lord Doto?" came a tremulous voice from the crowd.

"Ah. I am very pleased that you asked this question. I have a song that will explain everything about him."

Doto didn't really understand why Clay was so apprehensive about having his people learn the song of praise. It was a little hurtful, after he had composed one so brilliantly written and accurate. And why should Clay not want to see those people he favored most in the world dancing around him and singing the songs of praise he was due? But when Doto suggested this might be a good idea, Clay got very quiet and withdrawn and then he had to go back into the forest and sit alone for a while.

While he was gone, Doto took it upon himself to teach all the fire bearers the song of Doté, first in the language of Clay's people, and then in the language of the sea people. And then, once he judged that they had learned it successfully, he taught them the song Clay had invented for him. Whatever difficulties Clay was having with this, they were both new gods and needed all the worshipers they could get.

These were the first fire bearers that Doto had met other than Clay, Laughing Dog, and the two nasty ones that had captured them long ago, and he decided that, in general, he liked them. They were nothing like the terrible monsters his father had conjured up to terrify him throughout his childhood, though they were a bit smelly and liked wearing pieces of animal. While Doto had been forced to do this recently when traveling through the cold weather, he could not fathom the reason for it when no protection was required. Perhaps they enjoyed decorating themselves since they had no temples to craft.

They reminded him of Clay—in the way they spoke, laughed, gestured with their hands, the expressions of their faces, and their general awe around him, which he appreciated. Also, they were very curious and asked many questions, and learned things very quickly, especially the elderly, fat one they called the Teller, and the small cub at his side. Doto was pleased to answer his questions and give him a great deal of information on the forest and life and death and the gods.

The one they called the Matron, the one who had done so many terrible things in the story they had heard, did not ask any questions. She stood to one side, scowling at the ground, but Doto could tell that she was listening, too.

Clay came back after a little while, and if there were dark streaks in the fur beneath his eyes, they vanished when he stepped out of the forest and into his fire bearer form again. He told everyone that he'd missed them, and he insisted on moving among all the people to greet and talk to each one of them, which took some time because there were so many.

The fire bearers smiled a lot when they talked to him. They told him of their lives and their relatives and children and how things had been in the village since he left. They talked about his father and brothers and how sad they had been about everything. Many assured him in strong tones that they had never believed the lies that he was a demon. They told him about the hardships of their journey and captivity in Bogana. They told him that they were proud of him, that they loved him and missed him.

And it all seemed friendly and genial. But Doto could see the awe and fear in their eyes. They knew that Clay was not one of them anymore. They kept saying how tall he was now, how different. None of them ever argued with him or disagreed; whatever he said was met with hasty enthusiasm. Some would stare endlessly into his face and babble on and on meaninglessly. Others would stammer. Clay noticed it too; as he moved through the group a shadow fell across his countenance.

"A bonfire!" he exclaimed at last. "We should have one last council fire and feast!"

"But Clay," one of the fire bearers interjected, "we've lost everything. We have no food to prepare, and no tools to prepare it. There are no caterpillars or nuts or seeds, no game or fruit or vegetables. We would need knives and other tools, gourds and fresh water and wood for the fire."

Clay looked in Doto's direction. "Well, we *are* forest gods. That has to be good for something."

"Yes," Doto answered, feeling a little bewildered. "It is good for living forever and being strong and fast and being able to create life and nurture the forest and protect it and also imprisoning Ogya and saving the life of someone that you love."

Clay blinked at him. "Y—yes, of course, but—but *also* good for growing food, making tools, and gathering game and firewood, yes? We could do that for everyone."

"Yes, all those things would be very easy," Doto agreed.

And so they did. They asked the people what they wanted, taking requests from everyone, and then grew a wide variety of food plants—many fruits, including figs and dates, but also bushes with starchy roots, melons and gourds, palms for oil and wine, and a patch of high, seeded grains. They called forest pigs and deer to their glen and slaughtered them painlessly, following Clay's instructions for how to gut and drain them so that the blood would not sour in the veins. This was something that was never a problem for Doto, but it seemed fire bearers were choosy about flavors, even if it was a waste of a lot of good blood. And Doto thought about the hog he had found long ago, dying in the forest, the stone tooth broken off in its body. How terrible the fire bearers had seemed then.

Now he and Clay made tools for the fire bearers, shaping them out of dense, hard blackwood and treating them with resin to make them last. They gave the fire bearers wooden knives so sharp and shiny that once people had tested the first few, everyone wanted one. They made bowls and awls and needles, and Clay even elected to shape a variety of beads out of brightly colored wood.

The firewood was the simplest to create, since Doto did not have to be taught what its shape should be nor try to understand what plant one of the fire bearers was describing. He simply had to select a few larger trees and fell them, drain the water from them to make them burn more easily, and then separate them into manageable chunks so that the creatures could construct their fire. This task, however, he found the most distasteful. He did not enjoy felling the giants of the forest merely so that the fire bearers could commit them to Ogya.

Then they assisted the fire bearers in preparing the food; a meal that they claimed would have taken many hours to prepare took Clay and Doto far less time, for the forest moved to their will. Hard wooden blades could slice and scrape, trunks could crush and mash, plant fiber could sift, all far more rapidly than the fire bearers could with their fleshy hands and tools.

This too felt wrong to Doto, and as he worked, he sent his thoughts to Clay. *This is not what we should be doing. The forest should not be used for this. We are gods of the forest, and we should uphold its ways. Not twist it to the ways of fire bearers.*

*I know*, Clay sent back. *It doesn't feel right to me either. But we can't let them go hungry. That's wrong, too. Gods ruined their lives, their village. It's only fair that gods put things right again.*

*One time. But after this, no more of this moving the forest around to do the work of fire bearers. Their world and ours must be separate. Yes?*

Clay did not answer, but the shadow across his face deepened. Doto thought he knew what he was thinking. He wanted to stay with them. He felt that he was one of them, still. Even after everything that had happened, he still couldn't let go. Doto wasn't afraid Clay would leave him; Clay had promised he would always come back to Doto. And besides, the lure and the comfort of the forest was too strong. His home was there now, whether he understood it or not. His heart, his temple was there.

But what if he couldn't leave his people, either? What if he couldn't let go? Doto had often wrestled with this fear, but this was the first time he had seen Clay among his people first-hand, the first time he truly understood. Through his whole journey through the forest and savanna, Clay had never stopped speaking of them, yearning to return to them. No matter the suffering, no matter how many times he had been killed for their sakes, he had never given up trying to fight for them. And now, finally, he was among them again, and they were safe. Who could leave behind so many people who loved him for one small forest god?

~

The council fire blazed high, and it was hard for Clay not to search for traces of Ogya's figure in the flames. It had been a long time since he'd felt so hot or so full of good food. He suspected that the People had offered the choicest and largest portions to him and Doto. With Doto, at least, it was appropriate, since he was a guest, and hospitality demanded such generosity, but Clay hoped he was not considered a guest as well. More than that, he hoped they didn't consider this feast a sacrifice to visiting gods. Perhaps it was simply because he and Doto had provided nearly all the food. That was an explanation he could live with.

And his belly was taut to the point of discomfort. He half-considered sneaking back into the forest to allow his other form to deal with it more comfortably but stopped himself. That wasn't right. That wasn't human. Humans had to tolerate discomfort, especially when it derived from their own foolish choices and indulgences. You had to live with all the parts of life, the good and the bad. To be able to make all the little discomforts of the world go away whenever you wanted to, that was both more and less than human.

He could have done it. And he chose not to. But even having the choice set him apart from them.

He sat next to Doto, as close to the fire as Doto would tolerate. And then he had to put up with snorts and wrinkling of the nose and complaints about the heat and the stinging of eyes and the stench. Doto was never going to like fire. He had enjoyed the food, though.

No one sat very close to them, and every time Clay scanned the crowd, he caught people staring at them. Now, though, he was drunk enough not to care. He hadn't had *that* much palm wine, but this freshly made fire bearer body didn't have much resistance to it, and a couple of calabash servings had sent the world into a slow but pleasant spin.

Doto had had a bit as well and had quite taken to it; when he wasn't grousing about the fire or some other fire bearer custom he found silly, he kept nosing and pawing at Clay in a decidedly amorous fashion, and didn't seem to understand that rolling around rutting in front of everyone would be indecorous to say the least.

"We *are* gods," he reminded Clay for what must have been the ten-thousandth time in Clay's life. "If we do it, then it must be right. And then—and then *they* will have to change because they saw us doing it. Besides—" And here he paused for a long, drawn-out belch. "Besides, it's nature's way. All animals… all animals…" He scowled. "Why does that tree juice make everyone stupid except me?"

Clay patted him on the shoulder. If any of Doto's libidinous suggestions had been appealing, the thought of all of the People of the Savanna following suit and descending into an orgy around the council fire burned them right out of his mind. It was bad enough in the forest, when all the animals and plants did it, affected by their power.

"I think if they did that tonight, they'd never worship either of us again," he whispered to Doto. "Except in certain more secretive circles, maybe."

The Teller made his way into the ring of people surrounding the fire. He was limping, still. He raised his arms. "People of the Savanna! Honored guests from Bogana! Welcome to our council fire! Tonight is a night of celebration! Of feasting and drinking and dancing! We have much to celebrate. For yesterday, we lived in fear of three gods! Lady Mpo the Wrathful, who would have swept us away in the great water! Lord Kwaee the Spurned, who would have punished all mankind for our unfaithfulness! And Lord Ogya the Hungry, who wished to devour us all! Yesterday we ran! Yesterday we cowered! Yesterday we had no hope! And today? Do we run?"

"No!" the crowd shouted at the top of their lungs. Clay shouted with them, and Doto gave him a bemused frown.

"Do we cower?"

"No!"

"Do we have hope?"

"We have hope!" the people chorused, except for the ones who were confused about what to say next and shouted, "Yes!"

"Three gods, three! Once enemies of the People of the Savanna! Once angry with us! And now, Lady Mpo the Wrathful has withdrawn into her sea, repelled by the power of Lord Bew the Mountain god, Lord Bew the Lost, who will forever be remembered and recalled by the People, so that once more he may walk the high places and bless the faithful! Lord Kwaee has forgiven the People and given us leave to walk under the shade of his branches and through his still glens, where food is abundant, and the water never stops flowing! And Lord Ogya has been shut away forever by the bravery and valiance of the forest god Lord Doto, and his lover, one of our own people, Prince Clay, Lord Doté the Compassionate, ascended to godhood as reward for his kindness and generosity."

And there it is, thought Clay. Little inaccuracies, little exaggerations. This is how it starts. One day the name Clay would be forgotten, and there would be wild and ranging fictions told about Lord Doté of the forest.

"What story would you hear tonight, my people?"

Shouts rang up from all around the fire, suggestions of old favorites mixed with nearly forgotten, esoteric tales. Then the cry went up for the tale of Doto and Doté and how they won the clemency of Kwaee and the imprisonment of Ogya.

The Teller beamed and drew himself up to his full height. "Perhaps then we should ask our honored guests, for we will all remember this night, will we not, my people? We People of the Savanna are blessed beyond measure, privileged more than any in a thousand rains, for we have two gods here tonight!"

Clay could feel himself crawling backward into the ground as the Teller approached. *Guests*. Not one of the People. Not anymore.

The Teller bowed low. "What do you say, oh lords of the forest? Would you hear the tale of your own triumphs?" And as he bowed, he looked up at Clay and winked.

The rising tension melted out of Clay's bones. "I think we may already know that one," he managed, and the crowd exploded in laughter.

"Ah, our guest prefers a tale he has not heard? Then we have a special treat for you tonight, for also gracing our council fire is Elder Tobosu of Bogana, and he has a new tale you have not heard. This is the tale of Bogana and the Lost Cave of All Gods, and there will be a surprise guest in this story, I promise you that!"

An older man than the Teller, older than Cloud, got to his feet and began to tell, in thickly accented plainstongue, about a Bogana of long ago, and a people who worshiped all gods, and secret caves beneath the city full of temples, where priests practiced their hymns of praise to all the gods of the world, and called their magic into being. Clay was growing a bit drowsy with wine by the middle of the story, which, being new, had no call-and-response from the people around the fire yet.

But in the middle of the story, the old man mentioned a name familiar to Clay: Two Broken Hands, a woman cast out by a city already comfortable with sacrifice, but which could even then not abide her cruelty. And she fled not empty-handed, but with a young son. She disappeared, never to be seen again by any in Bogana, but one day her grandson returned and brought with him the secret to the lost temples.

Mirage.

Clay certainly knew that name. And he followed the people's stares around the fire until he found the face he recognized. Only a boy when Clay had first been taken from the village, but now a young man, sitting toward the back of the group, his expression guarded. Clay bared his teeth instinctively; Mirage had been one of Laughing Dog's fire hunters, and fiercely loyal to him. And if the gossip Clay had heard from other villagers was true, Mirage had done something terrible: he had killed poor, sweet Left Rabbit.

Clay wanted to leap to his feet, to demand that Mirage be expelled from the council and exiled from the People, that he justly be sent to wander the sahil for all his days in punishment for the crime he had committed. In a fit of drunken certainty, he stood.

A ripple of whispers and movement went through the crowd, like a breeze through a glen. Everyone turned to look at him. The elder's story faltered.

"I—" Clay began. He could do it, now. He could condemn Mirage. And it wouldn't be the words of an angry, hurt boy. It would be the words of a god. Whatever chance Mirage had to know peace or to find a way back to himself and his people would be gone. Not because of a judgment of a council of elders. Because of Clay.

"I—" Everyone was staring at him. They had to know why he stood up. Surely they could see the anger on his face. Maybe that would be enough. Maybe everyone's belief in him, in his divinity, could make this moment change everything for a people for a thousand years. Mirage would become part of another story, one that condemned all killers without any room for nuance or understanding, one that could start a new dogma, light a new fire.

And what right had Clay? His own mate, Doto, had killed a man. He had slaughtered Ulu in fury and righteous vengeance. Clay had not condemned Doto. He had told him to be better. And Doto had.

"I need to make water," he managed weakly, and stumbled away from the council fire amid a round of uneasy laughter.

He found his way to the edge of the forest easily and stood outside it, unwilling to go in and have the mantle of godhood fall around his shoulders again. Instead he leaned against a tree and looked down across the landscape. The nights weren't as dark as they'd once been. The bonfire was a bright orange flower in the distance.

Someone had followed him from the fire and picked their way awkwardly up the slope, tripping every now and then over roots and stones. When the person drew closer, Clay saw that it was Mirage. He bristled at the sight. What did he want?

The young fire bearer stopped a little distance away. "Clay," he started. "L—Lord Doté?"

"Clay."

"When you stood up at the council fire, I thought you were going to punish me."

Clay said nothing.

"Maybe have me killed? Maybe just… exile me?"

The distant sound of cheers came from the fire.

"I'm sorry about… what I did to Left Rabbit."

"Why did you?"

"I don't know! I keep thinking back to that moment, when King—when your brother told me to, and I—I just *did* it. I wanted to show I was loyal, I guess. Show I believed in what he was doing. I didn't understand. I thought he was right. About… about fighting the forest. Fighting the gods. It was a beast from the forest that killed my grandmother, and I was tired of feeling helpless. And Laughing Dog said we could fight back. I didn't know how wrong he was."

Clay sighed. "He wasn't wrong."

A puzzled silence. "But… but yes he was, he—"

"How he did it was wrong. That's my brother. Being right makes him awful. But he was right, and I was wrong. We shouldn't blindly obey the gods. If they're cruel or unjust, we shouldn't bow and grovel, we should… well, not fight them, but find other gods to worship. Better ones. No god deserves unthinking obedience."

Mirage kicked at the dirt. "That's a strange thing to hear from a god."

"I'm not a—" Clay paused. The denial was so easy. So instinctive. He needed it, he needed to feel that his past wasn't gone.

"You are, though. I guess you can't see it, but the rest of us can. Do you not understand how amazing everything you did today is? You gave us all food and supplies in… in no time. We would be starving tonight. And everyone listens to you. They'd do whatever you said."

Clay watched him for an uneasy moment. "Even forgive you." That was part of all the old stories of criminals and murderers. They were either unrepentant, and punished, or they were remorseful, and graciously forgiven by the gods. Clay had never found either outcome satisfactory.

"Yes. They would. And that's the reason I came up here."

"You want me to go down there and forgive you for killing Left Rabbit? In front of everyone?"

"No!" Mirage shouted. He rubbed at his head. "I mean, after you didn't punish me, and everyone was calling you 'the Compassionate,' I… I was afraid you might. I thought you might come back down and tell everyone to forget about it, that, I don't know, the gods should be more forgiving, and people should too, and that maybe I deserved a second chance."

"Don't you?"

"Not from a god. It shouldn't be that easy, should it? What I did—it doesn't go away just because a god says it's all right. It doesn't bring Left Rabbit back, does it? Unless that's something you can do?"

"No."

"So you can't make it go away. And saying I'm forgiven doesn't change it. It doesn't make his family happy again. Doesn't put him back walking around. And doesn't change what I did. That moment when I held the arrow, and let it go. That arrow didn't hit only Left Rabbit. It hit everybody. And you can't make it go away. Forgiveness has got to come from the people I hurt, not from a god. And I can't ever get it from Left Rabbit, so I've got to live with that. And try… try to put some good back in the world. To replace some of what I took out of it."

Clay didn't know what to say to that. Finally, he managed, "You're wrong about one thing. You did hurt me. Left Rabbit was my friend too. And you killed him."

"I'm sorry. I wish with all my spirit I could undo it."

"I…" The words *forgive you* wouldn't come. Maybe someday. "I believe you."

"Thank you, Lord Doté." The young man bowed low, turned, and walked back down the hill, carefully feeling his way in the darkness.

Clay didn't want to go back to the council fire anymore. The wine was beginning to ebb from his mind and send his thoughts down gloomy pathways. He could have taken a couple steps backwards into the forest and purged the effects from himself in an instant, but he didn't. This was part of it, too. He sat and watched his people from afar.

After a while, Doto found him, slinking up from the woods behind him. "There you are. People noticed that you didn't come back."

Of course they did. "I can't go back, can I?"

"What are you saying? It is right down the hill. No one is angry that you left. They only want you there for tonight. You should go. It is very interesting, and we have been promised a humorous story about an animal called a camel."

"No, Doto, I mean… *I can't go back.*"

Doto watched him in puzzlement for a moment, and then sighed in understanding. "Oh. Oh, I see. No, my Clay. You can't. Not anymore."

Clay clung to him, buried his face in Doto's chest, and wept.

# 36 Homeward

Mirage woke in dewy grass, feeling rested and energetic. The previous night felt like a dream, but the remnants of it were everywhere, uneaten food still piled high, the council fire embers still glowing. All about him, people were sleeping, though some had stirred and were milling about or whispering to each other.

Clay and Doto were gone. Had the people really celebrated with gods last night? The memory was too unreal to hold in his mind, like warm butter between the fingers. It had been real, though. He had an elegant, smooth wooden knife hanging from fresh leathers to prove it. But the night itself, being in the presence of drunken gods, one of whom he'd known as a boy? That felt like a dream.

Their victory against Mpo, too, seemed unreal, but in a different way. The outlines of that memory felt chiseled, engrained deeply, like those of an image he'd seen or of a story he'd heard many times.

Now they all had to go back to being real. They had to prepare for a long journey back to their village. He wondered what Laughing Dog would say when he saw them. If they would still have to fight, or if there would be more long arguments about the right way to live. Shuddering, he thought of the imposed order of Bogana—the strict laws, the worship, the ritual sacrifice. Arguing was preferable to that.

He was too full of food and drink. He needed to relieve himself. He stumbled among the people sleeping in the grass, making his way toward the woods where he could hopefully find a little privacy. And a bush with soft leaves.

He saw his mother lying asleep near Ant With a Leaf. They were both snoring loudly. His father wasn't anywhere in sight. There was Cloud, lying curled on her side, her head on the Teller's chest, his arm around her. That was somehow more shocking to him than the revelations of the previous night; he'd never known Cloud to be close to anyone at all. The Boganans had found a place to rest near the outside of the group, clustered together where they could share a language. And in the midst of their group was... He stopped.

"Hey. Hey," he said, crouching down to shake at Oru's arm with one hand.

"*Ara? Ara?*" she asked sleepily. She blinked up at him. "Mirage?"

"Where's the Matron?"

"Oh, she's... she's..." Oru faltered, and then in an instant she was on her feet, shaking the others awake, speaking to them in Boganan. The group roused quickly, and all of them looked around.

"I thought you were supposed to be watching her!" Mirage searched the area, but looking for tracks was useless; the grass had been trampled many times over the previous day, and the flood of the great wave had rendered much of the terrain unreadable.

Oru shook her head. "We were all... we didn't think she would dare... not when the gods were..." and she trailed off. There was a broken, numb look to her face and he cursed himself when he remembered that she had lost her father and possibly her home yesterday, that her city was in ruins. Perhaps all of the Boganans had had other things on their minds last night.

But there was no time to think of that now. The rest of the people were quickly roused, and they made a quick search about the council fire area. The Matron was not to be found.

Of course, there was only one place she would go.

As one group, the People of the Savanna and the Breakwaters made their way along the wave-scoured slope of the coast toward the cliffs of Bogana. The great doors hung open. The city yawned with a slack jaw. There was little activity this early in the morning, but a few tiny shapes moved in and out of the city. Rubble had been piled in large, slouching heaps around the gates, and the little shapes were pulling carts with more of it, tossing it onto the piles.

As they drew closer, they saw the Matron, the rags of her once-white robes flapping in the morning breeze. She was on her knees, staring at the ruins of the city. At first, Mirage thought she gazed at the city itself, but then he noticed that while much of the rubble was made up of broken furniture, carts, and pieces of building, there were whole piles of shattered stone.

Here a stone arm, there an outstretched foot, there a wedge-shaped face with a triangular mouth filled with teeth. There a hand that had once been a fist thrust upward in triumph, now lying in the dirt. The statues of Mpo lay broken. As they watched, several people gathered around one of the remaining statues poised atop the city wall, and a moment later, it tipped over the edge and dropped onto the rocks below.

The Matron didn't turn when the people approached. "How quickly their faith falters," she said. Her voice was flat and hard. "How eager to turn on their goddess."

The Breakwaters gathered around, looking at the ruins of their city. "What will you do?" Mirage asked Oru and Elder Tobosu.

The old man shook his head. "We cannot break a thing and not put it back together. We must try to help Bogana find a new path. We must restore the cave of temples and rebuild our city." He gave a mirthless laugh. "Perhaps this time not quite so close to the edge."

"Have you thought about rebuilding atop the new mountain? It might be good to have a foundation provided by another god. And to be out of Mpo's reach."

The old man nodded. "Perhaps. It will be up to the people to decide. I suspect the days of one leader are gone along with the days of one god. We will have to choose together."

Oru bit her lip. "I don't even know if I have a home there anymore. My father is gone. He may have been guilty, but he was still my father."

*That doesn't always mean much,* Mirage thought. "You could come with us," he said. "I couldn't promise it would be better, but at least it would be… different. All of you could come, if you wanted to."

"How kind of you to offer, Mirage," Cloud said dryly. "But he's right. We came out here seeking help and wisdom. We've found the latter but could still use the former. If you wanted. I don't know what we'll be facing when we get back, but you could teach us much about your crops and your clothing, and our people would surely be eager to hear of the people that fought a goddess and won."

In the end, a delegation was sent to Bogana. No People of the Savanna went with them, as Cloud swore she would not make that mistake twice, but a few of the Breakwaters went. And after a long while, all of them came back. They told of the ruination of the city: the western edge with the houses of priests and city officials had fallen into the sea, carrying many of its inhabitants with them. Those most devoted to Mpo and her tyrannical laws had been destroyed by her fury. Much of the rest of the city was unharmed, though there had been some flood damage. The Boganans had taken the destruction of the clerical sector as a sign, and statues and idols of Mpo were being defaced and broken all over the city. The Matron was presumed dead, punished by the gods for heresy, her name spat in the streets.

When she heard this part of the report, she turned around and without a word started walking, heading north along the coast. No one followed her, and she did not return.

~

After three days, the People of the Savanna finally left Bogana for home. They brought with them nearly a score of Boganans who had elected to come with them, and among them was Oru, who had been chosen as translator and one who could help teach the People the Boganan language and plainstongue to the Boganans.

Their journey back to their village was much swifter than their journey out, for all their heavy carts and tents had been destroyed in the wave. They also no longer needed to avoid the forest, and so were able to bypass the Stone Wastes. And somehow, every time they were ready to stop their journey for the day, they found a cozy glen where fresh fruit and vegetables grew and where game had been freshly slaughtered and hung waiting for them. They slept in hollows sheltered from rain, unmolested by beasts.

These wonders astonished the Boganans from the city, who had not shared the feast at the council of the gods and found the tales of it difficult to believe. But even they could not deny that the forest was looking out for the People of the Savanna.

And one night, as Mirage was bedding down, he glanced up in the trees and thought for a moment he saw a lithe shape crouched on a limb, and the flash of eyes.

He spent his days trying to ease the travel of others, sharing a burden when it was needed, helping to prepare a meal or repair a water skin, or teaching the Boganans about local plants and their uses. When Cloud saw his interest, she told him to start visiting her in the evenings, and began instructing him in some basic healing and the preparation of herbs and poultices. The idea of becoming a healer appealed to him, he found. When he wasn't busy with that, he sat with Oru, hearing stories of her life and learning, word by clumsy word, her language.

Then one night, not more than a few days travel from their village by his estimation, he was wakened by a rough, clumsy hand across his mouth.

He struggled and clawed at the hand, but the man was strong. He knew the smell of him: Knife Strap. His father hadn't been seen since the night of the council fire, but he must have been following the group in secret, as Mirage had done on their trip to Bogana.

"Keep quiet, son," he rasped in Mirage's ear. "No need to make a fuss. No reason anyone has to get hurt." And Mirage felt the prick of a knife point in his back.

His father led him a good distance from the campsite and, in a little clearing where they were too far to be heard, backed away, though he still kept his knife held at the ready. It was a smooth wooden knife, one of the gifts of the forest gods. "Didn't want to hurt you," he said in a low voice. "But I couldn't trust you not to give me away. Them folks think me a traitor."

"You are a traitor!" Mirage hissed back, the heat of anger and adrenaline burning in his face. "You told the Boganans where we were. You nearly got everyone killed!" He patted at his side for his own knife and found it missing.

Knife Strap scowled. The wilderness had not been kind to him. He looked lean and unkempt. Desperate. "They oughtn't to have left me behind. That was your mother's doing. You know that, don't you?" He scratched at his patchy beard with the knife. "She told Cloud to leave me. Threatened her. I always knew she was unfaithful. I always knew she deserved what I give her."

The twisted logic of this statement left Mirage speechless.

"So I cried out. I was in my rights. They left me alone. Any man would have done it. It's a natural human emotion. Not my fault the guards heard it. I didn't want everyone to get caught. I just didn't want to get left behind. That's all anyone ever wants to do, leave me behind. You, your mother, the whole foul lot of you. But I'm a human being, by the gods. I got rights. I got to be treated like a person, not a thing. And I'm not going to be left behind again."

"We're not taking you with us," Mirage said. "I don't care how much you wave that knife at me."

"No, no, see, I got a plan. It'll work out for you and for me. See. The group is slow. But you and me, on our feet, we'll be fast. We can get back to the village before the others do. Report in, like you were supposed to all along. Go and tell the King what happened in Bogana and that the people are coming back. Then you tell him about all the songs you learnt back there. Offer him the power, right? And he'll be ready. He can do whatever he wants. Lift a mountain high beneath the village. Pour a river round it to protect it. And he's got more people, more fighters. He'll have no reason to let these exiles back in. And you and me, we'll know all the spells. We'll be his sorcerers, seats on his council, wealth, honor, everything. You don't have to go around slavin' away for other people who look down their noses at you and call you murderer."

He grinned, a hollow-cheeked jackal's grin. "Don't you see? You and me, we can still win. Knife Strap and his son. Sorcerers for the King."

"No."

"No, what do you mean, no? It solves everything!"

Mirage sighed. "So many reasons why not. But most of all, I don't want to go anywhere with you."

Knife Strap's sunken face darkened. "I'm your father."

"You keep saying that like it's enough. But it's not. I don't want to see you again." Mirage turned to walk back to the camp.

"Wait, boy. You'll regret it. Everyone back there knows you're a murderer. If you leave now… if you leave now, I'll find my way into the camp some night. And I'll cut my own throat with this knife. I'll do it. I got nothing left without you. I won't go starve alone in the wilderness somewhere. I'd rather die. And those judgmental bastards you been cozying up to, they'll say, 'Who do we know around here that's a murderer? Mirage, that's who.' And then you'll be exiled just like me. No more second chances, not for you. I'll use your own knife to do it, just to be sure."

Mirage looked over his shoulder. "No, you won't. You only know how to hurt other people. You'd never hurt yourself, not even out of spite." He kept walking.

There was silence for a moment and then footsteps ran up behind him. He turned in time to feel the searing pain of his own knife pushing into his side. He tumbled sideways into the leaves.

His father was atop him, his arm across Mirage's throat. His flat, yellow teeth bared in a wordless roar. He moved his arm and another sharp pain lanced through Mirage's side. "I'll kill you, you son of a jackal!"

Mirage flailed and kicked in terror. He'd been in fights before, but never with such rangy, desperate strength behind the attacks, and never with knife wounds, never with his hot blood running down his side. More by accident than by intent, his elbow slammed into the side of Knife Strap's head, sending the man rolling to the side.

He pushed himself away on one elbow, groping for anything he could use as a weapon—a rock, a branch. His fingers found only thin stems and handfuls of leaves. He tried to get upright, but as soon as he pushed, blinding pain gnawed into his side and commanded all his focus, so his arms and legs forgot what he was trying to do.

His father rolled to all fours and then rose into a crouch, advancing with the knife, waving it like the head of a cobra. "This is where it was always gonna end up, huh? You killing me or me killing you. It's in our blood, boy." He took a sideways step closer, aiming the knife low.

Mirage kicked out at his knee with one foot, but Knife Strap was ready for it. The knife slashed across Mirage's shin. His blood ran under his leg and *pat-pat-pattered* into the leaves. He moaned in pain and terror and pushed himself further away. "No."

"No? You think you're not a murderer? We all seen what you did. How quick you did it."

He found a fist-sized rock and hurled it as hard as he could at his father. Knife Strap ducked easily out of the way and advanced again. "No," Mirage managed. "It's not in our blood. I… chose. You choose. That's all."

His father took another step toward him. He kicked again but he was weakening, and Knife Strap was mongoose-quick. He stepped around Mirage's kick and crouched to plant a heavy knee on Mirage's chest. Pain flared down Mirage's side and he howled in agony. He scrabbled at his father's face with both hands, his fingers tangling in the man's beard.

Knife Strap placed the hard, wooden edge of his blade against Mirage's throat. "They want you to think that so you'll feel ashamed. But I know our blood." He thumped his chest with his free hand. "I know. I know how it felt every time your mother made me hurt her. Every time you made me. Just like you're doing now. It's no choice, boy. It's no choice at all. This is the blood. Our blood. And if you won't own it, you deserve what—"

"Stop." The voice was a woman's, from the edge of the clearing.

Knife Strap looked up, the pressure of the blade on Mirage's neck easing. "Wife?"

Mirage didn't dare lift his head, but he shifted as much as he could. His mother stood a little distance away, limned in moonlight.

"I will never call myself that. And you will never call me that again either. Let my son go."

Knife Strap blinked at her and then back down at Mirage. Uncertainty flickered across his face. "You can't stop me. You *won't* stop me. You're weak."

"Let him go right now. I won't tell you again."

He sneered. "You go off on your own and shave your head and now you think you can stand up to me? You can't. I know you. Quick with your tongue, but get you alone and you won't say or do a cursed thing."

"Knife Strap." Another voice. Ant With a Leaf stepped out of the forest, her bow raised and drawn. "She's not alone."

The hand holding the knife dropped it; the knee on Mirage's chest eased. "Look, I don't know what you thought was happening here, but—but I was only—"

"And she shouldn't have been alone." Cloud walked up behind Dry Grass. "Ever. She shouldn't have had to stand up all alone to the likes of you. We didn't know what you were like, Knife Strap. Or… or maybe we knew but didn't want to."

Mirage pushed himself away, clutching at the wounds in his side with one hand.

"Don't move, Mirage," Cloud snapped at him. "Not until we get that treated. Have you not been paying attention in our lessons?"

Wonderful. Stabbed in the dark by his father and he was still getting scolded.

Knife Strap backed up against a tree, head jerking from side to side as more and more of the People of the Savanna stepped into the clearing. "Well, what are you going to do to me that hasn't already been done. You gonna exile me? So what? I'm as good as exiled already, trailing after your group and eating up your scraps like an animal. What else? I won't go away. You gonna beat me? Kill me? You can't. You're better than that." He said the last in a mocking voice. "Take away everything I own? I already have nothing."

Cloud had moved into the clearing while he was talking and was now bent over Mirage, shaking her head at his wounds. "Bring me my supplies," she shouted to someone at the edge of the clearing. "And be quick!" She pressed her palms down on each of the stab punctures, making him dizzy with pain.

Then she looked up at Knife Strap. "You have something left we can take."

"What? My leathers? Fine, leave me naked in the wilderness, you nasty old crone."

"No. Your name. You are no longer Knife Strap. You are not one of the People of the Savanna. You have no name." She turned toward the people gathered in the clearing. "Does everyone understand? There is no Knife Strap. No one can see him. No one can hear him. We cannot help him because there is no one to help. There are no tales that carry his name, no histories of his deeds. He does not exist, so there is no death to mourn. If you must shed tears, shed them for this boy, who has no father."

"You—you can't do that. I know my name. I know who I am. You can't take it from me." No one stood with his back against the tree, his gaze drifting across the people standing there. "I'm Knife Strap, son of Two Broken Hands of Bogana. You hear me? I am Knife Strap, and that is *my* wife and *my* son."

There was no response.

"You can hear me! You see me! I see you looking at me!"

Cloud reached into the brush and withdrew something. "Here is your knife, Mirage." She placed it in his hand.

"Thank you, Cloud."

The nameless man lurched across the clearing, his fists balled and raised, charging at Dry Grass. He hadn't made it two steps before one of Ant With a Leaf's arrows whistled over his shoulder. "Hah! You're not supposed to be able to see me, so what's that about? It proves you can see me."

"Why, Ant, who are you shooting at in the middle of the night?" Dry Grass asked calmly. She had not even flinched when the nameless man had run toward her.

"You know who I am!" The man roared the words at the group. "I won't let you forget me. I'll follow you day and night. I'll sit in your camps. I'll follow your hunts. You'll always remember."

A small rock flew out and struck the nameless man on the temple. It wasn't big enough to seriously injure—barely more than a pebble, but it had to have hurt, and left a trickle of blood running down the side of his head. "Who threw that?" he demanded, turning in that direction. Mirage hadn't seen where it had come from, but he did see others feeling around on the ground for rocks of their own.

"Think we've got a baboon sniffing around," Ant With a Leaf said. "No point wasting another arrow on it. A few stones will run it off."

The nameless man whirled on her and another rock hit him in the back of the head. "How dare you?" he cried, and his voice cracked in fear. "How dare you all?"

Another small stone flew out of the group, and another, and another, hitting him in the back, the arm, the leg. "Stop it!" he screamed, but now he was being showered with small stones flying from every direction.

"Get out of here, baboon!" someone yelled, and another snickered.

Mirage, too, picked up a stone, a heavy one. He hefted it in one hand and raised his arm. A stabbing pain shot through his gut, but he ignored it. It was time, finally, to fight back. He hesitated, caught in the moment before throwing.

The beast that had once been his father sheltered his head with both hands as little stones pelted him. "Curse you!" he screamed. "Curse you all!" Ducking low, he scrambled away from the group, trying to escape his justice.

Mirage's fingers tightened on the stone. His shoulder strained. The moment seemed to last forever.

He lowered his arm. And then the beast was gone.

~

As the people traveled, the landscape changed. The forest turned duller and muddier with each hour of travel, the leaves and grass coated with a dusty film, the ground grey with ashy sludge. Laughing Dog and his fire hunters had ruined these lands. Everywhere they found the carcasses of dead birds, and occasionally sickly animals lying in gummy-eyed torpor, slowly perishing. A low horror crept over Mirage as he saw what the man he had once followed had wrought.

They came across the village sooner than they expected. It was not on a hill at the edge of the forest, with Gamewatch Rise at its foot. This was smaller, more condensed and hastily constructed. A ramshackle fence surrounded it. Cloud stopped and shook her head when she saw it. "Those poor idiots. They put it at the bottom of the hill. They'll all be sleeping in soggy tents. They exiled everyone who knew better."

"Even I know better than to put a campsite in a hollow," Mirage objected.

"Well, maybe. But Laughing Dog wasn't exactly a 'listen to others' kind of person. And neither were his pack of fire hunters. If they say 'put the site here,' that's where it's going. When we get inside, it will be in a sorry state. See if it isn't."

And Cloud was right. They weren't stopped at the gate; the scout there took one look at them and bolted into the village. They passed through the shoddy entryway unimpeded.

The village stank. People lay about the work areas, listlessly scraping hides, crafting tools or pots, and preparing food, but there was no life to them, no chatter, no engagement. They were merely surviving. Mirage was astonished. Even in the days of the worst thirst and privation, when they'd traveled across the savanna with little hope, people still found solace in each other, still laughed and worked together. These people looked as though they'd given up. Their faces were drawn and hollow, and their skin bore welts and sores. Flies buzzed everywhere.

Still, they looked up in interest when they saw the return of their exiles. Comparatively strong, rested, and well-fed, Cloud and the others strode through the village like a vision from the past. People slowly roused themselves and crowded around, asking questions and searching for friends and relatives.

Halfway through the village, they were met by Burning Star, who stood with his huge arms folded over his chest. He was trying to look imposing and serious, but Mirage could see the weariness in the slump of his shoulders and the bags under his eyes. His skin was clear, missing the characteristic striping of ash that would have marked him as a fire hunter. "So. You've come back." There was no accusation, no menace in the words. Only guarded observation.

"Yes." Cloud stepped closer to him, having to tilt her head to see his face. "We have been to Bogana and have learned new secrets. And surprises. And we have spoken to the forest gods. We know that the burning has stopped and Ogya has been defeated. So we have returned to discuss how we might restore this village, how to make the People of the Savanna one people again. Where is your King? We wish to speak to Laughing Dog."

Burning Star nodded as though he had been expecting the question, but he sagged a little further. "Laughing Dog is… gone."

Mirage looked up in surprise.

"Gone?" Cloud said. "What do you mean, gone? Where is he? Who is King now?"

"Just… gone. We don't know. He walked off more than a moon ago and no one has seen him since. And… there is no King. Not now."

Cloud turned and surveyed the village calmly. "I can see how the responsibility could be a little daunting." She looked up at him with a glint in her eyes. "I expect you all could use some help?"

And the question broke the last little bit of resistance in Burning Star. His hands dropped to his sides. "I think we need all the help we can get."

"Good. Then first we should talk about moving back to the old village site."

Burning Star shook his head. "It's no good. There's no living up there now. The ash has made it unlivable. It's dead land."

"Ah. As to that…" Cloud gave him a wide smile. "I *told* you we brought surprises."

~

And so Cloud and Mirage taught the People of the Savanna a new song. Together, they traveled to the site of the old village, where everything was black and grey and dead. The tree atop Gamewatch Rise had fallen, and the old village sagged like an empty carcass. The people followed them into the blackened forest, where the remains of foliage crunched under their feet and the skeletal fingers of burned-out trees scraped at the sky.

They gathered in a circle and sang the song of Kwaee, the god who had fought them for so long, who had split their people into two. And as they sang, green broke the burned crust of the forest, little fresh, baby shoots uncurling from the ash and stretching toward the sky, thickening, spreading limbs and branches, sprouting new leaves that fanned out to cover the dancers with shade. Some had to change their gait to step around burgeoning trunks or emerging mushrooms. Roots crawled over the surface of the ground, churning it up and burying the ash and char in fresh loam. Flowers burst open in mists of pollen and scent; lianas snaked up tree trunks and clung to branches. Trees sagged with fruit.

In the middle of a field of grey ash and death, amidst a dead country, an emerald of green bloomed.

As one people, they called to Kwaee, and their forest was reborn.

# 37 A Pilgrimage's End

Clay gripped tightly at Doto's hips as he pushed into him, groaning in pleasure. His mate braced his paws against the ground and leaned back into the thrust, arching his body, his tail curling around Clay's back.

They were in their temple, and all was right with the world again. Ogya was imprisoned, Kwaee was at peace, and the People of the Savanna were settled once more and regrowing the forest day by day. After so much time of conflict and worry and fear, Clay almost did not know what to do with himself. But he knew what to do with Doto.

He settled into a smooth, slow rhythm, planting kisses on Doto's back with each slide inward. Their temple pulsed around them with the movements, their little garden echoing with leaf and petal in an undulating throb. Insects copulated in the air, their fish spawned in the stream, and all about them was the heady scent of nectar.

Clay opened his thoughts to share them with Doto. They had both been doing so with increasing frequency in their temple, letting the boundaries between the two of them blur, each becoming more like the other. And of course the sex was almost always better. The suddenness of the sharing surprised Doto, making him squeeze tightly around Clay's shaft. The two of them groaned in unison, feeling both squeeze and penetration. Clay sensed a mounting tension and reached one arm around Doto's waist, cupping his tip just in time to catch the slipperiness of his precum splashing into his paw. The scent of nectar in the air grew almost cloying.

And now they moved as one creature, two gods in one, sharing every sensation: the tickle of grass across a belly; the gentle caress of young vines curling up a leg, an arm, one god eager to touch the other with every part of himself; the raw, aching pleasure inside them; the rough grip of a paw, the hot spatter of slick droplets against the earth; a solid chest against a back; hips bumping against rump with graceful but urgent need.

With their climax, their temple opened toward the sky and every living creature within shared in their ecstasy, but they were gods and did not need to rest; Doto turned on the ground and Clay gripped his shoulders and rocked into him again. Their mouths met in hunger and they shared the taste and curl and lap of each other's tongues. Again and again they climaxed, until they were lost in each other, their sensations so enmeshed that they could scarcely remember who was who, and they had to lie still in each other's arms and rest while they disentangled their thoughts and returned to their own minds.

As Clay lay in the delicate grass of their temple, staring up at the stars, he gradually recalled that he was Clay, and not Doto, and not one being with two bodies lost in its own pleasure. Each joining like this felt more intense than the last, and took longer to separate, and he wondered if one day they would simply forget how to do so, or why they should.

Perhaps someday, he thought, but he hoped not soon. There was value to knowing yourself—to knowing *another,* he corrected himself—from a distance. But perhaps once all life had been part of the same entity, all part of Father Wem, and he had fractured himself into infinite beings only to know himself better. He sighed upward at the stars.

Doto leaned up on one elbow to ruffle the fur of his chest with one paw. "Are you all right? I felt a sadness in you when we were together."

"Everything is wonderful," said Clay. "Except I still miss being with the fire bearers. It's still a part of me, you know. It always will be, I hope. But that last time with them… I tried so hard. I wanted to feel like I could go back. But there is no going back, not really."

"You are too different now. Even if you could give back all your power and return to them as a fire bearer, you would not be the same, not after the things you have done. The things you have seen. Those things have changed you just as much. You think you could return to your village and be a… a stone-tooth-maker—I do not know what your role was—after you have wrestled with gods and saved the world?"

"I—maybe I could."

Doto laughed and slid his paw down to gently cup Clay's sheath. Which began firming. Stupid god's body that required no rest. "You could not. First of all, everyone would be asking you questions about the gods all the time, as they did before. They would treat you differently, because they would all know what you had seen and done. And you would grow bored. You would not want to sit around and tell stories of the gods anymore. You would seek them out. And then, somehow or other, you would end up right back where you started." He gave a low, hungry rumble. "And in my arms again."

Clay kissed the smirk right off his face. "Well, maybe we should do that anyway."

Doto's ears perked. "Do what?"

"Go and find the gods. The other ones, I mean. We've met Fam and Sarmu and Atekye and Asubonten. And… And Kwaee and Ogya. But there are others, aren't there? Let's meet the god of eagles and learn how to soar on wings of our own. Let's go find gods that have been lost, like Bew, and then—then we can find a way to tell the people of the world about them! And Mpo is out there storming around the ocean. Maybe we can find her and calm her down. And Doto… maybe there are other lands, with gods we've never heard of. Maybe there are other forest gods, even. We could go and find them."

"You forget, we'd be in those terrible fire bearer bodies the moment we left our forest."

"That just makes it difficult." Clay leaned over to lick hungrily at his neck. "And everything here is so easy now. We'll get bored eventually. And if the sex is this good every time we come back…"

"It is still good now," Doto pointed out. "Better every time. Let us rest and learn to be gods together in the peace of the forest. Perhaps after a hundred years or so…"

"A hundred years?" Clay almost shouted.

"With you it will seem like no time at all, I promise. And besides, you want to stay by to look in on your little fire bearer nest, do you not? I suspect soon they will begin praying to you for things."

Clay groaned. "I am not ready for that. It was already so strange, the way they all looked at me, the way they treated me."

"You will grow accustomed to it."

Clay stared into Doto's gold-green eyes but looked past them and into a strange future. A hundred years. They would go by for him and he would be unchanged, but all the fire bearers he knew would be gone. Everyone who remembered him as one of them, left to join the ancestors—ancestors who now he would never see after death, if indeed that was what happened. He wasn't so sure, now. All he remembered about death was a world of lights.

Doto's awareness brushed against his. "You have your brooding face on again. But you are not sad."

With a laugh, Clay relaxed and fell against him, inhaling the rich scent of his fur. "No. I think I was trying to feel sad because of everything that I've lost. But my fate has changed. This world is full of wonder, and I get to see it. I get to watch it change and grow and maybe even help it. Not to mention, live here in paradise with my love whenever I wish to. For ages and ages."

"Do you think we will still love each other after a hundred years? A thousand? More?" Doto asked. There was no anxiety in his voice.

Clay ran his fingers through the fur of Doto's thighs. "If we choose to."

"Then—"

Clay looked up at the same time Doto broke off. They had both felt it: the tread of a foot—a *human* foot—inside their temple, crushing their grass. With barely a pause, both of them streaked toward the intruder, arriving before he could take a second step.

The man standing there startled at their arrival and stumbled backward. He was thin and haggard, his drawn face filthy, hair matted and clumped with mud and debris. His sunken eyes widened when he saw them, and he reached out one feeble arm. Loose flesh hung from him like cloth, as though he were a small man walking around in a larger man's skin.

In an instant, Clay and Doto had him bound with vines, lashing him to the spot where he stood, encasing his arms and legs so tightly he could not move.

"Who are you?" Doto snarled. "How dare you set foot in this place?"

Clay's nose wrinkled; the scent in the air was familiar. Muted beneath the stenches of old urine and stale ash, but he knew it. His ears folded back. "Laughing Dog?"

The man made a raspy, whispery noise in his throat as he found his unused voice. "Wh-who are you?" he finally managed.

Doto stalked around the man in a circle. "Impossible. It cannot be Laughing Dog. How could he even have come here without our notice? Or Kwaee's? We would have detected him."

"Doto." Clay pointed, trembling. The man wore very little, but around his neck, lying against his sunken chest, was a thorny circle of vines with a wooden leopard pendant. "I was wearing it the day they killed me."

The man's eyes widened, and beneath the dirty and the sagging skin, his expression was familiar. "Clay?" he stammered. "No. No, that cannot be. You're dead. Great Ram… no. Even though Ogya said, he said you were still… I never believed…" His eyes turned wet. "You cannot be here. I lost you. Ogya—he tricked me, made me mad, in my mind. I lost everyone. Everything."

Fear prickled up the back of Clay's neck. Ogya was imprisoned, but his brother had caused so much harm. "What are you doing here? How did you find us?"

"He told me where to go. He saw you. Saw your… your temple." Dull eyes shifted back to Clay. "Are you a demon now, too? Are you… like me?"

"A demon? No, I'm—"

"He is a god," Doto interrupted. "And you will speak to him with reverence."

Laughing Dog appeared to choke. "A god," he rasped. He bared blackened teeth in a weary grin and then coughed. Something dry and gray flew out of his mouth and floated slowly to the ground. "After all this. After all our arguments, and all I've done, here we are. You sought only to worship, and I fought for the strength of mortal arms. And now I am broken, and you have become… something impossible. And I must bow."

Guilt, though guilt for what, Clay could not say, tugged at his heart. "You don't have to bow, Laughing Dog."

He gave a croaking laugh. "I do. I do. You must let me go so I can show homage. You were right the whole time, and I was wrong. And now I do whatever the gods command. It is what we all must do. We all must… obey."

Clay eased the vines around Laughing Dog so as not to grip him so tightly. He felt Doto resist a little in disapproval, but what point was there now in punishing this desperate, broken man? What else could they do to him that was worse? A little gentleness could hurt nothing now.

"No, Laughing Dog. Back then, we were boys, and I didn't understand. But you were not wrong about any of it. You were right. At least… at least at the beginning. Not that we shouldn't be grateful to the gods for the gifts of the world, and we… we should honor the traditions of the people that came before us, but not if they're cruel. Not if we suffer under them. I learned about fire bearers, and the power we… the power *they* all have. You can fight back. You don't have to bend to every command. The gods can be unjust. They can be tyrants."

His brother stared at him for a moment, and then laughed again, a manic giggle that rose into a bray that wracked his body. "I—I was right?" he managed through the laughter. "I was right, and you were wrong? And here we are now! Why all this, brother? If you are my brother anymore, somewhere inside this enormous cat? Why all this suffering if I was right?"

Clay shook his head. "You really don't understand, still? After everything you did? It wasn't about who was right and who was wrong. It was about what we did with it. You never listened, Laughing Dog. You were smart and you thought it meant you didn't have to pay attention to anyone else." He stepped closer and put his paw on his brother's shoulder. Beneath the flesh it was rail-thin and bony. "Everything I knew about the gods was wrong, and that was difficult. But I listened. I learned. You… no one could tell you anything. And in the end, you thought being right was more important than being kind."

He sighed. This felt cruel. There was so little left of his brother now. Why heap blame on top of everything else? "Listen. We can talk later. Let us get you water. Something to eat. We don't have to—"

"I killed our father," Laughing Dog said, his head listing to one side.

Clay froze. He had known, of course, but to hear it from his brother's own mouth, in such casual tones…

"And I ate some of him. Ogya made me do it. He showed me what he did on the way here. He showed me because… because I was a good worshiper. Because I obey him and because I know my place. He showed me everything he did. He put my mind to sleep and he put a face in me, a beast in the back of my head. And then he used me to kill our father. He ate out our father's heart with the beast in the back of my head. And now that I'm here he's going to set me free. Forever. I'll be free if I show you."

Doto muttered, "Clay…" in an alarmed voice. Wisps of steam were rising from Laughing Dog's hair. And Clay could feel, through the vines encasing his brother, a strange warmth, rising higher and higher.

"Would you like to see it?" Laughing Dog croaked. "Would you like to see the beast in the back of my head?" His eyes bulged oddly. A smile like ecstasy twisted his face. He turned his neck to the right, his chin meeting his shoulder. And then he kept turning. His eyes stared in two separate directions; his jaw bulged. His shoulders, his back, his legs were unmoving, held firm in Clay and Doto's vines, but his head kept turning, farther than a man's head could go. Something in his neck twisted strangely, jutting out.

And then there was a popping, cracking sound. His shoulders went slack. The back of his head faced them.

Clay screamed.

Doto recoiled, hissing.

Laughing Dog was dead. They could both feel it through the grasp of their vines: the thud of his heart faltering, the ebb of blood in his veins. But his lifeless body was warming in their grip.

Something moved under the dead man's hair. A nose, a snout pushed out from beneath the tangled mass. Eyes of fire blazed. Jaws lolled. A tongue dripped drool that sizzled where it hit the vines encasing the corpse, a body growing warm, hot, an ember in dead flesh. The voice that spoke was like the crackle of a fire. "Now I will finally take my meal."

Doto clenched his fingers, cinching the vines tighter. "No. Ogya? We imprisoned you!"

Above the eyes of the beast, a clear, gleaming stone pushed its way through the hair. A diamond. "Not all of me."

Clay scrambled backward into their temple in horror, all his mind focused on lashing the thing down, keeping it from moving, preventing the horrible broken-necked *thing* in the corpse of his brother from getting any closer.

The gem in the forehead shone like the sun, blinding them. The heat grasped by their vines was intolerable. Clay felt the tug of Doto against his own powers, pulling against the vines, trying to loose them, trying to move them—why? "Clay! You have to let go! We have to get him out of here now, before he—"

Laughing Dog's body bulged all over, in elbows, legs, forearms, his forehead, his broken neck. Red, shifting light shone through his stretched flesh. And then he exploded.

Fire rained down all over the forest, sprays of it splashing across Clay and Doto. Agony tore through them, but the pain was not coming from their avatars. Their temple was burning. Liquid flame arced across trees and grass, catching in an instant. The flames spread as though they had caught dry grass, racing across the ground. They pooled in an agonizing circle, a hole eating into their shared soul, burning them out of existence.

No. Not out of existence. Transferring their divine being to another, who should have remained trapped for eternity. The tiny fragment of Ogya fed on them. And from the blaze, first one, then a second huge claw thrust upward. The body of a massive, fiery scorpion pulled itself out of the blaze and into the forest temple.

Ogya was free.

38

# An Incontrovertible Account From the REAL Hero In All This Mess

But enough of all that. Enough of flames and scorpions and wiggly plants and dramatic weeping and so on. It will all end badly, mark my words. Back to the story you actually care about, and the voice you love to listen to.

You know, there are some who say that the voice of a god can cause madness, but I say, what else is madness but certainty, a belief that cannot be changed by any force? We gods speak so loudly that we deafen our followers to everything but our own words, and that's as it should be. Can't have little worshippers running around *questioning things*, can we?

That's why they name me god of lies: so that none of you will believe my words, not fully, not truly, not enough to make you certain. Not enough to make you mad.

You think being a god sounds fun, do you? Envious of young Doté and his adventures with absurd powers and mind-blowing sex with his mate in the forest? Suddenly living forever with infinite strength and youth in a paradise that you can shape to your whim is so desirable?

...well, yes. All right. It is pretty wonderful, and if you ever need to tell yourself you're feeling *challenged* or you need to brood for a while you can always make up some nonsense about how you're lonely or disconnected or you miss home or there's a horrifying fire monster devouring you and your mate alive, but these little quibbles are trivial, don't you think?

So being one of the big gods is pretty great, to tell the truth, and we animal gods, we have the sweet life too, usually. I mean, imagine being able to be any hare in the world. Literally any one of them. Pretty keen, right? And you get to try to make a real difference in the world. For me, though, it's hard. Because, again, this vicious rumor that I am some kind of untrustworthy god of lies. I can't even talk to most mortals at all!

Take that Mirage fellow. There he is, gallivanting across the savanna with his parents, just a big happy family, and he's heading toward disaster! You folks saw Bogana, you know what I'm talking about. A city full of madness, and that madness was caused by Mpo, the goddess *everyone* believed. Not that I'm jealous. Just because every single mortal cowered before her and took every word as… well, there ought to be a word for it. Something important and written down on something. Like those tortoise shells. Ought to be a word for it. Someone will come up with something eventually, I'm sure.

Clearly, Mirage and parents and all those other little humans were headed toward big trouble. But what could I do? Just pop in and tell them? Not how things are done. You'll never catch me talking directly to a mortal, no sir. Either they don't believe me because of the whole "lies" nonsense, or they do and then, whoops, Adanko's made humans crazy too. And what do I tell them? *Not* to go? Not to uncover the great lost mysteries that could change the balance of power between humans and the gods in ways that might be crucial for all of us?

What? No, I have *not* known about the existence of the tortoiseshells carved with all those divine spells, hidden in caves for centuries! Who has been filling your heads with this malarkey? Was it Okore? That pesky eagle. Full of rumors. He likes to claim that I've been going around trying to get everyone to find the shells again and take their power back from the gods, but take a moment to think of that. What would I gain? I'm a god, too! I can't have mortals running around wielding power over me, turning my precious savanna into a swamp or a canyon or whatever ridiculous thing they think of. Suddenly a bunch of baby hares drowning because some upstart human wanted a lake where they were nesting? Intolerable. I always said, we must keep this power out of their hands forever. Mpo, I said, you must outlaw all these songs and destroy anyone who dares speak of them.

Naturally, I was only exaggerating a bit, because I'm not a monster, but she's a very literal-minded goddess, Mpo, and once she's set on something? Impossible to dissuade. You try sometime, if you don't believe me.

So. Yes, I did want to help all those poor people, but I didn't want them to find the shrines beneath Bogana! What a terrible outcome. I was worried about it from the beginning, when Mirage kept working on that game he played with the grass. Ah, that, I said to myself, that's the map straight to the forbidden knowledge. I'd better distract him. So I gave him a little wave, a little something to think about.

I followed, of course, keeping an eye on things. I am a generous and giving god. If maybe someone overheard a word that was helpful but attributable to none, that might have been me. If someone knew which path to take or which house to hide under, I might have lent a little assistance.

But I did not, I repeat *not* intend for anyone to find those tortoiseshells. And when Mirage ended up in the tunnels below Bogana, I knew we were in for trouble. So once again, I tried to distract him. Just a little wave, just a little nudge to try to dissuade him from following a path he shouldn't have. Didn't work, unfortunately, but that's how it goes being a god like me. You can't just *talk* to people. They won't believe you.

Like with that little upstart Doto, I told him, you are just like your father, and nothing you do can change that, and did he listen? No. He rebelled. Against me! Against my wisdom! Against the truth, which is that our fates are determined by our ancestors and by the gods, and that fighting them leads only to misery!

And yet he didn't listen. No, he stood up to his own wrathful nature and gave his divinity to Clay, and look what we have now: more misery. I was right, of course. I'm always right. The world would surely have been better if he had given in to his anger, just like his father, and smooshed all those fire bearers like the helpless little mortal insects they are.

But he didn't, and I kept waiting around for a good chance to tell them I told you so. It was that and that alone that led me to follow them through the forest while they set food and supplies aside for that little fire bearer group they like so much. Spying on them, I was. Looking for a chance to give them a piece of my mind. Why else would I spend days waiting outside their temple while they engaged in so many tedious couplings. No, I was not watching with lascivious interest, I'm a hare after all and we aren't known for such things, and even if we were, *even if*, I tell you, there is no law in nature for what animals may look at. We can look at whatever we like. That's just common sense and I distinctly recall Father Wem decreeing it when he shaped the world. No rule against animals looking at things. You might as well be angry at the wind for blowing.

Anyway, the point is that up until then, I had no interest in what Ogya might have been up to—he was imprisoned, wasn't he? He's not a clever god, not *scheming*. No, he's a force of nature, and the fact that he sealed up my lazy friend Sarmu in a volcano was simply a stroke of bad luck.

Were I a different god, I might have followed the powerful players in this game around, seeing what they were about. I might have nudged events here and there, but we hares are not social creatures. We are prey. We look out for ourselves, run whenever we can, and are never where you look for us. We do not *ever* fight back.

But if we see you doing something we don't like, we might tell on you a little bit. So when Ogya burst out of that poor sack of fire bearer, I did the only thing I could do: I rushed off to tell Kwaee. We hares are fast, and a god of hares? So fast that we're all very lucky my feet didn't ignite the forest floor through pure friction.

As usual, Kwaee was delighted to see me. "Why, come in, Adanko, how lovely to have you drop by for a visit, it's been *far* too long."

"Yes," I said in my most serious tones, "I appreciate it, and we really must do this more often, but just now I am here with the most salacious gossip. Do you know what that upstart Ogya has been up to?"

"Ogya, that old rascal?" Kwaee gave a chuckle. "Well, I doubt he's up to very much! I sent him to his room without supper, you know!"

"True, and that was very wise and powerful of you," I told him, because gods deeply enjoy flattery and praise. Especially that Doté, now I come to think of it. If you get a chance to speak to him before he's gobbled up by a fire monster, you really should just *smother* him with adoration and fawning. He eats that stuff up. "However," I continued, "have you noticed the forest being a bit on fire lately? Roundabout the location of your son's temple?"

And Kwaee thought for a moment, doing that thing the big territory-type gods do, where they look out through all the land they control. Best I can manage is to look through the eyes of any hare, and let me tell you, all you usually get is a terrified blur. Sometimes you see the ground very far below you because an eagle is carrying you off. But it only took Kwaee a moment to see the truth of what I was telling him.

"Well, well," he said after a moment. He was clearly quite distressed. "You are a noble and valued friend for having brought this to me, Adanko. Thank you so much." You know how Kwaee is. All politeness and smiles.

"But I fear there is nothing even my phenomenal powers can do in this case. It took careful planning and the work of many gods to trap him before, and he still broke free. My poor, poor son. And that other one, the one he likes fucking so much. Poor both of them. I wish there was something I could do."

Now, a god never likes to see such defeatism on the face of a fellow god. Especially a big important one like the Forest Lord. I gave him a good solid whap across the cheek with one paw, startling him so greatly that he stammered and stared at me. Then I gripped his shoulders in both paws. He is much taller than me, so I did need to climb up his body a bit to do it, but we hares are also excellent climbers with terrific balance. But I hardly need tell you such a well-known fact.

"Now listen up, Kwaee," I told him, and I used my sternest voice so he would understand how serious I was. "You *do* know what you can do. The power has been inside you all along. You simply need to decide to use it, no matter what it costs. You can stop this. You know you can." On my honor, those were my words, verbatim. I am a very serious and encouraging person when I need to be.

Then the great Forest Lord clenched his fist in determination. "You're right, Lord Adanko," he said. "You've helped me to see the truth. As always you have been my truest and greatest friend, and my most trusted advisor. I know what I must do. Stay here and look after my temple, will you."

And then he left me to take care of the forest until he got back. I know! I could hardly believe it myself. "Lord Adanko," he said, "you're in charge until I get back. And listen, if anything should happen to me—"

I cut him off. "Don't you even say that. You'll be fine. You can handle this without a problem."

But he wouldn't hear it. "Listen, this is important. If anything should happen to me, you're the god of the forest now. You understand? I am leaving it to you."

"But I'm no god of the forest," I protested. "Why not… why not leave it to your son, or his weird hybrid boyfriend?"

"They have too much sex," he said, and I could tell that he disapproved a little but was also kind of envious. It has been a *long time* for Kwaee, let me tell you. "And they're not as serious and responsible as you, Lord Adanko. I name you my sole heir."

And then he ran off in a majestic blur to do something heroic, presumably.

I tried out the moabi throne a little, but that thing is uncomfortable *and* it itches. Not my speed at all.

# 39 Burn For You

Doto's whole world was agony. Their temple burned, and as it burned, so did he and Clay. They lay writhing in the grass, fire slathering hungrily over their bodies, smoking fur and crackling in their flesh. Above the sound of their screams and the flames came Ogya's booming laughter as he devoured their temple. He made his way deeper into their sanctum and they felt the fires of his footsteps bore into them as he unmade them.

Through the pain, Doto managed to push himself onto paws and knees, trying to look past the flames. He found Clay rolling in the flickering grass and grabbed him by one foot, dragging him all the way back into their temple. They were dying; he didn't want to miss another moment with Clay waiting for his avatar to be reborn in the center of their temple. No. If they were to die, they would die in each other's arms.

Clay pushed himself upright. Fire had already seared away the side of his head; his left ear was gone, his teeth exposed in his jaw, one eye dark. The other squinted, running with tears from the smoke. He got to his feet, helping Doto and leaning against him at the same time.

They stood in a chamber of flame. Above them, the branches of the temple crackled and blazed, raining red-licked leaves and twigs down around them. The fire roared up the side of the mountain and coughed thick billows of sickly yellow smoke into the air. A hissing came from their stream as it boiled in the heat, clouds of steam rising to mix with the smoke. And above it all loomed Ogya, roaring in satisfaction as he broke away trunks of trees with his clacking claws and crammed them into his greedy, chittering mouth.

"Ahh shhhhooooa…" Clay tried to say something but could not articulate the words with his ruined muzzle. Sparks flew between his bared teeth.

*I'm sorry I didn't get more time with you. I'm so sorry we failed.*

Doto leaned on him, resting his arms across Clay's shoulders. The right one had already gone skeletal, blackened bone still burning. The pain was terrible, but it was nothing in the face of this, watching Clay, his love, his savior, burning away, dying.

Ogya was free—had freed himself using *their own power*—and would devour them. And then, Doto thought, he would have the power of a forest god within him. That's what he had always wanted. He would consume them, then Kwaee, and then the savanna, and the swamps, the lowlands, the mountains. Two little forest gods would whet his appetite for the whole world.

Doto didn't care. The world didn't matter. Kwaee didn't matter. The forest didn't matter. All that mattered was Clay, and he was suffering. Dying. He needed something good. He needed to know that he was loved.

So Doto danced for Clay. It was not an energetic dance, because the air of his temple was choked with smoke. It was not a big dance. It was a slow sway, turning in a circle, his cheek to Clay's so that Clay could hear his rasping voice whisper, "All may love you, but none can own you."

He felt the magic move through him, the magic not of gods, but of fire bearers, calling the world to them, calling the gods to them. Not ash here, but forest floor. Was it spell or prayer? "Where you walk the world changes, and old laws die and are forgotten."

Beneath their feet, the fire flickered and died. Green pushed up through the ash. And in his arms, Clay healed. Just a little. Golden color traced through the burned fur. A gold-green eye opened in a darkened socket. Lips regrew over charred teeth. "You are Doté the compassionate." New growth rippled out through the temple beneath their feet, but still the fire spread. Still they burned.

Desperate, he clasped Clay closely, trying to dance faster, trying to sing louder, trying to do something to make the magic work better. "You give voice to the people the gods forgot." Tender vines twined up Clay's legs and then disintegrated, burned with fresh fire. "Joy—" Doto's voice cracked, rasping in the smoke. "Joy to those who have never felt it."

Joy. Running when you might fall but not caring. Loving even if it meant you might get burned. Fearlessness when there was everything to fear. "Life to hearts—" He stumbled. His legs were burning away. One foot was gone, a charred stump at the end of his leg. "To hearts that had tired of beating…"

He couldn't stand anymore. He hung helplessly from Clay's arms as the growth stopped and the magic faded. Steam rose from his cheeks as his tears burned away.

They were still turning, even though he could not feel the ground anymore. Clay was carrying him. And then he was singing back, through the smoke, his voice small but strong amidst the roar of the flames. "He is Doto the Mighty…"

His love sang back to him the song from so long ago, when they had been two lonely travelers lost in the fictions of their people, each seeking their own truths and finding them in each other. And Clay's song gave a little life back to him; feeling came back to his toes; he found the ground; he stood again, he moved, he had enough air in his choked lungs to sing.

And so they swayed in each other's arms, singing their songs of love to beat back the fires that would consume them, circles of green and new life radiating away from their feet, spreading, and incinerating again.

Ogya sensed what they were doing and roared in annoyance; just as he consumed, they robbed him of the sustenance, and he turned toward them, his claws clattering as he scrambled down the mountainside, his segmented feet breaking rock and snapping branches as he barreled to them.

*It's not enough,* Doto sent wearily to Clay, still singing his song of praise. *We can't heal each other faster than the fire spreads. We will still die, just more slowly.*

*If it gets me a few more minutes with you, then it's enough.*

*It is* never *enough. An eternity would not be.*

The power of the magic was fading now, unable to beat back the greedy flames of Ogya, the circle of green around them narrowing, closing in. Too much of their temple had burned. There was too little of them left.

Doto clasped the back of Clay's head, holding him close, trying to see only the eyes of his lover and not their sanctum in flames around them, not the all-consuming vision of the giant scorpion storming toward them; he had been slowed by the stream, which had made his fires flicker for a moment, but now he had moved past it and charged, claws spread.

*There must be some way,* Clay sent. *This can't be it. There must be something that can stop him.*

*You know there is not. Mother Fam said so. The hunger in him will never stop. It is a wound that cannot heal.*

Clay stiffened in his arms. *A wound?*

Doto puzzled at his reaction for a moment, and then understanding washed over him. *A wound that cannot—*

*Heal.*

*Heal.*

Ogya filled their vision, a nightmare of fire and chitin, all arms raised, his massive pincers spread wide, his barbed tail swaying over his head, knocking burning branches from the trees.

*It will destroy us*, Doto warned, but it was a ridiculous warning. They were all but destroyed anyway.

*I won't do it alone. I promised you I wouldn't heal again.*

*It was wrong to make you promise that. Together?*

Clay smiled at him. *I love you.*

*I love you.*

And then, as Ogya reached them, they turned, their paws raised toward him, and they summoned every ounce of their divinity. Doto wasn't sure if they had even a fraction of what was necessary to heal the fire god, to undo the hunger, the hole that the great bargain had carved out of him. They would pour all of themselves into him. They would be gone, but if it was enough, *if*… then maybe it could stop him.

Doto felt everything in him, all the divine power, flow through him toward his paws, crackling. The air turned electric. Next to him, all of Clay's unburned fur stood on end.

"Out, out!" Doto roared. "My power to you, into hunger and hollowness, into pain, into desire—" And he heard Clay's own roar, the same words cried in defiance of all hunger in the world.

There was a rush of wind. It smelled of fresh forest.

"No!" a voice roared, and a golden blur swept past them.

Time slowed.

Kwaee was there, in the air, his arms spread, his claws and fangs bared. The feathers of his crown blew in the wind. Behind him, a trail of embers and burning leaves hovered and swirled in the air.

Ogya gaped his chelicerae, reaching for Kwaee with both sweeping pincers, their edges jagged lines of magma, sharp and powerful enough to tear the forest god apart like a cobweb.

But too slow. Kwaee landed on the scorpion's face, narrowly dodging the clicking of his jaws. He braced his feet against the scorpion's thorax, between the joints of surprised, grasping limbs. Flames licked up his legs and around his arms, but if he felt the pain, he did not show it. He gripped the sides of Ogya's head and pulled, clenching his teeth, arching his back. His tail lashed the air.

Ogya screamed, a chittering howl, turning in a circle, flailing, his pincers too large and stiff to reach the leopard clinging to his face. He stabbed downward with his segmented tail, the huge, curved barb plunging toward Kwaee once, twice, three times, but unable to reach the god past his own huge, blunt head.

And then, with a cracking, popping sound and a gurgling scream from Ogya, Kwaee wrenched backward with all the strength in his body and tore the scorpion's head away.

Segmented legs folded. The great, chitinous bulk of Ogya collapsed to the ground slowly, as if remembering how to fall. The broad, blunt head of the scorpion bounced on the ground once and then rolled past Doto, its mouthparts still wriggling in pain and bewilderment.

Kwaee landed on his feet, looking down at the astonished Clay and Doto.

"He will be back soon," he said. "We do not have much time."

# 40
# Songs of the Forest

Cloud walked slowly through the regrown forest with the Teller. Everywhere new life was springing up from the ash. With the help of the People, they had slowly begun to restore the damage wrought by Laughing Dog and his fire hunters. Still nothing had been seen of the would-be King in months, and she doubted they would ever encounter him again. By all accounts, he had been gravely ill at the end of it all. Ill and extremely mad. She wasn't sorry to lose him, but she didn't like to think of him out there, somewhere, lurking in the woods.

There was still no new King, and if she had her way, there never would be. A council of elders might be less efficient and decisive, but it also meant no one person was going to ruin everything with some mad vision for the people. It meant there would be discussion. It meant, hopefully, that people would begin to listen to each other again.

"Astonishing," the Teller murmured, leaning on his stick as he walked through the young forest. "That we should have this much power over the land, to transform it so completely. This will change everything, I think."

"Well, not only transform it," Cloud reminded him. "Take it from one god and grant it to another. It's not an ability to use lightly. Remember what Clay and the forest god said: gods don't much like it when you take away their territory. This is something that must be used very carefully."

The Teller nodded. "With balance. Of course. Once we have restored what we can of the forest, we will be sure not to sing any of the sacred hymns without deep consultation."

There was a gust of wind. "Funny you should mention that," a cheerful voice said.

Cloud and the Teller both stared. Before them stood a tall, rangy figure that could only be described as half man, half hare. And he hadn't been there an instant ago. He gave them a bucktoothed grin and waggled his brows.

Cloud clutched at her heart, not because it was actually hurting but because this was the sort of time when one normally clutched at one's heart, and when giant animal people appeared out of nowhere right in front of you, you found yourself suddenly craving normalcy.

The Teller almost fell backward. "By—by the gods, you can only be Adanko, god of—"

"Hares," the creature said in a flat tone. "That's what you were going to say, isn't it? God of hares?"

"...yes," the Teller lied.

Adanko leaned toward Cloud. "I like him," he whispered loudly out of the side of his mouth. "He reminds me of a very, very slow me."

"Why... why have you graced us with your presence, Lord Adanko?" Cloud stammered, remembering to dip her head into a halfway bow.

The hare cocked one ear high. "What's that? No, 'this can't be happening' or 'I must be dreaming?' Well, it's a little disappointing, but I suppose that does save time. So listen. I'm about to give you a Command From The Gods. It's very important that you obey it exactly. Your little friend Clay and his uptight forest god buddy have found themselves in a bit of a soggy pit, a wasp hive, a crocodile mouth, you understand? Trouble, and lots of it. Turns out Ogya was *slightly* less permanently imprisoned than everyone thought and as we speak, he's eating them alive. Just gobbling them up. Burning their temple, everything." He chuckled. "They're in so much pain right now. So much. You wouldn't believe it. Just... just sheer agony. Doing all these romantic bits about how they love each other, you know how it goes."

Cloud listened in a mixture of fear and bewilderment. Clay? In trouble? But could she believe anything this odd creature told them? "What should we do?"

"You should do—and this is very important, obey the gods or face eternal punishment, you know—absolutely nothing." Adanko flicked one ear and looked back and forth between the two of them. "Okay, yes, I see that look, but listen. This is gods' business. It's not for you humans to get involved. Strictly forbidden."

"But won't they die?" Cloud asked, bewildered.

"Oh, yes. Certainly. Their little temple is going to go up in smoke because they've got nowhere to move it. No other territory anywhere in the world where they can escape to be safe from Ogya's flames. Tragic, really, a terrible loss. I hated them both, but still, one hates to see young gods go that way. And then, of course, Ogya will have the power he needs to burn the rest of the forest. Probably the world. It's really what he's wanted all along." Adanko shook his head sadly, and then narrowed his eyes and pointed a fuzzy finger at first Cloud, then the Teller.

"But don't you go getting any ideas in your heads about singing songs or doing any of those fancy new steps you kids are all about these days. This is for gods to deal with. Not you pesky mortals. You understand?"

Cloud blinked in the Teller's direction.

"Hey. Hey. None of that," Adanko said, poking a finger under her nose. "What are you not to do?"

She peered up at him. "Sing—sing any songs in praise of… Doté?"

"*Or Doto*."

"Or Doto."

"Or do any little dances to them either. Especially not for both of them at once. And why not?" He grinned in the Teller's direction.

"Because then they might be able to escape death?" the Teller ventured.

"*And* the world could be saved." Adanko nodded and dusted off his paws. "There. Now no one can say I interfered with you mortals or put crazy ideas in your heads. And don't go looking for me in the future. This was a one-time only appearance. You got me? I was clear?"

Still fighting through her bafflement, Cloud stammered, "I—I think you were."

The hare snorted. "Like I care what a human thinks, anyway. Well. Got god business to tend to. Bye!"

Wind lifted the leaves where he had been standing.

~

The People of the Savanna answered the sound of the Teller's horn: first a few scouts, and then runners were sent back for more of them.

Cloud knew they didn't have much time; every second was additional pain and suffering for Clay. She picked a spot as close to the village as she could reach quickly, a wide circle that overlapped the old boundary between forest and savanna, still marked by that old line of stones they'd placed back when crossing the line meant the forest would try to kill you.

She and the Teller gave instructions as the People of the Savanna hurried in, reminding them of the song and showing them where to dance. They began singing before many of the people had even arrived, dancing in concentric circles, the song for Doté moving on the outside, in one direction, and the song for Doto inside, moving the other direction.

Strange to be singing praise to gods you've met before, Cloud thought as she moved with her people, lifting her voice higher. Especially one you cared for as an infant. One you've personally scolded on more than one occasion.

Strange, too, how neatly these songs fit, one phrase overlapping the other, the tunes in harmony with each other, as though they'd always been meant to be sung together. More and more people arrived from the village and joined one of the dancing circles, their voices rising in a chorus that rang with beauty. Not that the song was especially beautiful, or that the singers' voices were especially fine—many had faltering voices, and many could not keep pitch. But it was all of them singing together at last: one people, one shared voice, singing to save the gods, and save one of their own who had gone to meet them, and stayed.

# 41 Enough

Kwaee was triumphant for the moment. Ogya's enormous body lay slumped across their temple, but his liquid, fiery blood poured out of it and spread across the ground, igniting everything it touched, incinerating the protective circle of green that Clay and Doto had formed together.

Clay collapsed to the ground. His temple, his body was still burning, and he had nothing left in him to restore it. Even without Ogya's avatar here, the fire was still spreading. His vision faded in and out, not between light and darkness, but between seeing and not seeing. He saw Doto crawling toward him, blackened and scarred, half his side missing, his tail gone.

He reached for Doto, spreading the fingers of one paw. He clutched at the ground, managing to drag himself a little way before his arm stopped moving. His vision faded again, and when it returned, Doto was a little closer, little fires moving through his fur. He couldn't feel his legs to try kicking himself closer. In the earth beneath him he found roots, still unburned, and moved them, pushing the ground beneath him, using what remained of his temple to do what his charred body could not.

Doto's paw reached for his, fingers stretching out.

He strained toward it, trying to touch.

And then his vision was gone. He groped for Doto's mind in the darkness and found him in there, fading, dropping away. It was all right. They had loved each other. They had done everything they could. They would go together.

A voice from above and within them. Strong. Confident. But even though it was within their temple, it seemed to come from a great distance away. "I will not let this happen."

And in what remained of their temple, in the half-burned leaves and blades of grass, Clay felt a rising wind. It swirled and gathered, building up speed. The flames flickered and flared on the fresh air for a time, but then the wind blew stronger, too much for the fire. Heavy gusts pulled the heat of Ogya's lifeblood away from the fuel that fed it.

The flames were gone, but the wind was still rising. In the emptiness of near-death, Clay could barely tell what was happening, but he knew that what remained of the leaves were being torn from his trees, that loose earth and dead ash was being scoured from the floor of his temple. He could feel the shaking and vibrations in his roots. An electrical energy tugged at the ground, and in his charred avatar he felt burned fur lifting as though lightning were about to strike.

"Out, out," a voice roared above the gale. "Into copse and glen, into soul and bone, into tree and grass and stream, into spirits, into sons, into all forest not my own, take what is mine." The voice roared loud enough to crack the heavens. "*Take what is mine!*"

And then Clay's vision came back and it was filled with blinding white light. It blazed through everything, so bright he could see nothing else, but it didn't hurt. It poured into him, filling him with strength and life. He felt Doto near him, the feeble pulse of divine power that was all that had remained of him strengthening into a pounding, a surge of divinity.

All around them, their temple was being restored, regrowing, ash and ember flaking away from fresh bark, soil soaking up the char and becoming newly fertile, everything returning to them. And in the midst of it all, Kwaee, crouched by his limp body and Doto's, a paw on each of them, his head tilted back in a soundless roar as the healing magic poured out of him and into them.

The light faded. The wind died.

Kwaee dropped backward into the fresh shoots of young grass sprinkled with delicate yellow flowers.

Clay felt whole again, but weary. And changed once more. The power of the forest crackled in his fingertips; it was more deeply a part of him now. His toes were the roots in the earth; his fingertips scraped the clouds.

He reached for Doto and found him still lying on his side, but healed, his gold-green eyes cracked open, almost glowing in the sunlight. He lifted Doto to his feet—he felt so light now—and kissed him. Doto's arms wrapped around him, hoisting him into the air.

"I am pleased that you are well," Kwaee's voice came from beside them, "but we do not have long before Ogya returns."

They turned. Kwaee looked smaller. He still stood proud and strong, but diminished, no longer towering over them. Or perhaps… Clay stepped back to look at Doto and saw that he, too, was changed. Taller, more muscled, with an easy, confident stance. He looked, a little, more like Kwaee.

"Father?" he said uncertainly, and his voice had a new, resonant timbre to it. "Father, what have you done?"

Kwaee put a paw on both of their shoulders. "I have healed you. But it took much of my power to do so. I hope enough remains for what comes next."

"What *does* come next?" Clay asked uneasily, and was startled at the changed sound of his own voice.

Another voice piped up behind them, not far from the edge of their temple. "That would be me."

They turned.

"Hello boys," said Adanko. He shook his head. "Growth spurts are coming later and later these days." He sauntered right up to the edge of their temple but did not enter. "Nice temple you've got here. Shame if something were to happen to it. Too bad you've got nowhere else to put it, isn't it?"

Clay glanced at Doto. His mind was still whirling with trauma and healing and change. They had nearly been destroyed and been pulled back from the brink. He was very definitely tired of being killed. But amidst all the new—the power surging through his limbs, his changed body, the strange, brilliant vibrancy of their temple, there was something else, something he hadn't identified. Where was it?

He sniffed the air. There was still the scent of smoke. He turned, following it. How could there be smoke? The wind from Kwaee's healing had been so powerful it had extinguished every spark, blown every burning scrap of fuel far away. A thin, white wisp of smoke rose from the forest floor, where charred remains of his brother still lay, unidentifiable. Clay turned away in sickness and grief. Poor Laughing Dog. But he had looked long enough to see what glinted in the charred remains: Ogya's diamond. With a *whoomf*, a flame billowed between the trees.

"You know, somewhere else," Adanko said in a slow voice. "Somewhere far away from any kind of *Ogya* you might have lying around..."

A voice like an inferno roared on the wind. "Fools. I cannot be destroyed. My temple is in the belly of the world. I cannot be stopped. My hunger will never be sated."

And once again, the god of fire crawled up from the forest floor, setting everything around him ablaze.

"Oh, for—" Adanko muttered, and then he bounded into their temple. Clay felt each step like a footprint on his soul. He raced up to the two of them, ears folded back in exaggeration. "I can't believe you're making me tell the gods-damned truth. Don't you notice when your territory grows? Listen to me. I spoke to your people. They've danced for you near their village. There's a nice comfy spot where you can move your temple. You don't want to burn again? Get rid of it, *now*."

Clay blinked at Doto. They both looked down at the little hare. "Is he lying?"

They spread their senses out together and felt it: a new, wide space of forest that belonged to them. There were people there, singing to them. They could feel it now that they were listening. Through the ears of birds, they could hear the songs to Doto and Doté. Through crawling insects they could feel the vibration of many feet hitting the ground.

Ogya spread his claws, his small, circular eyes scanning the scene in confusion. "How are you healed? How are you changed? What have you done?" His mouthparts wriggled as he looked around. "No matter," he decided. "What is a feast without a second course?"

He took one fiery step toward their temple.

"No." Clay and Doto said the word in unison, and in an instant, their temple was gone, leaving only a gust of wind to shake the bare, unsanctified forest that remained. The headless corpse of Ogya's previous avatar began to slide gently downhill.

"Finally." Adanko stared at them in disgust. "You made me tell the truth. You *made me*. Despicable."

Ogya froze in midstep. His blunt, wide head turned from side to side. "Where is it?" he demanded. "Where is the meal that has been promised me? You cannot deny me forever! You cannot stop me! I will burn all! See!"

He spread his pincers wide and flames roared out to either side of him. "Stronger now than before, you see? Now that I have dined on godflesh."

"Time for me to leave," Adanko announced, and vanished. A moment later, he reappeared. "The *truth*," he said reproachfully, and then he was gone again.

Kwaee walked up between Clay and Doto. "I am ashamed," he said, "of how long it took me to understand." Red light from the rising fires colored his fur. Ogya approached slowly, clicking his claws. "My son, I asked myself constantly: how much is finally enough? I gave to your mother, but not enough. I gave of my forest to stop Ogya, but not enough. I gave my time, my attention, my very self in little bits here and there, portioning it out carefully, sparingly, trying to save what I could. Always more was demanded, for no reward. Always another sacrifice. Always more. I asked myself, if you truly value—if you *love* something, someone, how much must you do for them, how much must you give, how much must you sacrifice? How much is *enough?*"

He turned to Doto. "Take care of the forest. Protect it. When times change, let it change too. Let it grow."

To Clay he said, "Take care of my son. Make him gentle. Keep him wise. Both of you, take care of each other, whatever it costs."

Something cracked in Doto's expression. "F-father?"

Kwaee shook his head. Ogya reared up behind him, his tail rising for a strike. Kwaee's feathers lifted and spread on his brow like a crown. "Because of you two, I know."

Then he turned and raised both of his paws toward the blazing scorpion god. "Out, out."

And once more, the wind rose.

Ogya paused with his claws stretched wide, his tail barb dripping molten fire. "What is this? What are you doing?"

It was a wind stronger than Clay had ever felt. It pulled tears from his eyes, flipped his cupped ears inside out. The ground was denuded in moments, and still the wind rose. He found a solidly rooted tree trunk and gripped it with both arms, sinking his claws deep, and Doto found one next to him.

The wind was a cyclone with Kwaee and Ogya at its center, the two of them unmoving, Kwaee's paws raised toward the titanic scorpion who stood with claws still opened, tail still ready to spear the forest god like a frog. He jabbed once, twice, but the strength of the gale blew his tail aside and made him miss.

Rocks flew through the air, lifted by the wind, and now it picked up Clay and Doto too, pulling them off their feet. But Clay's arms felt strong, his grip on the trunk secure. His tailtip battered against his heels as he clung, and branches and twigs struck him as they flew through the air.

"Out, out," Kwaee repeated, his roar barely audible over the wind.

Great cracks and snaps echoed through the air as some of the trees began to split or were wrenched away from their roots.

Ogya stabbed again and again. His tail grazed Kwaee's arm, and then his neck, spilling droplets of liquid fire over him, but he could not skewer the forest god.

"Into hunger and hollow," Kwaee called.

The air was full of electricity. A lightning bolt struck the ground with a deafening explosion, spraying sparks and filling Clay's ears with ringing, the wind with a raw, stinging scent. Another struck just by him.

"Into rage and cruelty!"

A flying tree trunk whipped through the air and struck the tree Clay was clinging to, making the whole thing shudder. He nearly lost his grip, and when he recovered and looked up with eyes streaming in the wind, the trunk above him was gone.

"Into hatred and greed, into famine, into starvation, into destruction and devastation!"

Another lightning bolt struck, and this one hit Doto with a terrible boom. The body of a leopard soared away on the wind like a leaf, struck another tree, bounced off, and disappeared.

Kwaee stumbled forward into the great bulk of Ogya, placing his paws against one chitinous leg. "Into desire, into craving, into torment, take what is mine!"

A light rose between Kwaee and Ogya, swallowing them up. It grew brighter than the sun, so bright that even with Clay's eyes closed, it shone through his eyelids with unbearable intensity. It penetrated the trunk of the tree Clay clung to as though the wood itself were transparent.

Clay felt his grip on the tree trunk tear free, and for one terrifying, flailing moment, he was carried by the wind.

He hit something with a crunch.

# 42 The People of the Forest

Cloud sat atop Gamewatch Rise next to Basket, who was munching happily on a pouch full of jugo beans. He had found a whole glen full of them on one of his recent trips through the forest and had lately been making himself sick on them. Strange to find them there, as they were not native to this area. Nearly as strange, perhaps, as when Cloud had stumbled across a little valley full of all kinds of medicinally useful plants—roots, herbs, bark, berries, leaves for binding wounds and staunching blood flow. Very, very strange, considering that many of these plants were never found growing together. The forest provided.

Dotari Forest, they had taken to calling it. Rich with fruit, game, strong wood, and useful plants. It was hard now to remember how they had ever survived on the savanna. The people were growing fat and comfortable.

Basket caught her gaze. "Still no change in the sacred place?"

"Not that we can tell," Cloud said. It had been more than two rains now since the Day of Light. They had danced the forest for Doto and Doté, and marveled at the new growth, and then something had changed. The forest in their midst had transformed—still forest, but with strange, delicate light and colors too bright and vivid to be real. In its center, a massive baobab spread its branches. A brook had wound through it, and flowers opened everywhere. The scents that drifted out of it were intoxicating, making those who drew too near feel dreamy and light of foot. The light shifted through it in hypnotic beams, whether day or night. Even on moonless nights, somehow, within that place, the starlight shone.

But no one entered. They all knew, without being told, that it was holy ground, that no one was to set foot inside.

And the Day of Light. Moments after the holy place had appeared, a great white light rose in the southeast, over the treetops, growing brighter and brighter, until it became too painful to look at. People wept in fear and fled, hiding themselves in their tents or under hides to try to shut out the brilliance. It lasted for a very long time, and when it finally faded, night had fallen. No one knew the cause of the light, and no one had ever explained it, but Cloud knew from personal reports that it had been seen as far away as Bogana.

Some claimed it was the creation of a star. Others believed it the birth of a new god and traveled as far as they could in the direction they'd seen, tracing the lines from different locations, following them for moons to the point where they met deep in the heart of the forest. But nothing had ever been found there—only empty forest and broken trees like there had been a terrible storm there.

The morning after the Day of Light, the people had looked into the holy place and saw that it had changed. A great, earthen mound had risen in the center, covered in moss and bedecked in white flowers. No one could decide what it was, but rumors of burial began to spread. Many had begun to believe that the bodies of the dead should not be set to flame. Not after Ogya had harmed so many and threatened their lives. Instead, why not commit them to the earth, and feed their life to the trees on which they all depended.

No one was sure who, if anyone, was buried in the holy place, but some thought it might have been Kwaee, god of the forest, because after the Day of Light, the spells in his name stopped working. They had all gathered around ash to sing the song of Kwaee and restore it to verdant forest, but though they sang reverently and danced their praise to him as fervent as ever, nothing regrew, and the burned soil remained. Only the songs to Doto and Doté had any effect, and the forest that grew from those spells was richer, more welcoming, and full of food than any that had grown in Kwaee's name.

Kwaee's name was still spoken in prayer and story, but less frequently now than those of Doto and Doté. The younger people of the village had even begun to reject the name People of the Savanna. Why the harsh, difficult savanna when everything they needed came from the forest, they wondered? Some had begun calling themselves the People of the Forest.

Cloud worried sometimes in conversations with the Teller that this shifting of allegiance would anger Sarmu, but these were new days. No more Kings, no more edicts. You start telling people what they can call themselves or what gods they should focus on, and next thing you know, you're a few sacrifices away from becoming the Matron.

"New days," she said aloud with a sigh. "You'd think I'd feel older."

Basket gave her a sidelong smile. "If anything, you seem younger to me. You were old all those years shutting yourself away in your healer's tent. Perhaps you've lived your life out of order."

"Not a usual sort of tale you'd tell, is it?"

He kicked at the earth in mock irritation. "Tellers like stories with a single hero on a path from start to finish. And what did you do? Did you defeat a god? Did you stop a mad king? Liberate a people? Defeat your enemies?" He gave her a sly look. "Is it not true that you merely followed along?"

"Followed? As I recall it, I was leading. It was I who took our people to Bogana, and I who brought them back with secrets that changed the world."

"Secrets you did not discover."

"Secrets that would never have been discovered had I not set an impertinent young man on a better path."

"The people could have made it on their own."

"Ah, I see what's happening here, you surly old buffoon. You're envious. You wish it had been you who had rallied our people in the wilderness, who had roused them to defy the Matron and Mpo, who had—"

"Been thrown into a pit of flies," Basket interrupted with an impish spark in his eye.

Cloud thwacked at his knee with her stick. "It was the Matron's mistake. She took away my fear. I fought her, leader against leader. And I brought my people home." She sighed. "But you're right, of course, it doesn't look like the old stories. But maybe we're done with those, too. Those types of stories."

With a creaking of joints, Cloud got to her feet. She was moving slower these days. The trip to Bogana had strengthened her, but life was a little too pleasant now, and she a little too plump, and so the old knots had worked their way back into her limbs again. A pretty complaint to have, though—life being too easy.

"Where are you going?" Basket asked. He tucked his pouch of jugo beans onto his belt and pushed himself upright using his stick.

"Back down to the holy place. Might as well look in on it."

"I will come with you."

Together they walked down the hill and into the village. They did not need to find their way to the gate, for the walls had never been rebuilt, and were eventually scavenged for tools or firewood. Animals didn't bother them here. Who needed walls?

They walked through the work area, which was well-equipped now; the forest had yielded materials for better tools and better-crafted supplies. Everything lasted a little longer and worked a little better, and people spent more time with games and sports than scraping leather or preparing food.

"Mirage is still doing well with his studies?" the Teller asked, spying him carding out medicinal seeds from plant fiber on one side of the work area.

"He's not as sharp as Yellow Bug," Cloud admitted, "but he works harder than she does. He cares more. And it'll take him farther than she'll go, I think. And Baobab? She is becoming quite the little Teller these days."

He gave a good-natured grimace. "If only I could get her to stick to the tales she knows. I've told her not to speak about Doto and Doté so lightly. Those stories are… unrefined. Dangerous. But whatever I tell her to do, she finds a way around it."

"Her father's daughter, then," Cloud said with some amusement.

"Unluckily for her."

She nudged him sharply with her elbow. "No insulting the man I love."

"Well, all right," he answered with a good-natured smile. "I wouldn't want to be rude."

They climbed the little incline in the village. Without walls, the people were free to place their tents where they wished, but for practical reasons, craftsmen wanted to live close together so as to share tools and conversation, and hunters grouped together to avoid waking everyone when they rose early. But the top of the hill was no longer reserved for the wealthy or those with status, and anyway, the village elders preferred to live at the bottom of the hill so they weren't having to climb up and down all the time.

These days, the tents at the top of the hill tended to belong to Boganans, who moved frequently between their coastal city and the village, finding life here a restful and welcome break from the stresses of city politics and the challenges of rebuilding a community fractured by the rise of many new thoughts on religion and government. Compared to arguing with new priests, engaging in heavy construction, carving countless new statues, or rewriting laws for trade and commerce, a stay among the People of the Forest represented a restful vacation. And they brought with them crafted stone goods, salted fish, pearls, and fine dyed clothes in exchange for leathers, precious wood, and arboreal spices and delicacies.

Cloud and Basket spoke briefly with them, making their greetings as they passed through. The Boganans were quickly learning plainstongue, though the villagers were a bit slower at picking up Boganan, with only Mirage among them becoming truly fluent.

"Still beautiful as ever," the Teller said, as they strolled out of the village and toward the garden temple at the edge of the Dotari forest.

And it was. Sunbeams drifted across the floor of the glade, flowers craning toward them, their petals catching the light. Birdsong drifted on the air, and the heady scent of sweet nectar filled their noses. They ambled toward it, enjoying the shade in the hot afternoon. The rain would come soon.

"Would you ever dare step inside?" Basket asked Cloud.

She immediately shook her head. "Not even if invited. It would feel wrong. Like disturbing a calm lake or startling a nest of fawns. It's their place, not—" She frowned, peering. "My eyes are not so good anymore, but..."

They ventured closer. "It's open," Basket breathed.

The mound in the center of the glade had two large holes in it, the moss pulled apart, earth sifting down the side, buried roots pulled free, jutting upward like an unfinished basket.

"What do you think came out of it?" Cloud asked. "What happened?"

"I don't—" Basket began, but there was a sudden *whup* noise and a gust of wind that nearly blew them over.

When they recovered and looked again, the entire glade had gone. There were no flowers, no gentle brook, no shifting shafts of sunlight. No sweetness of nectar on the breeze. Ordinary, empty forest.

Cloud and Basket stared into the trees and back at each other in bewilderment. "What happened?" Cloud asked again, flabbergasted.

The Teller shook his head, searching the trees as if he could spot the sacred place skulking behind a large acacia or creeping into a valley somewhere. "I don't suppose we will ever know," he said. "Well, should we go back and tell everyone what happened?"

Cloud shrugged. "Nothing here now," she said. "I guess we should." She turned to go and for a moment thought she saw, at the edge of her vision, two tall figures standing arm in arm, deep in the woods. And she thought in that same moment that one of them waved to her. But when she turned her head to look, there was nothing there.

# 43 Tracks of a New God

Ogya moved through the forest, little crackles of flame following him.

"I feel him," Doto said when Clay looked in his direction. "It has been a while. I thought perhaps he would not burn anything this year."

Clay stretched his back and legs lazily, arching his tail. "Well I'm glad he's bothering this time. Remember five years ago when he wasn't to be seen anywhere? The growth really suffered. I had to go around opening the seeds and clearing away underbrush myself. It took forever and still nothing grew the way it was supposed to. The soil really likes the ash."

"Fire and forest together," Doto sighed. "It still seems unnatural to me."

Clay drew himself to an imperious height. "Nothing a god does is unnatural," he declared in his best imitation of Doto's voice.

Doto groaned, and then curled his wrist and flicked a fallen thorn tree at Clay. Clay ducked it easily—the thing flew over his head and bounced down the hill before splintering to a stop against a large boulder.

"Don't be so grumpy," he said before settling down against Doto's side and stroking his chest. "The forest really has changed, that's all. It needs the fire now."

"Well, I still do not care for it," Doto declared.

Clay nuzzled up to his neck. "You still miss him, don't you?"

"There is no reason for it! I did not like being around him at all when he was here! Why should I care only now, when he is gone?"

"It's good that you care."

Doto sighed and turned to nibble at Clay's ear. "Did you go back to the village?"

"Yes, but I didn't go in. Even if I chose my human form, they'd have known me. Still, I could see well enough once they brought her to the forest."

"They put her in the ground, like you thought?"

Clay nodded. "They stopped burning their fallen after… everything with Ogya. I'll grow something nice over her. Maybe a big willow. For medicine."

"How long did she live?"

Clay thought about it. After the fight with Ogya—the Day of Light, the People of the Forest called it—they'd been in the ground, recovering and healing, for two years. And when they'd finally climbed out and moved their temple, Kwaee had been gone, and they'd been the principal gods of the forest, though they shared that title with Ogya in part. But since then, the years had begun to blur. He and Doto had been so wrapped up in adapting to their changes—and in indulging in their love for each other with no more fear or worry—that one year passed much the same as the last.

The village had grown in that time, and thrived, and even split, with many young people forming new villages all along the boundary lands between savanna and forest. Some had even begun to take boats up the Asubonten, though where the crocodile goddess reigned, the lands were a little less friendly to humans.

It must have taken some time for all that to happen, but Clay could not work out how long. And he'd looked in on his village year after year, watching the young grow old, and the old grow stooped and ancient. The Teller had died at least two rains back, but Cloud had kept on, looked after by his daughter Baobab, now a woman with children of her own, by Dry Grass, and by her staunch ally Ant With a Leaf.

"I don't know," Clay admitted finally. "But she was very old. It was a good life, I think. Eventually."

"While you were there, I looked in on my father's temple."

"It's still there, then?"

Doto switched the tip of his tail. "Barely. It is like a place abandoned. The pond is all dried up. Most of the trees are dead."

"You could regrow it, keep it how it was, if you wanted."

"Like he did with Abansin?"

Clay thought of the ruined, forgotten city in the middle of the forest. "No, I suppose not."

"It is better to let things pass. Look at everything that has changed. You and I are together. Ogya no longer devours the world, but helps the forest. Your people are happier and fed."

"Thanks to us."

"Yes, thanks to us. And now many of the gods are better. We talk to Asubonten, and we visit Atekye."

"Mpo is still a terror, though, I hear," Clay said. "When I look in on the Boganans. We were going to go seek her out, remember? We were going to see the world."

"And I told you after a hundred years or so," Doto reminded him. "I told you the time would go by quickly, didn't I?"

"You did," Clay admitted. "I didn't believe you, but you're right. A hundred years is plenty of time to wait. And then we can go and find out what happened to Bew, perhaps. Or the other lost gods."

"Or…" And Doto turned toward Clay, folding him up in his arms and rolling across the grass. "Or we could just give it another few hundred years and see what happens."

Clay nipped at his neck and licked up under his chin fondly before kissing him. "So is this it?" he asked. "This is what our life will be?"

"Until the world changes. That is what Kwaee could never understand. Things will always change. It's trying to stop everything that hurts everyone. Trying to hold it in place. But you and I know better. The world changed, and we changed with it."

"And what about when it changes again?" Clay asked, wrapping his arms around Doto and kissing him again. "Will it change us?"

"If we love it, I think it will. I think that is what love is for."

And Clay held Doto tighter and let his awareness spread out through the forest, from the storm-soaked cliffs along the ocean in the west, across the misty forests broken by cold mountaintops, to the gentle slope into the plains of the south, and beyond that, shores he had never seen, bathed by marine breezes scented with the fruits of other forests from far away, ruled by other gods. His senses blended with those of Doto, and they spread out through their forest together. Cutting through their belly, silvery-quick, was Asubonten, splashing in her clear river and sending a cloud of birds into the open, blue sky. On their borders, Atekye wallowed in lazy splendor, sprawling into their territory with an indolent grin. Baboons raced through their treetops. Elephants gabbled to each other in scandalous tones as they plodded beneath the canopy. Ants wandered aimlessly in search of fallen fruit. Baobabs, once unseen in the forest, now swelled their thirsty trunks among the older trees. And here and there, fire flickered, consuming and returning to the earth and air what it took, clearing away the brush and making room for new growth, new lives, new gods, new stories.

## About the Author

**Ryan Campbell** writes and works in Northern California with his husband, David, and their bunny, Biscuit. He is a graduate of the Clarion Science Fiction and Fantasy Writer's Workshop and the author of numerous short stories and novels, including *The Fire Bearers* series, *Koa of the Drowned Kingdom*, and whatever comes next.

## About the Artist

**Zhivago** is a lifelong self-taught artist and product designer from California. Over the years, they've grown to see the creative process in it's many forms as an important part of life; and enjoy seeking out new ways to encourage others to pick up a pen, pencil, or any other tool as a means to express, explore and create. Online, Zhivago plays the role of a sushi-rolling cartoon cat, bringing together a diverse international community focused on fostering positivity, acceptance, and the uniting of people pursuing a personal mission to be the good they want to see in the world.

Offline, you can find Zhivago roaming the earth with their partner, eagerly seeking to experience and learn more about its various wonders. More of Zhivago's work can be seen at their website *www.cat-bird.com*

## About the Publisher

**Sofawolf Press** was founded in 1999 to provide a venue to showcase great anthropomorphic storytelling and promote the genre to a wider audience.

Since the debut of their first publication, the short-story anthology *Anthrolations*, they have produced over 75 publications including: novels, shared-world and thematic anthologies, short story collections, graphic novels, artists' sketch books, and some things that defy categorization.

Their publications, and the talent featured within them, have been the recipients of numerous nominations and awards, including: 23 Annual Anthropomorphic Literature & Arts awards, one Russ Manning Promising Newcomer nomination for Teagan Gavet's work on the graphic novel *Nordguard: Across Thin Ice*, and both the 2012 Hugo Award for Best Graphic Story and the 2013 Mythopoeic Society Adult Literature award for Ursula Vernon's fantasy graphic novel *Digger*.

Visit their website at *www.sofawolf.com* for more information about their titles, submission guidelines, and upcoming events and releases.

Milton Keynes UK
Ingram Content Group UK Ltd.
UKHW020748111223
434160UK00016B/889

9 781936 689712